# THE ELITES OF WJ PREP ACADEMY

---

## THE COMPLETE SERIES

### REBEL HART

# Reckless RULES

# PROLOGUE

## BOOK 1

I wasn't here to fuck around at the Arcadia Invitational. I was seeded 17th in the Girls 300 Meter hurdles, and I was here to kick ass and take names.

I looked to my left. Carly Richardson was the girl I needed to beat to get to the finals. Our times were milliseconds from each other. Our lanes were four and five, and I was ready to ignite like fire out of the blocks. Coach had told me that I didn't have the acceleration to outrun her in the first 100 meters. I needed to outlast her in the last 100. I watched her jump, slap her thighs and sail through her pre-race routine. Her muscles rippled with effort.

Okay. Enough bullshitting.

I cracked my neck, did a couple jumps, high knees. Adrenaline pumped through my veins, visceral and real, and my heart rate was elevated. I took a couple calming breaths.

*Okay, Ophelia.* I told myself. The official mounted. It was time to get into the blocks. I did another jump, feeling my legs quiver like jelly. I slapped them. *No.* Now was not the time for nerves to make me weak.

I was a fucking bull.

Just before I knelt to my knees on the track, I glanced at the sidelines. Coach was there, giving me a stern look. His look of determination fueled me with confidence. We'd worked on my kick for the last 100 so many times these past weeks. He'd pushed me to my very breaking point. My mouth tingled with the remnant tang of vomit – if I did this right, I'd beat Carly. I knew what I was supposed to do. My gaze drifted to my mother and my step-dad who were pressed against the railing, smiling.

And then, there *he* was.

My stomach dropped. He was looking at me like he was hungry.

Over the past two days, I kept seeing him. He wasn't a competitor, but his muscles strained against his shirt. Fit. Just how I liked them. His dark hair was artfully tousled. And his light-colored eyes kept finding mine across the crowd. It was as if everywhere I turned, my eyes found his form like a magnet. Behind me in the bleachers, waiting at the concession stand, drinking at the water fountain. Basically everywhere. Something about him told me there was something not *quite right* with him being here. But try telling that to my hormones and that fucking dream I had last night...

The guy smirked, and my body flooded with heat.

*Fuck.*

I couldn't be distracted.

I settled my feet into the blocks. A rush of familiarity calmed me. These were just like the blocks at my high school. Though Nike was branded across them, they served the same purpose.

I tensed, waiting for that gun shot. Waiting for my time to spring. A sense of calm soothed my whirring brain, and my body stilled, tensed, waiting. This was instinctual. This was mechanical. And I was waiting...waiting.

---

"You did great," came a voice from behind me.

I froze. My body, already weak and tired and achy and sweaty, clamped up. I whirled around, my bags swinging, and my eyes met *his.*

He was even more perfect in person. He had thick dark lashes that framed his stormy gray eyes. His lips were plump – totally kissable. And they were curled into a panty-dropping smirk. His face wasn't quite symmetrical, but the crooked nose and thicker bottom lip added to his edgy look.

"Thanks," I said, trying to keep the bitterness out of my voice. "I didn't make it to finals, but yeah."

Just thirty minutes ago, I had run my fucking heart out. I

wanted to make it to finals so bad, I could fucking taste it. I'd had my eyes trained on Carly, and I passed her right at the 200-meter mark like Coach and I had planned out last night. But then, out of nowhere, some girl in lane 8 put on the blasters and passed both Carly and me right at the finish line.

She'd run a personal record of 41.55 seconds. Enough to slide her into the finals and boot Carly and me to the curb.

I'd exited the field, given my mom and stepdad a hug, talked to Coach about what went wrong, and then escaped to the girls room to avoid everyone. I'd sat in the last stall sullenly, listening to the flushes of toilets and the chatter of happy people.

I was so fucking disappointed. And angry.

I'd found a quiet corner against the back of the stadium. I just needed like ten minutes to myself to compose my face before I confronted my family and Coach again.

Until *he* had found me. Mr. Mysterious Good Looking.

"You're only a junior," he said. "You've got next year to make it up."

I jerked my chin up, narrowing my eyes at him. "Stalk much?"

"When I see a pretty girl? Nah, I just use the roster." He smiled as he pulled up a crumbled roster from his pocket. He offered it to me, but I declined. "Suit yourself."

I sighed. "Yeah, but who knows what will happen next year. I probably won't have enough money to go here again."

Bitterness soured my words. My body pulsed with irritation, disappointment and sadness. It crushed my soul to not be good enough. I clenched my jaw and let out an irritated growl.

"Ridiculous," I muttered to myself.

"Mmm," he said, nodding and pursing his bottom lip. For a moment, my eyes fixated on that lip. I wanted to bite it. Every nerve in me was short-circuited either from desire or anger, and I didn't know if I wanted to punch the wall or kiss him. "That makes sense. Kinda unfair though."

"Life's unfair," I ground out, shrugging my bag farther up my shoulder. "That's how it is."

"I'm Emmett, by the way" the guy said, extending his hand. I eyed the heavy veins that snaked down his arm to the back of his hand. I took it, delighting in the shivers creeping up my arm as his warm fingers enclosed around mine. "And you are?"

"You already know," I snapped, then realized I was being a

dick. *I shouldn't take my disappointment out on him.* I smiled up at him. "But Ophelia. Ophelia Lopez."

"A pleasure," he said, bringing up my hand and brushing his lips against the backs of my knuckles. My stomach dropped. *Holy fuck.*

His gesture was old-fashioned. But holy fuck, it was sexy.

And it made the swirling knot of disappointment and anger in my chest dissipate with the press of his lips.

Our hands dropped but remained entwined by the fingers. Flickers of warmth skated across my chest, and I stared at Emmett. Why was I responding so strongly to him? This was insane. His eyes, I noticed, were dark, forbidding, like the Midwestern storms I was all too familiar with in the middle of buttfuck Oklahoma.

"So what are you doing here?" I asked, looking at him under my lashes. "You aren't a runner."

He stepped closer, and a delicious scent of expensive cologne filled my nostrils. Who was he? He gave off a different vibe than I was expecting. Something more...suspicious.

"I'm supporting my little brother," he said. His fingers left my hand and trailed up the inside of my wrist. I sucked in a sharp breath. With my response, he stepped closer, and an electrical current built between us. "But that's not important."

Suddenly, his elbows were positioned by my head, his face leaning close to mine. His masculine scent flooded my nostrils – heavenly. I pressed back against the stadium wall, shocked at how my body both wanted to be next to his and far away. His eyes raked my face, and I couldn't decipher the expressions in them. Curiosity, desire...and something else churned in the icy depths.

I jerked when warm fingers touched my cheek. His eyes heated. But my body was frozen, wanting more of his touch, craving it. His fingers trailed along the cut of my jaw, fiery tingles. I'd thought about this last night, dreamt of kissing the hot guy who kept popping up, but this was real. His body before me was real and warm and – my hand unstuck itself from the wall and trailed itself across his pectorals – hard.

"You're different and odd," I said, licking my dry lips. There was something just *off* about him. I couldn't pinpoint any outward sign or anything that told me this. But I felt it. "But I like it."

He made a small sound in the back of his throat. He grabbed my wandering hand and placed a soft kiss on the inside of my palm. The tender touch zapped me out of my stupor.

"Let me kiss you," he said, locking eyes with mine. He was demanding rather than asking. "Let me."

My mouth dropped in astonishment, drawing his heated gaze. He stared at my lips like an addict.

I should have said no.

But what was the harm?

My hormones were practically begging me to kiss him.

So I went up on my tiptoes and touched my lips to his. It was a small connection of flesh, but my senses went haywire, my body lighting up like a firecracker.

"Fuck," he murmured against my mouth. His hand wound into my hair, tilting my heated face toward his. His gray eyes were delirious with desire, and my breaths came in short pants at just his taste. "You taste fucking delicious."

His lips came down on mine again, and he deepened the kiss, opening my lips, sucking, nipping. Heat poured off him in waves. The kiss turned demanding, and I grabbed his soft shirt to press him against me. I whimpered into his mouth as his kiss sent me skyrocketing.

Emmett kissed like he was confused. His lips were soft, but as he grabbed for my body, his fingers dug into my sides. Almost punishing. Almost brutal. But I rolled with it, matching each sweep of his tongue with mine.

"Ophelia!" came my mother's voice.

I shoved Emmett away, finding my mother's shocked face over his shoulder. *Oh shit.* Coach, my stepdad Brendan and my mother were staring at me with a mixture of confusion, disappointment, and amusement.

"Sorry," I said to them, wiggling past Emmett's still form and walking up to the trio. "I got distracted."

"I'll say," Coach said, fixing Emmett with a glare. "You look like a tomato."

I brushed my hot cheeks with the back of my hand. I decided to roll with it and dismiss their ogling. "Whatever. I just needed to get it out of my system."

But as I walked away from Emmett, I felt his heavy gaze on the nape of my neck. Shivers wracked my body and I ached to run back and finish what we had started. I couldn't help it – I sent a backward glance to where Emmett lounged against the stadium wall. When our eyes met, a flash of desire took hold of me.

Emmett was decidedly *not* out of my system. I shouldered my bag again, trying to brush off the sexual images burned in my brain.

Well, he needed to get out of my system. I was heading back to Oklahoma, and I wouldn't see him again.

# CHAPTER ONE

## BOOK 1

I hate running.

I do.

It's painful. It's hard. It's monotonous.

But then again, there's always been some sort of thrill, some sense of accomplishment that I feel when I push myself to the brink of passing out. It makes my thoughts numb, everything focused on pulling my burning muscles forward, expanding my heaving chest, and feeling the sweat trickle down my back or off the bridge of my nose.

So maybe, yeah, I fucking *love* running.

I love the sweet satisfaction that comes from every cell in my body burning with this intense heat.

I love the pain.

I love the delirious effect of a good race.

I love the sound of my feet slapping concrete, track rubber, grass, dirt.

I love that however I do in a particular moment boils down to me. There is nobody responsible for my failures or successes other than *me*. I am the sole determinant of how good or bad I perform.

I'm damn good at running. Just not *that* good. I'm nationally ranked in the top 50 of the Girls 300 Meter Hurdles. Thoughts of the Arcadia Invitational sour my steps. Even though it was months ago, I still can't get it out of my head. Just how hard do I need to work to run those thoughts out of my head?

Too hard.

I shake off the tendrils of disappointment that threaten to falter my stride. I obviously wasn't ready to go to finals. Nameless Lane 9 had showed up to kick my ass in gear.

Today's a long day. Seven miles.

I usually don't mind the length. Back in Oklahoma, I switched between three different routes depending on what Coach ordered. However, I'm not in Oklahoma anymore. And the streets of Jameson, Massachusetts are unfamiliar and sometimes bricked. They are windy, confusing and different. But I like the change in scenery.

As I race through unfamiliar streets, the houses get more impressive and old, and I think about the surprising turn of events following Arcadia.

Not a week after the meet, I'd received a phone call from the Headmaster of Weis-Jameson Preparatory Academy. He had an offer that made my jaw drop. A full-ride scholarship if I attended my senior year at WJ Prep. A little digging and I was hooked; their track and field program was nationally ranked, and they churned out an Olympic athlete every couple years. Their coach, David Granger, was legendary. A former Olympian hurdler himself, he'd gotten bronze back in his heyday.

Mom couldn't believe it. She'd grown up in Jameson when she was little − she hadn't been back for twenty years. She'd actually attended WJ Prep herself, where she'd met my bio-dad.

It didn't take a lot of convincing to move. Mom's ties to Jameson plus my scholarship and the opportunity to train under a former Olympian… Fuck, I could be set for life with just this one year stint at WJ prep.

And now I'm here. A week before the semester starts. In a strange town with the opportunity of my life. Pre-season workouts would start a couple weeks in, but David had emailed a 'suggested' workout. He wasn't technically able to supervise practice so early before the season starts in February.

Jameson is hilly, and I'm not used to hills. I push myself, feeling the remnants of my strength ebb as I struggle to put one leg in front of the other. With another right, I face an ornate gate: Crescent Hills, it reads. And holy *fuck* do these bitches have money.

I slow my pace, entering the community. The homes I pass get bigger and bigger as I go along. Immaculately landscaped yards feature fountains, perfect grass, trimmed hedges and sparkling driveways. Each one is breathtaking – clearly, this is the Mansion District. Many have gates across their drives, which lead up to columned porches framing massive wood or glass doors. Large stone potted plants decorate the porches, and I wonder what else these luxurious homes could be hiding behind their large windows and rooftop terraces.

As I run, each house rises into the backs of the mountain, and the road winds higher and higher. The steep elevation crucifies my legs. Jesus. My breath is painful, ripping an agonizing tear through my chest each time I inhale. What if I stopped here? I'm close enough to halfway.

I pause at a bend in the road. It overlooks the city before winding behind me, to further houses buried into the hills. Excuse me. *Mansions.*

Jameson sprawls below me. It is lit by the waning late summer light. I take a moment to bounce on my toes, feeling sweat dry on my calves as a cool breeze hit me. It's a gorgeous place, that I can admit. My town back in Oklahoma was flat, with concrete buildings and concrete roads and concrete fences. It was a concrete jungle, with little style and no beauty points. Only in the spring months did the flowers contrast the gray.

Time to go.

I start down the hill, letting gravity doing most of the work. Ahead, the first car that I've seen emerges, slowly driving toward me. It's a fucking fancy car. I stare at it. It glimmers a fire engine red, and as I get closer I notice the Lamborghini logo.

Fuck, these people are hella rich.

Suddenly, the car revs. It beelines toward me. A rush of red. The engine roars. A loud engine. It barrels down. Its lights aren't on, I notice. I can barely register what's happening before I dive out of the way. My foot dings the headlight as the car swerves just at the last second.

I land in the ditch. My feet are instantly soaked from the days-old water. Tremors shake my legs as I inch myself down to the sweet, sweet ground.

They just tried to run me over!

Cold adrenaline shocks my system.

I could have died.

"Oh my fucking gawd," screams a high-pitched voice.

A wafer-thin girl appears above me. Her manicured nails

are gripping her sharp hipbones, and she looks *pissed*. Her honey-blonde hair falls in heavy curls, and her face is Instagram-beautiful. Her pouty lips are curled into a sneer.

"You fucking dinged my car, bitch," she says.

I frown. She's wearing a pencil skirt and pink blouse. But she looks my age, around seventeen.

"Your car?" I ask. The red sports car is pulled over, idling. There's another girl lounging on the trunk. Her red hair is pulled back into a severely high bun, her lips as red as blood. She's also beautiful, but in a kinder, softer way. "The one that tried to run me over?"

"Don't get smart with me, bitch."

I start to stand up, but before I can even register movement, her platformed heel hits my shoulder. Hard. I tumble down, my butt landing in the water. A sharp pain radiates up my arm. A breath stills in my throat as I pull my hand up, cradling my wrist.

Great. Now I'm soaking wet and my wrist is sprained.

"What the fuck, bitch?" I snarl, pulling myself out of the ditch. She's shorter than me by a couple inches, and I've got at least twenty pounds of muscle on her. She doesn't look as intimidating now. Her blue eyes, still haughty, flash with momentary fear. "What's your problem?"

"Vivian and I are just needing to clean up the white trash in the street," she snaps. "So next time you go running, make sure to watch where you're going."

She turns on a heel, stalking back to her car.

"Who the fuck do you think you are?" I call after her. My wrist throbs. Goddammit. I'd just gotten over a thigh strain, and I was looking forward to running without pain for once. "Hey, you!"

"I'm sorry," said the red-haired one. Vivian. Yeah, the name suits her. She purred with disgust. "We don't acknowledge dripping garbage."

They pile into the car. Then reverse. I jump out of the way, glaring daggers at them. The girl who shoved me rolls down the window.

"What is your fucking problem?" I ask. "Who are you?"

"Oh, you'll learn about us pretty soon," says the girl named Vivian. She leans across the console, giving me a patronizing wink. Her eyelashes are so heavily layered in mascara, it's a wonder she can even keep her eyelids open. "Very soon."

"Look, new girl. I know *all* about you," says the girl in the driver's seat. "And you're going to wish you'd never even heard of WJ Prep."

"Why do you care?" I ask.

"You're scholarship scum. And if I ever see you running through *my* neighborhood again... " She breaks off with a laugh then fixes me with a glare that turns my insides cold. She smiles, her tone now hauntingly playful. "I won't miss you next time. Ta-Ta!"

With a peal of tires, she spins out, the red lambo taking off down the street with a scream. The smell of exhaust lingers in the air.

I stand there for a few moments, letting the waning sun bake my feverish skin. My heart rate calms its erratic pounding. I close my eyes and tilt my head up to the sky. What the heck just happened? Suddenly, all the beautiful houses I had been passing look ominous. It could be a combination of the darkening sky or the recent interaction I'd just had, but I notice that the windows are dark. Of nearly all the beautiful houses, only a few have their lights on.

The need to leave strikes me. I start running again. My wrist has recovered somewhat, but each jarring step reminds me that I'll need to ice it tonight.

Who was that girl? And how did she know who I was?

---

My step-dad, Brendan, is cooking dinner when I arrive home. It smells heavenly, and my stomach is growling.

"Hey, Dad," I say, giving him a kiss on his gruff cheek. "Whatcha making?"

"Hey, Ophelia. Spaghetti and meatballs," he says, looking at the timer on the oven. "Just a little over ten minutes on the meatballs. Sauce is simmering. Hand me that packet of pasta by your left hand. Please."

I do as he asks. "Here. I need to shower."

"Yeah ya' do," he says, not looking at me. He's a focused cook, and I can't help but smile when he says, "You absolutely *reek*."

"Thanks," I call out sarcastically. Brendan has been my dad since I was ten, though he's been with my mom much longer than that. He's more of my dad than my bio-dad, who I've never met and who I never really want to meet. He skipped out on my mom just months after I was born.

Brendan is a large teddy bear. His physically imposing form throws some people off – not to mention his tattoo sleeves and scruffy beard. But in my entire life, I've never once considered him anything other than my dad, and he's loved me as he would a daughter.

The duplex we are renting has two bedrooms and one bath, but it's cozy and recently renovated. I grab my shower stuff and a change of clothes before hitting the shower. The hot water works out all my knots. But the strange, uneasy feeling that's twisted in my gut doesn't go away. As I towel off, the blonde girl's cruel smile flashes in my mind.

*Next time I won't miss.*

Jesus, what kind of girl goes around threatening to run people over?

Apparently rich and entitled assholes.

My wrist aches a little, so I pop a couple aspirin from the cabinet. After I change, I join Brendan in the kitchen.

"When's Mom getting off?" I ask.

"Her shift ends at 8:30, so pretty soon."

As a Registered Nurse, Mom sometimes works odd hours. But she was able to get a job lined up at Golden Hills Community Medical Center even before we left Oklahoma. For the past week, she's been in training. Brendan has a couple of interviews lined up this week. There was always a demand for an Electrical Power-Line guy, but I can tell he is getting antsy playing domestic.

I play with my phone as Brendan finishes up cooking. He hands me a plate and I fill up. The first thing we did when we moved in was to finish unpacking the kitchen. Mom doesn't like eating off plastic plates.

"How was your run?" he asks around a mouthful of meatball.

"Horrible," I say before I can catch myself.

He frowns, concerned. I've never been super negative about my workouts before. "How so?"

"Some asshole teenagers tried to run me over," I say. "Fucking teenage little shits."

"You are a teenager."

I roll my eyes. "Are you missing the larger point, here?"

"Did you get the license plate?"

"No, I was too shocked to do anything. She also got out of her car and shoved me into a fucking ditch and I sprained my wrist." I stab a meatball viciously. "And now I'm going to have to work out around a fucking sprained wrist and I was *just* getting over my strained hamstring."

"Where were you?"

"Crescent Hills. Apparently the place for rich people."

"You know who it was?"

"Nooope," I say, extending the word with irritation. I stab another meatball and fit the whole thing in my mouth. "Ah, ah, hot hot hot!" I chew with an open mouth and swallow the meat when I can. I take a gulp of milk. "But if it helps, she drove a flaming hot red Lamborghini."

Brendan snorts around his beer. "A kid? Jesus, no kid needs such an expensive car. That insurance must be through the roof!"

Practical Brendan. Thinking about things in terms of money. "Like how much?"

"An insane amount. I know we spend 450 a year for you with your Good Student Discount. I can't imagine adding a teenager to an insurance policy with a Lambo on it."

There's a rustling at the door, and Mom enters, carrying several grocery bags.

"Ophelia," she says, stumbling over to the counter. "There's several more bags in the back."

I grumble but oblige, heading outside in my stockinged feet. I grab the rest and let the door slam behind me.

"Ooh, meatballs," I hear my mother say. "What's the special occasion?"

"I figured Ophelia's first day at school is celebration enough," says Brendan. I enter right as they kiss, and hide my smile.

Brendan is huge. My mother is decidedly *not*. She's full on Mexican-American – thick black hair, tanned skin and short. She passed on her light-brown eyes to me, though I inherited my height and athleticism from my wayward bio-dad. When my parents kiss, Brendan has to hunch to reach her lips.

I have always found it comical. With my mom barely reaching five foot and Brendan well over six-four, they're quite a pair.

"Okay, okay," I say, "Let's eat. I almost got ran over today and I'm not feeling very in tune with the world right now and just want to eat my spaghetti."

"What?" Mom rounds on me, her eyes widening in surprise. She's still in her blue scrubs, and she rushes up to me. "Are you hurt?"

"Nope," I say. She hugs me like I'm the last lifesaver in the ocean. "It's fine. It was a one-time incident."

It takes some time to convince Mom that yes, I'm unhurt, and yes, I'm not going to run through Crescent Hills again. She finally calms down enough so we can finish eating. I have to reheat my food in the microwave, piling on seconds. As I wait, my phone buzzes on the counter.

I look at the number.

Unknown. (617)-722-0000.

I watch it ring until it stops. It's not from Massachusetts, but something nags me in the back of my brain. I frown.

"Something wrong, Ophelia?" asks Mom.

My phone buzzes with a Missed Call Notification. I watch it to see if a message will pop up. "No," I answer. I take my plate out of the microwave. "Motherfucker!"

"Ophelia!"

"Sorry," I say, waving my hand in the air. My fingers burn. "The plate was hot."

As I join my parents at the table again, I stick my phone in my pocket. It vibrates against my thigh. I sneak a peek.

The Unknown Number has texted me: "Ophelia."

A cold chill spreads through my chest. No way. It has to be that fucking bitch who tried to run me over. I'm almost certain of it.

"Sorry," I say, pulling my phone onto the table. My mother has a strict no-phone policy when we're eating together. I see her eyebrows dip in disapproval, but I'm too busy deleting the text message and blocking the number to care.

Whoever that girl was – and her stupid friend Vivian – I'm not going to let them get to me. Never mind how they got my number or know who I am.

"So, Mom," I say, putting my phone back into my pocket. "Tell me about your day."

As Mom talks about her first full day of work, my mind runs at a million miles an hour. Tomorrow is my first day at WJ Prep, and for some reason, these two rich girls hate me. It wasn't getting off to a great start, but I was sure they would forget me by tomorrow. Don't rich girls have attention spans like goldfish? I'm sure I read that somewhere. Besides, I'm only here to run and get good grades. I don't want to make a stir, and if I stay out of their way, they'll stay out of mine.

My fingers play along the screen of my phone. My unease returns. How did they find my number so quickly? A chilling feeling settles over my skin. Suddenly, I'm not excited to attend school tomorrow.

# CHAPTER TWO

BOOK 1

Weis-Jameson Preparatory Academy is a private Catholic school.

The tuition? It'll replace the cost of a nice new Honda Accord with *all* the nice finishings.

The endowment? In the millions.

It's not surprising that given the cost of attendance is so high, only around five-hundred students 9th-12th grade attend. From what I read on their website, tuition-waiver scholarships are rare.

I've never worn a uniform in my life. A couple days ago, a large box with my name on it appeared on the front door. Inside it was the most uncomfortable apparel I've ever seen. I live and breathe athletic and comfortable. When I opened the box, I was greeted with five sets of pants and skirts, two "spirit" tees, three different types of jackets and cardigans and four uniform polo shirts. Each top had a monogramed WJ logo on it.

They were a surprisingly good fit. Clearly they'd taken my size from the publicity photos at the meets. But still uncomfortable.

I sit in my car in the parking lot – the lady at the front desk instructed me to park in the visitors' lot until I got assigned a space. This morning was hot, and I put on the khaki skirt and blue polo shirt.

I regret choosing something that exposes so much skin. I should have bundled up. The students... They are intimidating at first glance. The ones streaming by my car to enter the cavernous front of WJ Prep somehow look cooler than I do.

I watch them, fingering the hem of my skirt. What makes them different? Is it the stylized bags the girls have draped over their forearm? Is it the one-hundred-dollar hair-cuts the boys are sporting?

It's like I've entered a different universe where everyone is gorgeous and perfect and look cut out from a magazine. At my old school in Oklahoma, the dress-code was whatever you could get away with. Miniskirts, crop tops, see-through leggings, fishnets, baggy pants, wife-beaters, baseball caps – anything went so long as you avoided the stricter teachers in the hall.

I steel my nerves. Okay, so I'm uncomfortable. The tag of my polo itches my neck. My beat-up sneakers are a far cry from those expensive-looking ballet flats that girl is sporting.

But so what. I'm here to run.

I open my car door and step into the throng, making my way to the front office. When they'd offered me the scholarship, I'd done a campus visit. I'm not as in awe this time as I walk through the sparkling glass doors and enter the office.

There's a slew of students hanging around the front desk, so I join a line.

"Ophelia Lopez," I say to the secretary. Her manicured nails type my name into the system.

"Your liaison is Jason," she says, handing me a freshly printed schedule. "He'll take you around to all your classes today."

"Jason?" I echo.

"That's me," comes a masculine voice behind me.

I turn around. Jason is tall, intimidating and *angry*. A flicker of unease builds in my belly. Who spat on his cornflakes? His eyes flick up and down my figure before landing on mine with disgust. He's got a shock of blonde hair that's shorn on the sides, and his face is thin, pinched.

He almost reminds me of Draco Malfoy. I want to see his sneer to confirm.

He snatches my schedule out of my hands. "What's your first class?" He groans, then shoots me a look of contempt. "Fucking Calculus. Way on the opposite side of where my class is."

Jason's bitter attitude sours my expression. "What is your

deal?" I demand, grabbing my schedule back. He takes off, presumably to direct me to the Math wing, and doesn't answer.

"I'm Ophelia," I say to his back.

"I don't care," he growls. Suddenly, he whirls around, his hand finding my chest and shoving me back. I stumble into a girl, who glares at me.

What is wrong with the people at this school?

Jason steps close, but I stand my ground. I can't let these people see that I'm weak. This is obviously some sort of first day harassment.

"Look, New Girl-"

"Ophelia," I remind him.

"Tragic," he sneers flippantly. Boom. Draco Malfoy look-alike contest won. And I don't know if he's referring to the fact that my name is old and out-of-date or of the horrible, tragic fate of my namesake, Ophelia from *Hamlet*. "You'd best start to understand some rules around here."

"What's your policy on bullying?" I quip. "No-tolerance?"

His hand comes up again, but this time I dodge his shove. Fast reflexes thanks to track. But he cooly places it on the locker, leaning and bringing up his other hand to pick at his fingernails. Almost as if planned. *Smooth*, I think.

I glare at him. "Clearly not."

"There's a few things you need to learn," Jason says, ignoring my jab. His haughty look makes me roll my eyes. Where does he get off? "There's a hierarchy here. Older than you will ever understand. And we follow it to the 'T', just like our parents did, just like our grandparents did. And bumfucks like you, rednecks like you…." He leans in, but I jut my chin out. Even though I'm starting to feel ill about the absolute *loathing* in his eyes, I try to channel confidence. "Are at the very bottom."

"I don't care," I say. And part of me doesn't. But when his eyes flash darkly, I wonder if I said the right thing. "If *you* don't like me. I don't know what your fucking problem is, but you better check the attitude."

He barks a laugh, and its cruel edge lodges a sense of suspicion in my chest. "Oh, baby," he says, leaning in close. He smells delicious – a woodsy scent – and it's deceptive. "It's not me you need to worry about not liking you." His voice lowers, almost as if confiding a dark secret. "It's *them*. And if *they* don't like you, then nobody does."

Jason dropped me off at Calculus like it was a court-ordered community service act.

His sinister smile as he said, "Enjoy" made me feel like he wasn't talking to me but the bunch of wide-eyed rich kids I'd just stumbled on. When I walk through the desks to the back, each of them bends their head furiously over their phones. An eerie sixth sense tells me they were texting about *me*.

*Lucky me*, I think sardonically.

"Hey," I say, sitting down in the second to last row. The girl sitting next to me is pretty in a girlish type of way – round face, freckles and big green eyes. "I'm Ophelia."

"Hey," she says softly. She doesn't look at me though. Nor does she introduce herself. She looks at her desk like it's the most interesting desk in the world, that it will soon transform into a shuttle and blast her off into the moon.

*That's* how interested she is in that desk.

Okay, what the fuck. I've been the new kid in school before – before Oklahoma, Mom and I had lived in Kansas. But maybe fourth-graders are different than seniors, because clearly nobody is interested in being my friend.

Jason, those two girls last night... What vipers' nest have I stumbled into?

"What's wrong with this place?" I ask, pulling my backpack out and readying my supplies.

Her hazel-green eyes meet mine for the barest of seconds. "It's just how it is."

"Well, it's weird."

"You have no idea," she says, and she suddenly comes to life, twisting in her seat and motioning me closer. "It's basically hell."

"How so?"

She seems to war within herself, looking up to the class to see if anyone else was paying attention. "You know how this town was founded?"

"No."

"Well, okay." She pulls out a notebook and starts scribbling. In a few seconds, a diagram appears with lines and names.

The teacher walks in, and the girl's eyes glaze over. Something about him sets her off. She starts rapidly firing information so quickly and so quietly that I nearly cut myself in half leaning over the desk to hear her.

"Look, so the town is called Jameson. Basically they're the founders. The Jamesons, you know, back in the 1800s. And then, one of the Jameson sons got together with a bunch of other sons of these families" – she points to the words written: *Weis, Blackwater, Whitworth, Nikelson* – "And they created the Jameson Automobile Corporation. You know, luxury cars. Like, for the ultra-rich. Now, though, only these three"– she points to Blackwater, Whitworth and Jameson– "are still in town. And they've founded this school, and their children think they're God's Gift to Humanity."

"You're tripping."

She rips the piece of paper and hands it to me. *"Don't* get on their bad side."

She's circled many names and called them "The Elites". I almost want to snort – this is absurd! – but the serious look on her face makes me pause. I scan the list.

*Emmett and Bernadette Jameson.*

*Vivian Blackwater.*

*Trey and Vincent Whitworth.*

Understanding lights up inside me. Vivian Blackwater. No wonder she had such an ego complex last night – she's got a fancy little name and a fancy little history. But my bet is on Bernadette being the skinny bitch who almost run me over.

Things start to piece together.

"And where is Jason in all of this?" I ask.

The girl frowns. "Jason?"

"The guy with his stick up his ass."

Her lips wiggle wildly, as if she wants to smile but physically can't. What is up with this girl? She grabs my paper and scribbles some more words on it, just as the teacher starts talking to the class. I hadn't realized the tardy bell had rung.

"Satellite Elites – think of them as wingmen," she says, then turns in her seat and ignores me.

I inspect the paper. More words. More names. My head is spinning. The girl next to me – I still don't know her name – ignores me for the rest of class. I'm uneasy and on edge, and I can barely remember what the teacher has said. When the bell rings, I find Jason lounging outside the door, picking at his fingernails.

"That's a bad habit," I say, because I want to rile him. He's one of those Satellite Elites, and while I don't know what it means, I'm betting it means he's easily riled up.

"Shut your whore mouth," he says, "and follow me."

"Wow, good one," I say sarcastically.

But instead of getting angry, he smiles at me. And his smile is *sinister*, ominously spreading across his face.

Suddenly, understanding knocks me on the head. The weird phone call last night. Obviously these people have money at their disposal. Finding out my name and identity and contact information is probably easy when you have a tech army at your side.

The more I think on this, the more I realize I should probably delete my Facebook and Twitter accounts. I don't use them, but if they can easily find out who I am, then they can probably hack into my accounts. Safety first... But my Instagram account – I can't delete that. Probably should just change my password often.

"You're a good little whore," Jason says, dropping me off at my next class. "You kept quiet the whole way."

I throw him the bird and stalk into my class. Jason is the least of my worries now. I need to think of ways to protect myself.

I bury my head in my hands, and a little chuckle escapes my lips. What was I thinking? This is ridiculous. I was all wound up from that girl talking about a stupid hierarchy. The Elites. I chuckle again. What a fucking pretentious name. It wouldn't even work as a band name.

The morning passes quickly, and by the time it's lunch, I've pushed out all thoughts of The Elites from my mind. This was probably just first-day harassing. Nothing more. And Jason can suck my dick for all I care.

I stop by the girls' bathroom, taking a quick look in the mirror. I tried to style my chocolate brown hair nicely this morning, but the waves are now poofy in reminiscent eighties style. I redo my hair into a bun, applying chapstick and wiping away smudges from my mascara.

There's a piercing scream. "No, no, I'm sorry!"

My feet rush me into the hallway, and I'm met with a confusing scene. The girl from the morning is on the ground, covered in trash. One guy finishes dumping the trash-can over her, and I watch, horrified, and some nameless black sludge drips onto her head.

"I'm sorry, I'm sorry," she blubbers. "I was just trying to help her."

There are three boys. More like men than boys, as each one of them is tall and muscular from what I can tell of their backs. The one who throws the trash-can across the hall, he's the tallest, with dark blonde hair and a cruel glint to his eyes. Another one – a thick-shouldered guy, built like a footballer – grinds some sort of horrible concoction of trash, sludge and food into the girl's thigh with his foot. The girl doesn't do anything, whimpers escaping her mouth as she keeps her eyes closed.

"Please, I was just trying to let her know."

My shock dissipates, and I feel my limbs slowly thaw to life. Rage flows through me like lava, and I nearly sprint to the group, shoving away a guy and standing in front of the girl. I am nearly quivering with fury, and I feel loose, like a cannonball.

"What the fuck do you think you're doing?" I demand, giving them each a hard gaze.

Until. . .

Until I meet *his* eyes.

"*Emmett*-Emmett?" I stutter, looking into his beautiful gray eyes. They're as reckless and dangerous as a tornado storm. "Like Emmett from Arcadia?"

"I'm glad you remember, Ophelia," he says as his eyes rake over my body. Goosebumps pepper my skin as a hot coil of desire reaches low into my stomach. *Fuck.* "You haven't changed one bit."

"Arcadia was a couple months ago," I say, almost lost.

How can *Emmett* be here? My thoughts are beating against my brain, and a firestorm of emotions fight for dominance.

Emmett Jameson was one of these "Elites."

I'd tried to fuck him out of my system, but my hand didn't do the intense *need* that thrummed through my body justice. Each time my fingers ventured down there, his face popped into my mind. And I was left wanting the real thing.

And I hadn't remembered him clearly. He's as every bit as handsome, but his hair is now shorn on the sides and flipped to the right. I can feel my hormones taking over, quickening my blood at just the sight of his lips, wanting to tousle his hair with my fingers, feel him groan against me.

*No, Ophelia.*

There's a small sound behind me, and I look at the girl struggling to stand up. I extend a hand, but she waves it off. I'm kinda glad – her hands look sticky and wet.

"Lily," says Emmett, his eyes never leaving mine. "You're free to go."

I open my mouth, but before I say anything, Emmett glares at me.

"You say one word and you'll end up like her." He whips his head to the sodden, trash-riddled Lily. Her mousey brown hair has a gum wrapper in it. "Come with me."

Okay, so Emmett is a hot fucking jerk.

"What the actual fuck," I say quietly, looking at the two guys who've now circled around me. Emmett pauses about ten feet away. "You're all fucking insane."

One of the guys, the footballer-built guy, cracks his neck. "You clearly don't know what's going on."

"Clearly," I say sarcastically. "I do. You're fucking bullies."

"Ophelia," says Emmett loftily. "You'll *follow* me, or Trey and Vincent will help you."

"I'm not going anywhere," I growl, and when I say this, something glints happily in Emmett's eyes. It is almost as if he was wanting me to deny him. "So fuck off."

Rough hands grab my shoulders, wrists, and suddenly I'm being pulled. My hurt wrist screams with pain. My feet dig into the tile but the two guys are too strong for me. With a yank, I'm jolted forward and only avoid falling on my face thanks to their death grip on my arms.

"Fucking hell, stop!" I scream. Panic bubbles into my chest. I seriously cannot get out of their hold. I struggle, trying to bend my arms this way and that. They're dragging me to a door, and a fresh burst of fear fuels me. I try to trip the one to my left, but he just laughs, grabbing my leg so I'm hopping on one. My skirt bunches against my hips and I'm certain I'm flashing Emmett, who waits inside with a smarmy grin.

"Stop stop stop, what the fuck?" My voice is breathless and panicked. Teeth! Why didn't I think of it before!

As I struggle, I bite down on a forearm. There's a yowl of pain, and suddenly I'm flying, weightless. Pain cracks my skull, and for a moment I'm dazed, feeling my body being dragged. Everything is fuzzy, and the dull click of a lock barely registers.

"Oh fuck," I say, touching my head gingerly. Before I can move, arms scoop under my armpits and haul my limp body up.

My butt lands on papers and pens, but it's nothing compared to the headache I have. "Ow."

Warm hands press down on my thighs. Emmett appears in front of my face.

"Knock it off," he says harshly. "You didn't hit your head that hard."

"Fuck you," I growl through the haze.

I'm unprepared for the hand that grips my hair and yanks. Sharp pain radiates from my skull and I gasp as Emmett's lips touch the shell of my ear.

"We can do that, baby," he murmurs darkly. "You just need to be a good little pet and do as you're told."

"Get off!" I yell, placing my two hands on his chest and shoving. It's enough to get him off me, stepping away. His two cronies watch with beady eyes and salivating mouths. I realize my skirt is up, my blue lace panties being shown off to these creeps. I tug it down, glaring daggers at them.

"Who the *fuck* are you?" I say.

"You know who I am," Emmett says, sitting on a desk in front of me.

"Who are your cronies?" I jerk my thumb to the idiots who dragged me into this room. My body aches from their manhandling.

Emmett whistles softly. "You don't know much about us, do you?"

"I'm Vincent," says the football-looking guy.

"Trey," the blonde guy adds.

"They're fraternal twins," Emmett offers, carefully watching my face. I don't know what he expects from me, but he's disappointed I don't react more. He sighs. "My, my Ophelia. What are we going to do with you?"

"Let me go?" I grind out. I play with my hands like an idiot, struggling to maintain my composure. I can't let them know they've got to me. Bullies thrive off fear. "Like, obviously?"

"Oh, we can't do that." The ominous tone in his words... It's down-right chilling. My heart rate spikes as he slowly stands up. "You've gone too far."

"I don't see how," I say.

"Oh, you don't, do you?" says Vincent, crowding in on my personal space. His legs brush my knees, and it's all I can do to not wither into a ball. "I think you know *exactly* why you're here."

We look at each other. He towers over me, and the sheer *strength* he exudes reminds me of Brendan's. But far, far more menacing. Trey's eyes are black, and they suck me in like a vortex. I have a feeling he hides many secrets behind them.

He seems to be waiting for a response. "Uh." My voice is tight. My tongue is dry, and I tumble around the words. "Lily?"

Vincent and Emmett look at each other. Trey has taken up residence on a desk, looking bored.

"Come on, you guys," he says, "Let's move on with it."

"You don't belong here," Emmett says slowly, as if he's explaining something important to me. "You are a fucking *cunt* who doesn't deserve to lick the bottoms of our shoes. But you're here. And we need to make sure you understand just how things are around here."

His words don't hurt. They fall upon deaf ears, because all I can hear, feel and see is a raging tidal wave of anger.

I fucking hate him. I barely know anyone in this school, and they're trying to make me miserable.

"You interrupted our assertion of power. Lily was under strict orders not to talk to you. And you bust in, upsetting the balance of things. You don't *do* that around here without expecting to pay."

"Pay what, an exorbitant tuition fee?"

"You've got a fucking smart mouth for a charity case," Trey sneers.

"Your school *wanted* me," I snap back. My temper is flaring, and I struggle to rein it back in. "I didn't go seeking you guys out – you did *me*. A lowly, poorer than shit girl from buttfuck nowhere. And *I'm* who your preppy little entitled fucking school wants." I pop off the desk, landing me chest to chest with Emmett. "So remember *that* when you jerk off to the mirror tonight."

I ram my shoulder into his, wanting to run for the door but not wanting to seem scared. I can feel knives being dug into my back, but I'm almost to the door, I've almost made it when-

*WHAM!*

The knob is jerked out of my hand. I feel a body press against mine, locking me against the wood. Emmett's scent floods my nostrils as his hands grip my wrists and pull them above my head. I yelp in pain, but that causes him to grip harder, digging in a way that I know will leave a mark.

"All it takes is one word from me," he whispers in my ear.

His breath tickles. "And you're gone. You'll walk these hallways alone, invisible. Your grades here will tank that precious GPA of yours. Your coach will turn a blind eye to the bruises you wear. The colleges you think you can go to? They'll be warned away. Your life will become *nothing* if you displease me."

"Get off me," I bite out, but he presses against me, securing me tight.

"I can make your life hell, baby," he murmurs, dragging his lips up my neck. His touch makes my skin crawl.

"I won't let you." I try to move again, but it's like he's a boulder. I'm strong, but Emmett makes me feel helpless. "You can go ahead and fucking try."

A dark laugh curls out from his chest. "Oh, I'd love to, baby girl."

I stay silent, closing my eyes. *Just wait it out.* Emmett's face nuzzles next to the sensitive hollow of my ear. A warm breath cascades down my throat, and suddenly his body softens against mine, pressing against me gently, bringing my wrists down, though still clasping them in his hands.

"It seems she likes you," remarks Vincent, and his tone is amused.

"Maybe," Emmett says, and his nose trails along the side of my face.

*Stay still.* I must stay still. I cannot move. Maybe he'll lose interest if I stop responding. Maybe he'll just let me go. I squeeze my eyes and fiercely pray he'll just move on.

I can play dead like a fucking opossum.

I won't give them the satisfaction of a response. I'm done. Even though I feel violated and assaulted, I can still leave with the high ground.

"Let me kiss you again," he demands, and memories of that day flash back to me. Of the hot press of his lips, the warmth of his invading tongue, the press of his chest against mine. "Let me."

I can feel his hard length pressed against me, growing larger and harder. It scares me. How helpless I could be if he decided to... But he doesn't grind into me. Thank god for small miracles.

*Ophelia, sit through it. Document it.* I go into my head, taking stock of the situation, remembering all that has happened up until this point. Then I'll report it.

He reads my tense, still body as a no. I almost want to sag with relief when he lets go of my wrists.

"Do you promise to be a good little pet?" he murmurs in my ear.

I want to lash out at him, claw his eyes out, rake my nails through his skin, yank his dick off. A fresh swell of rage courses through me.

I want to hurt him like I have never hurt someone before.

He waits for an answer. I can feel his breath against my neck. Elevated. Quicker. The longer I wait, the more aroused he becomes. His dick is now full-on hard, and because of our position, it's pressing into my back.

What kind of fucking monster gets off on this?

But I wait, tense, and ready to fight when he tries to pull something. I just want to leave. I almost cry out – *please just let me go*. I'm scared and I'm done with this fucking game.

He bends his face and presses a kiss on my shoulder. I flinch, terror shooting me straight in the chest. What if I was wrong? What if this whole situation turned south? What if he and Trey and Vincent pinned me down and raped me?

"You know, Ophelia," Emmett says into my ear. His voice sounds tired. "You'll be a good little pet." He kisses my ear, and I try to think of anything, anything but the absolute *need* to turn around and punch him. "And I always treat my pets very, very nicely. I give them what their body wants. I *never ever* take."

His next words send a true shock of fear through my spine.

"And soon, pet, you'll be begging for me."

# CHAPTER THREE

## BOOK 1

David Granger must delight in his athletes' pain.

I can't remember the last time I've been so exhausted. Sprint drills push me to the brink. 300 meters at 95% effort. 100 meters at 100%. Rinse and repeat, until I'm dripping with sweat and the lactic acid build-up in my legs is killing me.

David Granger isn't present – he stopped by for a quick hello at the beginning of the session. He reiterated that these pre-season workouts were on our honor. He'd open up the track for us every day after school ended at 3:15 pm and expected us to be done by 5pm. We could only log so many hours.

I'm by far the best in-shape of the girls – even the girls who were nationally ranked last season took a couple months off. I didn't. But, nearing the end of workout, the assistant extends our rest period by a minute, and I find myself greedily sucking in lungfuls of air.

Sweat slicks my skin when the assistant walks away, signaling the end of our group session. The assistant really isn't an assistant but a fellow WJ Prep student, "suggested" by David to hold a timer and stand in the field. A couple of the long jumpers and high jumpers meander to their pits – they'll practice their form.

The track is fabulous. State-of-the-art, actually. Almost as good as Arcadia. And much better than the weather-beaten, warped track at my old high school.

I grab my bag and chuck my spikes into it. I haven't really

gotten to know my teammates yet, but I figure that as we suffer together, we'll bond. It always happens. Pain does that to groups.

I don't dally – I'm hungry and tired, and I want to shower. I head to the parking lot, but my eyes pick out three figures hanging around a car parked next to mine. Anxiety knots my stomach – it's *them*.

I won't talk to them. I want to run to my car, but my legs are too exhausted to even walk. I can barely hold myself upright as I beeline straight to the driver's door. I see Emmett move smoothly out of the corner of my eye.

He slides in front of the door just before I get there. My jaw ticks with irritation. *I just want to go home.*

"What do you want?" I grind out, staring at his chest. I will not give him the satisfaction of my gaze – I don't want him to see the fear in my eyes.

He must've been working out while I was training. He's changed into a tight muscle shirt that strains against his chest, and I can faintly smell his sweat. There's a leftover droplet clinging to his Adam's apple. My fingers itch to wipe it away.

"You're taking a ride with us," he says.

"No, I'm not. Please move."

"Seems like she's not cooperating," comes Trey's voice, winding around the side of my car.

"Ah, I do like the struggles of a woman," Vincent muses, sliding around the other. "So...appetizing."

The two guys stand on either side of me, too close for comfort, but I know I can't outrun them now.

"You're a sick fuck," I tell Vincent.

He smiles. "Aren't we all?"

"So, are you coming?" Emmett asks like I have a choice.

"I'm not getting into a fucking car with you three psychos." If only my phone wasn't in my bag, then I could call the police. But I don't want to alert them. "Never."

He shrugs, and my blood both chills and heats – it's a weird combination. I'm both full of fear and hatred, and I don't know which one will win out.

"Suit yourself."

Vincent and Trey pounce, and my body gives a half-hearted dodge backward. Steel-like hands grip my arms, and for the second time today I feel my feet leave the ground. I hiss in pain and I know I'll have bruises tomorrow.

"What the fuck!? Stop!" I scream as they rough me up to the car. I'm completely useless. "This is fucking kidnapping!"

"Stop screaming," Emmett says almost patronizingly, like scolding a child. He opens the back door. "No one from the track will help you."

His words send tendrils of deep fear into my chest. I'm shoved into the backseat, and my wrist stings from breaking my fall. Fuck, this thing will never heal.

Emmett gets in behind me, and I scramble for the other door, furiously pulling the handle.

"Child-locked," he says.

Of *course* it is, I think grimly to myself.

He moves to the middle, and I squish myself against the soft leather interior. Thoughts torpedo through my mind. What the fuck am I doing here? What do they want with me? I can't get out of the car, which is now backing out and pulling out of the parking lot.

"So, what do you want?" I demand. I'm trying to keep my fear locked tight – I don't know what they can do to me, but in my weakened state I know I can't put up much of a fight. I can't escape them either.

"Oh, nothing," says Vincent, twisting around and giving me a sick grin. "Just a little Jameson hospitality."

I don't want to know what their definition of "hospitality" is.

My track bag is shoved between my legs. My phone is in the side pocket, but it's pointed toward Emmett. *If I could just call 911 without them noticing...*

Emmett is on his phone, seemingly oblivious. I move my fingers to my thigh. No indication he notices. I move them to the zipper, trying to fiddle with it inconspicuously. His eyes flicker over, but when he notices I haven't done anything, he goes back to scrolling through Instagram. I casually try to gather my bag into my chest, but his fingers whip out and wrap around my forearm.

"Drop it," he says, still looking at his phone. A painful squeeze. "Now."

I do several things at once, one singular thought in my mind: 911. I reach over and knock his phone out of his hand. It bounces on the seat next to him. I put my back against his shoulder, and use my body as a shield, rummaging around in the side pocket. My fingers brush the cool glass of my phone before suddenly I can't breathe.

I choke. Emmett's fingers tighten around my neck. Panic stops my heart – I cannot *breathe*. The feeling is all-consuming and terrifying, and I grasp for purchase on his fingers, clawing at them. I need air. His fingers *dig* and I cannot make a sound. The air is muted around us. There's a rushing sound in my head.

Is he going to kill me?

"Phone, baby," he says in a low voice.

I'm seeing spots. My limbs are heavy. Somehow, I manage to pull my phone out and hand it to him.

Blessed air surges into my lungs. My vision returns and tears rush to my eyes. I bend at the waist, chest heaving and burning, and what just happened shoots through me with frigid awareness.

He could have killed me.

I rub my neck, feeling heat rise from the indentations his fingers left. I choke again, then suck in air like a fucking vacuum.

"You okay now?" Emmett's voice is distant, far away. Briefly, I'm aware of a hand on my back, rubbing soothing circles. I wrench myself away, pushing back against the door.

"Are you fucking insane?" I rasp – I sound like a smoker.

He reaches out, gaze fixed on the hot tears rolling down my cheeks. His eyes are a dark gray, but they're filled with a soft emotion. If I didn't know better, I would call it concern. I smack his hand away.

"Don't touch me," I say weakly. My throat is still fucked. "Ever."

Emmett stares at me. His gaze sends a bad taste in my mouth. Then he turns to Trey, who is driving, and says, "This is good enough."

I look outside – I hadn't realized we'd traveled outside of the city. The forests of Massachusetts rose up on both sides of the road. I don't recognize the road at all. I curse myself for not paying attention.

"Out," Emmett says. I look at him like he's crazy. Deliberately, I pull the handle.

"The child lock, genius," I snap at him.

A flicker of anger crosses his handsome features. Then he

scoots to his side, opens the door, and steps out, motioning me to follow.

I grab my bag and exit into the cool evening air. It's quiet. The road is one of those roads that needs some tender loving care, with black tar patches crisscrossing everywhere.

If they try something, I'm sure I could outrun them now. But Vincent and Trey stay seated in the car, and Emmett closes the door behind me.

"So, what now?" I say. I tense, ready to run, ready to fight for my life. I don't know what he's got hidden under his clothes, what his diabolical plan for me entails. But I won't go out easily. "What the *fuck* do you want with me?"

My voice breaks ever so slightly, and he hears it, eyes roving curiously over my face. I grit my teeth – I wish I could incinerate people with lasers. Emmett Jameson would be the first to go.

I wait and see if he moves closer, but instead he rakes a hand through his dark hair, meeting my eyes again. They're impassive, blank. Again, I'm reminded of how fucking handsome he is – his gray eyes are stormy clouds, framed by thick black lashes I would kill for.

I instantly clamp down on a flicker of desire. He's choked me, manhandled me, and hurt me. I don't want to even entertain a *positive* thought about the bastard.

"Not anything right now, Ophelia." Emmett looks into the trees. "When we do want something from you, you'll know. For now, we ask your total and complete subservience."

I don't respond. There's nothing to respond to. His words hammer the final nail into my coffin. I wonder if it is too late to move – surely other schools haven't started yet.

"But it doesn't have to be a bad thing," he says.

I give him a withering look, raising my eyebrows. "You're kidding."

"It can actually be quite okay," he insists.

"In what world is you kidnapping me and bringing me to the middle of the woods 'okay?'" I cut harsh quotation marks in the air. "Or trying to choke me out? Because in my book, that's assault."

"We're just giving you a little insight to what will happen if you don't comply."

"Comply with what?" I snap. I'm tired and irritated, and

this whole situation doesn't make sense. "What the *fuck* am I supposed to comply with?"

He gives me a hard look. It's like he doesn't believe I don't know.

"The whole hierarchy code?" I suggest. It sounds ridiculous when I say it. It's like I've stepped into some sort of weird drama series.

"My family built this town," Emmett says slowly. He's still got that curious look to his eyes. "And there's a certain expectation surrounding that. A certain sort of-"

"Hierarchy?" I suggest, but I can't stop my voice from lilting with humor.

"Respect," he finishes, grey eyes narrowing. "That comes with it."

"Like what?" I challenge. My hands find my hips, and I try to send him a contemptible smirk. "What more respect could you *possibly want* other than me staying out of your way?"

"You can't just escape, Ophelia," he says, and his warning gives me shivers. "You can't just try and avoid this."

"What is *this?* Look, I said I won't bother you. Great. That's what I was doing all along." Lily's face flashes in my mind and I wince. I realize I'd given these guys fodder to mess with me. "And I won't interfere."

"You're not the type to sit by idly."

He's right, but I'm not going to tell him that.

"Please," I say, lowering my voice. Great, I sound like I'm begging, "I just came here to run. That's all I want to do. Run and then leave."

"And that's all you're here for," Emmett says, but his tone seems more like he's trying to convince himself than me.

"I'm just here to run," I reiterate. I want him to get that into his pea-sized brain. "I just want to run."

We eye each other, sizing each other up. I notice he has the faintest of freckles speckling the bridge of his nose. It's cute, in a sort of devilishly innocent way. Like the rabbit from the Holy Grail.

But something in his gaze... It's the smallest speck of confusion.

Why would Emmett be confused?

"Back in Arcadia," I say, and the moment I do, his gaze locks on my mouth like a heat-seeking missile. "What was your brother competing in again?"

And there it is – his smile twists knowingly, and I suddenly understand. A breeze picks up, and suddenly I'm cold all over.

"You have no brother," I whisper, and it's like a knife has cut my sense of safety. My sense of understanding this world. "You were there for me, weren't you?"

He doesn't answer, but he's given me enough proof already: Emmett had been watching me. For *months* now.

"Why?" I ask.

I need to know why. I need to know why he was there, watching me, scouting me.

He finally opens his mouth as he shrugs. "I picked you. The school sent me there."

I don't buy it one fucking bit, but I keep my mouth shut.

"Yo, Emmett," says Trey, sticking his head out the window. "We need to go."

"Bye, Ophelia," he says, stepping into the car. For the first time, I notice that it's fancy. Sleek. And dangerous looking. I don't recognize the logo, and realize with a jolt it must be a car from the Jameson Automobile Co. "Have fun on your walk back."

With the snap of a door and the rev of an engine, the car does a U-turn and heads back into civilization. I feel an urge to stomp out their taillight, flip them the bird – do *something* to them – but I'm completely out of my league.

A chilly breeze hits me right now. The sweat has dried on my body, and goosebumps light up my skin. I shiver.

There's a reason for all of this, I think dully. There's a reason for Emmett showing up at Arcadia, for the scholarship offer. Emmett has some sort of ulterior motive for me. And I don't like it one bit.

And there was a reason they brought me out on this road, I think as I start walking.

Nobody ever fucking drives it.

# CHAPTER FOUR

BOOK 1

I sit in my assigned car spot – the very last spot at the very back of the lot. Yards away from anyone else. Figures. Even though there were plenty of open spaces before me that I could have, they assigned me the last one.

I can't help but think Emmett and the others are behind this. Clearly, it's some sort of status thing.

Last night, I did my research on Jameson, Massachusetts.

What Lily had given me proved accurate.

The Jameson, Blackwater and Whitworth families were the remaining founders, and their kids, Emmett and Bernadette, Vivian, Vincent and Trey went to WJ Prep. The Whitworths had another son still in middle school.

There was no record of a Jameson from Jameson, Massachusetts in the Arcadia track attendance.

Emmett was a lying sack of shit.

But yeah, a Forbes article last week had done an exclusive interview with Thomas Jameson. I promised myself I would read it, but I was so exhausted after coming home that I just went to bed instead.

Mom and Brendan had bought my "going out to dinner with the team after practice" bit. I wanted so badly to tell them everything, but I didn't want them to worry. They have enough on their plates as it is. Though they had been disappointed I hadn't told them about dinner. I tried to bite my tongue, and the hole in my pocket where my phone normally occupied... I knew they were doing shitty things on it. That phone has sensitive information.

I'd done my makeup that morning. An extra application of mascara, a dash of highlighter and a fresh coat of cherry chapstick. There were deep bruises on my arm, starting to turn dark purple, as well as marks on my neck. A hardened part of my heart told me not to cover them up. To bear what they had done to my body loud and proud, to stick it to them that I wasn't afraid of their bully tactics and assault.

So I rushed out the door that morning, my neck red and my throat swollen, to avoid Brendan's offering of cereal and eggs.

I flip down the car mirror and gingerly touch the marks. The ghost of Emmett's fingers are swollen and perfect indentations. The more I look at them, the more they distort and twist, and my mind flashes back to silent suffocation, the primal desire for air, the sinking feeling that I was at his mercy. I hadn't been able to move or make a sound, my breath lodged in my throat, Emmett's fingers stopping it.

Fuck them.

Fuck this place.

Fuck this weird sort of world I've entered.

I want nothing more than to scuttle back to Oklahoma. At least there I have friends, and I have Coach.

But for now, I need to show they haven't gotten to me. Honestly, how hard could it be to get through a school day?

***

Lily looks up when I enter, but then she quickly looks down at her desk. She's cleaned up, and she smells fine. I wonder how many showers it took to get rid of the smell.

I open my mouth to say something, but then close it. Lily got in trouble for talking to me. I look around at my classmates. They're talking to each other, writing things in their notebooks, but they keep glancing back at me.

What little snitches. They probably tattled on Lily yesterday.

So throughout Calculus, I ignore Lily. She does the same. Not even a glance in my direction. It stings a bit – it's not like I'm expecting a thank you, but it seems like we're caught in the crosshairs of the Elites.

When the bell rings, Lily jumps up and nearly sprints away. All heads swivel back to me – even Mr. Brayburn stares. There's a feeling building up inside me – *What!* I want to shout. But instead, I slowly gather my things and exit, refusing to give them the satisfaction of a backward glance.

---

I keep my head high throughout the morning. I get strange looks. Pitying looks. And I hear my name in whispers. I don't see any of the three guys, nor do I see the two girls. I do pass by Jason, though, and he breaks up laughing. My senses are on high alert – something has happened, and I don't know what.

During a bathroom break after third period, two girls fall silent when I enter. The sneers on their faces are mixed with contempt and pity. My cheeks redden– I know they're talking about me.

When I enter the stall, I hear one of them whisper to her friend. "Do you think she knows?"

My pants are halfway down my ass. I pause, hoping they'll say something else. But they titter out into the hallway, leaving me with my heart in my mouth.

*Do I know what?*

They have my phone. Maybe they unlocked it, maybe they discovered how to access my data without it. The sinking feeling grows. I try to think of the things I have stored on my phone, but I'm running a blank.

And then the door opens, and I hear the distinct sound of a *click*. Someone's locked it. My heart races, and I look underneath the stall, but it's just a pair of nice girl loafers.

"Ophelia?" comes Lily's voice. "Ophelia, I know you're in here."

I open my stall door. Lily's hazel-green eyes fall upon my neck, and she winces, giving a small sound of sympathy.

"Do you want makeup to cover it up?" she asks, nodding to my injuries.

I shake my head. Her sudden gesture of affection and sympathy unsettles me. "No. I won't show them I'm afraid."

Her eyes meet mine. "Good," she says. "You're much stronger than I was."

"They did this to you too?" I ask, intrigued. I wonder how Lily got mixed up in all this mess.

She winces. "Not exactly. It's hard to explain, really."

"I'm all ears," I say, walking to the mirrors. The bruises are becoming darker, and I feel a sick sort of satisfaction wearing them. I will not cover them up. Lily joins me, and our eyes find each other in the mirror. "I've literally got nothing else to lose."

Lily winces again, and she bites her lip. "It's complicated."

"Do you want to tell me or not?" I try not to sound irritated, but it comes off harsher than I expected. I sigh. "Sorry, I'm just very... I'm in a weird spot right now."

She nods like she understands, and again, I try and think of what she's gone through. "The Elites don't exactly like my family."

"Okaaaay."

She looks at me. "That's it. The Elites don't like my family." She sighs at my raised eyebrows. "More specifically, my dad. When we first moved here, he rejected an offer to work with the Jameson Co. And the rest was history."

"What do you mean?" I ask slowly. "Because he didn't accept a job offer, they hate him now?"

Lily runs a hand through her hair, frustrated. "I know it sounds weird, but in this town, either you work for the Elites, suck dick for the Elites, or are valuable to them in some other way."

"And if you're not?"

"If you're not and you're poor, fine. If you're success-ful...like my dad, then you're basically Blacklisted."

"Are you going to get another trash-can dumped on you for talking to me?"

Her eyes meet mine, and for the first time I see a flicker of worry. "Perhaps. But I'm hoping not."

"What a fucked up town," I mutter.

"It's going to get a lot worse before it gets better," she says, comforting me with a hand on my shoulder. "But if you make it through, you'll be okay."

"How old were you?"

"It was just freshman year. The Elites train their children well."

"Train?" I bark a laugh. "Like dogs?"

She looks serious, her hazel-green eyes unblinking and steady. "If they want to inherit the shitload of money their parents have, then yeah, they do whatever their parents want."

Jesus. What sort of cult have I stumbled into? Where beauti-ful, frightening and dangerous teenagers walk around, doling out violence and at the mercy of the will of their parents.

Where money is their only love in life, and they don't care who gets crushed under their giant egos so long as they inherit the millions their parents possess.

"What did they do to you?" I ask suddenly.

Lily's face transforms into a blank mask. It was so quick that I almost didn't see it − one moment, she was wearing her emotions on her sleeve, the next she was an impenetrable wall.

"So, do you know?"

I face her. "Do I know what?"

She rummages in her bag and pulls out a gold-cased phone − it's the latest Iphone, I notice. In fact − I scour Lily − she's got the look of a rich kid. While not flashy, her uniform is ironed, her shoes are undoubtedly expensive, and the earrings in her ears... I lean closer... are diamonds.

Lily is rich.

But why is she not with those idiots?

She pulls up an app. "The school... We have an app. Basically, the Elites run it. It sort of serves as a blackmail list − if the Elites have dirt on you and you displease them, this app sends a text to everyone in school." She bites her lip again, and she offers me a pleading expression. "Please, Ophelia, don't get mad-"

"What did they send?" I ask, and the cold, hard truth blankets my body.

She closes her eyes and then hands over her phone. The color leaves my face. I stare at the picture. My hands begin to vibrate. I can't feel, can't think. All I feel is dead.

One of my nudes.

They sent one of my nudes.

I'm laying back across my bed, looking up seductively at the camera which my ex, Mark, is holding. My eyes are hooded and you can tell I've just had sex. Mark's hickey claims my neck, just above my collarbone. My breasts are pushed up in my hands and my bush peeks out from between my crossed legs. I remember this picture − it was the first, and only time, I've taken nude photos.

I want to die.

I want to disappear.

And then I scroll through the chat. Disgusting comments about my body, boys declaring what they'd do to a girl like me, girls slandering my small boobs. The more I scroll, the more I feel heat burn my face.

*Everybody* has seen this intimate moment of mine.

This *thing* has been downloaded fifty-seven times. I feel my breath start to accelerate. Fifty-seven boys are going to jerk off to my picture and distribute it amongst my friends.

I want to cry.

"Ophelia, I am so sorry," Lily says. And she sounds sincere, she really does. But she also just spent an hour in Calculus with me and didn't say *shit*.

"Please leave me alone," I hear myself say. I realize, vaguely, that my voice is weak, breathless.

She looks like she wants to stay, but she nods and leaves. When she does, I hear her whisper, "oh, no".

I take a look in the mirror, but all I see is that fucking seductive, cringey as fuck photo of me. So that's why they took my phone. I close my eyes, rest my hands on the sink. I consider going home. My body sags with the weight of too much shit.

What kind of monsters are these people?

I've done *nothing* to them!

Hot tears prick my eyes, threatening to expose my weakness. I tilt my head up, willing them to go back in, willing myself to not give a shit.

I will not be broken.

I am strong enough to face this. *The sun will rise in the east and set in the west, and I will be okay. I will be okay. I will be okay.*

When I open my eyes, they're red with unshed tears. But it's better than nothing. I straighten my shoulders and smooth out my polo shirt and skirt.

I will fucking *end* The Elites.

The door swings open and a girl says, "*Oh. . .*"

I look at her. She's young, probably a freshman, but my eyes are drawn to the *things* littering the hallway behind her. She looks downcast and she starts to back away.

"Move, please," I say, maneuvering beside her.

It can't possibly be. . .

I look up and down the hallway. Thousands upon *thousands* of my nudes have been printed out and scattered upon the floor. Curiously, I realize that on these photos my face has been blacked out. Why? At the very end of the west wing, I can see a janitor start to sweep them up. My cheeks burn – he probably has a family.

Just then, the bell rings. I want to scream at it – *make them go back inside!* Time slows. My classmates stream out of their classes. Some boys whoop, grabbing pictures left and right. Most of them get trampled. I watch as my dignity and my respect crumble before my very eyes.

Emmett and Vivian appear in the throng. Her red hair is in curls this time, and when he wraps an arm around her tiny shoulders, he twirls one with his finger. His eyes catch mine, and the smile he sends me is positively *vile*.

I school my face into a mask, but inside I can feel my composure shattering. I race back into the bathroom and lock myself in the farthest stall. It takes every reserve of strength to not break down. The commotion of the hallway settles down, and when the tardy bell rings, I inch back out after the last girl leaves the bathroom. I want to make a break for my car. Screw school today. I just want to go home and have a good cry under my blankets and never see anyone ever again. But when I peek out, there are several lingering groups.

I shut it, sweeping the manual lock into place.

*I will not cry. I will not cry. I will not cry.*

There's a jiggle on the handle. A polite knock.

"You can't have the door locked, dearie," says the female on the other side. "It's a fire hazard."

I don't respond. I can hear the woman waiting for my response. But I can't trust my voice or I might start crying.

I open it, and it's a nice little lady. Probably from the front desk.

"You got a hall pass, sweetie?"

My throat is mute. Before I can form a remark, my feet are sweeping past her and I'm speed-walking down the hallway. I keep my eyes to the ground. *Walk. Walk. Walk.*

"Oh my god, did you see her *face?*" comes a high-pitched squeal.

Nope nope nope.

I pivot on my heel and race back to the bathroom. I slide in, almost startling the sweet lady as she exits. Taking refuge in my stall, I pray that I mistook the voice.

"-but like seriously, it was like beet-red *and* totally fucking hilarious," says Vivian.

My soul crashes to the tiled floor. Just my fucking luck.

I can't hold my tears back any longer. Unbidden and vicious, they pour down my cheeks. My face's screwed up, and I try to hold back my sobs.

"Good, she's like, super ugly." Bernadette has a distinctly

higher voice, more nasally. "And such a slut. Like, seriously, what fucking blowjob lips."

There's some ruffling around, and then Vivian takes the stall next to me. They continue talking. My feet are pulled up onto the toilet seat, and I hug my knees. I feel small, contained. Trapped. Tears continue to well and fall, and I wish I could make them stop.

"And like, did you see her try and make her boobs bigger? Like pushing them up would make *any* guy fall for that trick?"

"Right? They're like fucking tiny grapes."

"And, like, also, her bush. Like, a bush is so gross. It smells, it's nasty. No respectable guy would ever want to bury his face into that bear of a pussy."

"I bet she smells horrible."

"Ugh, totally, right. She runs all the time so it must reek."

"Do you think she went home?"

"Probably." There's a smack of lips popping. I imagine them doing their makeup in the mirror, but I'm too terrified to move. "I hope she's embarassed and ashamed as fuck."

"She looked pretty mortified," Vivian chuckles, flushing the toilet. She doesn't wash her hands. "Like, completely horrified."

"Good." There's some more ruffling, a spray of liquid, and the scent of coconut and vanilla fills the air. "Maybe now she'll be a good little pet and stop fucking this up."

*Pet.* There is that word again. It has such sinister connotations, and I shudder to think of what the word means to them.

"Emmett says she has no clue," Vivian says. At the mention of Emmett's name, my heart stutters a bit.

"Emmett's got his dick in a twist," Bernadette says. Almost flippantly, like she's mentioning some sort of mild affliction. *Oh, he's just got a cold.* "My brother can't be trusted with her. She's gotten under his skin already."

"She's such a fucking bitch!" Vivian's tone becomes enraged, and I wince. Clearly, I'm some sort of threat to her. Well, she can fucking have Emmett – they're made for each other. "I hate her."

Right back at you, Vivian. Less than seventy-two hours and you really can learn to hate someone.

"Calm down, he'll be right back in your lap when this whole thing is over," Bernadette soothes. "He won't lose sight just because she's a talking pussy with legs."

"But you just said–"

"Look, I know my brother. Once he fucks her, he'll toss her aside." She pauses, and then adds in a thoughtful tone: "Actually, it'd probably be good to just mess with her that way. Toy with her feelings, you know?"

"I don't want that bitch near him," Vivian snaps. "She'll probably give him a disease."

"Ooh, that's good for the next rumor," Bernadette says, almost like she's excited. "What should she have, like herpes?"

"Genital herpes." The snideness in Vivian's tone makes me sick to my stomach. "Like, that's a permanent one, right?"

"Yes, Viv." Her tone is exasperated. "It's fucking gross. Here, look at this picture."

A pause. "Oh fuck, gross!"

"Yeah." Bernadette moves a couple things around on the counter, almost like she's arranging her makeup. "Like, total fucking gross. Some of them even ooze I bet."

"Ugh, fuck, that gives me such anxiety!"

"Yeah, so let's go tell the boys we've got the next rumor down pat. I'm tired of Emmett just controlling all of this."

My ears perk up. Emmett was the one in charge? I cast my thoughts back... Now that Bernadette mentions it, it did seem like he was the one who was directing Trey and Vincent. I bet he was the one who found my nudes and decided to leak them.

Resentment and anger coil in my chest. I want to burst out of the stall and drag them around by the hair, but something stops me. Whispers that maybe, instead of rushing into things, I should instead observe.

Clearly, this is their version of some fun game. Fuck with the new girl, destroy her reputation and self-esteem – it's all fun and games and cocktails and something to do in their free time. Almost like a hobby – *Let's crush Ophelia, how can we ruin her today!?*

I have never, in my entire life, been so mortified and humiliated before.

But I cannot let them get to me.

If they get to me, they win. They've shown who is better, who controls who. They've shown me my place, which is exactly what they want. Emmett's soft words whisper in my ear: *your total and complete subservience.*

Suddenly, Bernadette's phone rings. It's some gawdy classical music song, and I cringe as she answers it with a chipper, "Hello, Daddy!"

My tears have dried. Listening to Bernadette and Vivian

slash me apart is enough to show me that clearly these girls have no shred of empathy or kind emotion in their bones. They shit on compassion and tear apart kindness – all in a day's work for two rich shitheads.

"Oh yes, Daddy, it's all going very well," Bernadette simpers, her voice like poisoned honey. "We're all just having a blast." A pause. "Oh, he isn't? Well I'll tell him then! Bye, Daddy!"

"Bye, Mr. Jameson," Vivian chimes in.

Mr. Thomas Jameson, their father. I cringe to think of ever responding to Brendan like that. He would laugh his ass off at the fake, honey-dripped sweetness and demand I speak to him like a normal human. Not to mention calling him *Daddy*. I shudder – what gross perverted relationship they must have.

Either that, or Bernadette is *actually* the living embodiment and stereotype of a rich Daddy's Little Girl.

She probably is. Her shoes, which I can see from under the stall door, are that sort of causal rich. The ones you *know* cost thousands of dollars.

She probably gets an allowance larger than Mom and Brendan's mortgage. She probably spends the kind of money someone earns in a *year* in a week. Her "Daddy" probably bought her that red Lamborghini for her sixteenth birthday. She's probably never had macaroni and cheese with cut-up hotdogs in them.

The sound of Vivian and Bernadette fade away – the door opens and closes, and I'm left in silence. Alone. Finally. But I don't feel like crying any more. I don't feel like hiding.

Suddenly, I'm bitter. I feel the bitterness and anger eat away at my humiliation, hardening my skin. People like me are just ants for her to squish. For her to hold a magnifying glass and say "oh, how cute" as she burns us to death.

A cold, dead sort of anger hardens my heart. I will not be intimidated. I will not back down. And I certainly won't let them show that they've cracked me. So what, the whole school has seen me naked? So what, they think I'm a slut?

I'm *not* going to bow down.

I grit my teeth and wipe the sticky tracks of mascara from under my eyes.

I'm going to fight back.

# CHAPTER FIVE

## BOOK 1

"Hey, little whore," a slimy voice whispers too close to my ear, and I feel the heavy presence of a boy beside me. My elbow connects with the soft tissue of his stomach, and he gasps.

I step aside, slamming my locker and watch the sophomore clutch his stomach. He groans. He's on the larger side, with a gut spilling over his khakis. He wears glasses, and when he recovers, he squints his beady little eyes at me through dorky rims.

"You were saying?" I prompt sweetly.

His eyes zero in on my boobs, and the disgusting lust in them almost makes me gag.

"I'll pay you twenty bucks to let me fondle them," he salivates.

"My rate is too expensive for you, sweetie," I grind out. "You couldn't even afford me."

With a twist of my heel, I walk away. It's lunch period, and many students are gathering in the cafeteria. That's where the Elites will be. I know if I show up, relatively unfazed, I'll have one notch up on them. They may think it's humiliating to walk in front of my peers, but if I do it with enough of a *fuck you* attitude, perhaps it'll come off differently.

At least I hope.

The cafeteria at WJ Prep is ridiculous. There are several buffet options available and one grill station that produces hamburgers, hot dogs and even fucking steaks on demand. The meals are all inclusive in the tuition fee – when I looked over their menu, I noticed they even have a sushi chef come in twice a month, and their in-house pastry chef provides at least five different desserts. They boast vegan, gluten-free, lactose-free and sugar-free options for the girls who like to calorie count or who've adopted a serious allergen diet as a "lifestyle choice".

There's a minor disturbance when I walk in, but the cafeteria quickly resumes normal activity as I walk around and select my food. I'm starving, unsurprisingly. I need to eat a minimum requirement of calories in order to maintain my figure, and I've forgone breakfast because I didn't want Brendan to see the marks.

*Okay,* I think as nobody is throwing things at me. *This is fine.*

The Elites occupy the center table. I can see them laughing and enjoying themselves. Their artfully styled hair, perfect teeth, immaculate uniforms – it's like they were born to be the center of attention. Either that or made to be. My mind casts back to Lily's comment – *trained.* Trained probably since birth to be in the spotlight, to gather attention effortlessly and to find ways to keep the spotlight on them at all costs.

I select mashed potatoes, green beans and two salmon fillets, grab two cookies and wade through the sea of tables to get to theirs. They see me coming, and Bernadette and I make eye contact. But it's like she sees through me – I'm beneath her, I realize, to even acknowledge. Suddenly, Vivian stands up and slides around to where Emmett sits, curling her body around his.

"Hey, baby," she says into his ear. Her eyes meet mine in show of dominance.

It's laughable, how she thinks I want him. I smile sweetly at her – he's all hers.

Yet, some part of me notices that Emmett, while he still lets her cling to him, doesn't react in any way. He's deep in conversation with Vincent when I arrive.

"Is this seat taken?" I ask, pointing to the empty one next to Bernadette.

Her eyes find the seat, then flick up to mine. She cocks her head. "Obviously."

"Well, I can't stay," I say, " So I'll get right to it. Where's my fucking phone?"

"Don't have it," Trey says, shrugging nonchalantly. He's

seated next to Bernadette, who is rolling her eyes. "Don't know where it is."

"Unlawful possession of pornography of a minor, tsk, tsk," I say sweetly, loudly, placing my tray at the edge of their table. "What will the authorities say?"

Trey laughs. "Oh, you think we'd be as stupid as to download your nudes onto our phones?"

"What are you, stupid *and* a whore?" Bernadette sniggers.

Trey holds a french fry between his fingers, twirling it like a pencil. "We didn't upload the photos from *our phones*. You did."

"I did no such thing."

"Try proving that," Bernadette says haughtily. "It's all from *your* phone."

I want to punch her. They made it look like I committed social suicide. Though we all know who was responsible, there's no way to prove that I didn't upload the photo myself. Or printed the hundreds of thousands of printouts.

"What you guys are doing is harassment," I point out. I jerk my fingers to my neck, and then pull up my sleeves, exposing the angry bruises. "And you think that they don't have camera footage of you dragging me into a room against my will?"

Trey's smile is almost pitying. "And who's going to go look at it?"

"The police."

I was hoping that the mention of the police would cause them to pause. But Bernadette's pealing laughter upsets me. Clearly, I had said the wrong thing.

"You think you can go to the police?" Trey says in between barks of laughter. His face turns red from the effort. "Oh my god, that's rich."

"We basically own the police, honey," Bernadette says with an irritating, condescending smile. "So that's cute."

"I love self-admitted extortion rings," I mutter to myself. But for some reason, I believe her. I'm starting to realize there's much more influence behind their names.

"Now you're learning," Trey says with a wink.

"Where's my phone?" I snap, voice rising.

Emmett, as if he's just noticed my presence, procurs my phone from his pocket. He dangles it in front of him, his long fingers playing with it. Vivian watches it like it's some sort of magic trick.

"Ooh," she says, "Look, it's her phone."

I almost expect her to start clapping.

"Give it back to me."

Emmett's cool gray eyes follow my outstretched hand up to my boobs. Heat rises in me – he knows what they look like, thanks to that fucking photo. When he finally finds my eyes, I feel violated.

"My," he says with disapproval, "were you raised in a crack-house back in Oklahoma? Where are your manners?"

"Where are yours?" I fire back. I extend my hand again. "Phone, please."

"Not even a full sentence?" Vivian laughs. "Did your crack-whore mama teach you that?"

She's trying to bait me, and just a couple hours ago it would've worked. But this is a new Ophelia. They might try to go for my Mom, but I know she would want me to take care of myself first.

"'Your Mom' jabs? Wow, what are we in, sixth grade?" I laugh, and I think I nailed the whole patronizing tone of it because Vivian scowls fiercely. Emmett, on the other hand, gives a small twist of his lips. Almost like approval. "I didn't realize that's the level we're playing at."

"You're sassy today," Emmett remarks.

"Having a very private photo of me leaked to the entire school will do that to you." I flash him a blinding smile, and I wonder if he can see the cracks in my facade. "But no harm no foul. Give me my phone please."

"Emmett, don't give it to her," Vivian snaps.

It dawns on me that they are under no obligation to give my phone back. They don't care – phones are like rocks to them: they probably have the latest models. They don't play by normal rules, but they might recognize that they can use it as a weapon against me.

I certainly don't have anything as humiliating and degrading as more nude photos.

But I'm sure they could find a way to twist the information on my phone to their advantage.

"Beg him for it," Vincent says. It's the first time he's spoken, but the sinister expression on my face causes my stomach to drop. "Beg him for it like a good pet."

The moment the words are out of his mouth, my heart pauses. Like a dog. They want me to beg him like a fucking dog.

"I'm not opposed to the idea," Emmett muses, and his eyes rove over my body.

"She'll look good on her knees," Bernadette intervenes, smirking at my open mouth. "I'm sure she's used to it."

Heat colors my cheeks. She can't be serious.

"I'm not getting on my knees," I say, and I look at Emmett. His handsome face tilts to the side, almost as if studying me and he finds my reaction curious. For once, I just want a speck of decency to shine through him. For once, I want him to do the right thing. "Emmett, please just give me my phone back."

He licks his lips, and the heat in his eyes warms me in all the wrong places. "On your knees, Ophelia."

"I'd rather die," I say ruthlessly. And it's true. I would rather die than show them that they have one iota of power over me. I will not bow to them. I scoop up my tray and give them a sour smile, and their expressions are hard to decipher. "See you around."

I walk away from them.

"Let me handle this," I hear Emmett say, and I increase my pace. He's following me.

My fingers grip my tray – should I whip around and hit him with it? But I'm hungry, I want to eat. I want to be left alone. My feet carry me toward the exit, and I can feel hundreds of eyes on my back, at the girl that Emmett is following to teach a lesson.

I'm just about at the double doors when a hand grips my elbow. I'm yanked back, my food flying, and suddenly my back is pushed against the milk dispenser. The cold of the metal is nothing compared to the absolute ice in his gray eyes.

I gasp at the sudden change. Emmett looks *murderous*. His jaw is clenched, sharpening the hollows of his cheeks, and his nostrils flare. His expression accentuates just how handsome he is, and I'm at the brunt end of his fury.

"Kiss me," he whispers harshly, just centimeters above my mouth. His breath is hot and smells like the hamburger he was eating. "Kiss me and you can have it back."

"What?" I gasp at the sudden warmth and pressure of his body against mine. He leans closer, and amidst the fury I can see it.

How much he wants me.

It burns within him, is eating him from the inside out.

Emmett Jameson wants me. And he's angry.

And I don't know anymore. Is his anger from my defiance? From my refusal to bow, from my refusal to let him intimidate me? Or is he angry at how he wants me? The fire in his eyes, the parted kissable lips – he wants me. I search his face, dumbfounded, wanting to know.

"What if I begged you," he murmurs, softer this time. "I just want another taste."

His words are for me and me alone, though our audience is the entire cafeteria. They don't know what he is saying to me, or know what he wants – they think he is putting me in my place.

"You know you want to," he teases, and his tongue darts up to wet his bottom lip. "You feel this too. You want this too."

I'm drawn to the movement, and my pulse quickens, desire pooling in my stomach. I hate how he makes me feel – both wanton and helpless, both filled with desire and repulsed by him. He's handsome and he scares me. He's done nothing but make me miserable.

And yet, I'd fuck him in a heartbeat if I had no control.

I want to pull him down to me and forget how angry he has made me feel.

"In your dreams," I finally rasp, and his eyebrow quirks at my quivering voice. "I will *never* kiss you."

His fingers come up and when I don't flinch, he presses his palm along the side of my face. His touch is tender, though I know inside hides a cruel monster.

"You will," he says with certainty. Again, the tip of his tongue wets his lip. The action sends a thrilling response to my core. "You want this just as much as I do."

His hand comes to my stomach, and I frown. A hard rectangular object is between us. My fingers come up and grasp my phone. As I take it from him, his thumb presses into my bottom lip. A dizzying rush of desire clouds my thoughts – *I want more.*

"Remember who this is from," he says, before breaking the spell by stepping away.

I don't want to remember. I'm tingling and dizzy and my core is throbbing. Emmett knows how much his presence affects me. As he gives me a wink before loping away, I realize that Emmett will always remind me.

I do want him. And I shouldn't. It's all sorts of wrong. There's nothing normal about this situation. There's nothing normal about Emmett Jameson.

That one sophomore kid is back at my locker. I almost groan with frustration, but I bite my tongue and walk up to him. I need my books for next period.

"Hey, little whore," he says, eyes glued to my boobs.

"Get lost, perv." I'm not in the mood to deal with him. He and hundreds of other horny male teenagers have seen my boobs, and I don't want word to go around that I can be harassed.

That role, it seems, is exclusively for The Elites.

And I will not tolerate this shit from anyone else..

"I thought you'd say that," he says, and I notice he has a slight speech impediment. There's Cheetos dust on his fingers and around the collar of his polo. Gross. "So I propose a proposition. I mean, we all saw what just happened in the cafeteria."

"I said get lost. Or are you just braindead?"

His hand reaches out, and in a flash I've got my elbow on his neck and his back up against the locker. My movement surprises me. His fleshy neck bends under my pressure, and his eyes bulge.

"What the *fuck* do you want, you twisted fuck?"

It actually feels good to take back some control.

"Let him go," comes Vincent's voice from over my shoulder. I freeze. "You hear what I said or are you just braindead?"

My words come spitting back out to me, but this time they drip with malice and promise. Vincent will hurt me if I don't do as he asks.

I drop my elbow and step away, but Vincent grabs me. My wrists are behind my back before I know it.

"Let me go," I growl, trying to struggle out of his hold. "Ouch, fuck."

"Shut up," Vincent says, and I stop, chest heaving and my wrist reminding me that it's still fucked up. "Go on, Nico, what was your proposition?"

The kid suddenly looks greedy, and he's looking at my chest like I'm the last cheeto in the world. "Boobs, under the bra, thirty dollars."

"Nah, I think he can touch them for free," Vincent whispers in my ear like we're conspiratory partners. "What do you think, Ophelia?"

"Over my dead fucking body," I snap.

I struggle violently, putting all my weight and strength into freeing myself. One of my wrists gets free, and I twist around. I will fight until my very last breath. I must have surprised Vincent though, because his dull eyes are widened. My foot comes up, connecting with his crotch, and he hisses in pain. He lets go of my other wrist, and I take off running down the hallway.

My feet slap the tile as I pick up speed – I race past doors and lockers and dodge other people. When I look back, Vincent is nowhere to be seen. My breaths are sharp and frantic – Vincent was going to help that kid assault me.

What a sick fuck.

---

The rest of the day, I'm propositioned by at least two other weird kids. I brush them off, but I don't touch them. In the hallways, Vincent passes by and wiggles his eyebrows at me. He thinks this is hilarious. I'm just some sort of object he can toy with.

I desperately want the day to be done already.

I just want to go home and sleep.

In seventh period, I debate whether to go to practice or not. It's what's expected of me. It's what Coach Granger wants. But my body is bruised and tired and achy. I'm mentally strung out, from being on high alert each moment, waiting for the next thing the Elites throw at me. The teachers are looking at me different – that is to say, they won't meet my eyes.

I'm betting the teachers are under the Elites' thumb just like the police. Figures why I haven't been called into the principal's office to talk about the blatant nudity and minor pornography littering the hallway. The trash-cans are full of the pictures – I see them everywhere I walk.

Screw practice. I need a nap.

There's a small form waiting for me at my car after school. I almost turn around and call a cab before I recognize Lily.

She has a hood over her head, and when she sees me, her eyes light up.

"Come on," she says, nodding impatiently to my vehicle. "Get in."

"Lily, I can't talk," I say, and my voice cracks with strain. "I'm exhausted."

"I-I-I know," she says. She looks at her loafers. "I just wanted to say that I'm sorry. And that I can't imagine how rough it's been. And that I'm glad you're staying strong."

Her kind words touch me, and unshed tears burn my eyes. I want so desperately for things to stop, for everyone to just leave me alone. Lily doesn't understand just how much her words mean to me.

A tear spills over and slips down my cheek. I hastily wipe it away.

"Thanks, Lily," I say, struggling to keep my composure. For some reason, just knowing that Lily is rooting for me makes me inconsolable. "I just want to go home and nap. Besides, for whatever reason, you're still talking to me and I don't want you to get dragged into this again."

She nods, like that makes sense. "I was going to offer to let me cover that up for you. You know, since I'm sure your parents don't know."

It's a cruel sort of world when Lily looks at me like she knows. They've done this to her too, long ago. I nod feebly, and we clamber into my car. She pulls out some heavy concealer. The color is lighter than my skin tone, but it'll have to do.

I close my eyes as Lily gingerly covers up my mark. Her touch is kind and gentle, and again I feel the onslaught of emotion nearly overcome me. I've been nothing but trouble for her, but she's still willing to help me when she can.

"There," she says after a couple minutes. "All done."

I flip down the mirror. It looks as good as it can get. "Great job, Lily."

"Thanks, I just figured you would need it."

Her small act of kindness means more to me than she'll ever know. I swallow the lump in my throat and just nod wordlessly. We stare out the windshield silently for a couple seconds before Lily shifts uncomfortably.

"What did Emmett tell you at lunch today?" she asks.

I look at her sharply. "He's just trying to bully me."

"Oh," she says.

I realize that I'm being unduly harsh, and I try to soften my words. It's not her fault I'm hurt and angry and sad. "I'm just tired, Lily. I'm sorry."

"It's fine. I should probably get going here pretty soon, but do you mind if I wait until we see The Elites leave?"

I nod. "If you want, you can get into the back – it'll be harder for them to see you there."

After a minute of shuffling and scooching around, Lily is settled into the back seat. I touch the freshly applied makeup with my fingers. "Thanks again, Lily."

She nods curtly. "No problem."

"Oh, there they are," I say, twisting over the back of my seat to see out the back window. Lily and I watch the Elites mosey out of the school. Emmett's arm is slung over Vivian's shoulder, and Bernadette is nestled into...

"Are Trey and Bernadette a thing?" I ask, watching him jostle her against his side as she laughs, tilting her head.

Lily's nose crinkles. "Sort of. They've had an on-and-off thing for a while."

It's just one huge Elite Orgy. Maybe they're all inbred. But they're all ridiculously gorgeous, so probably not.

We watch as Emmett's black car and Bernadette's red Lamborghini speed out into the main road. Vivian, it turns out, drives another one of those black cars with the Jameson logo on it. A flickering steam of jealousy heats my face. She probably got gifted one of those cars. Maybe for fucking Emmett. The Whitworth twins drive away in a sleek sports car – yellow and indistinguishable from this far away.

"Okay," Lily says, opening the car door. "Thanks for letting me hide out."

"It was the least I could do," I say, and when I reflect on what those words mean, I wish that I wasn't so sincere. What kind of world do we live in where she needs to thank me for hiding out in my car? "Honestly."

---

When I arrive home, it's silent. Mom won't be back until 8:30, and I take Brendan's absence as a sign that he's occupied with an interview. I hope he gets it.

Exhausted, I slip into a pair of comfortable panties and an old track meet shirt. I turn off the lights and flip over onto my back. My room is still bare, and the only things out of their boxes are my clothes and sheets. The rest of my nicknacks – photos, memorabilia, posters and track medals – are still packed away. I know I should at least hang my golden and purple tapestry I found at the flea market back in one of the cities I had a meet in. But the effort seems trivial.

What's the point in trying to make my room feel homey when clearly nobody wants me in this town?

For the first time, I take a look at my phone. It's fully charged — they must've plugged it in for me. The thought of them going through the effort of keeping my phone charged strikes me as odd. Why would they care if it died?

I put in my password and the home screen is just how I left it. I view my recent google history — nothing. But since my phone is linked to my computer, they clearly saw my efforts to research them last night. Of all things, the idea makes my cheeks heat with the barest hint of shame.

Emmett Jameson had added himself as a contact. He even had the audacity to put a little heart at the end of his info.

Suddenly, I receive a text from Emmett. My phone dings just a second too late, and my heart leaps. The good thing about this phone is that I can read the messages from the notification alert.

**Check your notes, pet ;)**

Like a zombie, I go to my note sections. There's only one note there — I don't make a habit of leaving notes in my phone. It was created yesterday at 1:12 am. The title is: To Ophelia, From Emmett.

*You're going to give in, pet.*

*You want me to fuck you. I can see it in your eyes. I can feel it in your body every time I touch you. You shiver when I come close, and you can't stop staring at my lips.*

*I'm going to bury my cock in your sweet pussy. I'm going to pound in you until you come, screaming my name. You're going to want me to do it. You're going to beg me. And I'm going to enjoy it so much. I'll eat you out like you've never been eaten out before.*

*Arcadia was just a taste. I want more of you. All of you. Writhing and screaming beneath me, milking my cock because I feel so good inside you.*

*You want more of me. I know it. We both do.*

*I'll see you tomorrow, pet. ;)*

My breaths come in quick pants. There's a liquid lava heating my core, and I feel like I can't think straight. Emmett's face flashes in my mind, and a strike of desire lights me on fire as I think of his tongue wetting his lip.

No no no no no.

This cannot be.

I cannot let this happen.

I quickly – even though I want to read it again, even though I want to memorize the words, even though I want to feel how hot and bothered they make me – delete his note. But the damage is done. Just thinking of us together is sending me off the rails. Just knowing that he also feels the same way makes me want to think that it's okay.

But it's not okay.

This is ridiculous. I cannot be having these thoughts and feelings about him. He's perverted and disgusting and hurtful and cruel and everything I don't want in a partner.

He'll do nothing but use me and abuse me.

I need to seriously get Emmett Jameson out of my head.

# CHAPTER SIX

## BOOK 1

They're planning something.

I just don't know what yet.

The rest of the week passes by uneventfully. I eat my lunch in my car. Whenever I passed by one of The Elites, they didn't look at me. Whispers followed wherever I went, but it seemed the horny fuckfaces had backed off on the propositions. I gave the sophmore the middle finger a couple times, but he didn't react.

My teachers, it seems, are oblivious. Either that or too scared to do anything. To them, the first two days of school were completely normal. Absolutely nothing happened.

Coach Granger doesn't say anything when he sees the faint marks around my neck. Instead, he runs me into the ground every day. Or, the assistant does. But I know he watched me kick ass. When he left after the start of practice, I watched him go and sit in his car. It was strategically placed on the Visitor's parking lot, an elevated lot right behind the main office. He stayed there for the entire practice, every practice, and I couldn't help but smile.

Sometimes, coaches are as obsessed with the sport as the athletes.

Practice is going generally well. I'm performing at top-notch, and my body feels strong and capable. But school still nettles me.

But what bothers me is the absolute absence of anything.

No acknowledgement. No side glances. No pointed glares. No shoving. No sexual touching. No nothing.

The Elites are ignoring me. Hard. And I can't help but think this is part of their diabolical plan. Their "ruin Ophelia for life as no one clearly gives a fuck" plan.

They don't seem like the kind of people to just back off. No. There is a reason behind everything they do.

The last bell on Friday rings. I'm free.

"There's a party at the Whitworth Mansion tomorrow night," comes a small voice. "They'll be distracted."

I know it's Lily, but she's trailing behind me. Her voice is lost amongst the hundreds of others excited about finishing the first week of school.

"And?" I say, staring straight ahead.

I feel like I'm in a movie. Lily shadows me close, but not close enough to be suspicious, and the hairs on the back of my neck rise.

"They'll be there. We should hang out somewhere else."

"Ah," I say.

I still don't understand Lily. She's taken a trash-can over the head for talking to me. Yet she still keeps coming back.

My curiosity burns. I want to know more about her.

"Come on," I say, scanning the hall for The Elites. "Let's go to the bathroom."

We slip into the nearest bathroom, and Lily takes off her hood. Her mousy brown hair goes to her mid-back, and as she shakes it out I laugh. She then goes to check under the stalls, then marches right back to the door and latches it.

"You had your hood on?" I can't help but chuckle.

Her eyes narrow at me, daring me to deny the obvious. "Clearly – it's just easier to keep under their radar."

I search her face. She's dead serious. "You're serious."

"More serious than a heart attack," she says, watching the remnants of my smile fade. "You still think this is a joke." Her voice turns dark, her eyes hard. "The Elites don't fuck around. They are ruthless and they are cruel, and they *will* hurt me and you if they see us together again."

"So why are you still talking to me?" I ask. "I don't understand."

"That's what we should talk about," Lily insists, extending her hand. "Give me your phone number and we'll meet up this weekend, away from all of this."

She heads to my messages, then pauses. Her eyebrows shoot up. "He got your phone number?"

Emmett had been the last one to text me, aside from Mom and Brendan. I run an anxious hand through my long dark hair, trying to push the note out of my mind. "Yeah."

Before I can say anything, she clicks on it. "Check your notes, pet," she repeats, then looks at me, expecting an answer.

"I deleted the note." Is it warm in here? I feel hot.

"But not his contact information or his text?"

I rub a hand down my face. "What would be the point? I'm sure if I block him he'll just find another way around it."

"True." She nods. "True, yeah."

She quickly types out a message with her contact info, then sends it. A few moments later, her phone buzzes in her pocket. It's one of those high-pitched dog sounding buzzes that teachers apparently can't hear.

"Why?" I ask, nodding pointedly.

Lily's eyes meet mine. "You'll soon understand that if The Elites don't like you, neither do the teachers. And I've had enough stupid fucking detentions for texting in class."

"Ah," I say.

"Anyway," she says, adding my contact information. "Do you have a fake?"

Her question throws me off. "A fake ID?"

"Yeah," she says, waving her hand in the air. "A fake ID. You know, a driver's license that says you're of age to drink."

"No need to sound patronizing, jeez," I tease her, but then turn serious. "No, I don't."

"Oh." Her frown is momentary. I wonder what sort of activities Lily gets up to in her spare time. Something tells me she isn't having tea parties to drown out the stress. "That's fine. We'll just go to a place I know."

"What do you mean?" I ask.

She looks at me, and her hazel-green eyes are insistent, almost like she wants me to understand. Her demeanor changes, and she's stiff. Her hand comes up and rests on my shoulder, though it feels weird since I'm several inches taller.

"There's only a few places in town that you can still go to where The Elites don't have eyes," she says slowly. "And I can't bring you to my place, and I'm sure you want to keep where you live quiet. At least until they figure it out. They probably have figured out where you live, now that I think about it." She shakes her head, refocuses. "Never mind. My point is, you need to be careful of where you go. And we need to be careful of where we meet. The Elites like to keep tabs on the people they hate."

"You're kidding," I say, a bone-chilling coldness settling deep into my body. I thought I'd left them every day once I was off school grounds.

Of course not.

The Elites are everywhere. They are like fucking God, and they sure play the part.

"Unfortunately, I'm not," Lily says, watching the information take hold, her hand squeezing my shoulder sympathetically. "You'll need to leave your phone at home. They've probably installed a tracking device on it."

---

The place Lily gives me directions to is a renovated warehouse. As the sun goes down, I drive through the shadily lit streets until I land on number 127.

It looks decent enough. Light streams out of the bottom floor windows, and a couple people mill about the uncut grass and weeds out front. Cars are parked haphazardly on the gravel lot, so I pick one far away.

The sign across the open double doors says: *The Rooster Cafe.* Below it is a sign: "Jameson's Number One Growler Fill Station and Family Restaurant."

I step in to see the place is literally split in two, a low half-wall extending through the back, zigzagging here and there. From the ceiling, heavy curtains of beads fall, reflecting the disco lights and pulsing purple lasers. It stops halfway at a railed balcony with even more seating.

It's a weird concoction of family restaurant and club, but with the dim lights and low-playing EDM, it somehow works. It's heavily packed when I go inside, but to my surprise, I find children lurking about the stools, cuddled up against their parents. Their parents are young – clearly this speaks to a certain crowd.

I find Lily to the left, nestled into a deep booth, picking at a plate of fries. She's dressed in a nice t-shirt but nothing fancy. I slide in across from her.

"Hey," I say, looking around. I spot the large neon blue sign that says *The Rooster Cafe.* "Weird place."

"It's got a certain quirk," Lily says, munching on a fry. "You know they don't cut the grass deliberately?" She shoves the basket in front of me. "Want some?"

I take a few and dip them in ketchup. I feel like a fish out of water, and when I strain my head up over the half-wall, I'm greeted with a group of twenty-somethings ordering craft beer.

"So, how's it going?" Lily asks.

"Oh, fine," I say. I'd spent the day lounging around in sweats and a dirty t-shirt, and I showered just before I came to meet her. "Literally did nothing."

"How are you holding up?"

I blow out a long breath, grab more fries, and stuff them into my mouth. When I swallow, I admit, "I'm okay. Not the best, but it's whatever."

"Has he tried to text you?"

"Nope," I say. "Thank god for small miracles, huh."

Lily gives a sad smile, like she agrees but doesn't want to. "Yeah. You want something to drink?"

"Sure," I say, and now that I think of it, my throat is a little parched.

Lily stands up, and her eyes land on someone behind me. Her face breaks into a genuine smile, and she beckons whoever it is with a dainty hand.

The waiter comes over, dressed in all black with a neon glow stick necklace around his neck. His face is sour, and he glares at Lily. "What can I get you?"

"Hey, Luke," Lily says, smiling up at him. "I'd like some more fries." She then looks at me critically, a sneaky smile on her lips. "You want a beer?"

"Uh, sure?" I say. I try to look at Lily. Surely they wouldn't serve alcohol to minors? She doesn't look at me, but her smile is still blindingly happy.

"Two Pilsners and fries please," Lily says to Luke, waving him off with a dismissive hand.

Instead of answering, Luke huffs and stalks away. My eyes widen – what was up his butt? She clearly knows him. Lily sees my expression and gives a chuckle.

"Luke's my brother," she explains. She gestures to the place around her. "And this is our weird restaurant."

"Oh shit," I breathe out. I cover my face with my hands briefly. "Sorry, I didn't mean to-"

But Lily is grinning, more amused than offended. "I know, I didn't design it. My mom did. Apparently this style is all the rage in New York."

"She's an architect?" I ask.

"Yeah, she designs buildings and stuff."

"What does your dad do?"

"He's a stock-broker."

"I don't know what that means."

"Neither do I," Lily admits, and we grin at each other. "What do your parents do?"

"Mom's a Registered Nurse, and my Dad is like a technical electrical guy."

"Nice," she says, and the genuine warmth in her tone makes me feel happy.

"So how exactly do you guys own a restaurant?"

Lily shakes her head. "Sorry, I should've been more clear. Dad buys properties and rents them out. He normally does like duplexes and things like that. This is one of his first commercial buildings, and Mom cut them a deal on the designing. And basically we eat here for free, and Luke gets me drinks." Her eyes cut past me, and she grins. "Don't you, Luke?"

Luke appears with our drinks and another basket of fries. He sets them down before me and sends his sister an acidic glare. She simpers and blows him a kiss. It's all I can do to refrain from laughing, and I hide my smile into my shoulder.

"If you guys basically own this place, why are you working?" I ask Luke.

He looks like his sister − he's got mousy brown hair that's shorn close to his head. There's several tattoos on his arms, and the tail end of one on his neck, and he looks like a rich kid trying to be gangster. Both of them are delicate, with thin wrists and narrow chests.

"Work ethic," he says. "Dad says it's good for us."

"Luke also skipped out on college when he graduated last year, so Dad says he needs to work until he goes to Yale."

The casual mention of Yale sends dollar figures before my eyes. Luke doesn't look like the kind of person who wants to go to an Ivy League college. But hell, I know that attending a place like Yale means legacies are first priority.

"So you went to WJ Prep?" I wonder what his experience was with The Elites.

He wrinkles his nose. "Unfortunately. I take it you do now?"

"Yeah," I say, but then fall silent. I want him to offer up his own interactions with The Elites, but the way he's holding himself – cornered, with his arms crossed and his body leaning away from me – tells me that he's not going to divulge his story freely.

"Thanks, Luke," Lily says. "Ophelia and I are gonna chat now."

He nods curtly. "Good to meet you, Ophelia."

"You too."

Luke walks away and heads to another table, and I direct my attention back to Lily, raising my eyebrows.

"What's his story?" I ask.

Her face darkens, and her eyebrows lower into a frown. "That's for him to tell."

I back off. "Sorry, I just was-"

"Don't say you're sorry," Lily says, but her eyes are thousands of miles away. "It's just...it's just something he should say on his own time."

A blanket of seriousness drapes over us, and I twiddle a warm fry between my fingers. The air is heavy, and even though there are people talking and laughing and enjoying themselves around us, it's like a switch has been flipped and we're left alone.

"So my dad is a stock-broker, right?" She looks for confirmation, and I nod. "Well, apparently there's this thing called day-trading in the stock market. My dad's pretty good at it." She makes a face. "Well, he's actually super good at it."

"That's nice," I murmur. "But where are you going with this?"

"The Jamesons, Whitworths and Blackwaters approached him. They wanted him to day trade some of their companies' money. You know, the Jameson Automobile Co money. I don't know how much, but it was a ridiculous amount. My dad refused."

"Why?"

She shrugs. "Part of the reason we left New York when I was younger was to have a slower lifestyle. Dad's got enough reserves to keep us going. He wants to retire here soon. He just didn't want to take on such huge clients...and be responsible for their money."

"So now they hate him."

"Hate is a strong word when it comes to The Elites," Lily says.

"What else could it be?" I bite back too harshly. "Sorry, I'm just angry."

"It'll dull over time," she says, swirling a fry in ketchup. When she pulls it up, the fry sags from the condiment weight. "Trust me, eventually it'll just feel like a dull ache."

"So what happened to you?"

She goes silent. A dark shadow crosses her face, and she sips her beer. I have yet to touch the beer. Lily's hazel eyes snap to mine, and the fury in them surprises me.

"What didn't they do?" she says bitterly. "It wasn't like they had any morals or human decency."

I stay silent. I don't feel like this is the time to interrupt.

"In the beginning, they toyed with my feelings. They brought me into their inner circle, and I was treated like a friend. Vivan and I actually became super close. Or so I thought. And then Emmett turned his attention on me."

I watch her quietly, and her fingers start racing up and down the beer glass, wiping away the condensation. She stares at it intensely, like she's trying to unlock the secrets of the universe.

"I had a crush on him, big time," she confesses, and there's color on her cheeks, spreading down her neck. "Like huge. And he knew it. And...he used it against me in the worst possible way."

Thoughts flash through my head, none of them good. Most of them are worse than the last, and Emmett's cruelly handsome face mixes among them.

I don't want to hear what happened. But I do.

"And so, basically Emmett invites me to the homecoming dance. I'm like, so excited and happy and I can't believe it. Vivian and I like, even go dress shopping together. And then the night of the dance, everything just...shatters."

"What happened?" I ask.

She gives a curt laugh. "What didn't happen? Emmett and Trey and Vincent start screaming at me. Vivian and Bernadette tear my dress and steal my shoes. Emmett starts kissing Vivian in front of the whole school. When I try and run away,

Bernadette grabbed my hair and dragged me to the punch bowl and dunked me in it. But that was only the beginning."

"Why didn't the chaperones do anything?" I'm incensed on her behalf – cruel, heartless monsters don't deserve shit, and The Elites clearly aren't human. "Why the fuck did anyone let them do that?"

"The school is *funded* and *ran* by their families. *No one* has the balls to go against them. They have ways of ostracizing people and running them out of town. Sometimes, overnight."

"What the fuck?" I say. "What the actual fuck is wrong with them?"

"Money does shitty things to shitty people." Lily leans back, and gives a strained chuckle. "But that wasn't the end of it."

"What else happened?"

"Vivian and Bernadette started sending me hateful texts. Telling me to go kill myself, to just do the world a favor. Every morning, they'd try and douse me with water or slushies or coffee or whatever they could get their hands on. Emmett started spreading rumors about me being easy, as if that's why he broke it off with me. And then..."

"And then what?"

"Then they planted a joint in my locker second semester of high school. Told a teacher. I was suspended, and thankfully my dad was able to convince them that this was a setup, otherwise I would have been expelled."

We fall silent. Lily's experience – no, torture – hangs between us, a giant reminder of who not to fuck with.

"They will remind me every so often to stay out of their way," she says quietly. "They like to, you know, resort to public humiliation or rumors or physical intimidation. Really just what they're feeling like that day."

"That's fucked up," I say. Lily's experience juxtaposes against mine – she's had four years of constant harassment and bullying, and I've only had two whole days. I dread what might come next. "How'd you get through it?"

"Therapy," she says. "But I had to go to a therapist in Boston. Anyone else is connected to them, and they would've found out. Also, lots of chocolate. I gained a lot of weight my freshman and sophomore years. That certainly didn't ward them off."

My heart hurts. I feel like I'm confined in a box, trapped on all sides, and The Elites just keep pushing and pushing and waiting until I break down. Until I beg to be let out.

My eyes find Lily's. She's pensive, looking at me with concern, wondering how I'll react. I want to tell her that there must be some way to retaliate against them, some way to get them to stop.

"That's hella fucked, Lily," I say, shaking my head.

"Yeah, but what are you going to do?" she says. "This town has been built around them. This place is *theirs*. It has been theirs for centuries, and it's not like it's going to change any time soon."

Unfortunately, I'm worried Lily is right. I rub the condensation on my glass – is this just what I'll have to deal with?

"Okay," she says, "enough about this. Let's go have some fun. Chug, girl!"

I laugh – Lily is a little crazy. Sure, I've had my fair share of drinks before, but it's always been in a controlled setting. At someone's house, at home – never in public, where we could get in trouble for being minors.

"How about we just sip and talk?" I ask. "I'm not really feeling up for getting drunk."

Lily rolls her eyes, but she smiles at me. "You'll stop being bummed by them soon. You'll soon realize that it's just a stupid fucking game and that it doesn't matter, even if it hurts all the time."

"That's morbid," I tell her, taking my first sip of the Pilsner. It goes down nice and easy. I don't like the taste of beer, but this is tolerable. "I don't think, you know, that's okay."

"It's not okay," she says. "It's the farthest thing from okay. But what can we do about it? We've got one year left, and then we can get the hell out of here."

She's using "we" even though I met her six days ago. But I like that she's included me in her statement, and I realize that Lily is on her way to becoming a friend. A friend of circumstance and coincidence, perhaps, but a friend nonetheless.

"Hell yeah," I say, cheering her. I lift my glass and we clink to celebrate. "One more year."

"Less than three-hundred days, actually," she says. She pulls out her phone.

"Hey," I say, eyeing her. "How come you could bring your phone?"

"This is a burner phone," she says, wiggling her eyebrows at me. "I just bring it when I go out – nobody except my family and now you know I have it."

"What the fuck," I mutter, more in awe of the fact that she's had to use a burner phone, and her family most likely put her up to it. "And your family knows all about The Elites and stuff?"

"Yeah, they do." She's busy pulling up an application on her phone. "Luke and I are very close with our parents. Anyway, here, this is what I wanted to show you."

I grab her phone and eye the countdown box. It's surrounded with glitter and fun little animations that look like stringers and confetti. *Days Until June 5th: 279.*

"Graduation," she points at the phone. "That's when we graduate and we're done. We just have two-hundred-and-seventy-nine days left."

I groan. All I see is two-hundred-and-seventy-nine days of potential pain and torture. But the happiness and glee that Lily has when she sees that number... I don't have the heart to tell her that none of this is normal. We should be counting down the days happily, in anticipation of our next step in our journey.

Instead, we're counting down the days until we escape *them.*

---

By the time I get home, it's almost midnight. Mom and Brendan are sitting in the living room, watching Office reruns. Mom's holding a glass of red wine in her hand, and when she turns at my arrival it nearly spills over Brendan.

"Honey!" she says, excited. "You're home!"

"Eh, watch it woman!" Brendan says, taking away her glass and gingerly placing it on the side table. "You almost spilled on me!"

I roll my eyes and walk over to give them a hug from behind. "The Office? Haven't you guys watched that like seven times through already?"

Brendan gestures to Mom, who is quietly giggling. "It's her show! And I just let her do what she wants."

"Clearly," I tease, giving them both a kiss on their cheeks. "Okay, I'm going to bed. Love you."

"Love you too," they chime in, my mother's a little slurred. She breaks into a fit of laughter at some joke, and it follows me into my bedroom.

I'm half-naked, only in my running shorts, when my phone

rings on top of my bed. I glance at it – Emmett is calling. Just seeing his name pop up gives my heart a little jump. A flicker under my stomach. Why would he be calling? What could he possibly want from me? I press my hand on the green phone icon before I come to my senses. What did I think I was doing?

I quickly swipe the red phone icon. Ha. Take that you pretentious prick.

He's quick. A text pops up: **I want you now.**

He probably wants a ton of people, I think to myself. My stomach constricts. He's probably drunk and horny – Lily did say the Whitworths were having a party today. The urge to text back almost takes over, but then he shatters the lusty build-up in my stomach.

**I guess we'll see what happens Monday.**

Nope. Not going to give in. Anger starts to build in my chest, eradicating any sort of sick lust I had. My fingers vibrate with frustration and anger, and I want to text him a paragraph that he'll never forget. But I resist.

I do what I should've done earlier: I delete his contact info. I know it's a short term solution, but I don't care.

As I curl up under the covers, I try and think what will happen on Monday. Lily's shown me their scope of cruelty is limitless, and it takes me forever to fall asleep.

# CHAPTER SEVEN

BOOK 1

S chool goes by slowly.

Like, if a snail was drunk and stuck on a glue mouse trap.

That kind of slow.

The slow that burns and aches and makes you want to tear out your hair from boredom. The slow that whispers *this isn't supposed to be happening.* The slow that is cloaked in tension so thick a circle saw wouldn't cut through it.

The slow that said: Ophelia, just you wait.

I caught Emmett's eyes two times in the hallway. Once, when I was exiting Calculus. He'd lounged against the lockers across the door, his hair ruffled, his gray eyes piercing. He wore his polo shirt half-untucked, and his collar was half-flipped, and he was making me half want to fix him up and half want to kick him.

He'd smiled at me, waggling his eyebrows suggestively. I gave him the middle finger, but his musical laugh followed me down the hall. My back broke into a sweat and my body tensed – for what? I didn't know. To be tackled, to be squished against the wall, to be hauled up against his warm body...but nothing happened, and soon a headache pounded at my temples.

The other time had been when the bell dismissed us for lunch. The Elites normally join up at the end of the hall and sweep toward the lunchroom together. Like some weird show of power. All walking in a straight row, forcing everyone to move out of the way. I didn't exit the building to my car fast enough, and I got caught walking toward them on my way out.

Emmett and Vivian, in another gross display of couply romance, were walking side by side. His arm was slung over her shoulder, and she had her hand looped into the back pocket of his pants. I noticed they didn't hold hands – perhaps too gushy? Too romantic? Too much softness for them?

I pressed to the side, like all the other good peasants did, but they'd already noticed me. It was like some attitude had been switched on – one moment they were laughing and joking with each other, the next I was at the full-front of their attention. I felt my skin, hair, outfit be torn apart by Bernadette, whose cutthroat gaze sliced me raw.

But then, I couldn't help it.

Emmett's face was blank. Clinical. And he studied me like I was some sort of object under a microscope. No hostility, no desire. Just...curious apathy.

It sent shivers down my spine.

My headache developed throughout the rest of the day, and by the time I'm at practice the pain is nearly unbearable. I try to stretch out my shoulders and neck, and while it helps, the throbbing comes back in full force.

I pinch the bridge of my nose, trying not to grimace.

"You okay, Lopez?" comes Granger's voice.

I open my eyes. Coach Granger is looking down at me. The big black watch on his hands shows 3:33 pm. We're waiting for the assistant to arrive.

"Yeah," I say, trying to add some pep to my voice. "I'm great."

"Come over here, Ophelia," he says, gesturing me over to the stands. He climbs up to the second row and pats the metal beside him. "Sit, sit."

I do as I'm asked, bouncing my toes a little. The pounding matches the beat in my head, and when I look at him, I'm surprised to find deep concern in Coach's eyes.

"Look," Coach starts off with a low voice. He clasps his hands between his knees. He always sports a ball-cap – either Nike or WJ prep – and it hides the graying sides of his head. "I know we haven't known each other for a long time, but I think we both know that something is going on."

I stay silent – what is he talking about? I don't want to give anything away. If he knows something, he'll have to be the first one to say it.

"And I don't like the looks of my athletes getting hurt," he says. "It's not right, and it isn't good for your performance."

"If I've been slacking- "

He holds up a gnarled hand to stop me. "You haven't been slacking. You've been kicking ass. As far as I'm concerned, you're the best athlete on this field. My concern is that this whole thing – whoever has hurt you, and whoever is probably giving you that migraine right now-"

"How do you know I have a-"

He smiles, his teeth a bit yellowed but straight. "Kid, I know a thing or two about migraines. And looking like you're going to throw up is one of those things."

"I'm hoping it'll go away during practice."

"My point is, kid, is that I want you to know that I'm here for you. I'm your coach. I'm here to support you."

I nod, looking at my Nikes, hoping he doesn't see just how touched I am by his comments. "Thanks, Granger," I say. "That means a lot."

He pauses, almost like he's waiting for me to say something else, but when I don't, he slaps his hands on his thighs. "All righty then, Lopez," he says. "Time to get on back out there. Short practice today."

When Coach Granger says short practice, what he really means is that it's your own tempo. The faster you can get through it, the faster you can go home.

---

The moment I see a darkened figure at my car is the moment I realize that Monday has twenty-four hours in it.

"Ophelia," Emmett says, his grin spreading as his arms open up wide. He looks sinful, his lips pillowy and his cheekbones high. When he smiles like he means it, it sends a zip to my core. "How was practice?"

I check around us – my teammates are slowly driving away, their windows down and looking at us. But I don't see any of the other Elites.

Emmett is alone.

Which is unusual.

And bad.

For me. Very bad.

I stop about five feet from him. He's parked his black car next to mine, on the drivers side. I can't help but think that's not a coincidence. Sweat has cooled my skin, and my need to brush away my wayward hairs is stemmed by my desire to not look like I'm primping in front of him. I'm wearing my sports tank that's a razorback, exposing my collarbones, shoulders and shoulder blades. My shorts are high-thigh and tight, and I know my legs and butt look good in them.

I wish I'd brought sweats and a sweater. His eyes flick down to my toes, meandering up my body, and settle on my lips. He stares at them a little too long.

"What do you want, Emmett?" I demand. I don't want to walk closer to him or to my car, so I stay put. "I'm not in the mood."

He unhitches himself from the car, and I contemplate making a break for it. But instead I'm rooted to the concrete, a tiny voice in my ear saying *bad move, Ophelia.*

"You know," he says, "I've been trying to think of how to punish you for hanging up on me on Saturday night. And then blocking me."

"Oh great," I say sarcastically, but inwardly a twinge of fear strikes a chord. "You know how I just love to be punished."

His lips twitch. "You've been a bad girl."

"That's relative. I'm great, actually." He's getting closer, but it's like he's approaching a wild deer, and his movements are slow, coordinated. I step back. "Why are you walking toward me? Please stop."

"Then don't back away," he says, stepping forward again. "Come on, I just want you to take a ride with me."

The normality of his voice chills me. Almost like the blank stare he gave me earlier in the day, with Vivian draped around him. None of the lust from our first encounter. And none of the sadism of every encounter after that.

"What the hell makes you think I would willingly go anywhere with you?" I snap. My voice cracks from the uneasiness. I had gotten used to the cruelty, but this strange, calculated, yet distant, eerie deadness in his eyes is shooting straight to my gut. Everything in me is telling me to run, but I know that will only make it worse.

And then…there is the other part of me that feels sucked in like a moth to a flame. His gaze is locked on to mine as he steps closer and closer, too slowly. I can almost hear the Jaws theme playing through my migraine, but that's too comedic for a moment this dangerous.

He freezes, inches from my face. A disturbingly cold breeze hits the strands of my loose hair ever so slightly…seemingly freezing time right along with his body. Everything slows.

His hand reaches for my face, and for the first time since I arrived, I don't feel the urge to flinch or bolt. It's like I'm suspended in some magnetic hold.

"You can try to ignore me, block me or whatever else you like," he says softly, his fingers brushing along my jaw. "But we both know what's going to happen. It has to. Sooner or later."

I give my best sarcastic laugh, but it's too thinly veiled. I know he sees straight through me. My defenses are officially tattered.

"And just what is that?" I tilt my head, trying to sound as harsh and uninterested as possible. But the seriousness in my face is giving me away.

"When two bodies are drawn to each other like ours," he whispers in his low, grumbling voice that ripples straight through me, "we have no choice but to act on it eventually. Why torture ourselves like this?"

He is close. Too close. His lips so close to my neck I can feel his hot and heavy breath burning into my skin. I swear I hear a growling snarl between each inhale and exhale.

I hate myself for it, but I want to give in. I want to believe he's right…That however fucked up it may be, our bodies are meant to meld together, in violence or in sex. And obviously I'd prefer the sex, if he'd actually behave like a decent person.

"I could never be with someone like you," I snarl against his neck. "Not after the things you've done to me."

"Oh no?" he smirks, completely unfazed. "So, you're telling me when you read that note…and my texts…you didn't linger on them? Think about it all…even just a minute longer than you meant to?"

His fingers trail through the back of my hair. I want to turn into him more, push my body against his. Break through all of this sick tension that has been building.

But memories of the cruel and vicious side I'd seen of him stop me. I can't move.

I wish I could run, or that he couldn't read my mind so well. It sickens me that for all he has put me through, he knows that some part of me deep down still can't deny this primal attraction to him.

"You know, no answer is an answer," he murmurs with a cocky smile.

I am paralyzed. I have no energy to fight back, to deny him. And I don't hate myself enough to surrender to him.

He finally takes several steps backward, leaving the places along my face and neck that he just touched cold. A loud and trembling exhale escapes my lungs, just for the simple relief from the pressure of saying or doing anything. For a brief moment, I'm free.

His hands go up in a surrendering motion as he continues stepping back. It's not like him to give up. To show any sign of caring for my comfort. It only unhinges me even more.

What the fuck is he up to?

His eyes dart down to specks of gravel scattered across the pavement as he kicks them around with his shoes. "Look...I know we've made it hard on you. *I've* made it hard on you. The way things work here...the hierarchy...the system... It's not easy to adjust to."

He has to read minds. Has to. Or maybe just mine. He knows when I'm at my breaking point. And when to back off just enough to make me think I could maybe...maybe not be filled with rage and an intense desire to knee him in the balls. Or worse.

"I want to make it up to you," he says, still not looking up from the rocks he is fiddling with across the black tar. "Give you a chance to...I don't know." He looks up and away, almost bashfully. "Get to know me. The real me." For once, his smile almost looks like one a normal teenage guy would flash when he's talking to a girl he likes.

I can't stop myself from laughing out loud...until my laughter almost turns to tears of frustration. Then I stop real quick.

"That's rich." I look away, trying not to cry.

"Just take a ride with me," he insists again. "I promise I won't hurt you. I mean, it's a beautiful afternoon." His hand flails toward the almost ready to set sun.

It is a beautiful afternoon. The air is perfect – not too hot or too cold. A breeze rushes through every few minutes, urging you to do something to keep up with the fleeting warmth. It's my favorite running weather.

It would also be a wonderful afternoon for a girl's crush to take her for a drive. If my life was still anything close to normal. The realization of just how far from normal I've been since arriving hits my gut like a knife.

Memories of my life before coming here start flashing before my eyes. How simple everything was. And moving here… That plays like a cheesy movie montage. One where I am blissfully naïve and optimistic. I had no idea how wrong things were about to go. I want to walk straight up to my former self and shake her. Warn her that this wasn't some dream come true. It was going to be a nightmare.

To my horror, the tears don't hold back with the thought. My eyes burn as they begin to pool.

I quickly shoot my fingertips up, pushing the drops away too roughly. Enough to tug the skin in pain and poke into my eyes. I deserve it. I'm angry with myself for letting any weakness show.

He's getting to me, and he knows it now.

His hand is suspended in midair, beckoning me to follow him. Get into his car. Surrender my safety and freedom. Trust him.

And like an idiot, I do. I know it's the wrong call. Everything in me screams to stop stepping forward. Stop following him. Don't slide into the passenger seat as he opens the door.

But my body follows him like a zombie. A dumb zombie.

I resentfully note the cleanliness of his car. Psh. Probably pays someone to detail it for him at least once a week. These people's cars are perfect, clinging to that new car smell for dear life.

Nothing like my beat-up old car, littered with empty water bottles and protein bar wrappers.

A blur of something in the back seat catches my eye. Something that makes me feel foolish for thinking about petty things like paid help or clean cars. It is a passing nothing at first, but quickly turns into a blaring alarm. A siren going off in my brain telling me to run. My pulse pushes to an impossible speed as my muscles tense and my jaw slacks. I'm unable to move, frozen with bulging eyes through my quickening breath.

Rope. Gloves. Other random things I can't make out…but whatever they are, it can't be good. Not with our history. And the fact that I am so completely alone out here.

By the time my mind absorbs the warning signals, he's plopping into the driver's seat as I tuck into myself and lean toward the door, as far away from him as I can manage. I know I only have mere seconds before he's going to lock the doors. My head shakes reactively with my mouth frozen in a panicked circle as my hand smashes against the door handle, blindly fumbling for a grip to fling it open. My shaking body prevents me from being able to pull the handle fast enough.

Just as the tiniest light seeps back through the door as it swings to open, a sharp blaring pain sears into the back of my head, causing me to cry out in pain. His fingers are digging into my scalp, catching a big enough handful of my hair to yank me backward. The door, and any hope I have at escape, slams shut. I beat mercilessly at it anyway, thrashing wildly against it with my hands and feet to no avail.

My heart started racing the moment I made that lunge for the door, and now it only quickens, the sound thrashing in my ears, as his tires screech across the parking lot, pealing away from everyone and everything that can help me.

I know the roads around here are long, winding and empty. Once he starts driving down them, I am completely at his mercy. And given everything I've seen so far, I can't convince myself he wouldn't kill me…after putting me through unspeakable torture for who knows how long.

My head hangs low and my teeth gnaw into the side of my mouth as I keep a side-eyed glare glued onto him with a need to see any other lunge for attack before it happens. I can't let him out of my sight for a single second, but my mind races for some kind of solution. An escape. I fight through the voice in my head telling me I deserve whatever happens for getting in the car in the first place.

The only thing I know to do is move and fight and try to escape this in any way I can.

The car. He's in control of the car. If I take back that control, even if only for a second, maybe I can find a way to escape.

My hand juts out to the steering wheel, mindlessly jolting it in any direction opposite from where he thinks he's taking me. My scream is the only thing I can hear when the streetlight post appears in front of the windshield. It sounds foreign and far away, as if it's not even coming from my mouth. But I feel it ripping through my throat all the same before there is a terrible, deafening crunch of metal and everything goes dark.

# CHAPTER EIGHT:

## BOOK 1

*You're being punished. Just like he promised.*

That's all I can think as I come to. My head wobbles around as my line of sight fills with indistinct blurs of harsh light and red spots. I feel like I've been punched in the chest and my head is throbbing. There's a hiss of smoke and dying car parts croaking in the background.

I look over to Emmett's foggy silhouette. His head is hanging limp and heavy from his neck. He's still out. I want to think over my options for killing him…making it look like it was from the accident.

But an urgent need to get out of the car takes over. The seatbelt buckle sticks at first, causing me to panic. I don't want to be stuck in here…with him. But my frenzied jiggle of the contraption finally sets the buckle free. My chest burns as the belt loosens. I can imagine a big red and purple strip across my skin from being flung against it so hard. I begin pushing on the car door which sticks at first – the same as the seatbelt. But once again I am able to pry it open. Some sort of adrenaline-powered strength, I figure.

I realize all of this is being made more difficult by the giant white balloon pressing against me. It whistles as I awkwardly maneuver around, not deflating fast enough to make this any easier.

By the time my feet finally touch the ground again, I nearly fall over. Everything aches and hurts. But not with the rewarding swell I am used to feeling from running. These pains are blunt and sharp. Unnatural.

I manage to find my footing as my eyesight slowly readjusts. That's when I realize my ears are ringing. The sound takes me back to what I saw just before the crash.

What was this fucker going to do with that rope? Just how was he going to punish me?

But then my heart begins to beg a different question… What if he wouldn't have hurt me at all? For once. What if he really did only mean to take me for a nice, innocent drive.

I remind myself of how he yanked me back into the seat as I tried to run. *Don't be stupid, Ophelia. There was nothing sweet and innocent about this.*

This is punishment, I think again.

For letting my guard down. I *willingly* got into that car. I let him know that all he had to do to get me where he wants me was pretend to be nice for a few minutes. Looking back, it wasn't even that convincing of an act. I only made him put forth the bare minimum effort of a show.

How could I be so easy and stupid?

I tell myself it's only because I was exhausted. But that's not good enough. No excuses. I don't get to run slower or cut the miles short…no matter how tired I am. I don't get to cave into these Elite fuckers just because they're wearing me down.

*Toughen up.* I clench my fists and repeat it to myself over and over.

I hear Emmett rustling out of his door. My feet immediately begin to bounce, needing to run far away from him. But the sight of blue and red lights stops me.

There's blood dripping from his forehead as he shoots his eyes straight to me. They're filled with rage and confusion, but I can tell he's blaming this all on me. Taking in the sight of his car and his banged-up body, he has the nerve to look to me with a *What did you do!?* victimhood.

I shake my head, snarling at him through my own bloody lip. How dare he look at me as if this was my fault. *Don't stalk girls, trick them into getting into your car, and then hold them by the hair when they try to run. Then your car won't get smashed up.*

Thankfully before he can say or do anything, he has the police to answer to.

"Are you two okay!?" One of the officers yells out as their doors swing open.

Oddly though, they both run up to Emmett and immediately begin giving him all of their attention. Wrapping him in a blanket, propping him up on their arms to help him over to their car to sit down.

I am left standing with the sickening reminder that everyone in this town is shoved up the Elites' asses. Even the cops. They did warn me but standing here now…just as bloody and beaten as my perpetrator…while the two cops that should be helping me are fawning all over the town's golden child. It reminds me just how alone I am in all of this.

"What happened?" they ask him, willing to get his side of the story before they even so much as acknowledge my existence.

I wait for him to blame this on me. Find some way to twist it all around to make this completely my fault.

"It's my fault," he confesses. "I feel so stupid… I guess I was showing off doing donuts and dumb shit like that…But I was distracted having a beautiful woman in my car. You know how it goes."

One of the cops laughs, "Oh, son. Believe me, I do. No sweat. Just be glad you're okay."

The other cop finally comes over to me and helps me over to lean against their car…too close to Emmett. I guess they can acknowledge me now that I'm not considered to be a problem or an enemy. I wonder if he had told them he was just getting ready to rape me if they would have helped him finish me off or dumped me somewhere.

More flashing lights emerge from the nearby winding roads. This time an ambulance. Each new arrival makes me feel safer, no matter how entrenched they all are in the game of the Elites. Safety in numbers. The more people who are here, the more likely it is that someone will make sure I'm okay.

I lean into the back seat of the cop car, their door wide open. Emmett is in their passenger seat. Our bruised and cut legs are perched out the side of the car on the pavement. I try not to notice his eyes burning into me every chance he gets. But I can feel the weight behind them.

I can practically hear his voice warning me telepathically… You just wait. You're really in for it now.

The EMTs get to work on us like busy bees – patching this, sanitizing that. Just enough to get us ready for a trip to the hospital. The reality swirls around my swaying head, my vision unable to focus. But my mind intact enough to piece together what's about to happen. There's only one ambulance. They're going to make us ride together.

The thought of being crammed into that tiny space with Emmett makes my stomach churn too quickly for me to hold anything back.

Chunks of whatever I managed to eat that day crash into the back of my throat as I thrash forward, puking onto the ground right there in between my legs.

I'm instantly plagued with embarrassment…that I puked in front of Emmett, which only makes me sick again.

I want to ask the doctors what is wrong with me. I must have a brain tumor. Why the hell do I still care what he thinks? How I look in front of him?

They barely let my stomach settle before piling us both into the back of the ambulance. I want to feel comforted by the additional presence of the EMT guys but knowing they're probably just as much on Emmett's side as the cops lessens my hope.

No one asks my side of the story.

It only gets worse at the hospital. We're both treated in the same room, our beds side by side which I'm sure Emmett is getting off on. I fight off any positive feelings I have about getting to stay close to him.

This is Stockholm Syndrome. Has to be. I wonder if that sort of thing shows up on a brain scan.

I'm treated for a concussion and a sprained wrist. I want to scream at the doctors that my wrist wasn't from the car accident, but I know better. I bite my tongue. Emmett is treated for whiplash which brings me a sick joy. It's about time he got hurt for once.

Once we're all bandaged up and our hands are stuffed full of printed papers for aftercare instructions, we're left alone while the doctor draws up our discharge papers.

"You fucking bitch," he grumbles the first chance he gets, with no one around to hear.

"Oh yeah…" I scoff. "This is my fault, right?"

"You grabbed the steering wheel."

"Why didn't you just let me go!?" I cried, my voice cracking from frustration.

He slowly stands to his feet and makes his way over to my bed, taking a seat right next to me. His arms wrap around me, squeezing too tight. He envelops me, towering around me with a threatening eeriness.

I keep my eyes glued to the passing nurses and doctors in the hall, hoping one of them will barge in and stop him, but of course to them he looks like a caring guy, merely comforting me.

His lips sink down to my ear. "But the fucked up part is… you're wondering what I planned on doing to you. And not just in a terrified way…but in a curious way, huh?"

I struggle to push him away, "Fuck off!" But his grip is too tight. I barely move a muscle.

"You're dying to know how I would have hurt you in all the right ways… How I would have had my way with you, not giving you a choice…then you wouldn't have had to feel guilty about wanting it. You wouldn't have had to blame yourself for not trying hard enough to get away."

"Obviously," I retort sarcastically, barely able to get the words out as he tightens around me like a boa constrictor. "That's why I was willing to risk our lives and slam us into that telephone pole before you could get away with me. Because I was *so* excited about whatever sick shit you had planned."

I crash my foot down onto his, brutally pinning his toes beneath my sneaker. He winces and accidentally loosens his arms, giving me the chance to run to the other side of the room.

We're both panting like wild animals by the time he stands up and starts to close in on me. His eyes and nostrils flare with rage with each slow scary step he takes. Like a lion about to pounce.

And he does pounce. Too quickly for me to react. But just as soon as his arms are around me again, his lips are against mine. I tense up, refusing to melt into his kiss. I turn my head away as much as his grip will allow and crash my hand into the side of his face.

The slap only encourages him. He glares into me, burning on nothing but fumes of adrenaline, anger and lust. I take in the sight of those gorgeous plump lips, sickened by the fact that I only find them to be more enticing with the giant gash from the accident.

An urge to fight back surges through me, but it's coupled with longing. Before I know it, our mouths collide once more.

The doctor barges in, ignoring our teenage horniness,

rattling off directions for leaving the building and filling prescriptions.

I can't stop thinking about the kiss as we walk through the halls and ride on the elevator. I shudder to think what I would have let him do to me if we had been alone on that elevator. I wonder what will happen when we leave. Will we run away together?

But just outside the elevator doors, we're met in the parking garage by his stupid posse.

Vivian races to Emmett's side, pummeling him as far away from me as she can get him.

"Oh, you poor thing!" she squeals in an alarming display of concern.

I was beginning to think the two of them didn't know how to feel and express genuine emotions like concern for others. Even each other.

"Are you okay?" she asks softly, her hands gripped tight into his face, shoving her tongue down his throat before he can even answer.

My heart pangs. I want him to shove her away, but instead, he kisses back even harder, flashing his eyes to mine to make sure I was watching. I did it again. I keep forgetting who I'm dealing with.

Vivian's humanity quickly shatters as she whips around to me like a viper. "What did you do to him, you stupid fucking bitch!?"

"Why don't you ask him?" I quip back, hoping she tasted me on his lips just then.

She's unbothered, stomping toward me, venom practically spewing from her clenched teeth.

"Listen here, you little cunt," she sprays, getting so close to me I catch the spit of her rage on my cheek. "You stay the fuck away from him. I've had about enough of your skanky white trash ass always getting in the way."

Before I can respond or expect Emmett to defend me in any way at all, another car pulls up. My mom and Brendan, thank god.

My mom races toward me, sending Vivian recoiling into the sweetest body language she could muster – her shoulders drawn up, her hands clasped to her side like a precious little doll. It was so over the top. She didn't even know how to *pretend* to be decent.

Mom and Brendan fawn over me incessantly, asking a million questions.

Emmett watches me closely, waiting to see if I'll corroborate with the bullshit he fed to the police. I do for fear of what will happen if I don't, and because some demented part of me wants to please him. Wants to leave myself in his good graces enough to see what could come after that kiss.

"Emmett was just picking me up from practice," I lie. "We were goofing off. His car hit a light post."

"Well, I hope you learned your lesson," she scolds. "And at least you're okay."

I am filled with joy to see Brendan's eyes dart over to Emmett's. He'll let him have it. He's about to tear him a new one, and then maybe, just maybe, the only thing Emmett will have left for me will be any remnants of sweetness he may have buried within him. Enough to make me feel okay doing all of the things I want to do with him.

But Brendan's papa bear rage is cut off before it can even erupt past a dirty look.

"Trey!? Vincent!?" my mother's voice squeaks in surprise, stopping my heart cold.

They both smile and nod to her like schoolboys sucking up to their teacher.

"Oh my gosh! Your mom and I were friends in high school!" she squeals. "How is Cheryl!?"

"Mom, you know these people?" I ask, half terrified, half heartbroken. It feels like a betrayal.

She completely ignores me, making her way over to them to chit chat. Vivian hangs on every word, inserting her own bullshit fake niceties when she can. I am forced to stand there and watch as my worst enemies win over my mother.

My concussed head tries to work harder than it should to process what this all means. If this twisted hierarchy system has been around for ages, and my own mother was best friends with someone at the very core of its roots, does that mean she once played these games too? Was she one of them?

I try to stick close to Brendan, who now feels like the only person left on my side. I am still hoping he's going to pounce across the parking lot and tackle Emmett.

But, to my horror, Emmett marches confidently over to him and extends his hand.

"Sir, you must be Ophelia's step-dad. I'm Emmett," he offers politely.

"You can call me Mr. Lopez," he replies sternly, tightening my stomach as he graciously shakes his hand.

My eyes dart from my mom playing pals with the twins and Vivian back to Brendan treating Emmett so respectfully. I want to transfer images directly into their brains, showing them flashes of all the things these assholes have done to me.

"Just goofing around?" Brendan finally presses Emmett.

I want to believe this is it. This is the moment he puts him in his place. Scares the shit out of him.

"I feel terrible," Emmett lies. "I should have never been so careless with your daughter's safety. I care for her a great deal, and this was a poor example of that."

He's laying it on thick. I feel like I might puke again.

Brendan nods in acceptance, but before one word of reprimanding can begin, we're all interrupted by our doctor coming out from the elevator.

"Mr. and Mrs. Lopez!" he yells as he scuffles across the pavement. "I'm glad I caught you. My nurse just gave me your message about the questions you had. She said you were on your way here so I thought I'd talk with you in person."

"Yes! So glad you found us!" My mother exclaims, rushing over to shake his hand. "As I said in the message, Ophelia is a runner. She's on scholarship and on a pretty strict practice schedule. Just wanted to review how it might need to be adjusted."

My mom and Brendan get swept to the side with the doctor. I try to avoid eye contact with the Elite gang who are circling around like sharks. I stick close to my mom, clinging to safety, but they begin flipping me off so that only I can see.

I want to fly across the parking lot and pummel them. Their faces and attitudes are nauseating on a good day. But watching them go from sweet talking my parents straight back to their heartless little antics in the blink of an eye takes things to a whole new level of despicability.

They go right back into their fake polite smiles and manners the minute my mom and Brendan turn to say goodbye. But as soon as their backs turn again, the Elites are frantically shooting me every crude gesture they can think of.

My mom and Brendan lecture and fuss over my wellbeing the whole way home. But their words melt into distant buzz. I just stare out the window at the passing houses, which get notably smaller the closer we are to home.

I realize just how many times Emmett has made me fear for my life and I feel like I am drowning. This is too much for me to handle on my own. Even with Lily's support…I feel like I am completely alone. After all, she never found any relief from their wrath when they were torturing her. She simply had to wait it out. And I'm beginning to wonder if I'm strong enough to do that.

Every few seconds I inhale sharply as if I'm about to start speaking. The entire story is so close to spilling right out of my mouth, but as I review it all in my head…I wonder if they would even believe me. And then what? They go to the police? I am already terrified that any action they might try to take would prompt the Elites to bring our whole family down. The way they tried to with Lily.

More than spilling everything to them, I begin to think I need a therapist. Amidst all of this there is still my lingering attraction to Emmett, which I hate myself for. And somehow the accident and the kiss in the hospital has only intensified my sickening desire for him. That's not the kind of thing I could explain to my mom. Only a professional could psychoanalyze me through that one.

# CHAPTER NINE

## BOOK 1

I head straight for the stairs the moment we get home, refusing to eat dinner. My stomach is in so many knots I can't even seem to get down a glass of water. My duffle bag flies from my careless hands, landing across the large chest that sits at the foot of my bed as I collapse down onto the mattress.

I feel like I'm coming down with the flu. My body is still sore from the crash but coupled with a relentless nausea. There is a pain in the back of my throat that swells every time I remember kissing Emmett in the hospital room or how things felt for just a few brief moments when I first followed him into his car. Before I saw his torture tools in the backseat.

I squeeze my favorite blanket against my body, clinging to it for some sense of safety and security, as I rock gently on the edge of my narrow, unmade bed. I feel the conflicting pull of wanting to be far away and out of reach while also close and protected all at once.

The brush of it against my skin sends a shiver of memories washing over me. Emmett's crushing grip followed by his kiss. My body releases, wishing I could have melted into his lips, but even the stinging recollection of my hand across his face turns me on in ways I wish it wouldn't.

That look in his eyes, fueled by so much pent up rage and lust, struggling in an all-out internal brawl against one another. Creating tornadoes that tunneled up behind our eyes, before our lids flickered and we kissed once more.

I shake my head and turn to the Bluetooth speakers on my nightstand. With a flick of my wrist, I turn the volume knob to blast over the rage that is rapidly bubbling up inside. Underneath the shroud of blaring music, I clutch my pillow and scream into it at the top of my lungs, wishing the feeling of release was enough to fix the actual problems at hand.

"Ophelia!?" My mom's voice breaks through my refuge with a light tap at the door, interrupting the muffled scream ripping through my lungs. I should have known turning my music up that loud would bring her to my door. My hands clench at the sound of her voice. All I can hear from her mouth now are the ghost tones of her speaking to Vincent and Trey.

"I want to be alone, mom!" I reply through grinding teeth as my jaw tightens.

"We saved you some leftovers from dinner," she persists gently. "They're in the fridge, but I could get them back out and heat them up if you like?"

"I'm not hungry right now! Please, I just want to get some rest!" I try to yell over the emotional cracks in my voice, fighting against the giant lump in my throat. I just want to be alone.

She carries on from the other side of the door with explanations of logistics for the week. Which practices I could and could not go to. A reminder that the doctor says I shouldn't run for a couple of days. Follow up doctors' appointments, pharmacy trips and her work schedule. Boring logistics that could all be just as easily reviewed in the morning, but she's worried and desperate to find some way to stay near me.

I answer her in one-word responses, knowing anything more than that will give me away. If I engage or let on to how upset I am, she'll barge right in and never leave until she's convinced I'm okay.

I do want to run to her. To lay my head in her lap and cry as she strokes my hair like a child. But it would only comfort me if I could tell her everything that was going on. And I can't find a way to play that scenario out in my head that ends in actually helping me or effecting any real change at all.

So instead I stay alone and silent, wishing she would just go.

Once she says goodnight and I finally hear the gentle click of her bedroom door down the hall, I sit up on the bed and cradle my legs in my arms, gently rocking back and forth. Her interaction with the Elites in the hospital parking garage is all I can think about now. Which quite honestly is a relief in the midst of my unrelenting sexual attraction to Emmett.

Even after luring me to his car with a backseat full of evidence that he was up to no good. The yank of my hair jerking me back into the seat, unable to escape. Leaving me feeling safer slamming the car into a telephone pole than to be carted off alone with him. All of that and I still buckled under his kiss.

Shaking it all away once again, I return to my unanswered questions about my mom. I know she keeps a box of her old yearbooks and high school photos in the attic. I don't know why I hadn't thought to dig into it all sooner. Really I should have the moment I was invited to WJ Prep, but for some reason none of it seemed relevant until I saw her talking to them in the hospital parking garage.

When the house has been quiet and still for a while, I creep slowly toward my bedroom door, overstepping dirty clothes strewn across the floor.

On my way out, I catch sight of myself in my tall bedroom mirror hanging against the wall. Turning side to side, I can see the effects of WJ Prep on my body. My muscles are still firm, but the rest of me is gaunt. As if I'm wasting away. My skin is ashen with dark circles under my eyes, the skin around them is red and bunched up into a pained stare.

The sight only motivates me more as I head for the attic door, taking care to step as quietly as possible around my mom's bedroom. I'm not going to let these assholes waste me away to nothing. I will not lose everything I have worked for so far on account of their sick and twisted games.

Ignoring their rules and social structures and chain of command hasn't worked. So now I have to find something that gives me the upper hand in their game long enough to find a way out of it. Suddenly, my mom's mysterious connection to them seems like a potential light at the end of the tunnel.

I pull down the rectangular hatch door and fold-down staircase of the attic and make my way up, my hand reaching blindly in the dark for the pull string to bring some light. The bare lightbulb buzzes as it clicks on, revealing dusty floorboards that creak as I step across. Pipes and wiring twist up above me in between exposed wooden beams.

The moonlight is filtered through a grimy windowsill littered with dead bugs, casting an eerie glow on the room as I search through the faded boxes labeled with marker until I spot the one I had in mind. My mom's high school relics, yearbooks included. I push past the smell of insulation and stale air filling my throat as I pull the box down from its stack.

Clouds of dust shoot out from the sides of the box as I shove it with my foot to the light in the middle of the room, causing me to cough into the sleeve of my hoodie from the tickle it creates in my throat. I crouch down to open the box, the masking tape squealing as I peel it from the dusty and bent cardboard.

I pull out the glossy hardcover book and begin carefully flipping through the pages that catch on the stomach of my hoodie as I go. Briefly, I freeze at the muffled footsteps of my mom and Brendan echoing through the air vents, and I hope they can't hear me in return.

I need to be alone right now. I have no energy for putting on a face for anyone. Not even them. Especially not while I have this rush of persistence to fight back. I need to ride this wave of energy for as long as it lasts and find out everything I can.

I almost flip right past a photo of my mom and have to go back several pages to look at it more closely. There she is in a puffy eighties-style prom dress, complete with permed hair. Standing next to her is a man captioned as Theodore Nickelson.

I race to my feet, shaking the grime from my jeans as I run over to another box of photos. One I haven't looked at in years. Old baby photos, some that feature my father still lingering behind, though my mom had thrown most of them out.

I find one of him by my mother's bedside in the hospital, her cradling me in a receiving blanket with him looking down from above, flipping it over to see the handwritten names…Lala and Theo with baby Ophelia.

Theo. Theodore. It couldn't be.

My body stiffens at the sight of it. It never occurred to me that my mom could have met my biological father at WJ Prep. All she had ever told me about him was that he was complete scum who wasn't worth her breath to speak about. Anything about him always brings on an uneasy feeling in the pit of my stomach, which only worsens now that I know he also went to WJPrep.

More than that, there is the haunting missing piece of the puzzle. Theo's full name. I feel like I know it, but I have to see it. My eyes dart between the yearbook and the baby photo of me featuring my dad. I can't deny the resemblance, but I won't accept what I fear to be true until I see evidence.

I remember Lily's run down of everything. Weis, Blackwater, Whitworth, and…Nickelson. The founders of the Jameson Automobile Corporation and the cornerstones of the Elites.

Now my trembling hands hold two photos… One of the man I know to be my father. The other of a man with the same first name…Theodore Nickelson standing next to my mother at prom. Nickelson being the only name Lily mentioned no longer being around town.

I turn back to the yearbooks, needing to find every photo of Theodore Nickelson that I can. A few pages later, I really feel sick. First there is just one, but then a flood of photos quickly follows after. This man who looks like my father cozied up with Thomas Jameson and Walter Whitworth. The three of them with an arrogant lean against lockers or the side of the school. Football games, swim meets and even in the background of other people's pictures.

They were obviously a clique, doing everything together. Meaning, if Theo was in fact Theodore Nickelson… My father…was an Elite.

Visions of my mom play on repeat through my brain. I analyze anything and everything I can remember for some kind of sign that tells me what this means. Was she with them too? How could she be so closely entangled with this sick society of games and hierarchy?

Her kind, smiling, caring face now seems like a mask, but even that conclusion is clouded in doubt. If I could get sucked up into this mess, surely she could have been tricked or forced just as easily.

I try to move through my baffled state well enough to clutch a couple of the most relevant books and photo boxes close to my chest and make my way back to the safety of my room.

I quietly race back into my retreat, locking the door behind me and collapsing across my rug with everything I collected. I open up the yearbooks again, spreading everything across my bedroom floor and staring for a long time. Scouring the pages for each and every mention of my mom or Theodore.

Soon the black and white images are running swirling circles around my head, pulling my hands to my temples. I can't believe it. I throw the book across the room, wanting to be far away from it. It flies across the top of my dresser, sending makeup and hair products raining down in a clatter.

The sound is like the crumbling of whatever I thought I knew about my mom and her past. How I came into this world. It's my own fault for not asking more. But she never seemed to want to talk about it, so I took her silence as all I needed to know.

My face melts in shock, my eyebrows drawing together in an inward stare. A forceful breath escapes my mouth, and suddenly my thoughts are a jumbled swirl. I can't make out a single coherently clear one amidst the scattered and muddled pieces. I need more information.

I place my fingers in a pinch across the bridge of my nose, pushing out slow, deep breaths to try and calm down enough to think of my next move. I need the library, but it's too late and I'll never make it out of the house without being caught. Brendan and my mom would assume I was trying to sneak in a forbidden run and send me right back to bed.

All I have at my disposal is the internet. I scramble to clear the stacks of school papers, pens, pencils and phone accessories from my desk so I can get into my laptop, nearly knocking my lamp over as I move in a frenzy.

My music stopped playing long ago, leaving only the taps of the keyboard to fill my silent room. My fingers restlessly tap against the mouse in between clicks, as I dig for any confirmation I can find of my mother and father's attendance at WJ Prep.

The sound of a flushing toilet from down the hall causes me to jump, as if I know I am uncovering dangerous top-secret information. Things that someone would want to protect and could jump out at any moment to punish me for even trying to uncover it all. A thought that seems absurd in the comfort and safety of my own home, but nothing feels safe right now. It hasn't since my first day at that damned school.

Digging through every free record available to me on the internet, I am finally able to locate several that both relieve and terrify me. I find the original certificates of my mother's marriage and my birth. Both featuring my mother's name as... Lala Nickelson.

My eyes narrow at the name on the screen, the glow of it burning into my pupils until they start to water. The laptop slams shut and then open again. I can't decide if I need to look straight at it for two more hours before I believe it, or if I'll throw up from staring a second longer.

I fly into a manic pace around the room, muttering names and dates as I rub against the back of my neck. I feel stupid. Why had I never asked what my father's last name was? A name that surely would have been both mine and hers at some point in time.

But then I wonder...even if I did have the name Nickelson floating around in my brain, would I have even thought of it when Lily told me about the Jameson Automobile founders?

I go to take a hurried seat at the edge of my bed but stub my toe on the frame, only making me angrier and more frustrated.

Shit!

My hand clutches around my throbbing toe as I bounce around in circles, screaming silently beneath my breath, still trying not to wake my mom and Brendan. I am no more ready to face them now than I was before my detective work.

Then the moment I sit down I can't help but jump up again. For how drained and despondent I felt only an hour ago, now I'm unable to sit still. My muscles feel like they're jumping underneath my skin.

I rub my hands against my arms, my hairs standing on end from the coursing adrenaline. My vision blurs in a sudden heat-wave across my skin as I try to push away my biggest fears. My father was an elite, meaning I was more than just some rat caught up in their game. I was tied to it by blood. But just how deep that tie is...that's what I can't figure out.

All I have is the tree of hierarchy spelled out to me by Lily and these photos and records that indicate my parents attended WJ Prep, with at least one of them being an Elite. But a few of those things are more than what I had at the start of the day, and that's something. Right?

Up until now it felt as if I had no options. No choices for recourse or any way to fight back. And anything that could be pursued, who was I to even try it? I'm nothing around here. Worse than nothing, I'm hated by the people who run this town.

It baffles me even more to think my father was once one of them. Shouldn't that mean I'm on their side? That I inherited a sort of white flag or magic key?

But he isn't on their side anymore... He isn't even in the

same town. Bringing a burning flood of more questions barreling up into my throat.

What went wrong? Why isn't my father still here living it up with his high school Elite buddies? Raking in the profits of the Jameson Automobile Company?

Worse than that…is he the reason I'm here? Why I was offered the scholarship in the first place?

Another thought sticks to my brain…the most irrational one, but the one my hormonal lusty side is distracted by the most. Did all of this somehow make my attraction to Emmett more justified? Was there something buried beneath these new revelations that excused his behavior?

If my mom could get past whatever my father's horrible faults were as a member of the Elites enough to marry him and have me, then surely, I could ignore Emmett's confusing hatred for me enough to give into our urges.

But that doesn't take away the fear. All he has promised is punishment…punishment I would supposedly enjoy and want more of but abuse all the same. So why do I still want it? Why am I grasping at straws in the middle of this new evidence that would give me an excuse to act on my inescapable attraction to him?

After all, Vivian is more of an Elite than I am. Her parents are still all tied up in it and had never left. If bloodlines were to determine who went to bed with Emmett, she's obviously the front runner. Which is why he was kissing her in the garage… but then he was looking at me the entire time.

I try to shake my sexual fantasies away as my body shivers again. Really, I have no idea what any of this means, but it feels like the start of something. A foot in the right direction, and I am desperately willing to cling to anything that hints at an end in sight. I try to keep my grip on the momentum rather than tumble back down under the weight of what felt like a mountain in front of me. One where I can't even see the path up or down.

My eyes glint across shelves of trophies and medals, all of my running accolades that used to make me feel so big and proud. Now they just taunt me. They tell the story of all my potential that is now completely overshadowed by this Elites nightmare.

I look to the posters of Shalane Flanagan and my other favorite runners tacked against my wall and wonder if they ever had to deal with this kind of stuff. I have prepared myself for every kind of typical challenge or obstacle a runner could face. Shin splints, runner's knee, stress fractures, meniscus tears. A bad run at the worst time, like the one I had the day I met Emmett just before coming here.

But I had put so much energy into my sport, I had forgotten to prepare myself for the possibility of whoever my real father was coming back to haunt me. The missing chapter to my story I thought I might make time for some day…when I'm older and in the middle of an illustrious running career. Not now. But it seems I have no choice.

Suddenly, the ding of a new text causes me to jump. I look to the message from an unknown number.

*Figure it out yet, bitch?*

# CHAPTER TEN



The next day, I am instantly hit with an uneasy sense of foreboding as I apprehensively walk into school, pushing strands of my ragged hair from my face. With a deep breath, I clutch my backpack and sweater and push myself forward.

My stomach turns in anticipation of what will be waiting for me today. I am expecting something awful in the wake of the crash with Emmett.

I am immediately caught off-guard at how unnoticed my entrance is. Everyone carries on like normal, not even glancing in my direction. I pull my jacket tighter, looking down as I navigate around other passing students in the halls.

But I don't have to do much to work my way through the crowd. Quite the opposite of being the center of attention as I expected. I keep my eyes glued to the floor, the tips of sneakers coming into view promptly step away as I move forward.

I glance up, expecting a sea of snarls and angry glares in my direction. But cheeks are turned with noses high, looking everywhere they can except for at me. It's like I have the plague.

I faintly hear one girl whispering to another, "Here she comes. Look away."

The elaborate game continues. What new way can we fuck with Ophelia today? Having run out of all their other tricks in their books, they seem to be waiting patiently for an idea of what to do next. Maybe that means I finally found some sort of advantage. I have, at least temporarily, outran their schemes.

Shoes squeak across the floors through the echo of everyone laughing and talking, clicking through their combinations and slamming lockers open and shut with thuds of their belongings being thrown inside. The moment the bell rings, the crowd disperses. But I'm in no hurry to rush off to class today.

The hair on my arm raises as my fingers graze my cold metal locker, taking the weight of the combination lock in my hand. The metal shows traces of my sweaty hands. Once I've thrown a few things in and taken a few things out, I look around again. Expecting the Elite mob to be stalking from a nearby corner, waiting to find me alone.

But I see no one. Everything is completely silent except for the muffled sounds of teachers starting their lectures.

My palm presses against the soreness of my neck as my eyes cut around the silent, empty halls. I roll my shoulders back against my neck, my fingers trailing up to fiddle with my necklace as I slowly step toward my first classroom.

I feel no better once I settle into class, the teacher and students around me carrying on as usual. I raise my hands a few times, even though I don't know the answers, just hoping to be called on so someone will have said my name or looked in my direction enough for me to know I'm still alive.

Did I die in the car crash? Was everything after that just my brain's weird way of fantasizing my life into continuance? And now reality's set in, my existence is fading into nothingness?

My mouth fills with the taste of wood from the pencil I have been gnawing at relentlessly, sparking an idea. I let the pencil fall to the floor, thinking someone will look up or pick it up to hand it back. But nothing. It quietly clicks against the floor as it rolls right out into the middle of the room, completely untouched and seemingly unnoticed.

My foot bounces wildly underneath my desk, my eyes darting to the clock on the wall every few seconds. I can't stop reaching down to dig through my purse, forgetting what I was looking for each time.

I blow out several short breaths, trying to steady my heart rate, but my fidgeting and noisy exhales don't bring a single darting glance my way. Even the teacher seems to be actively ignoring me.

I jump at the ring of another bell, following closely behind as everyone floods back out into the halls. Stopping at the edge of the door, my finger presses the button to light up my phone screen, wondering if another mysterious message will come through with a clue. Or even a menacing text from Emmett. But nothing.

My stomach churns and time moves too slow as the halls of the school seem to wind down to nothing in front of me, closing in on me. Normally I would welcome getting lost in the tide of students between classes. This is the kind of isolation I had expected when I first came here. But in this context, it feels wrong.

My hair is matted in the same ponytail as yesterday, tangled from restless tossing and turning in my bed all night. I keep my facial features blank, hoping that if I don't show any emotion they'll give up on the whole charade.

For a few periods, I tried looking as happy as can be. Smiling wide and whistling as I walked. But with no one to even notice, it started to feel ridiculous. So, I resorted back to calm nothingness. Apathy. Indifference.

For as calm as I look outside, inside I am falling apart. Frequently retreating to the bathroom to lock myself away in a stall. It feels better to be truly alone than to be surrounded by people who don't see me.

After an endless daze of morning classes, it's finally time for lunch. I'm certain something will happen in the cafeteria. The Elites had pounced on me for merely existing up until now. There's no way they'll leave what happened with Emmett unpunished.

At the very least, Emmett's car is mangled and in his warped mind, it's my fault. I expect to be punished. The silent build-up has to be part of their plan. Making me wither away in dreaded anticipation before they strike.

In the cafeteria, the bright florescent lights overhead flicker with a horror movie style buzz. I scan the rows of long tables and plastic chairs, ducking between lines of teens carrying their plastic trays. The double doors sway open and shut as more people flood in, each one's eyes looking everywhere but at me.

I know I can't eat, but I get lunch anyway, only to sit despondently and shove the food around on my tray with a fork. I guzzle down several bottles of water. Taking in liquids is the one thing I can do right now. I am parched no matter how much I drink.

I feel like an animal on high alert. Everything seems to be moving in slow motion under the gaze of the entire cafeteria. I hear every tiny little noise amplified…someone dropping silver-ware, the slop of food on someone's tray, students shuffling in their seats and clearing their throats. People chewing their food and the hiss of opening cans.

It gets to be too much, sending me bolting for the privacy of a bathroom stall yet again to eat alone. I duck into the first stall I can and flick the lock shut.

I quickly forget about my lunch as I hear a few girls flinging open stall doors that slam shut behind them with the flush of toilets followed by water streaming from faucets. They laugh as they fix their hair and makeup. The smell of perfume and hair-spray fills the air as they gossip in hushed tones.

Finally, I hear my name. I half expect them to be discussing my tragic death. I study the sounds of their voices and their shoes from under the stall to try and discern who the girls might be, but I can't place them.

My eyelids blink rapidly as they talk, my body closing in and growing still to better hear them as the whirring hand dryers finally quiet down enough for me to make out their words.

"Can you believe it?" One girl chirps with a pop of her gum. "She's nuts. She was so determined to blow him right then and there that she made him run his car straight into the damn telephone pole."

Resentment and anger bubble up in my chest. I want to come barreling out and tell them everything that really happened. But once again I find myself stilling to see what else I can hear. Hoping for some hint at what to expect next.

"Tragic," another girl answers dryly. "So what now? We just ignore her?"

"That's what Vivian says. We're supposed to act like she doesn't exist. Which I'm happy to do. That'll teach her a lesson. Maybe the bitch will think twice before trying to blow someone else's boyfriend."

Jesus. What sort of punishment is that? I would take the relief of being shunned over the torture they had been doling out any day.

I bite my lip to hold back the questions bubbling up inside, nodding and blinking as they continue. That's why there's a lull in my torment. The Elites have told everyone to ignore me at all costs. For the rest of the semester. No talking. No looking. I am essentially a ghost.

My lips purse with raised brows, my fingers pinching against my chin. I obsessively check my phone once more, feeling half tempted to text last night's unknown number back. At least it'd be someone to talk to if nothing else. Still nothing.

The girls shuffle their plastic cosmetic cases back into their bags in a flurry of maniacal cackles as they exit the bathroom, the door swinging shut behind them to leave me in silence.

It couldn't be so bad, right? So, no one talks to me. Who cares? It'll be a relief in comparison to what I've been experiencing.

The isolation carries on throughout the day. I catch a few glimpses of Emmett, each time renewing my urge to feel his lips again. To hear the breathless groans he makes beneath my kiss. But the surge of hormones always dissipates into knots of anxiety as he effortlessly continues to not see me.

I choke down my desire for him, running through the list of everything he's done to me so that maybe I will finally come to my senses and be glad that I am exiled.

Walking through the halls, I feel the emptiness in the lack of strange and pitying looks I had grown used to. In their effort to shun me, even the whispers of my name have vanished. I'm not even a topic of gossip anymore.

Under doctor's orders, I still can't run for a few days. So, I'm relieved when it's time for gym. I need something to do to work off this anxiety. Some physical activity might calm my nerves.

I walk past the cinder block walls of the gym, scoffing at the school's name painted along the shiny wood floor. I hate that my name is somehow wrapped up in the legacy of this hellhole with the new knowledge of my father's attendance and former Elite title.

But his involvement disturbs me much less than my mom's. She is supposed to be a cornerstone in my life. One person I can fall back on when I have no one else. But now even she is tainted by the WJ Prep sickness. Not knowing to what extent only makes it worse, somehow.

My back aches from the lack of support on the bleachers retracting into the walls as I anxiously wait for the teacher to announce what we're doing today. I slump my shoulders at the revelation of dodgeball, the basket of balls quickly rolling in behind the words.

Great, that will be heavenly for my already sore and aching muscles. But honestly, I'll take it. The thrash of balls into my painful joints might be soothing somehow. Something to jolt me out of this haze of nonexistence. A reminder that I am alive.

With the blow of the teacher's whistle, the gym quickly fills with the sounds of sneakers squeaking across the floor and students calling out to one another. But my state of exile worsens. Every ball I try to snatch up is quickly taken right out from under me. Not a single one is thrown in my direction.

I stand with my hands on my hips, watching as the entire game races by without me. A comedic image of the bullied kid being a target and getting pounded with everyone's balls at once flashes through my mind. A scenario that I would almost welcome at this point. Somehow being ignored is worse.

Realizing my participation is null and void, I retreat to the water fountains to lap up as much as I can take in, partly to soothe my sudden unquenchable thirst, but mostly to avoid the awkwardness of being invisible.

The locker room is another place most girls would gladly accept a shroud of invisibility, but once again I am surprised at how much it bothers me. I sit on the long wooden bench in the middle of the lockers and stare down to the faint mildew spots staining the grout between the plain beige tiled floor, wishing I could find relief in all of this.

Surely being ignored is better than being tortured. I wanted an end to it, and now here it is. Served up to me on a silver platter. But it doesn't feel like a break at all. It's like the silent ghost town in a movie with crows cawing ominously in the distance, tumbleweeds blowing past. Quiet should be good, but you know it's just making space for whatever bad thing happens next.

Suddenly, I see a familiar pair of shoes in the corner of my eye. My heart leaps as I look up to see Lily huddled in the corner, drying sweat from her hair.

"Lily!" I rush over like an excited puppy, my voice cracking under the hours of not speaking out loud. "There you are!"

She doesn't respond at first, looking to her phone instead before finishing her preparations to head back out into the hall.

"Oh, come on," I huff with a laugh, assuming she's just messing with me ."Not you too."

My smile wavers as she looks straight through me, refusing to let her eyes meet mine. My hands wrap around my arms as I feel my face blanch. Before I know it, she's whirling right past me, stepping to the side to avoid our shoulders bumping. She is pointedly ignoring me right along with everyone else.

Left alone again, I tensely pace the locker room tiles, wringing my hands across the back of my neck. For the first time today, I want to cry. The one person I consider a friend is now against me. Everyone is avoiding me. I am completely alone.

My world quickly feels like it's closing in. With even Lily refusing to speak to me, I officially have no one outside of my parents. Between this new discovery about my mom and biological father and their ties to WJ Prep, mixed in with feeling like I couldn't tell them anything that was really happening at school, they feel like they're a million miles away even if they're right next to me.

I stand with my hand spread across the wall, my head bowing to take in a series of deep inhales and exhales, before reentering the halls to exit the building. My heart rate finally slows when I'm outside again, feeling the warmth of the sun on my cheeks. But even the cloudy blue skies seem ominous in my exile.

I hesitate in my pace with each person I pass in the parking lot, thinking someone will cave in and acknowledge me. But they've obviously done this before. It's like the Elites control a switchboard in everyone's brains and can simply flip it on anyone at any time, making them completely unperceivable.

I debate going to practice. I can't run away. But I had planned on at least stopping by to talk to Coach Granger. My mom had already called to let him know I'd be absent for a couple of days as I recovered, but surely he's above this vow of silence? He might be the only person left who would still speak to me.

A glimmer of hope shines through the clouds at the thought of him. He had said I could come to him for anything, and while I wasn't prepared to even begin explaining everything that had happened, a simple smile or hello would suffice. After this day from hell where every other teacher played along as Vivian's pawns.

It was disgusting the way the entire school staff, and even the police, just sucked up to the Elites, going along with whatever new dumb thing they demanded. Even if it meant pretending I didn't exist. It was that extent of their power and influence that kept me silent. Especially after seeing my mom playing chummy with Trey and Vincent.

By not telling anyone, even my parents or coach, I still have some distant hope of confessing to them as a last resort. If I play that card too soon only to find it did nothing, I would feel too hopeless to go on.

I can't find Coach Granger at the track, and of course no one will answer me when I try to ask around for him. But finally I catch a note on the billboard informing everyone that he'd be absent today and to run the usual laps.

Fucking of course. Of all the days he could be absent, it had to be the one when he might have been the only person who would acknowledge me.

With each new instance of being shunned, I want to take off running to my car. But I'm too sore and tired. I walk slower than a turtle, kicking pebbles as I go. By the time I do reach my car, I decide to keep walking. I already feel claustrophobic with a lingering shock from the crash. I can't stand the thought of getting in. I'll walk home.

My mind races as I go, drenched in self-loathing of my own hypocrisy. From day one all I wanted was for everyone to forget me. Move their target to someone else's back. I just wanted to run and focus on my grades, hoping if I stayed out of their way they'd stay out of mine. And now that my wish is finally granted, I can't stand it.

When I get home, the house is dark and quiet, only worsening my feeling of seclusion. I remember Mom saying she would be working late. I collapse into bed, not even bothering to change out of my uniform. Sprawled out across the bed, my hand grips the phone, waiting for any kind of message. Even a bad one. Anything at all.

The long, gray day fades as I drift into a light nap. The kind that comes from boredom and restlessness, where every tiny sound or thought wakes you up again. Denying you the escape of sleep.

# CHAPTER ELEVEN

## BOOK 1

I don't know how long I've been awake before I finally resign to having to open my eyes. I had half-hoped I would just fall asleep again and wouldn't have to worry about it, but it became apparent that wasn't going to happen this time. The room is still mostly dark, but the harsh rays of light darting through the openings in the curtains tell me it isn't early morning anymore.

I look over to the nightstand. 12:00pm. Shit. I slept in again. This is becoming a more frequent pattern, seemingly beyond my control. I lay here for hours, tossing and turning, not falling asleep until it's almost dawn. Then I'm unable to stay awake when I should be getting up.

One week has gone by. Still nothing. No one will look at me. No one will talk to me. Aside from the moments I desperately cling to with my mom and Brendan, which are scarce around their busy work schedules, I am completely alone.

I slide out of bed, my still-tired body aching with each movement. My legs seem to buckle underneath me, not wanting to cooperate. I go downstairs, finding the house to be empty. My parents have already left for work.

I make it into the kitchen and see that it is mostly empty. Well, not exactly empty. There are eggs and bacon and bread for toast. A normal person would jump right in to making a nice breakfast, but the thought of cooking right now repulses me. I have zero appetite or energy to prepare food.

I throw on a t-shirt, secure my hair up into a sloppy bun and put on a pair of leggings and tennis shoes. Most importantly, I put on sunglasses to hide my tired eyes from the world. Walking out into the sun is painful. It burns into my eyes, my head and every bone in my body.

Once I'm at school, I wander through the halls, accepting my fate in exile. At least no one cares that I'm late. I look around and see a gangly kid approaching me with an apologetic look on his face. Finally, this is it. Someone is going to talk to me. But instead he just rushes past to his friends on the other side of the hall.

Coach Granger has been absent for a family emergency. And none of the other teachers will acknowledge my existence. Even when I try to corner them with direct questions, the other students always find a way to distract them or steal the attention back.

I am completely and utterly alone.

A state that at times, especially recently, I thought I wanted. But now that it is happening, I am more miserable than I have ever been.

I understand the concept now of children misbehaving for attention. Because negative attention is better than no attention at all. They would rather be punished than be ignored, and that is exactly how I feel right now.

I miss the punishment of the Elites. That's how insane isolation has driven me.

It's lunchtime, and I am over hiding away alone in the bathroom. I thought if I faced down being ignored, something would change. But then I realized it didn't matter if I tried to hide or put myself out in the middle of everything. The result is the same. So there's no use in hiding.

Instead I sit here in a room full of people completely alone. I can hear cackles from the Elite table. And it makes me want to smack each one of them in the face until there's nothing left to laugh about.

That's it. I have reached my breaking point. Finally, I'm so desperate for human contact that I decide to do something drastic. Something that can't be ignored.

I scan across the room, inevitably landing my sights on the Elites' lunch table. I hate how happy and arrogant they look. They don't deserve to be so carefree with the misery they inflict on other people's lives, and I've finally had enough.

I can feel my muscles quake as I stand from my seat and

charge straight for them. My nostrils flare as sweat beads across my skin. My shoulders bump against people as I go, which they still do their best to ignore, and I don't stop until I'm at the edge of their table.

They keep looking everywhere but at me, but I see their eyes give the faintest glint in my direction. Everything closes in around Vivian in pure tunnel vision. She is the only thing I can see now.

I bare my teeth and with one sweeping, swift motion, I slap Vivian right across the face. A violent clap echoes through the silent lunchroom as my flat and stiffened palm strikes her cheek.

Vivian looks up to me with a vicious growl, her hand still pressed against her red cheekbone in shock. Her eyes bulge out of her head so far, I think they might burst.

Before I can think or do anything else, she is pummeling toward me. My body slams to the ground beneath her attack, her hands pinning my arms down long enough for her to break free and go for a punch.

I am too high on jealousy and anger. My adrenaline is pumping, giving me what feels like special powers. I am alert and sharp enough to catch her blow midair with my hand gripped around her wrist. I roll over, reversing our positions so that she is now the one pinned below me.

I go into a flurry of punches. One right after the other. Anywhere I can manage. Her face, her ear, her side. She knees me a few good times, but other than that is completely helpless beneath my rage. I can't even feel the scratches she manages to get in across my hands and arms in defense.

I stare ahead blankly, cold and hard as jeers and taunts swell up around us. Finally, I think. At least they're acknowledging that they can see me. I don't even care that they are cheering for Vivian, encouraging her to get the upper hand again.

I'm surprised that no one jumps in to stop me, but I imagine I look like an absolute mad woman running on nothing but pure anger. They're afraid of me. I also like to think everyone secretly wants to see Vivian get the shit beat out of her.

Finally, an arm across my chest snaps me from my red blur of fury, but barely. I feel a man's firm chest push to my back as I'm raised into the air, my arms still flailing viciously. Just before I'm hauled through the swinging cafeteria doors, I see Vivian glaring as she's left to pick herself up off the floor.

I don't know who is carting me off until he's pushing me up against the wall of an empty classroom. Emmett.

His hand grips around my neck, his own neck muscles bulging and his breath heavy through his nose. I don't recoil as I normally would. I'm so desperate for his eyes to be burning into mine. His hands across my skin, even if they are holding on too tight. Instead I melt into him, drawing my chin up to meet his gaze.

The desperation in my eyes softens his touch, drawing the curve of his finger across my jaw.

"What the hell were you thinking?" he hisses, his skin roiling with desire. I can feel it coursing through his fingertips, and I know how it is burning into him because I feel it too.

"You can't do this to me," I respond breathlessly, his fingers clutching harder into my neck as I speak. "You can't just pretend I don't exist."

"You did this to yourself," he groans, his head swaying with the rhythm of my squirms. "If you had just been a good little pet and done what you were told…"

"Enough of that shit!" I try my best to shout, but it cracks into a whisper. "I'm no one's pet. Not even yours. All I've done is defend myself."

"Oh no?" he grins devilishly. His hand drops below my neck, forcefully pressing down every inch of my chest before resting across my abs. "You're not my pet?" His eyes move hungrily over me from top to bottom, taking in every inch of me.

I want to scream no, but I can't say anything. I'm too high on the ecstasy of human contact.

"I like you like this," he croons softly, leaning closer to my ear. The soft graze of his lips sets my skin on fire. "Broken down…desperate. I bet I could do anything I wanted to you right now, couldn't I?"

"Key word being *want*," I shoot back in a moan. "You do want me. You have wanted me this whole time."

I don't even care anymore how sick and twisted this whole thing is. His desire is all I care about right now. I need the validation. I need to know I am real after this week of feeling nonexistent. And I know that's what he gets out of all of this. I don't know if his motivation for making my life a living hell is the same as Vivian's or any of the other Elites, but I know the benefit is that it leaves me like this…putty in his hands.

When he doesn't answer, I push forward to run away, but his palm quickly juts across my chest and slams me back again. His breath quickens even more, and I can see him trying to resist as his finger trails across my face.

All at once we both surrender, our lips colliding and opening wide as our tongues crash across each other in firm waves. I can't help but whimper into his mouth, sparking an earnest groan from his in return.

"When I saw you storm up to our table, I was hoping we would end up like this," he mumbles into my lips, barely breaking us apart to speak. "I was expecting you to put up more of a fight. We really did get to you this time, huh?"

I almost think I can sense a tinge of pity in his voice. Not the degrading kind, but a sincere sympathy for what they have put me through. It makes me lose myself in him even more, my hands sliding across his back, up his neck and clenching into his hair. His hips push against mine, keeping me pinned firmly to the wall, and I can feel his hardness straining against his paints.

"Touch me," I plead, biting his lip.

He pulls back, his eyes lighting up with a yearning fire as he studies me. He's surprised I'm so willing right now. I saw it in the moment his eyebrows raised ever so slightly.

But rather than give in to what we both want, his grip tightens around my neck again, pulling my lips from his.

"You know I can't just let you get away with what you did to Vivian," he says almost apologetically. "They'll never let me."

"So...what? You're just their puppet?" I tease defiantly, expecting a swift reprimand for challenging him.

The way he stills suddenly frightens me. I can see a new touch of humanity in him. One that really does feel sorry for me and all he's done to me. Could it be that none of this is Emmett's choosing? Is he just caught up in the game like I am and doing what he's told?

His hand loosens from my neck, falling limp to his side as he steps back in surrender, still saying nothing.

My mind flashes with all that he's done. The physical and emotional abuse. And all at once I remember there's no way he's just an Elite pawn. He is one of them through and through. And even if part of him feels regret now, he was completely in charge all the times before when he caused me harm.

And it all served the exact purpose it was intended to...to leave me so fucked up and desperate for anything that I would willingly give myself over to him. Admit to the things he makes my body feel, no matter how much it repulses me.

I'm overwhelmed with it all. I can't believe this sad puppy act he's putting on all of a sudden, and I don't want to fall for it. Unable to fight the single tear spilling down the side of my face, I push past him and run away down the hall as fast as I can.

I don't stop until I'm halfway to my car. Fuck this day. Fuck school. The way the teachers have been acting I'm not even entirely sure they're counting my attendance or grades anyway. I might as well give up and go home.

But once I reach my car door, I still don't stop. Running feels too good right now. It's what I need. I keep barreling forward, right past my car, all the way to my house. I'll figure out the rest later. Right now I just need to run.

The cold sting of air bursts in my lungs as I go, burning with tears that I try to fight back as hard as I can. Every time I feel the pulse of his lingering touch, I run faster and harder. Hoping the swift wind against my body will blow it all away.

By the time I collapse on my bed in my room, all I can feel is the need for his warmth against me again. The fantasy of him falling on top of me in my bed is so palpable that I almost reach for my phone to message him. Beg him to come finish what he started.

I swear I hear a drum beating in my ears, but I quickly realize it's just the steady severity of my own heart. Pounding through me as the most tangible images of Emmett flash through my mind. I can see exactly what he would look like right here right now…towering above me in this light as he takes off his shirt.

I roll into my hands, covering my eyes and wishing it would all go away. Somehow my desperate need to punish Vivian and to get some kind of attention rapidly crumbled into a completely unhindered lustful need for Emmett. More strong than I have ever felt before.

The way he sounded so sorry… It reminds me of how he sounded before I got into his car. I remember now that's why I followed him in the first place. He sounded so sincere. So normal. Maybe even kind.

It was the same boy I met at that track meet before coming here. Maybe I don't have to beat myself up so much, or maybe I'm just grasping at straws. But I have seen small glimpses of a decent human being in him. Ever so brief moments when he doesn't seem demented or sadistic. And each new taste of it seems to cause my longing for him to erupt. It clouds my judgment. Makes me do everything I swore I couldn't.

It makes me surrender completely to him.

Completely exhausted, I close my eyes and hope to dream of something…anything else.

My brush with Emmett was exactly what I needed to set my head straight in a weird way, because now I am more than happy to embrace my isolation. I'm resting in it like a shroud.

I gladly walk alone and eat alone yet again when I return to the lunchroom. But it seems now that I want the isolation, they're ready to take it away again. Because I can see the Elite pack marching right toward me in the corner of my eye. I don't look at them, staring down at the sandwich in my hands instead, hoping they will just walk right past.

And at first, they do. But then Emmett's hands reach around and spread out on the table before me, his chest leaning into mine with his lips next to my ear. Reawakening every spark I felt the day before and had worked so hard to erase. Only now, Vivian is just a few feet away, watching our every move.

"Get up and come with us," he demands with the best growl he can muster, but I can still hear the lingering pity and reluctance. I tell myself he doesn't want to be doing this. He said he couldn't let me get away with it…that they'd never let him.

Before I can protest, his hand grips my arm and lifts me to my feet with a subtle jerk. Just enough to let me know I don't have a choice without outright manhandling me in front of the entire cafeteria. My sandwich drops to my tray and before I can say or do anything else, I'm being led back to the same classroom he and I took refuge in just the day before.

He pushes me inside as the rest of them file in behind him. I catch one last subtle "I'm sorry" look from him in my direction before he turns to lock the door and close the blinds. Instinctively, I start stepping back away from them, quickly meeting the edge of a table that stops me from moving any further.

I lean back to brace myself and consider attempting to dart away between the table and chairs, but they're surrounding me like a pack of hungry dogs. I know it's no use. Trey and Vincent surround me on either side, each grabbing an arm and carrying me to the wall.

The memories of Emmett pinning me to this wall almost make me immune to my fear of whatever is about to happen. I glance over to him, but before our eyes can meet, he quickly looks away. By the time I look back up, Vivian is storming toward me.

I brace myself for a revenge slap and am instead met with the blow of her fist, shooting straight into my nose and up between my eyes with streams of tears. Followed by a warm trickle of blood from my nostrils.

I feel the physical sensation of the pain, but barely. I am numb to them now. My apathy scares me more than they do as I look back to her blankly, unmoved by the punch. It only eggs her on. She delivers another swift blow to my gut.

"You had enough yet?" she growls into my ear. "You ready to talk?"

"Talk about what?" I shoot back, defiantly spitting the blood from my lips in her direction.

Her palm strikes my cheek, the sting echoing into my eardrums.

She steps back with a half-hearted smirk and looks me up and down, nodding to Trey and Vincent to let me down. I collapse to the floor, but quickly pull myself back up. Ready to stand and take more of a beating if that's what she insists on. I'm over backing down to them.

"Well?" Vivian snaps expectantly.

I don't know what she wants from me, but I'm positive I wouldn't give it to her even if I could.

"What!?" I cry back in frustration. "What is it you want from me?"

"You know damn well what we want," she sneers, pacing in front of me. "Don't play dumb."

I consider telling her what Emmett and I did in here the day before, and again before that in the hospital room. My eyes glint toward him at the prospect, but he still refuses to look in my direction. His hands are in his pockets shamefully, looking down to the floor as if he has nothing to do with any of this. But I know, no matter how sorry he may be, that's not entirely true.

And anyway, telling her about those moments will only ensure they never happen again. However fucked up it may be, it's not a bridge I'm willing to burn just yet.

"I don't know what you want!" I bark back at her, clutching the ache in my gut. "I haven't known what you've wanted this whole time! You're all fucking crazy! Ganging up on me for no reason!"

"Is that what you think?" she smiles arrogantly. "That we don't have better things to do with our time than chase you around? Get over yourself. We'd be happy to just forget you ever existed like the meaningless nothing you are. But we have to protect ourselves. So here we are."

"Protect *yourselves*!?" I scoff in disbelief, my voice betraying me with too high of a pitch. "What the hell do you need to be protected from? I'm the one that's being treated like some kind of prey. You've gone after me relentlessly from day one!"

"I'm not an idiot," she growls back. "You know more than you're letting on." She nods back to Vincent and Trey who promptly scoop me back up against the wall, my stomach muscles still clenching in pain from the time before.

I grit my teeth to bear another round of blows to my face and stomach, punctuated with a crippling kick to my shin. The sting sends me into a panic.

"Stop!" I scream in anguish. I can take a beating anywhere at this point, but not my legs. I have lost enough time on the track because of these assholes. I won't lose any more. "Not my legs! Please! I don't know what you want from me…but whatever it is, I'll try. Just please not my legs."

Vivian's lips curl. She's pleased that she struck a nerve. Found a weak spot. She steps forward, her foot rearing back again, but Emmett grabs her.

"Vivian, no," he commands, shaking her by the shoulder between his hands. "She said she'd talk."

Her eyes burn into him, giving me the feeling that he'd pay for that later. But for now, she complies and turns her attention back to me.

"You're gonna have to do more than try," she grunts. "When's the last time you talked to him? I want to know everything he has said recently. About us."

"What the fuck are you talking about?" I sob in exasperation, feeling completely clueless. Like they have the wrong girl. I'm being framed. I have to be. I don't know whatever it is they think I know.

"Give it up already, Ophelia! Your fucking dad!!" She barks back, my heart stopping as the words roll from her tongue.

My fucking dad, indeed. I should have known this entire vendetta against me had something to do with him from the moment I found out he was once an Elite. I suddenly wish I had kept digging. That I knew more by now. But I was too distracted with the exile they placed me under.

I can feel my blood boiling beneath my skin. Of course this man who my mom considers to be the scum of the earth…who has been completely absent from my entire life…is now somehow responsible for all the torture I've been enduring.

# CHAPTER TWELVE

## BOOK 1

My brain sparks, rapidly trying to connect everything enough to make some sense of her ranting. Wrapping my head around my dad being an Elite in the first place was hard enough. But that was in the past…and he seems to be long gone now. But Vivian is acting like he's still around…playing all of their games. I'm screaming inside, wishing I could escape being involved at all.

My eyebrows gather with a heavy sigh as my mind drifts to all the places I'd rather be. Anywhere but here. Running. Laying in my bed. Eating in the cafeteria.

I hate myself for slapping Vivian yesterday, even if it was rewarding. And even if it did get Emmett's lips pressed back to mine, if only for a few moments.

I knew there would be a price to pay. But I'm not so sure the benefits were worth the cost as I stand here now with the Elites circling me like vultures, working my stomach into knots.

My feet point toward the door as my dull eyes drift to its window, wishing I could catch sight of a teacher passing by. Or another student. But I know better. Even if someone did walk by, they wouldn't help.

I'm completely stuck. Cornered. The only way out is to bend to their will, and even that isn't a way out. It's just more of the same. No matter what I do…I am their pawn. Or, their "pet" as Emmett likes to say.

I want nothing to do with the Elites, especially if it helps them. The only thing I can think I want less than working with the Elites in any way…is to have anything to do with my biological father. In fact, it seems more and more that those two things are one and the same.

The sun is shining in through the classroom windows, and I can see the track field off in the distance. I would do anything to be out there running right now instead of in here being threatened and tortured.

I think back on Coach Granger's offer…when he told me I could tell him anything. I am kicking myself for not having the balls to talk to him then.

But now here I am piecing this all together on my own. All of this has something to do with my dad.

I guess it's better than having to think the Elites are so incredibly bored and desperate for something to do that they make people's lives miserable just for fun. These people have power and money, and they're willing to do whatever it takes to protect their positions in life.

I want this new motive to redeem Emmett. All of them, but mostly him. I know I wouldn't have liked Vivian and Bernadette even if they hadn't attacked me before I even set foot on campus.

But my crush on Emmett was strong. I thought we had potential…until I realized who he really was. Does having some insight to the motive somehow excuse everything he has done?

I can't believe my father used to be one of them and that he is apparently still chasing after them in some way. Enough to have them all riled up.

My mother is completely the opposite of anything the Elites stand for. She's worked hard to give me a good life. Brendan does too. But at the end of the day, all they care about is family. Money and things have never been top priorities for them. And they would never betray their friends or family, or bring physical harm to someone, just to protect some perceived entitlement to social and financial standing.

I look to the clock on the wall, gulping as I realize lunch period lasts for another twenty minutes. Then the students will crowd back into the halls and this classroom will need to be used.

It's a relief to know there is an end in sight. They could have thrown me into one of their cars and drove me off somewhere. At least this way I know we have to be done in twenty minutes or less. But a lot can happen in that amount of time.

"Just tell me what you want," I hiss with tired eyes that are dead and flat. I'm over the secrecy and vagueness. Maybe if I hear them out it will give me more information on what my dad has to do with all of this.

"You're just collateral, sweetie," Vivian answers smugly, her voice chiming sweetly in a mocking tone with her pinched face and sour expression. "Just be a good little bitch and do what we tell you, and we'll take it easy on you."

"Ha!" I scoff, finding it hard to believe they'd ever take it easy on me. "Now I really don't know what you're talking about."

They've hurt me. Humiliated me. I've suffered greatly at their hands and now…they want my help? I look away, feeling at a loss for words.

"Let me put it this way," she continues menacingly, jutting out her chest and crossing her arms. "If he doesn't stop playing games, you're dead. So, you might as well save your own ass and help us."

"You're out of luck, Vivian. I've never talked to my dad. I don't know the guy. He doesn't even know I'm here, so this is just a waste of your time," I fume, rolling my eyes, my head hanging heavy, in hopes that this will be the end of it. But I know better. They'd never give up so easy.

"I find that hard to believe," she fires back with a look of superiority, projecting her voice just to show she has the upper hand in a determined strut around the room in perfect posture. "We know he saw the press release about your scholarship and you attending WJ Prep."

"And how would you know something like that?" I groan with an upward glance, a dramatic breath rattling my lips.

"Because we sent it to him, you dumb bitch!" she shrieks impatiently, her fingers retracting into claw-like fists.

"Well then that's on you, isn't it? Still has nothing to do with me. And if anything, it just proves my point more. So, you made sure he knew I was here, but he still hasn't contacted me," I explain condescendingly, settling my back to the wall and crossing my arms.

"Trust me, he knew exactly where you were long before we sent that release," she continues with a loud blusterous voice. "We just wanted to make sure he knew we were on to him. I think he's been more present in your life than you originally thought. And if it comes down to it…we'll kidnap you and use you as a bargaining chip. He's not going to get away with his bullshit."

"This has nothing to do with me, Vivian," I plead cluelessly. "I don't know what's going on with you and my dad, but whatever it is…it's just between you two. He's not in my life and I'm not in his. And I'd like to keep it that way."

"You don't have a choice, Ophelia. Just by existing, you're wrapped up in this. You're the only key we have to him, and we'll use you however we have to." Vivian turns away snidely as Trey and Vincent circle me.

"Use me for what!? What is it that he's doing!?" I keep looking to Emmett, but he is still and blank. No one answers me. "I'll just go to the police," I try to reason uselessly. Knowing as soon as the words fall from my mouth that it's a futile remark.

"The police work for us just like everyone else in this town," Vincent sneers with a crack of his neck.

"Of course, how could I forget," I say sarcastically with a sharp, hopeless exhale. "This is fucking useless."

"You're still dumb enough to think everything is just happening by coincidence," Vivian sneers. "There's a reason you're here, Ophelia. At this school. Your father waged war with our families before you were born, and it's still going."

"How!? What did he do? I don't know anything!"

"I'm sure you'll figure it out in time," she smiles. "But for now…you have one job. Get him to stop coming after our parents."

"Great…except I have no clue how to do that," I fire back dryly. "You don't seem to be getting it. We have nothing to do with each other and I don't know anything about this supposed war he's in with you and your stupid fucking families."

"You don't have to know anything. You just have to get him to respond to our messages. Or else you're dead," she turns her back to me impatiently.

"Ophelia," Emmett finally chimes in, practically begging me to comply. "You'll help us. Or we'll kill you. And that's the end of it." It almost sounds like he wants me to give in so I'll be spared any more torture.

"I'm not helping you with anything," I growl, sparking a pleased grin across Emmett's face. It's as if he wants to kill me.

Maybe that'd be easier for him than dealing with whatever's going on between us.

Trey and Vincent lunge forward again, their rough hands twisting into my shoulders and wrists. I'm still sore from Vivian's beating, but try to buckle down and brace myself against the wall the best I can, but they're too strong. My teeth grind as their hands circle my arms tightly, burning and pinching the skin as they go. I wince and take tentative steps beneath their grip, my eyes watering up from the sensation. They don't stop. My head flails back against the wall with my face twisted into a grimace.

"Let me go!" I scream in a panic in between grunts and pained hisses, wondering if they really do have the balls to kill me right here and now. That might be better than having to help them or have anything to do with my father. Their fingers twist into my skin with a burning sensation. "Stop! Just leave me alone!"

My breath saws in and out rapidly as Vivian marches toward me again, sending her foot back into my shin despite Emmett's disapproval. I yowl out in pain as I crash back down to the floor.

"Fuck!" I cry, rubbing my hand across my stinging leg bone that is already turning purple. Within seconds, I am lifted back into the air, propping me up for more of Vivian's blows. But to my surprise, Emmett appears just a foot away from me. I wonder how he felt about Vivian denying his orders to leave my legs alone. After all, he enjoys looking at these muscular legs of mine. If I can't run, they go to flabby shit…which just isn't in his best interests.

He scowls toward the others, prompting them to back up. It's as if he watched for as long as he could, but now he has to have me to himself again. Whether Vivian is watching or not.

"Quit fighting us," he barks. "Just make sure your dad responds to our parents. And do what we tell you."

"I don't even know how to reach him," I growl, fighting back sobs.

His feet inch closer to me, propelling me back to the day before. We were exactly like this. Him seething before me as I was pinned up against the wall. My eyes dart over to Vivian as I wonder if I should kiss him again right in front of her.

"We can take care of that," he murmurs into my ear. "You just need to be a good little pet and do as you're told."

My eyes dart back to the ticking clock hands every few seconds, noting how painfully slow they are moving. Almost backward.

I hate that we're back to this and I feel stupid for believing even for a moment that he could be innocent in all of this. Just as stuck as I was. No, he was a willing participant. Getting off on it all just as much as the rest of them.

But as I consider how trapped I am, the bigger questions at hand flood my mind. What could my dad possibly be doing to have them this riled up? And what kind of ultimatum was he being given?

"And if I can get him to respond?" I test lightly with my brows raised, purposefully keeping my face too close to his in hopes that it will drive Vivian insane. "If I do whatever you say and get my dad to do what you want…when all of this is over… do I ever get to be free from this bullshit? Are you ever going to leave me alone?"

"Do you want me to leave you alone?" he whispers boldly into my ear, his hot breath rolling down my neck. "Don't waste your time asking what happens if everything goes right. You're better off focusing on what's going to happen to you if it doesn't."

"But I don't know how to help you," I try again through gritted teeth, spurring him to push into me harder.

"I think you do, baby," he jeers in a low tone that burns straight into my gut.

Baby. The sound of it on his lips used to make me sick. And it still does, but now my stomach twists with nauseating desperation.

I sigh dejectedly, slumping my shoulders. My eyes meet his with blank features, stooping below him as my feet shuffle to steady myself against the wall. "Okay, so what happens next?" I resign with a monotone voice, my chin trembling.

Emmett's lips curl into a pleased grin, his gray eyes piercing across my skin as he looks me up and down, violating me with his gaze in a way only he can.

"Emmett!" Vivian barks disapprovingly from over his shoulder. "Let's get on with it already!"

I can't help but smile at her impatience. She can't stand to see Emmett lusting for me so fearlessly, right in front of her and everyone else. We struck a nerve, and for once she wasn't able to hide it.

"What's wrong, Vivian?" I fire back with a cocky grin, placing a hand on Emmett's arm. "Jealous?"

"Jealous?" Vivian laughs. "I could never be jealous of a little worm like you. I have nothing to worry about. I'm just bored and ready to see you bleed some more."

The faintest crack in her voice tells me that she is trying to convince herself just as much as she's trying to convince me.

"You don't sound so sure, Viv," I tease back, buckling my hips forward subtly. Just enough to be closer to Emmett's body with my hand still draped over his arm. "Maybe we should ask Emmett if you have anything to worry about."

My eyes turn to his with a devilish spark. My hair may be a dirty, disheveled mess, and I can feel the drying blood caked above my upper lip. But a flick of his tongue across his lip tells me all I need to know. He still wants me. And restraining himself with his girlfriend in the room is torture.

"Stop causing trouble," he remarks apathetically, his smile betraying him.

"But you like me when I'm causing trouble." I flash him a smile, and I wonder if he'll smack me or kiss me. "Or at least you sure seemed to yesterday."

If I have no choice but to play along with their games, I at least want to have some fun at my own funeral.

I watch Vivian's confidence crumble. "What is she talking about!?" she snaps.

"Nothing, baby," Emmett dryly responds, not even bothering to look at her. His eyes are glued to me, and I know he's getting off on my defiance.

"Yeah, Vivian," I smirk. "Nothing at all."

"Emmett, I don't know what she's talking about, but if you don't make her shut up right now, I'm going to kick her fucking ass," Vivian threatens, desperately wanting to cling to her ignorance.

The Elites think they need me for something, which means momentarily they are going to avoid killing me at all costs. I know it must be driving Vivian insane. But I am loving getting to torture her some in return.

"How will you make me shut up, Emmett?" I provoke him coyly.

His fist slams next to my face so hard that the vibration in the wall hurts my skull. He is growling through his throat, holding back desire.

"Come on, Emmett. You've had no problem roughing me up in the past. I don't know why you're having trouble with it now," I continue, causing his face to wince. He's torn between Vivian's demands, his need to hurt me and his want to fuck me. I dart my eyes over to Vivian and then back to his. "You wanna tell her what happened in here yesterday, or should I?"

"Shut your fucking mouth, Ophelia…or I swear to god," he fumes, leaning in closer to intimidate me, but it only intensifies the heat between us.

"Make me. Or is that something you can only do when your girlfriend isn't watching?" There's a hard lump in my throat reminding me that I shouldn't be so bold.

They are going to make me pay for every cocky word coming out of my mouth. But I can't help it. Now that I know they need me…I can't resist taking advantage and turning the tables for once.

"Emmett, I swear to god…," Vivian grumbles viciously. "If you've been messing around with this filthy whore you're never touching me again."

"I don't think he'll be missing out on much," I quip softly, smirking to myself.

"Enough! We're not here for some stupid catfight," Emmett snaps, slamming his hand to the wall next to my head again. "Though I'd love to watch you two fight over me all day. We're here to get you to get your father under fucking control."

"You're going soft on us, bro," Trey mocks from the other side of the room. "She's not even scared of you anymore. That's why she's giving us so much trouble."

"Yeah, let's just get on with this already," Vincent adds in agreement, looking bored. "Just hurt her some more and she'll do what we ask."

"You're all good for nothing," Bernadette chimes in suddenly from the other side of the room, slamming her cell phone to the table in exasperation. "Let me take a crack at her."

She sways her hips in a dramatic fashion as she strolls up to me, popping her chewing gum in a big bubble. "You think you're tough as shit now, huh?" she taunts in my face, trying to squeeze in between me and Emmett but he's not budging. "Well regardless of whatever gross pussy magic you think you've worked over on Emmett here…the rest of us still see you for exactly what you are. Disgusting white trash. You don't belong here. Your father didn't belong here. And when we're through with you…you'll go right back to whatever dump you came from, penniless and worse off than before you came here."

All I can do is smile, reigniting the flames in all of their eyes. Funny that they think running me out of town is some form of punishment. At this point, it's what I'm praying for.

Fuck my scholarship. I just want to be done with these assholes.

# CHAPTER THIRTEEN

BOOK 1

"I'm done with your bullshit," Vivian huffs, marching up to us and flinging Emmett and Bernadette out of the way, wagging her fingers viciously in my face. "As long as daddy dearest responds to the ultimatum our parents sent, you won't get hurt."

"What ultimatum?" I ask, wishing I had more of a clue as to what was going on. "If my life depends on my ability to help you, wouldn't it be better for all of us if you told me what was actually going on here?"

"I don't buy this little innocent naïve act of yours for one second," she barks back, practically spitting in my face between her gritted teeth. "I'm not going to stand here and waste more of my time and energy explaining things that you probably already know. You're just trying to get more out of us so you can tell your shitty dad how much we know. And *that* is a biiiig mistake, you little rat."

"I wouldn't know how to reach him to tell him anything anyway!" I remind her, my voice shrill in frustration. "Much less how to reach him and tell him to do whatever it is you're wanting. I don't even know where to begin."

"Well, you better start figuring it out, princess," she walks away carelessly. "I'd hate for your first meeting with Daddy dearest to be at your funeral. That's if he even makes it out of this alive. Which is doubtful at this point."

My blood chills. She's not fucking around. And she's also

not budging. Her death threats make me want to threaten to go to the police again, but I know that means nothing to them. They're completely fearless.

Well, almost. My dad has managed to do something that has them afraid. Something I know nothing about but am somehow expected to stop.

She tosses a phone in my direction, sending my arms flying to catch it so it doesn't hit me in the face. Once my hands wrap around it, I lower my arms to study the device.

It's not just any phone. It's *my* phone. Again.

"How did you get this?" I murmur in confusion.

"Oh, I hope you don't mind…" Emmett answers tauntingly. "I borrowed that from you yesterday."

"No…you couldn't have…," I reason out loud, but then I start connecting the dots.

I was so upset after our encounter I had raced straight home and never even bothered checking to see if I had my phone last night or this morning. I slept straight through and then came to school in a daze. He had it the entire time.

Had that been the only reason he got so close to me? Why he kissed me again? Was it all just a ploy of distraction so he could swipe my phone right out from under me?

I shake away my doubts, filing them for later, as I bring myself back to Vivian's demands.

"Well, can you at least tell me when my dad needs to respond to the ultimatum by?" I try again, hoping for any small hint of where to even begin.

There's no response. Vincent and Trey are approaching once again with frightening smug grins. This isn't just another round of roughing me up. They're closing in on me with a purpose, one that they're too pleased with.

My eyes dart to the door as I contemplate making a run for it. They may be stronger than me, but I doubt they're fast enough to outrun me. But I know I won't be able to build enough speed between where I stand and the door. They'd have me back in their arms before I could make it out.

And even if I did get away…they don't sound like they're going to let all of this go easily. I'd escape only to be haunted by the constant looming threat of when they'd try again. And since this business with my dad seems to be of a time-sensitive nature, I might as well try to get this over with.

"I'll just ditch my phone!" I jeer, swallowing down my fears about how pricey a new one would be. "I can get a new one. You're not going to keep tabs on me."

"Oh, don't worry," Vivian grins. "We've got a back-up plan."

Trey and Vincent snarl and cackle as they grab onto me again, Bernadette joining in. They sound like wild hyenas who've just landed their prey.

"Get away from me!" I protest hopelessly as they each take an arm and lift my feet from the ground. I kick aimlessly into the air, but it's no use. My struggling doesn't doesn't faze them and I'm at the mercy of their hard grip around my shoulders.

With a painful thud, they slam my chest and face down onto a table. One hand spreads across the side of my face while another set of hands holds my arms behind my back.

"Move over," Emmett grunts. "Let me do it."

"I'll do it," Vivian protests. "I don't want you putting your hands on this filthy little cunt anymore."

Her jealousy gives me a momentary thrill, but I'm quickly brought back to the danger I'm in.

I hear a scuffle from the two of them fighting over something, but barely. One of my ears is sharply pressed down beneath the weight of my head, and my other ear is being crushed underneath Vincent's hand. All I can hear is the fierce and rapid pounding of my own heart in fear of whatever it is they're getting ready to do.

With a quick and sudden pull to my top, I hear the fabric rip around my right arm. I assume their motives are perverted and sexual, but then...

"What the fuck!" I cry out in a shrill sob as a sharp, searing pain cuts into my shoulder.

I can tell by the size of the hands that Emmett won out over Vivian, which I want to take some small comfort in. He seems to be leaning toward taking it easier on me. After all, if I'm dead, he can't fuck me. So, in a weird, twisted way, he's on my side, right?

But it doesn't feel like he's on my side as a cold blade digs deeper into my skin. I try not to notice the way his hips press against my ass as I squirm beneath him, but I feel a hint of that familiar bulge from yesterday. He's holding back, but he can only do so much. He's getting off on pinning me down from behind like this.

I can't believe my mind is even going there with the cold pain slicing into me deeper and deeper. A warm trickle of blood causes my skin to shiver and flinch as it trails down my side.

"What are you doing!?" I cry out again, jerking harder in their hold.

"This is a tracking device," he responds coyly, tinged with satisfaction. "Tucked away under your skin. So, you could ditch your phone…but it'd be no use. We'll still be able to keep an eye on you."

I scream and cry, kicking more violently, as I feel the distinct tug of a needle and thread working its way around the incision.

"Now, do yourself a favor and don't bother trying to get it out," he rants like a mad scientist at work. "It's too deep. You'll never get it on your own. And I don't have to tell you what would happen if you were stupid enough to try and get someone to help you."

"A doctor!" I protest. "I'll go to a doctor! Whether they work for you or not, they'll have to help me!"

Vivian laughs wildly from behind Emmett. "You go to a doctor whining about tracking devices being implanted in your skin and they'll have you committed!"

With a painful pull of a knot followed by the snip of scissors, they loosen their hold on me. My hand reaches to feel the wound, but it's just out of my reach. And the more I try to stretch around to it, the more everything hurts.

"That's all for now," Vivian chimes with a deceptively innocent smile, looping her arm into Emmett's before turning on her heels to exit the classroom. Trey, Vincent and Bernadette follow closely behind.

Emmett flashes one quick subtle look over his shoulder in my direction, but it's unreadable. And I can barely stand the sight of him right now with Vivian draped back over his arm like nothing happened.

My chest heaves in hyperventilation as they leave me struggling to regain some semblance of composure. I have given up on trying to feel my way around the implant in my shoulder. My uniform is still ripped and I'm covered in bruises. My shin has turned black from where Vivian's foot struck against it.

What was Emmett thinking, standing up for me like that? It may have been subtle, but it was a bold move on his part. One that leaves me even more confused than before.

I wonder if Vivian will continue their conversation about me later. If she'll ask him about what I implied over our private encounters. I'm just happy I managed to do something that got under her skin for once…no matter how briefly.

But none of that changes the spot I'm in now. Once again, I feel stupid for getting caught up in this high school romance drama over the same guy who is threatening my life, with his girlfriend by his side.

I look around the room in disbelief, blowing sharp breaths through my cheeks as my fingers press to my temples. I try to collect my thoughts.

All I gathered from our little encounter is that my deadbeat dad is somehow responsible for the entire nightmare. The hell I've endured since coming here is all because of him. And now I'm expected to do something to get him to respond to the Elites. What that is…I have no idea. Not only do I not know how to pull that off, but I don't even know how much time I have or what it is he's responding to.

Regardless of all that, now my every move will be tracked. No escape.

Fuck. I can't imagine things getting much worse than this, but I'm learning not to even dare to think such a thing. Before I could so much as blink, the Elites would be rushing back in here to find some way to prove me wrong.

I try to shake it all away as I snake over to the doorway, peeking out to see if anyone is in the hall. If I thought anyone would help me, I'd march right out in front of them with my wounds and distress on full display. But knowing it'd be no use; I decide to try and sneak to the bathroom with at least a tiny shred of my dignity intact.

Once the halls are empty and silent with the last few stragglers disappearing around the corner, I limp across the scuffed floors in between the walls of lockers. I stare ahead resentfully, blazing right past the trophy case commemorating the Elite scum who built this school.

But something about the case of school accolades stops me. I turn to the sea of carefully pinned metals and plaques and study the framed photos for a moment, skipping across the black and white faces in vintage sports uniforms.

I locate Theodore Nickelson in a few different places. Just another face in the rows of other clean-cut young gentleman.

Thomas Jameson and the other Elites usually only a few spots away from him. My fingers graze the glass that rests in front of his face.

"It's easy to find you in pictures," I mumble under my breath. "Now if only I knew how to find you in real life."

A renewed surge of rage bolts through me as I consider how absurd it is that some man I've never even met is so influential on my life today. The contribution of his sperm aside, he's had nothing to do with me…that I've known of. But now it seems his entanglement with the Elites didn't end whenever he left town. It was still alive and well and fucking up everything in my life.

My hand falls back to my side as I turn to continue my listless walk to the bathroom. The classroom doors shoot past the corner of my eyes, one after another, but I keep my eyes glued to the floor, noting the random bits of food wrappers and crumpled papers. The janitor up ahead will work his way to these things by the time I've reemerged from the bathroom.

Nothing in this ridiculous school stays dirty for long…at least not on the surface. The smell of his mop solution wafts through the halls, mixing with the lingering food smells from the cafeteria, creating the most nauseating aroma.

As the adrenaline rushes from my body, leaving me cold and shaky, I half wonder if I'll need to puke by the time I make it to the bathroom. I never was able to finish my lunch.

Aside from the nearby custodian, a few teachers make the trek between offices, classrooms and their lounge. Not a single one even bothering to notice how roughed up I am, much less stopping to ask if I'm okay. The occasional stray student I pass here and there ignores me just as adamantly.

I want to scream out, "Haven't you heard!? The Elites won! They made their point! And now I'm working with them! You can admit that I exist again!"

It's just as well. I'd rather not be seen in my current state. But then…

I feel a sudden hard tug to my side as another body pushes past.

"Watch where you're going, cunt!" A guy spits at me as his shoulder bumps into mine.

Wow, I guess word does travel fast. Guess I'm out of exile after all. Which is a relief, but I don't know if being held hostage as a bargaining chip in my father's charades with the Elites is any better.

His choice of words are ironic, I think with a half-hearted chuckle to myself. I actually don't have to watch where I'm going anymore. The Elites are doing that for me now.

The reality of it is daunting. Wherever I go, they can find me. There's no escape now. No retreat. No hope of losing them. They can show up anywhere at any time and continue my torment.

For the first time, I notice all of the safety signs around the halls. Yellow a-frames cautioning for wet floors. Print outs alerting us what to do in case of fire, flood or tornado. Even a few posters warning of the dangers of unprotected sex and STDs.

But nothing that could have prepared me for any of this. Nothing that tells me what to do to stay safe from the Elites. And from my father.

Once inside the bathroom, I don't even bother looking at my reflection before bending over the sink to take in handfuls of cold tap water. It's stale, but anything is better than this dry, hot, iron taste. Toilets gurgle with refilling water behind me as I look across the pink soap specks dripping down the sink.

The simple task of washing my hands becomes meticulous and important. Any small little chore to make me feel in control. I move through the motions slowly and carefully.

Fucking absurd. I glance up just enough to notice my hair sticking out in every direction, matted into nests. My skin is blotchy and bruised around my bloody, ripped uniform. And here I am, washing my hands of all things, like it's the most important thing in the world.

*Get it together, Ophelia. You're cracking. Don't let them get to you.*

When everything falls still and silent again and I've turned off the faucet, I hear the faintest whimper from the corner stall.

"Hello?" I call out timidly, convinced whoever it is won't answer me anyway. I'm too newly released from exile.

Two feet appear with a plop under the stall door as the lock slides slowly, faintly covering the sound of sniffles. Finally, the door opens, and I see Lilly standing there with black mascara circles under her bloodshot eyes. Her cheeks shine with wetness under the fluorescent lights.

As upset as she looks, I know I have to look worse. And I'm kind of glad. I can't help but feel angry as I remember the way she ignored me right along with everyone else. I had my ass beat when I stood up for her, and she couldn't be bothered to do the same for me in return. I hope my bloody and bruised image makes her feel remorse.

But she stands there frozen and blank, not saying a word, and I can't tell if she's angry with me or just afraid.

# CHAPTER FOURTEEN

BOOK 1

The moment the Elites left me, I slowly sank into a pit of numb hopelessness. Too overwhelmed to fully feel anything. But now that Lily is standing in front of me, my heart surges with emotion. Hope. Maybe she can help. Whether she can or not, I need to talk to her. She's the only one who can even begin to understand any of this.

I contemplate telling her everything. All that I've learned about my father and his ties to the Elites. How they think I am somehow their key to getting him to leave them alone.

I can feel the desperation rising too quickly in my hot chest. If I pounce on her like this when she's already upset and hasn't been speaking to me for over a week, she'll shut me out. I have to tread lightly. Handle this carefully.

I calm myself down and focus. My hand reaches for the faucet again, turning it on to muffle my voice as Lily walks over to the row of sinks. Her movements are rigid, her head and shoulders pointed straight ahead as she tries to avoid eye contact with me.

"You ready to talk to me yet?" I offer, extending my hand to give her some paper towels.

She snatches the crumpled tissues from my hand, huffing toward the mirror without a word. "That's the last thing I need to do," she barks.

"Why? What are you talking about?" I ask, blotting my own bloody lips. "What did I ever do to you?"

"Oh, absolutely nothing, Ophelia," she sings in a resentful, sarcastic hum. "You've only ruined my entire fucking life!"

"Whoa!" I smirk, too traumatized and desperate to feed into her misguided anger right now. "Do I look like someone who is ruining lives? Or isn't it more accurate that my life is being ruined right alongside yours?"

My eyes cut over, watching her shake her head and scrub her hands furiously, muttering under her breath. I decide to try again, more gently this time as I reach out to place my hand to her shoulder.

"Come on, Lily. You know I'm on your side here…" the words purse my lips as I remember how she had very recently not been on my side, but I try to push down my bitterness. "We're all just doing the best we can in this Elites hellhole."

"They've ruined my life," she sobs, blackening the same spots under her eyes she had just cleaned up. "Every college I had lined up for piano scholarships has rescinded their interest. I know those Elite assholes did this as punishment because I was nice to you."

"I'm so sorry, Lily," I blurt out, not even fully grasping the magnitude of the situation before the words spill out. I just want to say something…anything as fast as I can to comfort her.

I guess it shouldn't be so surprising that people of their financial and social standing would have the power to sway such prestigious institutions. But it angers me the same way the cops and teachers around here do. Certain things should be above social sway. A girl's entire education shouldn't hinge on whether or not she's in some rich teens' good graces.

"I can't believe they'd stoop so low," I add, brushing my hand on her arm as she cries over the bathroom sink. "I mean…I guess I can. They're monsters. But still….fuck."

She doesn't answer. I can see the lump in her throat and the tightness of her chest, and I know exactly how she feels. The Elites are especially skilled at reducing people to their lowest low. Taking away the things that matter most to them.

Or hitting your most sensitive nerves…as they are currently doing with my dad.

"My parents insist they can just send me to a West Coast school…somewhere far away. A place they maybe won't be able to have an impact on," she continues through her tears, her voice rasps in a way that only comes after several straight days of crying. "But I had my heart set on Julliard. Now that's completely ruined."

She slams a paper towel into the sink, but it catches in the air and lands with a disappointing lightness.

We're silent for a few moments as I think over all of the new developments. I want to tell Lily what they've done to me. How they're forcing me to help them negotiate some mysterious thing with my dad. But somehow, it doesn't seem like it will help either of us right now. I worry it will only upset her even more. Though I do wonder if she may know something that could help me understand exactly what it is I've signed up for…even if I didn't have much of a choice.

"Listen to your parents," I encourage her softly. "The West Coast will be wonderful. You'll be far away from all of this bull-shit. I mean, just look at everything they've put you and your family through. Aren't you ready to get away from it all?"

"Yeah and go running off to the other side of the country like a cowering dog," she scoffs. "It's exactly what they want."

"Don't think of it like that…"

"I wish you had never stepped in that day!" she snaps suddenly, turning her anger to me.

I recoil, thinking back on that day in the hall when they were covering her in trash. Her only offense was that she tried to help me. An unforgivable sin in their minds…which makes more sense now that I know they have some sort of vendetta against my father.

"I had to, Lily," I defend, knowing it's probably no use. "I couldn't just stand back and watch them treat you that way any more than you could stand by and let them harass me without at least explaining who they were."

I shiver at the memory of realizing Emmett was at WJ Prep…and that he was with the gang of offenders. That brief moment when I didn't fully know what was going on. When I thought I was just lucky enough to end up at the same school as my biggest crush. The guy I thought I had met purely by acci-dent, but now I know it was all set up.

"Well, we both should have kept to ourselves!" she shouts, crying harder and snapping me abruptly from those memories of Emmett.

"But I can't imagine how I would have got through any of this without you," I argue back, the idea of it causing my bottom lip to quiver.

Lily was the only thing keeping me sane at times. In fact, her shutting me out during my exile was what pushed me over the edge. That was what made it so unbearable.

"It wasn't worth losing my dreams over," she answers with a low groan, her face stilled with seething anger.

"Lily…there's so much I want to tell you," I hesitate, my hand frozen in midair. "You have no idea what's going on. It's so much worse than I thought."

"I don't care what's going on with you, Ophelia! That's what got me into this position in the first place!" she turns her shoulder to me, trying to be strong and cold. The way she wishes she would have been from the beginning.

"But don't you see this is what they want!?" I persist. "If we let them isolate us and pull us apart then we don't stand a chance. We have to stick together. I know what they did to you was terrible…but it's not my fault."

She whips back around, her eyes big and wild with anger. "The Elites were bored and done with me before you showed up. Now I'm one of their main targets again and have been ever since your first day. How is it not your fault!?"

"Because you know I would have stopped them if I could have. Just like I'm sure you would stop them from everything they're doing to me if you could. But even if we can't stop them…maybe we can at least help each other cope with their wrath…" my voice trails off, breaking. More than anything, I just need someone to talk to, and I wish she would listen.

"There's nothing to cope with anymore," she says softly, her head shaking. "I'm being ran off to the other side of the country, and everything I've been dreaming of since I was a little girl has been taken away from me. I don't care anymore. I just hope they're done with me and talking to you will ruin any chance of that."

"Lily, please…don't shut me out. I need you more than ever now. Maybe if you can help me get to the bottom of this, we can undo some of the damage. Find some way to get them to take it back so you can go to Jilliard and…"

"Enough, Ophelia!" she cuts me off. "Just let it go, okay? Game over."

"Please, Lily. You're the only one I can trust," I beg with tears streaming down my face.

I want to argue back more. Tell her to stop giving them so much power by giving up that easily. To stop letting them come in between us. Say again that by isolating ourselves out of fear, we only made it easier for them to fuck with us. But I can see she's in no mood to fight back. They've completely broken her.

Just as I part my lips to speak, not even entirely sure of what else I can say, she snatches her purse and storms out. I know better than to try and follow her. The Elites can track my every move now, and it will only make things worse.

I watch despondently as she storms out, leaving me feeling more alone than I ever have before. Even during exile. Lily is even more against me now than she was before. Now there is no one I can trust. She is the only one who can understand and relate to what I'm going through and she hates me.

I try to fix myself up the best I can. Just enough to make it home without being questioned by my parents. On the way home, I drive recklessly, my music blasting. I need to feel the vibrations of the music. The rise and fall of my heart as I speed too quickly around each and every turn, accelerating more every chance I get.

I need to feel anything intense I can get my hands on to fill this gaping hole and fear and powerlessness. I have never been so irritable in all of my life.

My mind goes through the possibilities. I could run away. I could catch a bus out of town and just ride it until it stops somewhere interesting. I could drive my car until it runs out of gas and just stay wherever I break down at.

But no, that would never be far enough away to keep me safe from the Elites. I have a feeling no matter where I try to run to, they'll hunt me down and find me. Especially now that I know they're motivated by some vendetta against my father.

I think again about telling mom and Brendan. But that thought is quickly squashed by the memories of her playing nice with Trey and Vincent. She was friends with their mom. I doubt she has any clue what these kids are really like.

Unless of course the Elites were like this back in her day too. I hope she never treated people like this. I can't imagine it. But then again, I can't imagine her being with an Elite either. Then of course I have to kick myself, knowing full well that if Emmett could be kind to me I would be his in a heartbeat.

I feel like if I even try to tell anyone outside of the Elites' range of influence, they'll think I'm lying. Or that I encouraged Emmett's assault in some way. I am convinced my attraction to him is written all over my face.

The thought of explaining what is really going on with Emmett to anyone makes me sick. Even Lily would judge me for that, especially now. My mom would probably think I'm a freak and disown me. Brendan would be ashamed. I'm sure they think I'm smart and strong enough not to fall for someone so fucked up who treats me so terribly. Hell, I used to think I was too smart and strong for that, too.

When I get home, I hear my mom and Brendan rustling around in the living room. They're home early. It sounds like they're putting on a movie and settling in with some popcorn. I want more than anything to join them, but I'm too upset. I can't hide it, and I can't tell them anything.

I feel completely helpless. And as tired as I am of going through this alone, the only time I feel safe is when I'm alone. And even then, I'm plagued with paranoia over what will happen next. Especially now with this tracking device in my arm. I feel broken. Like something is wrong with me. I don't know how I can ever go back to living a normal life after this.

Thankfully, I'm able to avoid my parents as I race to my bathroom. The spot on my shoulder where they sewed in the implant is still bleeding, and I have to bandage it up just to keep the blood off of my clothes.

I decide to take a bath to soothe my aching muscles, filling the hot steaming water with every bath product I can find that might bring me some peace and comfort.

I lay back into the bath water, my body still tingling and my legs feeling almost numb. The lavender scented steam rising up should comfort me. But nothing seems to be able to do that anymore.

I think back on the life I had before coming to WJ Prep and this Elites nightmare. I had friends to hang out with. People to talk to and go to the movies with. We goofed off at the park. Took bike rides. I had friends to jog with. I had fun. But now it all seems so far away.

I would give anything to have my regular running schedule back. I thought I knew what torture was. With what I used to put my body through. The hard, painful monotony. But those kinds of words have taken on a new meaning for me now.

I miss the thrill and sense of accomplishment. Since the Elites got their hands on me, I haven't felt like I could do anything right. I remember the way I would sweat and the way my muscles would ache. Those sensations come for very different reasons these days.

God, I miss running.

I miss the satisfaction of it.

The pain that was gratifying…not relentless and out of my control like what I've come to know.

When I ran, I was in control. How fast and far I went was all up to me. A kind of freedom and responsibility that has become almost foreign to me.

I wonder when all of this is over…if it's ever over…how hard I'll need to run to wash all of this away.

I miss my old routes in Oklahoma. The newness of Jameson wore off quick. Any thrill of it was chased away by the Elites. And I can't let myself forget the role that Emmett has played in that.

I should have known better when I first received that phone call from the Headmaster of Weis-Jameson Preparatory Academy. That scholarship was too good to be true. I wanted to think I had earned it. But now I know better. It was all just a part of the set up. The game.

I miss how hopeful and surprised I felt before school started. The exciting challenge of Coach Granger's workouts.

Those memories all vanish before my eyes into some far-off distant haze, like the Epsom salts in my bath water.

Once I'm clean, I stare despondently around my room. Unsure if I should try to sleep or face my parents long enough to get some dinner. Nothing sounds appealing right now.

Instead, I find myself staring blankly out the window at some kids playing in the yard across the street. I watch as one kid takes the other's two before they break out into a playful, but angry, wrestling match. I wonder if it's just human nature for us to be greedy and hurt others to get what we want. It sure seems to be around here. In the land of the Elites. Where no part of the town seems to be untainted by their evil ways.

I finally collapse back onto my bed, my eyes glued open wide but blank. I know I won't be able to sleep even though it's what I want the most. Instead I am stuck in a state of waiting. And I don't even know what exactly I'm waiting for. I'm at the mercy of whatever gets thrown my way next.

# CHAPTER FIFTEEN

## BOOK 1

I am so close to finding escape through sleep. At least I think I'm falling asleep and starting to dream. I'm back in the classroom, pinned to the wall by Emmett. It's just the two of us. He's kissing me, but this time he doesn't stop. I push his hand away as his fingers trail between my legs, but he slams my wrist to the wall and carries on with his other hand. I should be angry. I should feel violated. But instead I'm just incredibly turned on.

When suddenly my phone starts ringing, jerking me awake.

"Great," I think, rubbing my eyes as my hand blindly fumbles for my phone in the dark. "My only vacation from this nightmare is sleep, and I don't even get that."

I try to ignore the pool of wetness in my underwear as I answer.

"Hello?" I grumble, pressing the phone between my cheek and shoulder as I stretch.

Nothing. The line is silent aside from the faint shuffling that tells me someone is on the line. They're just not saying anything.

It beeps and disconnects just as I am about to speak again.

Emmett wouldn't call from an unknown number. He'd want me to know it was him. Any of the Elites would. And yet some mysterious person keeps contacting me. I'm fed up with not knowing who.

My heart stills with a chill that rolls over my skin. Vivian's words echo through my ears. She had said my father was more involved in my life than I thought. What the hell was that supposed to mean? She obviously knows something I don't.

He has to be the one calling and who sent the cryptic messages before. I used to think it was the Elites, but they have no reason to hide. They'd be much bolder in any attempt to make contact. They don't fuck around.

No, this has to be my father. And I am not going to brush it off this time. After everything that's happened, this fucker owes me an explanation. More than that, he owes it to me to do whatever it is the Elites are asking of him. Whatever it takes to get me off the hook. He has never done a thing for me, and I sure as hell don't deserve to go down for whatever mess he's gotten himself into.

My phone dings again. This time with a text. I race to light up the screen and read it, certain the message will be from my father.

**You're being watched. Close the blinds. Put on running clothes. Go to the living room and await further instructions.**

What the fuck. I hesitate to do anything some random mystery texter tells me. Especially without any kind of explanation.

My hands shake as I quickly type my response. **Who is this?**

No response. I look around nervously. Sure, I know the Elites are tracking me. But now I'm being watched by someone else too? I'm not even safe in my own home anymore.

I try again. **Who the fuck is this?**

Still nothing. My nerves get the better of me, and I decide there's no benefit to the risk of ignoring their guidance. The Elites said we're on a time limit. I don't know how long they'll give me to produce some kind of result, but right now I have nothing to work with. I'll take what I can get. Any kind of stab in the dark to get some momentum.

I walk in the darkness and rush to close all of the blinds, looking up and down the dark streets as I go to see if any cars or people look suspicious. I see nothing out of the ordinary. The neighbor walking his dog. A woman taking her trash bin to the curb. Only the usual cars parked in their driveways. People carrying on with their ordinary lives. People who don't have to worry about being stalked, tortured and tracked. I'm filled with envy.

I flip on my lamp and scramble to snatch up my nearest pile of running gear. I feel sick as I slide the clothes over my trembling body.

"Get it together, Ophelia," I huff to myself as I shake my hands, wishing they'd steady themselves.

I check my phone again anxiously, but there's still no further reply. With a few more paranoid, narrow-eyed glances out of my blinds, seeing nothing that gives away who could be watching me, I reluctantly make my way downstairs to the living room.

Mom and Brendan are still quiet and distracted with the couch and TV in the den. I try to be as quiet as possible, so they don't rush in and start asking a bunch of questions.

My phone dings again almost the moment I enter the room, causing me to jump. Fucking ridiculous. They're warning me I'm being watched while they're watching me.

**Drive to a McDonald's and start running.**

Perfect. That's just what I want to do. I wish I could take comfort in knowing the Elites are tracking me. At least someone would know where to find me if I came up missing. And I have to assume they would come find me since they need something from me.

I blow a long, sharp breath from my cheeks, closing my eyes as I picture getting into my car at night and running from a dark and empty parking lot. With my luck lately, it's the last thing I want to do. I'm convinced someone will be waiting to attack, but it feels like I have no other choice. I may be scared shitless, but I'm tired of being a pawn. This could be a way out, or at the very least, a way to get more information.

With a deep breath, I clutch my keys to my chest and swing my bag over my shoulder before heading out to my car. I don't even turn on the radio as I drive. My thoughts and nerves are loud enough as it is. Any more noise would only make my never-ending headache worse.

Just as I was instructed, I drive to the nearest McDonald's, park, and get out to look around. With no obvious threats around, I take off running. In a way, it's exactly what I need. All of this drama has been leaving me too exhausted at the end of the day to take any evening runs. I have been longing for this kind of release ever since I laid soaking in the tub earlier this afternoon. And now here it is. If only it wasn't under such crazy circumstances.

I relish in the feel of the night air swishing past me. The wind is numbing, biting at my ears and cheeks, but I love it. Right now I'll settle for any kind of physical sensation that doesn't come from the hands of the Elites…the hands of Emmett, specifically.

With each step, I want to feel like I'm closing in on something with this strange new development. This mystery caller. Maybe this will lead to a light at the end of the tunnel. Either that or finally put me out of my misery.

As soon as I get into a good stride and feel a moment of release, an expensive-looking black sports car rolls up beside me, speeding my heart to an alarming rate. As it squeals to a stop, I half expect the window to roll down and a gun to just start shooting. That's how paranoid I've become.

I slow down and look over to see the driver's side window rolling down, revealing a familiar face.

Malcolm Henderson. A satellite Elite from school. And he doesn't appear to have a gun. So at least there's that.

"You!?" I yell out in exasperation, feeling even more confused than before.

"I've been sent by your father," he explains curtly.

Of course. I knew it. I knew this whole thing had to be his doing.

"How the hell do you know my father!?" I quip back, feeling too strung out for niceties.

"Everyone here knows your father, Ophelia," he glares ominously. "I thought you would have figured that much out by now."

"I guess I'm starting to. But you'd think that'd make things a little easier on me. If he's such a big and important guy around here," I lament bitterly.

"Well…I said everyone knows him," he raises his brows, tilts his head and lifts his fingers briefly from the car door. "I didn't say people like him."

"And what about you?" I ask, leaning over with my hands on my knees as I catch my breath. "Do you like him?"

"My father and your father are very close. So, I suppose you could say I like him. Or rather, we're helping each other out at the moment." He reaches to his passenger seat and grabs a bottle of water, quickly tossing it in my direction.

"I didn't think my father had anything to do with this town anymore," I explain, twisting the cap of the bottle with an appreciative nod. I know I should be more hesitant and distrusting with Malcolm, but I'm too tired to put up any airs. "I thought he was long gone."

"Get in," he commands with a flip of the car door locks. "It'll all start to make more sense if you come with me."

I roll my shoulders and step toward the road to walk around the car, but something stops me. I remember the last time I followed a boy into his car. I duck down and peek into the backseat for an arsenal of weapons or any sign that he plans to torture me the way Emmett would after inviting me to take a ride with him.

It's spotless. I take a deep breath and get in, against my better judgement.

The car speeds off, leaving me at Malcom's mercy. I watch the familiar increase of house size fly by my window. The landscaped yards and all their pretentious ornaments. Giant mansions. Filled with haunting secrets, most probably connected to the Elites. Everything in this town is, especially anything bad and hidden away.

I grow nervous as he takes a dark side road, avoiding a fallen powerline. I wring my clammy hands around my cell phone, noting its loss of bars as we drive further away from civilization. What have I done? I am completely screwed.

"Relax," Malcolm says, his eyes darting at my shifting arms and legs as I squirm in my seat. "I'm not going to hurt you. Nothing bad is going to happen, I promise. Quite the opposite actually. This will shed some light on a few things for you."

"Oh, forgive me for not being so trusting," I quip back sarcastically. "This town hasn't exactly treated me well since I arrived." My fingers graze across my bruised arms before I turn to look out the window again. "So, the calls and texts from before? Were they all you?"

"Well there's no telling what all has been sent to you, but yes. Most of them probably were. I was hoping you'd catch up to things in time," he explains, shifting the gear to accelerate faster down a dark and winding road.

"Catch up to what!?" I groan, stroking my forehead in exasperation. "Everyone is acting like my role is so important in whatever is going on. But I don't know anything. And no one seems to want to tell me anything."

"Be patient," he insists with a frustrated huff. "I said this meeting will help with all of that."

"Can you at least tell me who you're taking me to meet with?" I ask earnestly, but he shakes his head in silence.

I press my head to the window in exhaustion, trying to push down the nervousness bubbling in my gut. I wrack my brain for what Malcolm Henderson and I could possibly have to talk about on this little road trip, since he seems intent on not discussing any of the things I need to know.

"I guess the Elites did all of that?" He nods toward the bruises I had been fidgeting with just moments ago.

Well, I guess that solves the issue of what we should talk about. But it's also not a very fun topic of conversation.

"You say 'the Elites' like you're not one of them," I grumble resentfully, remembering Lily's little chart of hierarchy that featured Malcolm and his family prominently.

"I'm not," he states bluntly. "We're tolerated by the Elites. More so than someone like you that's blacklisted, but definitely not regarded warmly. My family's fortune was built from the ground up in more recent generations. We can't touch the old money of the Elites. But they work with us so long as we provide them with something profitable."

"And what is it that your family provides for them?" I ask curiously, secretly delighting in a conversation with someone that doesn't involve beating or shouting. But of course, it still has to revolve around the great and mighty Elites. That seems to be all my life is about anymore.

"We own a software company that services the Jameson Automobile Corporation," he explains. "Open the glovebox." I pull the compartment open, grabbing a brochure that he motions to. "That tells you about our company."

I nod in a sort of stunned silence as I flip through. The ties to Jameson Automobiles really are endless. It's like the whole town is just one giant web with that one company smack dab in the middle. You either work for them, are controlled by them or hated by them. There doesn't seem to be any other way to fit into this elaborate social circle.

Something resting beneath where the brochure just was catches my eye. It's a strip of photos from the booth at the mall, featuring Malcolm making a series of funny faces. He must be a few years younger in them. But then I notice the face next to his in the photos that causes my hand to shoot out and snatch the strip up to take a closer look.

"What the fuck," I whisper, thumbing over the second figure in the photos. "Is this Emmett!?"

"Yeah. That feels like ages ago," he answers dismissively, shaking his head.

"You and Emmett are friends? I never see you together at school," I study the pictures more closely, taken aback by how happy and carefree Emmett looks. A side to him I have yet to see.

"Used to be," he replies with a tinge of sadness. "When we were younger, our parents didn't care if we were friends or if we hung out. My family has money after all, and that's all they care about. But his dad and my dad had a falling out. And then as we got older, it became less socially acceptable for us to be seen together as much."

"A falling out about what?" I ask, knowing it's a reach, and am met with another quiet shake of his head.

"Their businesses," he grunts, brushing a finger to his nose. "That's all you need to know."

"Asshole," I grumble disdainfully, tossing the strip back into the glovebox and slamming it shut.

"It's not his fault," Malcolm shoots back sharply.

"What the fuck do you mean it's not his fault!?" I shriek with more emotion than I mean to. "Don't tell me you're brainwashed by them too. Everyone's so afraid of them they just go along with their bullshit and let them get away with whatever they want. Treating everyone like shit."

"I'm not saying the Elites aren't capable of horrible things," he defends. "You don't have to tell me. I grew up with them. Vivian, Bernadette, Trey, Vincent…they're no good. But Emmett's always been a little different. That's why we were buddies. He's not like the others."

"Maybe he wasn't," I answer lowly in disdain, tugging at my shoulder. "But he had no problem writing you off when he got older. And some time after that, he became a monster just like the rest of them."

"He hurts you?" Malcolm asks, his face slightly twisted.

"They all do."

He shakes his head, turning briefly to the driver's side window with his lips pursed before refocusing on the road. "That's not like him. I know it's going to be hard to convince you…but anything he's doing is just out of fear. He didn't ask to be born into that fucked up family of his. He's just as much of a pawn as the rest of us."

I stare at him as he drives, searching for some sign of an ulterior motive. Doubt. Anything that tells me he doesn't know what he's talking about. But he's filled with resolve. Completely confident that Emmett is somehow different than his flock of abusers.

My head flings back against my seat. I can't handle this right now. The last thing I need is another gnawing voice in my ear trying to convince me that Emmett's behavior is excusable.

I've watched him dump trash on Lily's head. He manhandled me in front of his asshole Elite friends. He's verbally abused me. Humiliated me. Threatened me. Not to mention whatever he planned to do with me with that rope and gloves before we crashed his car. The list goes on and on.

I clench my fists, needing the reminder of it all to dig into me as deep as my fingernails dig into my palm. I don't care what Malcolm says, or what flash of pity I saw in him recently. He's one of the bad guys. He's hurt me. And my fucked up attraction to him is just that. Fucked up. It has to stop. I have to make it stop.

"I promise you, Ophelia," Malcolm continues, jolting my attention back to him. "Things are about to change. The days of the Elites' reign are numbered. They're on thin ice. And when their little hierarchy starts to shift…you'll see the real Emmett."

Emmett's angry snarling face flashes before my eyes. I have plenty of memories of him like that. Staring me down with pure rage and hatred. Saying terrible things to me. I can't let myself believe that there's anything more to him than that.

"We're almost there," he announces, pointing a finger over the steering wheel to an ominous looking vacant lot in the distance.

I gulp down a hard knot, unsure if I should be relieved or terrified. Either way, he claims this will be informative and good. So I try to hold on to that with any ounce of capability I have left to trust someone in Jameson.

# CHAPTER SIXTEEN

## BOOK 1

Malcolm drives us to what looks like an abandoned warehouse on the outskirts of town. The parking lot is dark, lit up by only one streetlamp that rests near the large garage door entry. He flips a switch, causing the metal door to clatter as it rolls up.

I am certain I should be afraid of dying. This could be how I go. But Malcolm doesn't seem threatening. His meager and slender build makes me think I could take him if it came down to it. But it doesn't make him unattractive. He has creamy pale skin and long legs leading up to a well-chiseled narrow chest. His light sandy blonde hair is cut and styled into spikes, complimenting his pale blue eyes that seem kind.

It's a shame I can't be attracted to him instead. He's shown me more kindness than anyone else around here, aside from Lily.

Or maybe my concept of kind has just shifted after enduring the torture of the Elites. In my book, he is still one of them by proxy after all, no matter what he says. Now it seems anyone who doesn't instantly attack me seems nice in my book.

The inside of the warehouse is even darker, with only the moonlight shining through a large opening in the back to give me any clue as to where to step. Malcom places his arm through mine, startling me as my eyes dart to his in suspicion.

"I told you I'm not going to hurt you," he assures me, nodding to his gentle, friendly touch.

"Sorry. I know," I groan, letting him lead me. "I'm not used to someone being nice to me. Trying to help." My mind drifts to Lily. I wonder if he knows how risky it is to be doing anything but treating me like shit. "In fact, you may want to be careful. The Elites tend to make anyone that helps me regret it. They may turn on you."

"I'm not afraid of them. At least not in the way you think," he huffs, guiding me toward a figure standing in front of a window so that all I can make out is the silhouette of what looks like an older man in a suit.

His tall slender legs mimic Malcolm's build, but he has a much bigger gut jutting out from his suit jacket. I can see a glare across his balding head as he wipes his forehead with a handkerchief.

I look up to him nervously, hoping and praying I haven't been duped yet again.

"Ophelia," the man calls out. "Thank you for coming. Sorry to have to drag you out of the house so inconspicuously, but as I'm sure you've gathered by now…there are some dangerous forces at play around here."

"Who are you?" I ask, squinting my eyes to try and make out his face.

"This is my father," Malcolm explains. "Meet Liam Henderson."

I have no idea what to think. What on earth could both Malcolm and his father want with me in this abandoned warehouse out in the middle of nowhere?

"Your father could not be present, but he says hello," Liam adds, firing the synapses in my brain.

My father. Of course he wouldn't bother actually showing his face, but at least he's making some form of contact. It's about damn time for how much trouble as he's caused.

"Well, that's a first," I jeer in bewilderment. "I've never even met him."

"I'm afraid this will have to be brief," Liam continues, ignoring my bitterness. "We can only block the signal of the tracking device in your arm for so long."

My eyes widen and glance toward my shoulder. I'm amazed that they can do something like that…and that they even know it's there in the first place.

"How did you…"

"I'll get straight to it," he carries on after clearing his throat, cutting me off. I still can't see his face as he stands in front of the backlit window. "Maybe you're aware that I write code and create software for a living. The programs I've designed have been used by many fortune 500 companies for many different purposes. I've been very successful."

"Yeah, Malcolm filled me in on some of that on the way over," I nod, still confused as to what this has to do with me. Or my father.

"Unfortunately, the Jameson Automobile Corporation has been using my software to run extortion rings of politicians," he continues with a disappointed sigh. "It's also been modified to create a black market for underage girls. I'm sure a smart girl like you can understand why that's big trouble for me."

"Sex trafficking?" I blink, staring ahead blankly. I want to be as smart as he thinks, but I'm too taken aback to piece anything together on my own right now.

"Since I'm the creator of the program and one of the top employees of the company, my reputation and career would be seriously harmed if this information came to light. Which is what brought us to the aid of your father, Theodore Nickelson."

His name hangs in the air like a plague. I hate the sound of it.

"I can't say I'm making that leap with you," I confess. "What does any of that have to do with my father? Or better yet...me?"

"How much do you know about him?" Liam asks, slightly stunned.

"Nothing," I shrug. "I told you. I've never even met him."

"Ah," I see the shadow of his brow wrinkling in the light as his head drops. "As I said, we don't have much time, but have a seat. I'll explain what I can for now." He motions to some nearby shipping crates and follows me over to take a seat. "Your father, Theodore Nickelson the Third is the only grandson of one of the Jameson Automobile Company's founders."

I shake my head vehemently, excited to finally be getting some kind of real information. I'm so wrapped up in every word he's saying, I can barely process the scope of it.

My father. One of the Jameson Automobile bigwigs.

"Therefore, he inherited a quarter of the company's shares," Liam continues. "But in the early 2000s, he misman-aged millions of the company's funds. He had used the money to fund his own private gambling problem. So, the Elites cut him off. He tried to go public with Marissa Jameson's affair with the gardener, which only got him blacklisted at every public establishment, sued for every penny he had, and his entire reputation was completely tarnished for good."

"Wow," I marvel out loud, still hanging from his every word. "All of that for a gambling habit."

"He fled town with your mother, Lala," Liam continues. "Theo trained as a private detective on the West Coast, but he could never let go of his hatred of the Elites. He built his fortune from the ground up through stocks, purely out of vengeance. And he vowed to come after the Elites in whatever way he could to make them pay for taking away all that he had."

"Seems ridiculous," I blurt out dryly. "It was his own gambling problem that put him in that spot. And he ended up making it all back anyway, so…why not just let it go?"

"Maybe you can ask him that yourself one day," Liam replies dismissively. "But for now, you can see why we would want to work with him."

"You both hate the Elites?" I offer.

"If this sex trafficking and pedophilia thing breaks, it could be a huge federal case," he barks, growing impatient with my seeming lack of interest. "All of the Jameson founders could be found guilty and sentenced to life in federal prison. But we need a verbal confession to really tie the case together. The evidence now is compelling, but it could be overwhelming with such a confession. And according to Massachusetts recording laws, it's illegal to record someone without their consent. This is the only reason there hasn't been any movement forward. Thomas Jameson isn't stupid enough to go to other states and say 'Yes, I'm the one who has done these horrible things'."

"So that's why the Elites are trying to get him to back off?" I think out loud. "They know he's not going to stop until he puts them all behind bars."

"Precisely," he nods, scratching his fingers across the five o'clock shadow on his chin.

"Well, now the Elites are up my ass," I commiserate, rubbing my bruised shin. "So you can tell my dad he has to respond to whatever ultimatum they gave him or else they're going to make me pay."

"I'm sorry they've been so cruel to you," he says softly, his face grimacing at the bruises shining in the moonlight. "They are ruthless. And will stop at nothing to protect their power and money. Which is why this situation is so perilous. I can't be dragged down for their wrongdoings, but that is exactly what they will make sure happens if we don't build a strong enough case against them."

I nod, believing all too well that the Elites will stop at nothing to protect their own asses. I would be scared too if I was in the Hendersons' position.

"Well, this has certainly been enlightening," I grunt as I stand from the shipping crate. "But I still don't see what any of this has to do with me. How am I supposed to help?"

Liam grows quiet in deep thought for a moment, leaning forward and running his palm to the back of his neck with what looks like remorse. Regret. He's sorry for something.

"Your father is sorry he hasn't been involved in your life," he offers as he stands, pacing in front of me. "But he wanted you to understand what was going on. So that maybe…you wouldn't feel so…helpless. He hoped the context would help."

His words suddenly sound more menacing. Something is about to happen, and the fear I was numb to before is creeping in full force. "Help with what?" I ask softly, taking a few steps back.

He answers with a silent smirk, nodding to Malcolm. "You can take her home now."

I pull away from Malcolm at first, wondering if he really plans to take me home or if something terrible is about to happen. I don't have a good feeling about any of this.

"But wait!" I shout, jerking away. "I still don't understand. What is it that I'm supposed to do!? If he doesn't do what they want, the Elites are going to kill me. They said they've sent him messages, but I don't know what they've said or what they're trying to do."

"They're likely telling him to back off," Liam deduces, tucking his hands into his suit jacket.

"Will he!?" My voice grows shrill with urgency. "Because like I said…they're going to kill me if he doesn't! Can you at least promise me that he'll respond? I mean…can't you all just work it out between yourselves without dragging me into it!?"

"All you need to know is that your father has a plan," he offers grimly, sparking more fear than reassurance. "Malcolm. That's all for now."

He steps toward me again, but I pull my arms back. I can't

believe I'm getting shuffled off again without knowing what this all means for me.

"Come on, Ophelia," Malcolm says reassuringly. "I promise nothing's going to happen. I'm just going to take you back to your car."

My heart pounds as I follow along, convinced that at any step everything could change. He could turn on me. Someone could come after us. Liam was eluding to something. That much I'm certain of. But to go through all this trouble just to set me free again…something's not right about it.

My anxiety keeps me quiet on the ride home, my senses on hyper alert as I note every last turn the car takes. I'm ready to bolt the moment it goes any direction that is not toward the McDonald's I parked at.

But to my surprise, Malcolm keeps his word and drops me off at my car. Flashing me a sweet smile as I exit his vehicle.

"So, what now?" I turn back to ask him from the sidewalk, rubbing my arms as I look around cautiously.

"Go home," Malcolm answers dryly, not looking away from his steering wheel. "Like my father said, your dad has a plan. You just have to wait."

"What if there's no time for waiting!?" I shriek back. "What if the Elites kill me before he carries out his little plan?"

Malcolm is unmoved. "Go home and get some rest, Ophelia."

Without another word, his tires squeal and he's flying off down the street. I stand and watch as the obnoxious buzz of his car engine drifts further and further away, eventually vanishing altogether.

Not knowing what else to do, I turn to walk back to my car. It's easy for him to say. Wait. Rest. I can't do any of these things. Not with all of this hanging over my head.

My dad has it out for the Elites, and not surprisingly they have plenty of skeletons in their closet for him to play with. I've seen the rage of their entitlement. No one questions them or fucks with them in any way.

I'd be glad my dad is giving them a run for their money if it weren't for me getting dragged down into it all. And the fact that his motives are no different than theirs. He messed up, and he's mad at them for putting him in his place.

I wrap my arms around my chest, shielding myself from the

night air chill as I climb back into my car. Everything around me is quiet to the point of being unsettling.

My car engine starts, and I drive back to my house as fast as I can. I'm in desperate need of some place that feels safe. With so many people watching me and keeping tabs on me, I'm not sure such a place exists anymore. But my room is the closest thing I have, so I'll take it.

All I want is to be curled up under my covers. Now I just have to hope that when I get there, dreams of Emmett don't come back to haunt me.

# CHAPTER SEVENTEEN

BOOK 1

My mind is on overdrive as I head home, but I'm relieved to finally understand what my father had to do with the Elites. And what all of it has to do with me now. But there is still a lingering fear that the Hendersons and my father aren't through with me yet. I'm able to push that further and further away as I get closer to home. At least for now.

I think about how badly I want to be able to ask my mom everything. I know my dad's side to the story, but I can't help but wonder what all of that must have been like for her. And I still have no clue what actually caused them to split up. Though I guess a gambling habit that ruined their lives would be reason enough.

As my car pulls into my driveway, I see movement behind the blinds. I consider marching in and asking my mom everything right away, but I'm too tired. I've taken in enough for the evening, and I just want to crawl back into my bed.

So, instead, I sneak past my mom and Brendan who are talking in the kitchen, bolting up the stairs into my room.

My heart plummets the moment I open my door. Emmett, Trey and Vincent are all standing right there in the middle of my bedroom, seething with anger.

"What the hell are you doing here?" I stammer nervously. "This is my house. How did you get in!? You can't be here. My parents are right downstairs. I'll scream."

"Where the hell have you been!?" Emmett growls, his

nostrils flaring in anger. "We know you met with someone, but we couldn't track you after McDonalds."

"I just went for a run," I offered as innocently as possible. "It's not my fault you stabbed a faulty tracking device into my body."

"Bullshit," he fumes back, racing up to skillfully push me to the wall hard enough to hurt, but without making too loud of a sound.

I'm back to squirming beneath his violent grip and I want to spit at everything Malcolm tried to say. There is nothing good about Emmett. He's no different from the rest of them.

Unless…he's worried about me? Upset that he didn't know where I was? But if that was the case, he wouldn't have needed to drag Trey and Vincent along with him.

"We've got to stop meeting like this," I quip defiantly, staring straight into his eyes from an angle that was becoming all too familiar.

"Oh, did you miss this?" he growls, his eyes taking me in with hunger. "Is that why you misbehaved? Just to get me here?"

"You wish," I roll my eyes, sparking a new rage behind his stare.

His hand jerks to the top of my head, gripping a fistful of what's hanging loose from my ponytail and pulling it back to raise my chin to him. The sting of it causes my eyes to water, and I have to blink away tears.

He pants over me, half with sexual desire, half with pure anger. I don't know whether to expect him to hit me or kiss me. All of my conflicted feelings are back in full force in only a matter of seconds of being in his presence.

"Let's see if you really know what it means to be a good little girl," he groans. "You broke the rules, so now you know we have to punish you."

Before I can even begin to guess what he's planning to do, he whips me around toward the door. I am shocked as he leads me out into the hall, Trey and Vincent following behind.

"I told you my parents are downstairs," I remind him, thinking surely he won't be so bold as to march me right out in front of them.

"Good," he retorts, unfazed. "I would like to meet your mom. I've already met your dad of course. Your real dad."

"Well, that makes one of us," I muster through a gulp as he practically pushes me down the stairs. I pray my mom comes around the corner and catches the way he's handling me, but he's too smart for that. He'd never let himself get caught.

"Ophelia!" she cries in innocent excitement as we round the corner of the kitchen. "I didn't even know you were home! Much less that you had company!"

Emmett's fingers pinch into my spine, just out of her sight. His fingernails sting the thin skin against my bone, causing me to wince. I am tempted to show how much it hurts. To jerk away from him and see what my mom actually does.

"Oh yeah," I play along, deciding to keep them out of this. If the Elites can take down millionaires and convince major universities to deny a potential student, it would be nothing for them to ruin everything my mom and Brendan have worked so hard for. I can't be the reason that happens. "I went out for a run. I just got back."

Her eyes look to the three guys expectantly, causing Emmett's fingers to twist even harder into my back.

"These are my friends!" I shout quickly, hoping he'll ease his pinch. "I ran into them while I was out."

"I remember you from the hospital," she shakes her head, looking like she feels foolish for not remembering sooner. "Emmett, right?"

I see Brendan's ears perk up from the kitchen at the mention of his name.

"And of course I know you two," she nods politely to Trey and Vincent, making my stomach turn.

"How are you, Mrs. Lopez?" they chime in almost comedic unison.

"Wonderful! How are you? And how is your mother!?"

My mom's small talk with them fades into the background as I look up to Emmett, searching his face for any clue of what's supposed to happen next. But he just smiles and plays along.

"It's kind of late for houseguests," Brendan finally jumps in, taking an authoritative stance behind my mom. His eyes are glued to Emmett. He still doesn't trust him after the accident.

"Yes, of course," Emmett agrees politely. "We were actually hoping we could take Ophelia out to a movie. If that would be alright with you?"

"Are you driving?" Brendan quips back, not missing a beat.

I smile up at Emmett in anticipation of his temper emerging, blowing their whole cover. But he's too smooth for that.

"Actually, no," he laughs. "Vincent is this time. I promise

we'll take good care of her. And we'll have her home as soon as the movie is over."

"What are you going to see?" my mother asks sweetly, causing my heart to drop as I realize they're actually going to let them get away with this.

"There are a few things starting soon," Trey explains. "We were gonna decide when we get there."

My mom looks up to Brendan for final approval, but her eyes seem to be trying to convince him to say yes. I want him to look at me instead of her. To somehow telepathically read into my suppressed dread.

"I do have school early tomorrow…" I remind them gently, fully prepared for Emmett's responsive twist into my back. But Brendan seems to read it as some kind of reverse psychology, much to my disappointment.

"Well then…don't be out too late," he says finally, sparking an erupting of nervous sighs from the guys around me. "You haven't gotten out much with friends since you got here, Ophelia. You've been working too hard. It'll be good for you to have some fun.

Ha, I think. Fun. Somehow, I don't expect much fun to come out of this. At least not for me.

"Great, thanks so much," Emmett says sweetly. His façade of innocence and niceness making me sick. "We'll bring her home as soon as the movie is over."

I eye my mom desperately as they turn and push me toward the door, but she must be mistaking my fear for nerves or something else. Some other kind of normal teenage girl behavior. She responds with a wink and a wave before the two turn back for the kitchen.

They laugh victoriously as they shove me out to the car. We're all dead silent as we drive with me sandwiched in the backseat between Trey and Vincent. I catch Emmett glancing back at me every few seconds through the rearview, and I can't help but laugh about his blatant lie to Brendan about not being the one to drive tonight.

I hold my breath in anticipation of whatever happens next. Did this have something to do with what Liam seemed to be hinting at? Whatever it was he looked so sorry for? What my dad was worried I needed help with? But that can't be. The Hendersons and the Elites are working against each other now.

But to my amazement, they take me to the movie theater. I

still expect it to be a front, even as they approach the counter and buy us tickets.

We file into the theater and find seats. I follow along like a lost puppy, completely at their mercy. I know it's no use to try and get away. This whole town is full of their puppets, and no one would help me when they inevitably caught up to me.

Trey and Vincent even bought popcorn. They try to sit on either side of me the way we were arranged in the car, but Emmett snaps at them, demanding them to move aside so he can sit next to me.

"Move over, idiots," he hisses, pushing them out of the way and sitting down next to me. I search his face for some kind of emotion, but he's blank and avoiding eye contact.

The whole thing is chillingly normal. Just a group of teens going to the movies. I want to rest in that, but my nerves won't settle enough to let me. I know something is coming.

Vincent sits on the outside with Trey next to me. Once the movie starts, I can feel his gaze burning into me.

I almost laugh when I realize we're watching some old slasher horror flick. Of course that's the kind of thing they'd bring me to see. Forcing me to sit here and watch them get off on half naked girls running away terrified in the night, screaming in terror before they inevitably get slashed to bits.

I side-eye Trey as I realize he's still watching me instead of the movie. I try not to make eye contact, but his sneering lips are practically drooling as he grins at me.

"What?" I snap in a whisper, wishing he'd move the fuck over. But his arm inches further across the arm rest, taking up even more of my space.

He says nothing, and Emmett is distracted, looking straight ahead at the screen. A few seconds later, his arms inches even closer. His hand touches my knee and swiftly moves upward.

"Get off of me!" I hiss, trying to push his hand away.

"Come on," he whines. "I'm bored. Let me touch you. I'm tired of watching Emmett have all the fun."

His hand persists, trying to catch a handful of my breasts. I kick him away, the shuffle prompting a series of shushes from the back of the theater.

This catches Emmett's attention as he snaps to, looking over just in time to catch Trey's hand recoiling from my chest. Suddenly Emmett's hand darts out across me, catching Trey's hand in a tight grip. I can see their skin turning white and red from the force of his grasp.

"Don't fucking touch her," Emmett growls, his neck bulging with wide eyes as he stares Trey down.

Thinking back on one of my first encounters with them, and how Emmett seemed to even encourage other guys having their way with me…whatever it took to humiliate me, I am surprised at his sudden protectiveness.

Trey finally fights his hand free, glaring at Emmett with wrinkled brows as he rubs to self-soothe the bright red skin of his wrist. "Jeez, man," he yelps. "Chill out."

Emmett's eyes barely cross mine as he turns back to the big screen. I try to ignore how much it turns me on to feel protected by him in some way. Even if he's also my attacker at times, it's almost sweet in a sick and twisted way that he wants to be the only one bringing me harm.

*Jesus Christ, Ophelia. He has really fucked you up in the head.*

Even still, I can't help but glance up at him every so often, wishing this could be like a normal date with a guy I'm attracted to. That all the bad history between us and crazy events at play could just suspend in time temporarily. He could brush my hand over a shared bucket of popcorn. I could jump and scream when the killer in the movie pops out, sending his arms around me in protection with a comforting laugh. Maybe we'd even hold hands and kiss.

But that's not for Emmett and I. Or at least not for him. He's too fucked up, as Malcolm would say. And I'm just the idiot girl caught up in it all. Not knowing what's good for me enough to be able to stop these feelings.

The rest of the movie is uneventful, but I never feel at ease with them. I'm on high alert the entire time in anticipation of what comes next. It almost scares me more that we make it through the rest of it without incident. By the time the credits are rolling, I realize I've barely paid attention to a single second of the film. I was too caught up in a daze of uneasiness and dread. Expecting them to do something crazy at any minute.

But no. The credits roll and we stand to exit the theater. I realize whatever they're planning will probably happen now and my heart pounds so hard I can barely breathe as we approach the car again. I wish I could be back inside, not paying attention to another movie.

This time, Vincent drives and Trey sits in the passenger seat, leaving me alone in the back with Emmett. At least there's some distance between us.

As soon as I have the thought of gratitude, his arms wrap around me tightly, one hand wriggling down to unbuckle my seatbelt before he drags me into his lap.

"What the fuck are you doing!?" I shout, kicking and squirming to get away.

"We're gonna take a little drive," he explains in a hauntingly snide tone. "And I want you close to me."

All I can think of is the last time these fuckers took me for a drive, and the time after that when Emmett tried again to lure me away in his car. My hands and arms flail frantically for escape, but he quickly grips onto me in every direction. He holds me down long enough to secure his stretched seat belt over the both of us. With one arm held firmly across my chest, holding my arms down, a black cloth falls over my eyes.

"No!" I yell hopelessly, not wanting to be blindfolded. But the cloth ties tight across my vision, blocking out the outside world. "Emmett, please…don't do that!"

Vincent and Trey cackle. They love it when I'm struggling.

I finally give up and grow still, surprised by how quiet Emmett is beneath me. His hands move up my arms, making their way to either side of my head as he strokes my hair.

"Shhhh," he hisses into my ear like a snake, smoothing down both sides of my face in some twisted form of comfort.

I remain perfectly still, my pounding heart beating through both of us as I'm forcefully latched in his lap. Like a scared rabbit who finally gives up and goes limp in the arms of its captor.

The car drives off into the night, me bouncing around in Emmett's lap with every bump of the road. I can feel the stiffness in his pants against my thighs as he keeps his mouth close to my ears so that I can hear every deep, hot breath that burns against my skin.

I stay focused on trying to time how long we've been driving. I know it's an impossible task, but maybe even if I don't know where our final destination is, I can have some idea of how far it is from the theater in any direction. It's the only thing I know to do. But even that seems futile as Emmett's hands move over my skin in the dark.

"Hey man, let us have a go at her," Vincent blurts suddenly, sending chills down my spine. "We can pull over somewhere on the way."

Well, at least I know they would need to pull over on the way, meaning that's not the end goal when we get to wherever we're going. But I should know better anyway. The stakes are higher now as things are coming to a head with my father. Their fucked up sexual assault games are on the back burner now. Just a fun side perk for them as they hold me captive.

"Drive," Emmett demands coldly, stern enough to scare me. I can only hope it's as effective on his friends.

"Maybe we should just tell Vivian then," Trey taunts, staring us down threateningly in the rearview.

"She knows what I have to do," Emmett answers despondently. The threat doesn't stop his hands from creeping across me. He keeps my hands sandwiched at his sides, in between his chest and arms. Leaving me helpless as he runs his palms across my knees and up my thighs. He lingers too long at the tops of them, in between my legs.

In the darkness, knowing it would be undetectable to anyone but Emmett, I give in. I cave under his touch, leaning my head back against his chest in submission as he explores my body. Maybe it's because I don't have a choice anyway. Or because of all the tension that has been building since the first time we met. Or perhaps it has something to do with knowing I mean enough to him to stir up trouble with his girlfriend. Whatever it is, I decide not to fight it. He says nothing to acknowledge my sudden willingness. We both seem content to steal the time we have.

The muscles and folds between my legs swell with warm wetness as he clenches my inner thighs. I wish he'd move up higher, forgetting for a moment that we're not alone. But he moves up to my stomach, working his way under my shirt and sliding up across my abdomen. My hips buckle and my back arches, sending my tense abs further against his hands as his lips graze my neck and ear.

"Good girl," he whispers so soft that only I can hear it.

It almost kills it for me, causing me to recoil slightly. But as his hands move up to my ribs, I melt back into the touch. I'm putty in his hands. Just as his thumbs graze my bra across my hardened nipples, causing me to bite my lip to suppress a moan, his body straightens. He goes tense beneath my body and pulls his hands away. My shirt is swiftly tugged back down over my breasts, feeling cold in comparison to the warmth of his touch.

"We're here," he blurts coldly with a gentle smack to my thigh.

I am left unfulfilled and reeling. So much that I almost forget to be afraid of what happens next.

# CHAPTER EIGHTEEN

## BOOK 1

I find my way down from whatever crazy plane of existence I was just on with Emmett as the car rolls to a stop, crunching across a driveway. I laugh once he slips the blindfold away.

They've brought me to Jameson Manor. Everyone knows where it is, meaning they never needed to blindfold me at all. It was just a fucking power move. Another scare tactic to mess with my head.

But if they hadn't done that, I wouldn't have just been felt up by Emmett. And judging by the dampness between my legs, I enjoyed it much more than I'd like to admit. Which only makes me hate myself. Especially as he yanks my arms behind my back and shoves me toward the door.

There's an ornate iron fence lining the property, enclosing a large circular driveway in front of the main manor. A series of statues surround a huge fountain in the center of the drive, and there are several other smaller buildings in the back. Probably guesthouses and other quarters for their staff. I assume one of them is a pool house with the large bean-shaped swimming pool that peaks out from behind the house.

In the distance I can spot gazebos, a tennis court and putting greens for golf. Sprinklers are sputtering away as they mist the perfect green grass. I can only imagine what expensive cars must rest behind the garage doors. They really have it all.

The yard is huge and well-kept with big, perfectly trimmed trees. They lead me past brick walls covered in sprawling ivy and manicured hedges up to the thick white columns and large brick steps leading to the front door.

The manor towers above us as we approach the entrance, my neck craning to make out the multiple balconies and rooftop patios. I hope to god we aren't headed for one of those spots once we're inside. One drop down from any of them and I'd be a dead woman.

We enter into a foyer with high vaulted ceilings that are covered in ornate gold leaf patterns that match the crown molding. A large chandelier sparkles up above the wide spiral staircase. It's more classic than I expected, but I guess it makes sense since they are such old money. I imagine the Hendersons' mansion is more modern.

I am too taken in at the sight of it to say a single word as they lead me up the stairs and into a bedroom. Each door we pass on the way reveals another spacious room perfectly decorated with giant velvet curtains draped across tall windows. The hallway is lined with expensive-looking paintings and sculptures. I have never been in such a nice house before. Every room I've seen so far even has its own fireplace.

They say nothing as they file me into one of the bedrooms, before promptly leaving and locking me inside.

"Just wait here," Emmett calls out from behind the door. "I'll be back soon enough."

"Great," I grumble sarcastically. I'm still for a moment, in shock from the sheer size and decadence of the house. I quickly begin to look around the room, hoping to get some clue as to exactly where I am.

I recognize the backpack thrown on the floor in the corner, but I quietly look inside to confirm. The name scribbled across the notebooks and homework assignments tells me I was right. This is Emmett's backpack, meaning this is probably his room.

I scan the framed photos scattered across his dresser and nightstand, confirming once again that he's featured in each one alongside smiling friends and family. I even spot one of him and Malcolm together. They're younger. Probably close to the same age they were in the photos Malcolm kept in his glovebox. It tugs at my heart.

Why would Emmett keep this around after deciding he was too good to be close friends with him? What if what Malcolm said was true? Emmett's just as trapped as any of us are. That would at least make me feel better about the way I surrendered to his touch in the car, which I am still reeling from.

There's something intoxicating about being in his room, especially when he's not in here with me. I feel like I could learn so much about him and uncover so many of his truths, if only I knew where to look first. And if I wasn't terrified of them returning at any second and catching me.

His room is nothing like other teenage boys' rooms I've been in. It's missing the musty dirty sock and sweat smell, but that's probably just because they have maids. Even still, it's meticulously neat. In a way that seems impossible even with hired help cleaning once or twice a day. I speculate on what this could mean. Is he a sociopath? OCD?

Even his trashcan is spotless, only littered with one fresh apple core.

I realize I can't remember the last time I've eaten. I'm kicking myself for not grabbing something from that McDonald's before heading home. That was the last chance I've had to eat since the Elites dragged me out of the lunchroom this afternoon. I've been running on nothing but adrenaline ever since.

The smells of popcorn and simmering dinner from home rush through my memory. I wonder how long they'll keep me here. Mom and Brendan will wonder where I am. I hate the thought of them worrying, but I can only hope that somehow saves me.

The door flings open again, sending me stumbling back innocently to the center of the room as the three of them re-enter with a pair of handcuffs in hand.

They're silent as Emmett walks over and handcuffs me to his bed, staring straight into my eyes the entire time. I wish more than anything that Trey and Vincent weren't standing right behind him.

The smell of his cologne fills my nose as I feel his hot breath bearing down on my neck. That smell is one that has haunted me. One that strikes both fear and arousal deep inside.

It's completely fucked up, but there's something incredibly erotic about him chaining me down in his room. It shouldn't be so fucked up. All sorts of regular couples do kinky shit like this, but Emmett's history of being rough with me makes it twisted. I can't help but admit that it somehow only makes it sexier to me. Maybe he has just completely worn me down.

"What are you doing?" I ask finally, reluctantly breaking the spell within our locked eyes. I imagine we're both thinking the same thing. I can see the desire glinting across his eyes.

"My father has put me in charge of watching you twenty-four-seven," he explains casually, as if it were the most normal thing in the world. "Your dad still hasn't responded to any of our messages, and his time is running out."

"How much time is left?" I try asking again, recalling that they refused to tell me when they first put me up to this and started tracking my every move.

They still don't answer. Probably just another power move, just like the blindfold. The only reason they could possibly have for not just coming right out with their deadline is to fuck with me.

"We're gonna go check in with the old man," Trey grumbles as he and Vincent turn to leave the room. "Don't do anything I wouldn't do," he winks disgustingly.

Emmett watches them leave with an excited but subtle grin, making a point to shut and lock the door behind them.

"This isn't necessary," I tell him as he turns back toward me. "You don't have to handcuff me. I'm not stupid enough to try and escape. I know you'd catch me."

"I have to do what my father tells me," he explains, not seeming too upset about it. Stirring up Malcom's words once again. I decide to try and play to this supposed good side he promised me is there.

"You always have a choice, Emmett," I beg. "You've done terrible things to me, but I know I've seen a glimpse of something good. Or at least I've wanted to, anyways. You don't have to do this. You could help me and they'd never know."

"It's getting late," he sighs, ignoring my pleas. "You want to sleep on the bed? You're already on it after all," he winks, eyeing my cuffed hands.

"You're sick," I bark back, my heart turning back over with hatred for him. I knew Malcolm was wrong about him. "I'd rather die than sleep anywhere you've slept." I let the sting of the words hang between us, wishing they sounded truer.

He pounces on me, pinning my cuffed hands beneath his hand as he towers over my body sprawled across the bed. His grip causes the cuffs to cut into my wrists against the hard bed frame.

"You're hurting me," I gasp with a squirm beneath his hold.

He's unconcerned. If anything, he's turned on. His nostrils

flare as his eyes light up in anger and lust. His hand moves up to my neck, lifting my chin up to him. I blink and stare straight back, ready for whatever comes next.

All at once he takes my mouth to his, still fuming and breathing heavy as our lips crash together. I bite his lip defiantly, too hard, causing him to jerk back for an instant. But his hands quickly secure their grip again, jerking my head back to the center of his attention.

"You bitch," he growls, licking his bright red lip.

I soften under his stare, closing my eyes and leaning up again to invite him in for another kiss. He obliges, more gently this time, moaning into my mouth.

We melt into each other, losing ourselves as our tongues explore each other's mouths. This is all I've been able to think about since I ran from him in the classroom the other day. The drum of my heart picks up again, taking me back to all the fantasies I had of him in my bed. Everything that was stirred up again in the car ride here. Only this time, we're completely alone.

His hands trail down my arms that are chained behind my head, not breaking his mouth from mine as they travel down my chest. I groan as he gropes my breasts, unconsciously spreading my legs wider.

Suddenly, he stops himself. He pulls back in a frustrated gasp, looking at me helplessly. He looks just as powerless to this as I am. And for the first time, I realize if he is only obeying his father's orders, how much easier all of this would be for him if he wasn't so inexplicably drawn to me. I guess we could both say that.

He is pulled back down to me, perched next to me on the edge of the bed. His hand runs through my hair in shocking tenderness.

"Why are we so attracted to each other?" He asks breathlessly, his eyes lingering on my lips as I wonder if he'll give in and dive back down for more.

I can't answer him. I'm suspended in lust, wishing I could hate him as I know I should. If I can't have that, I just want him to take me. Just get it over with. But he's fighting it just as hard as I am.

In my silence, he moves back to the edge of the bed, collapsing his forehead to his hands in exasperation as he tries to collect himself. We sit like that for a long time. Unable to move, I am completely at the mercy of whatever he decides to do.

I swear I can feel his breath on my skin even though he's all the way at the other edge of the bed. I want more than anything for him to come to me. Take advantage of our situation. Have his way with me. I don't know what's stopping him. Maybe he only wants me when I'm resisting. I consider telling him I don't want him the way I have in the past. Maybe that would pique his interest again.

My thoughts halt as my stomach growls.

"Emmett, I'm really hungry," I finally speak up reluctantly, wondering if he'll exploit it to further my torture or if he'll actually try to help.

"It's late," he says again, running his hands back through his hair. His eyes are bloodshot, and I can see how tired he is.

"My lunch got interrupted, remember?" I remind him bitterly, crossing my legs, closing myself back off to him.

"I can't help," he insists bluntly, staring at the floor.

"Don't you have chefs or something?" I scoff. "You could just tell them you want a late-night snack. And bring it to me instead."

"And when I leave you alone," his brows raise, cutting his eyes back over to me, "what then? I'm not the only one in the house. You know that. Those other guys are like vultures. They'll be at my door the moment I leave your side, trying to get at you."

I'm quiet for a moment, taken aback with his concern. "I'm surprised you care," I hiss, jingling the cuffs behind my head. "You've watched those two try to feel me up before and did nothing to stop it."

"Shut up!" He snaps, jumping to his feet and hinting that I've struck a nerve.

I decide to continue trying to appeal to his nicer side. "I'm sorry," I lie. "I'm just hungry, like I said. Starving actually. It's making me cranky."

He looks over me again, looking hungry himself. But in a different way. "Maybe I can take your mind off of it," he suggests coyly.

I want to be intrigued, but it's no joke. "Emmett, if I don't eat something soon, I think I might pass out."

"Well, you won't go far," he jokes coldly, nodding to my position on the bed.

"You fucking asshole," I gripe, turning my head. No matter how hard I try, he never fails to remind me that there can't be another side to him. He is nothing beyond the guy who has tortured me. Who continues to torture me.

He sighs in exasperation. "Alright, hold on," he says with an irritated tone. He goes to his dresser and fumbles around in the second drawer, pulling out some sort of small electronic device. He opens the door and attaches it inside the lock and then moves a switch on a small remote around.

"What are you doing?" I ask, craning my neck to try and see.

"Making sure no one bothers you," he assures me, trying something on the lock a few more times. "I'll be right back."

I can't tell if I have physical symptoms of emotional whiplash or if my neck is just aching from the suspension of my arms dangling from my hands. One minute he's as cold as ice. The next he's worried for my wellbeing. Or maybe it's just that he sees me as his property. He doesn't care what happens to me, as long as he's the one to do it.

*Some boyfriend you've found yourself, Ophelia.* And he's not even that. He's Vivian's boyfriend. He's just my kidnapper.

My eyes grow heavy as I wait for what seems like forever. I jump at the sound of the door, worried Emmett's contraption failed and someone else is coming in like he warned. But he appears with a tray of fruit in his hands.

"The cooks are gone for the night," he explains, taking a seat next to me. "This is all I could rustle up."

"I'm so hungry, I don't care. I'll eat anything," I state anxiously, moving my hands forward in anticipation. But he shows no signs of setting me free.

Instead, he takes a grape between his fingers and holds it to my lips.

"What are you doing?" my face twists in disbelief. "You're seriously not going to uncuff me long enough for me to eat?"

"It's more fun this way," he says mischievously, brushing the grape to my bottom lip, begging for me to open and let him feed me.

"This is ridiculous!" I protest, clenching my jaw shut tight.

But his eyes spark with that same strange tenderness. The one that keeps popping up suddenly out of nowhere and surprising me. A bead of moisture drips from the fruit across my lip and down my chin.

My stomach growls again, forcing me to give in. I part my lips slightly, letting my tongue brush the cold purple surface as he moves it closer into my mouth. The taste of it is too much to refuse. I unclench my teeth, letting him inch it in so I can take a bite. He watches intently, continuing to feed me slowly and sensually for what feels like hours. First grapes. Then strawberries.

I don't want to be turned on by it, but I am. Like everything with him. He stops every so often and runs his tongue along the edge of my mouth, collecting the juice of the fruit as it pools.

Once the tray is empty, things get awkward and silent. We're both breathing heavy, weighed down by all of the sexual tension and staring at each other with expectant "what now?" expressions. But we say nothing. Afraid to ruin it.

Finally, he stands and leaves the tray on the top of his dresser. He pulls some pajamas from the drawers and looks to me, as if he's about to say something. By the way he eyes my clothes, I think he might offer me something to sleep in. But he stops himself. I don't know why it's so hard for him to be kind and decent to me. Even offering me food has to be done on his fucked up terms.

"Well, we really should try and get some sleep," he grumbles half-heartedly. He knows that's going to be impossible. We're both too riled up and anxious about everything that's happening.

"How's this going to work?" I concede. "Where will you sleep?"

"The floor," he replies, pulling some spare blankets and pillows down from his closet.

I have to admit I'm disappointed that he plans to sleep on the floor. I've already come this far in surrendering to him. He might as well put me out of my misery and finish the job. But more than that, I'm afraid. I wish I was home. I don't know what kinds of fucked up things tomorrow has in store for us. I just want to be close to somebody…anybody for comfort.

"Emmett?" I call out softly after he's turned out the light and settled into his sleeping bag on the floor. He doesn't answer, so I try again. "Could you come to the bed?"

"That's not a good idea," he answers in an almost whine. For once, maybe I'm the one torturing him.

"Why not?" I persist. "I would just…I'd feel better."

"Ophelia," he says sternly into the darkness. My heart

tightens with the way he says my name, so earnest and desperate. "If I come up there and lay next to you, I won't be able to control myself."

His words hang in the air, teasing me. Daring me. I want more than anything to tell him I don't care. That I'm counting on him giving in. But I take his restraint as an opportunity to remind myself what he's capable of. I'd hate myself for letting him fuck me. I'm chained to his bed for christ's sake. I'm his prisoner.

I don't answer him. Instead I try to settle down onto the pillow as far as I can, forcing myself to close my eyes. I'm exhausted, but nothing happens. Hours go by. I look over at him every so often and see that he's just as miserable as I am. His eyes wide and glaring at the ceiling. The room is pitch black, but the glossy whites catch the moonlight coming in through his window.

We both stay like that for the rest of the night, unable to fall asleep for more than a few seconds.

# CHAPTER NINETEEN

## BOOK 1

I wake up with Emmett sleeping at the foot of the bed. I don't even remember him crawling up there or falling asleep at all. Last night was torture. The only sleep I did manage to get was when my body completely shut down for a few minutes at a time before I jerked awake again. Squirming with a need for Emmett. He must have finally had too much and thought being at my feet would be safe enough.

There's a strange beeping, which I quickly gather to be the alarm clock on his phone. I laugh as I watch him stir awake. It's time for him to go to school. Such a normal thing to be happening under such bizarre circumstances.

He sits up and rubs his eyes, avoiding eye contact with me.

"I guess you're off to WJ Prep?" I sing casually, still amused with the idea.

"Not today," he grumbles, checking for messages on his phone after he silences the alarm. "We've got something to take care of. Someone wants to meet you."

Fear falls over me again as I straighten up, my hands and arms filled with pins and needles from being handcuffed all night. "Are you coming with me?" I ask helplessly.

He smirks and nods, seeming pleased that I would want to keep him close. It surprises me too. But somehow, he has become a point of safety in all of this. At least when given the choice of all the Elites.

"But we have to get going now," he barks, jumping up to

grab some clothes and straighten his appearance in his bedroom mirror.

"Can I at least take a shower first?" I ask, desperate for anything to postpone my meeting with whatever terrible thing comes next.

He shakes his head at first but looks around in consideration with his hand clenched into his hair. He is torn, grappling with another crossroads between being my tormentor and being attracted to me. If that's even what you call it. I've lost words for describing what's happening between us at this point.

I willingly grip his arm for support as he leads me, my whole body feeling completely broken down. I don't see any chances of escaping on the short walk to the bathroom anyway.

"Okay, fine," he agrees reluctantly. "But it'll have to be fast." He comes over to unlock my handcuffs. My wrists burn and ache with the release, and I'm seriously concerned for what the extended loss of blood flow will mean for me later down the road. If I make it through this.

I bend my back and hunch my shoulders as he squeezes my elbow and leads me down the hall and into the bathroom. I walk stiffly, my limbs trembling. He's completely blank and unreadable as we go. Once we're inside, he follows me in and locks the door.

"I can't have any privacy?" I whine, hesitating to remove my clothes.

"Prisoners don't get privacy," he scoffs arrogantly, refusing to move from his spot in the corner of the bathroom. I see the Emmett I'm used to has returned with the light of day, which doesn't bode well for whatever we're preparing for.

I keep my arms wrapped around my body tight under his gaze, not wanting to undress right in front of him.

"Come on," he insists. "You were more than ready to take your clothes off for me last night."

His cockiness pisses me off, prompting me to stomp into the shower fully clothed before undressing and throwing my clothes out onto the floor, not letting him see a thing. But I can see his silhouette watching me through the curtain.

I notice the way my body responds to him lingering on the other side of the curtain. My nipples harden and there's a warm swell deep in my core, rising with the yearn to feel him inside of me. I wish I could make it go away, but it's insatiable as I stand here completely naked and wet. His tense figure stalking me from outside.

I know he has to be feeling the same way, but I refuse to give into this. It's too fucked up. Last night my resolve was broken down, but if his cold heartlessness is back then my resistance will be too.

I go through the motions of lathering up with soap, carefully keeping my eyes pinned to the side at his shadow.

"Hurry up," he barks at me as I wash my hair.

"I'm going as fast as I can," I whine back, trying to hurry.

He huffs over, slinging back the curtain and reaching in to turn the faucets off.

"What are you doing!?" I cry, looking at him in shock. "I'm almost done. Just give me a minute."

"You're out of time, princess," he sneers, throwing a towel at me, but not until after he takes a good long slow look at my wet and naked body. I'm quick to cover up from his gaze, figuring if he can't even have the decency to give me a full five minutes in the shower, he doesn't get to see me naked.

Anger sparks in his eyes as I cover up, robbing him of his eye candy. His hand grips my elbow tightly as he yanks me out, banging my arm harshly against the sink countertop.

"Shit!" I shout, looking down to see fresh red blood pooling out into the beads of water still dripping across my skin. Just another reminder of who he really is, making me kick myself for every moment of weakness I had last night.

"We don't have time for all of this," he moans impatiently, snatching the towel and sloppily blotting down my skin himself. I cringe and recoil under his harsh touch. He seems completely unphased, wrapping the towel around my shoulders and leading me back into the hall with his hand gripping firmly to the base of my skull.

He takes me back to his bedroom and pulls out a dress in my size. "You have to look nice," he orders, ripping the garment from the hanger and throwing it in my direction.

"What's the occasion?" I quip back dryly as I reluctantly step into the dress. I'm frightened that he has something like this waiting for me. Whatever is about to happen, he's been prepared for it.

"You'll see soon enough," he spins me and quickly yanks the zipper, making me worry my skin would catch in the ferocity of it.

He pushes me out into the hall and back down the main stairs. He's tense and sweaty, his skin jerking every time it brushes up against my arm.

The more I take in of the decadent mansion, the more it disgusts me. What a waste for such beautiful things to house such ugly creatures. But really that sums the Elites up perfectly. Shiny and pretty on the outside, complete shit on the inside.

We walk into what looks like the parlor. Maybe some kind of office or study. His sneakers squeak across the glossy hardwood floors as we enter the sitting area arranged before a backdrop of thick velvet drapes across large French windows. The walls tower high above us, accented with crown molding that reflects the tiered crystal chandelier hanging in the center of the room.

It looks like a scene from the Godfather, decorated in dark mahoganies and olive greens and deep burgundies. There's a bar cart that mimics what you'd see in a Mad Men office, complete with a silver ice bucket and various bottles of scotch, brandy and bourbon. The room is dark and smells of cigars.

He leads me in, my hands pinned behind my back, to find a man sitting in a desk chair with his back turned to us. As the chair swivels around I see Mr. Thomas Jameson is the one waiting for us, instantly sparking fear in my heart.

I can already tell he is no different, not that I would have expected him to be. His lips snarl in a viciously sexual grin at the sight of me. I feel the slightest hesitation within Emmett's arms as he notices how he's looking at me, but he quickly pushes any reluctance back down dutifully and does nothing.

My guts churn as Thomas stands to walk over to me, forcing Emmett to hold his grip on me as he trails a finger across my cheek. Emmett forces my hand to his father's for a strong, businesslike handshake.

"I hear you've been quite the naughty little girl, Ophelia," he teases, his voice making me nauseous.

"Don't touch me," I whimper, jerking my arms away from Emmett.

He laughs at my protest, his nostrils snarling with gross heavy breaths. "I can see why you've been such a handful," he jokes, reaching out toward my breasts. I try to step backward, but Emmett blocks my way. I cringe under his touch, my face wincing and screaming silently as his hands move lower toward my stomach.

"Get your hands off of me you fucking old perv!" I snap, unable to hold it in any longer. The words spill out over my fear.

My face is instantly socked with the bluntness of his knuckles. He laughs as I press my fingers to my cheek, my brow wrinkled in pain.

"You may be able to outwit my son and his little friends," he sneers with a crack of his knuckles, "but you're no match for me, you little cunt."

He steps away and pulls a handkerchief from his desk, wiping his hands down. Funny how someone so sexually interested in me can quickly turn violent enough to punch me in the face. Both acts apparently being repulsive to him, sparking the need to wash my germs from his hands.

"It's time to send a message to your beloved father," he explains mockingly as he paces before me, motioning to his cronies as they deliver a video camera and tripod to the center of the room. I watch him pace the room, his speech accelerating as he barks orders at everyone around. "We're going to record a little video."

I blink, processing his words, and focus on him intently. Clinging to any hint of what to expect.

Emmett pulls me from behind, pushing up a chair that I am quickly shoved into as he grabs my arms and ties them behind me. The rope burns into my wrists as he squeezes the knots securely, cutting off the circulation of my hands. My eyes narrow, peering into them as if I look hard enough all of this might start making sense.

"You're going to beg for your life," Mr. Jameson commands. "Let him know that if he doesn't stop, we have other ways to help make him." He speaks slowly and forcibly, trying to sound in control, but I can tell he's coming apart.

"I had never even heard a word from my father up until a few days ago," I protest. "I don't think I'm your best bet at getting him to do anything. He doesn't give a shit about me."

"Oh, I like a girl with daddy issues," he taunts, sweat gleaming on his face. "You let us worry about that and just do what we tell you."

Once the camera is in place, one of the men holds his finger over the red record button, waiting for his cue to start the video.

"Now, keep in mind, dear…the success of this message really is up to you," Thomas explains snidely. "Whether or not your father responds accordingly, allowing us to spare your life, will depend entirely on how convincing you are." He stops in front of me, leaning over to perch his hands across the arms of my chair. He winces, his face twisting into disapproval. "I don't know…you don't look afraid to me." He turns to Emmett. "What do you think, son? Does she look afraid to you?"

I see Emmett turn away in the corner of my eye, refusing to answer. Suddenly my head whips around with a painful sting across my cheek. Thomas is laughing as he stands back, proudly admiring the redness of my face as I whimper in pain.

I rock back and forth in the chair, trying to control my heavy panting as I tell myself over and over that this will all be okay. It has to be. My back arches as I squirm in discomfort with deep, shuddering breaths that make me feel lightheaded.

Emmett doesn't make me feel the least bit safe anymore and with Thomas's looming presence, already having hit me twice just in the few short minutes I've been in the room, I feel like I'm having a panic attack.

*Stop panicking, Ophelia.*

*Calm down, Ophelia.*

I see starbursts behind my closed eyelids. I focus on keeping my breaths steady and normal, but my muscles are rigid, my tendons standing out on edge. My head still swimming from Thomas's blows.

A man walks over and places today's newspaper in my lap to show the date. This really is a full-blown hostage situation. Out of all the things I thought I'd experience in my life; this was not on my radar.

"Now you'll tell your father to stop. And that he must answer to our ultimatum immediately. Or he'll never get the chance to meet his precious daughter," Thomas commands cavalierly.

"What if he doesn't care?" I propose, knowing all too well how possible that is. "Haven't you already sent him similar threats and got nothing? He's gone this long wanting nothing to do with me. Whatever he has against you seems to be more important to him than my life."

"Oh, don't be so cynical," he mocks condescendingly. "Even the most detached father wouldn't want to see certain things done to his baby girl. You see…I've put girls just like you in some pretty horrid conditions. There's good money in it. I doubt he'd want you to vanish into that kind of life."

I remember Liam's warnings about what the Jameson Automobile Company was fronting through the use of his software. Underage girls on the black market in sex trafficking rings. All this time I've been afraid of dying. It never occurred to me that my potential fate could be much worse. Maybe Emmett's sadistic sexual torture is just preparing me for what will happen if my father doesn't come through and meet their demands.

I look to Emmett again, desperately. He watches blankly. I want him to stand up for me. To say or do anything to intervene, but he cowers in the corner. Not lifting a single finger in my defense. Now I worry for how involved he might be in his father's business. Maybe he's just as sick and guilty of the same crimes.

"What do I have to say?" I ask finally, my voice cracking as I realize I have no choice but to give in. His scare tactics are working. Mostly because I know he's ruthless. Cold. Heartless. He doesn't make idle threats.

"Speak from your heart, my dear," he sneers. "I'm sure once we get started, you'll feel inspired." His menacing tone and grin frighten me even more as his men gather behind me.

I watch one of them press a button on the camera, causing a red light to flash. Thomas waves his hands through the air dramatically, like a maestro conducting an orchestra. His callous coldness is chilling. Enough to cause me to tear up in terror, but I hold back. Not giving them my tears is my last possible act of defiance. The only part of myself I can still hold onto.

"Dad," I begin, my voice already wavering more than I'd like. Even saying the title, addressing him directly, feels foreign and wrong. "You have to do what they say," I stammer, feeling at a loss for words. My mind is blank.

Still refusing to cry a single tear, one of Thomas's men crouches down behind me with a pair of pliers in hand, squeezing my knuckles in their grip tighter and tighter. I hope the lack of blood flow to my hands dulls the pain, but I can feel the cold metal cutting into me intensely. I still don't give in. My face winces in pain but I don't shed a tear.

"Dad!" I cry out louder. "Please…I don't know where you are or how far you're willing to go with this. But these people aren't fucking around," my sentiment sparks a maniacal, taunting laugh from Thomas. "You have to stop coming after them. Respond to their messages and let them know you'll stop. Please. They'll…they'll make sure I disappear forever if you don't." My throat tightens with even more building cries, threatening to forcibly erupt as I contemplate what could happen if this doesn't work.

"Are you sure you have nothing else to add? Nothing else to inspire your father to help you?" Thomas beckons, like a parent to a toddler. His tone soft and inviting in a chilling way, completely mismatched to his intentions.

I know he is encouraging me to cry, but I stay strong. Shaking my head. Liam promised me my father had a plan. And that I shouldn't feel so hopeless and powerless. It's all I have to cling to for now. I just have to hope he was right.

Thomas motions for the recording to be stopped and then nods to Emmett. He comes over and unties me, forcing me to my feet. He restrains me by the arms once again as Thomas approaches, coming too close.

"It was lovely meeting you, dear Ophelia," he groans with predatory eyes. "I'm sure we will meet again. Very soon. At least I hope it's soon…for your sake."

I want to spit in his face, but he hits harder than any of his younger Elite counterparts. I'm still weak, tired and panicked. I don't think I can withstand another blow. So instead I bite my tongue and turn my head, wishing Emmett would just hurry up and take me away.

Once we are to the top of the stairs, my tears flow like rain. I'm completely unable to hold them back a second longer now that it's just Emmett and I alone again.

"Thanks a lot," I sob, my throat tight with anger. "You really had my back in there."

"What do you want from me!?" he rumbles in a low, tired rage.

"Oh yeah…what could I possibly have wanted from you?" I fire back sarcastically. "What kind of guy lets his dad treat people that way?"

Suddenly I am thrown against the wall. Emmett's hands are digging into my shoulders, shaking me violently.

"Do you get it now, Ophelia!?" he shrieks in a hushed tone. "If you think my father was terrible just then…imagine the kinds of things I've…" He chokes, unable to say another word.

I bite back everything building up inside, feeling a new wave of pity for him. But he quickly pushes me along, both of us desperate to be back inside the privacy and safety of his room.

"Finish your sentence," I beg once we're hidden away behind his locked door. "What kinds of things…" I'm afraid to ask, but I need to know. It's his only chance at redemption. The possibility that he's just an abused fucked up kid who is too damaged to know how to treat people.

But he refuses to answer. He won't even look at me. He retreats back into his closed-off shell, staring despairingly out his window.

I'm certain Malcolm was right. There had to be something more to Emmett once. Something kind. But maybe as the years of his life went on in this fucked up house, in the world of the Elites, he was broken. My blood chills at the thought that he may never be restored. No matter what happens. Maybe he is fucked up beyond repair. And my biggest fear is that once he's through with me, I will be too.

# CHAPTER TWENTY

### BOOK 1

"I have to cuff you up again," Emmett says finally, brushing a finger across his upper lip before reluctantly turning back to me from the window.

"Emmett, my arms are killing me from being cuffed up all night," I lament in exhaustion. "Can we just skip that part this time?"

"You saw him in there," he offers up dryly. "You know I have to do this."

I'm too tired to argue. I take my seat on the bed and offer my hands over freely. My mind racing as he secures the handcuffs once again.

I'm getting desperate for some way out of this. I know time is running out. If my dad doesn't give these people what they want, they're going to kill me. Or worse. Sell me off into some sex trafficking ring. And since I have never been able to count on him for anything, I'm not going to hang all of my hopes on him.

I study Emmett as he sits in the corner, listlessly tossing a ball up to the ceiling and catching it again. Out of everyone I've seen in this mansion, Emmett is my best shot at manipulating my way to freedom long enough to hunt down some shred of evidence.

I know there has to be something somewhere in this place. Something that my dad and the Hendersons can use in their case. It can't be spotless. Then maybe I would have something more than these ransom videos to count on.

"I gotta say…out of all the times I imagined being locked alone with you in your room…this is not exactly what I had pictured," I attempt to joke with him with a half-smile.

His eyes spark with interest. "So, you have fantasized about me?" he asks with a suggestive note to his voice.

"Don't be stupid, Emmett. You know I have. And you've fantasized about me too," I state plainly.

He catches the ball a final time and sits up to look at me. His eyes trail over my body longingly and then settle on the cuffs around my wrist with a tinge of pity. Blood is still dripping down my arm from where it banged against the bathroom counter this morning.

He raises to his feet at the sight of the blood and steps toward me. "How's your arm?"

"It's alright I guess," I sniffle. "After everything with Thomas…I guess I forgot about it."

Both of our eyes turn dark with the memory of Emmett being forced to stand there and hold me down while Thomas felt me up. I watch the memories roll around in his mind, sending him into a sudden manic pace across the room.

"It can't be easy to have a dad like that," I offer softly.

He turns but doesn't answer me. His face twists slightly with a flood of suppressed emotions.

"You don't know what you're talking about," he mumbles half-heartedly. "You don't know anything about us."

I kick myself for having crossed a line, closing him off. But his voice is blank. He's lying to protect himself, and he's not even that adamant about it. I can tell he's tired and worn down from everything. Maybe just as much as I am.

Without another word, he leaves the room. His feet march toward the bathroom down the hall before returning a few minutes later with first aid supplies in hand. Taking a seat near me on the edge of the bed, he leans forward to clean my wound.

"I didn't mean for you to get hurt," he says softly, gently blotting a cold, damp cotton ball to the cut.

"I know you didn't," I lie, looking deep into his eyes.

His head raises with my words before he kneels back down to put a band-aid over the cut. "What's got you playing nice all of a sudden?"

"I'm just done playing games," I explain. "I'm tired and scared. And you're the only person I care about in any of this."

He laughs mockingly. "Care about?"

"You know I care for you, Emmett," I soften my voice. "And you care for me too."

"What makes you so sure of that?" he scoffs through a thin veil. I can see everything stirring up inside of him.

I strategically uncross my legs, revealing a slight view from where my dress is riding up my thighs, and move closer so that we are touching. His eyes drink in the sight of my hiked skirt and everything peeking out from underneath. Putting us right back in the tempting spot we were the night before.

"You made me sure of it," I explain, lifting my leg to rub against his, sinking beneath my hands that are chained behind my head. "All the times you knew you were supposed to beat the shit out of me, but you were too turned on to really hurt me. The classroom after I slapped Vivian. And again, when she was standing there watching us. I could tell how badly you wanted me by the way you looked into my eyes. It took everything in you not to take me last night."

He shifts uncomfortably, trying to look away but unable to.

"You didn't have to kiss me when you tracked me down at that meet…before I came to WJ Prep," I continue, wearing down on his defenses. "You know I'm not so gullible that I'd melt for any boy who kissed me. You did it because you couldn't help yourself. And I fell for you because I couldn't help myself. You can't deny that there's something between us."

My throat hitches as I realize everything I'm saying is true, even if I am only trying to butter him up. All of the tension between us amplifies with every word I speak. My lips part as I rest my eyes firmly on him, my suspended hands growing moist. "I didn't know what to say when you asked last night…but I feel it too. We are so attracted to each other."

His fingers trail across my arm too slowly as he tends to the wound, his legs spread, opening slightly wider as mine do. He leans forward, continuing to bandage my cut. Not saying a word. But I can see a million things going on in his head.

"What are you thinking?" my tone is soft and low. I relax into my captive state, turning my chest straight toward him.

His eyes soften and gloss over with desire. "You don't want to know what I'm thinking."

"Don't be so sure," I dart my tongue across my lips, loosening the tension in my muscles. "I don't have the energy to fight this anymore."

He shifts uneasily, clenching his hands briefly before tugging at his ear. I feel the skin on my chest grow flush as I swallow hard with a slow smile that builds. "How long do you think it will be before they want me again?" I ask as I lift my chin, holding my breath. "Can you let me go? Just for a little bit?"

He eyes me suspiciously before tensing up again, moving away as if he's trying to break the spell. "It's not a good idea," he insists. "My father will kill both of us if we don't do what we're supposed to."

"He'll never know," I protest, pulling at the cuffs eagerly. "Emmett, I won't try anything. I just want to be able to talk to you without being all chained up."

He scoffs with a dismissive smirk. "Fuck off, Ophelia. I know you too well. You may be attracted to me, but you also hate me. This is just a game so you can pull some kind of shit over on me. Which wouldn't be good for either of us."

I back off, shifting to make myself uncomfortable as I resign to being handcuffed longer. I wrack my brain for anything I can say to sway him as I feel the building intensity of time running out.

"Do you remember when we first met?" I try again. "I thought you were so hot. But then again I also thought you were normal."

I catch a faint smirk on his lips. "So, I'm not normal?" he teases.

I answer with my brow raised sharply, letting him figure that one out for himself. "The way you kissed my hand," I laughed. "And then you demanded that I let you kiss my lips."

He plops into a chair in the corner as his leg starts bobbing up and down. He presses his palm to his mouth and looks anxiously around the room, fighting hard not to let my words affect him.

"I can't believe I let you," I mused. "Something about the way you commanded me…I just couldn't refuse. I guess you still have that power over me somehow."

"I wasn't expecting to feel like that when I kissed you," he responds with a surprising tenderness.

His recollection of it makes sense. The way he seemed confused and tormented as he grabbed at my body with an almost punishing touch. He hated me for the feelings I stirred up inside of him. He was just doing what he was told, scoping me out and luring me to WJ Prep. He never meant to feel anything for me.

"I still never expect to feel that way when I kiss you," he added in a disappointed mutter.

"But you do," I offer optimistically, thinking maybe I've found my way into him. "And I do too. There's something between us, Emmett. Enough that…surely you can trust me to let me go for just a little bit. My arms are still sore from sleeping like this all night."

He eyes my red wrists in concern, rapidly already turning white and red with numb tingles that hurt much more than the first time around.

Springing to his feet like he might actually let me loose, he stops again. Eyeing me suspiciously.

"Come on, Emmett," I encourage him, sounding as innocent as I can. "Part of what made that first kiss so fucking delicious was the freedom of my hands. Do you remember how I explored your body? Trailed my fingers through your hair?"

He turns with a growl, growing more frustrated. "You drive me crazy, Ophelia. Just stop it!" he snaps finally. "When this is all over…"

He stops himself, and I'm surprised at his subtle implication. He's hinting at an end to this. One in which I'm maybe still alive. Does he know something I don't?

"I think a lot about those first couple of times we met," I carry on, mostly out of bored resignation at this point. "The way I saw you before I started piecing everything together. Before I knew about the Elites…or that you were one of them."

"Oh yeah?" he mumbles, doing a poor job of hiding his interest.

I part my legs again, spreading the tight black dress as my head falls back in a nostalgic moan. "I wish things didn't have to be so complicated."

He's started throwing his ball again without saying a single word in response. Just a frustrated sigh and quick glance in my direction.

"Do you remember the other day in the classroom? The things you did to me against that wall," my voice trails off into an almost whisper.

He coldly pushes back, "Ophelia, stop it. Everything's different now."

I grow still, feeling embarrassed. And also afraid, worried about what's happened since then that's changed everything so much. I have to remember he has the upper hand. He knows more than he's telling me.

I have to stop thinking about him like this anyway. It makes no sense. There are much bigger things going on. My life is in danger. I shouldn't be pining for some boy…especially when that boy is one of the people tormenting me.

He hangs his head in exasperation and heaves a sigh, "I don't know what you want from me. I just want this all to be over with. I have to be careful or…"

"Or what?" I try again, needing him to look at me – to want me the way he used to. The way he did just last night. I need a distraction from everything that just happened with his father. The fear of the unknown and what happens next. "I know you're keeping something from me. Just tell me."

"I can't do this right now. Why can't you understand that? You don't listen to me," he grumbles. It's a relief to see him angry but calm. To know he's capable of less than the extremes I've seen up until now.

"Where's Vivian been this whole time?" I ask finally. I'm curious, but also seeing how many different nerves I can strike. Hoping one of them will make him spill whatever it is he's hiding.

He shakes his head, not answering me.

"Did you two break up?" I ask lightly, trying to sound indifferent.

"Oh, just because she's not around for your kidnapping you assume we broke up?" he snaps back with an arrogant grin, his brows raised. "What's it to you anyway, Ophelia?"

Now I grow silent, angry that he even needs to ask why I care with everything I've said to him. He thinks it's all just an act. I wish it was. Mostly I just wish I didn't say anything at all.

"I need to go to school," he finally relents, giving up on his fight against me. Needing to retreat somewhere far away from me and this whole mess. I know he doesn't need to go to school right now. He's just looking for an escape.

"Take me with you," I beg urgently, cringing at the thought of being left alone in the same building as his father. "Don't leave me here alone."

"I can't," he insists sternly. "There's no way that's going to happen."

"Then at least let me loose," I cry sincerely, feeling unable to bear another few hours of my arms being suspended this way. "Please, Emmett. My arms are killing me. I won't leave your room."

"I know you won't," he huffs as he marches over, pulling the key from his pocket and unlatching the cuffs. "This door locks from the outside, and I'm the only one who can unlock it." He holds up the small remote from last night. He clicks the button a few times, prompting the latch of the door to move to and from.

After demonstrating the lock, he finally unlocks my handcuffs again. My arms shake as I groan with their release, wringing the soreness of my wrists.

He gathers his things, refusing to look at me, stopping once before he reaches for the door with a subtle glance over his shoulder. I pray for him to turn around and do whatever is going through his mind, but with another exasperated grunt he carries on his path. The door is swiftly shut and locked from the outside.

I'm relieved to be alone again as he leaves for school, but I would still give anything to be able to go with him. Though I know in reality I am no safer out there than in here, the illusion of freedom, even only for a brief afternoon, would restore me. Give me the strength I need to maybe gain a new perspective. Some new idea of what to do next.

My hands and arms still ache, and I wonder if I can use this time to sleep it off. I am exhausted. Being left alone finally, I try to make the best of it and rest in a way I couldn't when Emmett was just a foot away. But a strange longing for him lingers. I am once again left with frazzled senses, not knowing if I want to run to him or away from him.

I lay down, relishing in the relief of tension in my body. Time passes slowly as I'm unable to fall asleep. I'm too afraid of what might happen while he's gone. I know Thomas is lurking out there somewhere, and I can only hope he is too distracted to realize I'm up here all alone. Maybe my dad has responded to him. Maybe he's finally giving up and giving them what they want. But I know better.

The clock on his bedside table says it's close to noon. Every time I close my eyes, I swear I see someone moving in the corner of the room, jerking me back awake. Great, I think. Now I'm hallucinating.

I try to stay perfectly still, thinking maybe if I don't make any noise, Thomas will forget I'm up here all alone. But I can't lay on the bed anymore. I'm too anxious to stay still.

I pace the room in dreaded anticipation of what happens next. My skin is crawling from the memories of Thomas's hands on my body, and I swear I can still feel him touching me. I shake it all away, trying to bring myself back to reality. I am alone and safe. For the moment.

But then footsteps thud down the hallway, sending me back into panic.

Anyone would want to run if they were in this position, but being a runner at heart, it's that much more painful to be so trapped. My legs moving as fast as they can, the wind brushing against me as I leave everything behind, is the only thing that could make me feel better right now.

I just want to go home, far away from this hellhole. I wonder if my mom and Brendan have started looking for me yet. I never came home after the guys convinced them to let us go to the movies together. Surely, they would have contacted the police by now. I figure the Elites must have warned the authorities that they'd be up to something and not to look for me. They'd do whatever they asked. They could literally get away with murder.

The footsteps draw closer and suddenly there's a knock on the door that causes me to jump.

"Ophelia?" Thomas' voice calls out from behind the door, sending chills down my spine.

I'm too afraid to move. I stand there hopelessly, thinking maybe if I'm quiet he'll just go away. I know all about his preference for underage girls.

"Let me in, sweetheart," he croons, his voice making me sick. "I only want to talk to you."

"Go away," I answer softly, my voice cracking. "I don't want to see anyone right now."

"Now, is that any way to treat your host?" he taunts me, jiggling the door handle. "Emmett doesn't have to know we've seen each other. And I can make you much more comfortable… if you'd only let me."

"No…no thank you!" I stammer out. "I'm fine in here alone."

"Suit yourself," he jests finally. "But I'll be seeing you soon." I hear him cackle as he turns down the hall. The moment I hear his footsteps starting down the stairs, I race for my phone and open it up to Emmett's number.

**Thomas is trying to get into the room. Please help.**

I sit on the edge of the bed and wait anxiously, but there's no response.

Suddenly I hear the lock on the bedroom door click. My heart pounds as I think it must be Thomas. He's returned with a key. But the hallway is silent. I peek out and see no one. I quickly dart across the hall and lock myself inside the bathroom, only for that lock to click open a few minutes later.

A scream rests on the tip of my tongue as the handle turns and the door slowly creaks open, but I'm relieved to see Emmett on the other side.

His hair is disheveled, and he looks distressed.

"Are you okay?" he growls, fuming with anger. "I can't believe my dad tried to get at you again. I can't take this. You're *mine.*"

"Please let me go to school with you, Emmett," I plead again. "The moment you leave, he'll be back. And I don't think he'll give up so easily next time." I can see him considering it as he grazes his palm across the back of his neck.

"Convince me," he demands, for his own sake just as much as mine.

I step closer, leaning into his chest. "I'll stay by your side at all times," I argue. "For better or worse."

My head lifts, my eyes meeting his. They furrow narrowly, reading my face and body, before he blinks and leans back into my stance. My eyes are glued to his lips, begging him to make a move.

"Oh god, Emmett…please. Just fuck me," the words spill from my mouth in a breathless stream, surprising both of us.

He tenses, a faint smile turning up the corners of his lips as his fingers skate across his jaw. A faint jumble of syllables escapes his lips, but quickly trail off as he clears his throat.

My head tilts and my lips part as I slowly breathe faster under his gaze across my body. He moves even closer, as if he has no choice. We're both at the mercy of the magnetic pull between us.

My heart rate quickens as my body heat rises. I can't stand it anymore. I dig my fingers into his forearm, pulling him closer. The tension melts away with each touch, giving us release.

We've kissed so many times before, but we know this time is different. Once we start, we won't stop.

I swallow hard, alert and waiting for what he will do next. My muscles tense as I note the sweat beading across his brow. It's taking every muscle in his body to resist me right now.

Finally, he gives in, sliding his hand across my thigh under my skirt, gripping my ass as he lifts me up onto the bathroom counter. His hips push in between my legs, pressing the strain in his pants against the warm wetness between my legs. I can feel the stiffness through my panties.

His hand tugs at the back of my hair, pulling my head back and my mouth wider for his kiss. His tongue fills my mouth in slow steady waves, groaning so deep that it vibrates through my throat.

He pins my hands to the counter, frantically plunging his tongue in and out of my mouth. We kiss so hard and quick, drinking each other in so desperately that we accidentally scrape our teeth together a few times. Kissing each other with such urgency it's as if our lives depend on it. His tan fingers grab at my breasts, rubbing my nipples in tiny circles every so often – just enough to make them hard and send shooting signals down to my clit. I'm so caught up in lust, and wetter than I thought possible, enough to soak my underwear, which are now completely exposed from my skirt that Emmett has hiked up over my thighs.

I lift my arms, begging him to slip the dress over my head. He does slowly…too slowly. Torturing me with his soft touch and the hotness of his breath meeting my exposed skin.

His hands pull at the clasp of my bra, releasing my breasts into the open air as he kisses me harder. His palm stretches over one of them, squeezing it firmly before his fingers trails across my nipple. The curls of his hair brush my cheek as he drops to my neck, biting and kissing ferociously, working his way down to my breasts.

I moan as his tongue darts across my nipples, and I consider pushing him away as memories of the abuse I've suffered at his hands come back to haunt me. But the sensation of his warm mouth shoots straight to my core.

"Stop," I offer weakly, but the desire dripping from my tone betrays me. I'm unable to resist any further.

His fingers move my folds in circles, almost too roughly, but the force is just right. The burn of it only pushes me closer as he pushes the sharp zipper of his pants against his grip. He pushes my panties aside and slides his fingers inside of me. The roughness of his skin gliding into me is like nothing I've ever felt before.

I'm no virgin, and I've certainly been fingered before, but no guy's touch has ever felt like this. My eyes roll to the back of my head with a deep moan as I brace my arms against the counter.

He steps back to unzip his pants, staring me straight in the eyes, pulling out the most gorgeous long, hard cock I've ever seen. I lick my lips and can't stop myself from breathlessly exclaiming, "Oh, Emmett." He keeps staring me straight in the eye as he reaches down and begins stroking himself. "What is it, baby? Is it this?" he rasps in a deep sexy voice, "Is this what you want?"

"Oh god, Emmett, yes. Please, give it to me now. Fuck me."

He drops his pants and inches closer. Once he quickly manages to pull on a condom from the bathroom drawer, I grab his hips and pull him back toward me. He slams me back up against the bathroom mirror in a wave of excitement. I frantically remove my underwear.

As his big strong arms hoist my hips up in such a perfect way that his dick slides perfectly into me from just the right angle. I'm so overtaken by his strength and how good those first few deep thrusts are, sliding his hard cock inside of me. He fits into me perfectly. Big enough to hit all of the right spots without hurting me. Every thrust of his hips puts him deeper inside of me than the one before. He's large and the size stretches me, but I'm so wet that he goes right in. My muscles tense in pleasure around him as he growls into my ear. His rhythm speeds, his fingernails digging into my ass. Any brief sharp pain he causes me now isn't from hatred. He's just as overcome with passion as I am.

I cry out, "Oh Emmett! Emmett, fuck yes!"

He grips his arms under my legs, reaching around and tightly squeezing my ass, as his long dick slides in and out of me. He thrusts hard and deep but pulls out so slowly each time – sending ripples of sensation through my entire body.

Everything about it makes me more wet – the smell of his cologne, the sweat dripping from his tan gleaming chest, the way the muscles in his neck tighten and bulge as he moans with each thrust into me. His voice is smooth like honey, and it excites me to know that I can bring sounds like that out of him.

The stretch of skin and muscle just above his dick is sweaty and smooth and gliding across my clit pushing me close to climax.

"Emmett," I whimper against his neck as he moves faster, pushing me closer to the edge.

His eyes meet mine, burning straight into me as he moves faster. His breath quickens and catches with the rhythm as sweat beads across his upper lip, dampening the strands of hair hanging in his eyes.

I almost don't hear him at all as I cry out in pleasure, but the softness of his voice catches my attention. He whimpers tenderly, in a way I've never heard from him before. We're suspended for a moment, frozen with our bodies pressed together. He slowly pulls back, his eyes studying me as his face turns.

"That's it, baby. Come for me. I want to feel you come. God, I'm so close…I'm going to come too. Are you ready?"

I'm so overwhelmed with the strange feelings surging inside of me, I can barely answer him, "I…I think…fuck, that's so good…" I cry out as I realize how close I am to coming.

His hand spreads over my mouth to muffle my cries.

"Fuck, yes, I'm going to come…don't stop…right there… that's it!" I manage to say, muffled against his hand.

His groans in my ear grow deeper and entangled with a slight growl as he slams into me harder and faster over and over… He hisses through clenched teeth against my ear. He lets out a few manly grunts and final thrusts before vanishing, as if he disappeared into a cloud of smoke, vanishing to some other forgotten part of my brain.

We both lose ourselves, crashing over the edge in ecstasy. My head drops to his shoulder, both of us damp with sweat.

But suddenly, he pulls away, tossing my hands off of him and back down to the counter. Like a switch, I see the old familiar Emmett return almost instantly as he turns cold. I'm left alone and frustrated. My body feeling completely void of the desire I felt only moments ago.

He shakes his head, his lips ruffling like a horse. As if he's trying to shake me away. His shoulders roll with a crack of his jaw. I'm waiting for him to kiss me, to turn back to the way he was before. But his eyes turn distant and cold.

I suddenly feel vulnerable and ashamed, my naked body perched on full display in front of him on the bathroom counter. He pulls the full condom from his dick and tosses it into the trashcan, wiping himself down with a towel before tossing it to me callously. I jump back as it slaps against my arms.

"So…that's it then?" I ask in bewilderment, shocked that such an intense encounter could fade off into such ordinary awkward teenage behavior.

"What do you mean?" he asks as if everything is normal, but his refusal to look at me tells me what I need to know. He's hiding from me. Hiding from this.

"Is something wrong?" I try again.

"Ophelia, I don't know what you're talking about," he smirks with a perplexed grin that implies I am crazy. "We fucked. We're done. And now I need to go."

"Bullshit!" I cry out, clutching the towel around me to cover myself up. "You're acting weird. What's going on with you? How can you just shut off like that?"

"Maybe you've forgotten why we're here," he growls. "You're our hostage. My father is waiting downstairs right now, trying to decide when he's going to kill you or sell you off into his sex trafficking rings. It's not exactly a romantic time."

"Then why did we do it?" I huff, wishing I could take it back.

"You begged," he replies arrogantly.

I want to slap him across the face, but I'm afraid of what he would do in response. Instead, I curl into myself, making my body small. Wishing I could just disappear. I thought giving myself over to Emmett would make me feel better about the chaos and danger around us, but his quick withdrawal of feeling is only making it worse. I feel even more alone than before.

I stare with empty eyes at my feet dangling from the counter, turning the same shades of red and white that my hands and arms have been up until now. I wonder how long it will be before I'm chained up again. And how long after that before they finally kill me.

That's it, I think. He's gone. Everything I thought was between us was just his urge to get what he wanted. And now that I've given it to him, I have no more power over him. Not only am I disgusted with myself for caving in, I've endangered my life. He's the only one who's given me any hope of maybe helping me. At feeling something for me enough that I might be able to get out of this. But now I've lost that.

But it isn't a conclusion I'm prepared to come to yet – I don't have the energy. I let out an exasperated sigh and tuck away all of my thoughts to some other part of my brain, as I've grown so used to doing.

"Well…thanks. I guess," I grumble awkwardly in the face of his sudden cold detachment as he fumbles to put his pants back on, refusing eye contact.

"I really do need to go to school," he replies dryly. "I never made it before. I had to come back when you texted."

"Emmett…please, please let me come with you," I try begging again, forgetting about the rest of what just happened for a moment. "You know as soon as you leave that your dad will come for me again."

He nods knowingly, his eyes deep in thought. "You're right," he resigns. "But it's too risky."

"You told me to convince you!" I cry out, losing my composure. "And I gave myself over to you. Which I realize now was a fucking stupid thing to do. But the least you could do is have the decency to take me with you now that I gave you what you wanted."

"You think that was a mistake?" he asks, almost looking hurt.

I am stunned and silent. Does he not think it was a mistake? Could have fooled me with the way he immediately pulled away. Unable to look at me. All I can do is shake my head in exasperation.

"Alright," he mutters. "I'll take you."

My heart surges with renewed hope. I know it means nothing and that we'll end up right back here afterward. My fate being no more certain than before. But at least I can have a few brief hours of escape. And outside of these walls, the possibilities of being saved or helped in some way are a million times stronger.

I awkwardly put my clothes back on, too tired to think about this thing with Emmett anymore. All I care about right now is getting the hell out of this house.

# CHAPTER TWENTY-ONE

## BOOK 1

As Emmett's car pulls up to WJ Prep, the sight of the kids gathered in front of the school in between periods gives me hope. Though my situation may be completely fucked, there is still a normal world carrying on without me. And maybe, if I play my cards right, I can find some way to rejoin it all soon.

It's strange to be back at school, pretending that everything is fine. No one knows that I'm being held hostage. If this school wasn't so fucked up, I'd try to ask for help, but I know all too well how futile that would be.

I try to convince myself my life *is* normal for a moment. I think back on Emmett's and my encounter in his bathroom as I watch him kick a few pebbles around on the ground on our walk to the front of the building. I want us to just be normal teenagers. A guy and a girl who like each other, who've just had sex with each other for the first time. We should be giddy and all over each other, but instead we're caught in our parents' traps. He's too damaged to ever truly feel anything for me, which he made obvious by his behavior when he was finished with me.

I have to remind myself of everything Emmett has done. He is not so innocent, and I'd be dumb to forget that. I feel dumb enough for the times I've forgotten it up until now. But it's tempting. That's how desperate I am for things to feel ordinary.

Emmett escorts me to my next class, refusing to leave me as he takes a seat next to mine. The teacher eyes him questioningly.

"You're not even in this class," I hiss into his ear.

"I'm not letting you out of my sight," he barks. "They're not going to do anything."

I shouldn't be surprised when the teacher starts the lesson as normal, ignoring Emmett's unexplained presence. Neither of us can focus on the lecture. This is just a way to kill time and keep up appearances until everything comes to a head.

After class, we meet Bernadette out in the school yard. We all stand in a silent daze. We only made it in time for the final period, and it's time to go home now. But I can only assume Bernadette and Emmett are just as eager for an escape as I am, avoiding going home. At least that's one thing I can take comfort in. They're all just as stressed as me, just for different reasons.

Emmett's phone dings, and whatever he receives causes his features to twist. "I'll be right back," he announces suddenly, prompting me to shake my head in protest. But he ignores me, turning to Bernadette. "Don't let her out of your sight," he tells her sternly.

"Where are you going?" I ask desperately, afraid to be left alone without him. But he ignores me and disappears around the corner of the building.

Bernadette and I are left alone in awkward silence as she scrolls around on her phone. As much as I hate her, it feels strangely good to be around anyone who understand what our lives really are right now.

Anxious and unsure of what else to do, I pull out my own phone, thinking surely my parents have called and messaged me a hundred times asking where I am. I'm surprised they're not at the school looking for me. But of course, my phone is dead. Leaving me completely detached from anything outside the bubble of the Elites.

"My parents are going to be looking for me," I say without thinking to Bernadette, wondering how she'll respond with no one else around.

"We've taken care of that," she states plainly without looking up.

"How?" I gape, shaking my head. "What could you possibly have done to make them okay with me just vanishing and not coming home?"

"The principal talked to them," she smiles with creepy

confidence. "You don't have to worry about them. In fact, that should be the last of your worries. You need to be more concerned with your biological father and whatever he decides to do next."

I look back down to my phone and then around the schoolyard at the other students and teachers. Everyone is decidedly ignoring me once again, even though I know my appearance must be rough. They've got everyone playing along with their game, and I guess it makes sense. Everyone seems to be tied into Jameson Automobile Company to some extent, and if it goes down…the whole town goes down with it.

Before I can muster a response, I hear Emmett's voice from around the corner. He sounds upset, but I can't make out the words. I know Bernadette won't let me out of her sight, so I try inching far enough away without looking suspicious…just enough to get a better view of him.

I step a few feet away casually, looking around at random things in the parking lot before darting my eyes to the side of the school. I see Emmett's arms flailing. He's talking to someone. As he moves to the side, I'm able to make out Vivian standing next to him. They're having some kind of argument.

I assume she must be in the loop. Steering clear this whole time to let Emmett do what he has to do, by orders of his father. If she only knew just how well he was doing it. How serious he took his orders to look after me. I bite my lip with the memories of him taking me over the bathroom sink. The sounds of his moans and hot breaths as he came.

I look back to Bernadette to see if she's alarmed by my distance, but she doesn't seem concerned. She's too wrapped up in her phone, but she glances up every so often to make sure I'm still within her sights. I should be trying to run away, even though I probably wouldn't get very far. But instead, I'm drawn to Emmett's conversation with Vivian like a moth to a flame.

As I boldly wander just a few steps further, hoping to get close enough to hear them, Vivian's eyes bolt toward me, sparking the moment they meet mine. She looks furious. Without another word to Emmett she pushes past him and barrels toward me furiously.

"You!" she growls. "Don't fucking move."

Emmett rolls his eyes and follows slowly behind as she marches forward. I do as she asks, not moving, trying to hide the curious grin sparking across my face. I don't know what I expected, but of course Vivian parades right up to me and punches me square in the face. I buckle over from her blow, trying to straighten and hit her back, but she grips my hand in midair.

"You have some balls, you little whore," she hisses at me, full of hatred. "You're lucky I don't kill you right here."

"Vivian," Emmett groans, doing nothing to step in and make her loosen her hold on me. "I told you she has nothing to do with this."

"You think you can come in and steal my boyfriend?" her fist shakes, twisting my arm around. "If you survive this shit-show with your dad, I'm going to make you wish you never even looked at him."

I have no idea what's going on, but I can only assume Emmett has told her about us. Maybe he broke up with her. The thought makes me happier than it should.

"Enough, Vivian!" Emmett barks, coming over and ripping her hands away from me. "You're being paranoid. I told you I don't want anything to do with her. I love you."

My heart plummets. How stupid I was to think, even if only for a second, that he would actually leave her for me. Of course, he wouldn't. I'm just his hostage. Everything in me screams as I watch him try to pull her in for a reassuring kiss. I have to stop myself from going over and socking him in the face.

Emmett is sick. Just a couple of hours ago he was fucking me in his bathroom. And now here he is telling Vivian he loves her right in front of me.

"Get it together, Vivian," Bernadette chimes in, looking around in embarrassment. "What the hell are you thinking?"

Vivian huffs over to her. "What am I thinking!?" she scoffs. "What is your stupid fucking brother thinking!? He hasn't answered my calls or texts. I've had no idea what was going on. My parents won't tell me anything. I can only assume this little bitch has been whoring herself out to Emmett."

I press my hand to my cheek, still sore from Thomas and now even worse off thanks to Vivian. I ache with disappoint-ment, having thought Emmett might have told her something. Broken it off. But no. She just jumped to conclusions in a frenzy of feeling left out of the loop. And he's doing nothing to let on that her suspicions are true.

"Emmett doesn't want anything to do with her," Bernadette

defends half-heartedly. "He's just looking after her for Daddy. You're making a fool of yourself."

Vivian turns back toward me, her arms crossed in shame now that her friend isn't backing her up. It's strange to see her slip from her pedestal. Humbled into being worried about her own position in things. They're all acting on edge, and it's making me nervous. I'm used to seeing them calm and in control. Always one step ahead of the game.

I should be comforted that my dad's threats have them so afraid, but it only makes my position less certain. They could get tired of waiting at any moment and follow through on their own threats.

"Bernadette's right," I offer dejectedly. "Emmett doesn't want anything to do with me. And I sure as shit don't want anything to do with him."

I don't know why I say it. Maybe as some last desperate attempt to hurt Emmett back. It looks like it might have worked as his eyes glint over to me in subtle surprise.

"I don't need you to placate me," she barks back. "Soon this will all be over, and you'll go back to whatever little white trash hole you crawled out of." Her voice wavers with doubt. "Emmett, take a walk with me."

"You know I can't," he walks over to her, keeping his voice down while cutting his eyes over to me. "I can't let her out of my sight. I'll call you later, okay?"

She looks to him with an almost comedic pout, but her phone rings, pulling her attention away. "Hello?" she picks up, pressing a finger to her ear. "Daddy?" I watch her face wrinkle as she steps away. She's quickly distracted with her call, leaving Emmett and I in a stand-off.

I lift my chin and straighten my shoulders in resolve. I don't know what I expected him to do with Vivian, but at least now his intentions are clear. I was just a convenient fuck while he has me as his prisoner. And I'd say as much to him if Bernadette wasn't standing right there. If I make it out of this, I don't need Vivian's jealous wrath to worry about afterward.

Suddenly a black car whips around in the parking lot, screeching to a halt right in front of us. The back window rolls down as Thomas hangs his head out in a seething rage.

"Get in the car! Now!" His voice bellows with sharp command, and we're all too afraid to hesitate to obey him. I'm not supposed to be outside of the manor, and Emmett looks terrified of the consequences. We quickly file inside.

I start to follow into the back seat behind Emmett, hoping he'll protect me in whatever way he can. But Thomas suddenly appears behind me, clenching his hand around my wrist and yanking me to the front seat. Emmett and Bernadette comply, but I can feel Emmett's rage that he can't be near me.

Regardless of whatever he told Vivian, or whatever he feels for me, he still has a sense of ownership over me. He thinks I belong to him.

"Daddy, what's going on?" Bernadette asks from the backseat.

"The Whitworths tipped me off," he growls, his eyes darting over to me in disdain. "It appears the Hendersons are working with your father now.

I tense up in fear that they somehow know about my meeting with the Hendersons. I don't want to know what the repercussions for that will be.

"The feds are closing in," he continues. "My guy on the inside says I have less than twenty-four hours to leave the country."

Vivian's phone call makes sense now. Her parents must have been catching her up to speed with this new development. I can't help but smile slightly at my father's jump on the deadline. "Well then maybe that's what you should be doing," I offer coyly. "Instead of wasting your time with us."

He slams on the brakes so suddenly my forehead shoots straight toward the dash, but I'm saved with a searing pain to my scalp as he violently yanks back my hair. His lips snarl as he looks over to me.

"Watch your mouth," he sneers. "We told your father our terms. If I have to leave this country, you're coming with me and you'll never be back."

After glaring into me for a few moments, his nostrils flaring with hot and angry breaths, he finally lets me go and returns to driving the car. We screech around every turn as he flies down the streets back to the manor. I bring my knees to my chest, making my body small as I press my forehead to the window.

He doesn't take it any easier on me once we're back to the manor. Before I can pull the handle to get out of the car, he is yanking the door out of my hand and reaching in to pull me out by my hair. I clasp my hands to his grip, trying to lessen the pull to my scalp, but he's moving too fast for me to keep up. My eyes water with pain as he marches me back into the parlor and flings me back down into the chair.

He takes long and smooth cavalier strides over to this desk, his sudden calmness frightening me. With a tug of a drawer, his hand grips something and pulls it up into the light. My heart plummets at the sight of his pistol. He grins as he holds it up and cocks it before marching back over to me with purpose.

With another yank of my hair, he puts the gun to my head. "We warned you," he growls into my ear. "We told you if he didn't stop, we'd kill you."

"I told you I don't know him," I plead. "I didn't think he'd listen to me! He doesn't care about me! This is a waste of your time!"

"He'll listen," Thomas barks. "At least you better hope he does. Now…what do you say we try again? Maybe this time with more feeling now that you understand we're not fucking around?"

"It's no use!" I argue with clenched fists, my voice trembling.

I look to Emmett hopelessly. He cowers, refusing to look up from his feet. His jaw is tight and clamped.

My teeth clench and grind as I grab at the finger marks on my arms. "Emmett, please! Do something!" I cry, but he just turns away and does nothing. I'm getting reacclimated to his indifference now. It was silly for me to think he would ever be some kind of savior. He's just his dad's puppet.

Thomas's angry eyes turn to Emmett. He looks completely disgusted with him. "What's this, son?" he calls out in a chilling tone. "Why is it that she's turning to you for help?"

"I have no fucking idea," Emmett lies in a low grumbling tone, shifting uncomfortably.

"You sure about that?" he continues, looking at his son with such hatred. "You haven't been sampling the goods have you, my boy?"

"No, Dad!" Emmett defends with a nervous shriek. "I swear! I haven't touched her! I just did what you said!"

"Well then, maybe you'd like to come over here and prove it?" Thomas calls his bluff.

Emmett's fists clench, his lips snarling as he glares at me. Ready to pounce and do whatever his father says. He doesn't even look like himself anymore. He's running on fear. Whatever his father would do to him is enough to put him back in his place.

My breaths are so quick and shallow, I'm certain I'm hyperventilating as his grip in my hair tightens. I shudder to think what Thomas might make Emmett do to prove his loyalty. It shouldn't matter right now, but I realize this is how he maintains control. Calling anyone out the moment they question him or go against his wishes.

I squeeze my eyes shut as the cold metal barrel pushes into my temple, Emmett's stand-off with his father quickly being filed away for later. Thomas clicks the pistol with what I can only assume is the removal of the safety.

"Wait" I cry, desperate to do anything to get out from under the barrel of his gun. "I'll do the video! Please! I'll do it!"

He throws me back to the chair, nodding for his men to come and hold me down as the video camera is brought out again. I'm overwhelmed with sudden dread as I calculate the likelihood that I will die in this mansion. I try to think of anything else to calm myself, but it's no use.

"He has two hours to respond," Thomas barks. "He puts a stop to this or you're dead."

I rub against the bulging veins in my neck as I try to steady my voice. He leans against the edge of his desk, adjusting his cufflinks calmly. He's too confident. Whimpers escape my lips in between each breath.

My trembling fingers dig into the seat of the chair as I straighten my spine and brace myself, my leg bouncing uncontrollably with adrenaline and panic. I note my flushed, sweating skin on the screen as I gasp to control my breathing.

One of his men pushes the red button and flails his hand at me to start talking. I jump from my seat, desperate to wipe the tears from my face as I step backward, wanting to feel a wall behind me for security, but they quickly barrel toward me and fling me back to the chair as I cry hysterically.

I want to call for help, but I know that no one here will save me. My eyes dart around the room in desperation for anything that could inspire an idea for how to get out of this.

I gulp down acceptance. I have no other choice but try to plead for my father to save me once again. Feeling even more hopeless now than I did the first time.

"Dad, please," my pitch spikes and cracks as I sob. "We

don't know each other, but I'm your daughter. And they *will* kill me. Just do what they ask."

"Is that all you got!?" Thomas bellows from behind the camera. "This is your life on the line, Ophelia! Better make this one better than the last!"

"Please!" I scream out again at the top of my lungs. "Please, dad, I'm begging you! Stop all of this and let the Jamesons be! He's not going to go down without taking me with him."

I scream and cry every plea I can think of until they're finally satisfied, taking the camera away again. As the recording stops, my muscles twitch and there's a cold silence. All there is to do now is wait.

My heart races in palpitations as adrenaline shoots through my body, and I think I might choke on my breaths…short and out of control. I can't get enough oxygen and my limbs are tingling. My fingers and toes going numb. I think I might pass out as spots dance across my line of sight.

Thomas wipes down his pistol but doesn't return it to the drawer. He keeps it close to his side. His eyes are glued to Emmett, and I can see him contemplating bringing up the issue of our involvement again. Emmett has braced himself against the wall, blowing sharp breaths from his cheeks.

"We'll come back to you later, son," he announces grimly. "I can't have you making friends with the enemy. You know that."

"Dad, I promise…," Emmett tries to defend weakly, his voice trembling. "I didn't…"

With one swift raise of Thomas' hand, Emmett stops cold. Not bothering to say another word. No wonder he is so afraid to step in and help me. Why he never even tries to defend me. He wasn't kidding. His father would kill him or make him do something terrible to me to prove himself.

Thomas has him completely under his thumb, and he's too afraid to question him or go against him in anyway. For a second, I almost feel guilty for tempting Emmett. For putting him directly in the line of his father's wrath. But remembering all of his inappropriate touches from before, I wonder if it even would have mattered how willing I was.

Thankfully, Thomas seems to let it rest again. Huddling with his cronies as they discuss what happens next, leaving me to try and control my crying. I hate that I let my last ounce of control slip. They saw me break down on camera. The composure I clung to the last time completely vanished this time, solidifying that when it comes down to it, they really can make me do whatever they want me to.

If time could just slow down somehow, or if I could just go back to a different time when I felt safe. But now, life feels like a broken hourglass in my hands, with the sand slipping through my fingers and blowing off in the wind. Time is running out. All I can do is hope my pleas appeal to something in my father.

# CHAPTER TWENTY-TWO

## BOOK 1

The room stills as my cries slowly quiet, trailing off into nothing. I notice Bernadette perched in the corner of the room, looking bored. She pops her gum as her pastel pink nails flip across the screen of her phone. As fucked up as Emmett may be, at least he is feeling something in the middle of all of this. She looks completely apathetic and indifferent.

Thomas turns to his cronies and whispers instructions in hushed tones. They look to me with evil grins, nodding as he tells them what to do. I know he's preparing them for the time to kill me. A time which I know is quickly approaching. I can feel the desperation in the air.

"Let's hope this last performance inspires more than your last one," Thomas announces to me coldly. "Makes no difference to me. I'm getting out of this one way or the other. It's just a matter of how hard it will be on everyone else."

He probably does have back-up plans galore. Anything to save his own ass, but I see the subtle panic in Thomas's eyes. His life is just as much on the line as mine. If my father succeeds, he'll be in prison. And for underage sex trafficking at that. An offense that I imagine all the other cons don't take kindly to, with their own troubled daughters waiting for them on the outside.

I want to believe this video could save me, but given my father's lack of response so far, I'm not hopeful. The most frustrating part about their entire plan is that it hinges on my father giving a shit about me enough to stop in order to save my life. He had to have known the risk he was taking by continuing, even after Vivian and the other Elites made sure he knew I had been uprooted to WJ Prep. If he hasn't stopped before now, I have no reason to believe he'll have a change of heart in time.

The room is tense, filled with impatience. I worry Thomas will grow restless and just shoot me before fleeing. I look to Emmett once more, but he's still and silent. Doing nothing to intervene.

With a father like Thomas, I know his life has probably been fucked up in more ways than I could ever understand. But I have even less sympathy now that I have learned my father isn't so different. Maybe he did me a favor by not being around.

I remind myself I'm not so above it all. Not now that I've given myself over to Emmett willingly. Even with my life hanging on the line, resting in my father's hands, the haunting memory of his touch still plagues me. The torture and the pleasure all blurs together. The times he inflicted violence on me didn't seem so different from when he was moving inside of me. Our movements and noises were almost the same.

I meant everything I had said when I was trying to convince him to release me. There was an undeniable connection between us, but it obviously wasn't strong enough to inspire him to save me. I watch him shift uncomfortably, his hands in his pockets, looking almost as dejected as his sister on the other side of the room.

What a strange world these people live in where torture and hostages and death threats are so normal. No wonder Lily tried to warn me and was so scared shitless of these people. Seeing how cold and cavalier Thomas can be with a young girl's life on the line, I'm not surprised his kids and friends' kids are so sadistic.

My disgusted gaze drifts from Emmett, who is decidedly avoiding me. And I realize all at once that no one is within a few feet of me. They're each distracted and dispersed into their own corners of the room. It's now or never. If he's not going to do anything to help me, and my dad's intervening isn't guaranteed by a long shot, I might as well try to make a run for it.

My eyes are bright and feverish as they dart around the room, noting everyone's position one last time. No one is paying attention to me, probably assuming I'm surrounded enough not to try anything. My fingers twitch against the edge of my chair, and my heart drops knowing if I don't do something right now, I won't have another chance.

I leap out of the chair and bolt toward the door, my heart plummeting to my stomach. I instantly hear Thomas shout behind me followed by feet pounding in my direction, but I don't stop. My throat chokes as I race for the front door faster than I have ever ran in my life.

I feel a surge of hope as my hand grips the handle, flinging it open so fast I almost hit myself in the head as I waver with the surge of adrenaline and panic. I come to a dead halt at the front doormat. A figure is blocking my way, and I look up expecting to see an unfamiliar guard or house staff member ready to snatch me up and return me to my captor. I scream, thinking I've been caught. I know the reprimand for an attempted escape will be brutal.

But instead I see a familiar face. One that I know but am unable to fully comprehend. I am almost too panicked to fully take in the features, but my brain slowly pieces it together.

Standing before me is the man responsible for all of this. My father. Theodore Nickelson.

There's a quiet rage burning behind his eyes. He's alone with only a gun in hand for protection.

"Ophelia," he announces in an unreadable tone.

I never expected to meet my father. I had no intentions of ever trying to find him. But if I ever did have some kind of fantasy about us meeting for the first time, this was definitely not one of the scenarios I pictured. Not by a long shot.

"Theodore…" I blurt. "Or I guess…Dad…" I am overcome with anger, wanting to lash out at him for never being around. For being such a shit loser that he started all of this mess and nearly got me killed over his pathetic gambling habit and need for vengeance.

I never noticed in pictures, but now that he's standing here in front of me, I can see the resemblance between him and I. Though I certainly favor my mother, our eyes are the same shape. And the curve of his lips is the same as what I've studied in my own reflection every day. It stirs a strange tenderness in me, but it's squashed by the threat lurking behind me. And the fact that he is the reason I am here in the first place. Any ounce of curiosity or kindness I could feel for him quickly fades back to anger and resentment.

"I'm surprised to see you here," I gulp. But I quickly remember my life is still in danger. There's no time for any of that now.

His eyes dart to something over my shoulder as the army of marching feet rapidly approach. His hand brushes my shoulder, pushing me aside.

"Kill him!" Thomas's voice shouts from behind me suddenly.

I am barely shoved aside just enough to gauge how far away Thomas is from me when a deafening crack shoots through my ear drums, following by an incessant ringing. I can hear nothing else as I look to my father's hand, raised and on the trigger, smoke trailing from the barrel of his gun.

My eyes dart over in Thomas's direction, but everything is moving in slow motion. I see him falling to the ground. Blood instantly pools around his head. I take a couple of steps back from my father, my eyes bulging as I look back and forth between my dad's gun and Thomas's body. I am deaf and speechless, my eyes blinking rapidly as I try to process the scene before me.

Thomas is dead. My dad shot him. My brows raise as my mouth falls open, my palm shooting up to cover it. I step back again, searching for something behind me to steady against, but there's nothing there. My gaze wanders around as my brain struggles to settle on my next move.

I feel suddenly heavy as my muscles get weak, my head feeling dizzy with a tight feeling in my chest. I replay it in my mind over and over, what bit of it I actually saw. My father's hand raising, the crack of the gun, Thomas falling to the ground.

This is definitely not the first in-person impression I wanted of my father. But at least if he was going to kill a man right in front of me within seconds of us meeting, it was a terrible man who was going to kill me first if he had the chance.

I look to Emmett who is standing in the parlor doorway, keeping a safe distance from his father. But his wide eyes are glued to the lifeless body laying there. The rest of his cronies and the staff stand there frozen, just as shocked as everyone else.

I study Emmett further, waiting for him to fall apart the way

Bernadette is in the corner of my eye. I think I hear her scream, but my ears are still ringing so it's hard to tell.

Emmett is strangely calm. Shocked, but not upset. I assume it has to be the shock that is keeping him so collected, but then I catch a subtle nod between him and my father. Did Emmett know this was going to happen?

# CHAPTER TWENTY-THREE

BOOK 1

We all stand there completely clueless as to what we should do next. Thomas is dead. I'm dumbfounded and have no clue what the fuck is going on. Emmett doesn't look the least bit bothered that his own father was just shot right before his eyes, but Bernadette's screams and cries grow more vivid as the ringing in my ears fades.

"Come with us," my father states suddenly, causing me to jump as he takes me by the arm and leads me to an adjacent room. Emmett follows behind.

"What's going on?" I ask, plopping into the nearest seat, taken aback by how comfortable the two of them seem.

They hesitate and look to each other for a moment, not saying a word.

"Someone better start explaining things real quick!" I snap. "Do you two know each other!?" My features twist with an impending sense of betrayal.

"Your father approached me three weeks ago," Emmett starts. "His terms were simple enough. I grant him access to the manor grounds when he asked, and I wouldn't lose Jameson Automobile Company. He'd no longer hurt you, and my mom and sister would be safe."

I'm frozen under his explanation for a moment, my face contorted in shock. I quickly shake it away. "Wait, so you've been working with my father!? You son of a bitch!"

"Ophelia, please," he begs. "I was so desperate to get out

from my father's thumb, I was happy to do whatever he asked. You don't know Thomas like I do. Even with what you saw… you have no idea what kind of monster he was."

"So you think mine is any better!?" I fire back, ignoring my father standing in the corner.

"I was trying to help you," he defends desperately, kneeling at the foot of my chair. "That night you met with Malcolm and Liam, your father planned to kidnap you. We barely got you in time before his guys showed up to take you away. I convinced him you'd be safer with me."

"Liam's warning," I mutter under my breath. Now it all makes sense. The ominous threat dripping from Liam's words. That his explanation of things, by order of my father, would somehow make things easier on me when I was taken captive by him. "What would you have done with me?" I ask him timidly, afraid of the answer. "If Emmett hadn't intervened…what were you going to do when you had me as your prisoner?

"The Elites thought they had too much bargaining power with you around," he defends weakly. "I just needed to remove you from the game. So they no longer had you to hold over my head."

"Take me out of the game how?" I ask, my voice trembling. "As in keep me somewhere safe until this was all over? Until *you* decided it was over? Or take me out as in…kill me?"

My mind freezes, unsure if I was better off with Emmett, right in the hands of danger and so close to his father. Or if I would have been more screwed in my own father's possession.

"None of it matters now," Theo says dismissively. "It all worked out. Thomas is dead. I'll make sure his death is labeled as a suicide," The flippance of his voice chills me. "The investigation into the extortion rings, child prostitution circles and illegal arms dealings will continue on the Whitworth and Blackwater families. But now the Jameson family is free. As promised."

"I can't believe anything you're saying." My fingers rub into my temples as Emmett stays at my feet, looking to me desperately for approval or forgiveness. We exchange a knowing look. My father isn't denying that he would have killed me if it came down to it. Maybe I was better off with Emmett. Especially if he knew the entire time we had my father to fall back on, hoping he would come in and take care of Thomas.

"You both seem like lying snakes to me," I snap. "I can't

trust either of you. Your solution to learning my own father wanted to kidnap me…was to just do it yourself instead?" I muse in disbelief to Emmett. "You've got to be kidding me," is all I can manage to say, as my hands rub absently against my arms. "You're like a bunch of children fighting over candy. But you don't even care that real human lives are at stake." I step to the other side of the room, needing to be as far away from them as possible.

"We would have never let you get hurt," my father protests dryly. His calmness makes me sick. As if this whole thing was just some minor blip.

"I did get hurt!" I scream, jumping to my feet. "I have done nothing but get hurt from the day I got here! And you're both to blame!"

"I did what I had to, Ophelia," my father responds coldly.

"We both did," Emmett adds.

My mouth slacks as my eyes widen. I have to look away from them. I can't stand the sight of either of them. I rub my eyes, trying not to see them, and am at a loss for words.

"You didn't have to do any of this!" I scream back to my father. "You're the one who fucked up when you gambled away all of that money! You could have just accepted your fate and left things alone. You had plenty of money. You didn't have to come back here and…," I turn away and cover my mouth. My face blanches, turning white, as I shake my head.

"But the lives that matter the most made it out unscathed," Emmett offers with a startling indifference to the death of his own father, leaving me to wonder how I'd feel if my own monster of a dad had just been shot right in front of me.

I pivot on my heel, my brow raised as I tilt my head. "I am hardly unscathed," I scream. "You've both caused irreparable damage. I'm not just some toy or game piece for you to toss around. I'm a human being! Your daughter!" I turn to my father with tears in my eyes, and then back to Emmett. "And I'm your…" I stop myself, unsure of how to finish the sentence, but his eyes look to me hopefully. My eyes blink rapidly and unfocus as I my hands carve back through my hair before my arms drop limply to my sides. "Someone that you should care about, but then again…I guess that makes me sound stupid. You've done nothing from day one to indicate you care about me at all."

"That's why you're here, Ophelia," he argues back. "Because I do care about you."

My chest tingles as my stomach hardens. I feel lightheaded. I try not to excuse any of Emmett's behavior, but knowing he was intercepting my father the night he kidnapped me almost makes his actions more tolerable. I shudder to think what my father had planned if he had been the one to kidnap me instead.

"What the hell is wrong with you, Emmett!?" I ask, shaking my head. "I may not care for my father...but I don't know if I ever could have willingly assisted in his murder."

"You don't get it, Ophelia," Emmett fumes. "Thomas Jameson was enough of a monster to justify me being an accomplice in his murder. We're all better off. You'll just have to trust me on that one."

"So, what now?" I blurt without thinking, frightening myself with my own question as it hangs in the air. No one answers, but my mind skips across the possibilities.

I can't imagine ever having any kind of relationship with Emmett. If that's even something he would want. Everything up until now was a product of force. And now that I know he's been working with my father for weeks; I can never trust him again.

Now that I am not being stalked by a pedophilic murderer and he's not perched on a doorstep with a gun in hand, I am finally able to study his features more carefully. My father is a handsome man. His dark brown hair is wavy, similar to my mother's and my own. But with touches of blonde, giving him a more Caucasian shade. He's tall and slender, and his words are sharp. Intimidating. But I could see him turning that over in a second, becoming a complete charmer.

My mother always said I had a mischievous smile, and I wondered why when she said it, she sounded sad. Angry at times. I can see now it's because that smile came from my father. He has the same devilish spark to him. I can picture them as teenagers, both young and attractive. Falling in love with each other. But then I remind myself they were in Jameson surrounded by the Elites, and I can only hope my mother's experience wasn't anything like mine.

There is nothing to be salvaged between my father and I. Knowing what I know now, I would have been fine never meeting him. And now that I see firsthand what having him around brings, I am eager to put him back out of my life. But while I'm here, I think I might as well try and get some answers.

"What happened with you and my mother?" I ask him suddenly in desperation. "Tell me everything. I deserve to know after everything you've put me through."

He takes a seat with an exasperated sigh, running his hand across the top of his hair. I study his hesitance, but finally his lips part as he braces himself. "We went out west after the Elites took everything from us," he explains. "Lala started a bakery and you were born, while I worked trying to rebuild my fortune. But then I found out your mother was cheating on me. I did things I'm not proud of. I flew into a rage. I beat her. That's when she took you and left."

"My mother would never do something like that," I defend.

"She didn't cheat on you," Emmett blurts suddenly, shocking both of us. "That was my father and his friends. They set her up. They weren't going to stop coming after you because of all the money you squandered." His head hangs sheepishly in fear of my father's reaction. The words spilled out faster than he meant, sounding too accusatory.

I see the dots connecting in my father's eyes, but any regret is quickly shrugged away. "She went back to her maiden name, Lopez, after that," my father finishes, looking as if he's fighting away the new information.

"So it turns out you laid your hands on my mother for no reason, forcing her to leave," I gaff at the whole idea. "The Elites strike again. Stopping at nothing to destroy anyone who crosses them, even if children's lives are destroyed in the process. Though I can't really say we were so bad off without you around. Brendan is ten times more honorable than I think you could ever be."

"Yes…Brendan. Your stepfather," he concedes with a knowing nod. "I looked into him when he and your mother got engaged. He is a good man. That's why I never intervened."

"You've got some nerve," I shriek. "So you've been keeping tabs on us this whole time!? And what do you mean…that's why you didn't intervene!? What makes you think you'd ever have any right to try and influence her life after everything? And my life too."

"She belonged to me before anybody else!" he roars back in a sudden show of emotion. More than he's shown this entire time, even after having just killed a man. "I promised to take care of her."

Funny, I think. Girls really do go for men just like their fathers. Apparently even if they don't know their fathers. I could imagine Emmett saying the exact same bit about me belonging to him. He has several times. Always pointing out that I am his.

"So, you were taking care of her when you beat her?" I square up to him, too pissed to back down, even though he towers above me in height.

"I don't expect you to understand any of it," he resigns, turning to calm himself. "I loved your mother. I was furious when I thought she had betrayed me and been with another man. And it was right after everything that happened with the Jamesons and Whitworths. I was humiliated. Desperate."

"I wonder if your family and their friends were pleased with themselves, Emmett," I channel my anger back to him. "They had already ran my father out of town. He was completely broke. You'd think they could have just let him be. But no…you just had to come and put one last nail in his coffin."

I am angry about it, but I'm glad in a way that things happened as they did. I can't imagine what my life would have been like if my father had stuck around. I want to say as much, but I can see he is already reeling from Emmett's confession about their responsibility in breaking up my parents' marriage.

"I'm going to give you two a moment alone," Emmett responds, his eyes hopeful and desperate.

"I don't have anything else to say to you," I bark as he exits the room.

"I'm going to do everything in my power to make sure you don't leave without seeing me again," he states calmly before turning to shut the door.

It almost makes me want to crawl out of the window just to prove him wrong, but I'm left alone with my father who is coldly staring off into the corner.

"So…do you have anything else to say for yourself?" I sneer, crossing my arms expectantly.

"I can leave you alone now, if that's what you want," he offers sympathetically. I can't tell if the softness of his voice is out of respect, or just a manipulation tactic. "I can walk away from all of this now that Thomas Jameson and the rest of them will be going away."

"And what about Emmett?" I ask, my voice wavering. "What makes you trust him so much more than the rest? How do you know he won't come after you for revenge?"

"I could tell Emmett was scared shitless of his father from the moment I first met him," he explains. "His father would have dangled the company over his head for the rest of his life, threatening to snatch everything away any time he didn't comply with his whims. Thomas would have made his son do terrible things. Turned him into a monster just like his dad. Emmett could see it coming and wanted no part of it. Now he'll walk away with his father's fortune. Free to call the shots without the Elites pushing him around."

I roll his explanation around in my mind, wanting it to be true. But I don't know who I can trust. "How do you know he's not already just as fucked up as Thomas Jameson?" I propose. "He sure has put me through hell. Something I'd think my own father would take issue with."

"Things are different around here," he answers flippantly. "You're dealing with generations of ruthless entitlement. Emmett is salvageable though. I can tell you that much." He stands and begins to button his coat.

I study his movements in confusion. "You're leaving!?" I belt out unexpectedly. Moments ago, I was praying for him to just go. Now I'm offended that he would just walk off. "You're just going to leave things like this? What about me? What do I do?"

"You and Emmett will tell the police you ditched school and came back to the house to fool around and found Thomas Jameson dead. I'll take care of the rest. After that, you're free to go."

Free. I don't even know what that word means to me anymore. Now that it's so close, it's almost frightening.

"Talk to the police and go home, Ophelia," he orders me, turning for the door. "I won't be bothering you again."

"It doesn't make any sense," I mutter, my eyes darting to connect the dots. "You said you loved my mother. But what about me? Does finally meeting me mean nothing to you?"

I see him shake his head with his back turned, but he won't look at me. "I know I've done too much damage," he answers with quiet resolve. "You and your mom are better off with Brendan. Without me. I've been working your whole life toward what transpired today. And now that it's over…it's time for me to go."

"What will you do?" I ask, fighting back bewildered tears. I don't want to care, but some primal part of me still does.

"You don't need to concern yourself with that," he reaches for the door handle, pausing one last time to glance over his shoulder, his eyes still not meeting mine. "I'm going to make sure you're taken care of, Ophelia. You'll go back to WJ Prep on scholarship, and if you need anything after that for college…I'll see that it gets taken care of."

"What do I tell Mom?" I suggest, wondering if she has any idea he's been lingering around Jameson this whole time. But he doesn't answer. Just like that, he's gone again.

I liked it better before when I never thought twice about him. Now I'll always be afraid of when he might pop up again, and what kind of havoc it might wreak on my life.

My mind jolts back to action mode. I am ready to go home, but first I have to talk to the police. Which means talking to Emmett. I pull myself up from my chair and head for the door, not surprised to see him waiting for me just outside.

I'm just about to fly right past him when he yanks me back, pushing me against the wall. His icy gray eyes burning into me intensely.

I try to look anywhere else. I'm too raw to look him in the eyes right now. But he desperately bobs his head to force himself in my way. I still can't deny how handsome he is, even after everything. Even though he is a sweaty, disheveled mess just like me.

"Kiss me," he pleads harshly, pressing his face to mine. His breath is hot and frantic. "Please, Ophelia. Before we go back out there. I need to feel close to you again."

"You're fucking crazy!" I cry and squirm in his arms. "I'd rather die."

He leans into me anyway, the strain in his pants giving away how much he wants me. I see it burning him from the inside out, and I feel the same way. Whatever this thing is between us will eat us both alive if I don't put a stop to it. Especially now with no outside forces standing in our way.

Is he angry because he can't have me? Because I'm not giving in to him as easily as he is probably used to? The moment he had me before, he turned cold again. Without my resistance, he's uninterested. I still and search his face, exasperated with how much I still don't understand about him.

"I'm begging you," he murmurs softly. "Please, just one more taste of you. Before we have to face everything out there."

His words draw me in. I can't deny how nice it would be to give in to him one last time before we walk out into whatever happens next. When I intend to fully put him out of my life altogether. Nothing about my feelings for him have changed. Still just as wanton and helpless as day one. I need him and am repulsed by him all at once. He scares me, but I want to give myself over to him completely.

My heart stings with an afterthought. I want to torture him the way he's tortured me. And that desire rises quickly above everything else. "You'll never taste me again," I growl sternly, looking straight at him in pure coldness. His brows raise to my quivering voice. "You'll never have any part of me again."

He raises a hand, and I don't know if he'll hit me or force me into his kiss anyway. But instead his forehead drops to the wall above my shoulder. Like he's completely broken.

"Never say never, Ophelia," he whispers into my neck before pulling away. "There's too much between us for you just to walk away from."

"Is there?" I question defiantly, steadying my voice. "There's nothing between us. You've tormented me, Emmett. Your family and friends did too, and you're no better than them. I see that now. I don't care what anyone else says. I've looked into your eyes and have seen nothing. The same cold, empty, blank stare of your father."

"That's not true," he snivels, shaking his head to block out my words. "You know it's not true. Everything I've done up until now…none of that was the real me. Just the small moments we shared when we both gave in…when everything else fell away. That's all you really know of me. And I can show you so much more."

His words instantly slice through my resolve, pulling me in as his lips brush my cheek. I want so badly to make him hurt, and I can't seem to convince myself that what he's feeling now is hurt enough. It can't be if he's still insisting he's entitled to me somehow. A truly sorry man would just walk away and let me be, just like my father did.

His lips melt to mine as I surrender one last time. Everything inside of me screaming to push him away, but I'm paralyzed. Finally I hear sirens wailing outside, and I'm surprised it's taken this long. "We have to go soon, Emmett," I remind him, thankful for the escape as our lips part. "Do you know what we're supposed to say?"

"I want to talk to you after," he insists again.

"Emmett, no!" I beg against his persistence. "Please…why can't you just let me go…"

"I don't know," he rasps. "But I can't. Not like this."

I see the red and blue flashing lights reflecting through the front windows and know we're out of time. My fingers pull to the wet circles under my eyes, and I try to smooth back my hair. It's no use. I'm a mess. We both are.

"I'll explain everything," he maintains, pulling back to straighten his shirt and put on a composed face. "You'll see. You have to listen to me."

Without another word, he walks confidently out into the foyer. I want to remind him he'd do well not to act so put together this time. He did just see his father die. A fact that will make the police suspicious if he's not distraught enough, even if it's fake. But I quickly remember he doesn't have to worry about things like that. Not really. Whatever his own personal sway and power doesn't take care of, my father's influence will.

I am left alone in shock once again. Still amazed that I'm so intertwined with this world of powerful and ruthless men. It's too much to take in. All I can do for now is prepare myself to give a statement, putting myself that much closer to freedom at last. It will all be over soon.

# CHAPTER TWENTY-FOUR

BOOK 1

I follow behind Emmett to face the sirens wailing outside of the manor. Bernadette is still hunkered over his body, crying in mourning. It's a relief to see her feel something, even if Emmett would argue it's misplaced. The room goes dark as the sun's rays disappear from the windows behind cloud cover.

The police don't waste any time explaining they'll need to take us into the station to give our statements. I don't feel too nervous about it, knowing our story will be backed up with whatever contact my father has in their department. Plus, I have Emmett on my side for this one. They assure us it won't take long.

The police escort us from the manor as the sun starts to go down. On our way to the station, a thick fog falls over everything and I can hear thunder rumbling in the distance.

The wind howls around us as we approach the front of the building. Buzzing doors and jingling keys echo out through the sparse waiting room of the station as we are both led through long winding back halls of officers speaking to each other in hushed tones, tucked away into different corners.

We are, of course, separated. I'm taken into an interview room that is gray and plain with one small table scattered with pens and notepads. I note the handcuff rings implanted in the surface, wringing my wrists that still ache from my own time in cuffs.

My stomach is uneasy as I rub my arms, nervously giving

my statement to the police. I stick to the story made up about ditching school and coming back to this house to hook up. That's where we claimed to have found his body dead on the ground. Anyone can see plain as day that he was shot directly in the forehead from the direction of the front door, but my father will make good on his promise. He has contacts who will still by some miracle get this written off as a suicide.

Even though I don't give two shits about whether it's coined as suicide or murder, I must admit there is something satisfying about my own father having his sway over this town. Maybe for his sake some of that will be restored with Thomas Jameson out of the way. But I still have every intention of staying as far away from him as possible.

"So, you and Emmett Jameson returned to his residence around four o'clock in the afternoon. Is that right?" The officer asks me again after he's collected my statement and asked me to repeat it.

"That's right," I say as confidently as possible.

The officer scribbles a few more notes, scratching his head, and then whispers a few things to his partner. "Thank you, Miss Lopez," he states, dropping his pen to the pad of paper. "We won't be too much longer here."

I try to hide a sigh of relief that they're buying everything. Either that or they've already been bribed and aren't even going to bother with a real interrogation. I've been warned countless times that the cops around here can't be trusted.

"You haven't been attending Weis-Jameson Preparatory Academy long, have you, Miss Lopez?" he stands to pace the room, changing his tone.

"Just started this semester," I reply glumly, feeling weighed down by everything that's happened in such a short amount of time. "I'm attending on a track scholarship."

He nods, biting at his lip. "And you live with your mom and dad?"

"My mom and step-dad, Brendan. Why?" I am starting to grow nervous with how personal the questions are becoming. What does any of that have to do with Thomas Jameson's supposed suicide?

"What about your biological father..." he proposes timidly. "Do you know him?"

"No." I blurt too curtly, causing his brow to furrow suspiciously.

The room is suddenly cold. My heart starts to race. No one told me I should be prepared for questions about Theo. I don't know whether to deny everything, or if they already know he's been poking around in the Elite's business recently. What if I incriminate myself by lying about something they already know?

"You don't know him at all?" he asks again, his tone peaked.

"No, not at all," I confirm nervously. As long as he keeps phrasing it that way, I'm fine. Because I can honestly say I don't know my father. But if he gets any more specific…I'm going to freeze up.

"You seem nervous," he observes, towering above me with his hands rested on the table. "Does it make you uncomfortable to talk about your father?"

"I just don't know him. Like I said." I bite my lip and stare to my hands, falling into a snowball effect. The more I know I look and sound nervous, the more nervous I get.

He concedes with huff of breath, taking a seat once again. "Miss Lopez, I don't want to be the one to have to tell you some of these things," he continues gently, "or maybe you already know some of them and just don't want to say… That's fine too. I understand. But…your father is a pretty dangerous man."

"How so?" I try to plea ignorantly, the image of him shooting Thomas fresh on my mind. But that's the last thing I need to be thinking about right now.

"He's been investigated by the FBI for quite a few hefty crimes," his fingers clasp and open as he speaks. "Insider trading. Money laundering. Extortion. Blackmail. The list goes on and on."

"Oh, I had no idea," I mutter truthfully. I thought my father's only crime was his relentless pursuit of the Elites, and whatever gambling trouble he had from before. I guess I should have figured there was more to it than that.

But as the two officers stare me down, the weight of all the warnings I've been given about the local police looming right above them, I wonder if I can trust anything they're saying. My father just took out the central figure of the Jameson Automobile Company…the town's livelihood. Leaving everything in the hands of Emmett…a teenage boy.

If they have any inkling at all that he's responsible for Thomas's death, they might be eager to take him down. I know my father has contacts in the police, but I'm clueless as to how far his reach extends.

"Do you know where your father is right now?" they ask bluntly.

"I have no idea," I reply, once again grateful that I am telling the truth.

"I understand," he says again, only this time he seems to know there is more that I'm not saying. "Listen, you've had a hard day, I'm sure. We don't want to keep you any longer. But could you do us a favor and let us know if your father tries to contact you?"

"Why?" I protest, not wanting to commit to that position. "You said he was investigated for those crimes. But that doesn't mean he's guilty, right? Is he wanted for arrest or anything?"

"Nothing quite like that," he answers with a cocky grin. "We just want to let you know…if he pops up again…you can come to us. It might be in your best interest to keep us informed of any communication. To protect yourself."

"So…we're done here?" I ask, already posed to exit. I feel like I'm lost in a minefield. One wrong word and the whole thing will blow up in my face. This was supposed to be a simple statement. Not an interrogation about my father, and I have no idea who to trust.

"For now," he leans back smugly, pressing a button that sparks a buzz and shoots my escape door open.

"Thanks," I huff as I bolt for the door. I start marching through the winding halls back out into the lobby. I need to be outside and free. My heart is still pounding in my chest, and I desperately need to run far away from here.

I walk down the sidewalk away from the police station, trying to add everything up in my head. The police can't be trusted. I don't know who is on my father's side and who isn't. I don't know who is playing for the old gang of Elites and who is rooting for whatever is on the horizon for Jameson Automobiles. I definitely don't know where Emmett stands in all of this.

My walk turns into a sprint the moment I'm back in a residential area. I decide to run home. I need it. I don't even care that it's starting to rain.

I haven't been running for long when I hear footsteps plodding up from behind. I glance over my shoulder to see Emmett racing behind me.

"Ophelia!" he calls out breathlessly. "Can I talk to you? Please!?"

I don't answer. He is the last person I want to talk to. But with him following behind, I don't want to go home. I don't ever want him in my house again. So instead I keep running.

He keeps stride with me, holding back by just a few feet. His stalking presence makes me feel like I am being held against my will, hitting the nerves of trauma from everything I experienced when I was being held hostage. All that his father did to me.

Every sudden movement startles me, my brain jumping back to the abuse I endured at the hands of the Elites, Emmett and his father. It just makes me run harder as the rain pours down around us.

We run like that for miles before finally stopping in a parking lot. I buckle over, resting my palms to my knees as I catch my breath.

I notice clumps of feathers scattered across the ground nearby, sticking to what remains of a dead bird. I have to laugh to myself, thinking it's a fitting representation of my life right now. Pieces of me still sticking around but maimed beyond recognition. All I can do now is try to reassemble the pieces, and I can't do that with Emmett around.

"Ophelia, please," he pleads between gasps for breath. "Can't you see now? I'm one of the good guys. I'm on your side."

"Are you fucking kidding me!?" I fire back with an angry laugh. "Is that why you beat me? Threatened me? Humiliated me? What was your excuse for all of that!? That was long before you supposedly started working with my father."

"I had to," he defends softly, his eyes glinting with regret. "I had no choice. As far as I could see, my father was going to get away with everything and be fine. I couldn't go against him or the other Elites."

"And you and Vivian?" I shoot back, still unconvinced of a single word and rapidly piling on more offenses in my memory. "What was all that about?"

"At first I didn't know any better," he defends adamantly. "I mean, it'd make sense for Vivian and me to be together. It's practically an arranged marriage with the way our families are. But then I met you…"

"You met me, and you continued seeing her…flaunting it in my face," I argue, still somewhat in disbelief that I'm even worried about his relationship status with everything else he's done.

"Vivian knew I had a thing for you," he explained, flailing his arms in the air. "If I had broken up with her she would have told everyone it was because of you. I would have been black-listed. If my own father didn't kill me for thinking I was in cahoots with you and your father, I definitely wouldn't have been able to help your dad. We'd probably both be dead right now."

"I'll never be able to forget the ways you've treated me," I continue, unmoved. Shaking my head at the memories flashing through my mind. "Then you sided with my father to get what you wanted. For all I know, you're still working for him. It's unforgivable."

"I had to, Ophelia," he continues pleading. "If you just give it some time…I think you'll understand that I had to. I had no choice."

Maybe he's right. Maybe small parts of his behavior will seem better once I've had some time to think. But there's too much of it staring me right in the face. The way he roughed me up with the other Elites. Sexually humiliated me. Acted like Vivian's little puppet and did nothing to stop my torture.

"Please let me try and make it up to you," he asks softly with a painful sincerity.

"What will you do now that your friends' families will fall and yours won't?" I ask bitterly, figuring he must think he's hot shit right now. The Elites have been upgraded to a one man show. The rest of them are going down and he gets to walk away with everything. "I can't help but think your motivations weren't as centered on my safety and well-being as you claim. I mean, you ended up with a pretty sweet deal out of all this."

He moves closer in slow cautious steps, his eyes trained to me. "Not if you won't talk to me," he protests. "I don't care about the money and all that other shit. The Elites can kiss my ass. I've always hated the whole fucked up game. None of it means anything if I don't get you in the end. Please, Ophelia. You're *mine*."

I want to scream. I don't belong to anyone. Especially not him, but I can't deny the way my heart warms and swells at the thought of it. What he used to always say…his little pet. I'm tempted to give in to it. Curl up right in his arms. Submit and give myself over to him the way I did in his bathroom. It felt so good to stop fighting it for once.

He can sense my hesitation and takes it as an opportunity to inch even closer, placing his hand to my cheek. My lips part beyond my control and everything in me yearns to feel his lips against mine again. I am so close to giving into him. My eyes close and I want to melt against his body, but I force myself to pull away.

"I can't, Emmett," I whimper as my voice cracks, taking a few steps back and looking off into the distance. "I don't see how I can ever trust you."

Maybe if I just try to forget any of this ever happened, I can move forward. It's too painful to face straight on.

It's not just about Emmett. I don't know how I can ever trust anyone ever again now that I know the kinds of things my father is capable of. My own father. His greed and maliciousness could be hereditary. Maybe it's in my blood. Either way, even my own father would kill me to serve his own desires.

I don't let myself feel certain of anything anymore. I've learned my lesson well enough to know I'm not in control of what can happen. I have to trust my gut now. And I can't shake the feelings of unease that plague me when I look into Emmett's eyes, no matter what other feelings I have for him.

But his moans of pleasure haunt me. The way his face wrinkled in ecstasy. I want to go back to that place with him, where I was able to let go as my body did the talking. Responding to him without hesitation. Surrendering to the sensations of how he felt inside. The touch of his hands. I half consider begging him to take me somewhere so we can have sex again. That made sense to me. But I know when it's over, it would only confuse me more and leave me worse off than I am now.

"I know you deserve better than me, Ophelia. You deserve better than your father too," he insists, speaking to my hesitation.

"I have better, Emmett," I remind him bitterly. "I have a whole life outside of this shitstorm you're wrapped up in. I have a mom and stepdad that love me. I had a promising running career ahead of me, if that hasn't been ruined by everything that's happened. I was just fine before you, and I'll be just fine after you. If you'll just leave me alone."

"But that's just the thing," he rasps. "I can't. I knew this whole thing was fucked from the moment I first saw you. I knew

I'd never be able to do the things I was expected to do. I feel too much for you."

"It sure didn't stop you in the beginning," I sneer.

"Come on…you know you want this just as bad as I do," he pushes toward me again, his touch begging me to melt into him. "Give me a chance to make all of that up to you. We're both fucked up. But…maybe we can find some way to make each other better. Look, Ophelia, I'm sorry. Just please try to understand – I'm not perfect. Neither are you, okay? I'm not going to stand here and lie…"

"For once." I cut him off. "I didn't do anything wrong, Emmett. That's the difference," I growl, resenting that he could even begin to suggest I am as fucked up as he is.

"I'm not going to stand here and pretend like I have all my shit figured out or that I knew what I was doing this whole time," he carries on, rain dripping down his face. "I just…I just didn't think and got in over my head and…and I really didn't mean to ever hurt you. I was selfish, I know that. I did it all wrong. But I'm lost too, okay? That's why you and I get along… because we're both just lost and fucked up and trying to figure it out."

"I wasn't fucked up until I met you," I hiss, making him recoil finally. He looks genuinely sorry. I want more than anything to tell him it's all okay and we could keep trying to figure it all out together. But then my father resurfaces in my mind, and I just know this can never work.

"So…what now?" He looks at me eagerly.

"It just…it has to be over now. That's it. It's ruined. I can barely look at you now, knowing what you were doing this whole time…working with my father behind my back," my words trail off into the sounds of the rain, my head shaking in exasperation.

He hangs his head and I think I see a tear streaming down his cheek, surprising me. But the downpour makes it too hard to tell. "I'd take it all back if I could." His voice is cracking.

But knowing so many lies have been told by this point, I don't know whether to believe his tears or not. It is still so hard to walk away. Half of me wants to run away and never look back. The other half of me would let him take me again right here, right now.

"Emmett…" I walk over to him and touch his cheek, as we both sob uncontrollably. This is the only time in my life I have ever cried so openly with another person. "I wish you didn't do all of those terrible things, but…maybe this just wasn't meant to be."

He leans his forehead against mine and we're both paralyzed in the pain for a moment. I realize if I don't leave now, I might lose the strength. I pull away and start walking down the sidewalk.

"Ophelia…" I stop and face him, afraid of what he's about to say. Afraid I won't stick to my resolve. "Do you think…maybe after some time has gone by…maybe you could give me another chance?"

"I think it's better if we just let it go. Just let me go," I turn to run away before he can say anything else. Before I can change my mind.

I run through the dark streets, my wet cheeks freezing in the wet wind. I don't stop until I'm home. The heat in the house burns my face when I walk in, and I find mom sitting at the kitchen table leaned over with her head in her hands.

"Mom?"

She jerks up, her eyes bloodshot. "Ophelia, sweetie…hey. I'm glad you're finally home." She notices my face and looks concerned. "Are you okay? You're soaking wet!"

"No, not really. Are you okay?" I respond breathlessly, still confused as to how she is so calm about how long I've been missing. I join her at the table. "We have to talk, Mom."

"I know we do," she nods, wringing a tissue in her hands. And yet, we sit in silence for what feels like forever.

"I'll start." She says with a heavy sigh, "Ophelia, there are some things I need to tell you about your father."

I blink, my eyes wide and blank. Out of all the times for her to bring this up…

I have no idea what lies the Elites have fed to her or how. "Wait, Mom…" I stop her. "Before you start talking about him…about me being gone…"

"Oh sweetie, don't worry about that," she waves her hand with a sniffle. "The principal called and told me Coach Granger had been keeping you late for practice and that he saw you leaving every day with that Emmett boy. I tried to call and tell you to come home, but your phone was dead. Then the police called and told me what happened at Emmett's house. Are you alright, honey? That's a terrible thing to go through. That's part of what I wanted to talk to you about."

A sarcastic grin eases across my face, out of my control, and I look down to my hands, shaking my head. I don't know if I'm more surprised that they went to such lengths to keep her from interfering or that she actually bought all of that so easily.

"You weren't mad?" I gaff, peering into her. "You didn't try to come find me?"

"I wanted to, but Brendan said we should give you some space," she explains. "You've always been so responsible and well behaved. You were bound to get a wild streak at some point. When the police called…I felt terrible for not coming to find you. Maybe if I had…"

If she had. Suddenly I'm relieved she didn't try to find me. If she had tried to, the Elites may have taken care of her just to get her out of the way.

"That wasn't your fault, Mom," I clasp my hand to hers, unsure of what else to say.

"When the police said Thomas Jameson was dead, I… well…this will sound terrible, but I thought your father had done it," she confesses through sobs. "But then they said it was a suicide, and I just felt so guilty. I felt bad for not telling you more about your dad in case he ever did try to come back into our lives. For not protecting you from the possibility of something like that."

I have to bite my tongue to keep from screaming out that she's right. My father did kill Thomas Jameson, and if she had warned me about what kind of person my father was…it might not have done any good or changed anything. But maybe I would have made different decisions along the way. I could have had somewhat of an upper hand.

"Mom, I know all about my real dad," I blurt out finally, searching her face to see how she'll respond. She looks completely shocked, her bottom lip trembling. "The kids around here…they know the story of his family and everything that he did. They told me."

"You should have come to talk to me!" she shrieks. "Ophelia, you never should have had to learn about all of that on your own!"

"I guess that's why I was gone for a bit," I murmur, knowing she'd never understand what that really means.

"I understand," she nods, blotting the tears from her eyes, squeezing my hand tight. "So then you know he had it out for the Jamesons. That's why when I heard about Thomas…I just jumped to conclusions."

I look at the regret and sadness in my mom and wish I could take it all away for her. She deserved better than my father, and so did I. The thought stings as I think back to what Emmett said earlier. Even he admits I deserve better. Part of me wants to see if he can be better for me, but I'm not going to let myself go there.

If I meant what I said about wanting him to let me go, I needed to do the same and let him go. I'm eager to find my way back to the person I was before I ever met him. Before enduring all the torture of the Elites. But I don't know if I will ever shake this feeling of unsteady ground beneath my feet. Now that I've seen firsthand just how wrong it can go and how fast, I will always be worried that around any corner…everything could go to shit again.

I'm quiet, afraid if I say too much else everything will spew out of me. "Mom, should we be afraid?" I ask timidly. "Of Dad I mean. In case he ever came back around. I…I heard he had hurt you once. When the Elites framed you for that affair. Do you think he'd ever do anything like that again?"

"No, sweetie," she replies confidently. "I don't think he ever meant to hurt me. But…who are the Elites?"

"Oh," I stammer, pinching the bridge of my nose. "That's what they call them. The Jamesons. The Whitworths. The Blackwaters. They're called the Elites. They didn't call them that back in the day?"

"Ah. Well…I don't think so. But I don't really know. I stayed out of all the high school cliques as much as I could. Which is how your father preferred it. He said it was all too cutthroat for someone like me. As long as I was with him, no one messed with me. Other than that, I mostly stayed to myself," she explains, her eyes drifting to distant memories.

"But Trey and Vincent's mom…," I puzzle out loud. "You seemed so friendly with them at the hospital. You had said their mom and you were friends. I thought…"

"We were friendly with each other in school," she twists her lips glibly. "Like I said, no one had the nerve to be unkind to me when I was with your father."

If only it could have been like that for me. The only perk that came with Emmett being attracted to me was being tortured, kidnapped, beaten and having my life threatened. And my dad sure didn't do anything to help me. I still wasn't even entirely sure he wouldn't have killed me if it came down to it.

But I guess the kind of protection my mom was talking about was reserved for Vivian in my case. The real girlfriend. I'm suddenly overwhelmed, unable to swallow away the hardness in my throat.

"I'm tired," I whisper. "I'm going to get some rest."

"I understand, sweetie," my mom says sweetly, standing to hug me goodnight. I head for the stairs. "Ophelia," she adds as I walk away. "Don't disappear like that on me again, okay?"

"Come hunt me down if I do, Mom," I smirk, trying to pass it off as a joke. But I mean it with every fiber of my being.

My father and I aren't so different in some ways, I think as I shuffle to my bedroom. He refused to bend to the Elites' intimidation when they ran him out of town. They stripped him of his shares in their business, cast him out into society and made my mother leave him, taking me with her. He never stopped trying to jail them for all their crimes, and then he came charging back after all this time to make them pay.

I may not be able to do much of anything to make the Elites pay for what they've done to me. I guess he took care of that for me in a weird way. But I didn't let them break me. And I only fully realize that now. I may have been afraid and had moments of weakness as anyone would in my position, but I stayed strong. I never let them fully break me.

Except for Emmett. I don't feel strong when it comes to him. He got to me more than anyone, and now I have to walk around haunted with the memory of him being inside of me.

My shoes are still squishing from the rain across the carpet of my bedroom. I would collapse on my bed right now if I wasn't soaking wet. I peel the heavy wet clothes from my body, tossing them into the bathtub with a plop. My fingers trail across the bathroom counter, and I wonder if I'll ever look at one of these the same again.

I try to push it down. I'll never sleep if I start thinking about Emmett, and I'm in desperate need of rest. But his words haunt me anyway. My stomach turns to remember the way he suggested over and over that he had no choice in all of this. For all that I've been through, it never made me do horrible things to the people around me. The only horrible thing I've done is fall for him. One thing that I'm certain of is that I never have and never will be as messed up as he is.

I slide on some clean underwear and an oversized shirt, blotting my hair with a towel. I probably need a shower, but I'm too tired. Now that I'm dry, I instantly collapse into bed

It's an intense feeling to return home when you never thought you would again. Everything feels different. The sheets feel softer. My mom's cooking wafting from downstairs smells stronger and more inviting than ever before. I'm free. Something that I worried I would never feel again.

I relish in the feeling of my own bed. I am certain that once I fall asleep, I will sleep for a million years. But neighborhood dogs are barking, prompting me to shove my pillow around my ears to block it out. They sound louder than they should, giving me a headache.

The police station. Emmett. My mom. My dad. It all swirls through my head, making me nauseous. I can't shake the feeling of dread that this isn't over yet. Emmett won't give up so easily. It seems my father may not either. Everything between my mom and I will be different now. Especially as I try to recover from this nightmare.

I feel like my chest is caving in from the weight of it all, but thankfully I am so exhausted that my body takes over and goes into autopilot. At some point, I finally drift into a deep and heavy sleep.

# CHAPTER TWENTY-FIVE

## BOOK 1

Things have almost gone back to some semblance of normal. Coach Granger is back and working me harder than ever. I'm happy to have running back as a form of distraction and therapy as I'm still reeling from everything that's happened.

Brendan and my mom bought into my story, writing off my disappearance as reckless abandonment. I just got so swept up in my feelings for Emmett that we ran off together. They're of course not happy that I would be so careless, but my mom mostly just seems relieved.

But I think she suspects my father may have reemerged and is somehow responsible for the Elites' demise. No matter what the police say. I see her frequently reminding herself to write it off as paranoia. She's just so happy he doesn't appear to have got to me, that she's welcomed me back with open arms, just asking that I never do it again.

I still desperately want to ask her more about her side of the story. Especially now that I know they tried to accuse her of adultery to ruin my parents' marriage. My mom is the most loyal person on the planet, so I have no doubt that it was a set-up. And even if it had been true, it wouldn't have excused my father's behavior. She had to be so afraid and alone. Punished for something she didn't do and then left on her own to raise me.

But I know it's too soon to start digging things up with her. She's already suspicious and on high alert, and I could use a little more time to process what I already do know.

I wish my lies were true. I wish this has all just been normal teenage misbehavior. And that my father really hadn't got to me. If she only knew just how much he did…or how close she came to losing me, I don't know what she'd do. I have to convince myself my alibi is the true story sometimes, just to make it through the day.

It's been a few days since the news started spreading about the investigation into all of the Elites' dirty dealings. Emmett and Bernadette coming out on top, completely unscathed as promised. But word is that Bernadette is so distraught from the loss of her father that she's completely hysterical and inconsolable. She obviously didn't know her father the way Emmett did.

My heart hurts for Bernadette in a way. To see her own father be murdered. I remind myself that she'll have it out for me. After all, it was my father who killed him. But maybe Emmett will protect me. I have no idea how he feels about me now that I've refused to give in and give him a chance at redemption.

I've heard nothing from my father, thankfully. I know he never really cared about me. I was just as much a pawn to him as I was to the Elites. Emmett claims I was more to him, but I haven't heard from him either ever since I asked him to leave me alone. I told him only space and time would determine if I could ever find some way to forgive him. It was a fib I threw out to get him to leave me alone, thinking I would never really be able to trust him again.

But secretly, I did wonder if I could bring myself to open up to him. I am still fiercely attracted to him, and there aren't many parts of the day when he isn't taking up at least some portion of my brain. I worry it might be some kind of Stockholm syndrome, so I am grateful for the space to sort it out.

I fire through track practice, leaving all the other girls in the dust. Though the nightmare I've been through took up a lot of time, putting me out of practice, I have a new fuel out on the track. Now running is a mission to escape everything I have been through. I tell myself if I run fast enough, maybe it will all be so far behind me that I won't see it at all anymore.

Every slam of my foot to the ground is the crushing of another memory. Each mile behind me puts me further into the future. Every pained breath in my lungs washes out more of Emmett. I am taking it one day at a time, but at this rate… everything will be behind me in no time.

The other girls can't even touch me now. No matter what hell they've seen in their lives, I doubt any of it holds a candle to what I've experienced. Emmett and I are connected in that way now. The strange isolated privileged life of wealth he's known makes him so different from everyone else around him. And now I feel different too.

As I'm finishing up, I can't help but think how happy I am that Coach Granger is back. I don't pry into his personal life to ask what pulled him away, but I suspect the Elites had something to do with it. Maybe he was the only person they couldn't sway, so they caused some kind of trouble in his life that forced him to be away.

"Good work out there today, kid," Coach Granger beams, patting me on the shoulder.

"It's good to have you back," I tell him, swinging a towel over my shoulder as I head for the locker room. "Is everything okay? You were out for a pretty long time."

His stare grows distant and stern. "Just some trouble at home," he answers lightly, with a strange unease about him. "It's funny," he remarks in a way that doesn't sound amused at all, "I had just mentioned to some people I know how worried I was about you right before everything happened."

"Before what happened?" I ask cluelessly.

"I heard you were absent for a bit yourself while I was gone," he continues. "According to the other girls on our team. If I didn't know any better…I'd think someone wanted me out of the way for something." He lets the idea hang there, studying me carefully.

"I wondered the same thing myself," I reply gingerly.

We exchange a knowing nod before he walks away. I think we both know better than to say too much more about it right now. But that brief conversation told me everything I needed to know. He was the only person in the school who would have my back over the Elites. And that's exactly why they made sure he was gone during the final stages of their plan. They knew I would go to him in desperation.

But what I really want to know is…could he have helped? Is that why they needed to make sure I couldn't confide in him when I needed it the most? I don't want to know what they did to make sure he'd be gone. I'm just glad those days are over. And that now I know he's a safe haven for anything that may come up in the future. Hopefully none of us ever have to be so careful again.

I walk across the black, cracked pavement navigating around cars that are coming and going from the painted white spaces. I have started parking closer to the building now, despite the assigned parking. No one seems to care now that the Elites are out of the way.

Much like my home has become more comforting to me than ever before, long walks like this are more precious. I close my eyes and lean my head back, feeling the warm sun on my face. Relishing in the freedom to come and go as I please without worrying who is waiting for me around the corner.

It's well into fall now and I have to wear a hoodie when I'm not running. I curl into the warmth and comfort of it around my skin. All of these small things have become so big after wondering if I would ever live to see another day.

Suddenly, I think I catch a glimpse of Lily in the distance, but she disappears around the corner before I can even think about catching up to her. I hope when the time is right, things will be easier to mend with her now. But I'm giving her the same space I requested of Emmett.

I wonder when Emmett will come back to school. And when he does, if he'll be different. He has to be. Everything is different now.

---

A few days later, I see Lily sitting alone in the lunchroom. The social dynamics of school have changed completely now. All of the Elites have still been absent, including Emmett.

Still dealing with the aftermath of all their families have been implicated in and Thomas' death. At least for a little while, none of us have to worry about being seen talking to the wrong person. Everyone is much more relaxed. The laughter echoing through the rooms sounds less menacing. Kids seems to be talking about normal things again now that they're not terrified and wrapped up in the game of the Elites.

I take the opportunity to approach Lily's table, thinking maybe things will be different between us now. I stand there for a moment, my tray in my hands, trying to read her receptiveness. "Mind if I sit?" I ask finally, after she tries to ignore my presence.

"Go ahead," she answers, not looking up from her sandwich as she takes another bite.

I slide in across from her and start picking at the food on my tray, cutting my eyes up to her every few seconds. "I guess you've heard about everything that's happened?" I question her carefully.

"Thomas Jameson is dead," she replies curtly.

I nod, hoping she'll say more from there. "I'm surprised you didn't come talk to me when you found out. It's big news after all." But we fall back to silence. "So, did it help your situation at all?"

A smile curls across her lips, giving me hope. "Actually...I got a call from Julliard a few days after it happened," she gushes, still holding back from being too warm with me. "I've been accepted on full scholarship. They claimed the rescinded interest was a mistake."

"Lily, that's amazing!" I shriek, wishing things would go back to the way they were before between us. "And the other schools? Did you hear from any of them?"

"That's what's funny about it," she continues, turning cold again. "Julliard was the only one to call."

"I guess that is a little funny," I nod cluelessly. "But good... because that's the only one you cared about, right?"

She looks back down to her tray, spitting out a bite of food in disgust before going quiet yet again. I am completely lost as to why she still hates me or why she's being weird about the school calling.

"Come on, Lily...the Elites are gone. There's no reason to be angry with me anymore. It's not like they can punish you for being friendly to me now. We're free," my eyes light up optimistically, but she seems unconvinced.

"The only person left who has the kind of sway to turn things around with Julliard like that is Emmett," she proposes in an accusatory tone. "And the only person who knew Julliard was my top choice was you."

"What are you getting at?" I cut my eyes upwards and shake my head. Refusing to believe that Emmett would do anything nice for anyone. Especially after the way he has tried to keep Lily and I apart.

"What happened with you and Emmett?" she sneers. "You two must have got awfully close for him to want to do something like that for me."

"There's nothing going on with us," I defend bitterly. "I didn't even know about any of this until you told me. I had nothing to do with it, I swear."

"Well…that's hard to believe, but I sure hope it's true," she bites back. "Emmett is a monster. I would hate for the Elites to get taken down just so you can become the new Vivian."

"Don't be ridiculous!" I snap, the tremor in my voice sounding too defensive. "I could never be like her! I can't believe you'd even suggest something like that." I watch her tear away pieces of a roll only to throw them down again, forming a tiny pile of torn crumbs. "A lot has happened, Lily. I wish I had you to talk to during some of it. You probably could have helped."

"I doubt it," she murmurs. "I don't want to help anyone but myself from now on. I've learned my lesson."

"I don't understand why you're still being this way!" I force myself to lower my head and speak in a hushed pitch, to avoid screaming so loud the entire cafeteria hears me. "The Elites are gone! Sure, maybe Emmett will still be around, but he hasn't been at school since his dad died. And if you do think he took care of the Julliard thing…don't you think that proves maybe he's different than the rest of them?"

I think to myself that it's a good sign that he would do something like that for Lily even while I'm not giving him what he wants. Maybe he does stand some chance at being redeemed. But I don't dare try to argue that to Lily right now.

"I knew it," her eyes cut into me. "I knew you were going soft for him. He got to you, didn't he? Buttered you all up to make you think he wasn't like his dad and sister? Don't fall for it, Ophelia. You're only going to get hurt."

"I've already been hurt plenty," I quip back. "You have no idea." I study her to see if there is any hope of this conversation turning with a positive spin, but she seems dead set on keeping me as her enemy for some reason. "Look, if that's how you want to be…I'll leave you alone. But I hope you come around someday. I'm not with Emmett. We don't even speak anymore.

And even if I do ever get 'buttered up' as you say…I could never be like Vivian."

"You keep telling yourself that, sweetheart," she answers coldly. "I know all about who your father is."

My blood runs cold. "What the hell do you know about my father?"

"I know he was one of them, and I heard he's back," she thunders.

The words of the police officers ring through my ears. If my father is still around, I don't want to know anything about it. I don't want to be held responsible for not reporting it or being faced with the choice of what to do with that information. As much as I want to pry into what exactly Lily knows, I want even more to protect myself and stay blissfully ignorant for as long as I can.

"I have to go," I quake, rushing up from seat without bothering to grab my tray. "Take care of yourself, Lily," I offer sincerely as I bolt from the cafeteria.

"You too, Ophelia," she calls out menacingly as I flee.

My chest burns as I race through the halls, looking over my shoulders in paranoia. Lily's words echoing through my brain with each step. He's back. What did that mean…he's back? What could possibly be left for him in Jameson? Surely, he was smart enough to know it'd never be safe here for him. He got his revenge and took out Thomas Jameson. Why wasn't that enough?

Unless…with Emmett's rise to power as the new alpha of Jameson…he latched on to work his way back up the top, taking back everything he lost and then some. Could they still be working together?

Why would Emmett do that for Lilly? Was that some sort of peace offering? An attempt to show me he's changed now that he's free from his father?

Lily's accusations rest sour in my gut. How could she ever think I would be anything like Vivian? I think back to what they did to her freshman year. How they took her in, treated her like a friend. All so they could humiliate her at the homecoming dance.

That was the same Emmett. Not too different from the way he declared his love for her in the schoolyard right after we had sex. Lily once had the hots for him too and even considered

Vivian a friend. Was it just history repeating itself with me? Only the torture tactics intensified with age?

But maybe Emmett really was just always doing what he thought he had to. Looking tough and cool in front of his friends, because if he didn't they'd destroy him. And make sure his father made his life more of a living hell than he already did.

Emmett said I would understand more if I gave him a chance. If I knew more about what his life had been like. But opening myself up to his side of things only opened me up to more manipulation. More risk of harm. And I just don't think I can do it again.

I make my way down the mostly empty halls, trying to keep my breathing under control. I go to get my things for my next class out of my locker. I stop for a moment, smoothing my thumb across the metal of my lock. I want everything to be open like that. To have all the answers so I can be free from worrying and not knowing who to trust. The moment I was freed from the Jameson's, I was thrown into the crashing waves of the mind fuck that lingers after.

I shrug my shoulders and slam the door shut, jumping at a figure that appears suddenly behind it.

It's Emmett. He has dark circles under his eyes and his hair looks damp from sweat.

"What the hell are you doing here?" I gasp, feeling uneasy with his disheveled appearance.

"Come with me," he barks, not bothering to explain before taking me by the hand and leading me into a janitor's closet.

I try to pull away, but he's too strong.

We shuffle in between shelves filled with chemicals and boxes of supplies. A cascade of mops and brooms clatter in the corner as we accidentally bump into them. He quickly turns me around, placing his hands across my shoulders in urgency.

I start to squirm to pull away, but I sense an urgency in him. He's looking over his shoulder in fear as footsteps echo beyond the door, but he seems to breathe more easily when he hears the unrecognizable voices of two girls laughing and talking about normal things.

"What's going on?" I shriek as he pushes me into the closet, locking the door behind us.

"Shhhhh, please," he's panicked, looking around with his palms suspended midair as he tries to quiet me. "Keep it down. I know I'm being watched."

I have never seen him so vulnerable and afraid. I don't want to buy into it, but a big part of me also just wants to take him into my arms like a scared little child.

Emmett's grown up in a life of privilege. He's never had to want for anything. He's intelligent, selfish and dangerous. He harbors a caged-in resentment toward everyone, and I am all too familiar with the violence he can inflict when he's angry. He's nothing like an innocent little child. But for some reason, as I look at him now, all I can see is a lost little boy. And I want to hold him.

"By who?" I answer in a more hushed tone to appease him.

"I don't know, but I need your help," he explains in terror. "Bernadette is missing."

"What do you mean she's missing?" I respond with a bored and dismissive sigh. "She's probably just hiding out somewhere. She doesn't have her precious Elite gang to back her up anymore and she can't stand to be on her own."

"No, she hasn't been home," he insists frantically. "I'm worried someone's taken her."

"Who!? Who's taken her?" I put my hands to his shoulders trying to calm him down. But I quickly stop myself from getting roped in. "Why are you coming to me with this? I told you I don't want to see you, and I definitely don't want to get dragged into another mess like before."

His muscular arms are tense beneath my touch. I realize this is the first time I've seen him in at least a week. It catches me off-guard instantly. Erasing all the work I've done to run him away. To sweat him out of my system.

Strands of his dark wavy hair hangs in his eyes, damp with sweat. His magnetic gray eyes burn into me, pulling me back into my undeniable attraction for him. I bite my lip, wishing it would go away. I thought I was past this.

Thankfully, his mind is nowhere near any of that. He is completely lost in panic, saving me from my desires.

"You're the only one I can trust," he heaves. "Will you please come with me? Can we go back to your place? I'll explain everything."

I look into his eyes, paralyzed with uncertainty. I don't know if I should believe he really needs my help or if this is some kind of trick. It's funny that he thinks I'm the only one he can trust, while he is the last person on earth I feel like I can trust.

"Okay," I sigh, against my better judgment. "You can come

with me to my house, but my mom and Brendan are home, and they're not going to be so easily charmed by you after what happened last time. You try anything and they'll kick you out."

He nods urgently, desperate to agree to whatever I ask if it means he finds some kind of sanctuary. He clings to my hand as we walk. He's afraid in a way I've never seen before, and I'm terrified to hear about what has him so shaken.

# Broken RULES

# PROLOGUE

## BOOK 2

I'm walking hand in hand with Emmett Jameson. Something I never thought I'd do again.

Torture. Humiliation. Assault. Threats on my life. Taking me hostage. Constant emotional manipulation and abuse—these are the things he has put me through. Not to mention he worked alongside my estranged biological father to plot the murder of his own father. Can't forget about that one. But there is also this intense attraction and sexual energy between us. A primal connection that keeps drawing us together no matter how hard I try to forget about it.

I swore that I never wanted to see or talk to him again—pleaded for him to let me go and leave me alone. But now the tables have turned, and he's the one who's afraid. Holding my hand like a scared little boy, and tugging me down the street to my house.

Emmett Jameson is drop dead gorgeous with thick, dark lashes, stormy gray eyes, and plump, pink, kissable lips that are always tormenting me with a faint smirk. His face has a slight crookedness to it that somehow only makes him more charming and irresistible.

My former friend, Lily, had just informed me my father is still hanging around town, scaring me into a frantic race towards my next class—anywhere away from her newfound hatred for me and the looming threat of my father's lingering presence—when Emmett appeared, scared out of his mind and begging for my help.

He's holding my hand too tight and walking too fast, sweating and looking over his shoulder in paranoia. I've never seen him this undone before.

"Slow down!" I bark at him, skidding my feet to a halt and yanking my hand away. "You're hurting me." My eyes glare at him with renewed rage as I tug at my stinging hand. I'm used to him hurting me, but I swore to myself it would never happen again, no matter what his excuse.

He looks back at me, his eyes welling up in desperate remorse.

"I…I'm sorry, Ophelia," he stammers, stepping towards me. But I am unmoved. "I know…I know," he tries again. "I know I promised I would never…"

"Hurt me again?" I snap back. "Funny how you've only been back in my life for ten minutes and you've already found some way to do that anyway."

"I'm just scared, okay?" he pleads with me. "Come on, I don't want to talk about this here in the middle of the street."

I clutch my arms tightly across my chest, studying his urgency for a moment before I finally submit with a groan, taking off behind him again. His pace grows more frantic with each step as we approach my house.

"Hey! Wait!" I pull him to a stop again, wrestling him off to the side of the house. "Remember, I told you my mom and Brendan are home today. You've got to pull yourself together before we go in there." Sweat is beading on the tips of his loose strands of hair.

"Okay." He nods, not seeming to be able to snap out of it. He blinks rapidly, his wide, bloodshot eyes looking at me in a daze.

"They already don't trust you after what they think happened before," I remind him, growing angry at the memory. Remorse returns to his face, piling even more strain on top of his already-stressed expression. "Come on, Emmett, I mean it! They're not going to like me bringing you here. If you act like this, they're going to know something's up. So, unless you want to tell them everything, you've got to calm down."

He steps back and leans over to rest his hands across his knees, puffing sharp breaths out through his cheeks. I have to fight the urge to rush to his side and wipe his damp forehead, straighten his hair, and tell him everything will be okay. I want to coddle him, but I can't let myself do that. Not after everything he's put me through.

Suddenly, he straightens up and mops the sweat with the sleeve of his shirt. Like a switch has been flipped, he composes himself and comes back to me with an eerily casual smile. His face leans close to mine and a heavenly masculine scent floods over me. The effect he has never ceases to shock me—how I can always want to be so close and so far from him all at once? He devours me with his haunting, icy eyes, always filled with curiosity and desire. But there is always a lurking tinge of hatred and malice, and I never know if it is intended for me or not.

Emmett leans against me, nudging the strain of his pants between my legs. We're both burning with desire. "I want you right now. Right here," he murmurs softly. "Don't you remember what it was like before? How good it felt to have me inside of you?"

He draws me in, and I am so close to caving. To risking getting caught or seen, and just wrapping my legs around him right here and now, hidden beside my house. The past couple of weeks have changed nothing—I still need him, even though I hate him. And no matter how much he scares me, it takes next to nothing for me to be ready to give myself to him again.

He stares at me and frowns. "I've always been able to see that fear in your eyes when you look at me," he says remorsefully. "I've always wished so badly that I knew how to make it go away." Before I can respond, he walks away.

"Okay, then," I mutter, half-stunned as we turn back to the front door. I have to remind myself that I'm dealing with a master manipulator. Aside from the many things Emmett's guilty of, his father was a monster, so he's used to detaching from his emotions to save face.

The smell of simmering meat and spices wafts through the air as we step into the warmth of my home. "Ophelia?" my mother calls out as soon as the front door opens.

My mom is a nurse, and had no trouble finding a job when my scholarship brought us to Jameson. My stepdad Brendan works on power lines. They both do their fair share around the house, with the cooking and cleaning and constant worrying about me. She has been especially overprotective since I went missing for those few days.

Her face drops the moment she rounds the corner and sees him standing there next to me. "Oh," she gasps.

"Hello, Mrs. Lopez," Emmett chimes brightly, with a polite smile.

"Ophelia…" My mom is speechless. She didn't expect to see me with him again after I told her I'd decided he was a bad influence.

"Emmett just needs some help with his homework," I offer as calmly as I can. "We're going up to my room, but he won't be here long."

She looks unconvinced, and won't stop looking him up and down with a seething, distrusting glare.

"Mrs. Lopez, I owe you an apology." He steps forward to interject just as her lips part and she seems to be gathering her words. "I can't imagine how worried you must have been when Ophelia was gone with me for those couple of days. I should never have allowed us to get so carried away."

The sincerity of his tone chills me. He is too good at lying, and any time I see him doing it to other people, I am reminded to be cautious of every word he says to me. I never ran off with him. He and his fucked-up family, along with the rest of the Elites, held me hostage in an attempt to get my estranged father to back off, but you'd never know that looking at us both now.

"Don't worry, Mom," I assure her, placing a hand on her shoulder. "I'm not going anywhere this time."

She looks at my hand, and then back at Emmett's face. She's not going to be so easily convinced. I see the rage building inside of her as her brow furrows and one fist rises to her hip. "You've got some nerve showing back up here," she growls, scowling. "And you expect me to trust you this time? Just like I did after you wrecked your car with my precious Ophelia inside?"

"That was an accident," he blurts, his lips pursing immediately at his poorly chosen words.

"An accident," she scoffs. "How do I know she won't 'accidentally' go missing again for a few days in your company?"

"Mom, really, it's okay," I interject, knowing Emmett can't hold up to an interrogation right now. "I promise you I'm not going anywhere. Just a quick study and homework session in my room…that's all." The confidence and assurance in my own voice surprises me. I am getting good at lying, too, now. Something I've picked up along the way in Jameson, I suppose.

Her face twists up with doubt as she looks us both over with narrow eyes. I'm thankful for her wariness. If Emmett is up to his old games, it could save me. But I straighten up under her gaze, holding strong to convince her I am fine. Everything is fine. I am working to convince myself of just as much.

"I don't want you two leaving the house together," she commands, her voice low and defeated.

"Absolutely," Emmett shoots back eagerly. "We won't go anywhere."

He is already turned away from her, racing up to the privacy of my room, but I linger for a moment and hug my mom tight. "It's okay, I promise," I whisper to her, side-eyeing Emmett boldly. I need him to make sure my words stay true.

"Please eat dinner with us tonight," she says dryly in reply.

"Of course," I chirp, sounding too cool and normal. I have to break away from this now, or I'll lose my nerve. I turn to follow Emmett, wishing more and more that I had just told him no, that I couldn't help him.

Our rented duplex is just big enough for the three of us. It's cozy and has become my only safe haven in this hellhole. And even then, sometimes the danger has found ways to seep inside. Like right now, with Emmett Jameson in my room yet again.

The second we start up the stairs, his panic returns. He's walking so fast, he stumbles as his sweaty hand pulls me along behind him.

His sister is missing, and he thinks he's being watched. He has good reason to be afraid. He has just played a part in taking down the Elites, the old money organization that founded this town and the owners of the Jameson Automobile Company, which employs just about everyone in the city. With his father dead and the rest of the Elites facing time in prison, he is the new king of it all. The only one, aside from his sister and mom, who got out of the scandals free and clear with his life and wealth intact. You don't pull off something like that without dredging up at least a few enemies along the way.

I can see all of this new reality written all over his face. The perfect ending my father promised him isn't all it's cracked up to be, and it's only just begun.

# CHAPTER ONE

## BOOK 2

Emmett storms into my room and plops down on the edge of my bed as if it's all so natural. But all I can think about is the last time he was here. His Elite buddies, Trey and Vincent, were with him. He pinned me to the wall before dragging me downstairs and sweet-talking my mom and stepdad into letting them take me out to the movies. I didn't come home that night. Or the next night. My heart surges with anger as it all replays in my mind, and his pathetic, slumping posture only enrages me more.

"Okay, so spill it," I demand, crossing my arms at a safe distance. "You got me here. What's going on?"

"Bernadette hasn't been home in days," he says through a long exhale, running his hands through his hair. "Mom won't let us call the police. She says she doesn't trust them with the investigation going on right now."

"Oh, so you mean the cops aren't in your pocket anymore now that your father's dirty dealings have come to light?" I snap, unable to hold back a grin of satisfaction. "It must be really hard on you, not having anyone to turn to," I mock him sarcastically.

"I know, Ophelia. You have every right to be angry with me," he murmurs as he breaks down into tears.

I have seen a lot of different faces on Emmett Jameson, but I don't know that I've ever seen him cry. I hate the way it weakens me. Every muscle in my body screams to stand still and hold my ground, but instead I find myself racing to his side, collapsing beside him as I pull his sobbing face against my shoulder.

"Calm down," I tell him gently, with a tinge of resentment, but my body betrays me, stroking his hair. I hate how quickly he can quash my anger. The hold he has on me is maddening. "We'll figure this out. Are you sure she didn't just run away?"

"She would've left a note," he sniffles, wiping at his eyes. "She likes attention way too much to just slip away quietly. She would've written something dramatic and made sure we found it."

The rumors from school circle in my brain, coupled with the image of Bernadette screaming over her father's body. My biological father shot him right in the entryway of their manor, leaving him flat and limp across the marbled floor with blood rapidly pooling around him. She was distraught. None of the Elites, including Emmett, have returned to school since, but word is that Bernadette is completely despondent.

"You don't think…" I start softly, immediately covering my mouth to try and stop myself from even saying it.

"What?" Emmett barks, desperate for a lead.

"Well…everyone's been talking about how much seeing your father shot in front her fucked her up," I continue, hoping he won't make me say it. "She wouldn't have…"

"Killed herself?" he interjects, too dryly.

"I hate to even say it…I'm sorry," I stammer and recoil, rubbing my hand against his shoulder. "I'm just trying to cover every possibility. I shouldn't…Shit, I'm sorry…"

"Same as running away. She would have left a note." He stands and walks a few feet away, distancing himself from me and my suggestions.

"You're right. I'm sure that's not it," I say too loudly with false confidence, but the possibility still hangs heavy in my mind. "You're all too full of yourselves to do anything like that anyway," I mutter under my breath.

"What?" He spins back around, too distracted with his own busy mind to have really heard me.

"So, you think someone took her?" I pick up the thread again, trying to placate him. He nods. "What about Trey and Vincent? The Whitworths?"

The Whitworths were key players in the Elite gang, along with Emmett, his family, Vivian Blackwater, and her family. All old money who'd founded the town, built the school, and controlled Jameson Automobile Corporation, a maker of fine, high-class automobiles that employs practically the whole city of Jameson. The Elite parents had dabbled in oil, stocks, and arms-dealing. All their kids had trust funds. But now that has changed.

"Or Vivian and her family?" I continue, knowing that any one of the Elites could have it out for Emmett, his mom, and his sister. They are the only ones who made it out from my father's vengeful wrath unscathed.

I hate even saying her name. While Emmett was making my life a living hell, despite our primal attraction to one another, Vivian stood by his side as his girlfriend. He doesn't flinch at the mention of her, and I am unable to bite back my curiosity regarding their status, even with everything that has happened.

"Have you talked to her?" I ask gently.

"She called once the investigation began," he explains, rubbing his jaw. His eyes dart around the room as he speaks evenly, without interest. "She thought I'd comfort her, but when I told her we weren't together anymore, she turned on me. Screamed and cussed me out."

"So, you helped land her parents in prison and then dumped her?" I quip, masking how happy I am that he didn't cave into her plea for sympathy. "That's cold."

I want to hate Emmett, but whether I like it or not, my mind still isn't made up about him. I've seen nothing but pure evil in Vivian and Bernadette since day one, though. I arrived in Jameson hopeful and excited about my track scholarship at WJ Prep, only to have them almost run me over and damn near break my wrist before I'd even had a chance to step foot on campus. And it only got worse from there.

"Would you have rather I stayed with her?" he asks coldly, his tone shooting straight to my core.

"I hate you," I fume in response. He's too cavalier, as if I was supposed to be left completely unphased after everything I saw happen between them.

"No, you don't." He flashes me an eerie, suggestive grin.

He's right. I don't. And that's the problem. "Let's focus, okay?" I fly to my feet and begin pacing the room. I can't let this spiral into a talk about us.

"I don't know." He sighs. "Have you heard from your dad at all?"

I shake my head. Up until a couple of months ago, my biological father was completely irrelevant to my life. But shortly after realizing he and my mom met at WJ Prep and that he used to be an Elite, my whole life fell apart.

Not long after the discovery of who my father really was, I was plagued by mysterious messages and endless threats from the remaining Elites. Their parents had been using the software company of the satellite Elites, the Hendersons, to cover up politician extortion and sex trafficking rings. My father, having been cast out of town and stripped of his fortune after he embezzled tons of money to pay off his gambling debts, returned with a vengeance. He killed Thomas Jameson, leaving everything in Emmett's control, and sending the rest of the Elites to prison only to supposedly disappear again once he was done.

"No. Nothing. And I'm hoping it stays that way." I shake my head, feeling sick from the all too recent memories.

When Emmett and I gave our statements to the police, framing his father's death as a suicide, they cornered me about my father. They told me he was under investigation for a slew of federal crimes and that I should report any contact I have with him back to them. But around here, you can't even trust the cops. I'd rather not be faced with the decision of whether or not to tell them, so I desperately hope my father stays away for good.

"Do you think he has something to do with this?" Emmett asks desperately.

"I wouldn't rule it out, honestly," I reply, my legs buckling underneath me as I plop back onto my bed. "I don't trust him. But that's what you get, Emmett. If you're going to make deals with people like him, you have to expect shady things to come out of it."

"So, you think he could have taken Bernadette?" he continues, reaching for any possible lead.

"I didn't say that, but…" I stop myself, remembering who I'm talking to. Emmett was the one who worked with my father, offering to kidnap me for him and then letting him onto his property to kill his father. Who's to say they aren't still working together? That I know too much about their scheme, and when I refused to talk to either of them, they decided I couldn't be trusted? This could all be some sick game to lure me back in close so they can take me out the way they did Thomas Jameson. My suspicions hang in a heavy silence.

"Have you thought about going to the cops anyway?" I ask finally, hoping to catch some hint of Emmett's truth in all of this. After all, teaming up with my father again would explain his hesitancy to go to the police. And Lily did warn me that my father wasn't really gone. "I know your mom doesn't want you to, but…maybe they could help."

"So many of them were close to my father," he says, shaking his head in stubborn refusal. "I don't trust that they'll have our best interests in mind. Everyone knows my father didn't really kill himself. They just got paid off and put that down on paper. They may be against me."

"Could they have something to do with it?" I sit up, remembering not to rule anything out when it comes to the town of Jameson and its Elites. "Are they so corrupt that they might have something to do with Bernadette's disappearance?"

"I can't rule anything out at this point." He collapses next to me, burying his face in his hands. "Which is the hardest part—I don't even know where to begin."

"Well, what we do know is that she is missing," I recap with intense focus, scooting away from him. "And that there are plenty of people who are upset and nervous about your father being gone and the changes happening with Jameson Automobiles. You taking everything over."

"People strike when you're weak and vulnerable." He groans. "When things are changing…when you're distracted."

"Tell me about it." I turn away from him, rubbing my arm sheepishly.

I was weak and vulnerable when I came here because of my sheer ignorance. I had no idea Emmett and the others would make it their sole mission in life to make mine a living hell. I want to be over it all, but it's too soon. And I'm afraid forgetting will only open me up to more trouble.

"I really am sorry, Ophelia." He places his hand on my knee, but I quickly push it off and move further down the bed. "I know I've told you before, but…everything you've seen of me so far…that wasn't me," he continues earnestly. "I was under so much pressure from my father and the other Elites. I hoped that after a little time, we could start again. That you could get to know the real me, but now, with everything with Bernadette…I didn't know who else to turn to. Who else I can trust."

"I'll help you figure out what happened to Bernadette," I say bitterly, knowing even that much is far more than he deserves. "But after that, I'm done. I told you I don't want you in my life."

"But you do." He reaches towards me defiantly, wrapping his fingers across my thigh. "You say you don't, but I know you do. That's why you're helping me."

"I'm helping you because it's the decent thing to do," I insist, closing in on myself and rocking back and forth. "But don't worry. I don't expect you to understand anything about the decent treatment of others."

He recoils against my jab, exasperated and leaving me to study him carefully. I wish I could see into his head and know exactly what's going on inside. So much of me wants to believe him when he says I don't know the real him, that with his father gone he can prove to me that he is a good person who has sincere feelings for me. But every time I think I can open myself up to the possibility, flashes of everything he has done to me pull me back into disbelief.

But he looks genuinely sorry as he watches me glare at him in distrust. More than that, he looks just as clueless and hopeless as I am. I have to remind myself that he is just a teenage boy, even if he is now the sole executive of Jameson Automobiles, with all the money and power that come along with that role. His sister is missing, and he has to know how big of a target is now on his own back.

"Ophelia, can we talk?" he asks with a pleading tone.

"We are talking," I snap back, crossing my arms again.

"No, I mean…can we talk about us?" His head is down, but his eyes are burning into me.

"There is no 'us' to talk about, Emmett." I shake my head in exasperation. I refuse to cave into him. "I said I would help you with Bernadette, but that's it. And this whole thing better not be some ploy to get back into my life."

He follows me as I rant and pace around the room. "Will you just look at me?" he begs, grabbing my wrists and pulling me towards him. "Just be still for a minute and listen to me. Please."

"Okay." I shrug finally, with an angry and impatient stare. "What is it? What do you want to talk about? Because as far as I'm concerned, you already said everything you had to say after the police station. It wasn't enough then and it won't be enough now."

"I don't know if I said everything." He reaches out as if he might touch my face, but then pulls back like he's not worthy. He steps away and looks at the floor, his shoulders slumping over his chest. "I don't know how to explain how I feel about you," he says slowly, unable to look at me. "It's like…from the moment I saw you, I felt sucked in. And everyone around me expected me to torture you and do all of these terrible things to you because of who your father is, but I just couldn't do it."

"Oh, you did," I retort bitterly.

"No, I didn't," he insists. "Not like I was supposed to and you know that. It was supposed to be so much worse. I tried to do what they wanted but…" He trails off and turns back towards me. His eyes are urgently taking me in. It's like he started to slip off into too dark of a place in his memories and needs to see me to anchor him in the here and now. "When I look at you, I feel whole. And I think I hated you for that for a while, because it showed me how empty I was before. But now that I know what that feels like…I can't live without it. I need you, Ophelia."

I push through the melting feeling, trying to envision my heart hardening into stone. I can't let myself fall for this again. Even if I can't fully control how I feel inside, I can't show any of it to him. I can't get sucked in again.

"It's great that you realized you need more in your life and that you want to be a better person and all that," I answer coldly. "But I can't be responsible for you in that way. What happens when I can't be there? You just slip back into being your old self? You can't put that kind of weight on me."

"And what about you?" he asks sternly.

"What about me?" I respond weakly, stepping away from him.

"You don't feel different with me? Something you've never felt before?" he asks daringly, his voice growing frantic. "You know you do. You need me just as much as I need you."

"No, I don't, Emmett," I lie as best as I can. "I have other people in my life who love and support me. You are not my only source of love."

"I'm not talking about love." He shakes his head vehemently. "I'm talking about feeling alive. The rush of everything that could happen. I know you feel that with me just as much as I do with you."

"But people get burnt out on rushes like that," I argue softly. "The rush can't sustain you. It just feels good."

"It's more than that," he insists. "It's more than just some temporary high."

"How would we know? Look at what we've been through together…All we've ever had are moments—fleeting highs." I shake my head, hating that I'm even admitting this much. "This is just too much." My eyes begin to water, but I quickly wrinkle my face and use my hands to hide them.

"That's exactly what it is," he agrees passionately, rushing forward to grab my wrists again. He pulls them down and forces me to look at him, watering eyes and all. "It's too much. But you want it, don't you?"

"No," I swear, clinging to every ounce of resolve I have built up in our time apart. "Too much is just that…too much. And I don't want it. I can't handle it."

"Oh, that's not the Ophelia I know," he dares me with a coy smile. "You can't handle it? You know damn well you can handle anything."

"Until I met you," I bite back.

His eyes spark at the challenge, and all at once he swoops forward and presses his lips against mine. I try to pull back, but the reminder of how sweet he tastes is the last straw. I crash back into him and lose myself completely. I don't know what it is that snaps me out of it. Maybe it's the way he growls against my mouth or the way his hand kneads into my skin desperately. But something gives me enough strength to push him away again.

"No, Emmett." My chin quivers. "I told you, I can't do this." I look at him and wait for my resolve to break again, but somehow I am able to stand firm.

The wrestling match inside of me continues, sending me flailing back on my bed with an enraged groan. One minute I remember everything from before and have no trouble hating him, the next I am softened by something inside of him and whatever this is that keeps drawing us together. I know my desire to help him goes beyond me trying to be a decent person. I don't owe him anything. I just want him.

"What are you thinking about?" he asks gently, lowering

himself beside me on the bed, but he's smart enough to keep a couple of feet between us.

All I can do is laugh and try to hold back tears, completely overwhelmed in a way that only Emmett can make me feel. "Where to even start," I scoff. "But I've said it all before. I told you how I felt when you chased me down outside of the police station."

He looks away with a soft and stern nod. I still have no way of knowing whether or not he's still working with my father. He claims he had no choice the first time, and he could just as easily be stuck in the same spot now. But he also claimed he didn't care about anything my father had to offer—everything that came along with his position as one of the last remaining Elites. He said all of it meant nothing without me.

I watch the edge of his face as he stares out my bedroom window, his eyes darkened by too many thoughts too like my own. I am once again left with a longing to go to him and trace my fingers along his jaw, drawing him to me for some kind of comfort. He used to insist that I belonged to him, and I've never understood how he could make me feel so afraid at times, yet still make me want to be his.

Always seemingly aware of what goes through my head, he never misses an opportunity to play on my momentary weakness. Right on cue, he turns back to me and reaches his hand across the bed, leaving it just a few inches away for me to take or leave. I was able to resist him before when he stood in the rain, pleading for another chance; I have to believe that I'm strong enough to do it again.

I roll away from his touch and refocus, straightening my hair and steadying my voice with a sharp breath. "So, what's next?" I ask. "I told you I'd help you find Bernadette, and I will. We need a game plan."

He sits back up on the edge of the bed, looking disappointed and tired. "Maybe I can look through her things," he suggests, raking his hands through his hair. "I know she keeps a diary. Maybe there's some hint of some kind in her room."

"You don't need me to do that," I snap back. "Why didn't you try that before dragging me into this?"

I worry that while his fears for his sister may be sincere, this is an all too convenient excuse to get to me. He's side-stepping my pleas for him to leave me alone, to give me time and space, and instead roping me right back into the dangerous games of his world——a world he knows I want to stay away from.

"Because I need you, Ophelia," he insists, looking up at me with pouting eyes. "It's not just about what you can do to help…I need to be close to you. Having you around helps me keep my head straight."

I laugh sarcastically and look away, shaking my head as my arms fold firmly over my chest. "Forgive me if that's just a little hard for me to believe," I sneer over my shoulder. "I've never known you to seem like you had your head on straight."

"What about now?" He stands urgently. "We've been alone in this room for how long? I could have done a million things to you. What about when I had to hold you captive in my room? I could have let Trey and Vincent have their way with you, or done things to you myself if I was really such a bad guy. I did my best to protect you and keep us both safe."

"Are you delusional?" I fire back, my voice growing too loud.

"Shhh…your mom!" he hisses at me, stepping closer as we both fight the urge to fall into each other's arms.

"I didn't feel protected when you held me down…when your father put his disgusting hands on me. Punched me. You tied me down and left me at his mercy," I remind him, my voice cracking from the pain of the memories.

"Stop it," he growls, turning his back to me. "I can't think about those things."

"Well, I certainly can," I shoot back bitterly. "Some days it's all I can think about. And if I have to live with those memories, then so do you. You don't get to just pretend like none of it ever happened. You have to face it if you want to be around me."

"I did all I knew to do at the time," he murmurs quietly, his voice dripping with conflict and regret. "I've told you before… you don't know what my father was like." He trails off into silence, looking at the floor in complete silence. But then, suddenly, he shakes his head and tugs at his shirt as he turns back toward me, snapping into a different state of mind far from the memories of his monster of a father. "Let me show you who I really am, Ophelia."

His eyes are heated as his warm fingers brush along my cheek. I am frozen under his touch, always needing and wanting more. He trails his index finger across the line of my jaw as I clench against his hard chest. I step up to my tiptoes and press my lips to his, lighting us both up with the heat of passion.

He murmurs something indistinct against my mouth as his hand winds through my hair, jerking my face upward, demanding that I be right where he wants me as I am left breathless and at his mercy. His lips come over mine in a deep kiss as his tongue opens my lips, sucking and nipping across my mouth in heated waves, growing more demanding and urgent. I tug him in closer, whimpering into his mouth and begging for more. He still kisses in the same confused way, always furiously switching between pulling me closer and pushing me away. Always punishing and brutal. I struggle to keep up and match the sweep of his tongue with my own. But it's an intoxicating dance that I can never get enough of.

"That," he blurts suddenly against my lips, with a groan of satisfaction.

"Hm?" I hum back.

"That's what I was talking about earlier." He grins. "The rush. Didn't you miss it?"

"No," I lie. "I don't know what you're talking about."

He pulls me back in, eager to face the challenge. He begins kissing me urgently, with greed, pulling and tugging at me and sucking my breath away. I can't help but whimper against the force of him as I feel myself surrendering.

"You still going to pretend you don't feel it?" he pants, his forehead pressed against mine.

It's too much. My chest tightens as I buckle under the overwhelming surge of it all. I push him away and retreat a few steps back. It's surreal to be standing here with him in my room, feeling everything rushing back over me. I hate the way it makes me want to forget about everything from before, so that I can crash into him and revel in the way he makes my body feel. The primal urge outweighs the consequences I know he should face. He doesn't deserve to have me again. I've already given him far too much just by letting him come here.

"You can try to run from it," he teases, "but you know you want it as much as I do."

The deep rasp of his sexy voice is killing me. It still excites me to be wanted so much by him. I'd convinced myself for so long that his attraction to me was just some fleeting curiosity, that I was just some fiery, unobtainable object that bruised his ego when I didn't melt for him. But he's still coming back for me, poking holes in my old theory.

"You don't know anything about what I want," I insist sincerely.

I am not as fucked up as Emmett. Yes, I want to give into our lust. I want the momentary thrill of having him inside of me again. It's only happened once before, and it was the best sex of my life. Of course, I want it again. But I also want the things that go beyond the awkward coldness he showed me afterwards.

It may be dumb to think that any guy I meet in high school could develop into someone and something that lasts in the long-term, but I still crave a relationship that can lead to a real partnership. Someone who can be there by my side when my running career takes off, and someone who can settle down with me once it's over. But Emmett isn't thinking about any of those things. He only lives moment to moment, taking whatever pops up in front of him when he wants it. He is not a little house with a white picket fence.

"Tell me what you want," he tries, moving forward again, his voice dangerously suggestive. "Tell me every…last…thing… you…want…" His words trail off as he kisses, bites, and sucks along my neck, sending chills down my spine.

He doesn't even know how far off he is. What he's asking for is not what is on my mind, but the more he moves his lips across my skin, I am beginning to forget everything else. I'm slipping, falling back beneath my physical yearning for him. I'm trying my best to resist, but he's breaking me down—just like he knew he would.

"We should stop," I beg, more as a reminder to myself than a real plea. "I don't want to do this."

"You don't?" All at once, his hand moves between my legs and pushes just enough to prove me wrong. He can feel that I'm already wet and pulsing with need.

"Fine." I bite my lip in defeat. "But just because I want it doesn't mean we should."

"You should have everything you want." His voice cracks with tenderness.

I want to scream at him. What I want is for him to be a good person, but that's something he can't give me. Can he? I feel dizzy from how quickly he's breaking me down and sucking me back in. My ability to push him away and run is quickly fading. I can't resist him.

I step back just enough to take him in, reminding myself that this isn't another one of my fantasies. He's really here right now, standing before me with hungry eyes. My eyes drop as my head bows. My subtle sign of giving in. He responds instantly, cupping his hand around my cheek and drawing my lips back to his.

"Don't hurt me," I plead.

"Never," he replies confidently, and we both know it's a lie.

He can't say never because he already has, more than once. But despite everything inside of me screaming to run away, I am melting into him again. Unable to fight it. A breathless moan escapes against his lips, too sweet and tender. I didn't want to give that to him. If this is going to happen, I want it to be brutal. Because I have made up my mind that he is brutal.

I bite his lip too hard and push him away again, my eyes brightening to match his. It's my way of showing him things are going to be different this time. I am not the same vulnerable, desperate girl he found before. I know exactly who he is now, and I've survived him once already. I have to be rough enough to make sure I survive him again.

"Maybe I should be telling you not to hurt me," he quips, touching his finger to the bite mark on his lip.

"Maybe."

"I know you've never thought I was any better than the rest of the Elites," he pleads desperately, "I know I just look like a monster to you...but I had no choice, Ophelia."

"I've told you before...you've always had a choice, Emmett."

"Well, the choice I'm making is to set things right with you," he announces confidently, puffing up his chest. "And to take over my father's company, and run it the way I always wished he would have. It's a business and nothing else. It doesn't come above people, it helps people."

# CHAPTER TWO

BOOK 2

My feet are glued to the floor as he walks towards me with less hesitation than before. He's determined now, and my ability to resist him is weakening with each passing minute. He tries to pull me into his arms, but I push him and turn away.

"I don't trust you or believe anything you say," I insist sharply, trying to remind myself just as much as him.

"So, let me show you with something other than words." His voice drops to a low, suggestive rasp as he lingers right behind me, facing my back. His fingers glide gently across my lower back, up my spine, sending chilling tingles through my entire body.

"Emmett…don't," I protest weakly, still unable to move away. "My mom is downstairs and probably listening to everything…She doesn't trust you either."

"We'll be quiet," he whispers against my ear, moving in closer behind me as I feel myself melting into him. Giving in. "Unless you want me to stop…" he offers as his palms glide up my arms, begging to explore other parts of my body.

"I can't." My voice wavers and is unconvincing. I can't fully give in, but I can't move away or ask him to stop either. The bad memories drift to the back of my mind, replaced with the haunting recollection of how he made me feel that afternoon in his bathroom. Emmett had tried to escape to school for a while, leaving me locked in his room—supposedly having no other choice. His father tried to break into the room, and by the time Emmett came racing back to make sure I was okay, we were both unable to fight it anymore. The way his fingers felt on my skin and inside of me, the taste of his mouth, the way his tongue and teeth devoured me, his smell, and the warmth of his body moving inside of mine…it's all painfully vivid.

My lips part in longing as it all crashes over me. Regardless of what has happened and what will, I want Emmett. Even if only physically, I am sure of that much. And he's standing here right now, offering himself to me. I desperately want to surrender and let us both feel good for just a little while, temporarily forgetting about everything else.

But I'm still frozen in fear as he pushes his chest against my back, gently pressing his lips to the back of my neck. An electric current flows through my veins at his kiss, lighting every part of me on fire with an uncontrollable desire for him. But I can't let myself forget what happened after we had sex the first time. As powerful as it had seemed, he turned cold the moment it was over, transforming back into the heartless, empty shell I feared he truly was, regardless of what he insisted.

A soft whimper escapes my mouth as his kisses grow deeper, traveling up and down the back of my neck, begging me to cave into him again. Suddenly, I don't care if he can be trusted or if he'll turn cold once he's through with me. I just want to feel him again, even if it's only once.

Without saying a word, I march over to my bedroom door and make sure that it's locked. I turn back around slowly, pushing my back to the door as I look at him with pleading eyes. My arms hang limply at my sides as I soften in submission. His eyes light up with hunger as he walks over to me, tunneling forward with a primal urge.

Our lips crash together in desperate kisses as he pushes me against the door. There is nothing slow or reserved about it as we drink each other in with all the same repressed desire that roared up between us the first time. Within minutes, he tightens his hands around my ass, lifting me up to wrap my legs around his waist as his teeth dig into the side of my neck.

"Oh god, Ophelia," he growls, urgently moving across every inch of my face, neck, and mouth that he can with rapid force.

A taunting grin curls across the corners of my mouth as I look up at him, relishing in how much he wants me. Suddenly I realize that this is my only advantage. He needs me as much as I need him, but the idea of making him think he can't have me fulfills a need for vengeance. I decide right then to torture him.

My fingers press into his cheeks as I spread my hand under his jaw, forcefully holding him back from kissing me anymore. His brows flicker in confusion as he tries to push forward, but I keep my grip firm. With my hands to his chest, I shove him backward, flattening against the door as I look at him with daring eyes.

I lift my shirt over my head and take off my pants. He tries to rush forward again, but I shove him back. One brow rises in defiance as I slowly drag a finger across the clasp of my bra. "Do you want me to take this off?" I ask him tauntingly.

He grunts and charges, but I push him away for the third time. "Tell me that's what you want," I insist.

I can tell he's infuriated that he can't just take control and throw me down to have his way with me. But he reluctantly nods, shifting impatiently as he drinks in the sight of me standing there in my underwear.

"Say it," I command, keeping my fingers still but close to the clasp.

"Please, take it off," he begs, his voice deep and heavy with unsatisfied longing.

"Good boy," I tease, taking us back to all the times before, when he called me his 'good little girl.' With one flick, the band around my chest loosens. I gently swipe at the stripes, letting my bra fall to the floor. I kick it away as it lands at my feet and stand there, forcing him to look at my bare breasts without being able to touch them.

"What about these?" I continue, sliding my thumb around the waist of my panties. "Should I take these off, too?"

"I want to take them off," he insists.

"No," I bark, shaking my finger in the air. "If you want me…we do this how *I* want."

His face softens in submission as he accepts my game, forcing him to be the one to give up control for once. "I want you to take them off," he answers breathlessly.

I pull at the elastic, stretching them down just enough to reveal the flattened skin that rests above what he wants to see most. But I stop and let the fabric snap back in place. "I don't know," I tease. "I'm not convinced of how bad you want me to do it."

"Ophelia, fuck…please…" he hisses with clenched fists. "Please take them off. I need to see you."

The pain in his voice fills me with an exhilarating desire. I slide the panties down over my thighs and legs slowly, keeping my eyes glued to his the entire time. He bites his lip as I straighten again, completely naked. I make him stand there as I run my hands up my bare thighs, across my stomach up to my breasts. I cup them and squeeze, watching him closely. I touch myself in all the ways I know he's dying to touch me. With one hand filled with my breast, I let the other travel back down. His eyes follow it closely as I inch between my legs.

"Do you want me to touch myself?" I ask him, circling just above my clit.

"Yes," he growls immediately, with sweat forming across his forehead.

"You know that's not good enough," I remind him adamantly. "How badly do you want to see me do it?"

All at once he drops straight down to his knees, completely helpless to my demands. "Please…" he begs. "Touch yourself."

His surrender causes me to tighten with excited yearning as I step past him to the bed with a coy smile. I lay back across the comforter as he follows closely, knowing to keep his distance. He stands with wide eyes at the foot of the bed as I spread my legs before him and gently push my fingers down to the throbbing folds. I moan with relief as I move in soft circles, leaning my head back to forget about his watching eyes for a moment as I just relax into the sensation.

I slip into a space where there is nothing but the feeling rippling from my fingertips and the thrill of knowing he is on his knees at the edge of my bed, watching me with longing. It doesn't take me long to feel like I might cum, but I stop myself. I want him to do it, and I am ready to feel him against me again.

"Come here," I demand impatiently.

Emmett grins and crawls across the bed, hovering over me as he bites at my bottom lip. His tongue crashes over mine as his hand skims across my stomach, taking in a handful of my breast that he had been eyeing so lavishly. He kisses down to my throbbing nipples, taking them into his mouth one by one. I moan and dig my fingers into his hair, feeling even more afire with need.

I push both hands to his chest once again, lifting him far enough off of me to grip his shirt and yank it over his head.

Excited by the sight of him, I rake my hands across his abs, digging in my nails as I go. He tightens beneath my touch, hissing between his teeth as his hand moves behind my head and pulls a clump of my hair.

We both fumble frantically at the zipper of his pants until finally, they are tossed aside, followed by his boxers. Finally, the hardened length of him is free and pulsing over me. The first time we had sex, I didn't have as good of a view. But now that I can see every inch of him perfectly, I want to taste him.

I sit up and crawl towards him, lowering between his legs with one hand gripped firmly around the base of his shaft. Broken breaths shutter from his mouth as I move my hand up and down, looking him in the eye as I tease the tip with my tongue. Slowly, I move my mouth over him, tightening my lips against his hardness. He lets out a deep groan as I push him further into my mouth, taking him in as deep as I can. His hand squeezes my hair tightly, encouraging me to move him in and out.

Emmett's groans grow more breathless and broken as I move my mouth around him, until all at once he shoves me back in desperation. I can tell I almost made him cum, but he wants to be inside of me. He shoves me back down onto the mattress with such desperate force, I almost slip back into a place of fear. But I know the place he is coming from—one of primal lust that is burning inside of me just as strong.

He turns for his pants and pulls out a condom, tearing the wrapper with his teeth before sliding it on. I have to wonder if he brought that over just for me, confident that this might happen, or if he always keeps one on hand.

He quickly flings my legs over his shoulders, and I brace myself, expecting him to slide inside of me with the same urgent force he pushed me back with. But instead I am surprised as his head drops between my legs, taking me into his warm, wet mouth.

I gasp out in shock as his hot tongue laps across my lips, dripping with desire. I cry out, melting beneath him. My back arches as I try to warn him how close I am, but the words trail off into nothing. Waves crash over me as my heart races from the pleasure of a rippling orgasm. He sucks my shaking bundle of nerves in even deeper, holding me close as I cum against his mouth.

Giving me no time to recover, he shoots back up and glides

into my tightened, still-quivering muscles. He moans desperately as he fills me. I'm so wet that he slides in completely with the first thrust. I take him in greedily, bucking into each movement. His hardness pushes against my G spot, instantly putting me close to another orgasm.

I can tell he is already just as close. He doesn't waste any time trying to tease me with slow movements. He thrusts in and out in a quick, steady rhythm, keeping my legs held up so that I am tight around him. We move together, trying to keep our cries contained so they don't echo through the house. He keeps my hips hoisted close to him so he can move inside of me without the bed making too much noise.

"Fuck, Ophelia," he gasps, looking at me with weakened eyes. "You have no idea how bad I wanted to be inside of you again."

I want to tell him that I do know, because I wanted it, too. All the emotional distance I felt I needed never once lessened the physical desire I had for him. I lie in this bed night after night, touching myself as I imagine everything that is happening right now. But I am too dissipated in the sensations to get out a single word.

He moves more rapidly as beads of sweat form on the tips of his dangling hair strands. My fingers clench into the sheets beneath me as I writhe against him, feeling closer to the edge. He pushes in even harder with each urgent thrust, growing faster and faster until finally we are both on the cusp. His moans crack in between panting breaths as my head throws back, trying not to scream as I cum a second time. I tighten around him as I feel the pulsing pumps of his orgasm rippling through me.

As the height of our pleasure slowly fades, he melts over me, gently pushing his lips to mine. I am hit with a sudden, over-whelming relief at his tenderness. My fingers cling to his hair, pulling him deeper into the kiss, hoping he won't pull away like he did the first time.

He kisses me until I let my lips sink away, my head crashing to the side from exhaustion. With his weight still supported on his elbows, he lays his damp head across my chest. I don't know how long we lay there like that with our bare chests pressed flat together, heaving up and down as our breathing slowly regulates.

"Emmett," I finally whisper after a while. "You'll have to go soon. My mom will come up here to check on us before too long."

He groans, lifting up to look down at me with a gentle smile. It's something I haven't seen in him before, and I can't help but pull him down for another soft kiss. There's something innocent and pure about him. Words I have never thought to use to describe him before.

I felt every bit as connected to him during this encounter as I had during the first, only this time he didn't turn cold afterwards. He is staying here with me, reluctant to move even though he knows that he has to soon. He looks at peace. Happy. And I want to feel the same way, but I'm not ready to let everything go. Holding onto that anger and mistrust feels like the only way to protect myself.

I look deep into his eyes as I stroke strands of hair from his face. I want to stay like this forever, and I have to admit how tempted I am to believe him now. He promised that the way he was before was all a product of his father and the rest of the Elites' demands. And now, for a brief moment, with all of that out of the way, he does seem to be different.

I don't want to let this side of him go, but we reluctantly peel ourselves apart and put our clothes back on. I straighten up the bed in case my mom comes knocking, as Emmett stands next to the window in still silence.

"Everything okay?" I ask him as I smooth out the sheets.

"Just worried about my sister is all," he mumbles grimly, bringing reality crashing back into the room.

I can't let go of my suspicions, not fully. But I can keep those in a dark, quiet corner of myself for now, and to Emmett's face, I can behave as if I am nothing but loving and trusting. As long as he continues to be kind, I can maintain that much.

I think about how things would have been if my mother hadn't left my father, if he hadn't been cast out from the Elites. I wonder if I would have been raised in the same way as the others. If I would be just like Vivian, or even Lily. While at times I wish I understood more so I could understand Emmett better, maybe even love him better, growing up the way he did is a level beyond what I want. I would rather stay here in our small rented home with my innocent, white spackled ceilings, where my parents are laughing downstairs, and the smell of home-cooked food wafts through the air.

I walk up behind him and wrap my arms tightly around his

chest. "We'll figure it out, Emmett," I assure him gently, kissing his shoulder. "Wherever she is…we'll find her."

He wraps his hands over mine and squeezes tightly, clinging to my words. I don't want to let him go, but the dreaded knock finally comes at the door.

"Ophelia?" my mom calls out nervously. "Are you okay in there? Open up."

I race over to the door, not wanting to worry her with any delay. "Yes, Mom. We're fine!" I say as brightly as possible as I fling the door open.

She peers inside, looking back at Emmett and the room suspiciously. "Well," she hesitates, still seemingly convinced that something isn't right. "Dinner is ready. It's time for Emmett to go home."

"Thank you, Mrs. Lopez," Emmett offers graciously. "Thanks for allowing me into your home. You certainly didn't have to…considering everything."

"I know I didn't have to," she snaps back. "But it's time to go now."

I can't help but flash him a smile over my shoulder at my mom's persistent hatred. Something about it is satisfying. He deserves it after all, and at this point I'd rather it come from her than me.

"Give us just a minute to say goodbye," I ask her, inching the door shut. "We'll be right down, and Emmett will go home."

She barely budges as I push the door closed. I'm laughing by the time he pulls me back into his arms.

"What's so funny?" he asks.

"She hates you," I reply.

"I think we were getting somewhere," he insists confidently. "It'll take some time, but I'll win her over."

"In all the years I've had people over to the house, she never, not once, *ever* refrained from inviting them to stay for dinner," I snicker against his shoulder. "You are number one on her shit list."

"Well, I was number one on yours, too, just a few hours ago," he suggests coyly. "Now look at us."

My smile fades, but I try to hide it from him. His statement scares me—as if this is all just a game of winning people over when you need to, not caring how you treat them when things change. "Don't be so certain," I try to say as jokingly as possible.

He's not worried and still has the same kind, innocent smile plastered on his face. One that I could very quickly get used to, but I'm worried that the moment I do…it will vanish.

Emmett gives me a long, slow kiss goodbye before we go downstairs. I have to stop myself from kissing him again just as he's about to walk out the door. I'm not ready for my mom to know for certain that something is going on between us again.

I watch him walk away down the sidewalk, in disbelief that all of this has happened. Emmett Jameson is back in my life. For better or for worse. I swallow a hard lump in my throat and force myself to go sit down with my mom and stepdad for dinner, trying to act as normal as possible.

# CHAPTER THREE

## BOOK 2

The next day, I return to school happier than I should be. Bernadette is still missing after all. But I can't deny how hopeful I am that something real is happening between Emmett and me. That maybe he really will prove himself to be a good person, who can treat me well now that he's out from under the influence of the other Elites.

Before WJ Prep, I had never worn a uniform before. Now, every day, it has become second nature to throw on a pleated skirt and monogrammed shirt and cardigan with the WJ logo. In the beginning it felt itchy and uncomfortable, but now I barely notice. I've even gotten used to carrying around a change of running clothes and can zip in between outfits like a superhero.

WJ Prep is like a cult where everyone is beautiful, frightening, and dangerous. Each at the mercy of their parents and committing the same acts of violence on the rest of the world that are committed on them at home. All the Elites care about is money and power.

This school is a different universe where the students are all perfect and gorgeous. You don't show up here on a bad hair day. It's nothing like my old school in Oklahoma, where everyone was frumpy and laid back. Most people there were poor like us, but here...I think our family is the only one without money.

I've learned to walk these halls with caution, but I'm still getting used to the feeling of that fear being gone. I can still remember being warned about them on my first day: "If they don't like you, then nobody does." The words have echoed through my mind endlessly since that first day. At first I thought I didn't care, but I quickly found out that not being liked around here is a lot more brutal than you'd think.

The Weis, Blackwater, Whitworth, and Nickelson families all teamed up with the town's founders, the Jamesons, and started the Jameson Automobile Company back in the 1800s. They make luxury cars for rich people. All of those families except one remain in the town and they are like gods around here. The only family that is left? The Nickelsons—part of which is now known as the Lopez family. As in Ophelia Lopez, my mother's maiden name, which she took back after leaving my dad… Theodore Nickelson, or Theo for short. Not that the connection has ever done me any favors. In fact, it has made my life much worse around here.

Shortly after Emmett and I met, I got a call from the Headmaster of Weis-Jameson Preparatory Academy offering me a full-ride scholarship for my senior year. My research found that their track and field program was nationally ranked and was responsible for numerous Olympic athletes. David Granger was the legendary coach of the team and a former bronze Olympian himself.

As I walk to class, trying to hide the persistent smile on my face, a pair of arms suddenly grabs me from behind. Given my past experiences at WJ Prep, I immediately shriek and try to break free from their grip, but I stop in shock when I see it's Emmett.

"You're back?" I gape, my heart still pounding from what I thought was an attack.

"Sorry, babe. I didn't mean to scare you," he answers casually, sliding his hands back around my waist and pulling me in for a kiss right there in the middle of the hallway.

"What are you doing?" I ask against his lips, looking around at the staring students passing by. It's too much to take in at once. Calling me 'babe,' the PDA.

"What do you mean?" he scoffs.

"People are looking at us," I inform him, cutting my eyes to the glaring girls in the corner.

"So? Are you embarrassed of me?" he laughs, pulling me to his side as we continue walking down the hall.

I remember Emmett and Vivian walking down these halls like this, side by side, their arms around each other and her hand in his back pocket. I refuse to mirror their image. I pull away from him and squeeze his hand in mine. Any small gesture to make me feel like we are different.

"I'm just...surprised is all," I explain, feeling like I'm experiencing some kind of emotional whiplash. "Guess I'm used to you keeping whatever this is between us under wraps."

"Things are different now. I'm not stuck with Vivian," he states plainly. "Besides...with all the rumors flying around about our family scandals...people need the distraction."

Any giddiness I felt rising inside me is quickly squashed. "Figures this would be a strategic social move for you." I roll my eyes.

"That..." he confesses reluctantly, "and I want everyone to know you're mine." He stops and whips me back around for another long, slow, unapologetic kiss.

"I never said I was yours," I tease him, biting at his lip. But the statement is true.

"Are you not?" he asks, with a deep voice and questioning eyes, but I can't bring myself to answer him.

Sure, he's broken up with Vivian, but I don't remember ever agreeing to take her place. And with that thought, Lily's words echo through my brain. The last time I talked to her, right before Emmett found me, she warned that I'd be the next Vivian—something I swore would never happen. No, agreeing to 'belong' to Emmett in some way does not automatically make me the same awful, shallow monster Vivian was. But I worry about what comes along with being his girlfriend. Does it open up a whole can of worms that leads to me being just as hardened and bitchy as she was?

As I stand there, trying to stammer through the start of a reply, my heart drops at the two figures leaning against the lockers down the hall.

"Oh, shit. Speak of the devil," I murmur. Emmett looks to me cluelessly. "Look." I nod toward Lily and Vivian's glaring faces. "I guess you're not the only one who decided to come back to school today. Why is Lily with Vivian?"

"Don't worry about them," he says, unconvincingly, but his head stays turned in their direction. He stares right back at them, and I can't tell if it's from interest or disgust.

"Oh, sorry...but the idea of you and Vivian in the same

building together is still pretty triggering for me…for a number of reasons," I reply bitterly, pulling his arm to regain his attention.

"Let's just focus on the present," he insists, turning too slowly to put his arm back around me. "Right now. The present, and moving forward."

"Easy for you to say," I mutter under my breath, but regrettably loud enough for him to hear.

"Hardly," he bites back. "You forget my sister is still missing."

"Of course, I haven't forgotten," I answer more softly, my head craning towards the two of them as we pass. "But what are they doing together? They don't look like they're fighting."

"I haven't seen them get along since freshman year." He keeps his eyes straight ahead now as we walk by, leaving them behind us.

"And even that was just a trick…so you could fuck with Lily," I remind him, feeling their eyes still burning into our backs.

"Well, she doesn't appear to have any hard feelings about it now," he states dismissively.

"She did with me yesterday," I snap, stopping to pull him around the corner. I put my arms on his shoulders to make him understand I'm serious. "Really, Emmett…if you could have heard the way Lily was talking about you and Vivian. Something's not right about this…they're acting like best friends."

"You're paranoid." He rubs my shoulders and kisses my forehead. "You have nothing to worry about with those two. They're basically outcasts now after the news of Vivian's parents' involvement in those sex trafficking rings. And Lily's been blacklisted for a while now. They don't have any more power here."

His words don't settle right with me. Outcasts. Blacklisted. Power. This is the kind of hierarchy Emmett is used to. I could be comforted knowing that by mere association, no one is going to fuck with me now that he's the only one left standing at the top. But these are exactly the kinds of things I want to avoid.

I let him walk me to class with my arms clenched tight around my chest as I try to wrap my head around everything. When I was the one being tortured by the old gang of Elites, it felt like time moved by in slow motion, but now, all at once it seems to have sped up and completely turned everything around.

We pass the can in the hall where I caught Emmett dumping trash on Lily just for talking to me. That was when I first realized he was the same boy who I'd met at the track meet earlier that summer. Only in the halls of WJ Prep, he didn't seem like the same boy at all. Nothing like the mysterious, funny, charming guy who lured me into a kiss even though I didn't know who he was. Here he was an animal with Vivian hanging by his side and their little pack.

I hate that nothing with him can ever just be what I want it to be. It's still hard to look at him without some bad memory popping up in my head. His sister's disappearance is looming, and now Vivian's back to make things even worse. But when he squeezes my hand and kisses my cheek before I walk into class, the thrill of it is almost enough to chase the rest away. At least temporarily.

My mind is like butter throughout the next period. Constantly sliding right over everything I'm supposed to be paying attention to and dripping back to thoughts of Emmett and the night before. It's a sort of daze I should be used to by now. For better or for worse, I've been in some form of it since the moment we first met.

After class, I can't help but frantically search the sea of scrambling students for Emmett's face. Caught in this distraction, I round the corner and accidently walk straight into another girl. I don't even have to look all the way up to realize it's Vivian, and of course she looks pissed. Just my luck.

"Well, if it isn't the little boyfriend-stealing skank herself," she jeers with cold eyes before I can even begin to attempt a half-hearted apology for running into her. It's no use saying sorry to her, anyway. She's going to hate me now more than ever.

Vivian is freakishly thin, yet still somehow curvy with perfectly manicured nails and a relentlessly pissed look always plastered on her face. She keeps her blonde, curly hair up in perfectly tight buns that frame her pouty, red lips. She is intimidating and beautiful. And Emmett's ex-girlfriend. A fact that seemed irrelevant until she was standing in front of me.

"Fuck off, Vivian. I'm not in the mood," I bark, turning to move past her.

"What's wrong? Troubles with Emmett?" Lily taunts, popping out from beside Vivian to block my path.

Lily is several inches shorter than me with long, brown hair that goes smooth and straight down her entire back. She has hazel-green eyes that used to be the only kind and friendly sight I would encounter in these halls, but now they've turned fiery and malicious. She wears a snarling grin that matches Vivian's.

Her dad works in real estate, buying properties and renting them out, and probably manages the very property my mom and Brendan rent. He also dabbles in stocks, like all the dads around here do. But her dad is especially skilled with it. Her family was blacklisted by the Elites when her dad refused to day trade a ridiculous amount of money from the Jameson Automobile Company. That's how Lily and I became friends, but apparently the standards have changed now that all the Elites are under investigation.

"What's gotten into you?" I scoff. "Why the hell are you with her!?"

"Well, since you turned out to be a backstabbing, lying cunt...I had to find an ally somewhere," she replies callously.

"This isn't a game of survivor, Lily," I insist, knowing this is a pointless argument to make. But this isn't the Lily I know. "It's just life. You don't have to be so calculating. I thought you were better than those kinds of games."

"I could say the same about you," she snaps back through pursed lips.

"I don't know what you're talking about. I haven't done anything to you," I defend myself, shaking my head in exasperation. I still don't have a clue as to why Lily hates me so much. Much less why she has joined forces with Vivian.

"My dad is going to prison, you dumb bitch," Vivian burns into me. "We're losing almost everything. And it's all your fault!"

"I didn't have anything to do with that!" I gawk back at her. "If your dad didn't want to go to prison, then maybe he shouldn't have been selling underage girls on the black market."

"Shut your fucking mouth!" She wags her finger in my face. "You don't know what you're talking about."

"I don't have to, but the police sure do," I reply bitterly, cowering slightly at her stance. I've slapped Vivian once before, and I'd gladly do it again. But I did not walk into school today prepared for a fight. I've grown too used to the peace and quiet of the past couple of weeks.

"What the hell is going on here?!" Emmett's voice booms out from a few feet away.

"There you are," Vivian coos, her voice immediately turning sickeningly soft and sweet as she races over to drape her arms around his neck. My stomach churns at the sight of it. "I knew it wouldn't take you long to come back around."

"Back off, Vivian," he growls, but he doesn't move an inch.

"I don't think either of us really want that," she says suggestively, trailing a finger across his jawline. I am just about to walk over and snap her finger until it breaks when Lily intervenes.

"Come on, Vivian." She tugs at her arm, keeping an angry stare glued on me. "Let's let the two lovebirds give each other all of their STDs."

"Clever," I snap sarcastically as they shoulder bump me on their way past. I am left fuming and glaring straight at Emmett. "Thanks a lot," I hiss at him with clenched fists.

"What are you talking about? I came as soon as I saw," he whines defensively.

"You didn't lift a finger to get her off of me," I grumble. "Much less to get her off of you."

"Because that's what she wants," he says with a subtle roll of his eyes, completely unmoved by all of it.

"What are you talking about?" I am still stiff against him as he puts his arm around me.

"She just wants my hands on her again. She doesn't care if it's good or bad," he explains casually.

"That's so fucked up," I reply, shaking my head. But I regret the words the minute they fall from my mouth, and of course he doesn't miss a beat.

"You used to be the same way," he reminds me as a hard lump forms in my throat.

Is this really all so normal to him? To have girls falling all over him to the point that they'd endure his anger and violent temper just to get his attention? I've known it was a fucked up state for me for a while now, but I never expected that Vivian could stumble so low just as easily.

"Don't remind me," I mumble. "So, wait…you're saying you get off on that? Is that how you like your girls to be?"

"Don't be ridiculous," he scoffs. "What you and I have is nothing like what was going on between Vivian and me."

"In what way?" I push him further, needing to understand exactly what I am signing up for. Or apparently, what I have already signed up for.

"You know what way," he insists as we continue walking. We've gone too slow and the halls are quiet now, with full classrooms behind the passing doors. These are the kinds of things Emmett can get away with, and I can only hope I am now granted the same privileges.

"Come on, stop torturing yourself like this," he continues in the face of my silence. "The only reason you don't have some crazed ex-boyfriend for me to be jealous of is because this is your first year here."

"So, we'll save that for next year?" I joke, desperately needing everything to stop feeling so heavy. But he's not amused.

"Don't joke like that," he snaps sternly. "I'm not letting you go any time soon. As long as we're under this roof together, you're mine."

"You didn't feel that way when I first came," I remind him, recoiling from the memories and my need to not only remember, but not to let him forget it either.

"Yes, I did," he blurts, turning and pushing me against a wall. "I just couldn't express it the way I wanted to. And now that I have you…you're not going anywhere."

He towers over me possessively as he slides a strand of hair from my face and leans into kiss me. I want to be turned off by his hypocrisy and the way he insists I belong to him. I want to tell him what I have said before, which is that I don't belong to anyone but myself. But my arms fall limp as I melt against his tongue. And suddenly it seems ridiculous to even try and convince myself that I don't belong to Emmett. It seems that I do, whether I like it or not.

Emmett sits with me at lunch that day and acts like everything is totally normal. But Vivian and Lily are sitting a few tables across from us, cackling like hyenas. They're staring so much I feel uncomfortable, and it's obvious they're making fun of us. Or rather, making fun of me. No matter how angry they are with Emmett, it seems he will always be the golden child who can't be subjected to the full force of anyone's wrath.

The WJ Prep cafeteria has buffets and grills that can serve up just about anything you want, ranging from steak to sushi. They even have an in-house pastry chef for desserts, and of course, keep vegan, gluten-free, lactose-free, and sugar-free options for certain girls' diets. Ahem, *Vivian*. And now Lily.

The Elites used to always sit at the table in the very center of the room, commanding everyone's attention as their cackles echoed out through the cafeteria that's more like a lavish dining hall in a fancy hotel. Always in the spotlight. Always the center of attention. The kinds of things that were beginning to fall by the wayside in the short period they were gone. But now here I sit with Emmett, and I have no fucking clue what to think about it.

"Why don't they hate you?" I ask bitterly, pushing food around on my tray as I glare back at them resentfully. "It was your dad that led everyone into this mess, wasn't it?"

"What makes you think they don't hate me?" he suggests, completely unbothered and chowing down on his sandwich.

I watch them more closely, noting how their expressions differ from him to me. They look at him with glinting eyes, hoping he'll glance in their direction. They jeer and taunt at me, and I know they're thinking I shouldn't be the one sitting here with him.

"They have stars in their eyes for you," I reply. "They look at me like a bug that needs to be squashed."

Emmett shrugs and continues eating. His cavalier attitude about it all is maddening. I would have expected his possessiveness to make him act a little more protective over me than this, but I guess that doesn't apply to ex-girlfriends. The growing uneasiness inside gets larger by the second. I'm not so sure I can carry on ignoring them if he's not going to lift a single finger to try and stop it.

"Couldn't you try some of the things you used to do to me?" I ask in frustration. "Blacklist her? Have everyone ignore her or make her life hell until she backs off?"

His eyes widen, and I cringe at the hint of disappointment in them. "For as much as you've shamed me for how I acted towards you, now you want me to do the exact same thing to someone else? That's rich," he answers harshly, throwing a crumpled napkin down on his empty tray. "You know I only went along with all of that because I had to. Those are Vivian's kind of tricks, not mine. Also…it's unnerving that you'd look down on all of those things until they serve whatever purpose you have in mind. Whatever benefits you."

I want to cry as he gets up and walks away without saying

another word. For one thing, Vivian and Lily saw him looking tense and angry before storming off, and they're currently delighting in the whole scene. Second, he's right. And that makes Lily right, too. One day by his side in this school, and I am no better than Vivian.

"Emmett, wait!" I call out, getting up to chase after him. Vivian and Lily erupt in mocking laughter as I go, but I do my best to ignore them.

He's already back in the hall by the time I catch up with him. I pull at his arm, but he barely stops for me. "What the hell!" I snap, taken aback by his behavior. "I know what slipped out from me was fucked up, but why are you acting this way? You humiliated me in there in front of them when you knew I was already on edge!"

He's fuming as he stares back at me, unable to respond.

"It's not fair," my voice cracks. "You two treated me like shit. Am I still bitter? Hell yes, I'm bitter. This whole thing is fucked up. But why are you acting like I'm the bad guy for being upset over all of this?"

"How long can you punish me for all of that?" He throws his arms up in exasperation. "I've told you…I can't change the past."

"I'm not asking you to change the past." I swallow hard. "I'm asking you to fix things right now! And you're too busy placating Vivian to even listen to me!"

"Look, you knew Vivian would probably be back at school eventually," he snaps back. "This is only day one. If you can't handle it now…how's this going to work? I thought you were ready to deal with things like this when you…"

"When I what!?" I thunder, slamming my fists to his chest. "When I got myself into this with you? Right, but I didn't exactly get myself into it, did I? You're the one who came to me and roped me back in."

"You knew what you were doing," he smirks coldly.

"Obviously not," I fume before turning on my heels and storming off.

He quickly runs up behind me and grabs me, spinning me back around to face him. He shakes me with both hands firmly gripping my shoulders. "You didn't know what you were getting into?" he questions. "Is that what you think? You didn't realize this was going to be hard? Fuck, Ophelia. I'm trying my best… but you know who I am. You know what comes with me."

"Vivian?" I raise my brow sharply.

"We have a history. Yes. But that doesn't have anything to do with you," he argues.

"It does when she's marching up to us in the halls and putting her hands all over you while you do nothing!" I scream.

He quickly puts his hand over my mouth to muffle my voice and jerks me over to a corner. "Stop acting this way," he demands. "Everyone is going to be talking about this."

"I thought you didn't care about what everyone thought anymore!" I shoot back, still defiantly loud. "You're right…this is just day one of her being back. Day one of you being back. And things are already like this. This obviously isn't going to work!"

"What do you need?" he softens and pleads with me. "Tell me what to do, Ophelia. I can't lose you. I just want you to be happy."

I look away, shaking my head. I don't even know what I want now. He was right. I knew what came with him and I knew what I was getting myself into. And I am just as stuck as he is. I don't want to lose him either.

"I just want her to know you're with me," I answer quietly. "That you don't want her anymore."

He leans in and pushes his lips to mine. I respond urgently, pushing my tongue in between his lips. He pins me against the wall as he's sucked into the kiss, and we both lose ourselves there for a minute before he finally pulls back.

"She knows," he pants, looking down on me intensely. "That's why she's acting this way. She knows what happened between her and me doesn't hold a flame to what you and I have."

"How do I know for sure?" I push. "How do *I* know what you had doesn't hold a flame to this?"

"How do you *not* know?" he gapes, looking disappointed. "You really think this is all just some game to me? That I'm just jerking you around?"

I shrug, looking down to my feet. I know he needs to hear me say I believe in him, that I believe in us. But everything's happening so fast with all of them coming back here on the same day. It's too much to take in all at once, and I'm terrified of things going back to the way they were before.

"I know you think it's terrible," I mutter. "But if you could just put her in her place somehow. Make her back off…"

His eyes widen and his hands pull back. I wince in anticipation of an explosion, but he freezes. His face drops in exhaustion. He purses his lips to the side as he looks around and then back to me, not knowing what to do. I am backing him into a corner—one he's not used to being in. I don't know what Vivian did when she was jealous of me, but it didn't matter. Emmett had already made up his mind by then that he'd be with me if he could. Now I have him, and I'm not going to let her take him away.

"I need everyone to know you're only with me now. That she doesn't matter to you anymore," I continue, rambling insecurely, pushing him closer to the edge. I know I should stop, but I can't. I am too exposed and afraid of her coming between us.

"I don't have time to worry about this high school drama bullshit!" he fires back through clenched teeth, the muscles in his neck straining. "I thought coming back here today and being with you would help take my mind off things with my sister, so I could think more clearly about what to do next. But now I wish I'd just stayed home alone!"

"I'm sorry," I offer lightly, still not entirely won over by his argument. "I know you're under a lot of stress, I just…I just wasn't prepared to deal with Vivian today, much less to see her teamed up with Lily. And I wish there was something you could do to make them lay off." He looks around despondently, still not offering to help in any way.

I do feel guilty and try to convince myself this is all trivial stuff I should just ignore. But I know Vivian and what she's capable of. If Emmett doesn't put a stop to it, it's only going to get worse from here. I stand in silence, deciding not to keep pushing him while he's like this. He murmurs something and walks off, leaving me standing alone and feeling terrible.

Of course, when I turn around Vivian and Lily are standing right there, watching everything. As I go to chase after Emmett, I accidentally turn my unzipped bag in the wrong direction, sending its contents scattering across the floor, including an assortment of condoms and tampons—the two worst things to be picking up off the middle of the floor with Vivian and Lily leering over me. They erupt into giggles, teasing me as I struggle to gather everything back together, but I drown them out.

# CHAPTER FOUR

### BOOK 2

I turn to face Vivian and Lily's pleased, judgmental faces, cringing over the satisfaction there after seeing Emmett and me fighting. Especially with me chasing after him as he stormed off twice in a row.

"Ready to give him up yet?" Vivian taunts menacingly. "Everyone knows he's only with you out of some weird survivor's guilt over everything that's happened. And it's only a matter of time before he realizes that, ditches you, and comes running back to me."

For once, Lily seems somewhat bothered by Vivian's remarks, but she still does nothing to come to my defense.

"You have no idea what you're talking about, Vivian. So just back off." I turn to walk away, feeling in no mood to get into another verbal sparring match with her.

"And you have no idea what he needs," she shoots back before I can get away. "Things won't stay like this forever, Sooner or later, Emmett won't be in the position he's in now. And he won't know how to live without that kind of money and power. My family will be back on top and he'll come crawling back to mooch off of us…"

She keeps rambling as I round the corner and push through the back doors of the school. I try to note everything she's said to bring up with Emmett later. She could just be blowing hot air on false, narcissistic confidence. Or she could be alluding to what's happening with Bernadette.

My stomach rumbles as I push through the chilly air, realizing I shouldn't have been so quick to abandon my lunch and chase after Emmett. Now I'm cold and hungry and really have no clue where I'm walking to. I only know I don't want to be inside of the school and run any risk of dealing with Vivian and Lily again.

Realizing I'm storming through the school yard aimlessly, I finally stop and take a seat beneath a large tree. Thankfully, the sun is angled in just the right way to provide some warmth as I rest my back against the bark. I close my eyes and lay my head back, feeling sick over how the day is going.

I didn't expect Emmett to be back today but walking through the halls with him all over me felt redemptive in a way. It felt like the rest of the Elites had fallen down to where they belonged—shamed, out of sight, and out of mind. But then Lily and Vivian had to pop up out of nowhere, and now Emmett and I are fighting. Right in front of them at that—giving them just the ammunition against me they needed.

Why couldn't Emmett have just told them off? Who cares what Vivian wants or doesn't want…what about me and my feelings? I'm frustrated that my needs always seem to come second to hers, even when she's not his girlfriend anymore.

When I first came to WJ Prep, I was captivated by the Elites and their endless, tormenting games. Caught up in their maze, never knowing what to expect next, but it was never good. Then Emmett took me prisoner, and I thought once I was free that would be the end of it. But he still has me held captive. I'm starting to wonder if I will ever be free. Even if things between us end one day, I can't imagine not being haunted by all that has happened between us.

"You're in my spot." A guy's voice suddenly pierces through my circling thoughts.

"Excuse me?" I shriek back, bolting my head forward in expectation of yet another bully waiting to strike. But instead I'm surprised to see Malcolm Henderson standing there with a gentle smile on his face. "Oh, it's you. I haven't seen you since…" I trail off, remembering the eerie night when he and his father, supposedly by order of my father, met with me in an abandoned warehouse out in the middle of nowhere. It was right after that Emmett and his cronies ended up taking me captive.

Malcolm Henderson and his dad, Liam, are the owners and

founders of a software company that services the Jameson Automobile Company. Malcolm and Emmett are already ex-friends who don't like each other, but I have been especially curious to see how things turn out now that Emmett is in charge of everything. The Jameson Automobile Company used Malcolm's software to run extortion rings of politicians, and modified it to create a black market for underage girls. A sex trafficking ring.

Malcolm is tall and slender with creamy pale skin, sandy blonde hair that he keeps spiked up, and kind, pale blue eyes. His chest is narrow, but chiseled, and sits on top of long legs that spider out around him.

"I hear it's been quite eventful for you since then." He smirks sympathetically, nodding to the sunny seat in the grass next to me. "Mind if I join you? I normally hide out here to eat lunch."

"Sure, but only if you've got enough in there for both of us." I eye his full and unopened bag of McDonald's, thinking how ironic it is for him to be eating that considering that's where I was ordered to go alone before he picked me up.

"I believe I just might." He smiles before spreading out on the ground and opening the bag.

"How did you have enough time to pick that up, anyway?" I ask as I accept a small handful of fries.

"One of our assistants brings it to me every day," he explains casually. "I promise it's not always fast food though. Sometimes they bring food from the cooks in our kitchen at home. You know, healthier stuff."

He talks about it all as if it's so ordinary. I wonder if he even has a clue that the average home doesn't come with assistants for food delivery or a kitchen full of private chefs. "Healthy is good." I nod awkwardly, feeling suddenly in way over my head.

"I'm just kidding." He bursts into laughter. "I skip out early on third period, just long enough to go grab something and bring it back here where I hide out to eat."

"Oh...sorry..." I laugh uncomfortably. "I guess I just thought...well..."

"That I was that spoiled and rich?" He grins.

"Aren't you?" I blurt coldly. I almost feel bad, but really, I'm genuinely curious.

He nods bashfully. "Okay, fair enough." His face lights up as he looks over at me with perfect shining white teeth. "True...my family does have enough money for things like chefs and assistants. And we do have those things, but we weren't always so rich. We never got into the habit of relying on those things too heavily."

"Ah," I grunt as he hands me one of the burgers from his bag. "New money?"

"It's what the Elites hate about us," he answers frankly. "But I'm sure you can relate. Your dad has money, after all. And he's just as despised by the Elites…especially now."

I shift in the grass, wanting to talk about anything besides my father. Especially because I have no idea if Malcolm is someone I can really trust, or how connected he is with Theo.

"My father probably does have money, but that doesn't have anything to do with my family," I confess bitterly. "My mom and stepdad have always worked their asses off to support me on their own. I'm sure our lifestyle is nothing like what your family has grown used to, but I'm not complaining. We're happy. At least as long as Theo and the rest of the Elites stay out of our lives, anyway."

Malcolm purses his lips in a grimaced nod before taking a big bite of his burger. We eat like that in silence for a moment until I finally start to feel a little pathetic for sounding so bitter.

"I'm sorry if you and your dad are really close to Theo or whatever," I add, embarrassed, realizing I've probably already said way too much. "I just don't have the best first impression of him."

"Just distant business partners," he says softly. "Don't worry. You're allowed to hate your father. I wouldn't like him either if I were you."

I'm taken aback by his understanding, which is more than I'd expected. "How much do you know about everything that happened after we met with your father that night?" I ask him, feeling on edge thinking about just where he falls into all of this.

"Well, I'm sure your perspective would take the cake." He raises his brows. "But I don't expect you to tell me anything. I wouldn't put you in that spot. I've heard enough to piece things together. My father and I didn't know everything Theo had planned, but after hearing about what happened to Emmett's dad…we made assumptions…ones that are probably pretty accurate."

I grow quiet, wishing we could change the subject. The fact that he said 'what happened to' Emmett's dad gives away the fact that everyone is well aware it wasn't a suicide, and he obviously has his own conclusions about my father's involvement. I want to stay as far away from it all as I can, so I go back to eating without saying a word.

"I guess it's no wonder I never see you around school much," I blurt finally, blotting food away from the corner of my mouth. "If you're always hiding out here for lunch."

"I try to stay out of all the bullshit around here," he replies.

"I thought it had all calmed down," I murmur. "Until today."

"Yeah, I thought I saw Vivian lurking around earlier," he offers empathetically.

"And Lily…who is apparently her new best friend," I add, with a resentful slump.

"Ah, so I guess the rules of who runs the school still change overnight." He laughs. "Why am I not surprised?"

"I don't know how all of you put up with it." I shake my head and crumple an empty burger wrapper in my hand before shooting it into the nearby bag. "I haven't even been here a full semester and I'm already over it. I can't imagine growing up like this."

"I didn't grow up like this," he reminds me. "But it wasn't much better where I'm from in California. Worse maybe, because there were more people with even more money. Imagine ten groups of the Elites all battling it out with each other."

"What a nightmare!" I gape. "How the hell did you put up with that?"

"Just like I do here." He motions around to our secluded spot on the edge of the schoolyard. "I keep my head down and stay out of it all as much as I can. I don't need to rely on the approval of the Elites. My father built his own fortune and has taught me everything I need to know to run it one day. Nothing we do is dependent on the Elites."

"Which is great, considering they just ran everything into the ground," I scoff, still surprised that Vivian can show up and be so bold after the scandal her family is facing. "How are you and your father's software company holding up, by the way? I take it the authorities don't suspect you two of having anything to do with the sex trafficking rings?"

He shakes his head quietly, seeming disturbed by just how close they came to going down with the rest of the Elites. "We're free and clear."

I study Malcolm leaning back in the sun, closing his eyes against its rays. He seems so above all the WJ Prep drama, and I can't help but wish Emmett could be more like him. Emmett claims to want nothing to do with any of it, but somehow he always finds himself at the center of it all. I guess there's no escaping it, considering his father was the Elites' ringleader, a role that has essentially been passed onto him, only now the rest of the Elites are facing time in prison.

"Hey, don't let Vivian and Lily get to you," he says suddenly, as I realize we've swapped roles. Now he's studying me as I drift away into my own tangle of thoughts. "Those two are just in rough spots because of everything that's happened. They're desperate and grasping at straws. They think you and Emmett are the easiest targets to get a rise out of so they can still feel some sense of control."

"It's working," I confess shamefully. "I know I shouldn't let them get to me, but that's why they're so evil. They know exactly how to push your buttons." It feels strange to be talking about Lily as if she's one of them, even though as the day goes on, I'm slowly accepting it as true. "I just can't believe Lily could turn like that," I add. "She seemed different. And her family has nothing to do with all this trouble the rest of them are in."

"Maybe her motivations are different," he suggests, just as we see a few groups of students huddling around outside for some last-minute fresh air before lunch is over.

Lily and Vivian are hiding out in an alley nestled in the middle of the building. Emmett is conveniently not far away, but he seems to be looking for someone. Hopefully he's looking for me.

We watch as Emmett's eyes search through the parking lot and outer campus, before he finally turns and freezes when he sees the two of us sitting together. I expect him to come over, but instead, he awkwardly turns and slowly walks back inside.

"I guess you two are officially a thing now?" Malcolm asks with a strange smile. I almost hear a tinge of jealousy in his voice, and I hate the way it excites me. I can't tell if I want Malcolm to be jealous because he is so nice and good-looking, or if I just want to get back at Emmett somehow.

"You must think I'm a monster." I shake my head with an embarrassed smile. "You probably know more than I think you do about how he's treated me…I'm sure everyone does. And now I'm with him like some sick girl with Stockholm syndrome."

"I don't think you're sick or a monster," he replies sincerely, with a subtle lean towards me. "People are complicated. Nothing is ever as simple as it seems. You seem like a smart girl, so if you're with Emmett…I'm sure you have a good reason."

His words burn me deep. A few hours ago, I would have thought I had a million good reasons—with just as many bad ones, too. But now the only things that come to mind to explain Emmett's and my relationship are uncontrollable urges. Like a car wreck I can't stop staring at. And I know trying to explain that to anyone else would sound like nothing more than teenage hormones that I just can't get a grip on.

"What if I don't have a good reason?" I murmur quietly, half-hoping he won't hear it. I feel terrible for even saying it out loud, and I wonder if it's some weird cry for help seeping out.

Our eyes lock for too long as our faces grow serious. I wonder if I wouldn't be better off going for someone like Malcolm, who manages to stay far away from the Elites' pull. Even when their software company was threatened by their wrongdoings, the Hendersons only got involved long enough to keep their names clear so they could focus on their work.

Malcolm is just as good-looking as Emmett, only nicer. He's kind in an effortless way that makes me feel safe…and has ever since the first night he took me to meet with his father. And he seems to like me. At least enough to share his food with me and to look at me the way he is now, as if he's waiting for any hint or sign that it would be okay for him to make a move.

The only thing that's missing is the powerful, inescapable, magnetic draw that emanates from Emmett. As much as I want to like Malcolm in my head, because it makes more sense and seems like it would be easier and simpler, my heart and body just don't feel inflamed in the same way as they do with Emmett. And maybe that's what makes it a healthier attraction, but it doesn't make it more appealing.

Any hint of a spark I want to exist between us quickly falls flat. "Forget what I said," I announce suddenly, as we both let out sharply exhale at the weakened tension between us. "I do have good reasons. Lots of them," I lie. "It's just been a hard day. Emmett's going through a hard time."

"So then maybe you should be with him," Malcolm bites back, sounding jealous and accusing as he stands from his seat and swipes the grass and dirt from his pants. He seems mad, but that doesn't stop him from extending a hand down to help me up.

I put my hand into his in surprise as he hoists me up. But once I am on my feet again, I quickly begin shaking the grass from my own pants and hurrying to gather my things. I don't want to risk any surprising moments that could happen if we keep looking at each other with my hand in his. I catch a subtle nod of acceptance in the corner of my eye as he begins to gather his things as well.

"Well, it's about time for our next class," I say too loudly, bobbing my head while still standing frozen to that spot.

"Guess so," he says, mocking my body language and tone.

"Okay, then," I breathe out, as I finally start to walk away, but I can't stop myself from turning to face him one last time. "Malcolm, you're a really nice guy."

"Hey, Ophelia." He throws his hands up in surrender. "You don't have to placate me," he explains with a nervous smile. "I mean, you're an incredibly attractive and sexy girl...with the brains and personality to match. I can't say that I wouldn't be happy if you and Emmett weren't a thing, but you deserve to make your own mind up about these things. And I'm not lonely or anything...believe me."

His tone turns cocky at the end of it, which should gross me out. But instead I am filled with a surge of burning desire. His complimentary confession makes my heart swell, and the implication that he has no trouble with girls sounds like a challenge. Like I am passing up on goods in high-demand. I shake my head, hating the way my own thoughts are beginning to sound.

"All of this entanglement with the Elites is fucking with my head, I think," I confess, blushing over my thoughts in combination with the things I suggested to Emmett earlier. "But you are a nice guy. And you seem like a good friend. Maybe one I need to have around to keep me grounded in all of this."

"Deal," he answers, holding out his hand. "Friends to keep each other clear-headed in this nightmarish jungle."

I shake his hand and practically sprint away as fast as I can, before any more revealing thoughts pop into my head, or worse...out of my mouth. The rest of the day feels off, but in a good way. I appear to be momentarily free from Emmett's sex-hazed state of mind, and instead find it easier than ever to throw myself into schoolwork as an escape.

For three more blissful periods, I barely think about him, Vivian, Lily, or even Malcolm at all. It's as if our short little encounter on the edge of the schoolyard, and the edge of the lingering Elites' drama, allowed me to come up for air and set myself straight again.

# CHAPTER FIVE

BOOK 2

I continue feeling clear-headed well into track practice that afternoon. There's no reason to feel this way, other than that little bit of time with Malcolm, which was surprisingly and inexplicably refreshing. I wonder if that's how it would feel all the time if Emmett was out of the picture and anything ever happened with Malcolm, or even just someone like Malcolm. Someone who hasn't tortured and kidnapped me, and then somehow roped me into forgiving him through his own family drama.

But it really doesn't matter. My clear head doesn't make things any less confusing. There are Malcolm's good looks and kindness to complicate our agreed-upon friendship, and Emmett is still mad at me as far as I know. And Vivian and Lily are likely just waiting for their next chance to strike at me. With Vivian at school again and Lily as her newfound sidekick, sharing a sudden and renewed hatred toward me, I'm forced back to beginning every day in dreaded anticipation of what will happen.

But all of that easily drifts away as I run through my laps. Fall is setting in, sprinkling orange and yellow leaves across the track that blow up in clouds around us as we run through them, our sneakers crunching across the ground with each sharp step. I love the way the cool breeze feels against my hot skin, and I can barely see faint traces of my breath in the air.

My thigh muscles ripple with power, my pounding steps in

rhythm with my sharp and heavy breaths. The chord to my headphones bounces against my chest as heavy rock beats boom in my ears, drowning out everything else around me. I feel like I could run even faster and keep going like that for hours. It may have been harder to run when things were at their worst with the Elites, but I'm back in full force now and can't seem to get enough.

Coach Granger watches me carefully, as he always does, as I continue racing through my runner's high. But he's been strangely quiet ever since his and my conveniently-timed, simultaneous disappearances.

Coach Granger has always been my glimmer of hope in this hellhole. He's always told me that I could come to him for anything, and I could always count on him for the warmth that everyone else lacked. Which is crazy because he is not what you would call a warm person. He is serious and stern, his eyes always wide and intensely focused, like his head is always in the sport, pushing through another mile.

We'd both subtly hinted at our suspicions about his family troubles happening right around the same time I was kidnapped, as if someone was trying to get him out of the picture so he wouldn't be able to help or protect me in any way. But ever since then, he has been strangely quiet towards me.

He studies me with a distant look in his eye, as if he's still trying to figure everything out before we talk about it more. I can only guess at what is going through his mind, as I still have no idea exactly what tore him away for those couple of weeks.

The unspoken words that still seem to hang between us only make me run harder. I need the release. Each sharp breath through my pounding feet and burning muscles seems to push everything a million miles away.

I am dreading the return of my anxiety once practice is over. I rush into the locker room and go through the motions, hoping to get changed quickly and then breeze through homework and dinner at home before crashing into bed. I've learned the key to outrunning my worries about everything that's been happening is to stay busy.

I step behind the curtain into the shower and turn on the water, which sends billows of steam up into the air to join what's rising from the other showers. I try to ignore the gross clump of stringy hair floating on top of the drain at my feet. I can remember when my own hair was coming out in handfuls like this in the shower from all the stress Emmett and the Elites had me under.

I want to think we've come so far since then. That everything is so different between Emmett and me now. But there is a daunting sense that the worst isn't over yet. I quickly remember these are exactly the kinds of thoughts I was hoping to avoid for the rest of the day and turn the water off, sending the returning cold shivering across my skin.

After patting myself down with a couple of towels and slipping into my clean, post-run sweats, I am out the door and back to thinking about normal things, like wondering what my mom is making for dinner. When I returned home after that short absence, she finally noticed just how much weight I had lost since starting WJ Prep and quickly took it on as her personal mission to fatten me up.

As a runner, I can't afford to be running on empty, and my figure is finally rounding back out to normal as she stuffs me full of her best dishes every night. Even on nights when she works late, she has made a habit of taking long lunches to come home and cook dinner. Of course, Brendan helps when he can. I have told them not to worry and that I'm more than happy to cook for myself, but they insist that it makes them feel good to take care of me in that way.

I keep a steady pace towards my car as I imagine what she must have baking this evening, but I quickly realize nothing will be as easy as I hoped when I get closer. Emmett is leaning against the driver's side door waiting for me. The closer I get, the more I can see the furious look on his face.

"Hey," I call casually once I'm close enough, hoping to gauge his mood before we're face to face. He says nothing but his eyes keep burning into me, making me slow down from caution. "Something wrong?"

With sullen eyes, I can see a suppressed growl roll through his throat. "Have you been avoiding me?" he asks, doing a terrible job at releasing his clenched teeth as he talks.

"No, I thought you were mad at me." I move past him to throw my bag into the backseat, wishing he'd move so I could get in and drive away. I want to see him, but not when he's angry like this.

"Is that why you were talking to Malcolm?" he fumes, clicking everything into place in my mind.

"You jealous?" I ask lightly, hoping to pass everything off as no big deal.

"Should I be?" he barks back. He sharply blows a string of hair from his eyes and crosses his arms. "Is that why you were with him? To make me jealous?" A gentle booming roar rises within every word. I can tell his rage is bubbling up, but he's trying his best to keep it contained.

My heart swells with shame as I think of what really happened with Malcolm. I didn't just flirt with him and think about what things could be like with him. I compared him to Emmett, and that feels like the biggest betrayal of all. He's already paranoid enough that he's not what I deserve, and I used his biggest insecurities to compare him to Malcolm.

Who's to say Malcolm wouldn't be just as fucked up behind closed doors? I know that's not true. Emmett is not my first boyfriend. I know not all guys are like this. There are plenty of them who don't get physically violent. Plenty who aren't as fucked up as Emmett. But I feel awful for even thinking about that. And now I am standing here swearing there is nothing going on, when I knew I was flirting with disaster the whole time.

"I was just having lunch with a friend, Emmett," I explain sternly. "I'm allowed to do that."

"So, you consider Malcolm to be a friend?" He looms over me, pushing his palm against the car on the other side of me, boxing me in with his arms and shoulders.

"What's your fucking problem?" I snap finally. "You're creeping me out. You were the one who got all pissed at me because I expected you to stand up for me against your psychotic ex-girlfriend. Forgive me for wanting a break from all of your mood swings."

His nostrils flare as he takes it all in. "A break," he scoffs. I immediately know I've crossed some sort of invisible line. He snaps suddenly, grabbing me by the arm and forcing me away towards his car that's parked a few spaces down.

"What the fuck, Emmett!?" I shriek, looking around to see if anyone is nearby to witness this. With no one in sight, he shuffles me to his car and pushes me inside. Instinctively, I look to the backseat expecting to see all the things that tell me I'm in trouble. The same kinds of things that made me try to get away from him when he lured me into his car once before. Rope and gloves. But thankfully it appears to be clear.

"You're coming with me," he demands as he slides into the driver's seat. "We need to talk."

"Going with you where!?" I yell out in shock. "Why can't we just talk here!? I don't want to go right you right now, Emmett! I want to go home!"

"No," he roars back, continuing to drive despite my obvious fear. "I'm taking you to my hotel room."

"What hotel room!?" I shout, feeling completely confused.

"Things were getting too intense at home with Bernadette being missing. Mom's been acting weird. I rented a room to get away from it all, and it makes me feel safer," he explains with a strange calmness, which is somewhat comforting. At least he's not seeing red to the point of wordlessly forcing me to go along with him whether I like it or not, except he *is* still forcing me along despite my refusal.

His hands clench around the steering wheel with wide eyes and flaring nostrils. He is completely on edge with tunnel vision focused on the road ahead. He's determined to get me away as fast as he can. To carry me off to some place where it's just him and me, and no one else can get to me.

"I need you to tell me right now if anything happened between you," he fumes in desperation. "I don't just mean if anything was reciprocated. Did he touch you in any way? Make a pass at you?"

"No! Nothing happened!" I insist, but my tone lacks the certainty he needs.

"I just can't stand the thought of it." The veins and muscles in his neck strain and his voice cracks with a guttural roar.

"Fine, you don't have to," I continue, shrugging pensively. "I just told you nothing happened. So just let it go! Better yet, take me back to my car so I can go home!"

"Nothing happened, but you suddenly don't want to be with me?" he suggests defeatedly.

"You're being ridiculous!" I shout back. I struggle for a moment to find the right words. "What happened to everything you were saying earlier? You think I'm supposed to be so certain that this thing between us is so solid and important, enough not to let Vivian get to me, but you're completely unhinged just a few hours later over the exact same thing. You're a hypocrite."

"It's not the same." He shakes his head. "Vivian and Malcolm are two totally different animals."

"Agreed!" I shout bitterly. "Malcolm is actually nice and was just trying to be my friend. Vivian is an evil, conniving bitch who is intentionally trying to stir things up between us."

"You don't know Malcolm the way I do," he replies grimly. "Nothing about him is nice. He's doing everything you think Vivian is doing and you can't even see it."

I look over to him shifting madly in his seat as he speeds along. The engine revs every time he raises his voice, like he is completely out of control. I just keep thinking this isn't good. I have just taken him back into my life and given this thing a chance, and so far it's been nothing but jealous shouting matches.

And I hate the way I'm getting off on it. It's like what he said in my room yesterday; it's the rush. The thrill of being together. It's intoxicating. Even now, as I'm furious and watching him spiral out of control, I want him more than ever. I would fight harder to get him to take me home, but I want to go with him to his hotel room. Because I know what will inevitably happen when we get there.

I inhale sharply in anticipation, but I try to maintain my scowl. I don't want to let him off the hook so easily. He should think I'm still pissed. That thought scares me. Now I'm being just as calculating and manipulative as Vivian. I really am turning into her. I feel a sudden urge to fling open the car door and take off running. I can't let myself turn into her. I have to be better than that.

Once again, Malcolm's kind, smiling eyes creep into my brain. Maybe he's the key to making sure I stay far away from the danger of the new Elites, which just might very well include me if things keep going this way. I don't care who my father is, I don't want to be like those people.

"Are you thinking about him?" Emmett asks suddenly.

"Who?" I blurt defensively, playing dumb. He glares over at me, not falling for it. My gaze darts around, trying to avoid his questioning stare. "No, I wasn't thinking about him. I was thinking about how messed up all of this is. This isn't going to work."

"Don't say that!" he roars. "Why are so quick to let go of this!?"

"I'm obviously not," I scowl. "I'm in the fucking car with you, aren't I? Not like you gave me much of a choice."

I look outside the window at the green trees sprinkled in between the turning golden and red leaves. Gushes of wind keep creating tornadoes of them, whirling off into the air with a hiss that feels as sudden and urgent as everything happening with Emmett and me. I brace myself against the seat and try to catch my breath, but I am too hyped up on emotion.

Maybe this rush we both feel isn't worth it. Nothing about it is healthy. And I can't help but think back to my mom and biological dad, and wonder if this is what things were like for them.

I shrink in my seat, growing quiet. I feel a headache coming on, and my body feels heavy from the tightness in my chest. My stomach is sinking, and I just wish we could find our way back to the way things felt in my bedroom last night. I want to run back to that place, and I can only hope that once we get to the hotel, we can find the same kind of retreat.

"I don't know what it is you want to talk about," I protest. "But I don't want to do this right now. Not when you're pissed like this. I just want to go home."

The sound of my own pleas is surreal and bring back way too many memories of the other times he has held me against my will. I can't hold back the tears and hate how vulnerable they make me feel all over again. I burst into sobs against my hands, trying to hide my face.

"Why are you so upset!?" he shouts defensively. "I'm not going to hurt you! I just need to talk to you!"

"Bullshit!" I scream, my voice cracked from the persistent crying. "You could have talked to me back there! You just need to feel in control of me and you're losing your temper…only this time you don't have your dad to blame."

I cry even harder as the words spill out, realizing he has no excuse for his behavior now. At least none of the old ones he's tried to fall back on in the past. I slide down into my seat from the disappointment of accepting that this is just how Emmett is, whether his father is in the picture or not. Any hope I had of Emmett redeeming himself or proving that he's a kind and trustworthy person feels like it's slipping through my fingers.

A painful reality sets in. I may have to leave Emmett behind. As much as I love him, this may be too much for me. I don't know if I can martyr myself for him. I feel like I have lost all of myself to him. And I don't know if I am strong enough to walk away from him, but part of me thinks that I should. But it feels like a betrayal to even think it. I promised him I wouldn't. I told him he would be safe with me, that I could never hurt him.

Why did I make such big promises? I made them because I wanted them to be true. I thought if I said them out loud that they would be. That I could will it into being no matter what, because I wanted it so bad. But as he seethes in the corner, I don't know if I can stay with him.

I can walk away from all of this right now. And pretend that I don't know that he would go to pieces the moment that I did. And my heart may go cold the moment I do, but maybe one day I would find someone else to revive it. But I can't imagine anyone ever making me feel the way he does. It's so cliché. Everyone feels this way about their first love, right?

"Malcolm just left school a few minutes ago," he says in a deep booming voice. "Were you planning to meet him after practice?"

"You're fucking paranoid!" I laugh with a shriek. "I was on my way home! And what do you mean he just left a few minutes ago? Were you stalking him?"

"No, I wasn't stalking him," he gapes defensively. "I was only trying to make sure you were safe."

"Safe from what? Malcolm has never hurt me in anyway whatsoever, which is more than I can say for…" I stop myself but it's too late. We both know exactly how that sentence ends as it hangs heavy between us.

Every muscle in his neck tightens and bulges as his hands ring around the steering wheel, making the leather creak. His foot slams to the gas as the engine revs in a loud whirring sound, sending us speeding off down the road.

"Slow down!" I demand, but he ignores me. "If you were so worried about Malcolm and I talking, why didn't you just come over and talk to us like a normal person!? You had no problem hanging all over me for everyone else to see earlier in the day."

"And yet that still didn't stop you from running off with him," he scoffs. "I saw the way you two were looking at each other."

"This is ridiculous, Emmett." I shake my head, feeling completely flustered. "We weren't looking at each other in any way other than friends having a nice conversation."

"Nice!?" he bellows.

I feel a small tinge of guilt knowing that the conversation did seem to get a little flirtatious, but I can't let that show. I'm too afraid of how Emmett will lose it if I let on that he could actually have something to worry about with Malcolm.

"You're being ridiculous! Why are you making me go off with you like this!? We could have had this talk back in the parking lot." I grip my seatbelt as the car drives even faster down the winding roads leading to the edge of town.

I can't stop the memories of our car crash from flooding my brain. I try to focus on my breathing and calm down. We kissed in the hospital after that. Maybe we can skip the crash this time and go straight to the kissing part, but not if he doesn't slow down.

"I just...I need..." he stammers through his words, which only makes him angrier. "I just need to be away with you somewhere for a minute."

"You just need to feel in control of me," I suggest once again, feeling even more confident in my conclusion. "You're overreacting."

He's silent the rest of the way until the car finally skids around a twitching neon sign for a run-down motel outside town. I look out my window as we park, noting the "rent by the hour" sign and the dirty, painted brick building. The windows to the rooms are cloudy and dark with broken blinds.

"I would have expected you to be staying somewhere nicer," I admonish as Emmett storms over to my car door to let me out, ensuring I don't try to run off.

"I want to lay low until I know exactly what happened with Bernadette," he explains as he ushers me to the front door of his room. "I could be in danger, too, for all I know."

As we step inside, I feel oddly calm. I don't know if I am not afraid because I see Emmett as less of a threat now, even though he didn't give me much of a choice in coming here with him, or if I am less afraid because I have become so used to this kind of treatment from him.

I want to remind him that this is exactly why I wanted space from him the first place. Because I deserve better than this. I can't help but wonder if Malcolm would ever do anything like this. Sure, he messaged me to meet him alone and took me to meet with his father inconspicuously, but even then, he never made me feel afraid.

Emmett slides several different locks into place once we are inside the room. It's filled with mismatched furniture and peeling wallpaper that reveals moldy, stained walls. The room is dimly lit behind the musty curtains, lightened in color from years of sunlight.

I collapse onto the edge of the squeaky bed, waiting to see what he'll do next as a faucet drips loudly in the bathroom. There are angry voices and crying children echoing through the thin walls with loud, obnoxious dogs barking in the parking lot. It smells like piss and stale cigarette smoke.

"It's disgusting in here," I comment, noting the mouse droppings lining the closet floor.

"It's cheap," he states plainly. "And far enough away from Jameson that I don't have to worry about someone telling the wrong people where I've checked in."

"So…still no word from your sister?" I ask lightly, pursing my lips to the side as I grasp for any change of subject. I secretly wonder if he's being just as paranoid about his sister and someone being after him as he is with his jealousy.

"You don't think I have a right to be upset about Malcolm!?" he barks back, ignoring my question.

"Not if I didn't have a right to be upset about you and Vivian," I reply bitterly.

"So, you *were* just trying to get back at me?" He shakes his head as he continues manically pacing.

"No!" I groan, rolling my hands through my hair in frustration. "I wasn't trying to do anything, Emmett! You humiliated me in front of Vivian and Lily so I took a walk! When I sat down, Malcolm came up and offered me some food. I left my lunch when I ran after you, remember? So, I accepted. We talked while we ate. That's it!"

It's exhausting to have to defend myself and watch him act this way, but I feel a slight flutter of satisfaction in my chest at seeing him so jealous. I hadn't done it on purpose, but after letting Vivian treat me that way earlier, it's hard not to feel like he got what was coming to him.

His dark brown eyes are glinting with pain and confusion as sweat beads across his forehead. So many things are bubbling up under the surface, and I am left waiting at his mercy, wondering when and how it will all come out. Emmett releases things in slow, furious waves, each completely unpredictable. He lets it all bubble up until it crashes out, usually crashing out onto me.

I wonder what he and Vivian were like alone when they were together. Could she get to him this way? Did he care enough about her to be this jealous? She has certainly always been jealous of me. I technically stole him away from her in a weird way. Do I deserve to be tormented by her now? Maybe I am just getting what was coming to me, the way Emmett is now with his feelings towards Malcolm.

I should be angry with Emmett for forcing me to come here like this, but I keep ending up only feeling angry with myself. I'm the one who can't help but fall for this whole fucked up relationship instead of going after a nice, normal boy who is every bit as rich and good-looking. Even now as I watch Emmett fuming in a furious pace across his motel room floor, I can't bring myself to just get up and walk away.

# CHAPTER SIX

## BOOK 2

There is something honest about Emmett being in this motel room. A dirty, cracked hole-in-the-wall seems fitting —more so than the polished manor where his family lives. I have always hated how deceptively beautiful everyone and everything in Jameson is. I lay in my bed at home and stare at my white ceiling, thinking that's fitting, too. I'm innocent. Less so now than I was before, but I can never fully know what it was like to grow up the way he did.

Suddenly, Emmett stops dead in his tracks and turns to me with an almost frightening sternness. "I can't lose you to him," he bellows, stepping towards my perch on the edge of the bed. "You're mine, Ophelia," he offers more softly.

His eyes spark with a tenderness that lures me in. He kneels down in front of me, pressing his head to my chest, running his hands across my thighs. I feel myself melting into his desire. His warm, soft hand engulfs my cheek and there's so much kinetic energy flowing through it that I feel like I could drown in it.

"This is so fucked up, Emmett," I whisper, closing my eyes against his skin.

"I know I'm not the best, Ophelia," he says softly. "But we've come too far together. I have too much of myself invested in you. I can't lose you."

I find myself thinking I could never hate Emmett, but then I have to remember who he was before. And now I am stuck in this haze…trying to save him from himself. As long as he keeps fighting for me, I know I can never leave. No matter how badly I want to.

I believe in Emmett's goodness. I swear that I can see it, and I want to hold out hope that it's real. Maybe if I believe in it enough, he will believe in it, too.

"You're not losing me. I'm right here."

"Are you?" He looks at me in desperation. "Are you here with me enough to feel this?"

I know what he is talking about. This thing between us that makes us both feel crazy. The thing that keeps drawing us together, no matter how much easier it would be if we could just go our separate ways. The spark in his eyes pulls me in, and before I know it, I am drowning in his kiss.

When Emmett's and my lips collide, it feels like time holds still. Everything slows and suspends—it's just the two of us and our heat. I could get lost in his mouth forever, just exploring his tongue with mine and feeling the gentle bite of his teeth against my bottom lip that grows greedier as we go.

I feel like my heart might stop with excitement when he lifts me up further onto the bed, digging his hands into my thighs as he takes in more of my mouth. He angles himself between my legs and presses his hardness into me, fitting perfectly and making me dizzy with lust.

"Ophelia," he hums against my lips, pressing deeper.

He pulls back in an urgent pant for air, taking in the sight of me with a carnal gaze, and I think in that moment that I have never seen a more beautiful guy, but before I can fully rest on that he lunges forward again, gripping his hands into my hips.

The push of his tongue makes me long to feel him between my legs. The ache in me rises as I claw at his shirt, catching his skin with scratches as I lift it away. His palms press against my breasts, twisting fervent handfuls but he grunts with dissatisfaction. He quickly slips my shirt over my head just as ferociously as I had with his, and moves to undo the clasp of my bra. He moans when he finally feels my bare breasts in his grip, trailing his tongue around my mouth with each squeezing motion.

My fingers clench into his messy curls as he moves down to take my hardened nipples in between his lips and tongue one by one. He releases breathless grunts as I pull his hair harder, urging him to keep going as my hips buck and rub up against his bulge, still nestled between my legs.

"Now, Emmett," I plead as he thrusts against me through

our clothes. "Please, I can't wait anymore. I need to feel you inside of me."

He jumps back and quickly removes his pants before grabbing a condom from his pocket and swiftly sliding it over his erection. I can't stop myself from pulling forward and taking him into my grip, sliding up and down as I tease him with my lips. I feel him shudder against my trailing tongue before he throws me back against the bed hard—so hard that it causes my vision to go blurry for a moment, but it's exactly uncontrollable wildness about Emmett that makes him so irresistible to me. Always keeping me on the edge between my fear of not knowing what could happen next and intense desire.

"Please come here," I reach for him, desperately needing to feel him slide inside of me.

He smiles proudly at my impatience and removes my pants and underwear. But instead of lowering to me like I had asked, he kisses down my legs in between my thighs. I am so wet and hungry that the moment his tongue flickers across my folds, I feel like I might cum. His hands creep back up to my breasts as he works soft circles around my clit with his mouth. He licks until I think I might scream loud enough to worry the neighbors, until finally his fingers slide inside.

I am so worked up that the added sensation of being filled with his fingers makes me lightheaded with pleasure. Before long I am gripping the pillow against my mouth and shivering beneath a tidal wave of ecstasy.

"Oh god, Emmett," I moan in the aftermath of my pleasure, yanking his head out from between my legs and writhing across the bed, begging for him to finally move over me. Any orgasm from him is earth-shattering, but nothing compares to the feeling of him moving inside of me.

He growls as he eases himself inside, bringing his fingers back to my clit as he pushes and pulls against my tight and pulsing muscles. I realize this is our third time together, and I must be getting more comfortable with him, because for once my excitement overrides any anxiety I might have felt before. I am so tight around his hardness that every thrust, combined with his stroking fingers against my folds, makes me feel like I will cum again instantly.

"Cum for me, baby," he commands, giving me permission to fall into another roaring orgasm.

He stays inside of me as I cum on his cock before he crashes over my quivering body, pressing his bare chest to mine as he slows down.

"I don't ever want anyone else to know you like this," he groans into my ear. "This is just for me." His hands slide across my body as he moves inside slowly, but deep enough to drive me crazy with pleasure.

"I don't want anyone else," I whimper against his neck, knowing in that moment that I've never said anything truer.

His head rears back suddenly as his pace quickens and he looks me boldly in the eyes with an almost threatening stare. "Promise me," he bellows. "Promise you belong to me."

He thrusts harder as he stares expectantly, needing me to devote myself entirely to him.

"Only you," I assure him breathlessly, not feeling a moment's hesitation as he pounds into me harder, pushing me to an edge of sensation I've never felt before.

He straightens and pulls my legs to his shoulders, angling himself into me and stroking all of the perfect places, moving faster with building need. I don't think it's possible to cum again so soon, but as he moans my name in his own mounting plea-sure, I crash over the edge yet again. He collapses across me again, pushing so deep into me I'd expect it to hurt, but it only makes me cum harder as he releases at the same time.

He lingers inside of me, slowly gliding back and forth to draw our orgasms out to the last possible second. He milks every ounce of pleasure we can get from it, moving so slowly I think I might die. Finally, we are too sensitive to keep going and his head crashes to my shoulder.

We lay in still silence for a long time as I stroke my fingers through his hair, cradling him against my naked body. I lean my head around to see if he's asleep, but his eyes are still open and glistening in the dim lamplight. He looks content, with a gentle grin settled into the corner of his mouth. I don't think I have ever seen him look so peaceful.

I bunch up the cheap comforter in my hand, watching the paisley pattern of it melt together. It's made up of the ugliest shades of maroon, emerald, and white, with touches of mustard yellow. It's also itchy and feels grimy. But I'm still lying here, wrapped up in it without a care in the world. My desire for Emmett makes me forget about these kinds of things for a moment. I forget where we are and how gross this room is. It all falls away before my need for him. Everything seems to fall away when I am face to face with him, maybe to a point of being unhealthy.

"Third time's the charm, I guess," I giggle after a while, breaking our quiet trance.

His head bolts up with an almost panicked look. "It wasn't good the first two times?" he frets with a pained smile.

The way his plump pink lips curl into a grin, matching the devilish spark in his eyes, is one of the most adorable things I've ever seen. Emmett's intensity is sexy and alluring, but this calmer, more playful side of him is new and even more attractive. I want to see more of it. I want to see him as just a normal teenage boy. The yearning for it makes me more determined than ever to help him find Bernadette. Hopefully she is safe and can come home soon so we can move forward.

"No, every time has been perfect!" I insist as a blush creeps across my cheeks. "But you know…you made me cum three times in a row." His cheeks light up with a proud smile as he leans in for a kiss. I want to ask him so many questions about how much experience he's had or the kinds of things he's done. But I am almost afraid to know the answers. "No guy has ever made me cum before you. Much less three times in a row." The smile quickly leaves his face as he stands and puts on his boxers.

"Something wrong?" I ask in alarm at his sudden change.

"I don't want to hear about you being with other guys," he grumbles.

"Jeez, you are so possessive," I hiss through my teeth, not realizing my remark would be so offensive. I playfully trail my toes across his chest, hoping to lure him back down into bed. "It was supposed to be a compliment."

I'm hoping he'll lighten up and smile again, but instead he drops to a seat at the edge of the bed next to my legs. His head drops as he runs his hands through his hair with a long exhale.

"I'm sorry, Ophelia." His voice cracks with remorse.

"It's no big deal," I assure him. "Just come back and lay down with me a little longer before you have to take me home."

"No, I mean…I'm sorry for everything," he persists. "I don't mean to be the way that I am. I just…I've never known anything different."

"What do you mean?" I straighten, realizing this is much deeper than awkward pillow talk.

"My dad was just so…awful. At least towards me. In ways Bernadette never saw," he explains with a pained expression. "I want to be different. I want to be better for you. I'm trying…I just…" He trails off and buries his face to his hands.

"Hey…" I coo, rushing to his side to wrap my arms around him with a flurry of kisses across his back. "It's okay."

"It's not okay," he insists firmly. "You deserve better."

I am speechless, knowing I have said those words to him too many times to try and take them back now. I thought them on the way here, and with our track record, I may be thinking them again in a couple of days. But in this moment, I feel more confident than ever that what Emmett has been telling me this entire time is true. He's not some sick monster out to manipulate me at every turn to get what he wants. He's not even acting purely on whatever this primal connection is between us. He has a good heart beneath all of his issues, and has genuine feelings for me.

"Everything's just been so messed up," I murmur against his bare shoulder, wishing I knew exactly what to say to make things better. "Maybe one day we'll have a chance to just be normal kids together. Having a good time. Maybe then things will be easier. Different."

"No, Ophelia," he says with a startling certainty. "Things will never be easy with me. Not with my life and the cards I've been dealt. Even if Bernadette is okay, I still have Jameson resting on my shoulders."

I think about insisting that he can run away from it all. Choose his own life that has nothing to do with the burden of his father's legacy. But what could I really know about his life? I didn't grow up wealthy, knowing that I would one day inherit the company my hometown depends on more than anything.

"Then I don't want easy," I offer, as I crash back down onto the bed, hoping he will follow.

His head perks up. "What?"

"Fuck easy," I answer loudly. "Easy is boring."

He eases across the bed, sprawling out beside me. "You should have easy," he says softly, caressing my cheek with his thumb before pressing it into my bottom lip firmly, as if it's a gentle reminder of the beast inside of him.

"I said I don't want it," I fire back. "I want you."

His lips crash across mine as a tear falls down my cheek. I'm terrified, but I mean every word I say. As much as I long for the simple life I once knew, I ended up here in Emmett's arms instead. Getting here may have been a nightmare, but somehow, we came out on the other side still mad for each other.

"I love you," he whispers suddenly into my ear, causing my entire body to tense up and swell with a gasp. He pulls back and studies my reaction.

I can't remember if he has ever said those words to me before, I only know that if he has it was unconvincing. Anything he has said until now felt like a ploy to rope me back in, to keep me where he wanted me. This is the first time it has ever sounded real and sincere, to the point that he might as well have never said it until now.

"What did you say?" I gape in disbelief.

"I love you, Ophelia," he says again, setting my heart back into an intense pounding.

The sound of those words and my name on his lips has to be one of the most forceful things I have ever heard. I can feel them emanating through my entire body.

"I love you," I barely manage to say back through my chest, tight with excitement.

I'd always imagined love was something permanent. Something that may change or fade, but could never fully go away. To say you love someone is to bind yourself to that person for life. Even if you are no longer with them, they will always be one of the important people in your heart. Someone you loved. The concept feels heavy to me, and I am scared for a moment to think about being attached to Emmett in that way. But the feeling swells in my heart and I know I have no choice. I do love him, whether I want to or not.

We kiss and talk, buying as much time as we possibly can. Playing songs for each other on our phones. Emmett may not be easy, but for a little while we forget about everything waiting for us outside. We even forget that we're locked up in a shitty motel room outside of town. I check my phone every so often for the time, until finally I know we can't stay any longer.

"You better take me home," I tell him reluctantly. "My mom will start to worry soon, and…"

"I know," he cuts me off, not needing a reminder of why she is so suspicious of him. "Okay," he adds with a heavy sigh. "Come on, let's get going."

I don't want this night to end as I slide back into my clothes, and I half-consider telling him to sneak into my bedroom window after we get back. I hate the idea of him driving all the way back out here and sleeping alone, and I need to be close to him right now. But I stop myself. Everything has been so perfect; I don't want to risk ruining it by pushing our luck.

"Hey, can I pick you up for school tomorrow?" he asks as we gather our things and head for the door. "Early. I was hoping you could come with me to take care of something before school."

"Sure." I shrug without giving it another thought. I'm too high on my feelings for him and his lingering scent on my body, which only intensifies as we step out into the crisp night air.

I almost fall asleep on the drive back to my house, but his hand keeps moving across my thighs inching up dangerously far and reawakening my desire for him. It doesn't seem possible to want more of him, but I do. By the time we reach my house, I am eager to kiss him and toy with how far we can get in my driveway before I have to go inside, but it's already late and I can see the heaviness in his tired eyes.

"You sure you'll be okay to drive back?" I ask with concern, curling a strand of his hair around my finger.

"I'll be fine," he assures me.

I lean in for one final kiss before giggling into his cheek. "Hey, say it again."

"Say what again?" I raise my eyebrows and look into his sparkling eyes as he realizes what I'm asking for. "I love you," he says breathlessly, before biting and kissing across my neck.

I finally pull myself from his arms and force myself from his car. He watches me walk to the door with a big smile, and I can't wait to see him again in the morning. I practically float up the stairs to my bedroom and crash onto my bed, still wishing he could be lying next to me.

For everything that has been wrong between us, tonight has been perfect. And it was all I needed to know, without a doubt, that Emmett and I are meant for each other.

# CHAPTER SEVEN

BOOK 2

The next morning, Emmett picks me up as promised, but reality quickly sinks in with the new day. My euphoric high from the night before has been dissipated by a string of the nightmares that still plague me regularly. As much as I want to throw myself into trusting and loving Emmett fully, the reality is that I have been traumatized during my time at WJ Prep and he's not entirely without blame for that.

It's the beating drum of my heart that only Emmett can conjure. He makes me feel fearless and terrified all at once. I wonder if I could just dive head first into this, never fearing or doubting anything, if things could be better. Maybe it's my own doubt that will destroy us.

I try to swallow down my renewed wariness of him, hoping that the moment I see him again it will all fade away. I notice my mom peering at him through the curtains as I'm heading for the front door.

"You okay?" I ask casually, as I swing my bag across my shoulders and zip up my hoodie.

"You two are spending an awful lot of time together again," she remarks suspiciously as she suspends the blinds between her fingers, eyeing his car in the driveway.

"It's nothing to worry about," I assure her. "I know you didn't have the best first impression of him, but he's not a bad guy."

She looks to me with a haunting expression, as if she can

instinctively see straight through to all of the doubts inside me. But she quickly softens with a half-smile. "I hope you're right," she says softly, before pulling me in for a hug.

"See you later," I answer quickly, pulling away to run to the warmth of Emmett's car. He tries to lean over and kiss me the moment I get in, but I can still feel my mother's eyes on us, so I stiffen under his touch. "Let's go," I urge him. "My mom is on high alert right now."

He nods as he looks back at her through the window and quickly puts the car in reverse. "Thanks for coming with me this morning," he offers as we drive off through my neighborhood.

"What are we doing anyway?" I ask as I fumble for my seatbelt.

"I was thinking I should look in Bernadette's room," he explains. "Maybe see what's in her diary. I just didn't want to go back to the house alone." He spreads his hand across my knee with a tight squeeze.

I'm half-relieved that we're focusing on Bernadette again. That's all I was supposed to be in this for when he first came to me, and things somehow quickly spiraled back into the throes of our relationship. At least now I know his sister's claimed disappearance wasn't just some scheme to rope me back in, and his willingness to finally go through her things lessens some of my suspicions about him in this ordeal—and will hopefully return some of my feelings from the night before.

"Are you still adamant about not going to the cops?" I ask once again, reflecting on how many days she's been missing at this point.

"Not until I know more," he replies grimly. "Mom is still against it."

It's hard not to be distracted by his scent as we go. One whiff of his cologne sends me into a haze of memories from our recent encounters, last night's especially. I hate how easy it is for me to be distracted by my lust for him, even while we're playing detectives for his missing sister. Maybe we're both eager to cling to sex as an escape.

Emmett flashes me a strange grin as we pull up to his family's manor, which makes me wonder if he was just thinking the same thing I was. But the grinding gears of the car going into park snaps us back to the task at hand.

Their ornate, blackened-iron fence towers above me, bringing back chilling memories. We walk down the long, circular driveway and around the fountain at its center as sprinklers sputter mist across the perfectly green, manicured lawn.

I try to avoid the vivid images flashing before my eyes of my father showing up on their doorstep as we walk through the entryway. I was running for my life and ended up face-to-face with him just before he shot Emmett's dad. I guess not every girl my age could say they watched their dad murder someone, especially not their boyfriend's father.

The Jameson manor is decorated in dark mahoganies, olive greens, and deep burgundies. The smells of Thomas Jameson still linger from his office. Scotch and cigars. Everything is dark and ominous and old. Not just old, but old and expensive. It's the kind of lavishness that makes you feel afraid to move, always afraid of what thing you might accidentally stain or break that's worth than your house.

The foyer has high vaulted ceilings with gold patterns sprawling across them to the start of the crown molding, with a large crystal chandelier in the center of the room that reflects dancing lights across the room, all the way up to the spiral staircase that leads to the hall where Emmett's room is. Every room of the house is filled with expensive art and draperies, antique furniture and linens.

Things only feel more surreal as we walk through the mansion halls I was once held captive in. Emmett leads me to Bernadette's room, which I hadn't seen when I was here before. I'm surprised by how far it is down the hall from Emmett's, but I guess the distant quarters explain how everyone in this family managed to be so different from one another.

The size of the room is somewhat surprising, though I guess it shouldn't be considering the immensity of the house. Her large king bed rests along the center wall, made up with luxurious bedding.

"I guess we know she didn't vanish too suddenly if the bed was made," I offer, trailing my hand across the soft comforter.

"Maids," he reminds me bluntly, making me feel stupid.

Emmett digs through her tidy nightstand, pulling out a red leather journal with a pen still attached to the outside. He sits on the corner of the bed and begins flipping through the pages as I look around the room. Everything is perfectly clean and in place, just as in Emmett's room. Nothing like my chaotic, messy bedroom. I think it must be a relief to live in such an orderly space without ever having to clean it yourself, but something about it feels too stark. And knowing some of their family secrets, I don't know if it's a worthy trade.

"Well, what does it say?" I ask after a few minutes, checking the time on my phone.

"I guess Vivian was really angry at her for everything that happened between our families," he explains. "She was mad that my mom and I made it out of everything unscathed, leaving both of her parents completely liable."

"So, could Vivian be a suspect in all of this?" I offer eagerly, wishing Emmett would hate her as much as I do.

"Seems like they were still trying to be friends," he continues. "And since Lily is sort of an outcast, too, I guess they wanted to take her back under their wing."

"Does it say anything about me?" I accidentally blurt out, immediately realizing that shouldn't be relevant. And judging by Emmett's face, whatever it says about me is not surprisingly unkind. Enough that he's not bothering to share, which is probably for the best. "It doesn't matter," I correct myself. "Anything else that might help us figure out where she went? What does the last entry say? Was she planning to meet up with Vivian or anything?"

He thumbs through to a middle passage that's followed by blank pages and begins to read carefully. "There's definitely nothing that sounds suicidal," he says with a relieved sigh. "And nothing that hints at wanting to run away."

"So, then we should question Vivian, right?" I suggest, clearing my throat and shifting uncomfortably across the plush carpet.

The last thing I want to do is encourage any interaction between Vivian and Emmett, but I can't help thinking she has something to do with all of this. The police would probably assume the same, since Vivian was already angry with her. And maybe if I can get Emmett to see that, Vivian will finally be put out of our lives for good.

"I know you don't like her," he starts, prompting a sarcastic laugh to slip from my mouth.

"Dislike is an understatement," I murmur under my breath.

"But it really doesn't seem like her or Lily are involved in anyway," he finishes, ignoring my remark.

"You've got to be kidding me!" I shake my head and feel an uncontrollable surge of jealousy bubbling up inside. "Does she talk about anyone else being angry with her in there? How do you not see she is the only feasible lead we have right now?"

"Read it for yourself," he answers curtly, shoving the book into my hands. "I'm not trying to protect Vivian and Lily. I'm only telling you what it sounds like."

"Well, she might not have known what Vivian was up to!" I insist. "Or Lily, for that matter. I mean, doesn't it seem odd? Vivian is heartless and only cares about social status. Being mad at Bernadette over what happened to her parents…do you really think she'd still try to be friends with her after that?" My arms are flailing as I rant, and I can't even bring myself to focus on the written words in my hands as he requested. "And taking in Lily all of a sudden. That doesn't seem suspicious to you?"

"I guess you just don't know them like I do," he defends. "You don't understand the dynamics of their friendships."

I scoff and stew in my building rage, pretending to finally start reading the diary. But the words all blur together in my line of vision. All I can see or hear is Emmett's misguided and blatant disregard for how guilty Vivian and Lily obviously look in all of this.

"You don't think it's at least worth it to talk to them about it?" I try again, my voice growing even more shrill.

"For what?" he grimaces. "They know Bernadette is missing. And if they did have anything to do with it, which I don't think they do, they're not going to just confess when we ask about it!"

Which is exactly why we should go to the police, I think to myself. But I don't bother suggesting it to him again. He's already refused the idea several times. I accept that it must be just another thing about their weird Elite world that I don't understand, but the way he said the words still burns in my gut. As if I am some outsider who could never fully know his world. Not in the way Vivian does.

"I still think we should talk to them," I persist fervently. "Even if they didn't have anything to do with it, they're our best possible place to start right now. And maybe it could lead to something else."

"This isn't some detective flick," he snaps back callously. "They're not going to have some magical piece of information that leads straight to her."

"How the hell do you know?" I argue. "And how can you be so quick to rule them out when we have literally nothing else to go on?" He sits and stares off, completely unmoved by any of my arguments. "Let's at least talk to Lily," I add more softly, feeling like I'm only talking to myself at this point. "She hasn't been over on the dark side for too long. Maybe I can get her to open up to me. Tell me anything she knows. Even if it's just the last time they saw Bernadette."

"It's all in her diary," he tells me, sounding frustrated.

"Unless they were the ones who kidnapped her. That entry wouldn't have made it into her journal, obviously." I roll my eyes and sink down onto the opposite edge of the bed, knowing it's a useless argument. His mind is made up and he's not budging no matter what I say, which only makes me more jealous of whatever his weird, lingering deal with Vivian is.

He disliked her enough to break up with her and seems to want to be with me instead, but he won't tell her off when she gives me shit and he wouldn't even dream of the possibility that she could have harmed his sister, even though he knows how brutal she can be! Suddenly, Vivian is some golden child who can do no wrong, and I'm becoming the monster for insisting anything different.

"I just don't think we should rule them out," I conclude quietly. "That's all I'll say about it for now."

"Fine," he grunts half-heartedly, just trying to appease me.

Bernadette's room is feeling creepier by the minute. It's too clean. Too still, quiet, and empty. And we're still no closer to finding out what could have happened to her. I realize part of me thought she'd turn up again after a couple of days. Probably returning from some wild bender like the one Emmett and I claimed I was on when I disappeared. But the more time that passes, the less likely of a possibility that becomes.

Even if Emmett doesn't want to go to the police, I wish I could bring myself to. She could be hurt or dead. And his fears are starting to feel heavier. We don't know who's behind this or why, so we have no way of knowing if they're coming after him next. Our fathers have left a big target on our backs, especially Emmett's. Nothing feels safe.

"Okay, okay," he repeats urgently. "Let's think. Let's really think about this. What are the possibilities of what could have happened to her?"

My mind immediately goes to the worst conclusions, none of which seem like good ideas to mention. She could have been kidnapped, murdered, or any number of other things. Terrible things happen to people every day. But welcome to Jameson, where any time someone is hurt or killed, everyone knows it was calculated with a very clear motive.

"Well, obviously…Vivian has a motive," I suggest lightly.

"Vivian was mad at Bernadette, but she was still trying to be her friend," he repeats dismissively.

"Right…but why? Does that sound like Vivian to you?" I question. "Maybe she was just pretending to be her friend so she could pull something over on her."

"You don't know Vivian like I do," he insists. "You're just going to have to trust me."

I seethe inside at the paradox of that. Statements like that about Vivian are exactly what makes me distrust him.

"What about your father?" he asks suddenly, sending chills down my spine. I was already feeling uneasy. My father is the last person I want to think about.

"I told you I haven't talked to him," I remind him.

"But don't you think we should?" he suggests in a hopeful tone.

"Why?" I cross my arms and look away, wishing this wasn't his grand solution. I'd much rather go after Vivian and Lily.

"Maybe he never intended on stopping after he took my father down," Emmett explains with a furrowed brow. "Maybe he wants to take over Jameson Automobiles for himself."

"Then why wouldn't he have just come straight for you?" I wonder out loud. "You're the one in control of it all now, right? Bernadette doesn't have rights to any of it unless you give them to her."

"I know, but it's not completely unbelievable," he continues to my dismay. "I don't know what exactly he'd be up to with Bernadette, but there is a motive there."

"There's a motive for Vivian and Lily, too," I remind him bitterly. I can't believe he'd rather go accuse my father than the two of them. "Lily did say my father was back."

"What? What do you mean?" his tone grows urgent.

"Before you found me and told me about Bernadette," I explain. "She was angry with me. She said everyone knew my father was back around."

"What do you think that means?" he pushes, but I only reply with a flustered groan. If I had known what that meant, maybe I wouldn't have rushed off and accidentally landed right back in Emmett's arms.

"So, we should talk to him," he persists, this time standing to look deep into my eyes as he caresses my arms. "I know it's scary for you. But I promise if we talk to him and nothing comes out of it, we can try with Vivian and Lily."

I collapse against him, pushing my forehead to his strong chest. The idea of talking to my father again terrifies me. He may have looked harmless the last time we parted ways, but the cops let me know he is definitely not some innocent guy to feel sorry for.

"What if it's dangerous?" I ask against his shoulder, feeling suddenly exhausted. "You said you offered to take me captive because you were afraid of what he might do to me. You made it sound like he'd sooner kill me than let the Elites use me to get an advantage over him."

His initial silence only makes me feel worse. He knows what I'm saying is true.

"I'll protect you," he promises in a deep rasp, brushing his hands along my hair.

"I know you'd try, but…I don't think any of us stand a chance against my father," I reply bleakly. "Your father didn't. None of the Elites did…except for you. And if this is just his way of coming back for you, I think we should stay far away. Or go to the police. They told me they were looking for him anyway."

"And why didn't you tell them how to find him?" he asks in a leading tone. "You may not have known exactly where he was, but you could have found out if you tried."

"Because I was worried I couldn't trust the police," I sigh, hating that he has to be right. Hating even more that this town has to be so fucked up.

He kisses my forehead, as if to apologize for making me eat my own words. "It's okay," he says softly. "I'll help you track him down. We'll figure out where he is during lunch and try to go see him after school if he's nearby."

Regardless of what Lily tried to say about my father being back, I have been clinging to this blissful notion that he had run back off to California or Spain or any other far corner of the earth that is nowhere near here. I swallow hard as I try to wrap my head around him lingering so close that we could pop by after school. I hope Emmett is wrong. I hope we can't find him at all, or that he's much too far away to be implicated in any of this.

"We better get going," he nudges me, giving one more soft kiss before we make our way out of Bernadette's room.

It feels wrong to be walking away from it, as if we're walking away from her. Her disappearance has apparently softened my feelings towards her, and I can't help but feel incredibly sorry for her. I stop and look back over the empty room once more. "Wherever she is, I hope she's okay," I pray out loud, grazing my fingers across her open bedroom door.

"You hate my sister," he shoots back with a cold smirk.

"That doesn't mean she deserves for anything bad to happen to her," I defend. Suddenly I feel tears welling up. "I'm sorry, Emmett. You were right. I was so wrapped up in my jealousy of Vivian and feeling hurt by Lily that I let it distract us from finding your sister. I shouldn't have been so selfish."

His hand reaches for mine with a tight squeeze. "I've been just as selfish," he confesses. "Probably much more so than you."

I want to stay in this moment with him, where we are both humbled enough to just be sad and afraid together without all of our fucked-up defense mechanisms getting in the way. But the sunlight sprinting across the empty room beckons us to get moving. Standing around won't do anything for Bernadette.

We go to school and spend lunchtime on the computers in the library, hunting down my father just as Emmett said we would. We don't find any clues, so I reluctantly sneak off and call Malcolm. He is able to give me a cell number to reach him, but I don't tell Emmett how I got it.

I ask him to call my father, not having the nerve to do it myself. He gets off the phone and gives me a nod and sympathetic grin, signaling that my father is close enough for us to make the visit that afternoon.

# CHAPTER EIGHT

BOOK 2

I can barely sit still in my next class, feeling overwhelmed by the looming meeting with my father after school. It is a small relief to know Emmett will be with me, but it doesn't stop my leg from bouncing rapidly under my desk no matter how hard I try to stop. I fidget and chew on the eraser on my pencil, unable to hear anything the teacher is saying.

My nerves build to a rising sickness in my stomach until I finally decide to go throw some cold water on my face in the bathroom, hoping it relieves my anxiety. I shoot my hand up and request a hall pass and march towards the bathroom, trying to outrun the twisting sensation in my gut.

The burst of water from the faucet sends droplets of water splattering across the plastic countertops. In moments like these, WJ Prep feels cursed. I have to wonder how many times I have leaned over this bathroom sink, desperate for some kind of escape from outside. But the threat of my father feels even greater than anything in this school.

As I close my eyes and splash another wave of water across my face, I hear the bathroom door swing open followed by a string of familiar cackles. I know those laughs all too well, except one of them didn't have much to laugh about not long ago. When she was on the other side of Vivian's wrath.

Vivian and Lily. Nothing good ever comes out of running into either of them in this bathroom. And the click of the lock on the main door tells me this time won't be any different.

I quickly realize they're standing on either side of me before I have a chance to wipe my face and look. I can feel them looming over my shoulders. My gut tells me this is going to be bad. This is the first time they've managed to corner me alone since Vivian returned to school and the two paired up.

"Things still going rough with Emmett?" Vivian whines in a mocking voice against my ear, crouching dangerously close.

"No, actually," I answer coldly, trying my best not to let her get to me. Maybe if I just give short answers and ignore them the best I can, they'll go away. I know that never works, but it's all I know to try. They've cornered me, after all. "Things are going just fine," I add.

"Just fine," Lily calls back to me. "Sounds…passionate." She smirks.

"Don't worry about us," I murmur with a shake of my head, reaching out for a paper towel to dry off with. "It's none of your business anyway."

But as my arm reaches out across the counter, Lily's hand tightens around it, holding it firmly in place. Vivian slides behind me, pinning my other arm down as she goes. I let out a scream and struggle to get free, but I'm stopped by a sharp stinging sensation digging into the veins in the middle of my arm, opposite my elbow. My teeth grind against the pain as my eyes strain and tighten, filling with tears.

"What the fuck!?" I shriek, still unable to get loose from their hands. The pain is quickly followed by several more stabs, then it switches to the other arm.

"Don't bother fighting it," Vivian hums.

I ignore her and continue flailing my arms, trying to get free. I want to punch them both when they finally let go, but I am overcome by a sudden rushing surge. My stomach flips as I lean against the counter and lose myself in a swelling daze. I have to assume they've left the bathroom because everything around me grows quiet and still again.

My breath slows and my ears pound with a popping feeling. I sway and look up into the mirror, noting my shrunken pupils. They've obviously drugged me with something, but I have no idea what.

"Emmett," I mouth to my reflection in a whisper. I want to go find him, but my motivation to move or go anywhere shrinks away.

I know I should be panicking over whatever they've done to

me, but I can't seem to feel anything bad. I am suspended in a strange euphoria, even though I know in my brain that I should be terrified. I look at myself in the mirror once more and know I can't face anyone like this. I'm too out of it.

I slink into the nearest stall and lock the door behind me. I want to move fast, but everything goes by in slow motion. My skin is heated and flushed as I smack my dry lips across my tongue. My arms and legs are so heavy I don't even know if I am sitting up straight. As afraid as I am, I can't deny how elated I feel. Even as Vivian and Lily's cackling voices linger in my brain, I feel nothing bad towards them. I feel nothing bad at all.

"What a strange punishment," I laugh softly to myself under my breath.

After a while, I'm unsure of how long I've been locked away on my own. Clusters of shoes beneath the stall door come and go in crowds, accompanied by the sounds of distant voices I have no interest in making out. I sit huddled up on the toilet, relishing the feeling against my will, until finally it feels like it has passed enough for me to face the world again.

But the moment I peel myself up, sickness rises with my body. I turn quickly and buckle over the toilet. Again, I have no idea how long I am stuck like that. Once my stomach has calmed enough for movement, I try to make my way out into the halls.

Everything is quiet and still, and I don't even want to know how much of the school day I've missed thanks to whatever Lily and Vivian have done to me. I slip into my last classroom, ignoring the daggers from the teacher's glare. The period I left during has passed and there's a new set of faces looking at me like I'm crazy as I slip in to grab my bag.

I return to the halls, slamming the classroom door shut behind me, barely looking where I'm going as I pull my phone out and try to text Emmett. I still feel out of it and am struggling to type the right words when suddenly a pair of large sneakers appear in the path before me. Following them up a long pair of legs, I see Coach Granger towering over me.

"Coach Granger," I mutter, swaying slightly as I speak. "I'm glad, I…I need to…"

"You okay, Lopez?" he asks sternly, looking extremely displeased.

I shake my head, unsure if I agreed or disagreed. Before I

can say anything else, he wraps his hand around my arm and begins marching me down the hall.

"Come with me," he orders. "We need to meet with the principal."

"I can't do that right now," I reply lethargically, wishing I had the power to pull away or ask what this is about. "I can't go in there with you and the principal. I don't...I'm not...not well."

He ignores me and continues shuffling me along as the swelling panic inside grows. I want to turn and run in the other direction, but my body feels too weak and lifeless to fight against his pull. Before I know it, I am dragged inside the principal's office and plopped into a stiff, leather chair.

"You don't look so well, Ophelia." Principal Brown peers over his glasses at me, his big, gray bushy eyebrows furrowed together.

I consider telling them that Lily and Vivian have done something to me, but I don't know if it's any use. Sure, they may not be official Elite status anymore, but I imagine they still have more sway in this school than I do. My mom and stepdad are poor, and my bio dad is hated by the entire town. Trying to speak too much makes my stomach turn again, so I just slink down in my chair and hope the feeling continues dissipating fast enough for me to catch up in the conversation.

"Do you know why you're here?" Principal Brown asks with his unrelenting stare. I look to Coach Granger, who is exchanging knowing nods with the principal. "It has been brought to our attention that you may have been using illegal substances."

I brace myself against the chair and push forward, swallowing down another surge of vomit. "No," I protest weakly, my voice cracking. "No, I'm not. Vivian and Lily. They...they..."

"They came to us and said they were worried about you," he continues. "They're good friends."

I eye his trashcan and think I might have to lunge for it at the sound of the words. "No..." I continue trying to speak against it with everything I have, but my words won't match the feeling in my chest. Nothing circling through my brain will come out. "I haven't done anything. They did something to me."

"We searched your locker, Ophelia," Coach Granger chimes

in, flicking away a piece of dandruff from his pants, not seeming to want to look me in the eye.

The principal pulls a plastic bag from behind his desk and sets it in front of me. I can make out several syringes and a rubber tie inside. I know exactly what it looks like and want to scream bullshit.

"That's not mine," I say gingerly, knowing how ridiculous that sounds.

The room closes in around me again, but I can make out enough of what they're saying to know they believe I've been using heroin. Suspension. Kicked off the track team. The words fall from their lips and hang heavy all around me as I rock in my chair.

"I don't use drugs," I persist through a shaky, cracking voice. I continue trying to argue against the accusation to no avail. "You have to…I couldn't…I'm telling you…Lily and Vivian…"

"You're high right now, aren't you?" he accuses, his voice hammering too loudly into my skull.

"No…I don't know…I…I didn't…They did this to me," I babble on, knowing I'm only making it worse.

"If we were to drug test you right now, Ophelia…" Principal Brown suggests accusingly. "Do you honestly expect us to believe you'd pass?" His eyes move over my disheveled appearance with waves of judgment. I caught my reflection as I was leaving the bathroom. I know exactly how I look right now and it's not good.

When I don't bother trying to defend myself any further, he finally stands to approach my chair. He pushes back the sleeves of my sweater, confusing me at first. But as the marks left from Vivian and Lily's attack are revealed, it all clicks into place.

It wouldn't have been enough for them to leave track marks and plant needles in my locker. They needed the actual drug in my system, so I'd have no leg to stand on. No chance at passing a drug test to prove my innocence.

"We're going to give you a chance to talk to your parents about this yourself," Coach Granger tells me, as I sense the meeting coming to a close. "But I'm calling them tomorrow night, so you only have until then to tell them." The two nod at each other with disappointed looks before Coach finally stands to escort me out of the room.

A rush of clarity finally starts to return as he walks me to my locker to gather my things before leading me out of the building. A few straggling students remain in the halls as I am marched out with his hand firmly gripped around my arm, just as last period is beginning. Judging by the way they're gaping at me with snickers and whispers, I expect the entire school will know what's happened by the end of the day. That's if Lily and Vivian hadn't started spreading the rumors before I even got pulled into the office. His long legs are moving so fast I almost trip, but I know he still has some heart for me. He's only trying to move fast so more kids don't see me being escorted from the building.

The moment the fresh outside air hits me, I feel almost back to normal. My hands are shaking, but my stomach has calmed down. My head feels groggy, but my thoughts are growing clearer. My brain finally feels connected to my mouth again.

"Please, Coach," I start pleading more coherently. "You have to believe me. I would never use drugs. Track means too much to me. You know that!"

He scrunches his face in my direction, squinting from the sun and from anger. "Well then, how do you explain the things we found in your locker?" His voice booms with accusing fury and disappointment. "And the marks on your arm. The way you're acting. Don't bullshit me, Lopez. Is it Emmett Jameson? Did he get you started on this stuff?"

"You've seen me in practice!" I cry back. "You know I haven't been messed up like this before today." His face softens as he considers what I'm saying. "It was Vivian and Lily! They cornered me in the bathroom this afternoon and injected something into me. I was stuck in there feeling out of it until I finally came out and you dragged me into the office."

I look to him with wide eyes, praying he can see the truth in my words. I know how it sounds. Every kid tries to plead innocent when they're accused of something like this. My heart stings with the betrayal of Lily being involved in this. When the Elites turned on her, they planted drugs on her, too, and also got her suspended. I can't believe that she'd pull something like this after going through it herself and knowing what it feels like.

I remember her sitting across from me at her parents' restaurant, explaining their history with the Elites. She seemed hurt, but so nice and kind. So human. I am baffled that she could turn so quickly and so completely. Maybe that's what this school does to people. Hits them over and over until all the corrupt ugliness finally starts seeping in through the cracks.

After all, I had just begged Emmett to treat Vivian the same way I had once been treated. I guess we all cave under the brutality of Jameson. Eat or be eaten.

Coach Granger blows a big breath out from his cheeks and pushes his fists into his hips as he turns and looks aimlessly across the schoolyard. I want to think he's struggling to believe me, but that doesn't seem right. Something more than that seems to be troubling him.

I know he's thinking about whatever happened when he disappeared from school. His mysterious troubles at home. I don't know what they have to do with this, but I can see that same gloomy look on his face now that he gets every time he's looked at me since he came back to school. I wish he could just tell me everything, but for whatever reason, he is keeping it to himself for now.

"You believe me, don't you?" I press desperately. I can deal with whatever else is going through his mind as long as I know he believes me.

He shakes his head and murmurs something I can't make out. "Dammit, Lopez," he finally blurts more clearly. "They cornered you this afternoon, you say?"

"Yes! You can ask my teacher," I explain. "I left for the bathroom and never came back. I knew they'd drugged me, but you know how people are with them at this school. I was all messed up and didn't think anyone would believe me if I'd told them what happened." He studies my face in silence, taking everything in. "You told me I could always come to you about anything. You said that because you knew what the Elites were doing to me, didn't you? You're the only one who doesn't bend to them! And I'm telling you this now: they're not done with me, even after everything that's happened. Vivian and Lily drugged me and set me up. Please tell me you believe me!"

His eyes grow dark with something unspoken before he finally straightens and speaks more calmly. "I believe you," he states. My heart swells with relief and adrenaline all at once, forcing me to steady my still-shaky body against the brick wall. "I have to go," he blurts suddenly. "I'll work with you privately for practice until I can get you back onto the team."

"Thank you," I reply through trembling lips, feeling so grateful that he's on my side that I almost forget how fucked up it is that I'm in this situation in the first place.

There's something haunted in his expression, letting on that whatever is going on in his mind is much bigger than what's happened today. There are a million things I want to say, but he quickly walks off, leaving me standing alone in front of the school I'm suspended from. I quickly pull out my phone and return to the draft of the message I'd begun to Emmett before running into Coach.

I know that as long as Coach Granger believes me, he'll do everything in his power to make this right. And work with me on the side until then, like he promised. But I need to be in Emmett's arms right now. Even though there have been times when he has been the cause of my torment, nothing compares to the comfort of being near him.

# CHAPTER NINE

## BOOK 2

I wait outside school for what feels like forever after texting Emmett, but my concept of time seems to still be off. I am still coming down from everything. Finally, I hear the side door swing open and shut before Emmett appears around the corner and comes running up to me.

I used to only feel safe when I was alone. But now I only feel safe when I'm with Emmett, even when he is the one I am afraid of. It's the thing that makes me feel the most broken. My love for him makes me feel sick, but it heals me at the same time.

"What's going on?" he cries as I collapse into his arms. "Your message had me worried. I came to meet you as fast as I could!"

"I'm suspended!" I sob against his shoulder. "Fucking Vivian and Lily did this. And don't you dare try to defend them! I told you they wouldn't stop coming after me until you stepped up and did something. Look!" I whip my sleeves up, revealing the forced track marks.

"What the fuck?" he growls, gently rubbing his thumb along the throbbing punctures. "What did they do?"

"They grabbed me in the bathroom and pumped me up with heroin," I explain rapidly, my breath quickening as I relive it all. "What if they had given me too much, Emmett? They could have killed me!"

I watch the heaviness of the situation settle across his face, and I don't know that I'd fully accepted the severity of it all until just now, with him standing before me.

"They suspended you?" he recaps with me as I feel the muscles in his arms tightening beneath my fingers.

"Yes, and kicked me off of the track team," I seethe. "Those fucking bitches. Running is my life, Emmett. It's the whole reason I'm here. I'll lose my scholarship and I can forget about college or any sort of athletic career I expected to have after that." My words quickly trail off into tears. "Coach Granger says he'll try to fix it, but I don't see how he can. He's the only one that believes me. He'll never convince Principal Brown."

"I believe you," he says, pulling me closer and stroking my hair. "So, Coach Granger offered to help? You told him what Vivian and Lily did?"

"Yes," I sniffle into his arm then grow still. Coach Granger. I have never talked much to Emmett about him, and the mistrusting side of me still wonders if I should have even mentioned our alliance. But then a new slew of questions come over me. "I need to ask you something," I announce, stepping back to look him in the eyes. "Do you know anything about why Coach Granger disappeared before you held me captive?" I ask lightly, almost afraid to know the answer. "Did you have anything to do with it?"

"No, Ophelia," he answers sincerely. "I don't know anything about that. I promise I would tell you if I did."

The possibility of him lying is too overwhelming for me to even consider it. I lean back into his arms and decide I have to believe him for the sake of my own sanity.

"I'm going to fix this," he assures me, as he straightens up and begins adjusting his hair and shirt.

"How? What are you going to do?"

"Just go home and get some rest," he commands, already stepping back to rush off into action. "I'll call you in a little bit."

"But what about my dad?" I ask reluctantly, hoping this somehow means we don't have to meet with him at all. But I know this doesn't change anything about Bernadette. We still need to find out if he knows something.

"Don't worry about that right now," he tells me, scooping me back in for one final kiss. "We'll go meet with him tomorrow. You're right. I should have taken things with Vivian and Lily more seriously. I have to fix this for you. I owe it to you."

My heart pounds with the same familiar, intense drum beat

that strikes every time Emmett looks at me like that. Really, any time he is near. He still looks like the same boy who stalked me down at the track meet before I came here, but nothing about him seems the same. Not after everything that's happened. He has shown me glimpses of redeeming qualities, just enough to keep me hooked, in hope of what could happen between us. Just enough to keep me entirely at his mercy—always.

Before I can say another word, he runs off and disappears back under the brick archway into the school. The day suddenly feels cold with him gone, so I pull my sleeves back down and quickly remember that I now have these awful marks to try and hide from everyone...including my mom. I'm hoping that Coach Granger won't still make me talk to them, now that he knows the truth. I don't think my parents could handle the idea of me using heroin right now. I can't even handle the idea of it.

I start walking to my car before remembering that I rode to school with Emmett this morning. I start to turn to remind him, but he's long out of sight by now. Pulling my zipper up the rest of the way and securing my hood firmly around my face, I resign to run home. It could do me some good. Maybe help sweat the rest of this shit out of my system so I can feel normal again.

My feet pound against the pavement, the muscles of my legs rippling with each step. A cold fire burns through my lungs, which would erupt in a cough if I wasn't so rapidly running out of breath. I'm outrunning the cough or anything else that could possibly slow me down. Move. Just keep moving. One leg after another as fast as you can, as far as you can.

But my legs wobble less than a mile into my stride and I go into a coughing fit that makes me feel like I might start throwing up again. The sweat is freezing against my skin, which starts burning with an intense itching.

"Dammit." I heave as I stop to buckle over my knees and catch my breath. "I hope this isn't permanent."

Slowing back down to a walk, I continue making my way home. I haven't made it far when sprinkling raindrops begin to fall, renewing my shiver. It's going to be a long, miserable walk home. Then I'll have to face my parents when I arrive.

I tell my mom I was late because I stopped for food on the way home, which she has a hard time believing. She was upset that Emmett didn't drive me, considering the rain, and she could see that I look like shit. I convince her that Emmett and I grabbed food together, and then I felt sick and asked to walk the rest of the way home. She still seems suspicious but lets me go to my room to lie down.

After a long hot bath, I climb into bed with my phone in hand and wait for Emmett's call. I am starting to doze off by the time it rings.

"Ophelia, it's me," his voice comes in across the line. "I took care of everything, okay? You don't have to worry."

"What do you mean…everything?" I ask in disbelief.

"You can come back to school tomorrow and you're back on the track team," he continues, explaining confidently.

"You're kidding me!" I exclaim in shock. "How did you fix it all so fast?"

"I run Jameson Automobiles now, which basically runs the town. All of which was founded by my father," he reminds me. "All I had to do was talk to Principal Brown. I told him I knew for a fact you were framed and that I would personally take care of the people who did this to you, as long as he fixed everything on his end."

"So…I don't have to tell my parents?" I sob in relief.

"It's like the whole thing never happened," he promises. "It won't even be on your record."

I cuff my hand over my mouth to quiet my happy cries, but then something he said stands out to me. "You'll personally take care of who did this to me…what do you mean by that?"

"I'm going to confront Vivian and Lily about this. They can't get away with it. They have to know things aren't going to be like they used to be. I'm in charge now," he says sternly, in a way that I have to admit turns me on. "I'm on my way to talk to them now."

"I'm coming with you!" I blurt, knowing I don't want him anywhere near either of them without me. "Come by and pick me up first."

Emmett agrees and I quickly hang up the phone to get ready. A few minutes later, he arrives, though it's no easy job convincing my mom I am well enough to go out again. But I manage to get past her and back into his car. He drives us to

Lily's mansion, which is almost as big as his. I can't help but feel uncomfortable knowing my house is the size of one of their living rooms, and these are the only people I have any contact with these days, outside of my parents and the occasional teacher.

"How do you know they'll talk to us?" I ask, as I unbuckle my seatbelt.

"For one, they don't know what it's about or that you're with me," he explains quickly, as he combs back his hair in the rear view mirror. "Two, they know they can't afford to piss me off more than they suspect they already have."

I'm not so sure I know what that means, but I follow along and feel the same surge of desire I felt on the phone. I've never really seen Emmett take care of things this way. At least not for me. It matches his actions towards Lily before she aligned with Vivian, the way he called and made sure the Elites wouldn't stop her from getting into Juilliard. But her actions after that make even less sense now.

Emmett rings the doorbell and I expect to see Lily or her parents behind the door, but of course it's some kind of butler. "Good evening, sir," he says in a ridiculously snooty voice.

"Lily is expecting me," he says coldly, breezing right past.

"Thank you," I offer gently as we walk by.

The butler rushes to close the door and show us the way to one of the many living room-type areas of the house. Lily and Vivian are huddled on the couch together doing homework, and I start to wonder if maybe Vivian is staying here because of everything going on with the investigation and her parents at home. They both jump up the minute they see us, their eyes planted firmly on me in shock.

"You didn't say you were bringing that skank with you," Vivian scoffs.

"Did you think he was coming over just to hang out?" I ask sarcastically.

Emmett marches right over to Vivian, getting closer than I'd like him to. But the anger surging through him puts all of us off, and no one bothers questioning him right now. "What the fuck were you thinking, trying to pull that shit on her!?" he growls into her face. "You know she's with me now. Did you really think I would just let that slide!?"

"Did you think I'd let what she did to my parents slide!?"

Vivian barks back, not cowering away from his intimidating stance.

Suddenly, Emmett lunges forward, taking Vivian with him. He pins her to the wall with his hand around her neck. I am horrified, but I don't know why. I've seen him like this plenty of times before, but I was the one in his grip.

"You're hurting me," she squirms against the wall, but he doesn't stop. Lily and I step back and stay out of the way, our mouths open wide as we watch it all go down.

"She didn't do a damn thing to your parents!" he hisses, viciously pointing his finger against her face. "Your parents and my dad all knew exactly what they were doing with that sex trafficking ring. They broke the law and now they're paying for it. The end. Ophelia had nothing to do with it, so lay the fuck off. Or you answer to me!"

"You think you're real hot shit now that your dad isn't around," she teases coyly with his hand still stretched across her neck. I grimace at the way she writhes in his grip and looks back at him defiantly. Like she's getting off on the whole thing. "Lucky us, Lily. The new Thomas Jameson is right here in your living room. How kind of you to grace us with your presence."

He slams his palm to the wall next to her head with an alarming bang. "I'm nothing like him and you know it," he bellows. "But I can act just like him if that's what it takes to make you back off."

"I've missed the feeling of you against me, baby," she teases, looking at me as he tightens his hand, cutting off her voice.

"Emmett! Stop it!" I cry out, scared of what he'll do to Vivian if she doesn't stop encouraging him. But mostly because I can't stand to hear her talk to him that way, and I don't want his hands anywhere on her body.

He's in a rage trance and doesn't move. I race over and pull back on his arms, forcing him to let go. "That's enough," my voice booms with a surprising intensity.

"Good job keeping your boy in line, Ophelia," Lily taunts from over my shoulder. "If you had let them go any longer, you may have seen some things you didn't like. I heard they get real freaky together in bed."

The words twist in my ears with a terrible ringing, and I wish I'd never heard them. I have done my best not to picture them together in that way, telling myself that maybe their whole relationship was just for show. I always knew that wasn't true, but it helped save me from torturing myself.

"Let's go, Emmett," I command softly, wanting to be anywhere but here.

"Not until she promises to leave you alone," he snarls, his body frozen and stiff as I try to tug him away.

Vivian flashes me a daring look, and I realize that Emmett was right all along. This is exactly what she wanted. To get Emmett's attention, good or bad. And me being here to watch only makes it better for her. This is what I did to her once upon a time. As much as I want to believe I am somehow better than Vivian, it's hard to feel that way now. In fact, I feel like I deserve this no matter how much it hurts.

Are we both just messed up girls who got roped into his charms? I have no way of knowing their relationship didn't start the exact same way ours did. And before I know it, maybe some other girl will come along and get him riled up like this all over again, if Vivian doesn't steal him back first. One way or another, the connection we supposedly share will mean nothing then, and I'll be cast aside just like Vivian.

"Say you'll let her be," he tries again, rearing back like he might pounce again. Vivian braces against the wall with a seductive gasp, one that's scared and inviting all at once.

"It looks like your man doesn't want to leave right now, Ophelia," she taunts, running her tongue across her bottom lip.

I keep trying to cling to my sympathy for her, but the more she carries on, all I can feel is anger. I've taken her once before in the cafeteria, up until Emmett pulled me off of her. I could do it again.

"Maybe he's remembering all the things he misses about me," she continues. "You and I should hang out sometime. I could give you some pointers about how to keep him satisfied. You know he likes…"

I'm convinced if she wasn't in the picture, everything would be perfect with us for once. Even if we were still struggling to figure out what happened to Bernadette. My mind goes to the darkest places, mulling over thoughts I wish weren't there. If only Vivian was gone. I shutter it all away. This town is corrupting me. Turning me into one of them, and I hate myself for it. But is it the town or Emmett? Maybe this is just what he does to girls.

I barrel forward all at once without thinking, shoving

Emmett aside. My fist slams into Vivian's nose, drawing blood. This is the second time I've made her nose bleed, and both times have been equally as satisfying. It's like a switch has been flipped in my brain, and suddenly I can't relate to her or feel bad for her at all. A primal jealous rage takes me over as I pull back to hit her again, but my fist is caught in midair. I turn to see Lily holding me back, but Emmett quickly rushes in to take me into his own arms.

"This isn't over," Emmett glares at them as he carries me away.

"Oh, I know it's not, baby," Vivian teases.

I start flailing in his arms, dying to have another go at her. I don't even recognize myself in the foyer mirror as Emmett hauls me towards the front door. Before coming to WJ Prep, I don't think I had hit another human being since grade school. And now I feel like these people are turning me into a monster.

My nostrils are still flaring when he pushes me into the passenger seat of his car. I slide down into the dark seat, saying nothing as he drives off into the night. I'm ashamed for not listening to him when he warned me this was exactly what Vivian wanted. But now I feel less protected than ever. Sure, Emmett reversed all of their damage at school, but it won't stop them from trying something again. Maybe something worse that he won't be able to fix.

More than that, I hate myself for losing my temper the exact same way Emmett does. It's the side of him that I can't stand, but apparently it's the side Vivian gets off on. Their terrible words ring through my head, and I have to bury my face in my hands to make it stop.

I remember Emmett once trying to tell me we were both fucked up. That neither of us were perfect or had it all figured out, and I was furious. It felt like he was trying to rationalize his own sins away. Everything he had done was far worse, and I didn't want to let him forget that. But now I'm wondering if he was right. Maybe I am just as fucked up, and that's what drew me to him in the first place.

"Take me to your hotel room!" I shout out suddenly, desperately needing to be back there with him.

I can't face my mom like this, and I need to feel close to him again. To erase everything that just happened at Lily's. They'll never let him come up to my room this late. Not after my mom's already been wary of him and my behavior all day.

I feel like I am letting her down. I promised Emmett wouldn't hurt me and that everything would be okay, but nothing feels okay right now. In one day, I had to track down my father, was forced to take heroin, and then watched Emmett threaten to strangle Vivian before jumping on top of her myself. I'm exhausted, but somehow still writhing with energy for one thing and one thing only.

I need Emmett. Now.

# CHAPTER TEN

BOOK 2

We're fueled on nothing but anger, frustration, and lust as I follow closely behind Emmett into his motel room. The second the door locks, I'm pushing him up against the wall with our tongues crashing together. Our hands grip around each other's throats in desperation. I try not to think about seeing Emmett strangle Vivian or the memories of him doing the same to me. My need to push it away just rushes my hands faster over his body.

"Fuck, Ophelia," he sighs against my lips as our hips grind together, throbbing with impatient need.

He grips into the back of my hair and pulls my head back, lifting my face up towards his, just out of reach of his lips. Suspended like that, he pushes me backwards towards the bare countertop space next to the cheap and broken TV. With his legs and his growing hard on pressing between them, he nudges me back until I am pinned against the edge before clawing too hard into my ass and hoisting me up.

We tear at each other's clothes ferociously, and then all at once he whips me around, tears off my skirt, and presses my hands to the counter. Then I feel his hardened bulge teasing against my ass. I bob against it, wishing he could just be inside of me now. His hands finally pull at the elastic around my waist and lower them down just past my cheeks, leaving them there so that my legs are pulled together.

"Take them off, Emmett," I beg. "Fuck me."

"No," he growls, gripping his hand around my neck from behind. In one swift motion, he moves his hands down before tightening them around my wrists and pinning them behind my back. With one hand holding my hands in place, the other travels across my stomach and down in between my legs, teasing my clit.

"You're so fucking wet," he groans into my ear. "Did you get off on that, you bad little girl? Did you get off on beating up Vivian?"

"No," I protest weakly, not knowing what else to say. I don't want to think I did, but here I am with greater need than I've ever felt before.

"You sure?" he taunts. "Maybe we should try it again and see how you feel." As he growls into my ear, he suddenly shoves his fingers into my wet pussy, making me cry out and try to reach around for a grip of his hair. With one hard tug, he spins me back around and looks at me with a teasing hunger.

I spread my legs wider and grind my hips against him, needing to feel him inside of me so badly. He finally pushes the soaked fabric to the side and effortlessly slides his fingers into my wetness, causing me to yell out. He covers my mouth and leans in, hissing into my ear. "You have to be quiet."

He keeps his hand there, muffling the whispers that continue to escape no matter how hard I try to suppress them. He lifts my shirt and kisses me urgently, rolling my hard nipples between his tongue and teeth. I moan out, "Fuck me, please… please." I grind against his fingers more and more with every thrust as his thumb trails up and around my pulsating clit in soft circles. He keeps his fingers expertly bent, pushing against every place inside of me that sends out a rippling surge and ache for more. I cry out as the orgasm builds, causing him to panic and shove his hand back to my mouth.

"Please," I beg. "I want you inside of me when I cum. I'm so close." I begin frantically unzipping his pants, jerking them down around his thighs and pulling his boxers down immediately after. I am overcome with the urge to be filled with his hardened shaft, skin on skin. I pull his hips towards me, guiding him in as he digs into my upper thigh, hissing in my ear. He lowers his neck and lets out a roaring moan, gliding in and out of me with slow but firm thrusts. I lean back, wresting my weight on my elbows, lifting my shirt so he can see my bare breasts bouncing each time he pounds into me. He yanks up my legs, angling me perfectly so he slides in even deeper, almost more than I can stand as my legs begin to shake in his hands.

"You're so tight," he groans as he looks me up and down, spread out across the table.

"You like that?" I tease, circling one finger around my nipples as his eyes light up. He begins moving more urgently, growing even harder inside of me. My muscles tighten around his cock as I am pushed to the edge.

He backs up slowly with a devilish grin and sits on the edge of the bed facing me. "What are you doing?" I ask in confusion, feeling vulnerable with my panties around my thighs, standing there alone and naked.

"Hit me," he commands.

"No!" I answer instantly, without even thinking about it. "I don't want to."

"You don't?" One brow raises. "Are you sure? Think about the things I've done to you, Ophelia. You've never wanted to slap me in the face?"

"I have slapped you," I remind him, not knowing how to feel about this sudden request. I only know I don't want to think about that side of Emmett right now.

"Do you think you did it enough?" he dares me, turning his head in invitation.

I want to resist whatever he is trying to bait me into, but I am still writhing with burning need and not thinking clearly. Whenever I am with Emmett, I try to push my bad memories of him as far away as possible. Intentionally thinking about them feels foreign and strange. But the memories never far from the surface, and I quickly find them flooding in, whether I like it or not.

"That's it," he encourages, noting the building fire in my eyes. "I know you've hated me before. Punish me for it."

His voice drifts into an unfamiliar sound. One that belongs to the other side of him that I've compartmentalized. That other Emmett is the only one sitting in front of me right now.

"Be a good girl, Ophelia," he adds with a vicious grin that sends me over the edge.

Those words. Things the new Emmett I have come to know would never say, but sadly this is the side of him that somehow pulled me in first, long before I even knew another side existed. I take several firm, decisive steps forward, my chest heaving with old anger. My hand rear backs and cracks across his cheek with a loud snap that almost startles me. The skin turns white, then bright red as his fingers lightly touch the source of pain, before he turns his face back to me with an excited smile.

His eyes burn into me and the throbbing between my legs grows. His hands bolt forward, grasping behind my thighs and yanking me forward so fast that I lose my balance and fall on top of him. He crashes back onto the bed, hoisting me up onto his hips. He lifts his ass from the bed, pushing far in between my legs with his hard and bare cock resting outside of my lips. His fingers wrap around my wrists and pin my arms behind my back once again, and he uses the grip to lift me up off of him, teasing my folds with his erection.

"Please, Emmett," I beg him, suspended over him and at his mercy. "I want you inside of me."

His other hand moves over his shaft. He looks at me as he hisses and strokes. "This?" he asks coyly. "Is this what you want?"

I try to struggle free and force myself down on him, but he keeps me in place. "I'm not wearing a condom," he reminds me.

"Where are they?" I ask impatiently. "I'll get one."

"I don't have any." He grins.

I let out an exasperated groan, thinking the relief I need is surely off the table now. I want to start bitching him out for not stopping to get more on the way, but I am distracted by him pulling me down. He grips my face and urges me to take him into my mouth. I need to feel some kind of satisfaction of my own, but I will settle for driving him crazy for now.

He tries to thrust against my lips but I grip him firmly and move down to trail my tongue up and down the length of him. He murmurs against the sensation, his hips bucking and begging to feel the warmth of my mouth. I tease the tip with my tongue and bottom lip, reveling in how he's squirming for more, breathlessly imploring me.

I can't wait to feel some relief, feeling overwhelmed by the intimacy of the taste dripping out from him. I slide my mouth around him and run my fingers down between my legs. His eyes spark at the sight and the moans that escape my mouth at my own touch.

"Wait." He sits up suddenly, pushing me to the side of him. "I want to watch you." He says it as a command, not a request.

I sit next to him on the bed, perched on my knees as he

watches my hand. I keep one hand gripped around him, moving up and down against the pulsing throbs that flow through him as I touch myself. My head thrashes back in cries of ecstasy as I stroke him and myself, loving the intensity of his glaring eyes. I start to feel self-conscious and vulnerable, but his excitement pushes all of that away.

My dripping wetness and the feel of his hardness in my hands makes me yearn to feel him inside of me. In frustration, I grab his hand and pull it between my thighs, coaxing his fingers inside of me. He hardens even before his fingers slide inside and I begin rocking into them to feel him more deeply.

I am in complete control of him, directing my own touch and his wherever I want it to go. For whatever I thought I wanted to happen in this room tonight, I realize now this is exactly what I needed. The relief of sex completely on my own terms. The return of control washes over me, allowing me to let go of any and everything else.

My hair falls loose as my head thrashes around and I lose myself in our hands, our breaths, and my primal cries. I rock my hips harder against his hand, moving my fingers in quickening circles that glide over my pulsating nerves. My climax builds as Emmett begins to grunt and strain in my grip.

"Wait," I barely manage to whisper as I yank my hand away from him.

He leans forward as our hands continue working me over, and takes my hardened nipple into his mouth, holding it with his lips and teeth as his tongue darts against the sensitivity of it and the sensation that shoots straight to my core. It sends me over the edge as I grind against our combined touch, rubbing against the rippling pleasure that crashes over me in a merciless wave.

As the tingling fades, I push his hands back to his sides, catching one hand on the way to take his fingers into my mouth. I wrap my lips around them and suck in the taste of my own juices. Something I've never done before, but I am so lost in the ecstasy that in this moment I feel like I could do anything that popped into my head or his.

I bring him back into my mouth and lower over him, taking him in as deep as I can stand it. I am overcome with a need to own him. To make him melt in my hands and belong to no one but me. He may have to put Vivian in her place, but I am determined to make sure no one makes him feel the way I do.

His cock pushes against the back of my throat before I pull back again, pushing him in and out until he is whimpering and his legs are quivering. His hand grips into my hair as his hips thrust against me until finally, I feel the taste of him spilling into my mouth. My hand continues working over him, sliding across my spit, as I milk every last throbbing drop of him into my mouth.

With my mouth full of his seed, I think of looking for a place to spit it out, but I want to drink him in. I take it all down with one swallow, leaving him breathless and stunned as he watches me. We're both speechless and breathless as I collapse next to him, nuzzling my cheek in between his muscular arm and chest.

We melt into a deep sleep until I wake up in a panic. I fumble for my phone in the darkness.

"Shit!" I yell out, jerking him awake.

It's after midnight and my mom has called three times. I don't know how long we were asleep, but my legs are still numb from my intense orgasm.

"We have to go," I tell him as I race to find my clothes.

He wipes the sleep from his eyes and stands to flick on the bedside lamp, but he doesn't look like he's in any hurry to get out the door. "Wait," he says, walking over to run his arms around me from behind.

"No, Emmett! We have to go!" I plead with him. "My mom is going to be pissed. I can't afford to be put on house arrest right now with everything that's happening with your sister. We still have to go talk to my dad, remember?"

"You're already late. The damage is done." He grins. "Might as well get as much out of it as we can while we're here."

I open my mouth to argue, but I'm silenced by the feel of him nibbling at my neck and ears. He kisses down my neck and down my spine, sending chills of renewed desire across my still naked body. One hand trails down and feels how wet I already am again as he lets out a grunt of satisfaction. Sure, I'm ready to go for round two. But everything in me wants to urge us to leave. I just can't seem to get the words out of my mouth.

Suddenly he whips me around and pins my face down to the mattress with a force that only excites me more. His erection presses against my ass, when I finally regain my ability to speak.

"There are no condoms, remember?" I groan.

His hands leave me for a moment and then I hear tearing paper. I lift slightly and look around to see him sliding a condom on. "You asshole!" I cry out. "You had one the whole time?"

He ignores my scolding, which makes me want to bitch him out even more. But I am quickly distracted by his hands squeezing into my hips as he effortlessly slides straight into me. No warm up needed. Wasting no time, he begins thrusting in and out of me at a quickened pace.

We are inexplicably restored to the same level of desire we had been suspended in earlier. He fills me completely as he pounds against me. I push against him as hard as I can, feeling like I can't get enough of him inside of me, even though I am certain nothing else could possibly fit. I slip back into an insatiable hunger as I claw into his thighs, urging him not to stop or slow down.

Our groans grow more demanding in between our heavy breaths until we finally we build to our release. I collapse against the bed as my muscles tighten around him, tensing with the roaring orgasm that crashes over me.

"Okay, now we really have to go," I laugh into the sheets as I try to regain my ability to move and speak.

His hands press into my ass and rub up my back, followed by a trail of long, slow kisses that drive me mad. "Don't get me started again," I quip.

I'm scared of losing myself in this. Everything about him is intoxicating. The winding curls of his hair, and his expressive eyes that give away everything that is going on inside of him. I see even more sparking inside of them every day. He's finally opening up, letting the real him shine through.

"Started?" he asks coyly. "My goal is for you to never stop."

We're all afraid of the darkness inside of us, but Emmett has a way of bringing mine front and center. I can't hide from it when he's around. He forces me to confront the darkest parts of myself. What I can stand, what I can forgive. I have been able to outrun everyone and everything else I have ever encountered… except for him. I can't outrun Emmett. I can't get away from him, no matter how hard I try.

"Let's just run away," he blurts suddenly. "Let's just get away from all of this."

"What about Jameson Automobiles?" I reply heavily, knowing Emmett could never run away. And I wouldn't run away with him regardless. I have a family here who loves me, but I don't throw that in his face right now.

He sighs and lets it go. I don't know if he was hoping for me to tell him it was okay to run away from the company, but I think we both know that can't happen. And he would never let himself do that, even if I did tell him it was okay.

"Why do you always look at me like that?" I look away, blushing.

"Like what?" he asks.

"With that crazy look in your eye."

"I'll tell you a secret," he says with a shy grin that quickly fades. "I have always wondered, if I stare at you long enough, if maybe you could read my thoughts. Know what's going on inside of me so I don't have to fuck it up trying to say it all out loud. Before…when my dad and the Elites were still around…I had to act a certain way. Say and do certain things that I hated. I used to wish you could read my mind. So you'd understand everything the same way I did."

"That's funny," I smirk shyly. "I never feel like I know what's going on in your mind, but I feel like you always know what I'm thinking. It scares me sometimes."

"I don't know what you're thinking right now," he quips.

"Yes, you do!" I laugh. "I just told you!"

"Oh, don't play dumb, Ophelia." He teases my chin with his finger. "You expect me to believe there is anything less than at least a thousand thoughts going on in your brain at any given time?"

"I think you give me too much credit." I smile.

"Or you don't give yourself enough credit," he quips back before rolling over.

It's strange. I'm not used to Emmett building me up. I can't understand why it's so hard for him to just say how he feels, but it seems maybe he feels so much it's hard to express. It's a possibility that I've never fully considered before. I was so busy convincing myself he was heartless and malicious for so long, I never considered just how many conflicting thoughts could be happening inside of him. Or that he feels he has no way to get it all out.

But it makes sense considering what I know about his father. Emotion wasn't allowed. It was considered a weakness. Emmett has been trained to suppress how he feels. More than that, he's been trained to convince himself those feelings aren't there at all.

"If only we could just hide away in some place like this for a few days. Or a month," I say with a smile as I peel myself up and reach for my clothes.

"I'm serious," he says with a kiss to my forehead. "I don't ever want to be too far from your mind. Think of this and me at least a little all the time."

"Ugh, I do," I assure him bitterly. "That's part of the problem."

My mind drifts back to his sister, still believing that once we find her, everything between us will be easier. Could Bernadette have just run away? Or even killed herself? Emmett is convinced she would have left a note, but he's not traumatized by his father's death in the same way she was. But then another thought crosses my mind.

"Do you think Bernadette knew about your deal with my dad?" I ask cautiously.

"No, how could she have?" he replies confidently.

"I don't know, but...do you think...she'd come after you if she knew?" I suggest. "Could that have something to do with this? What if she's plotting some kind of revenge against you?"

"My sister isn't smart enough for that," he quips.

"No, be serious." I lightly smack his arm. "Let's say she did know...would she understand what you did? Or would she hate you for it?"

"She'd hate me," he states plainly. "But the only people who know about that deal are you and your dad."

My eyes cut over to him. "And you know for certain she wouldn't have talked to my dad?"

He looks to me with fading concern. "Anything's possible." He nods. "But why would he tell her something like that? She could turn him in."

"She is a Jameson," I remind him. "I'm sure she doesn't trust the cops any more than you do. Do you think he would have tried to use her to come after what's left? To come after Jameson Automobiles? They could be allies."

"All the more reason for us to talk to your dad," he insists.

We finally manage to get our clothes back on, but only after stopping too many times to lose ourselves in each other's mouths. I am alarmed by my never-ending desire for him. No matter how much of him I get, I just keep wanting more and more.

"What should I tell my mom?" I ask him as we begin the long drive back to my house.

"That you fell asleep on my couch," he suggests.

"Good enough, I guess." I huff. "She's going to be pissed no matter what I say. That excuse is better than telling her anything that really happened today."

"How are you feeling?" he asks, glancing across my arms.

"I guess like someone who just did heroin for the first time," I grumble, realizing the effects of it faded long ago.

I still can't believe what Lily and Vivian did to me, or that Emmett managed to fix it so fast. Everything that came after that is far from my mind. It vanished between our bodies at some point in the motel room, and I am in no hurry to revive any of it.

"Maybe we should skip school tomorrow," Emmett suggests. "I can convince Principal Brown that you're still not feeling well after what Vivian and Lily did to you, and that I'm taking care of you."

"So, we can go back to your motel?" I ask longingly, with a dreamy tone of voice.

"Actually, so we can go see your dad." He sighs. "I'm worried if we go to school, something else crazy will happen and set us back again. We need to get this out of the way. If your dad doesn't have anything to do with Bernadette's disappearance, we need to start planning what to do next."

"Yeah…I guess you never know what's going to happen whenever you step into WJ Prep," I lament, feeling a dull ache of exhaustion growing between my eyes. "I'm not in any hurry to go see my dad, but whatever you think is best. I told you I'd help in any way I could."

He takes my hand in his and raises it to his lips. "Thank you," he says tenderly.

It's hard to reconcile the different faces of Emmett at times. A few hours ago, he was triggering some of my worst memories and asking me to slap him in the face. Now, he is sweet and tender and driving me home like any other boyfriend would. I want to think his dark side if just a symptom of his upbringing, and now that his dad is gone, he will eventually heal and those things will fade. But I also want to accept the very real possibility that all of it is the real Emmett, and that I may not be able to get one without the other.

I told him I didn't want easy, that I only wanted him. And today has put the truth of that to the test. But as he kisses me goodnight and tells me he will be back to pick me up in the morning, I know I'd make the same promise all over again.

# CHAPTER ELEVEN

BOOK 2

The time has finally come, and I can't put it off any longer. With my suspension from school lifted and Vivian and Lily seemingly scared into submission for the time being, we have to start getting some answers about Bernadette. Which means we have no choice but to go see my dad.

We drive to a small town outside of Jameson called Portville Bay. It's a coastal fishery area with lots of white-haired men who look like they're retired walking around. I hate how close it is to Jameson and wonder how long my father has been lingering so close by.

Theo is living in a modest house on the shore with a line of expensive boats tied out back. It's not the sprawling mansion I expected, considering the fortune he has supposedly built back up, but I get the feeling he stays on the move a lot if the FBI really is after him like the police warned me.

But within those small walls, it doesn't look like any expense was spared. We are greeted at the gate by one of the people working at the house and immediately taken around back to a lavish patio area you would never expect to see tucked behind this kind of house. Even with the fall chill and the even colder breeze blowing in off the water, we nestle into warm seats by an outdoor heater.

"Mr. Nickelson will join you in just a moment," the man cordially informs us. "Is there anything I can get you while you wait?"

"What more could we need?" I joke as I look at the arrangement of snacks and drinks on the table, including an assortment of strange-looking milkshake drinks. "What are those?"

"They're one of Mr. Nickelson's favorites!" he beams in reply, looking way too happy about his job. "They're a sort of spicy hot chocolate with alcohol."

The man walks away as we take our seats at the table. I note the three alcoholic beverages and turn to Emmett. "He does know we're teenagers, right?"

"You complaining?" he smirks as he takes one of the drinks into his hands. The liquid steams against the cold air as he puts it to his lips for a sip.

My stomach growls as I look over the assortment of fruit, vegetables, oysters, and crab legs. But after what happened with Vivian and Lily at school, I'm feeling oddly wary of consuming anything from people I don't trust. And I definitely don't trust my father.

I look over to the waves crashing against my father's line of boats. They crash with an alarming intensity in front of a darkening sky. I can see the storm rolling in across the sea, and it does nothing to settle my uneasy nerves about being here. The boats rock helplessly against them, tied up tight enough that they can't be swept away. What is keeping me tied up and safe from being swept away by the currents of these rich and powerful men who keep sucking me in? Emmett. My father. They're more alike than I want to admit, and I can't seem to escape either of them.

"Ophelia." My father smiles half-heartedly as he appears through the sliding back door of his home. "So good to see you."

My father has dark brown wavy hair that pokes out from under a straw fedora. It's almost as dark as mine, but with touches of blonde against his paler skin, giving away that my Hispanic side comes entirely from my mother. He's tall, like me. But my mannerisms are entirely from my mom. I am practical and to the point like her. That's what makes him so charming. Dangerously deceptive. He can talk his way around anything to get you back where he wants you.

I want to say something smart ass back, but we are here for answers. No use getting on his bad side. And anyway, his tone is unconvincing. I am guessing he is not actually happy to see me at all.

"Good to see you again, Theo," Emmett chimes in politely, half-standing to shake his hand.

I let out a sigh, seeing the two of them greet each other. A girl's boyfriend and her father. Something you always hope goes well, but also something I've never experienced outside of Brendan. Of course, these two already know each other too well for my comfort. Emmett has probably talked to my own father more than I have, with the deal they made in the past.

"How are things going with Jameson Automobiles?" he asks Emmett with genuine curiosity as he scoops up one of the hot chocolates in between his palms. "That's a big job for a guy your age."

"Plenty of good staff to help." Emmett smiles. "At least until I finish school and can start running things full-time."

"Any plans for college?" my father shoots back, and I hate how normal it sounds. Plus, we didn't come here for small talk. I'm eager to get this over with.

"Emmett's not exactly sure what his plans are yet, Theo," I answer for him, firmly directing my father's attention back to me. "His family is going through a pretty hard time right now."

"Oh, I'm sorry to hear that," he replies in smooth surprise, as if Thomas's murder wasn't enough of an explanation for any trouble they could be experiencing.

"Emmett's sister, Bernadette, is missing," I blurt out, cutting to the chase.

"Missing?" He raises his brows.

I study him carefully, looking for any hint of guilt. I may not know my father well, or at all really, but we resemble each other enough that I'm positive I could spot a lie on his face.

"Yes, missing," I continue curtly. "We've looked through her things and she doesn't appear to have run away or hurt herself. She's been gone for a week now. No one has heard from her."

"Such a shame," he commiserates. "She seemed like such a bright, pleasant young woman."

This guy's good. I don't detect an ounce of sarcasm or insincerity in his voice, but I know for a fact that he didn't see anything of Bernadette besides her screaming over her father's dead body. I wonder if he assumes we would have forgotten that much, or if he cares so little that he can't even bother to lie well. Unless…he has seen more of Bernadette than we realize.

"I wasn't aware that you knew much about Bernadette?" my voice raises accusingly. "You've only seen her once, right?"

He recoils, but not in a guilty way as I would have hoped. He just looks embarrassed over his social fumble. "Sorry, must have gotten her confused with someone else."

I flash a look at Emmett, wondering if it seems odd to him. "Obviously you know a lot of people in Jameson," he says to Theo, straightening in his seat. "You have police connections and you know a lot of people who, let's be honest…aren't entirely on the up and up. We were just wondering if you had heard anything? Any talk of someone wanting to come after what's left of my family?"

"I'm afraid not," he shakes his head before blowing on his drink and taking another sip. "Listen, I like you, Emmett. You have what it takes to run Jameson the way your father should have been all those years. Not only that, but you're seeing my daughter, right?"

I shift uncomfortably in my seat, not wanting him to act like a regular father. He's done nothing for me, and it feels insulting. But Emmett nods honorably, just as he would with any girlfriend's dad.

"If I ever hear of any threat to you or your family, I will come to you. You have my word," my father vows earnestly.

I can't sit still while he sits here and acts like this great guy. I restlessly fidget, prompting a slew of warning glances from Emmett. But who is Theo to care about threats on Emmett's family? He was the biggest threat of all when he barged in with a gun and murdered Emmett's father. Sure, he may have been a bad guy that Emmett was happy to see go, but my father didn't care about that. He would have pulled the trigger just as quickly if Thomas Jameson had been the greatest guy on earth. He was only looking after his own interest in getting revenge, and I can't stop myself from thinking he won't let things end there.

Maybe he really was planning to keep going until all of Jameson was his, which only makes it that much more convenient for him to sit here and lure Emmett into his pocket. It'll only make it easier for him to finish what he's started when he's ready.

"Spit it out, Ophelia," Theo blurts suddenly. "I see your wheels turning. You and I may not be close, but you're still my daughter. I can tell you're thinking something, so why don't you just come out with it?"

"Well," I straighten in my seat to meet his challenge with a daring stare. "If you must know, Theodore…I am just wondering how we can be so sure you don't have something to do with Bernadette's disappearance. You took out Mr. Jameson after all. How can we trust you?"

"That was a deal between Emmett and me, and you know it," he defends coldly.

"You would've found a way with or without Emmett's cooperation," I shoot back. "You took the Elites down. But maybe that wasn't enough for you?"

"Thomas and I had an old score to settle." He clears his throat and leisurely swirls the stirrer in his drink, as if murdering a man was no big deal. "That's over and done with, and I have no interest in Jameson now. Beyond you."

"Ha!" I laugh out bitterly. "That's rich."

"Ophelia," Emmett mutters under his breath, nudging my leg under the table.

"I'm sorry, but it's just a little hard to stomach, sitting here and listening to you claim to have any interest in me," I sneer, hating the way my voice wavers with overwhelming emotion. "You didn't want anything to do with me until the Elites tried to use me against you. And who knows how you would have solved that problem had Emmett not stepped in and offered to take me captive instead."

He sinks a bit in his chair under my accusations, but keeps a calm and collected demeanor. Overall, he seems completely unaffected by my obvious hurt, which I'm not surprised about. I just wish it didn't sting so much, and that he'd stop lying to our faces by claiming to care about me.

"I'm not proud of many things in my life, Ophelia," he explains slowly, staring off at his line of boats on the bay. "But that's in the past. All I can do now is try to move forward and make things right."

"And exactly how do you plan to do that?" I snap harshly, but the man who greeted us interrupts, whispering something into my father's ear.

"If you'll excuse me." Theo stands with a gentle smile, seeming relieved from the excuse to escape. "I have to take this call. It'll only be a moment."

I am still fuming when the sliding door shuts behind him. Emmett immediately hunkers down next to me, his breath smelling like chile liqueur.

"What the hell are you doing?" he hisses into my ear. "We didn't come here to berate the man!"

"This is pointless, Emmett!" I snap back in a hushed tone. "Just as pointless as talking to Vivian or Lily. If he did do it, he's not going to tell us anything."

"Do you still think he could have something to do with my sister?" he asks earnestly.

"I don't know." I bite my lip and shake my head. "We can't rule him out yet."

"Well, then…let's take a look around his house," he suggests.

"Oh, yeah, sure," I snort. "That's not going to seem suspicious at all. 'Hey, estranged dad who I hate! Can we just rummage through your house really fast, having just accused you of kidnapping!?'"

"Exactly why I wanted you to control yourself while he was here before," he scolds. "Just follow me."

I follow Emmett as he slides in through the back. We are of course quickly greeted by the man working in my father's home. "Need something?" he asks.

"Just the bathroom," Emmett replies.

"Ah, yes. Of course." He steps aside and motions down the hall. "Second door on the left."

We follow his directions, noting that my father's office is just to the side of us. He casually shuts his door for privacy when he sees us walk past. Once we're down the hall and out of sight, Emmett nods for me to go ahead into the bathroom.

"I'll look around first, then you take a quick turn and see if you find anything," he whispers.

I try to stall as much as I can in the bathroom, doing everything as slowly as possible. I would sample any bath products lying around, but my father is a classic bachelor. Only keeping the essentials on display, none of which include hand lotions or moisturizers.

After a few minutes, I hear a slight tap on the door. Emmett is waiting outside. "That's probably as much as I can look around without taking too long," he tells me, stepping inside the bathroom to take my place.

"Find anything?" I ask, but he shakes his head.

"Look for any sign that he may have been in touch with Bernadette. Look for notepads laying around that could have her number written down on it or something," he instructs in a whisper.

"My dad's not stupid," I hiss. "He wouldn't leave stuff like that just lying around. Especially knowing we were coming here."

"Take a quick look, but don't go through anything too much and don't get caught," he continues, ignoring my doubts. "Look for any weird doors or passageways with a lock on them," he orders before shutting the door.

I nervously step through the few small rooms lining the hall. There's a big living room on one end, and what appears to be my father's bedroom on the other. The space is clean and minimal, but I can see the line of expensive clothes in his closet with lavish leather shoes and designer sneakers to match. My father is trying to look like any ordinary coastal guy out here, but I can see the signs of the other side to his life.

There is another bedroom near his that looks like it hasn't been used any time recently. Nothing is out of place. There are no strange doors or anything that could hint at him holding Bernadette hostage. I try to take in as much as I can, but am only met with the occasional framed photo of my father standing alone at various places from his travels.

Emmett soon emerges from the bathroom, nervously smoothing back his hair. "Anything?" he asks, peeking around the corner to make sure no one is coming or looking for us.

"No," I huff. "This is hopeless. I don't know what you expect us to find. He knew we were coming. If he was up to anything, he would have hidden away any sign of it."

"Ah, there you are," my father chimes from down the hall. "I'm sorry, I feel rude. I should have offered to give you two a tour of the house." He swipes his palm across the back of his head with a nervous smile. "I guess I was just embarrassed," he confesses shyly. "This isn't exactly the nicest place I've lived, or really the first impression I wanted you to have of me."

"My first impression of you was putting a bullet through a man's head, remember?" I respond bitingly before shoving past both of them toward the front door.

I catch a glimpse of Emmett rolling his eyes and sulking behind after me with an exasperated breath.

"Did you want to stay for dinner?" Theo calls out, chasing us towards the door. "I can have my cook whip something up for us."

"No, thank you," I state plainly as I storm through the front door. I'm still exhausted from the day before, and I'm beyond ready to go and hopefully never see my father again.

I march out to Emmett's car and notice the two of them exchanging words in the doorway. "Nice to see you, Ophelia!" he calls out to me with one swift wave. "I promise it won't be so long until we meet again."

I want to think he's making empty promises, but there's something ominous in his tone. "What does that mean?" I whip back around to him.

"Just that I don't intend to stay out of the picture forever," he explains coyly. "I'll be seeing you around."

I release a huffy moan and give up, yanking the locked door handle repeatedly.

"Give me a minute!" Emmett snaps as he jumps into the driver's seat and unlocks my door. "I know you don't like the guy, but you don't have to be so hard on him."

"This whole thing was a waste of time," I lament, sinking into my seat and crossing my arms.

"No, it wasn't," he defends. "I think your father is innocent."

"What makes you so certain?" I ask in an unconvinced tone.

"I've met a lot of bad guys doing a lot of bad things when I was by my father's side," he explains. "I can usually spot a guilty man, and your father doesn't seem like one of them. At least not in terms of Bernadette."

"Then why was he acting so fucking weird?!" I argue, wishing he would be guilty out of pure spite.

"He's trying to charm us. I can't tell you exactly what his motivations are, but he's not a guy who's responsible for a missing girl. I just don't see it in him. You have to trust me on this." He stops and looks at me. "I'm proud of you," he says softly.

"For what!?" I shoot back, still feeling angry.

"I know it wasn't easy for you to come here and see him today," he explains.

I sink down in the seat. Emmett doesn't know the half of it. This about more than just my dad. It's about him and that stupid deal they made. Whatever way Emmett redeems himself, it's hard to reconcile with his partnership with my father. And I still can't shake the feeling that Theo will be coming back to get more out of that deal than was originally promised.

Seeing my father does scare me. I'm afraid that whatever part of him made him fit into the Elites is something hereditary that exists in me, too. What if I am just as capable of being selfish and vengeful? To the point that I'd sacrifice others to get what I want. Isn't that what I've been doing? Only feeling motivated to find Bernadette because of my own selfish need for Emmett? I don't think enough about the fact that she's his sister or what this is doing to him inside. I've been distracting him every step of the way, not helping like I promised.

We're silent for most of the drive back. Emmett eventually plays me an album from a band he's been telling me about, claiming he wants to take me to one of their concerts sometime. It feels good to talk about normal things for a bit, but I can't let go of the greasy feeling leftover from my father's visit so easily.

As much as I hate to admit it, I think Emmett is right. He may know more about bad people than I do, but I didn't see any sign of guilt in my father either. He's up to something, but whatever it is doesn't seem like it will lead us to Bernadette. And now I am left knowing that once all of this is over, I'll have to worry about my father trying to show up in my life again, thanks to his departing promise. I can only hope that he just feels bad about never being around and wants to make it right, but something tells me nothing in my life will ever be that simple again.

"Hey, what are you doing tonight?" Emmett asks suddenly.

"Reeling from everything that just happened," I quip. "Or at least that's as far as I've planned. Why?"

"There's a Halloween party," he announces casually. "Wanna go?"

"A party," I gape. "Wow...I wouldn't have thought you'd want to go to a party right now...with everything that's going on."

"We could use the distraction I think." He nods. "Maybe relaxing a little will set our heads straight. Give us some clue of what to do next."

"Sure," I shrug with a smile. "Let's go."

We stop by a second-hand store on the way home to scour through the clothes for some sort of Halloween costumes. We have a blast digging through the racks and trying stuff on.

"Where is this party anyway?" I ask, as I try on a wig.

"This girl from school, Diana," he replies, straightening the wig for me and planting a soft kiss on my lips. "Her parents are famous musicians. Very wealthy. She always throws these giant parties and makes everyone endure her own nasally performances. But I don't think she's going to be as successful as her parents." He laughs.

"I'm sure they'll just buy her fame," I joke.

Emmett and I settle on some vintage clothes that can let us pass as hippies. To him, this is just a way to pass the time and get our minds off of things. But I'm excited for so many other reasons. In my entire time at WJ Prep so far, I have never been invited to a party.

He shoves a pint of liquor into my purse before we walk into the party. The only Halloween decorations to be found are an unlit string of pumpkin lights half-hanging from the edge of the staircase in the living room, where a makeshift stage had been built to accommodate each of the musicians taking turns singing slow, steady acoustic songs.

Emmett quickly gets caught up talking to a group of guys, and I am left standing on my own awkwardly, realizing maybe I hadn't been missing out on much by not getting invited to these things. He finally turns back to me and says they're going to go check out Diana's brother's new car.

I'm not on my own long before a familiar tall, slender figure approaches. Malcolm. He's holding a PBR and his icy blue eyes light up with a kind smile as soon as he sees me. Everything seems to slow down a little.

"Didn't expect to see you here," he says coyly as he slides into a standing position next to me against the wall.

"Why's that?" I shoot back.

"I never see you at parties," he explains.

"I'm never invited," I scoff.

"Well…glad you got invited this time." He smiles, stumbling slightly as we both laugh.

"Somebody's drunk," I snort.

"No, I swear. Just hopelessly clumsy." He flashes an adorably sly boyish grin. "Okay, and maybe a little drunk."

"Hoping to join you soon," I reply as I raise the pint from my purse in cheers before taking a big, long swig.

He's standing too close with a light in his eyes that's making me feel uneasy.

"I like your costume." He points to my long-tasseled suede vest.

I peer at him from the corner of my eye, noting the way he's looking me up and down. I don't know if it's the swigs of liquor I am taking every so often, or just the desperation of feeling awkward and alone at a party, but I don't feel nearly as defensive towards him as I normally would. Which is dangerous, considering Emmett is right outside and could be back at any time.

"What are you supposed to be?" I ask, examining him and coming up empty at guesses.

"A computer hacker." He grins.

"Oh, so yourself…" I laugh when he nods, realizing that's why he's wearing his regular clothes.

Silence falls and I can feel him staring at me again. "Hey, you got something…" His hand reaches up towards my face, "Just, uh…mind if I?…" I awkwardly flinch back. He licks his index finger before pressing it to my cheek to remove a lone eyelash. He holds it out before us. "Make a wish."

Feeling a growing buzz from my drink and his suddenly handsome presence come over me, I press my fingers to the cold spot burning on my cheek. We both blow until the lash vanishes.

"Malcolm," a voice booms out suddenly.

"Oh, hey, Emmett," he replies innocently, rubbing his hand down the back of his neck.

"What's going on here?" Emmett thunders back, looking between the two of us as if we've just committed some kind of horrid sin.

"Nothing." I lower my head uncomfortably. "You left and Malcolm just came up to say hi."

"Funny how you never seem to be around until I'm not," he bites back, burning his eyes into Malcolm's.

"I should probably get going," he offers casually, shooting me a sympathetic grimace.

"Ha! And look…I come back and you conveniently leave again," Emmett continues.

"Well, it's not like we're friends," Malcolm reminds him, his smirk growing more arrogant this time.

"But you and Ophelia are?" Emmett questions with daring eyes.

Malcolm's chest bucks out slightly as his eyes widen. He steps closer, dancing shoulder to shoulder with Emmett briefly. I grow tense, bracing myself against the wall, certain that the two of them are about to fly into a brawl. But thankfully, Malcolm shrugs it off with an amused smirk before walking away.

"Let's go," Emmett huffs suddenly, watching Malcolm leave.

"What?" I cry. Not that I want to be here, but his sudden

reason for wanting to go is irritating. "We haven't even been here that long," I argue.

"We've been here long enough," he fires back, grabbing my arm.

I'm about to fight him on it, when I catch a pair of eyes glaring at me from across the room. Vivian and Lily are watching us intensely, their mouths tightened, not looking pleased that Emmett and I leaving together so suddenly—even though it's obvious that he's furious with me. But with them watching, I feel suddenly inclined to let him drag me along. I wouldn't want to miss this chance for them to see us going home together.

"Not that I was in love with the party or anything," I protest once we're climbing back into his car. "But did you have to flip out over Malcolm like that?"

"I saw the way you were looking at him." Emmett scowls. "I told you I don't want you around him."

"I didn't really know anyone else." I cross my arms in a pout. "He was the only one talking to me."

"And why do you think that was?" he jeers suggestively.

"Because he was being nice?" I suggest.

"That word again. 'Nice.'" He shakes his head in disgust. "I promise you, there is nothing nice about Malcolm Henderson."

I turn my head to the window, feeling too tired to argue with him. Malcolm would say the same thing about Emmett. But I don't really know what came over me back at the party. I was being dangerously flirtatious with Malcolm, and really, I deserve for Emmett to be angry with me right now. But the alternative was standing alone or following him around, pretending to be interested in their luxury car jargon.

The car speeds up as Emmett rushes me back to my parents' house. Once we park, he leans over to give one quick, cold peck to my cheek, then turns straight again over the steering wheel, waiting for me to get out.

"Are you serious?" I glare at him in disbelief. "That's it? You're that mad at me."

He doesn't budge at first, refusing to look at me. But eventually he caves to my questioning stare. "I'm sorry," he groans, dropping his arms and shaking his head. "I'm just stressed. You were right…we probably shouldn't have gone to that party tonight. I feel like I'm just wasting time. Another day is gone, and we're no closer to finding Bernadette."

I reach out and rub my hand along the back of his neck, massaging the tension gently. "You can't just go, go, go all the time, Emmett," I say softly. "You have to have some time to decompress."

"Well, I don't feel any more decompressed," he says through clenched teeth.

"Why don't you come inside?" I suggest with a grin, eyeing the dark windows of my house. "It looks like my parents are asleep. I could sneak you upstairs and think of a few ways to help you decompress."

"Not tonight." He shakes his head, still not looking at me. "I'm tired. I'll call you tomorrow."

The thought of not spending the night with him, or having a chance to make love to him after the night ending this way puts my stomach in knots. But my eyes are heavy, and I don't have the energy to try and persuade him. I pull him in for a quick kiss, but somehow it melts into something long, deep, and lingering. Next thing I know, we're making out heavily in his car, not wanting to stop.

He pulls me across the dash, straddling my legs on either side of him. I don't even care that the steering wheel is pushing into my back as our tongues passionately crash together in deep, sweeping waves. I forget about how tired I am, on fire with intense need for him.

My lips part, just as I am about to plead with him again to sneak back inside with me. But before I can say anything, a loud, blaring horn sounds out, causing me to jump. I must have accidentally leaned back too far, right into his horn. The noise stirs a flickering behind the blinds of my house.

"My parents," I groan, knowing I ruined our chances.

"It's okay." He smiles, breathing out as he presses his forehead to mine before hoisting me off of him. "It's for the best."

"I guess so," I shrug reluctantly, wishing he wouldn't act so responsible right now. I wish he would speed off for his motel and I could just face the angry wrath of my mom later. But instead, I reach for the door handle.

I look back one more time before I open the door. Emmett is staring straight ahead again with dark, haunted eyes. He looks troubled, and it brings back the knots in my stomach. I don't know if it's guilt over what happened with Malcolm, but I can't help but feel some of his discontentment is definitely directed towards me right now.

"Goodnight," I say grimly, knowing I have to go inside, hoping something in him will change for just a moment before I have to walk away.

"Goodnight, Ophelia." He smiles sweetly, just enough to restore a little hope in me. "I'll call you tomorrow."

I can't hide the grin on my face as I walk back inside, still smelling him on my clothes. Our relationship may have had a twisted start, but things are starting to feel good. Normal, even. And if everything else has to be such a mess all the time, at least for now I have him. I just wish it didn't feel like something was always popping up and getting in our way.

I tell myself that the thing with Malcolm was no big deal and that Emmett will be over it by tomorrow. But as I lay down to go to sleep, the words of my father come back to me, causing me to toss and turn all night.

# CHAPTER TWELVE

BOOK 2

The next morning, I wake up to my mom knocking on my door saying she wants to talk. I'm panicked as I climb out of bed to let her in. So many things have happened this week that she could have somehow found out about. All the sex in Emmett's motel room, the drug incident at school, the fight at Lily and Vivian's, skipping school, the visit with my dad. My defenses for all of it are racing through my mind as she comes in making small talk about work.

"So…things have been going well at work," she says with an awkward and heavy smile.

"Oh, yeah?" I perk up nervously. "Well…that's…good."

"Yeah." She nods earnestly. "Hard work as always. But I really like the medical center here. Even better than the one back in Oklahoma, I think."

She looks at me expectantly, but I am too on edge and clueless to what to say.

"Well…what about school?" she asks finally.

"What about it?" I snap back defensively, my eyes wide.

"Just…how is it going?" she prods. "We haven't really been able to talk about it much since we got here, you know? And I felt so bad when everything happened with Emmett's dad. I felt like I knew nothing about your life or what had been going on with you."

"Oh…you know…That was a crazy time." I laugh nervously, but quickly realize how inappropriate it sounds. "But, um…things are good at school. You know, better now…Sort of."

"Better how?" she shoots back brightly.

My mind races. How is it better? I'm not getting the shit beaten out of me anymore, but I have beat up Vivian again. And asked Emmett to torture her the way he used to torture me, and realized both Vivian and I seem to get off on it in a weird way. Yeah, Ophelia. Start telling Mom all about that.

"It's just boring," I offer finally. "I don't really know what else to say about it."

"Oh, okay," she recoils in disappointment.

She tries to ask me questions about school, but I only give her brief answers. Then her expression changes, and I brace myself for whatever is coming. I know she came in here for a reason, and I can only guess what it might be.

"How are things going with Emmett?" she asks gingerly.

"Oh!" I blurt. "Emmett? Good…You wanted to talk about Emmett?"

Truthfully, I want more than anything to be able to talk to my mom about Emmett. I want to ask if this is what it was like when she met my father. I know it's nothing like how it is with Brendan. He's calm and strong enough to keep his emotions under control. He's never threatened or hurt my mom in any way. I know I want what they share together. And I'm afraid that with Emmett, I am getting what she had with my father. That's more believable.

I want to ask her if she felt this way about my dad—if she had this hard of a time walking away from him, too. When did she know it was time to give up on him? The story is that he hit her once and she left. Emmett has done worse than that to me —more than once. And I'm still here. If I told her that, as my mother, she would be obligated to lock me up and never let me see him again. But I need her to help make me understand the way my heart feels about him.

I don't want to blame him for the way he is. I know no one ever taught him how to love someone. How to really love them. I don't know what his mother is like, but she was absent enough to let his father be a monster. I want to tell him it doesn't matter that he's so fucked up, as long as he loves me the best way he knows how. Maybe I can teach him. Maybe I can fix him.

"You've just been spending so much time with him lately," she says lightly. "Things must be getting pretty serious."

"I'm not going to run off with him again, if that's what you're worried about," I reply confidently, thinking in my head that what I really mean to say is, 'He's not going to kidnap me again.'

"No, I wasn't worried about that, Ophelia," she answers crossly. "I just want to know what's going on in your life. Be a part of it all. Since you are spending so much time with Emmett, maybe you could invite him over to dinner tonight? I mean, if he's important to you, then we'd like to get to know him."

I'm quiet for a moment, thinking through her suggestion. She has no idea just how important Emmett is to me, or how much we've been through together—how much we're still going through together. I want to deny the invitation, but I feel guilty that we've sat down with my dad and not my mom and step-dad...the parents who have actually been supporting me and involved in my life.

I'm also relieved that Emmett is the only thing she is concerned about right now, given how many other things are looming. So, I tell her that I'll ask Emmett to come over for dinner. The hard part is going to be telling him that.

"Okay, I'll ask him," I tell her finally. She lingers with a wide smile, just staring at me. "Well...not with you sitting right here." I laugh. "Go and I'll call him."

"Got it." She nods sharply, throwing her hands in the air. "Say no more. Here I go." She shoots me one more excited and giddy grin before shutting the door.

She calls over her shoulder on her way out to let me know that they'll have dinner ready at six o'clock, and once she's gone, I pick up my phone to call Emmett. He sounds groggy when he answers, and it takes a moment for us to really be able to hear each other.

"What?" he grumbles across the line for the third or fourth time.

"Dinner!" I yell back. "Come over to my house for dinner tonight."

The line falls quiet for a moment, making me wonder if he still can't hear me. "Tonight's not really a good night," he says finally.

"Oh." I wait for further explanation, but he says nothing. "Why not? What's going on?"

"What's going on is my sister is missing," he bites back, "and I still have no clue where she is or where to even start looking."

"I know that, and I'm sorry. But if we don't know what to do next anyway…why not come over for dinner?" I suggest. "We can talk afterwards and figure out a plan." There's a long pause on the call. "Listen, you sat down with my dad and played nice…it'd mean a lot if you could do that for the parents who have actually been present in my life. Besides, Mom is getting suspicious of how much time we've been spending together. If she doesn't start getting to know you, she may put a stop to all of our rendezvous."

"Fine," he says after another long pause. "I'm sorry…I just didn't sleep much last night. What time?"

"Six tonight," I tell him. "And don't be late, okay? My mom is really excited about this."

"Great," he grumbles and promptly hangs up.

"What the fuck," I mutter under my breath, staring cluelessly at the phone.

Emmett seems to have changed overnight. Aside from what's happening with his sister, things between us were fine. And now he's closed off. Like the well of everything that has been opened up to me over the past couple of weeks is suddenly dry. I try to ignore how terrible it makes me feel, and I'm hoping that by the time he arrives for dinner, he'll have snapped back into the new Emmett I have come to know. Or at the very least, the Emmett that knows how to charm people into getting what he wants. I've watched him work that magic on my father, and I want more than anything to see him please my mom and Brendan in the same way.

I'm surprised by how excited I am to be having Emmett over for dinner. He is charismatic enough when he's trying to win people over, and I think that given a second chance, my mom and Brendan will actually come to like him.

Mom and Brendan are nothing like the other parents in this town—at least not the ones whose children attend WJ Prep. Their world centers around family, not money. And ironically enough, it was bringing us here that has torn part of their family away. I have only grown distant since we moved, but not out of choice. I am just constantly being pulled off by some new disaster.

But my excitement fades that evening when it's nearly 6:45 and Emmett still hasn't showed. I call and text but get no reply.

My mom has made one of her specialties. They're just simple bean burritos, but her seasonings, the spices and sauces, are what make the dish. It's a rich and salty dish and it's one of my favorites. Now it's sitting here getting cold because my boyfriend couldn't bother to show up on time, even though I begged him not to be late. My heart sinks in embarrassment with each passing minute. I can't help but feel judged by my parents. Like they're wondering why I'm spending so much time with this guy who, in this moment, appears to be an asshole. If they only knew the things he has done that have been so much worse. Then they'd really judge me. I wanted him to impress them. I wanted to be able to feel proud of him and our relationship. Instead I'm sitting here feeling certain that they think I'm an idiot for falling for this guy.

"I'm so sorry," I offer shyly, pinching the bridge of my nose. "I don't know why he's late. You worked so hard, Mom."

"Oh, nonsense!" She waves my apologies away with a smile. "I would've made this whether he was coming or not. And we'll eat it whether he comes or not."

"You don't think he's coming," I state with a muffled sigh.

"No! Not what I said!" she shoots back confidently. "I'm sure he'll be here."

The smell of my mom's cooking is almost enough to calm my anger. She's right. We have this with or without Emmett, which is more than he has without me. I don't even know if he knows how to appreciate a family like mine. It's unfamiliar and foreign to him. Maybe that's why he's not here. Because he has no comprehension of how important this is. Meeting with my father was like a business transaction. He only went because he needed something out of it. I'm more afraid than ever that Emmett is too fucked up to merge into my world in the ways that I need. In the ways that I want.

"Well, I'm going to start eating," Brendan grumbles finally.

My stepdad Brendan is a big guy with full tattooed sleeves and a big scruffy beard. His stance is scary and enough to throw any guy off, but I know his warmth and sweetness. I just don't want Emmett to know about it. He needs to be afraid of something around here.

Brendan towers above my petite mom, with her thick black hair and tan skin. We share the same hazel eyes and small figure, but running keeps my muscles bulky, giving me more curves than her.

"No!" my mother hisses, smacking his fork down from his hand. "I'm sure he'll be here. Right, Ophelia?"

"No, go ahead," I answer despondently. "I'm hungry. It's going to get cold."

An awkward silence falls over the table as Brendan digs into his food without hesitation. I shovel my food around on my plate, but my mom keeps her hands firmly planted, refusing to take a bite without our guest.

"Emmett has been preparing to take over Jameson Automobiles," I explain, trying to make excuses for him. "Which is really like running Jameson. He has already started meeting with the advisors of the company and has been really stressed."

"I can't believe that so much responsibility would be placed on someone his age," my mom gapes.

"I know." I sigh. "But he seems determined to prove to everyone that he is capable."

Finally, the doorbell rings. I race to answer it and thankfully, Emmett is finally standing there with a bouquet of flowers in hand.

"Where have you been!?" I hiss quietly, yanking him inside and shoving him towards the dining table.

"So sorry I'm late," he announces, rushing over to shake their hands and give my mom the flowers. "I stopped for these and then hit traffic."

I instantly know his excuse his bullshit. It's all backroads and neighborhoods between our houses and the local stores. There's no where he could have hit enough traffic to make him almost an hour late. But I keep my mouth shut, still clinging to the hope that he can actually win my parents over.

"We just started eating," Brendan tells him, motioning for him to have a seat.

"Thank you," he beams. "This looks delicious."

"Does your mom cook a lot?" my mom asks him innocently.

"All the time." Emmett takes a big drink of water and clears his throat. "She's German, so she likes to make a lot of dishes from her home. Recipes passed down through her family."

"Oh! How lovely!" she chimes. "Authentic German cuisine. Huh."

I peer up at him over my plate. He's lying and I don't know why. Sure, it might be a lot for them to take in if he was honest and told them their house was staffed with chefs, but they know who he is. They have to know how wealthy he is. And I've barely ever even seen his mom, much less known her to cook a meal for her family.

What bothers me the most is that I want to know why he feels the need to lie about these things. Is it out of some sort of pity? Does he think we're so poor we can't handle the idea of someone rich sitting at our dinner table?

"And how have all of you been holding up recently?" Brendan asks, subtly referring to Emmett's father's supposed suicide.

"Well," Emmett answers curtly, shifting in his chair, "as well as could be expected."

Lying again. We don't even know where Bernadette is, but I didn't expect him to actually come clean on that one.

The dinner trails off into small talk. Emmett does a great job of deflecting everything back to my parents, asking a million questions about their lives and their jobs. By the time they've answered one thing, he has another question ready to go. They love it, taking it as very polite and stimulating conversation. But I can see he's only trying to keep from talking about himself.

Once we've finished eating, I offer to help with the dishes and suggest that Emmett and Brendan go find a movie for us to watch.

"Um, actually," Emmett turns to me quietly. "I may need to go."

"Go where?" I ask in a hushed tone. "I thought you and I were going to talk later tonight. We can't spend a little time with my parents first?"

"Look, I came for dinner. What more do you want from me?" he hisses.

"Mom, actually…I'll help you with those dishes later if that's okay," I stammer, quickly trying to come up with an excuse before the full extent of my anger becomes obvious. "Emmett just reminded me of a report we're supposed to be working on together and we're behind. We need to catch up on it. We'll be up in my room!"

I yank Emmett away as she reluctantly agrees. I know the tension between us is probably painfully obvious. I pull him upstairs and slam my bedroom door shut.

"What the fuck, Emmett!" I belt the moment we're alone. "My dad gets the nice, charming version of you, but they get the you that's almost an hour late and lies about anything you actually say about yourself!?" He opens his mouth to speak, but

I cut him off. "Don't use your sister as an excuse again, either! You have no problem putting that aside when we're making visits to your motel room. You could've given me and my parents a nice evening with you. Do you know how important this was to my mom?" I demand angrily. "She feels like she doesn't know anything about my life. And she doesn't…because of you and everything your fucked up friends and family have dragged me into since I got here."

"Hey, your dad is just as messed up and would have dragged you in, too, whether we did or not," he defends. "Need I remind you, you would have been his prisoner if I hadn't taken you instead."

"Oh, yes, I keep forgetting how you kidnapping me was some sick way of saving me," I sneer. "And no, Emmett. You don't need to remind me of any of that. I'm all too aware. Which is why tonight was important. I wanted you to see my real family. Not my stupid biological father. My mom and Brendan mean everything to me. And they wanted to know you."

"I'm sorry, Ophelia," he answers in frustration, "it's just not a good time. Let's just find Bernadette, and then we can try again. I'm just getting more and more worried, and I don't know what to do. What if I never see her again?"

"Go to the fucking police, Emmett!" I snap, knowing he'll refuse yet again. "We're wasting time trying to figure this out on our own, and we're no closer to having any answers now than we were when we started! Let's just please, please go to the police. Or hire a private detective or something!"

"The detectives all know the cops," he argues. "You know it's too risky. The cops in this town are no good, and I have a feeling they're out to get me. What if they try to pin the whole thing on me?"

"What if they're not as against you as you think and have nothing to do with Bernadette's disappearance? And by not going to them, you shoot yourself and her…and me in the foot by not reporting it. Do you have any idea how it would look if they found out we knew about this for so long and said nothing?"

"That's on my mom," he insists. "She's the one who swore it was the worst possible idea. She made me promise not to." I pace the room in silence, not knowing what else to possibly suggest. "I was thinking about talking to Vivian. Like you suggested. I did promise if nothing panned out with your dad that I would go to her and Lily."

I can't help but groan at the idea of confronting those two again, especially after what happened last time. "When?" I ask resentfully. I don't want to do it, but I knew from the beginning they'd probably be our best lead.

"I was going to go tonight," he mumbles nonchalantly.

It struck me as odd that he didn't want to come to dinner at all when I first asked. Then he was late. Now he's conveniently telling me he was thinking of meeting up with Vivian tonight. "Would you have gone to see her without telling me?" I ask through the lump in my throat.

"No, of course not," he replies unconvincingly.

"Okay, well, I'll get my things and come with you," I announce, turning to grab my purse. "Let's go."

He stands and purses his lips, shuffling towards me awkwardly. "Actually…I think it'd be best if you didn't come."

I laugh out loud, but he's dead serious. "What the hell do you mean I shouldn't come with you? To go see Vivian!? Why… so I don't step in to stop your fucked up foreplay like last time?"

Suddenly, I'm afraid that's what the weird, kinky stuff at the hotel was about. Is that the kind of thing Vivian and he used to do? Lily seemed to think so. Did he miss it so much that he tried to get me to play along?

"No, it's nothing like that. Don't be ridiculous," he insists. "Vivian acts different when you're not around. She won't be so confrontational if it's just me. And maybe you could meet with Lily while I see Vivian."

"You're not hearing me, Emmett," I say slowly and clearly to the point of insult. "I don't want you to be alone with Vivian. Period. I don't trust her. I just know something will happen."

"You don't have to trust her," he says, growing angrier. "You just have to trust me. Don't you?"

The words stings. Trust. How can I possibly trust Emmett after everything he has done to me? I am giving him a chance at redemption, but always with the lingering fear that at any moment, he will go back to the way he was before. Always with fear and hesitation. I keep the expectation of it happening in place to protect myself, but maybe that's what will be our down-fall. By not trusting and having faith in his ability not to mess this up, I'm manifesting his failure. My inability to trust him is what's dooming both of us.

My lips part but nothing comes out. I can't lie to him, but I don't want to say the truth. I want to trust him, but I don't. Not when it comes to Vivian. I know what our little violent encounters used to turn into when the tables were turned. And I can't stop myself from wondering what would have happened at Lily's if they had been alone.

"This isn't just about us, Ophelia!" he shouts after I don't reply. "This is about my family. You understand?"

"You said you loved me," I remind him. "Doesn't that make me like family? I'm sorry…I just can't be okay with you running off alone with Vivian. I can't. You don't want me to be alone with Malcolm. It's only fair."

"Do you think Malcolm knows anything about my sister?" he asks in a sarcastic rage. "Cause if so…then by all means go do what you need to do."

"Oh, how convenient…a sacrifice you know you won't actually have to make," I shoot back, rolling my eyes.

I want to be more sympathetic. Softer to him right now while he's stressing out, especially knowing he might still end the night with Vivian against my wishes. The last thing I want to do is make him think I don't care and then send him off to her while he's angry and questioning our relationship. But I can't seem to break through this wall I have about the two of them. It's overpowering everything else inside of me.

"I just have a terrible feeling about it is all," I try again, softening my tone. I walk over to him and try to take his hand in mine, hoping to stop our argument. "Just please let me come with you. I promise I won't let things get out of control like last time."

He considers it for a moment and then looks away. "I don't know," he mutters under his breath. "I'm so exhausted. I don't even know if I'm up to talking to her tonight. I just don't know what else to do." He looks at me again, his eyes distant in thought. "I think I'm just going to go to bed. I've felt so tired and lost all day. Let's figure all of this out tomorrow, okay?"

He tries to lean in for a quick dismissive peck to my forehead, but I flinch back. "What are you talking about?" I ask in an accusing panic. I know he's not going to go to sleep. This is just to keep me at bay so he can go see Vivian. Maybe it's paranoia, but I can't convince myself of anything different. "Stay here," I plead with him, trying to pull him close to me again.

"My mom won't bother us for a while," I add suggestively, standing on my toes to lure him in for a kiss.

"I just said I was tired, Ophelia," he groans. "I'm not in the mood."

My heart sinks. He's never refused me—not since we started this up again. The only time he has ever refused me was when he was still with Vivian.

"Are you lying so you can go see her?" I ask against my better judgment. I know it's only going to make him mad and push me away, but I can't stop myself. He feels like sand slipping through my fingers, and I am desperately trying everything I can to hold on. "Or is something else going on? Something you're not telling me?"

"No!" he whines, pushing me away. "I'm just fucking tired, okay? Let it go. I'll call you tomorrow."

"Please don't go," I mumble too quietly as he walks out the door. I don't want him to hear me. Not really. At this point I know he's going to leave anyway, and I want to save some shred of my dignity. If there's even any left.

"Wait!" I barrel after him, unable to hold myself back, yanking him back into my room.

"Ophelia, what are you doing?" he groans.

"Please just hold me," I plead with him. "Just for a moment. This doesn't feel right. I need to feel close to you right now."

"You're always close to me." He sighs, pulling me to his chest.

"It doesn't feel that way right now," I confess. "I'm scared something else is going on with you and you won't tell me what it is. What am I supposed to think?"

"I need to go," he insists, pulling away, leaving my arms suspended and reaching for him in midair. He doesn't look back once as he leaves.

If he would have just made love to me, it wouldn't have fixed everything, but I wouldn't be left feeling so empty and unwanted. It feels like a big red flag waving mercilessly in my face, begging for me to accept what is right in front of me. Something has to be going on with Vivian. Before, he couldn't see that she's the best possible suspect in his sister's disappearance, and now I'm positive he's sneaking off to see her without me.

I fall to pieces as he slams my bedroom door shut. I'm too embarrassed to even go downstairs with him while he says goodbye to my parents. Everything about this feels wrong, and no matter how hard I try to redirect my thoughts or explain away his behavior, all I can see is Vivian's snide face in my mind, looking pleased as she puts her hands all over him.

Not knowing what else to do, I race to my laptop and begin scouring social media. I look at every chat platform I can to see when Emmett or Vivian were last active, if there's any correlation. After making up a million different scenarios in my mind and imagining them all in painful detail, I finally collapse onto my bed in tears.

This isn't like me. I have never acted so crazy over a guy. And I hate myself for it because I know everything I'm doing is exactly what will drive Emmett away. I decide that no matter how mad this is driving me, I have to at least make it appear as if I trust him. I open up my phone to send him a text message.

**I'm sorry for everything. I love you. Please get some rest. Talk to you tomorrow.**

I pray for some kind of instant response that will calm my runaway thoughts, but there is nothing. The longest hour of my life goes by without a single word from him. I finally tell myself I'll just go to bed, but once the lights are out and I'm under the covers, all I do is toss and turn restlessly. I have to talk myself out of going for a late-night run…which would really only turn into me stalking different places around town to see if I spotted them out together.

The worst part is that Emmett has literally tortured me in the past, abused me emotionally and physically. And not only did I manage to forgive and still fall in love with him, but this honestly feels worse than any of that. At least then I could try to hate him. This new territory just makes me hate myself.

Every time I think things are getting better, everything goes horribly wrong again. Maybe that's just how relationships are supposed to be. The ebb and flow. The ups and downs. I had always heard that, but I never knew it could hurt this bad.

At first, I check my phone every five seconds, terrified that I won't hear the ding of a new message. But quickly it fades to every thirty minutes. Then maybe every hour. When I wake up the next morning with phone in hand, and see that nothing has been sent since I fell asleep, I decide all at once that I'll never hear from him again.

# CHAPTER THIRTEEN

BOOK 2

I'm a complete wreck by Monday morning. Everything's gotten so much worse than I would have expected. Not only did Emmett not text me back Saturday night, I didn't hear from him all day Sunday either.

Part of me is convinced beyond a doubt that he met up with Vivian Saturday night. They decided to give it another go and haven't left each other's sides since. When he arrives at school today, he'll be back to the old Elite Emmett I once knew, tormenting me with Vivian at his side.

I am so certain of this scenario I have made up in my mind that I flinch back with a shriek when a pair of arms wraps around me in the hall.

"Jeez, you're awfully jumpy," Emmett says casually as he tries to pull me in for a kiss.

I'm so angry now that he's actually in front of me, I can't bring myself to say a single word. I fling him off of me and keep walking.

"Ophelia!" he calls out. "What's going on with you?"

"What the fuck do you mean what's going on with me?" I hiss back through clenched teeth, trying to keep my voice down so everyone else doesn't hear. "I haven't heard from you since you stormed out of my room Saturday night. Do you think I'm an idiot!?"

I try to march off again, but he chases me down and grabs

my arm tightly enough that I can't run away from him anymore.

"Of course, I don't think you're an idiot," he huffs. "Your text made it sound like you understood how upset I was…So I thought you were giving me some space, which is what I needed."

"Bullshit." I try to hold back my tears. "You expect me to believe you didn't run off to see Vivian anyway? And tell me Emmett…how did that go? Has she told you exactly where Bernadette is yet?"

"I promise you…I didn't go see her. I haven't talked to her at all," he insists. "I was hiding out in my motel room making some calls and trying to see if I could track anything down online. I haven't found anything yet, but I didn't say a word to Vivian. You asked me not to. I thought we could talk to her together today."

I want to believe him, but I've spent the last twenty-four hours working myself into a frenzy, and it's not so easy to just snap out of it now. But he wouldn't invite me to talk to Vivian with him if he had already seen her or if something else was going on, would he?

"I thought you didn't want me with you when you talked to her again?" I throw in his face bitterly.

"Whatever I have to do to make you happy," he says, trying to pull me in again. "I do think it'd be better if I talked to her alone, but if you're not comfortable with it, then I won't do it." He holds his fingers up in a mocking scout's honor.

I'm silent and stewing, feeling dangerously close to caving in. I want to believe every word he's saying and just let this whole mess be over with. I'm tired of feeling jealous and threatened, but I can't get over his strange behavior on Saturday, or the way he just disappeared and shut me out afterwards.

"I just can't handle your mood swings," I sob. "One minute, you're madly in love with me and saying all these perfect things. The next, you won't even touch me and you're storming off from me."

"It's all the stress, Ophelia!" he urges. "I'm under so much pressure! I'm taking over Jameson Automobiles, and now all of this stuff with Bernadette. It's almost more than I can take."

"Well, maybe you'd be better off without me getting in your way," I suggest, studying his reaction carefully.

"No way," he shoots back, pulling me in. "You're the only thing keeping me sane in all of this."

"Then I'm doing a terrible job," I bite back.

"Please…don't be like this," he begs. "Just come with me to talk to Vivian. You'll see plain as day that there's nothing between us and maybe we can start getting some answers. Come on, baby," he begs in a low, sexy voice, trying one last time to kiss me.

"I'm just not in the mood," I sneer. "Isn't that what you said Saturday night?"

I storm off, wishing I could bring myself to turn around and run back into his arms. But that one wave of distant behavior sent me into high alert. All of my walls are back up, and I'm fearing the worst. I retreat around the corner, bracing my back against the wall as I try to breathe through angry tears. I don't know if I'm angry or glad he didn't try to follow me this time.

After a few moments, I peek around to see if he's still standing there. He's moved further up the hall, but of course Vivian is right there with him. I jerk back when I see him look in my direction and run to my next class. I can only hope whatever talk they were just having in the hall was the last of it, but I guess that's what I get for turning cold on him.

I'm completely on edge the rest of the day, hoping that by the time school is over, Emmett will know all the right things to say and do to break me out of this state. But things only get worse at lunch.

I'm stuck in class fifteen minutes over, trying to copy down notes I missed when we skipped on Friday. By the time I make it to the lunchroom, I'm disgusted to see Vivian, Lily, and Emmett sitting together. My heart stops, and I almost drop my lunch tray. I am left frozen at the edge of the room, not knowing if I should run away or march right up to them.

He's my boyfriend, after all. I don't know what the fuck he's doing sitting with them, but I have every right to join or pull him away. But old memories plague me. What if he's turning back into the person he was? What if he joins in with them, berating and bullying me? I keep trying to tell myself he would never do that now, but I couldn't bear it if it came true. Deciding it's too much of a risk, I retreat to the bathroom. Only by the time I get there, I'm so anxious I'm not even hungry anymore.

The final straw comes at the end of the day when I think he

and I can finally meet up. I can ask him exactly what he was doing with them at lunch, he'll say something to explain it all away, and I'll throw myself back into his arms. I'm more tired than I was this morning, and now that's all I want. More than anything. I know I wouldn't be able to resist him now, and I don't want to anymore. I just want to feel like things are okay again. Like he's still mine.

I'm excited to see him come around the corner at the end of the hall. We're both walking towards the double doors that lead outside, and I know I'll be able to catch up to him there. But then I see Vivian appear right beside him. It all goes by in slow motion. She leans in and whispers something in his ear, and then runs her hand down his arm, trailing her fingers across his as he pulls away.

Their briefly joined hands freeze in my mind, forming a silhouette in front of the sun shining behind them. Emmett does pull his hand away and hasn't initiated anything, but he doesn't pull it away fast enough. I can tell by Vivian's body language that she wants him, and as usual, he appears to be doing nothing to stop it.

I'm too tired to keep asking myself whether or not Emmett would cheat on me or go back to her. But one thing is certain—he's not fighting as hard as he should to stop her attention towards him, and everything in my gut tells me it's because he doesn't want it to stop. Maybe it gives him an ego trip. Or maybe it's because he still has feelings for her.

As I turn to run away, I run smack dab into Vivian's new best friend—the last person I want to see right now. Lily is standing there taking in the sight of my wet cheeks. She doesn't miss a beat, peering past my shoulder to catch a glimpse of Emmett and Vivian together. After seeing them, she just looks back to me with a menacing grin.

"We told you she'd get him back eventually," she taunts heartlessly.

"She doesn't have him back," I hiss defiantly. "He's with me."

"Then why are you so upset?" She laughs. "Admit it, Ophelia. He was never yours. It was just your turn. Welcome to WJ Prep. Guess I left that out of your little introductory course on how things work around here."

Her cruelty is too much. I push past her and rush out the back doors. I can't handle Lily even mentioning anything that happened between us when she was my friend, not while she's acting like this. I still don't know what I've done to make her hate me so much, but the switch in her personality is damn near sociopathic, making me question everything about the friendship I thought we had.

If Vivian is managing to steal Emmett back, and Lily is on her side now, then I am all alone again. And I'm certain it won't be long until the old Elite hierarchy builds itself back up. Which means everything Emmett said about things being different now has been a lie.

There's no practice today, but I go to the track field anyway and plop down my bag before spurring off into a series of laps. I get a thrill out of pushing myself to the limit. Everything else falls away and I only need to move. My burning muscles must keep going no matter how much I sweat. No matter how hard my chest heaves and feels like it's on fire.

I don't know how many laps I've run when I notice a figure sitting on the bleachers watching me. My heart leaps, hoping its Emmett. But the next time I come around, I'm able to see that it's only Malcolm. I run around once more, trying to shed my disappointment.

"Hey, stalker," I joke as I stop to catch my breath at the end of my final lap. But the joke only stings, reminding me of how Emmett and I first met when he practically stalked me at one of my meets.

"Not stalking." He laughs. "Just admiring."

I squint and raise my eyebrows at his suggestive tone.

"Everyone said you were fast, but I hadn't seen it for myself yet," he corrects himself. "You're pretty fucking talented."

"Thank you." I blush, wiping the sweat from my brow, realizing suddenly how ridiculous I must look running in my full school uniform. "It was a little unplanned," I try to explain, brushing at my outfit, but my voice cracks and I feel the rush of tears returning.

"Are you alright?" he asks, crushing any hope I had that I'd managed to keep my distress under wraps.

"Fine!" I call back too quickly, not sounding the least bit convincing. "Totally fine! Just...uh...just needed to run some things off."

"I actually looked for you at lunch today," he tells me.

"Really? What for? I thought you didn't eat in the cafeteria with the rest of us," I tease, still catching my breath.

"I was kind of hoping once you saw my secret lunch spot that you might join me there more often," he explains. "After you didn't show back up, I thought I'd come to you. But…then I saw you run off." He waits for me to respond, but I'm too embarrassed. "I take it you don't like Emmett having lunch with his ex."

"Not just any ex." I laugh bitterly. "Vivian. The wicked bitch herself who has made it clear she has every intention of getting him back."

"What does Emmett say about all of that?" Malcolm asks with a sympathetic smirk.

"Doesn't matter. He's still hanging around her," I mutter. I grow quiet, feeling like I shouldn't be talking to Malcolm about all of this. It's humiliating enough as it is and I don't need his pity.

Maybe I need someone better than Emmett. Not better… but more than him. Someone who can be wholesome and available. Someone easy. The thing I vowed I didn't want. I do want Emmett, and I don't want to change him. Not now that I understand him better. But I wish there weren't so many other things that came with him. I wish that being with him didn't mean feeling alone so much of the time. Always longing and yearning in a way that is hardly ever fully quenched. Maybe I love him too much. Could that be the problem?

He winces and looks to his shoes, realizing he's probably treading on a touchy subject. "Hey, sounds like you could use a break from all the WJ Prep bullshit," he says finally, after a long, awkward silence. "Wanna come to Ritzville with me?"

Ritzville. Jameson's cheesy amusement park that I have secretly wanted to go to the entire time I've lived here. It's high school date central, and I've spent many nights imagining riding to the top of the Ferris wheel with Emmett and making out with the nighttime view of the town lights twinkling behind us. Of course, it's just been one disaster after another, and it never seemed like a realistic dream until recently. But whenever Emmett and I haven't been on the hunt for clues about his sister, we've been fucking or fighting over Vivian.

And now Malcolm wants to take me. I know I should say no; it's too much like a date. I would have a complete meltdown if Emmett and Vivian went to Ritzville together, even if it was as innocent as me spending time with Malcolm. But as the memory of seeing them in the hall together replays in my mind,

I suddenly want nothing more than to go with him. I need the distraction, and Emmett needs a reminder of how jealousy feels.

"Okay." I nod with a smile. "Let's go."

When I was little, sometimes a carnival or fair would set up at the mall near where we lived in Oklahoma. We would drive past it and I would see all of the lights whirling around with screaming, laughing children. The smells of fried foods and cotton candy would waft through the air, luring me in. I would see little girls walking hand in hand with their dads and wish that I knew who my father was. By the time Brendan came around, I'd decided I was too cool for the carnival and wouldn't let him take me. He wasn't who I wanted to go with, anyway. Not then. It feels ironic now that once again, I can't come here with the person I want to the most. Only this time, I guess I'm desperate enough to go with whoever is willing.

I eye the giant spinning Ferris wheel as we pass, drifting back to all of my fantasies about it and wishing it was Emmett walking beside me right now.

"Do you wanna go on that thing?" Malcolm asks as he studies my face.

"No, that's okay," I lie. I do want to go. But going with him feels like too much of a betrayal somehow.

We pass twirling teacup rides and airplanes whooshing screaming kids around the air in a loop. The carnival workers heckle us as we walk past, daring for us to come shoot a water pistol at a target or throw darts at balloons. If this were a movie, I imagine Malcolm would play one of the games and win me a ridiculous, oversized teddy bear. And he probably would in real life if I asked him. He seems eager to cheer me up.

Malcolm tries everything to get me to let go and have a good time, but I turn everything down. I can't seem to pick myself up enough to be in the mood for anything. I finally agree to play that game where you throw a ping pong ball into fishbowls and win a goldfish if you land one in. I throw the balls listlessly. And of course, because I don't care, one of my balls swirls around the top of the bowl and plops right down into the surface of the water above the unsuspecting fish.

"Shit," I murmur.

"Hey!" Malcolm exclaims proudly. "Look at that!"

"One goldfish for the lady!" the worker announces. "Coming right up!"

"No!" I belt back. "No goldfish for me!" I turn back to Malcolm. "Come on, let's go." I tug his arm and rush him away before they can stick me with the fish.

"Wow," he chuckles. "I don't think I've ever seen someone run so fast from a fish."

"Everything's a mess," I groan. "I can't deal with a fish right now. I can barely keep up with the rest of my life. The last thing I need is a life depending on me to take care of it."

"It's just a fish," he reminds me with a smirk. "A goldfish at that…They live like thirty days and die. It's not a human baby."

I shrug. "A life is a life."

"I don't know." He looks away, taking in the passing sights of the carnival. "I don't know if all lives are equal. The Elites sure don't seem to think so, anyway."

"Well, let's not stoop to their level," I conclude.

As the night goes on, all I can think is that I want to tell Emmett everything, even though he'd be furious that I was here with Malcolm. If he could get over that, he'd think it was hilarious that I 'ran from a fish,' as Malcolm put it.

The smell of funnel cakes, hot dogs, slushies, and nachos pulls me in as we walk through the row of food vendors.

"Do you want something to eat?" He looks at me with an impish smile, knowing I've turned down everything he's asked since we got here.

"Food." I nod with a smile. "That I can get behind. I'm starving."

He looks ecstatic to have finally found something I'll agree to. I feel bad for him as he orders us some trays of food. He's been trying so hard to be a nice guy, and I've been weird every step of the way.

"Sorry I'm such shitty company," I offer as he returns with our grub and we settle onto a metal table lined with red rubber, and a red-and-white striped umbrella overhead. "Things have been pretty crazy lately. Or, really…I guess ever since I moved here."

"It has to be pretty crazy to go from being Emmett's target to being his girlfriend," he states frankly.

"You must think I'm a fucking idiot." I hide my face in my

hands, feeling certain that he's judging me. Hell, I'm judging me.

"No, not at all!" he assures me. "I didn't mean anything by that."

"It's more than that…" I offer lightly, unsure if I should open up about everything that's going on or not. "Have you noticed that Bernadette is gone?"

"Of course." He nods through a big bite of a burger. "I just figured she was upset about everything with her dad. That, and avoiding school now that she doesn't have the old Elite gang to back her up."

"Actually…Emmett and her mom don't know where she is," I reveal, feeling terrible for saying it. "I'm sorry. I shouldn't be telling you that. He really wants to keep it a secret."

"Why keep it a secret?" Malcolm asks.

Relief washes over me. Something about hearing another person point out how odd it is to keep this under wraps makes me feel saner and less guilty about questioning Emmett. But I still can't escape the nagging feeling that I should be defending him.

"He says he has too many enemies around here and doesn't know who to trust," I explain, swirling a fry in some ketchup. "He's worried the cops are loyal to his father and are working against him. But we haven't had much luck figuring anything out on our own, and it's just been…stressful. I guess that's what seems to be driving him straight into Vivian's arms."

"That is a lot to put on you." He nods, studying my face for any sign of resentment.

"I said I would help…so I am. The best I can. But I'm feeling pretty useless at the moment. I think I'm just making things worse." I slump down across the table, releasing a groan of exhaustion. "Sorry to be telling you all of this. Just promise you won't tell anyone else. Whether it makes sense to me or not, Emmett wants to keep it a secret and I want to respect his wishes."

"Of course," he replies reassuringly. "I won't say a word to anyone."

We're silent for a moment as we eat our assortment of fried foods. As much as I love my mom's cooking, this is exactly the kind of guilty pleasure I've been needing without even realizing it.

"Hey, I think I might know a way to help," Malcolm says after a while.

"With Bernadette?" I perk up, hoping he can. If we can get that mess squared away, Emmett won't be under so much stress and will hopefully stop finding excuses to run to Vivian. Maybe we can finally have some semblance of a normal relationship.

"Yeah, have you tried hacking her phone? Tracking her through it or anything like that?" he says with a tinge of excitement in his voice. I'd forgotten he was a software guy. This kind of thing is right up his alley.

"Neither of us have any kind of clue how to do that." I laugh. "I didn't even know that was an option."

"Oh, yeah," he says confidently. "As soon as we're done eating, I can take you back to my place. I have enough equipment there to pull it off, I think."

"Can we do that without having her phone?" I ask. "Emmett never found it."

"I can do it with just her phone number," he replies with a twinkle in his eye.

"That would be amazing!" I beam, jumping forward to give him a big hug. I ignore the lingering look in his eyes afterwards. "You would do something like that?" My eyebrows raise. "I know you don't like Emmett very much. And I shouldn't be pulling you into all of this."

"That's the difference between me and the Elites," he explains. "They may let their personal grievances get in the way of who they help and who they don't. But at the end of the day, a person is missing and could be in danger. If I have some assistance to offer, I will."

I smile at him and look away with flushed cheeks. This is the kind of thing that makes Malcolm so attractive, and I don't know why I can't make myself fall for him.

"It seems you're a better guy than me," I admit regretfully. "Sometimes I feel like the only reason why I want to find Bernadette is so I will have Emmett back all to myself."

"Don't beat yourself up too much," he offers, lightly placing his hand over mine across the table. "She's not exactly…a pleasant person."

I think back to when my father shot Thomas Jameson. The sounds of Bernadette's screams. She was mortified and devastated. Emmett was the one standing there with a calm, cool stare. But his determination to find his sister is somewhat redeeming. He can be loyal to his family. And protective. Just not towards his father.

I feel a renewed sense of hope as we drive to Malcolm's. Maybe I can finally get a lead on this thing and prove to Emmett that I do care about what he's going through. Originally, I'd wanted to find Bernadette so I could push Emmett out of my life again. But things changed quickly. Now I want us to find her so I can have more of him.

# CHAPTER FOURTEEN

### BOOK 2

Malcolm's mansion is nothing like Lily's or Emmett's. It's clean and sleek. Nothing like the old-fashioned classical architecture I've seen everywhere else around here. And the inside is the same, with carpets and marble flooring so white I'm scared to walk on it, and bright white walls broken up by modern, abstract art pieces in bright colors that pop against the starkness.

"This place is exactly how I imagined it would be," I marvel as I take in the clean, minimalist vibe, the big, open, almost too-empty rooms. He shoots me a discerning look. "I just mean…I envisioned it being really modern. With you and your dad being tech guys and all."

"My place is actually around back," he tells me as we walk through to the back doors. "I just wanted you to have a glance at the main house. My parents have great decorating taste."

"You have your own place?"

"My dad already has me doing a lot of work for our company," he explains. "Coding and developing. Things like that. So, they let me have the pool house so I'd have a quiet place to focus."

"You're really lucky," I gape, wondering if the Hendersons are even wealthier than the Jamesons. It's not too hard to imagine it by the looks of this place.

"I'm really busy," he shrugs. "They know I stay focused on work and school and am getting ready to take over the company one day. I don't fuck around. That's why they trust me to have my own place like this."

"Don't you ever make any time for at least a little fun?" I tease as we walk out into the backyard of sprawling greens decorated with elaborate landscaping and lustrous fountains.

"I just took you to Ritzville tonight, didn't I?"

"Oh, I'm so sorry. You did and I ruined it." I shrink in embarrassment. "I was a complete bummer and now I'm just dragging you into doing more work."

"No, I love this kind of stuff," he assures me. "It's way more fun than my real work. I want to do work with investigations and the criminal justice system one day. This is right up my alley."

"Oh…well, I guess I don't feel so bad then." He leads me past their glowing swimming pool to the house nestled behind it. The inside is a lot like his parents' house, but darker and with a more eclectic vibe. "This place is almost more amazing than the main house. It's so clean. Let me guess…maids? Everyone around here seems to have those."

"No, actually," he corrects me. "I clean it myself. It's part of my routine. Helps me keep my head together."

"Wow…new money really is different from old money," I accidentally blurt out.

"How so?"

"Your work ethic and sense of responsibility," I clarify, wishing I didn't have such a big mouth.

"You mean old Emmett doesn't have those kinds of things?" he chuckles back, making me feel terrible.

"No, he does. I'm sorry," I wince, squeezing the bridge of my nose. "I don't know why I said that. You seem to have that effect on me. I keep blurting out all sorts of things around you."

"Well, here it is." He waves his hands across the biggest desk I've ever seen, neatly organized with various screens and controls. "This is where I do all of my work."

"It's a lot more elaborate than my old laptop, that's for sure." I admire the setup, wondering what all of the different gadgets could possibly be for.

Malcolm sits down at his desk and goes to work. He babbles off a string of technical jargon that goes way beyond my under-standing of computers. I try to keep up, but I mostly just try and stay out of his way. But I'm relieved he seems so knowledgeable and has so many tools at his disposal. Maybe I'll leave here with something that's actually useful for Emmett.

"Is this legal?" I ask hesitantly, as he outlines the process of hacking someone's cell phone data.

"Not at all," he answers smugly.

It makes me a little nervous, but if you can't trust the cops around here…what else can you do?

"Okay, I've got all of her cell phone data from the past six months," he tells me after a long string of typing and clicking and speaking to me in what might as well be a whole other language.

"Wow, just like that, huh?" I gasp. "Anything recent?"

"No, it looks like all activity stopped about two weeks ago," he says as he clicks through pages of encrypted data.

"Sounds about right. Emmett said she had already been missing for a few days before he came to me. What about the last location?"

"It looks like the last traceable on the phone was the Jameson Mall," he replies, still scrolling through. "But that doesn't necessarily mean that's the last place she was. The phone could have died there and never been recharged. Or it could have been dropped."

"The mall? Huh." Not a surprising spot, but knowing it's the last place her phone was used feels important. "Well, that's more than we knew before. Anything else useful?"

"I can pull up her calls and messages," he trails off into more typing. "Looks like these were the last numbers she exchanged texts and calls with. The texts seem to indicate meeting up at the mall, which makes sense."

"What are the numbers?" I ask impatiently. He angles the screen so I can see. He flips through the contacts in his phone, letting me look over his shoulder as he compares them to the ones on the screen. It doesn't take us long to find a match. "Those are Lily and Vivian's phone numbers. You don't think… Do you think this means they have something to do with her disappearance?"

"Based on that alone, I'd be inclined to say no," he speaks candidly, pursing his lips. "Though you shouldn't rule it out. Whatever happened to Bernadette could have happened right after meeting up with them. But what's strange is…if I pull up the records from their numbers…Look at the timestamps here."

He angles the screen in my direction again and points to a transcript between two phone numbers.

"That's Lily and Vivian talking to each other, right?"

"Yeah…all the way past the meet up with Bernadette. The three of them were exchanging messages up until their locations were traced to the mall," he explains. "Then Bernadette's texts drop off. But Lily and Vivian's continue."

"So, Lily and Vivian kept using their phones to communicate with each other…" I try to follow along with him. "Even though the three of them were, in theory, all hanging out together in person?"

"It would appear so."

"Well, what do the messages say?" I ask eagerly. Not only could this be a crack in the case, but, out of wild curiosity, I would love to know what those three talk about when no one else is around. "Vivian and Bernadette still had some tension between them after the investigation and everything. Could Lily and Vivian just have been talking shit about Bernadette through texts while they were hanging out with her?"

"The texts don't look like anything out of the ordinary. But it's still strange." He makes a clicking sound against his teeth. "Makes it look like they were coordinating around something Bernadette didn't know about. Something they didn't want her to know about. Or maybe just one of them was hanging out with her while the other one kept tabs on them."

"Like to plan an attack or something?" My eyes dart across the screens, wishing I could keep up with it all.

"Possibly. With this being Bernadette's last known location and them being the last people she talked to…" he trails off, shaking his head. "It definitely doesn't look good on their part. The police would definitely consider them their best suspects based on this information. Have you or Emmett confronted them about her disappearance yet?"

"No. Emmett's been too convinced of their innocence this entire time," I scoff. "Now he finally has decided to ask them about it…but I don't know if that's actually happened yet, or if anything has come of it."

"Well, you should definitely tell Emmett about this," he announces as he spins around from his desk to face me.

"Definitely." I nod with my eyes still glued to the screens. "I want to tell him right away. Would you come with me to talk to him? He's so paranoid that I'm just accusing them out of jealousy. If you're there to explain the technical side of it, he might actually take it seriously."

"I don't know." He frowns. "I'd be happy to…but you remember Emmett doesn't exactly like me anymore."

"You said the Elites had a lot to do with that," I uphold optimistically. "I know things appear to be a little weird with him and Vivian right now…but hopefully that's nothing. And if so, Emmett has changed a lot now that his father's out of the picture. I know it's hard to believe, but he's really nothing like he used to be. Maybe he's let go of whatever he had against you back then."

Of course, I can't bring up just how bad Emmett's jealousy over Malcolm is. He'd never come if he knew how bad that was. I can only hope he'll set that aside in light of the news. After all, Emmett asked me to try and set aside my jealousy towards Vivian, considering everything that's happening. He should be able to do the same.

"If you say so." He finally nods hesitantly. "I'm willing to try."

Malcolm prints off large stacks of all of the data before we jump into his car and drive out to Emmett's motel. I'm relieved his car is outside. If it hadn't been, I'd have gone into a paranoid fit thinking he was still with Vivian.

"Stay here for a minute," I tell Malcolm as I unbuckle my seatbelt. "Let me catch him up to speed a little before he sees you."

"Sure." He nods with an understanding smile.

I take a deep breath as I walk to his door. I'm still angry with him, but I try to push all of that away in the hope that this will change things.

"Ophelia!" he shouts as he flings open the door, yanking me into his arms. "Where have you been? I waited by your car after practice and never saw you. I've been worried sick. I went by your house and everything!"

"Why didn't you just call me?" I cut my eyes into him, still wondering if he was really with Vivian all afternoon.

"I did!" he shoots back. "Like a hundred times."

I pull my bag around my shoulder and fish out my phone. The screen is black and not turning on. "Oh, I'm sorry…it's dead. I didn't realize."

But Emmett's eyes have already settled on the car behind

me—on Malcolm waiting inside. "What the fuck," he growls. "What is he doing here?"

"That's what I came to talk to you about." I wave for him to get out of the car and come to the door. "Can we come in?" I push past Emmett before he even has a chance to answer. "Malcolm may have found out something that could help with your sister."

"You told him about Bernadette?" he thunders, not taking his rageful eyes off of Malcolm.

"I know I shouldn't have, but we can talk about that later," I insist hurriedly. "But right now, you really need to hear about what we found."

"What the fuck are you doing hanging out with her, Malcolm?" Emmett fumes as he marches up to him. "You know she's mine. You need to back off."

"Listen, man…I don't mean any harm." Malcolm's hands fly up in surrender, but his tone is even and cool. "I don't want to cause any trouble between you two. I just want to help."

"Emmett, please…" I go over and place a hand to his chest, hoping to calm him down. "Just listen to him. It could help us find your sister."

"Alright, let's hear it, old buddy," he says condescendingly, crossing his arms. "Just what is it you think you know about my sister?"

"I traced her phone and went through her messages and calls. Here, I printed it all out for you so you could see for yourself." Malcolm holds out the stack of papers, but Emmett doesn't budge to take them. Malcolm tosses them onto the bed next to him instead. "Her last location before her phone dropped off was at Jameson Mall. And she was there with Vivian and Lily."

"Oh, wow…" he coos cynically "So you mean my sister went to the mall with her friends? Shocking."

"There's more," I insist, holding my hand up to get him to keep listening.

"There was some suspicious communication between Lily and Vivian," Malcolm continues. "Makes it look like they were planning something against Bernadette."

"Yeah…those girls are all malicious bitches to each other, you know that." He shrugs. "They were probably just planning a revenge prank or something like that. This doesn't prove they're behind her disappearance."

"Did you ask Vivian about it yet?" I ask him, growing frustrated.

"She says she doesn't know anything," he answers plainly, looking away from me.

"I guess it took her all day to tell you that," I mutter.

"What?" he bellows.

"Nothing."

"I want to know what the fuck you two were doing together in the first place," he demands, bucking his chest up. "Why did you tell him about all of this?"

"We're just friends, man," Malcolm offers lightly.

I put myself in Emmett's path, trying to redirect his attention back to me. "He came back to the track to say hi and saw that I was upset."

"I bet he did," he smirks with disgust.

"Stop it! That's enough!" I snap. "He was just trying to cheer me up, and that's when I let everything slip about Bernadette. I was upset for you and didn't know how to help."

"So, you help by hanging around with this dick?" He glares at Malcolm with hatred in his eyes.

"Malcolm was the only one around when you were off somewhere with Vivian!" I shout back.

"I told you I didn't want you hanging out with him!" he roars at me before turning back to Malcolm and charging towards him with alarming force. "But since that didn't sink in, let me try telling you! Stay the fuck away from her!"

"I better go," Malcolm announces, stepping back toward the door.

"No! You stay!" I command. "Emmett, you're being ridiculous! Are you not hearing what we're saying? Vivian and Lily were the last ones to see Bernadette! They can't just slip their way out of this one. They need to be seriously interrogated."

"I talked to them at lunch today. They don't know anything," he insists. "They're just as worried as we are."

"Did they say anything about the mall?" I ask in annoyance. "Or when they last saw her?"

"They mentioned something about the movies, but not the mall," he replies.

"See!" I shriek, flailing my arms. "Why would they lie about that? Unless they're not telling you everything!"

"Because they're airheads?" he sneers. "I don't know. They probably just forgot."

"Fucking insane." I shake my head, wrinkling my chin. "You're still defending them. This is the first real lead we've found on anything and it points straight to them. And you're still standing here insisting they're innocent!"

"She's right, man," Malcolm backs me up. "I don't think you should write them off so quickly."

"You get the fuck out of here!" Emmett charges again, taking him by the shirt collar with clenched fists as he screams in his face. "I don't want you having anything to do with this! And if you come near Ophelia again, I'll fucking kill you!"

"Emmett! Stop!" I scream, rushing over to try and pull him off.

"I'm gonna go." Malcolm tries for the door again. "Sorry for bothering you like this. I hope it still ends up helping somehow."

"Fuck you!" Emmett pumps his fist. "I don't trust anything you say or anything that comes from you."

Malcolm ignores him and turns to me, making it worse. "Do you want a ride?"

I feel pathetic. I know how this must look to him. I should just leave with him now while Emmett is behaving this way. Threatening to kill people in a jealous rage, all because he's too hung up on his ex to admit to himself that she obviously had something to do with this.

But I still fall back on blaming myself. I shouldn't have brought him here. I feel like an idiot for not listening to him and realizing how badly it would go. I knew Emmett didn't want us hanging out, I was just so desperate to turn things around for the sake of his well-being…and our relationship.

"No," I answer finally with a heavy sigh. "I'll walk you out."

"The hell you will!" Emmett lurches forward and grabs my arm.

"Let go of me!" I jerk away from him. "I'll be right there, Emmett…Jesus! What do you think I'm going to do? Hang all over him with you just a few feet away? Oh, wait…that is what you do with Vivian. So, I guess it's not that far-fetched."

With no defense and looking humiliated after being put in his place, he directs his rage back toward Malcolm. "Leave!" he fumes.

I ignore him and follow along outside, slamming the door shut behind me. "I'm so sorry, Malcolm. I should have listened to you. I had no idea he'd react that way."

He shakes his head and pulls his lips to the side, looking at me with wide eyes. I know he's judging me now more than ever. Emmett is looming in the window, tearing through the blinds to see us.

"Are you sure you don't want a ride?" he offers again, with a pleading expression.

"No. It's okay." I turn around to see the impatience growing on Emmett's face as he stares out at us. "Emmett will take me home. I'm sorry again."

He finally accepts my decision and opens his car door. "Take care of yourself, Ophelia," he calls out in a pitying tone as he gets in. "Call me if you need anything."

The room door flies open again as Emmett comes hurtling out. "She doesn't need anything from you!" he screams and kicks towards the car as it speeds away.

I grab him by the arm and pull him back inside. "What the fuck is wrong with you! I can't believe you lost your shit like that! I'm so embarrassed. He was just trying to help!"

He braces himself against the same countertop where we once made love, and I wish more than anything this was one of those happy times, though I have to remind myself that didn't happen for good reasons. I only came here that night to run from more of our problems, and while I don't regret it, I hate how complicated everything constantly is.

I sneak over to put my phone on Emmett's charger, thinking if I missed so many of his calls, I must have missed some from my mom, too. I know it's getting late.

I see his nostrils flaring as he breathes heavily, trying to regain control. I almost wish I had just left with Malcolm, but I can't let him off the hook so easily. I settle in for what I expect to be a long night, ending in another missed curfew—something my parents and I will both have to get used to as long as Emmett is around.

# CHAPTER FIFTEEN

## BOOK 2

The room is quiet, with nothing but the sounds of Emmett's labored breathing and muffled expletives. I am left waiting to see how bad the rest of his explosion will be.

I sit silently and stare into the dark corners of the room, waiting to see what he'll do next. I have never been a big drinker, even at parties back home, but right now I would give anything for a drink. Isn't this exactly why people drink?

What am I doing here? Why am I putting up with this? I only wanted to help. And he's acting like a crazy person, pushing away one of the only people who has been nice to me lately—all because of some old high school drama—a person who's been nicer to me than he has. I should have gotten into that car with Malcolm and ridden away from all of this without ever looking back.

Something has to end it. It can't last forever. Nothing does. Especially not high school loves, as hard of a pill as that is to swallow.

"Should we go to the mall?" I propose. "See if there is anything there? Maybe someone working there saw Bernadette that last day before she disappeared."

"Oh, come on," he scoffs. "You don't honestly believe anything Malcolm showed you, do you? Look at this shit he printed off. It's just a bunch of encrypted files! It could say anything!"

"Why would he lie like that?" I protest, stomping my foot. "I saw all of their phone numbers. I saw the timestamps. I can't believe you think he'd go so far as to make all of that up."

"I can't believe you don't see how he *would* make all of that up!" Emmett fires back, his voice growling with rage. "I told you I didn't want you around him, and I meant it! He's playing you. Convincing you that he's some great guy…Well, he's not. And I don't want you anywhere near him."

"Well, it still wouldn't hurt to try and go to the mall!" I continue. "What other options do we have? Emmett, each day your sister is gone…it just seems less likely that she'll ever come back. And I haven't wanted to say anything, but you know time is running out. We don't have time to be picky about what leads we follow. Unless you want to call the police."

"I just don't want you hanging around with Malcolm," he fumes finally, trying his best to keep his voice even and calm but failing miserably.

Some moments feel so much heavier than others. Emmett looks sabotaged and exhausted, cradling his head in hands, rocking back and forth as he tries so hard to cling to any sense of self-control. We both feel vulnerable and ashamed. The curls of his hair twist up around the light like winding tree roots, and I want to run to him. Hold him and tell him everything will be okay, the way I always do. He looks over to me expectantly, as if he's wondering why I'm not already by his side. He expects it now.

"I know, but I was just trying to put an end to all of this. I wanted to help you," I explain urgently. "I thought if we could just find out what happened to Bernadette…all of this shit with Vivian would be put to an end, and you and I could finally have a chance to see what this relationship can be. Without all of this other stuff always getting in the way."

"I don't trust him," he replies, his voice softening some. "Just promise me you'll stay away from him now."

"I'm sorry, Emmett." I slowly move towards him, being careful to make sure he's not going to lash out again. I don't even know why I'm sorry. I shouldn't be. I didn't do anything wrong. And everything I did was all for him. But I think he knows that. This is just another one of his fits of rage that he's trying his best to control and just can't.

I run my eyes along the edges of his face and the curls of his hair, glowing amber against the lamplight in the corner. His eyes are closed as he clings to some semblance of control. I feel the same way now that I did when he first found me after Bernadette went missing. I want to hold him and help him find his way. I want to make everything better for him. But I have been trying to do that for almost two weeks now, and am no closer to accomplishing it.

Emmett is still just as lost. The only thing that's changed is that now, I am lost with him. My need to take him into my arms quickly changes. Suddenly, I feel afraid and alone, and I am the one who needs to be held.

"I need to be close to you," I rasp across the room, not daring to go any closer until he shows me that it's okay.

His darkened eyes find me standing there, as if he has been in some far-off distant place. I see his face drop, realizing how he abandons me when he has his freakouts. He deals with his fears the only way he knows how, and leaves me all alone with mine.

The longer we stand there and stare, the more the electricity between us builds in the room. But it's not the intense primal shock I am used to. It's a tired, but thriving need. We need so much more than each other's bodies. We need to devour each other—mind, body, and soul. We can see it in each other's eyes.

I walk quickly to erase the distance between us, my lips parting with a slack expression. I reach out to brush against his lips, making steady eye contact with his as I lean forward. He smiles and releases an appreciative sigh, taking my hand and spreading my palm across his heart. I reach up with my other hand and skim my fingers along his jawline. He closes his eyes, savoring my touch. If only we could stay like this. I wish there was a pause button. I want to stop time and every other thing that keeps coming between us.

He lifts me up to wrap my legs around his hips, but we don't kiss. He keeps me suspended in the air, looking down into his eyes. I swear I can see straight into his soul, a place that has scared me in the past because I was afraid that I would find it to be empty. But right now, it looks alive and it's burning for me. Right here in this moment, it feels ridiculous to have ever been worried about Vivian. She can't touch what we have.

I finally lower my lips to his and we dive deep into each other, running our velvet tongues together. Melting into each other's mouths, seamlessly becoming one. At some point he lowers me to the bed, but I can't say exactly when. Time is completely lost. All I can feel is his skin and his warm tongue.

His lips moving over every inch of my body as I claw into him, telling him with my hands that I need more—always more.

The room is brown and yellow, lighting the silhouettes of our bodies up like fire as he moves over me. I'm not even aware of the exact moment he slides inside of me. I'm in a trance, and it feels like he could have always been there. Maybe he never left.

For what seems like hours, we roll around in the sheets. Soft and slow, but with desperation. I take him in as deeply as I can, losing myself in his eyes and his body. Our breathing and the sensations melt together, building leisurely. We don't even care about getting off—then it's over, and we have to face everything that waits for us outside of this room. So, we put it off, wanting to steal away every possible second that we can.

Normally there is a point when we're making love when I close my eyes and lose myself in nothing but the sensation of our bodies. But this time, we both make a point of keeping our eyes wide open. It's as if we're deciding not to hide anymore. To look each other straight on and face everything that exists between us without fear. The intensity of it takes my breath away, and I have never felt so connected with another human being before. His fingers interlace with mine and I could swear our veins are flowing together, sharing the same blood. Our chests are flattened against one another, our hearts beating in time, the rise and fall of our breaths loud and matching perfectly.

We say each other's names into the darkness like animals, calling each other closer. We can never get close enough. I swear I can feel inside of him as I claw into his skin—the heat of his skin is the heat of his organs, his veins, his soul. All pulsing just for me, in tune with my own.

I feel like I'm drowning in him, but I've lost all desire to come back up for air. I'm losing myself and don't even care. This goes against everything I always believed about myself. I thought running came above all else, aside from family. But didn't I tell Emmett we were family? Does that somehow excuse my obsessive love for him? I thought when he showed me some hope that he could become a decent person that things would level out between us. That I would feel more in control. But it seems to have only made things worse. His reciprocity has only fanned the flames, and they're devouring me faster than I can do anything about it. Not that I would if I thought that I could.

Eventually we can't stand it anymore, and his pace quickens. It's just enough to quickly push me to the edge, and I feel him moving there right along with me. Unexpectedly and all at once, we find ourselves digging into each other's skin as our bodies pulse together in perfectly-blended bliss.

We're speechless and fighting sleep by the time our orgasms are over. I don't want to move or say anything. I am out of it, still stuck in a lingering sex haze, but I think he is still inside of me as he lays on top of me. I want to stay like this forever— where it's just the two of us with nothing from the outside threatening to come in between. It feels like this is how we are meant to be. We're both perfect when it's like this.

Emmett and I are as close as any two people can be, bonded by tragedy, hope, and loss. He clings to the hope that he can run his father's business differently. That he can do things right and stop this town from being so fucked up. I cling to the hope that he can do all of those things and not crack under the pressure. I am scared of seeing him become the same kind of man his father was. Scared that there is no other outcome for people like him in Jameson.

If I could just get over this jealousy towards Vivian, I could be there for Emmett in the way that he needs me to be. But I'm afraid that letting go of my jealousy is a mistake. Then, maybe I will miss it when he begins slipping from my fingers. I don't want to be surprised. I want to see that hurt coming from a mile away. I don't think I could handle it if it snuck up on me. If I just walked into school one day to see the two of them back together, with me being the last one to know. I need to let go of it for Emmett's sake, but I cling to it for my own protection.

"I don't want to be safe with you, Ophelia," he explains desperately. "Maybe that's where we keep going wrong. You keep trying to make this small and comfortable, and it's not. We're too much for that."

The sound of Emmett's voice is smooth and deep like honey, and it has the magical ability to instantly shake me to my core. No matter what I think I have my mind made up about, it flies out the window the moment he says a word. I'll try to hold strong to whatever I've decided, but his voice carries on like a hammer to glass, and I always inevitably break. All of the feelings I have for him come flooding out in a big, overwhelming gush, swallowing us both whole. The release of it takes my breath away every time, and he is always left looking to me for more.

"You get off on it when things are fucked up between us," I answer decidedly.

"No, we feel too much for it to be safe," he shoots back. "That's what I'm saying."

"So, what do we do?" I ask, my voice drenched in fear.

"We hold on as tight as we can and never let each other go," he says softly. "Hold onto each other for the ride."

"Looks like I held on to you too tight," I snicker against his arm, my finger trailing circles around the scratch marks running down the sides of his body.

"Good," he says boldly. "I want to be branded by you. You can mark me up as much as you want."

"I've had my fair share of marks from you, too," I note resentfully, cringing at the slip.

"And you'll never let me forget it." He sighs.

"Probably not," I reply truthfully. "I don't know that it's fair for either of us to forget."

"Then how can you be with me?" he asks. "If you still think about it all so much."

"That's what I keep asking myself." I shake my head, looking hopelessly to the ceiling above. "Maybe it's not so bad for me to remember. Doesn't it say more about how I feel about you? That I've been able to move past it and see you for who you are now?"

"But have you moved past it?" he asks, as if he already knows the answer.

I don't want to tell him the truth. That I am always secretly waiting for that side of him to return. It has, though. I've seen it. He hasn't been perfect. I just don't know which side to believe—if the bad will always resurface, or if eventually, he can learn to move past it.

Emmett looks at me desperately, as if our lives are hanging on this moment as he moves inside of me again. He trembles against my body in breathless moans. I keep my hands planted on either side of his face, guiding him back and forth, letting him know that I am right here with him, feeling everything he is feeling.

"You're all I've ever wanted," he mouths to me.

I swallow hard from the pressure. I wanted to be the center of Emmett's world. Part of me has always secretly wanted that, even if only as a way to escape his tormenting. Now I am, and I don't know if I can bear it. The weight of it crashes down on me, and I feel like I might suffocate beneath it. But he sweeps my lips back into his, and I am lost again, unable to care about anything but him. That's how quickly he makes me forget that I have a choice, and I relish in the freedom of it. His prison feels like freedom. I know it's wrong and messed up, but I can't feel any other way. We belong to each other.

"I want to do everything to you, Ophelia," he murmurs in the darkness. "I don't think I could ever get bored of your body. I want to do everything there is to do to it…and once I've done it all, I'll start over and do it all a second time."

I shiver against his words, growing wet all over again. "That could take quite some time," I warn him jokingly.

"Planning on going somewhere?" he questions, raising his brows at me.

I hesitate in my reply, hating to kill the mood. "Well… Emmett…there's college and everything," I remind him. "I mean, who knows what will happen. I want to be with you, but…we don't know what the future holds. I don't want us to make promises we can't keep."

"Go to college near Jameson," he suggests cavalierly. "Or go wherever. I'll fly to come see you."

I laugh out loud at how easy he makes it all sound. "And what about you?" I ask. "Do Jamesons not have to attend college?"

"Not really." He shakes his head. "Not when we take over things this young. My advisors will hire private tutors from top institutions—enough to satisfy the requirements for a degree. Anything from an ivy league school that can be framed and hung on the wall above my desk for business meetings. That's all I really need."

"What?" I gape. "Are you serious?" He shrugs and looks away. "That's so fucked up. Isn't that basically just buying a degree?"

"Basically," he says quietly. "But that's how we've always done it."

"There are a lot of things your family has always done that you were hoping to change," I remind him. "What about what you want? Was there anything you ever wanted to go to college for? Even if it was just to learn a new skill or enter a new field?"

"Never had time to think about it." He shakes his head,

pursing his lips. "There was no point. I always knew that wasn't going to be an option for me. If my dad was still around, I would have gone off to some ivy league campus, but I basically would have just been fucking around until he was ready to retire."

I try not to think about how deeply his entitlement goes, overriding something as basic and fundamental as a college education. But for some reason, my brain is still stuck on the fact that he is planning our future. He intends on staying with me enough that he is talking about flying out to wherever I am if I go to college somewhere else. I can't deny the giddiness rising in my chest at the thought of it.

All at once, both of our phones start buzzing with incoming messages, breaking us from the space we fell into together. We give each other a knowing look. Whatever we just experienced was important, but we can't hide here forever, no matter how badly we want to. We have to go back to the surface and face all of it.

As we are putting on our clothes, Emmett comes closer and pulls me to a stop. We're both standing there in nothing but pants, bare chested, when he puts his arms around me and begins to sway to the music playing from his phone in the background. I love feeling the warmth of his skin against mine as I melt into him and match his movements. For a brief moment, we're frozen like that, dancing slowly in the middle of the room. I wish it didn't have to end.

# CHAPTER SIXTEEN

BOOK 2

Emmett and I peel ourselves away from one another and reach for our phones. The messages from my mom aren't as bad as I expected. She's not angry, she just wants to know when I'll be home. I tell her it should be soon, but Emmett cries out as he goes through his beeping phone.

"We have to go right away," he tells me sternly as his eyes glow against the screen in the dark.

"Go where?" I shoot back. "What's wrong?"

"To my house," he demands, as he keeps one eye glued on his phone and begins reaching for his clothes with the other. "Come on, I'll explain in the car."

I slip into my clothes, struggling to keep up with him as he bolts for the door. He's in such a hurry, I feel like he might leave me here if I'm not fast enough.

"Emmett, what's going on?" I huff as I slide into the car.

"Vivian texted me," he states flatly. "She's at my house."

"What do you mean!? Why? How did she get into your house!?" I know something serious is wrong, but I can't see past my rage that Vivian is texting him this late…from his house.

"She just said she was there and that we needed to come right away," he answers dismissively as he speeds along.

"Are you crazy!?" I cry, wondering if I heard him correctly. "This could be some kind of set-up! Pull over and ask her to tell you what's going on before we just barge in there."

"Ophelia, Bernadette could be home." He sighs and drags a

hand through his hair. "Or maybe she found something that could tell us where she is. I can't waste any time! Let's just go."

"Or maybe Vivian is the reason your sister is missing," I thunder back. "And all of this is just a ploy to make you disappear, too!"

He ignores me and continues driving. I wish I could do something to make him stop. Everything about this feels like a trap to me, but he just won't see it. Why is he so blind when it comes to her?

We pull up to the manor and park behind Vivian's car. It's strange to see all the windows lit up inside, knowing how little life is actually left here now. But the entire house is still buzzing with the staff, carrying about their usual business as if nothing has changed.

Vivian is curled up on the couch in the sitting room and perks up the moment we come in. Her cheeks are red and wet, and I realize I don't think I've ever seen her cry before.

"What's going on?" Emmett asks as he rushes towards her. She doesn't hesitate to throw herself into his arms, making me sick.

"It's your mom," she sniffles. "I think something could have happened to her."

"What? How do you know?" His eyes light up with panic as he hangs on her every word.

"I had borrowed a dress from her a few days ago," she explains, her voice cracking, "and we had plans for me to meet her here to return it tonight. We were talking just up until a couple of hours ago, but when I got here, she was nowhere to be found. The staff haven't seen her."

"Oh god, Emmett…" I groan too harshly. "This is obviously just an attempt for her to get your attention. That doesn't mean anything! Something could have come up, or maybe she just forgot you were meeting. You can't just assume something happened to her."

"Shut up, Ophelia! You don't even know her!" Vivian hisses at me, her eyes daring me to say another word. But then she softens and turns back to Emmett, like putty in his hands. "I'm telling you…something is off about this. She wouldn't have just run off without saying anything if we had plans to meet up."

"What are you doing still hanging out with his mom anyway?" I can't stop myself from interjecting again. "Jeez, you're desperate. When are you going to get it, Vivian? Emmett isn't with you anymore. He's never going to be yours again."

"Why did you even bring her with you!?" Vivian asks him with a furrowed brow.

"Because I'm his girlfriend!" I remind her vehemently. "I have every right to be here. You're the one who shouldn't be here."

"Just stop it, you two!" he barks, slicing his hand through the air in a demand for silence. "Vivian…you asked around the house? No one else has seen her?"

She shakes her head, staring off into the corner of the room. "Not since this morning." But her eyes turn back to his with a desperation that makes me squirm. "I've known your mom my whole life, Emmett. She's not the type to just vanish like this when we had plans. I waited around here for a while and tried to get a hold of her, but she's not answering any of my texts or calls. This just isn't like her. I'm afraid something bad has happened."

"Thanks for calling me," he says softly, laying her head on his chest to comfort her. I think I might scream, run over, and rip them apart. I know that just a short while ago, it felt like Vivian couldn't touch what we share together, but it worries me to see him fall for her scheme so easily.

"I can't believe you're falling for this bullshit, Emmett!" I shout out, unable to hold my words back. "You said your mom has been acting weird ever since Bernadette went missing. It's understandable. She's paranoid about everyone in the town… maybe even including you, Vivian. She has no one to go to for help, and she's scared for her daughter! Of course, she's going to do some things that are out of character. This is just a sick and twisted ploy to get Emmett to come running back to you."

"You don't know what you're talking about," she snarls, "so why don't you just run back to wherever you came from and stop trying to stick your nose in things you know nothing about! You don't know anything about Jameson, or Emmett, or our families!"

"I know enough to spot some desperate girl grasping at straws to get his attention," I bite back, refusing to let her make me feel small again. There are plenty of things about Emmett and me she could never understand, and I'm tired of her acting like she has a monopoly on suffering because her privileged life came crashing down.

I want her to fight back so he can see who she really is, but she's too smart for that. She has Emmett exactly where she wants him, and she's not going to let him go this time. She breaks down into tears, crashing her head back against his chest. I swear I see her flash a conniving smile over his shoulder, but I can't be sure if I'm just imagining it or not.

"I'm just upset. You understand, don't you?" she begs between tears. "Something doesn't feel right about this! I'm worried about her, Emmett. You know we've always been close."

"I know," he hums, rubbing her back.

"You've got to be fucking kidding me!" I explode. Every bone in my body wants to beat her right here in this living room until she shows her true colors. I'm not buying a single word she says.

"Enough, Ophelia!" Emmett scolds, but I'm not backing down.

"Fuck you, Emmett," I growl. "She's obviously playing you, and you're too blind to see it."

"Some winner of a girlfriend you've got there, Emmett," Vivian scoffs bitterly. "Your sister is missing and now your mom could be, too, and all she cares about is coming in between us."

"I don't have to come in between you! There's nothing to come in between!" I insist in a shrill tone. "It's over, Vivian! When are you going to get that through your thick skull?"

"It's not the time for this!" he demands, looking at me with angry, pleading eyes. "Can't you see she's upset? Have a heart!"

"You two have some nerve telling me to have a heart considering everything you've put me through," I snap back, my voice dripping with resentment. "But now that it's your family's lives that are in danger, you expect everything to stop and revolve around your problems? What about when I was the one in danger! Or when you two were torturing me!"

"Do you have any idea how selfish you sound right now?" Vivian accuses.

The whole room goes dark for a minute. I don't see or feel anything but rage. I feel like she is just pouncing on any chance to make herself look all sweet, innocent, and sad, while not missing a beat to make me look like a selfish monster. She's trying to reverse our roles. What's worse is that I don't remember Emmett showing me much sympathy when they were together and making my life hell. She apparently has some kind of priority and always will.

Before I know it, I'm shoving her down onto the couch. I'm about to jump on top of her when my feet are lifted from the ground and my whole body is moved backward. Emmett has one arm wrapped around my stomach to restrain me.

"Stop it, Ophelia! Please!" he barks into my ear. "If you're not going to help, then just go!"

I punch him hard in the arm, just enough to make him put me down. "Can't you see that's what she wants?" I shout as I pull down my shirt and blow hair out of my face.

"You heard him, Ophelia," Vivian says as she pulls herself up from the couch. "Just go."

At first, I think there's no way in hell I'll leave the two of them alone here together like this, but I quickly realize that this is the last place I want to be. I can't watch another second of her manipulating him. And he's falling for every bit of it.

"Gladly," I huff, my face so scrunched and angry I know I must look like a mad woman. "Call me when you realize I was right about her."

My phone beeps as I storm away from them, hoping Emmett will come after me. But I accept that he's not going to by the time I reach the end of the driveway. I glance down at the screen and see that it was Malcolm who texted me. I don't even know what it says, but my mind is already made up. I'm going to see him right now.

# CHAPTER SEVENTEEN

## BOOK 2

I pace the end of Emmett's driveway alone in the dark, resisting the urge to look at his and Vivian's silhouettes moving behind the windows. My mind plays tricks on me, making me swear I can see their bodies moving closer out of the corner of my eye. I shake it all away and try to keep looking anywhere but at that window.

Unlocking my phone screen, I scroll to Malcolm's message. **Everything okay? I'm worried about you.**

I remember telling my mom I'd be home soon before we left the motel. I know I should just go home like I promised, but the idea of hanging around my room having left things this way with Emmett seems like torture. With a deep breath, I type out a reply to Malcolm.

**Can you come pick me up? I'm at Emmett's.**

He messages back instantly, telling me he's on his way. I don't know what I want to happen when he picks me up. I just know I can't go home right now, and I can't stay here. I feel awkward standing just outside the manor waiting for Malcolm. I'm half hoping that Emmett will see me and come out just as Malcolm is pulling up. He'll fly into another jealous fit, but at least it would distract him from getting wrapped around Vivian's finger.

I spiral into a fit, trying to talk myself down. Flashes of our bodies moving together in the motel bed just a little while ago flood over me. I cling to them, hoping they'll give me the strength I need to text Malcolm back and tell him to forget it. I could still march right back into that house and buckle my emotions down so I can stay, no matter how insane it makes me.

But then I drift back to the sight of Vivian nestling herself into his arms. Him stroking her hair, telling me that I should be more sympathetic. Those moments in the motel fell away the minute he insisted on rushing to her side. I tell myself it's good that he brought me with him without question, but then again…he didn't stop to think about anything before racing off. I cringe to think it had less to do with wanting me with him, and more to do with him not wanting to be bothered with the inconvenience of arguing or taking me home first. It's like he couldn't wait to get to her.

I'm still at war with myself in my mind when Malcolm's car pulls up. I glance back one more time, wishing I'd see Emmett barreling out of the house to stop me. But he's not there. So, I open the door to reveal Malcolm's smiling face waiting for me to get in. Time has run out. I couldn't make myself go back inside to Emmett, and he never came out here for me. It feels like I have no choice but to get in this car right now.

"Hey, I'm so glad you texted me," I tell him as I slide into the passenger's side and buckle the seatbelt. And I mean it. This isn't where I want to be, but it's the best option I have at this moment.

"I figured you might need an escape," he explains, in that same pitying tone I am beginning to hate. "Things seemed pretty intense with Emmett back in that motel."

If he only knew how intense things got after he left—just in a completely different way. Yet somehow, we still ended up back where we started, in a jealous dance around each other, with Vivian playing him like a puppet.

"It's fucking Vivian," I seethe, shaking my head. "She's trying to convince Emmett his mom is missing now, too. But it's obviously just a trick, and he's too hung up on her to see it."

"Those two have a lot of history. That's hard to compete with," he says slowly. I clench my teeth. I don't need to be reminded of that; I am all too aware. "He shouldn't be leaving you to worry about this."

The love in my heart pushes through, reminding me that while Malcolm is right, Emmett has plenty of his own to worry about right now. The internal war continues as I start to feel guilty for getting so angry while they worried about his mom. Maybe they were right. Maybe I was being selfish.

"It's complicated," I huff, not wanting to talk about it anymore. I fight the temptation to ask what the hell he means by that. Is he so sure that's what this is about? That they just can't let go of their past relationship? That's what I think, but right now I just wish someone would tell me that I'm wrong.

"Not really," he replies curly. "If you were mine, I'd never give you any room to doubt what we had, or worry about some other girl."

I study his face as he stares at the road. His light hair and eyes turning shades of neon as the lights outside whiz past. No room for doubt. That is what I want. That's what I need, but I need it with Emmett. Not Malcolm. And I can only manage to attain that kind of security for brief moments here and there, before it inevitably slips away again.

"Thanks, Malcolm," I say with a half-smile, sinking down in my seat.

"Well, I'm happy to help you take your mind off of things." I see his hand rise hesitantly, as if he's about to reach over the seat for some kind of comforting touch, but he puts it back down. "Where to?" he offers instead. "Want me to take you home?"

Home. Yes, I need to go home. But right now, the only thing that word makes me think of is Emmett's arms. Even if I could go back there, I'd be watching him hold Vivian instead of me.

"No," I answer with certainty. "I don't want to go back home yet. I'm too anxious."

"How about we go back to my place then," he suggests. "We could watch a movie until you hear from Emmett."

The thought comforts me. He just suggested that Emmett and Vivian have some kind of unfinished business, but obviously he still thinks Emmett is coming back for me at some point in the night.

"Okay." I nod with a sharp inhale through my nose. "We can go to your place and watch a movie."

I'm quiet the rest of the way, hoping Malcolm stays the same. I don't want to talk about it anymore. I just want to kill time until Emmett comes to his senses and realizes the only person he should be with right now is me.

We pull up to the now-familiar mansion and follow the brick path leading behind the main house to Malcolm's spot in the back. I hate the feeling of knowing we were doing this exact same thing earlier this evening, but then I was filled with the hope that we were about to fix everything. I thought we'd find something that would lead us to Bernadette, and this would all be over. But now there's a hole where that hope used to be, and I am no less worried about Vivian.

"What are you in the mood for?" he asks as we file in and throw our things to the floor. He plops down on the couch and picks up the remote to begin scrolling through the selections on the screen. "Action? Comedy? Suspense?"

"No suspense, please," I reply bitterly. "I have enough of that in my real life right now."

"Got it. Light and funny," he concludes. "Coming right up."

As he's scrolling past the shows and movies, I am surprised by how foreign it all looks. I'm behind on everything. I have no clue what's come out recently, since I haven't had any time to do things like this. Normal things. Sitting and relaxing with mindless entertainment. I've been too busy chasing Emmett around, or being chased by him and the rest of the Elites.

I watch the characters on the screen float through life, dealing with the most trivial matters. A bad day at work. Trying to find a date. The date going well and then the tricky part of falling in love. Emmett's never even taken me on a date. Unless you could count our fucked up trip to the movies, with Trey and Vincent by our sides, trying to feel me up the whole time.

"Is this what life is like for some people?" I muse out loud.

"No, it's a movie," he smirks.

"No, you know what I mean." I moan with exhaustion. "Everything in Jameson is so…heavy."

"Maybe I should have picked a suspense thriller," he quips. "I know you said you've had enough, but you might be able to relate to it more."

"Do you ever get tired of it all?" I ask him.

"I told you." He keeps his eyes glued straight ahead, his tone growing cold and apathetic. "I stay out of all of it. Anyway, if the Jamesons weren't the ones in charge…things might not have been this way."

"What do you mean?" I shoot back, sensing a new hint of jealousy.

"Nothing," he states, not looking open to saying anything else about it.

"I can't thank you enough for being here for me, Malcolm,"

I offer. "Things with Emmett are always so fucked up, and with Lily deciding she hates me…I've felt so alone. It's really meant a lot to have you around as a friend."

I emphasize the word *friend*, feeling suddenly self-conscious about how this looks. I haven't been trying to run crying to Malcolm's shoulder every time something goes wrong with Emmett, but somehow he always seems to be conveniently planted in my path whenever the need arises.

"Well, I have to admit…I am being a little selfish in all of this," he answers coyly, leaning back on the couch and spreading one arm out across the back in my direction. If I were sitting close to him, his arm would be along the back of my seat. But I made sure to keep a few feet between us when I sat down.

"What do you mean?" I ask, wringing my hands together in my lap.

"You're fucking gorgeous, Ophelia," he blurts out. "And a hell of a runner. You're smart and funny—I'm not just hanging around you out of pity."

"That's sweet. Thank you." I say sincerely, feeling my cheeks grow flushed. But my heart doesn't swell with his words in the way that I wish it would. I take it the same way you'd take a compliment from anyone. Nothing like how I would feel if Emmett was sitting here, saying those things to me right now.

"I know that from what you've seen…my relationship with Emmett must seem like pure masochism," I explain, clinging to my need to defend him. "And maybe it is. I don't know." My hands swipe across my tired face. "But I can't let him go. Not yet."

"But you deserve so much better," he argues, no longer watching the screen. His eyes are glued to me, but I keep staring intently straight ahead. "And where is he right now while you're upset? He's with Vivian."

I feel a knife in my heart. I know he's right. "She may be playing him…I know that, and you know that. But Emmett's just feeling lost and trying to do the right thing to protect his family," I say with as much conviction as I can, but a waver of doubt creeps through my voice. "He does love me," I add confidently.

"Well, he has a real fucked up way of showing it," he grumbles, turning his head back towards the TV.

"I just can't wait for all of this to be over," I groan, folding over myself in exhaustion, realizing it was probably ridiculous to think I could just sit and watch a movie at a time like this.

Suddenly, I feel his hand on my back. "You know…there are other things I could do to take your mind off things until then," he says suggestively.

I know what is about to happen. I had hoped Malcolm would let me keep things friendly and platonic, but deep down I knew this was coming. This is the moment of truth. His pale blue eyes look to me expectantly, and I have a decision to make. Will I let myself believe that Emmett and Vivian are fooling around right now and use it to justify something happening between Malcolm and me? I don't want Malcolm in the way I want Emmett, but if I can't have Emmett, then being with Malcolm would be something to dull the pain. But I can't bring myself to let it happen. Maybe if things were officially over with Emmett, it'd be a good consolation prize. But I can't do anything until I know for sure. If Emmett is still mine, I'm not going to risk jeopardizing that out of spite when I'm not even sure if it's justified.

I turn in confusion and glare at his hand, smoothing over the back of my sweater. "Malcolm…" I trail off in a warning tone, looking at him with disapproval.

"I could make you feel good, Ophelia," he replies deeply, not shying away from my glare. "You may even forget about him by the time I'm through."

I inch several more feet away to the opposite end of the couch. "I can't do that to Emmett," I contend. "Let's just watch the movie." My arms cross and I glue my eyes back to the TV, hoping he'll just drop it and let us sit here in awkward silence. My phone rests beside me on the arm of the couch, and I am on high alert for any sound vibrating through it. Just please let Emmett text me soon, I think to myself over and over.

"You honestly don't realize he's fucking Vivian right now?" Malcolm says suddenly.

"What?" I start. "Don't say that. He's not." A lump forms in my throat, and I hate him for putting it so bluntly. I know he's not. He can't be.

"You're delusional," he scoffs. "It's so obvious that's what he's doing."

"Okay, well, this definitely isn't helping." My voice grows shrill as I squirm against the couch cushion.

He moves closer, erasing the gap between our bodies. "Stop

fighting for him when he's not fighting for you," he says sternly, staring straight through me.

Before I can muster up another defense, his hand is snaking across me to reach for my cheek. His fingers push into the side of my face, trying to turn it towards his.

"Malcolm, stop!" I snap, pushing his arm away. "I can't tell you what's going to happen between Emmett and me, but I'm not going to cheat on him. Even if I'm wrong and it turns out that's what he's doing…I can't stoop to that level."

"I know you feel something for me, too," he insists, not moving away.

"You're a great guy," I offer pityingly, as his hands keep grabbing. "But no…I can't, Malcolm…Stop it!"

"Come on, just let go…Give in…" he persists, trying to grab everything that he can in order to coax me closer to him.

"No, Malcolm!" I yell louder. "Stop it! I mean it!"

His whole body moves forward, positioning himself over me as I try to turn away. I quickly go into panic mode, realizing he's not going to back down with my refusal. He continues trying to grab at me, moving his face closer to mine as he tries to force me into a kiss. I keep telling him no, but nothing stops him. I struggle, trying to put all of my weight and strength into breaking free. I'm a fighter, and will keep fighting until my last breath before I let Malcolm have his way with me. I roll my body over, putting him directly on top of me, and instantly jut my foot out with force, nailing right between his legs.

His dull eyes widen just as my foot comes up and rams in between his legs, sending him recoiling and crashing off of me in hissing pain. He falls backwards, wincing as he grabs at his balls. "You fucking bitch!" he shrieks.

He recovers quickly, and I barely have enough time to jump up and grab my things before he lunges towards me. I race for the door, but he catches up behind me and tries to pin me against the glass pane. I ram my elbow back into his ribcage, buying myself just enough time to get the door open and run off into the darkness.

My feet pound along the cobbled sidewalk alongside the main house. My breathing sharp and frantic, I try not to run into anything as I look back over my shoulder, making sure he isn't following me. Now safe from Malcolm's attack, I want to run straight into Emmett's arms. I want it to be that simple. To know that he will take me in and hold me as the man who loves me should. But what I am fleeing from puts a shadow over the protection I need from him. I shouldn't have gone with Malcolm. And what has happened with Vivian since I've been gone? Did she get what she wanted? Was she able to seduce him while they consoled each other?

I don't stop running until I am at least a mile from Malcolm's house. Hot tears burn down my cheek as I heave, feeling so stupid for coming out with him. I should have just gone home. As awful as it seemed at the time, it would have been better than this.

I zip my hoodie up tighter so that it covers as much of my face as it can. I barely want to see. I want to hide in here, in the warmth, and use it as a barrier between me and this fucked up town. My tears sting in the cold night air, but I can't stop them. It hurts too much. They flow out seamlessly.

I don't even have a plan for what I'm doing, I just know I need to go, get as far away from him as I can. I know Emmett said he didn't trust Malcolm, but I never expected this. He seemed so kind and gentle. I have to fight against the tug in my heart that tells me this means I can't trust anyone. Even the good guys end up turning bad in the end.

All at once, I know I need to run back to Emmett. That's where I belong right now and I probably should have never left. Fuck Vivian. She can cry and play damsel in distress all she wants. I can't let it come between us. I probably played into her trap perfectly by leaving them alone like that while Emmett was mad at me. I gave her the perfect opening.

As I run with a fury back to Emmett's, I tell myself she won't be there by the time I get back. She told Emmett what she needed to and then he made her leave. That has to be what happened. For my own sanity, I need that to be true.

Emmett will be pissed that I was even with Malcolm in the first place, but I am prepared to admit how wrong I was. I should have listened to him, and now I've paid the price. I keep looking back to see if Malcolm is chasing after me, but the neighborhood streets are quiet and empty. I cringe at every black car that passes, worried it might be him.

I make it to the manor, but my stomach flips as I get past the gate and see that Vivian's car is still parked right out front. I almost hesitate at the front door, but I push through. I need to be in Emmett's arms right now and feel safe again.

One of the staff members lets me in, and thankfully

Emmett and Vivian are still right in the sitting room where I left them. Emmett is standing near a corner, facing the wall while she sits on the couch. I'm happy to see the distance between them as I rush in.

"Emmett! I have to talk to you!" I shout through my labored breaths. "Now."

But I can instantly tell I've walked into the middle of something. Vivian's lips snarl at me in a satisfied grin, and Emmett doesn't budge. He just stands there with his back turned towards me, looking off into the corner.

"Didn't you hear me?" I try again in confusion. "I have to talk to you."

Vivian holds back a snickering laugh, not saying a word. I march right up to Emmett and tug at his arm. Suddenly, he flips around, almost knocking me over as he flings my hands off of him. His eyes are bloodshot and glassy. The look of rage in his eyes surpasses anything I have ever seen in him before. The intensity of it sends me stumbling backwards, bumping into an end table.

I don't know what happened while I was gone, but judging by the way Emmett's looking at me, all of his sudden anger is channeled towards me. I wonder if maybe it's because he saw me leave with Malcolm, but the longer I stare back at him, I know this is about something much bigger than that.

# CHAPTER EIGHTEEN

### BOOK 2

I am cornered against the table lining the back of the couch where Vivian sits, with Emmett glaring at me in fury, having no clue what exactly I've just walked into.

"You've got some nerve showing back up here," Vivian sneers from behind me.

"What is she talking about?" I ask him, refusing to acknowledge her directly. "Emmett, please. Tell her to go or take me to your room. I need to talk to you."

"To tell him what?" She stands up from the couch and huffs over. "That you've been fucking Malcolm?"

My lips part to tell her how wrong she is, but before I can get out a single word, Emmett flies across the room suddenly and swoops his arms across the fireplace mantle, sending a flurry of vases and frames crashing to the ground with the loud, startling sounds of breaking glass. I flinch and push further against the tabletop, practically sitting on top of it.

"What!?" I cry. "No! I would never…"

"Check your phone, Ophelia," Vivian tells me, with a tired and irritated voice. "The whole school knows now. It was sent to everyone."

I want to argue back, but I'm too confused—and afraid of Emmett's unexplained seething rage. I fumble for my phone in my bag and look to see the notification for a text from an unknown number. I open it to see a photo has been sent to me and every other student at WJ Prep. I remember Lily telling me about the app—one that Malcolm helped design, no doubt. It served as the Elites' blacklist and had the ability to text every single person in the school, letting them know if someone had fucked up and was expected to be treated like shit now. But it hasn't been used since the Elites were taken out. Until now.

The file takes impossibly long to load, but my heart sinks in horror as it finally pops up on the screen. It's a photo of Malcolm and I on his couch, but it is nothing like what actually happened. I am topless, with one of his hands cupping my bare breasts. Our mouths are locked together, and the rest of our bodies are out of view, but imagination fills in the blanks. We are obviously having sex. I try to blink the image away, but it stares back at me boldly.

"No…No, no, no. This isn't what it looks like," I stammer, shaking my head cluelessly.

I fly into a panic. How the hell could this have happened? Even if it were a photo of me from back at his place before I came here, I was definitely never topless and definitely *never* kissing him back. The position could be slightly similar to that of me warding off his advances, but everything else about it is wrong. I feel a crack in my mind as I race to piece it together.

"Emmett, that's what I was coming to you for." I fly to him across the room. "I was with Malcolm and…"

"Obviously you were with him!" Vivian smirks. "We can all see that, Ophelia."

"Not like that!" I shout, my voice cracking into fearful tears. "We were just hanging out and then…"

"Don't listen to her shit, Emmett." She cuts me off, walking over and putting her hands over his arms in comfort. "You don't need this right now." Her eyes cut back over to me with an accusing stare. I'm the outsider now. I'm the one who has betrayed him.

"Fuck off, Vivian!" I snap. "Did you do this!? Are you the one who made this photo and sent it to everyone!?"

"She was with me the whole time," Emmett says coldly, refusing to look me in the eyes.

"Now who's just making desperate attempts for Emmett's attention?" she taunts. "Pathetic. You're so jealous and inse-cure…you have to run off and fuck some other guy while your boyfriend is sitting over here worried sick about his family."

"Will you please just stay out of this?" I beg. "I don't even know why you're still here!"

"Because I care about him. In ways you obviously don't." She rolls her eyes like a dutiful person sweeping in to clean up my mess.

I want to slap her, but it wouldn't help anything right now. I look back to the photo again, wishing I knew how to explain it and realizing nothing may help right now.

"Emmett, you have to believe me…that message…" I shove Vivian out of the way and try to force myself into his line of sight.

"I can't look at you right now," he seethes, pushing me away.

"Emmett, please!" I plead, grabbing for his arms and face, trying everything I can to pull him back to me.

With a vicious roar, he growls and firmly grips my shoulders before hurtling me off of him down to the ground. I fall back and land on my ass with wide, stunned eyes. I try to get up quickly enough to try again, but he is already storming out of the room and up the stairs.

"You better go," Vivian commands before running after him.

I am frozen, unable to move. I hear more crashes coming from Emmett's room, and I hate myself for unleashing this side of him in such force. I feel so guilty, I have to keep reminding myself that I didn't do anything. Nothing happened with Malcolm, and I know that. But how can I argue with what is staring me right in the face?

I imagine being sent that image but of Emmett and Vivian together, and I think I might throw up. It's hopeless. There's nothing I can do to convince Emmett the photo isn't real, and I am beyond certain of it because I don't think he would be able to convince me if the tables were turned.

I hear the echoes of Vivian knocking on his door, trying to coax him to let her in. His voice shouts back indistinctly, but I can't make it out. All I know is he's not letting her in, which gives me some small comfort. I am still right on the ground where Emmett left me by the time she comes running down the stairs and out the front door. I let out a heavy exhale as I hear her car starting and peeling away.

Finally, I reach for the edge of the couch and use it to pull myself up. I half expect one of the housekeepers to stop me as I round the corner of the stairs. I feel like an enemy in this house now. No matter how innocent I know I am, I also know how guilty I look.

From memory, I find Emmett's door and knock gently. It's quiet inside now, and I don't know if that's better or worse. "Emmett?" I call out gingerly. "Will you please talk to me?" There's no response. I flatten my palm against the door and wait, but after a few minutes I accept that nothing I can say will fix this. I need more than words. I need proof, and there's only one other person who can give me that.

I force my breathing to become slow and intentional, trying to control each and every exhale so I don't feel like I'm hyper-ventilating. I slowly slide down the wall until I am seated safely on the floor. I don't know how long I sit there. It's so hard to walk away, knowing that Emmett may never speak to me again. He has to come out eventually, and part of me wants to wait here until that happens. But seeing him is no guarantee that he'll believe me.

"I'm going to go now," I sob softly, my forehead collapsing against the frame. "I know you don't believe me and I'm sorry for that. But I'm going to fix this. I swear to you nothing happened with Malcolm, and I'm going to find some way to prove it to you." Still nothing. "Okay?" I try asking hopelessly. I don't know how long I linger outside the door before finally forcing myself to walk away. But Emmett never budges. Things are completely fucked up beyond repair.

# CHAPTER NINETEEN

## BOOK 2

I stop myself from calling a cab as I walk along the dark sidewalks in Emmett's neighborhood. I can't stand the thought of making small talk with a stranger right now, and I think the awkward silence would be even worse.

I ignore a few worried texts from my mom, not even beginning to know how to respond. It's almost two in the morning now, and she's furious. I can't even begin to think of any decent excuses for why I didn't come home four hours ago when I said I would. Then the phone rings. I try to ignore it, but another one quickly comes through.

"Ophelia!?" her voice calls out across the line in a panic when I reluctantly answer.

"Mom," I sniffle, not knowing what to say.

"Are you okay? Where are you!"

"Could you come get me?" I ask hesitantly. I don't want to, but I don't have any other choice. Although it would serve me right to walk the entire way back to my house in the cold. "I left my car at school."

Without pausing, she tells me she'll put Brendan on the phone to get directions to where I am. They don't ask any questions. All I hear is the shuffle of her gathering her things in the background.

Once I hang up, I know I can't just stand here and wait. I feel too awful to stay in one place, but I also don't want to wander too far from the spot I directed her to. So, instead I pace back and forth along the same couple of blocks over and over until her car finally slows down beside me.

I burst into tears the moment I get in her car and can barely hear her persistent questioning over my sobs. There are a million things I wish I could tell her, but it's all untrue. I wish I could say I had been drinking or smoking, that I was being irresponsible and having fun. But what actually happened is too heavy to even begin to explain.

"I don't know what is going on with you lately!" She finally snaps into tears. "I keep trying to give you space and let you figure things out on your own. But you won't tell me anything! How can I help you?"

"You can't!" I scream. "That's the whole problem! You can't possibly help me!"

"How do you know if you don't try?" she pushes. "I wasn't born yesterday, Ophelia. I know things about the world. Probably more than you think. I work in a hospital! I see all kinds of things. Not to mention what I've been through myself. Please… Just talk to me."

I shake my head and look out the window through my tears. "Tell me about you and my dad," I murmur, needing to say it for myself, but I hope she doesn't hear.

"What?" she demands. "I didn't hear you."

"I can't talk about it right now," I finally sob. "Tomorrow, maybe."

She forces herself to stop hounding me and drives. Once we're home, she rushes out of the car to wrap me in a long hug the moment I step foot onto the ground from the passenger's side. Her embrace sends me right back into an eruption of tears. Only one other time have I been so grateful to see our house standing there just a few feet away, and that was when I was finally coming home from the police station after everything happened with Emmett and our fathers.

She doesn't ask me any more questions as we go in, and instead leaves me be to retreat to my room. I toss and turn in my sleep, dreaming of Emmett's t-shirt. The way it feels over his hard chest as I cling to it with my fingers. The way it smells like his cologne, sweat, and the salt of his skin. The warmth of him that rests beneath it. I want to bury my face in his shirt again. I don't want that to be gone forever.

Eventually my dreams fade into a deep sleep. So deep that I sleep through my alarms the next morning.

I catch Brendan in the kitchen when I finally wake up and pull myself together. He drives me to school on his way to work, also not prodding about what happened the night before. I can only assume my mom asked him not to until I was ready to talk about it.

I stop outside the front doors of WJ Prep, feeling that same familiar sense of foreboding as I apprehensively make myself push forward with a deep breath, clutching my bag to my side. I walk into a familiar scene. I've already missed first period, but regretfully caught the rush in between classes. Everyone stares and snickers as I pass. They've all seen the doctored photo of Malcolm and me. I don't know if this is better or worse than the time a nude picture of me was printed onto hundreds of flyers and spread around the school.

I keep my head high despite the strange, pitying looks that I have grown used to. The whispers of my name that put me on high alert. I've done this walk before. At least this time I know what the offense is. Everyone thinks I've fucked Malcolm, and no one knows what to do about it. The hierarchy of things is completely thrown. Before the Elites were taken down, an offense like this would have made me instantly blacklisted. But Emmett hasn't commanded his old position of power since he came back, and now no one knows how to feel.

As I approach my locker, I don't notice the strange gleaming substance smeared across its surface until it's too late. I pull my sticky hand back from the lock and realize the whole thing is slathered in lubricant.

"A girl like you fucking two guys at once could use a little lube," some random kid jeers as he pushes past, shoving me straight into the sticky surface.

I almost chase after and pounce on him, but my focus turns to getting this stuff washed off of me. I head for the bathroom, laughing to myself as I realize something like this doesn't bother me nearly as much as it would have before. I guess the joke's on them. It seems someone took it into their own hands to decide how to handle the news about Malcolm and me. Even without the Elites commanding everyone, it's still the nature of high schoolers to bully or be bullied. And I guess my crazy life has given everyone more than enough ammunition.

Straightening my back, I hold my head high and breeze past everyone. They're not the ones I'm worried about. I only have eyes for two people. Emmett, in hopes that I can somehow convince him of the truth, or Malcolm, so that he can help me fix this.

But the day carries on without any sign of either one of them. I don't see Emmett in the halls or in any of his classes, and Malcolm isn't in his hiding spot come lunchtime. By my last class, I am crawling in my skin. I had hoped I could have fixed things at some point during school, but it quickly becomes obvious I have no hope of doing so until I can get out of here.

With the ring of the last bell, I fly through the double doors and decide I have to skip practice. As much as I would love to run right now, I can't focus on anything until I have found some way of making things right. I pull out my phone and call Malcolm.

"Why hello, beautiful," he says as he answers. I am amazed by how quickly his kind voice has flipped. Now it just sounds creepy and gross to me.

"I need to talk to you," I huff urgently as I walk to my car. "Are you at home?"

"Yeah…" He yawns. "I played hooky today. I was pretty worn out from last night."

"I'm coming over," I insist, hanging up before he has a chance to respond.

It feels good to reunite with my own car again, restore some sense of control. My music blares as I swerve around corners, relishing in the acceleration. It makes me feel like I am doing something. I am taking action, even though the situation with Emmett feels completely hopeless. I speed away from school towards Malcolm's, losing all sense of how fast I'm going until the flashing blue lights appear behind me just a few miles from his house.

"Shit," I mutter as I pull over to the side of the road. I've never been pulled over before. In fact, the only contact I've ever had with the police was when I gave my statement about Thomas Jameson's claimed suicide.

"License and registration, please," the officer says as I roll down my window with shaking hands. I nervously mumble something as I dig through my bag to collect everything. "Do you have any idea how fast you were going?"

"I'm so sorry." I blush. "I'm…I'm late for meeting a friend and I…I just lost track of my speed, I guess," I offer anxiously as I hand him my information.

"'Ophelia Lopez'," he reads off my license. "I know you. You're Theodore Nickelson's girl, aren't you?"

My hand grips and twists the steering wheel, wishing more than anything that wasn't how people knew me. I am not his girl. I'm my mom's girl. Brendan's girl. Theo can't claim any part of me beyond the role of sperm donor and recent life-ruiner.

"That's my biological father, yes," I answer with a tight smile.

"Ah." He grimaces. "You heard anything from him lately?"

"No," I lie. "Why?"

His eyes cut into me as he leans over my window. His stare is questioning, like he's waiting to see if I'll crack and say more, but I keep my lips clenched tight. Finally, the corners of his mouth turn up in an insincere smile. "Alright, well…this all looks in order," he says, to my surprise, without even returning to his car to look up my information. "I'll let you off with a warning. Just be sure to drive slower, okay?"

"Yes, of course, Officer," I promise urgently, ready to get the hell away from him. "Thank you."

I am shaking by the time he walks back to his car and watches me drive off. I am on high alert, driving as slowly and carefully as possible, hoping he won't come after me again.

Great—now on top of everything else, the police seem to still be convinced that I have ties to my father. I worry that sooner or later, it will come out that I met with him recently, making me look guilty of something because I lied about it. I knew that little meeting would come back to bite me in the ass. I should just run and tell the police everything I know about him, but of course I can't without telling them that Emmett struck a deal to have his father murdered. Also, if the police could be trusted, then this whole ordeal with Bernadette wouldn't be so complicated.

I have no way of knowing if I can make things right with Emmett. I won't know until after I talk to Malcolm, but I obviously can't get there any faster than this. And without him, the only thing I can think to do is call my father and come clean about the cops questioning me about him. I don't know what he can do to fix it, but if I can't be honest, then he at least needs to tell me what lie I'm supposed to tell.

My mind slowly comes back to the task at hand as I pull up to Malcolm's, surging with adrenaline.

"I knew you'd change your mind." He smiles arrogantly as he opens his front door before I even have a chance to knock. "You probably ran to Emmett and saw he was still with Vivian, right? I told you they were fucking."

I breeze past him through the door without stopping. "Have you seen that photo?" I ask impatiently. "Do you know who did this?"

"What photo?" He's playing dumb, but I know he knows exactly what I'm talking about. "Did you come back to finish what we started?"

"This!" I bark as I shove my phone in his face, the disgusting fake pic pulled up on the screen.

"It's a great photo." He smirks as he lifts his arms into a casual stretch.

"You know damn well nothing happened between us, Malcolm," I thunder. "Who took this? Did you have someone do this?"

"Obviously I had nothing to do with it...I was busy." He laughs, and I want to slap him in the face.

"Look, I know you're upset that I didn't mess around with you," my tone turns calmer, wanting to reason with him. "But I know you're a decent guy," I lie, feeling nothing of the sort anymore. "You have to help me fix this. Emmett saw this and thinks it's real."

"Oh, it's real," he replies boldly.

"Why are you acting this way?" I whine in distress. "I thought you were different...I thought you were better than this. You know this is doctored. It's fake. Somebody is trying to tear Emmett and me apart!"

Suddenly, a toilet flushes from the back of the room. "Who's here?" I glare at him, but he doesn't answer. I'm surprised to see Lily appear from behind the bathroom door.

"What the hell are you doing here?" I gape, flailing my phone in her direction. "Did you do this?"

"No, but I wish I had," she snickers, before plopping down on the couch.

"Since when are you two friends?" I admonish with a furrowed brow, shaking my head in confusion. "Is this why you were hanging out with me the whole time, Malcolm? Are you just working with Vivian and Lily to ruin my life?"

"No one has to work to do that, Ophelia," Lily answers coldly. "There's not much of a life to ruin to begin with...and the pathetic mess you do have…You do more than enough to fuck it up on your own."

"Why is everyone in this town so fucked up!?" I shriek, flying into a mad pace around the room, feeling like I'm wasting my time talking to these idiots. They're both lounging around looking bored and snide, and it's becoming more and more obvious that I'm getting nowhere. "Lily, I know you're angry with me right now," I try to plead, "but we were friends once. Surely some part of you feels bad about how you've been acting. Please, help me."

She shrugs. "You're beyond help. You cheated on Emmett, and you got caught. The end."

"I did not!" I cry back. "Malcolm and I were watching a movie. He made a pass at me. I fought him off and then ran away. The end. That's it. That's all that happened, and I don't know where the hell this picture came from!"

"That's not how I remember it," Malcolm adds snidely.

"So, you did this, then," I conclude. "You're the one who made this and sent it to Emmett!"

"You sound like a crazy person, Ophelia," Lily taunts. "Are you back on drugs?" She laughs.

I pace around Malcolm's house, looking back and forth between the couch and the front windows. I compare it to the photo and can see that someone clearly had to have been watching from outside the window. They must have snapped the picture when Malcolm forced his way on top of me, and then edited it in Photoshop afterwards.

This whole thing was planned. Someone had to have been waiting out there for him to make his move just so they could get the picture, and once they had it, they worked fast. Fast enough for it to have already been sent out by the time I made it back over to Emmett's.

I'm convinced that Lily had to have been the one to take it. Why else would she be hanging around here right now, acting just as delusional as Malcolm? I want to interrogate them some more, but it's obvious neither of them is going to own up to anything. But I am determined not to leave here until I have some sort of proof or explanation for Emmett.

My eyes dart across Malcolm's expensive equipment, and it hits me. He has to have security measures in place to protect all of this stuff. All rich people spend just as much money on protecting their things as they do on the things themselves.

"Security cameras!" I shout. "You have cameras outside?" I grasp desperately at this last straw.

"What are you talking about?" he grumbles in annoyance.

"The footage would show who took the picture," I insist. The two of them don't move. I know it's hopeless. They're probably behind the photo, even if I can't figure out why. Maybe Malcolm was just mad that I refuted his advance and decided to get revenge. Maybe he thought that once Emmett was out of the picture, I'd come running back to him. But I'm half-tempted to try and get a hold of the footage anyway. Just as I am inching towards the door to see if there are cameras, my phone rings. I hope it's Emmett calling. Maybe he's ready to listen to me. But it's a number I don't recognize.

"Excuse me. I have to take this," I explain as I step outside, but I know it's pointless. They could care less if I'm here right now or not. They've already had their fun, and at this point I'm just a source of entertainment. They're enjoying watching me go mad as I try to figure all of this out.

I step out into the backyard of the main house, which happens to be Malcolm's front yard, and answer the call.

"Ophelia, it's me. Granger."

"Coach Granger," I answer apologetically. "Sorry I missed practice today…I…I wasn't feeling well and…"

"Are you alone right now?" he cuts me off.

"Sort of," I answer lightly, looking through the window to make sure Lily and Malcolm are still in sight on the couch. I quickly realize he's not calling to yell at me about practice. "Coach, what's wrong?"

"Where are you right now?" he snaps back urgently.

"Everything's a mess," I groan, not knowing where to begin. Where I am right now doesn't feel as a simple question as it should be, but I try to get myself together. "I'm at Malcolm Henderson's," I say finally.

"Does he know you're talking to me?"

"No, I don't think so," I reply, the concern in my voice growing at the panic in his. "I stepped outside to take your call."

"I don't have much time to explain," he huffs. "I'm on my way there. But you have to be careful, Ophelia. Malcolm's dangerous."

My heart pounds. An asshole definitely, but it hadn't occurred to me that Malcolm could be more dangerous than refusing to take no for an answer. But Coach Granger doesn't sound like he's playing around, not even a little bit.

"What do you mean?" I question with caution, keeping my eyes glued on them through the window. "Lily is here, too."

"Don't trust either of them," he orders. I already didn't trust them, but it's becoming obvious that something much bigger than I realized is going on. "The reason I was away those few weeks…" he explains slowly, clearing his throat. "My son died."

"Oh my god…Coach…I'm so sorry," I gasp, my heart breaking for him and a lump in my throat. "I had no idea. That's terrible!" I feel awful for not knowing this whole time, for not being able to offer my condolences in some way. "But I don't understand," I continue carefully. "Why are you telling me this right now?"

"He was a recovering addict, Ophelia," he answers. "He relapsed and overdosed on heroin."

"Heroin…" I trail off, making the instant connection between what Lily and Vivian did to me and what happened to Coach's son.

"My son was doing better than ever," he explains vehemently. "We were very close. I knew what the signs of a relapse were, and he showed none of them. I knew the Elites had to be behind it somehow because of the timing of it all. I just didn't know how. Until you told me what Vivian and Lily did to you."

"I believe you," I offer immediately, needing to show him the same trust he showed me when I was in trouble at school. Ironically, those are also the same words I am longing to hear from Emmett right now. "You think they did the same thing to your son?"

"The stuff they found in his room around his body, Ophelia…it was all wrapped in a bow. Like someone planted it there just for him, knowing he wouldn't be able to resist," he illuminates chillingly. "After you told me what Vivian and Lily did, I called up a detective friend of mine and had him look into it. There was DNA on the items that matches two people from WJ Prep."

"Lily and Vivian," I announce confidently.

"No. Lily and Malcolm," he corrects me.

"Why would Malcolm do that to your son?" I exclaim into the phone, quickly softening to a hushed tone so they won't hear me inside.

"Ophelia, where are they right now?" he asks, the panic in his voice returning.

"They're inside," I reply. "I can see them through the window."

"It's not safe for you there, but I need you to try and make sure they don't leave until I get there," he instructs. "The police are on their way, and so am I. Can you do that for me? Without getting hurt?"

"I think so," I say timidly. "I can try. But I don't think either of them want to physically harm me...Just ruin my life."

"No, they're dangerous," he reminds me. "Be very careful. I'll be there as fast as I can."

# CHAPTER TWENTY

## BOOK 2

I walk back inside trembling, trying to hide my fear. I feel stupid for not realizing how much danger I could be in when I charged in the first time, and I am still having a hard time believing what Coach Granger said.

I never knew Lily to be vicious until recently. Same with Malcolm. I knew when the old Elite gang was together, they were capable of some pretty monstrous things, but Lily and Malcolm were never a part of that. They were supposed to be the good guys. But now it appears as though they may be the worst ones out of them all.

"So…you never said what it was you were doing here exactly," I say carefully to Lily as I shut the door behind me, wishing I could leave it open as a means of a quick escape. "I didn't know you and Malcolm were friends."

"What…you think you know everything about me just because we hung out a couple of times?" she shoots back coldly.

"Obviously not," I mutter, clenching my fingers around my phone before slipping it into my pocket.

"Who were you talking to on the phone?" she asks in a sly, questioning tone.

"Oh…uh…it was my mom." I laugh nervously. "Just wondering where I was." It feels like the energy in the room has shifted, but I can't tell if I'm just being paranoid. I swear they know that I know something, and I suddenly feel like a rat thrown into a snake's cage. "Can I use your restroom?" I blurt, needing some kind of retreat to collect myself.

They say nothing, but Malcolm lingers behind me, vaguely waving his arm towards the back of the room. So, I direct myself to the door I saw Lily coming out of before. I brace my back against the door as I close it behind me, blowing sharp breaths from my cheeks as quietly as possible. My shaking hands reach for the faucet, turning on a rush of water on to drown out the sound of my panic attack.

I lean over the sink and splash some water on my face. My heart is breaking for Coach Granger. Even though Lily and Malcolm didn't murder his son with their own hands, what they did seems worse somehow. To plant his weakness in front of him wrapped in a bow. They just left it there and waited, letting him take care of the rest. Coach sounded confident that his son would have never relapsed on his own, had it not been for their little gift.

I swallow down the sickness rising in my chest and try to regain my composure. With one last deep breath, I flush the toilet and turn off the water. I reach for the door handle to go out, realizing I have zero plan for what to do until Coach Granger gets there.

I frantically try to wrap my brain around some sort of explanation for my lingering presence and to keep them occupied, when I am frozen at the sight of both of them lurking on the other side of the door, waiting for me to come back out.

"Hey," I gulp innocently.

"Been talking to Coach Granger, huh?" Lily's voice burns as I blindly feel for my pocket and realize my phone is gone.

"Looking for this?" Malcolm teases as he holds my phone up in the air. He must have grabbed it just as I was walking past to the bathroom.

I lunge forward to grab it back, which is pointless because it's obviously too late. Lily pounces on me from behind and wrestles me to the ground as Malcolm swings his hand back, snatching the phone from my reach. I squirm as he joins in, helping her pin me to the ground.

I'm terrified of what might happen once I am fully restrained, but suddenly the front door bursts open, slicing through my fear. I expect to see the police or Coach Granger standing there, but I'm shocked to see Emmett instead. He freezes at the sight of them tackling me.

"Emmett, help!" I scream out as he rushes over.

Emmett pulls Malcolm back by the hair and punches him in the face with enough force to scare Lily off of me. Malcolm stumbles off to the other side of the room, holding his hand over his eye and cheek while I pull myself to my feet and cower behind Emmett.

"Coach Granger and the police are on their way here," I announce over his shoulder. "They know all about what you two did."

"Your girl has officially lost it, Emmett," Lily sneers, trying to play innocent.

"What's going on?" Emmett asks, looking at Malcolm like he could kill him.

"He found your DNA on the needles and drugs you gift-wrapped for his recovering son," I explain. "It's all over now. He knows what you did and can prove it. He's on his way with the police!"

Lily and Malcolm are still before us like deer in headlights, but Malcolm quickly bolts for the door. Emmett chases after him but doesn't catch up in time. I see him sprinting across the yard out of sight as Emmett quickly locks and blocks the door so Lily can't escape.

"What's all this about, then?" he asks as he instinctively guards the escape. He's smart enough to know to act and then ask questions. I'm glad he still has at least this much faith in me. "What are you talking about?" he asks again.

"I told you someone made sure Coach Granger wouldn't be around when things came to a head with the rest of the Elites," I remind him. "They're the ones who did it. They made sure his son would use again, and it's the reason he died." I watch his expression as he pieces it all together before turning back to Lily. "How could you do something like this, Lily? Why were you helping the Elites?"

A look of defiance comes over her for a moment, but it quickly fades. She knows I've talked to Granger and that I know everything. Emmett knows now, too, and the police will be here soon. She accepts that she's been caught. Her eyes close, and then she turns to Emmett in desperation.

"I did it for you," she cries softly in his direction.

"What the fuck are you talking about?" he thunders back.

"I've always loved you," she sobs. "Ever since freshman year. You knew I had a crush on you."

"What does that have to do with Coach Granger's son?" I redirect her, growing impatient. If there's any chance of getting a real explanation from her, it has to happen now, before the police show up.

"I don't have to tell you anything," she insists. "Malcolm promised nothing would happen to me."

"He's gone, Lily," I remind her with a pitying, reprimanding stare. "He left you. He's not going to help you."

"I was furious with you and the Elites for ruining my chances for college," she explains desperately. "And it was all your fault. All because I was stupid enough to try and help you and be your friend!"

I could never believe that those Elite monsters would stoop so low as to ruin Lily's entire educational future just because she wasn't in their good graces. It changed my entire view of the world, realizing that even the most prestigious institutions could be swayed by the right people in the right places. Nothing is sacred.

And now they have stooped even lower in the aftermath, reducing Lily to a love-raged murderer. She always seemed so bright and above all of the bullshit around here. But I guess maybe that was just an act. Maybe she was just trying to keep me close out of jealousy for Emmett.

I never realized how unhinged Lily was. To think she caused so much damage all because of me. "Why would you get mixed up in all of this, Lily?" I try to understand. "Emmett fixed your chance for that scholarship at Juilliard. But now that's over with because of this. Why would you do that?"

"You did that for me, didn't you?" she pleads with Emmett. "Because you love me, too?"

He shakes his head. "I'm sorry, Lily," he says lightly, but with certainty. "No. I did that because I thought you were Ophelia's friend. I was trying to make things right."

I see her recoil, but something stays persistent. I don't think she accepts his rejection any more now than she did freshman year. She has obviously been clinging to some hope of being with him ever since, refusing to admit that it was all just a cruel prank.

"I just wanted to make sure the Elites got away with whatever they had planned for you," she continues. "I knew Coach Granger was the only one who would have helped you."

"But I thought you cared about me..." I gape in shock.

"You tried to help me! Why would you want the Elites to hurt me? Why would you risk ruining your own future just to get back at me?" I shake my head in disbelief. "Jesus, Lily. Because of you, his son is dead!"

"Because it's not fair!" she screams through her tears. "I know Emmett had real feelings for me! Vivian just came along and fucked it all up! Made him turn on me!" she insists before reaching out to Emmett. "I thought if I just kept my head down and stayed out of the way, Vivian would eventually fuck off and you'd come back around. You'd realize that what you felt for me was real."

"That was just a prank, Lily," Emmett confirms with real remorse. "It was awful. I know. But I didn't feel anything for you then."

"Because Ophelia came along. Everything was fine before then. Everyone knew you were just with Vivian because of your families. You had no choice! It never would have lasted!" She flies into a mad and desperate rant. Her words spill out quickly, leaving no room for any other possibility. "But then you showed up and it was so obvious—the way you secretly fawned over him even when he treated you like shit!" she bellows at me. "And then I was stupid enough to help you and ended up right back as one of the Elites' main targets. You ruined everything! I wanted to make sure they took you out of the picture for good!"

"So you helped kill someone!?" I shriek, wishing she could hear how crazy she sounds.

"I didn't know he'd die!" she defends frantically. "It was Malcolm's idea! I thought he would just start using again and Coach Granger would be distracted trying to help him. I hated him for being on your side. Emmett, college—everything—all ripped from my hands because of you!"

"Lily, I had no idea you felt that way," I reply in astonishment. "You should have just talked to me."

"I wanted to punish Coach for going against the Elites. Both of you act so above everything. Like you can do whatever you want," she says, shaking angrily. "Like you're the only ones who can just ignore the way things work around here and get away with it. After everything they did to me and my family for not respecting the hierarchy of things!"

"But now you're going to be investigated for murder, Lily!" I try to give her a reality check. "Just because you were angry with me."

"That's not all of it," she persists. "I did it because I love you, Emmett. And I knew once she was gone, you'd finally come around to how you really felt about me. You do still feel the same way, don't you? Isn't that why you're hanging around Vivian again? Because of me?"

Emmett's eyes cut to mine with a knowing glance. We both know what he has to do. The sirens are wailing in the distance, but Lily is growing more frantic and anxious. He has to play along with her before she hurts herself or one of us. Or before she tries to make another run for it.

"Yes, Lily," he sighs. "You're right. I do love you. That's the only reason I have been trying to spend time with Vivian. So I could be around you."

"I knew it! I knew you felt the same way!" she shouts ecstatically as she throws herself into his arms. "Run away with me, Emmett! I can't stay here and go down for this. You have enough money. We could go wherever we wanted to. Away from all this Elite bullshit. We could start all over again!"

He says nothing but cradles her, keeping his eyes glued to me the whole time. I wait pensively until I see Coach Granger and the cops surrounding us outside. They burst into the room, but Lily is so far gone she doesn't seem to hear or see them. All she cares about is that Emmett just confessed his feelings for her and is finally holding her in his arms.

"She confessed to everything," I announce, almost hating to ruin Lily's delusional fantasy.

"I can prove it," Emmett says as he pushes Lily over to the cops. He pulls his phone from his pocket and begins playing Lily's recorded confession back to them. He must have clicked the recording on as soon as I said the police were coming.

Lily doesn't even flinch as it plays. She keeps her eyes squinted shut tightly, as if she's trying to stay in some mythical space where Emmett's feelings are real, and she's not about to be arrested. I am overcome with pity. I knew Vivian obviously still had feelings for him, or maybe she just wanted him back to restore some sense of her social status. But I couldn't see Lily's affections for him boiling beneath the surface this entire time.

Coach Granger nods to me before following the police out as they put Lily in their squad car. Emmett and I are left alone in shock, but I don't even know what to say to him. I'm almost more afraid of him now than before. I want to feel above Lily, like I am somehow better and could never be so delusional, but am I? Is this just what Emmett does to girls? Who knows how far he took things with Lily during their little prank, knowing he was with Vivian the whole time? I am becoming paranoid that all of the Elites are going to jump out from behind the curtains and announce that what he and I have is really just a prank, too.

"Did you have any idea Lily felt that way?" I gape at him from across the room, wishing I could run into his arms.

He shakes his head no, staying silent. He looks lost as his dark gray eyes dart hopelessly around the room and back to me. He looks like he's trying to decide if he can talk to me right now, if he can bring himself over to me. But his feet are planted firmly. He won't come to me, and he won't go.

"Emmett," I start, my face lifting in desperation. "There's so much I need to say. I…"

He holds his hand up firmly to silence me, and just like that, he turns to leave. I don't know why he came here in the first place, but he was exactly who I wanted to come bursting in after me. But now that he's gone, I don't think he was coming after me at all. Why else would he have left me?

I look around the empty room, feeling suddenly vulnerable and afraid to be here alone, not knowing when Malcolm will return or if he will at all. I don't want to risk it. I walk out of the house, hoping maybe, by some chance Emmett was unable to leave. Maybe he's waiting for me by my car. I don't see him when I get out there, so I linger for a while, thinking maybe he'll come back. But there's no sight of him.

I remember my thought about the security cameras and turn back towards Malcolm's one last time to see if I spot anything, but there are no cameras that I can see. Even if there were, I probably wouldn't have a clue how to retrieve the footage. Someone like him surely has every measure possible in place to protect people from getting into his system.

Feeling no closer to convincing Emmett the photo was fake, I reluctantly climb into my car and drive home. Lily's voice and face haunt me for the rest of the night. I'm beginning to question my ability to judge the character of a person. To think she was so desperately in love with Emmett the entire time, and I had no idea! Even when she paired off with Vivian, even after what she did to me, I never would have thought she'd be capable of something like what she did to Coach Granger's son.

After everything I have been through, I am grateful that I

still have so much to come home to, which is more than I can say for everyone else. Emmett seems to have lost his entire family. Lily has been arrested. Malcolm's been forced into hiding. The rest of the Elites are under investigation. I almost feel sorry for them, no matter how awful they all have been. They were raised to believe they could do whatever they wanted. That people like them never faced consequences for their actions. And now all at once, their worlds are crumbling down around them.

My world may feel like it's crumbling without Emmett, but I still have the warmth of my loving family to come home to. I give my mom and Brendan extra-long hugs after dinner that night, and think of Coach Granger and his poor family as I fall asleep. I hope that maybe he can find some peace now that he knows who sabotaged his son's recovery and ended his life.

# CHAPTER TWENTY-ONE

BOOK 2

I am dreaming about being on a sinking ship. Alarms begin to sound when the water levels grow dangerously high, but I ignore them. I carry on with ordinary things while the ocean rushes in. People around me rush past in a panic, heeding the warning of the alarms, but I refuse to move. My dream self has decided to go down with the ship. It's a strange moment when real life and dream life bleed together. The alarm of my phone leaks into my dreams as the alarm on the ship, and I choose to ignore it and stay asleep.

The Elites taught me about pain. I thought I knew all about it from running—pushing past the burning ache of my muscles to get in another mile and then another. But I didn't know anything about pain until I met them. Until I saw what Emmett was capable of. To still desire a person even as they are scaring you and physically harming you—that is a pain running could have never prepared me for. Just like this seizing feeling in my chest is something I have never felt before. I've seen what Emmett is capable of in both good and bad ways now, and the thought of losing him is still paralyzing.

I sit up in bed feeling a new kind of emptiness. A big, wide, gaping hole where Emmett used to be. At least when I asked him to give me space, it was a choice, one that I felt like I could take back at any time. Now the choice is his, and any attempt to chase after him will just look desperate. And before I asked for space, there were times when I wanted him, but the reality of him was so awful that I prayed that he would just leave me alone. And yet he invaded my life anyway. Always there when I wished he wouldn't be. Never in the way I wanted him.

I tell myself this is my way out. This is my chance at freedom. I should take it and run. In fact, I really should run. I should go out and run until I can't anymore, shedding away everything about this whole nightmare with Emmett. And maybe, by the time I'm done, I won't want him to text or call me anymore. I won't want him at all.

I imagine I can feel him next to me, lying in my bed, smiling at me from the pillow next to me. It may not be something I've had much here in this room, but I've experienced it enough in his motel room that I can picture it so vividly.

There's no telling where Malcolm is, or if he'll be back now that he's wanted by the police. I let out a scoffing smirk to myself as I stretch out in bed. Malcolm will probably find some way or another for his dad to fix all of this for them. They have enough money and power to do that sort of thing. Either way, there's no hope of Malcolm helping me prove the photo of us together is fake. If Emmett won't come to believe me on his own, then it's hopeless.

A frightening reality sets in. What if I never do convince Emmett of the truth? What if he never believes me, and everything we've shared is lost because of whoever made that photo and sent it out? I try to picture life without Emmett. Now he has become so ingrained in me that it's hard to imagine. Even when he was still acting under the influence of his father and the Elites, he was still devouring my thoughts for better or worse.

I think of his warm, tan skin and how the touch of it sets me on fire. It feels like home. I try to imagine never feeling that again, or seeing the spark in his icy gray eyes. My chest tightens. Feeling like it all might be lost forever only makes me want him more, even if just for a few minutes. Just to feel him against me one last time, to see his grinning face or to hear his laugh. Even his screaming fits—I'd take those at this point, too! Any part of him is better than none of him at all. But maybe that's the exact same kind of longing that drove Vivian and Lily to where they ended up.

During fourth period, a terrible noise blares through the classrooms and halls, jerking me out of my anxious daze. The fire alarm bellows relentlessly as the teachers quickly shuffle us out into the school yard. There are whispers and murmurs through the crowd that someone has pulled it as a prank. There are no signs of smoke or fire. As everyone gathers out front, I still can't see Emmett or Malcolm anywhere. As I'm looking around for them, something catches the corner of my eye. I turn, and swear I see someone who looks like Bernadette walking off to the side of the school.

"Bernadette!" I scream out instinctively, as everyone backs away and looks at me like I'm crazy. I take off running in her direction, ignoring the teachers around me who yell for me to stop and stay with everyone else.

By the time I reach the edge of the building, she is nowhere to be seen. I don't see anyone at all, not even someone who looks like her. Just like that, she's gone again. Like a ghost that's vanished.

The sighting leaves an uneasy feeling in the pit of my stomach. I try to call Emmett, wanting to tell him about it, but of course he doesn't answer. The rest of the school day feels strangely calm. I don't know if any rumors are circulating yet about what Malcolm and Lily did, but things seem to be back to normal. At least as normal as it ever gets around here. But I am still feeling distracted and out of it, and find myself racing through empty halls to catch one of my classes when I hear crying coming from behind the stairs.

I know I should keep going, but something makes me stop. I peek around the railing and see Vivian standing in a corner with her head tilted back. Her eyes are closed as she sobs quietly, hiding away by herself. At first, I feel nothing, thinking she deserves whatever tears she has to shed and then some. But for some reason, I can't bring myself to just leave her there like that, even though I know I should.

"Hey…you okay?" I ask from around the corner. My tone is apathetic, and I'm hoping she'll just say something rude, giving me permission to carry on.

"No," she laments.

Shit. Now I have to talk to her. Actually, I don't have to— she deserves nothing from me, but no matter how hard she tried to paint me as a monster to Emmett, I do have empathy. Even some left for her it seems.

"Wow…no biting remarks," I shoot back as I crouch to join her behind the stairs. "Now I know something must be wrong. Is this about Lily being arrested?"

"No." She rolls her eyes. "I knew all about what she and Malcolm did."

I want to hound her for that fact and make her feel as guilty as possible, but I try to push past that. "Is it Emmett?"

"My parents," she sobs. "The investigation into the sex trafficking ring is coming to a close. Trey and Vincent's parents are being sent away. Our lawyers say my dad is going to go away for a long time, and my mom will, too, because she knew about everything and helped him. There's going to be a trial." Her breath catches through sniffles. "Our family name will be completely ruined. The lawyers say there's nothing they can do for them and that they should just plead guilty. And then there's the sentencing."

I knew things had to be hard for her because of what's been happening to her parents, but I am still taken aback. I guess it just never occurred to me that Vivian would even care. That's how heartless she seemed to me. "I'm sorry, Vivian."

"I didn't know about what they were doing," she assures me, looking at me with deadened eyes, blotted with runny makeup.

"Really?" I reply, sounding too shocked.

"Don't act so surprised," she snips. "I know I've done some fucked up things. Made your life hell. But I'm not a monster, Ophelia. Neither is Emmett. Our families are just so fucked up."

"I'm realizing that pretty quickly," I grumble shrewdly. "And you all run around doing to others what has been done to you."

"I just feel so alone. We may have had to do fucked up things to stay on top, but that's what was expected of us," she explains in a wavering voice. "But I had my friends and I had Emmett. Then everything just crumbled down overnight." Her arms fly up dramatically. "I held onto Bernadette, even though my parents told me we could never speak to any of the Jamesons again. And we both realized what was happening to us was similar to what happened to Lily…We felt bad for her. Tried to take her back in. I even thought I could get Emmett back and things could sort of go back to how they were before. At least at school. Then I realized Emmett didn't love me anymore and that he was with you. Then Bernadette ran off. Now Lily is gone, too."

"I never realized you cared so much, Vivian," I offer sincerely. "I thought you were just a cold, heartless bitch."

"Well, that's how I'm expected to be," she barks. But then

with a sigh, she relaxes. "Ophelia, I really was worried about Emmett's mom the other night," she explains gently. "I know I tried to make things hard for you and Emmett because I was jealous, but I was just so scared of losing her, too. She's like a second mother to me. And with my parents going away and everything else that's going on…I just panicked when I thought she might be gone, too."

"I had no idea, Vivian. I'm sorry." It had never occurred to me that Vivian's emotions at Emmett's might be genuine. No wonder he got so angry and I ended up looking like a bitch. I was the one being heartless. But who could blame me after the way Vivian has treated me?

Worse, it pokes holes in everything I thought I had figured out. I was convinced that Vivian called Emmett and me over to wail about his mom just to distract me. That everything went as she had planned, putting me right in Malcolm's arms so Lily could take that picture, doctor it, and send it to everyone.

I figured she must have thought that after all of that, Emmett would be hers. It would have made perfect sense, and maybe part of it is still true. But regardless, Vivian was legitimately upset that evening. Afraid of losing one of the few familiar parts of her life that were left.

I think over all of her words, and then it hits me like a ton of bricks. "Wait a second…what did you say a second ago? Did you say Bernadette ran off?"

"I don't know. I don't know what I said." She waves me away dismissively. "I feel like I haven't slept in weeks."

I want to press her about it, but Emmett has already talked to her and is convinced she knows nothing. I am done sticking my nose too far into this thing with Bernadette. He asked for my help, but everything I've tried to do has only ruined things more.

"What will you do now?" I ask finally, willing to just let her slip go. Emmett's not even talking to me right now anyway. "After your parents' sentencing?"

"I have an aunt in New York," she states plainly. "I could go stay with her. Change my name. Try to start over and finish high school somewhere else."

"I hate that you have to do all of that. All because of what your parents did."

"Maybe it's for the best." She perks up her chin with a deep, optimistic breath. "This way I won't have to keep up this ridiculous charade. Treating everyone like shit just to protect some familial social status. It couldn't have lasted forever, anyway. No one gets to stay on top forever after treating people the way our families had."

I'm blown away by her humility and self-awareness. I'd always figured if the Elites had any understanding of the damage they caused to others, they must get off on it. I thought they were so entitled that they relished in other people's suffering. But now Vivian claims it was all just a farce, which matches what Emmett always claimed to be true.

"Want one?" Vivian asks, pulling a pack of cigarettes out from her bag.

I shake my head. "No, emphysema and lung cancer are kind of a runner's worst enemy," I joke dryly.

"Whatever." She rolls her eyes as she lights up.

"Won't you get in trouble?" I ask as she barely cracks the window to catch the wafting smoke. "We're not exactly in hiding back here. The teachers will smell it."

"You still don't get it, do you?" Her eyes spark at me. "We can do whatever we want, Ophelia. Even with everything that's happening to my parents, I'm still one of the Elites. Whatever that means now. The teachers aren't going to say a fucking word to me."

I purse my lips, not wanting to question her. I'm sure she knows better than I do.

"You could take advantage of some of that, too, you know," she adds. "Now that you have Emmett."

"I don't have Emmett," I remind her. "That fucking picture. You know it was fake, right?"

She studies me intently. I realize she didn't know it was fake. Her insistence with Emmett the night it went out was genuine. She truly was just looking out for him, convinced that I had cheated on him.

"I didn't know." She flicks her ashes onto the ground. "But it doesn't surprise me."

"What do you think will happen with Malcolm?" I ask.

"Nothing," she blows out a long stream of smoke. "Absolutely nothing."

"Is there anything I can do?" I offer finally.

"There's nothing someone like you could do," she scoffs. "You can never really understand all of this. What it's like to grow up here, the way we have."

"I might understand more than you think," I insist. "I've caught myself saying and doing all sorts of things over the past couple of weeks that I never would have thought I was capable of."

As Vivian swings her bag over her shoulder, the sleeve of her sweater slips, revealing a number of nasty, bright red, stinging cuts up and down her arm. I try to look away, but by the time my eyes move upwards, she is staring straight at me. She knows I saw them. We're frozen like that for a moment, our eyes locked together. Not only is Vivian not heartless, she's wounded. This really has done a number on her, maybe even more so than me.

"Do you need to talk someone?" I offer lightly, not knowing what else to say. "Someone other than me, I mean."

"Just another side effect of Jameson," she says casually, her eyes dark and haunted. Her tone turns to a warning. "Get out of this place if you can, Ophelia. Even if you think you're on top of everything, it can all change in a heartbeat. And it will eat you alive. Just look at Lily."

"Vivian, I have to ask." I stop her, knowing it's probably pointless, but I can't stop myself. "Are you sure you don't know anything about Bernadette? I know Emmett said he talked to you about it...but...I'm desperate. I have to hear you say it myself."

"I promise you Bernadette can take care of herself," she says confidently. "Wherever she is. Emmett shouldn't worry about her. She wouldn't worry about him if it was the other way around."

I know she's probably right, but it doesn't make it any less brutal. And worse, it makes it sound like all of this is for nothing. Like Emmett should have just accepted that she was gone and not even bothered looking for her. None of this had to happen. Vivian obviously knows something, enough to not be scared for Bernadette, but I realize I've gotten all I'm going to get out of her.

I think back to when Vivian had me cornered in the classroom and I first realized their vendetta against me was all about unsettled business between my dad and their parents. She was desperately trying to go along with what she was ordered to do, believing that I really was the scum of the earth for threatening the position of her family. All of the Elites' families. On top of that, Emmett was dying to have me, right in front of her. And I played on our attraction to drive her mad. She deserved it for the way she was acting, but I can see now she was really no different from Emmett.

"Emmett really does love you," she says after a long silence passes between us. "Nothing happened between us, you know. The moment you came here, he started slipping away from me, and once he got you…he didn't want anything to do with me."

I can tell that Vivian is telling me the truth. It comes with an odd feeling of being told something I already knew. I knew all along Emmett didn't want Vivian in the way he wanted me. But I had to keep convincing myself that there was still something between them—telling myself that kept me from falling too far. It kept me from feeling too safe with Emmett. It protected me from opening myself up to being hurt by him again. I needed my jealousy as an excuse to stay guarded. It was my safety net. But now it falls away before acceptance.

"Thank you for telling me that," I answer, believing every word she says. She has no reason to lie anymore. This is her accepting defeat.

"I better go," she says, peeling herself from the wall. But then she turns sharply with her old, familiar glaring stare. "You tell anyone you saw me like this, and I'll kill you. If I have to leave WJ Prep, I'm at least going to do it with what's left of my reputation intact."

I smirk. "This all stays between us, I promise."

I let go of any corny thoughts about how if only Vivian had showed me this side sooner, maybe we could have been friends. She's only doing this now because she has nothing left. She's completely broken and knows she has to get the hell out of Jameson. That's the only reason she can show her true self to me now.

# CHAPTER TWENTY-TWO

BOOK 2

After school, I know I have to see Emmett. Now that I know exactly where Vivian stands, I have to try one last time. I drive to the motel, but his car is gone. The front desk says he's checked out. So, I try driving past the manor and am relieved to see his car parked outside.

"Mrs. Lopez," the butler beams as he answers the door. "Is Mr. Jameson expecting you?"

"Nope!" I reply boldly as I push past him and race up the stairs. I'm not going to risk him asking Emmett if he wants to see me and getting turned away. He continues to call up after me, but I know if I can just get to Emmett, he'll back off and let him decide. It won't be as easy for Emmett to turn me away once I am standing face to face with him.

I knock on his bedroom door, and he looks annoyed when he peeks out from behind it. But thankfully, he throws his head back in exasperation and leaves it open for me anyway. I rush in, not knowing if I should jump straight into defending myself again. I decide to stay focused on my other concerns for him instead.

"Have you heard from your mom?" I ask, helping myself to a seat on his bed.

"I don't want to see you," he replies weakly. "I told you, I can't even look at you after what you did."

"Then why did you come to Malcolm's yesterday?" I raise my eyebrows at him.

"I was coming to beat his ass for putting his hands on you," he booms in his deep voice.

"Emmett, nothing happened between Malcolm and me," I say again. "I promise. I could never do that to you."

He groans. "I saw the photo, Ophelia."

"You know what Malcolm and Lily did," I shoot back. "That should be enough to prove to you that Malcolm is a terrible person and a liar. He made sure that photo got sent to you and everyone."

"But there was something for a photo to be taken of..." he insists.

"No!" I cut him off, flying into a pace around the room. "I was hanging out with Malcolm, yes. And I realize now that I shouldn't have been. But I was so convinced Vivian was luring you back in and I was upset. He offered to keep me company, and then he made a pass at me. I fought him off and came here to tell you everything. But by the time I got here, that photo had already been sent. Someone doctored it!"

"How am I supposed to believe you?" he persists in an aching tone, as if he's asking himself just as much as me.

"Because I would never do anything to hurt you, Emmett!" I cry earnestly. "You have to know that! I love you! I never even got to tell you about him trying to get me to fool around with him because Vivian was here! I didn't even have a chance to explain."

"You swear it was faked?" he asks. "Nothing happened?"

"I kicked him in the balls to get him off of me," I explain. "I didn't even want to be around him in the first place. I only ever wanted to be with you...but every time Vivian tried to come between us, he was always there waiting. I should have known he was up to something, that he was no good!"

"You're right. I'm sorry." He melts in exasperation, collapsing into the chair in the corner of his room, sliding his hands across his face and through his hair.

"I can't imagine what it must have been like for you." I shake my head, tears in my eyes. "To see that photo and think it was real. I don't know what I would have done if it had been a picture of you and Vivian."

"You would have broken everything in your room." He smirks in embarrassment, gesturing around to the lingering assortment of cracked and broken objects littering his floor. "I was so upset I wouldn't even let the housekeepers in to clean this mess up."

I start to argue with him, but then I realize he's probably right. I didn't used to think I had a temper, but lately I seem to be proving myself wrong on that one.

"I guess love makes everyone a little crazy," I suggest, running my palm across the back of my neck.

He steps towards me with an intense look in his eyes, whipping my body over to his. "You definitely drive me crazy, Ophelia," he coos in his deep, sexy voice.

My heart lights up at his sound and the feeling of being in his arms again. It's a wave of relief when his lips lower to mine, kissing me soft and slow before quickly picking up into a needy pace, the way all of our kisses are. Desperate and insatiable. This is all I have been wanting the past couple of days, and everything I thought I would never have again. I'd convinced myself it was over, but my heart refused to let go. And now that we are together again, I know why. I know why I can never seem to get away from Emmett. This is meant to be, and that is the intense pull we feel towards each other.

"I think we're soulmates, Emmett," I suggest softly. "Do you believe in that sort of thing?"

"I never thought about it before," he replies honestly. "But...I think you're right. I don't feel whole unless I'm with you."

The intense need scares me, but I know there's no use fighting it. It's never worked before. It seems as though no matter what we do, we're going to end up like this. Back in each other's arms, as we should be.

"Something weird happened today," I tell him finally. "The fire alarm went off at school. It ended up being some kind of prank, but I could have sworn I saw Bernadette walking away from the crowd."

"What?" he exclaims. "Are you sure?"

"No, I'm not sure..." I hesitate. "But it definitely did look like her. And just like that she was gone! I tried to catch up to her...but nothing."

His face wrinkles in confusion as he stares off.

"It's not your fault," Emmett continues. "I know what kind of guy Malcolm is. I should have realized it was all a set-up. That's why we're not friends anymore. He's a terrible person." I see acceptance washing over him. One side was telling him not to buy into that photo the whole time, just as one side kept telling me not to worry about Vivian, but he couldn't bring himself to let go of his insecurities.

"We used to be best friends, but he was sick. A sociopath," he continues. "Even when I was forced into going along with the Elites, I couldn't get over how fucked up and sadistic Malcolm was. He reminded me too much of my father."

"That's funny." I wrinkle my nose as I remember the first night I met with Malcolm. "He said the same thing about you."

"What are you talking about?" he asks.

"When I first met Malcolm," I go on. "It was right before you, Trey, and Vincent kidnapped me. I met with him and his dad, and on the way, he told me how you two used to be friends, but that you turned into a horrible person when you started hanging out with the Elites."

"What meeting with Malcolm and his dad?" Emmett's eyes dart back and forth cluelessly.

"My father sent them. They were the ones who told me who he was and what went down with him in Jameson," I explain. "They told me all about his gambling debts and how he embezzled money from Jameson Automobiles to pay them. How he got stripped of all his shares and cast out of town. They wanted me to help them collect evidence against you and the rest of the Elites, to prove their software company was being used in the sex trafficking rings, but that they were completely innocent and had nothing to do with it."

He shoots up in alarm. "When did this happen?"

"I told you…right before I came home and found you and the twins in my room," I stammer, not understanding why he seems so worried.

"How could you not tell me that!" he snaps.

"I didn't think it was important!"

"Ophelia, the Hendersons aren't innocent," Emmett states coldly. "The entire sex trafficking thing was their idea! Malcolm himself tailored the software to run it!"

"Well, then, why aren't they going down with everyone else?" I ask.

"They just wanted to pin everything on the rest of the Elites to get their hands on Jameson Automobiles!" he asserts. "They've always wanted control over the company. I wasn't just jealous of Malcolm. I didn't want you around him because he's dangerous! I knew he was just trying to use you to get to me. I wanted to protect you from him."

Now all of my comparisons between Vivian and Malcolm feel ridiculous. That's why Emmett was so adamant about me staying away from Malcolm, while being unable to understand my jealousy of Vivian. He wasn't being jealous and possessive. He was afraid for me.

"You know for certain they're behind everything with the sex trafficking rings?" I ask, needing to know he's positive.

"Yes!" he fires back without hesitation. "That's part of why we stopped hanging out. He was already making plans for the whole thing! Vivian kept trying to tell me it was all just a plan to take the rest of our families down in the long run, but we couldn't convince any of them. They all fell right into his trap. They've been setting things up to work out this way from the beginning."

"So…does that mean…my father?" I try to connect the dots. "Was he involved, too?"

"Think about it. Why would your father send Malcolm and Liam to talk to you like that when I had already agreed to take you in?" he proposes. "I don't think they ever had anything to do with your father at all. They were just trying to make you trusted them enough to get them the evidence. To help make sure nothing went wrong with their plan."

"It doesn't make sense." I shake my head. "Sure, maybe Malcolm was just trying to use me to throw you off this whole time so he could find some way to get control of the company. But what about Coach Granger? Why did he drag Lily into that?"

"Without Coach Granger around to offer you other solutions, you'd feel like you had no other way out than to help them find evidence," he concludes.

I nod in agreement. "But they didn't know I had you."

"And they didn't know your father was working with me."

"I'm so sorry, Emmett," I cry, feeling stupid. "I'm sorry I never mentioned the meeting with them. So much happened so fast! I should have listened to you when you told me to stay away from Malcolm. I thought you were just jealous."

"It's okay," he sighs, taking me into his arms. "I wish I had told you what kind of person he really was."

My cheek drifts across the warmth of Emmett's warm skin as he holds me, and the world feels right again. I'm so relieved he finally believes me and that I understand more about everything that has been happening. Emmett wasn't giving into Vivian because he still had feelings for her. He knew there was a side to her that I couldn't see—the side I saw under the stairs at school. And his rage towards Malcolm was all about keeping me safe.

Suddenly, he pulls back and whips out his cell phone.

"What are you doing?" I ask.

"I'm calling the police," he states sternly.

"What?" I cry. "Why now? I thought we couldn't trust them!"

"Don't you see? The Hendersons are behind Bernadette's disappearance. They have to be!" he explains assertively, but I'm not following him.

"How can you be so sure?"

"You don't have to believe me, but I know Vivian doesn't have anything to do with this," he continues. "And her parents are too wrapped up in the investigation to pull something like this off."

"No, I know that now." I nod my head in earnest agreement. "I do believe you."

"Trey and Vincent were sent off to stay with family on the other side of the country," he expounds. "No one has heard from them. Their parents are in the same boat Vivian's are. We know Lily was wrapped up in her own problems…nothing that had to do with coming after the company."

"And if we're certain my father didn't do it…then that leaves the Hendersons." I exhale sharply, wishing we could have seen it before.

"They must be trying to use Bernadette and my mom as some kind of leverage to get control over Jameson Automobiles," he rants with a certain clarity. "That's what they've wanted all along."

"Why wait so long?" I question, still not feeling as convinced as he is. "Why not just come straight after you?"

"I don't know." He shakes his head, his eyes darting around the room in thought. "I don't know what they're up to, but I'm convinced they'll know exactly where Bernadette and my mom are."

The Hendersons could have taken Bernadette, hoping to arrange some sort of hostage deal to get what Emmett inherited from his father, but it still doesn't make sense. Why would

Malcolm spend so much time goading me? Why wait at all? Why not just let Emmett know right away to try and get what they were after?

Emmett seems convinced, and he knows more about the dynamics of this fucked up town than I do, so I don't question him.

"But wait…how do you know the cops aren't just as much in the Henderson's pockets as they were your father's?" I propose. "You said we shouldn't trust them."

"I'm done playing games," he barks. "This has gone on long enough. You were right. We should have called them right away. I just needed to be certain of who was responsible for this."

"Just think about this first," I plead with him, worried he's acting too rashly. "You swore calling the cops wasn't an option."

"I'm not going to get wrapped up in the same endless stream of dirty games as my father," he insists. "I said I was going to do things differently, and now it's time to do that. I have to set an example for the Hendersons and anyone else who even thinks about trying something like this after them. Jameson is going to play by the rules now. These twisted games aren't going to work anymore."

"Wait!" I throw my hand around his to stop him from dialing. "I have an idea. What about Coach Granger? He knows just as well as you do that the cops around here are corrupt. But he said he has a detective friend or something that he can trust. They helped him find out Lily and Malcolm were behind his son's death."

"Do you think he'd help us?" Emmett asks me, his face bright and open.

I shrug. "We stand just as good of a chance with him as we would with the rest of the police."

"Okay. Call him," he commands urgently.

I pull out my phone and step to the other side of the room. I tell Coach Granger I don't have time to explain, but that I need someone within the authorities that we can actually trust. Without hesitation, he gives me the name and number of his friend, Detective Williams.

"Are you sure you want to do this?" I ask one more time before Emmett calls.

He nods assertively. "I'm sure." He puts the phone on speaker as it rings.

"Yeah?" A curt and raspy voice picks up.

"Detective Williams?" Emmett asks.

"Who's this?" the man shoots back, sounding like his mouth is full of food.

"Emmett Jameson," he replies. "Coach Granger told me I could trust you."

The line falls silent for a moment. Then, "Wow…Mr. Jameson himself," he marvels. "Listen, son, I don't know what you need…But I don't play into all the bullshit the rest of the force around here does. I can't be bought off for whatever trouble it is you've gotten yourself into."

"Then you're just the guy I need," Emmett pleads. "I need to report a disappearance. Possibly two. Mrs. Jameson and her daughter, Bernadette Jameson. And I know where they are."

Silence again, muffled by a big gulp and the ruffle of what sounds like a paper napkin against the guy's face. "Where?" he asks finally.

"With Liam and Malcolm Henderson."

We hear a pen plopping to a pad of paper, as if he's not even going to bother writing it down.

"The Hendersons?" he gaffs. "It's going to be pretty hard to go after them for anything. They're quickly becoming even more powerful than your father was."

"That may be, but this town still depends on Jameson Automobiles," Emmett insists. "And if they get their hands on my company, they won't look out for the people here the way I will. So, everyone's jobs and this entire economy rests on your ability to save Bernadette and my mother and stop whatever they're planning. Can you help us?"

Detective Williams tells us he will see what he can do. We sit side by side on the edge of Emmett's bed and anxiously wait for him to call back. I squeeze his hand tightly in mine as we watch the sun slowly set outside his bedroom window. We're both mulling over every possible scenario, the best and the worst. He could call back and say he has Bernadette and is bringing her home alive and well. He could call back and say everything has gone wrong.

Finally, the phone rings, making us both jump. Emmett flies from the bed, flipping the phone back onto speaker. "Detective Williams?"

"Emmett," he answers with a big sigh that makes our hearts sink. "Look, son, I gotta ask you: are you feeling okay?"

It's not a question either of us were expecting.

"Did you find my mom and Bernadette?" he asks frantically, shaking away the odd question. "Are they okay? Did you rescue them?"

"I'm afraid we couldn't rescue them..." he says grimly. "Because they weren't kidnapped."

"What are you talking about?" Emmett freezes. My mouth drops. His tone had us both preparing for the worst, but this... this is something different.

"They were with the Hendersons, alright," he clarifies. "But they said they were there of their own free will. To get away from you."

"What!" Emmett snaps.

"They said you've gone off the deep end since your father died. The Hendersons offered to take them in to get them away from you," Williams explains frankly.

"No...no..." Emmett massages the bridge of his nose in confusion. "You saw them!? You talked to them yourself, in person?"

"Of course," he confirms, sounding too chipper. "They looked perfectly fine. Said they were there of their own free will. They're really worried about you, though. Malcolm says you've been having some...girlfriend troubles? He mentioned that hasn't been helping things too much."

Emmett looks at me with wide eyes, and I look just as shocked. I've been to Malcolm's house twice now, and it never occurred to me that Bernadette and their mom could both be there—much less of their own free will. To make everything worse, they're inexplicably trying to pin all of this on Emmett, to make it look like they were escaping some kind of psychotic break down of his.

"I'm fine, Detective Williams," Emmett murmurs despondently. "Thank you for all of your help."

"You at home, son?" Williams asks suddenly. "Can I send someone over to check on you?"

Emmett ends the call without answering and looks at me with distant, lost eyes. With a breath of disbelief, he drops to the chair behind him. The phone thumps to the floor from his listless hand.

"I can't believe they'd do that," I say softly, not knowing what else to say. "Do you think he's telling the truth?"

"There's only one way to find out," he answers dryly. "We have to go to the Hendersons'."

"What? Emmett...no!" I protest, flying to my feet. "Out of the question. It's dangerous!"

"They're doing this for a reason," he explains. "And if they wanted to kill me, they would have done it by now. They're trying to fuck with me."

"But why would your own family do such a thing?" I cry, not wanting to believe it. "You've been worried sick about Bernadette this whole time. And your mom...she knew all along and didn't try to tell you things were okay? She played into your worrying! She made it seem like she was afraid, too!"

"Welcome to the Jameson family." He smirks sarcastically, swallowing hard as his eyes gloss over. "Let's go see what they want. They're waiting for us now. And anyway, we can't stay here. Detective Williams or some other cop will be showing up soon to check on me. They think I'm crazy."

Emmett stands and walks indolently out the door with me following behind slowly. I don't bother questioning him now. Everything he's said up until now has proven to be true. Malcolm is evil. Vivian isn't as heartless as she seems. And just as they both told me, I can never understand the weird world they've grown up in with their families. Something I believe now more than ever.

# CHAPTER TWENTY-THREE

## BOOK 2

The butler at the Henderson's manor doesn't say a word as he opens the door and directs us to Liam's study, proving what Emmett said to be true. They were expecting us after the visit from Detective Williams. This is all a scheme, but we're left guessing as to what its purpose is.

He leads us to a room that looks more like a billionaire's office in a high rise in a big city than someone's home office. The floors are black marble with crisp, clean white walls. The furniture is plain and sharply designed, with brightly-colored modern art sculptures lining the shelves, much like the rest of the house.

Liam is sitting at his desk, which houses a computer set-up that is almost as expensive as Malcolm's, with Mrs. Jameson standing behind him. Bernadette is sitting in a corner chair, filing her nails with Malcolm sitting across from her. They barely respond as we enter.

Liam is tall, with slender features and a big gut that juts out of his expensive suit. He is always wiping his balding head with a handkerchief, much like Thomas Jameson used to do. It's a strange idiosyncrasy that all of the old rich men around here seem to share. I guess with that amount of money on the line, there's a lot to sweat about.

"So, it is true," Emmett says blankly. "You're both here."

"I have to admit, Emmett," Bernadette sneers, "it took longer than I expected for you to catch up to us."

"Mom, what the hell is going on?" he snaps. "Why are you here? Why did you tell the police all of those things about me?"

"I'm afraid I have to tell you something…" Liam answers, as Mrs. Jameson smiles coyly over his shoulder. "…that's really not easy for any young man to hear. Especially not so soon after the death of his father."

"Somebody better start telling me what's going on real fucking fast," he seethes impatiently.

"Liam and I are in love, Emmett," Mrs. Jameson announces casually. Emmett's mother is frighteningly perfect to the point that she looks plastic. She has long, blonde sleek hair that curls around her face and back, leading down to a blue pencil skirt suit that accentuates her curves—courtesy of her personal trainer and decades of plastic surgery. Her face also looks like she's had some work done, looking impossibly young but still wrinkled and puffy from injections. She stands perched on top of stiletto heels and moves gracefully like a spider. "We're getting married."

"Bullshit." He laughs.

"Are you fucking blind?" Bernadette mocks. "They've been having an affair for years. Everybody knew."

"And you're okay with this?" he shoots back at her.

"Bernadette and Thomas always had a special bond," his mother reminds him. "Nothing like how you and I knew him, Emmett."

"I think most of us can agree it was a relief when Thomas Jameson 'committed suicide,'" Liam adds.

"This doesn't make any sense." Emmett shakes his head, refusing to accept it. "Bernadette…have you been here the whole fucking time?"

"Daddy said we have to protect the company above all else," she replies snidely. "It's our family's legacy. He always knew you were too weak to do it. Someone has to step up and make the hard decisions."

"We can't just sit back and watch you take control over Jameson Automobiles, son," his mother proclaims decidedly. "I'm sorry."

"You're too soft for this level of money and power, Emmett," Liam adds in agreement. "We can't let you have any part of your father's business."

"The fact that you turned to the police about us being gone proves that," Bernadette jeers.

"So…what? This was some kind of fucking test?" he fumes. "You see how long I would go without calling the police just so you can tell me I'm incapable?"

"No, not a test. But an insurance policy," his mother explains. "The police think you've gone mad now. It only helps our case against you as being unfit for running the company."

"Everyone knows you're unstable," Malcolm jumps in, adding to the circling ganging up against Emmett.

"Being unstable sure didn't stop Dad from running the company his whole life," he bites back bitterly.

"It's time for the whole town of Jameson to move into a new era," Liam continues, as he stands to glide proudly around his office. "Malcolm and I, alongside your mother and sister, are the only ones capable of restoring the Elites back to their rightful place. We're the only ones who can take Jameson Automobiles to the next level of success."

It sure does look like a new era. Their extreme modern décor is nothing like the old, musky halls of Jameson manor, which look more like something from the 1800s than the current century. My memory of comparing old money to new money with Malcolm carry a new sting now. The differences were more than I ever could have imagined.

"Oh, yeah, I'd like to see just how many lives you'd ruin with that kind of power," Emmett rants. "How much damage you'd do around here. I'm not listening to another second of this nonsense. Jameson Automobiles and everything in my father's name legally belongs to me now, and there's nothing you can do to change that."

"I was afraid you'd feel that way," Mrs. Jameson sighs.

Malcolm suddenly appears behind me and yanks me from Emmett's grip, just as another man enters from the side and restrains him. Before we can even take in what's happened, I feel something terrible and all too familiar against the side of my head.

"Emmett! Help!" I scream out, feeling the cold barrel of a gun against my temple.

For a moment, I see red. I'm angry that I'm standing here screaming and begging for my life with a gun to my head. This is the second time this has happened to me, and both times have been directly related to Emmett! I swore I would never let myself get into a position like this again. I want to hate him for bringing these kinds of things into my life, but this time I can see clearly how it's not his fault. It's his family that endangers people in this way. It's why he resisted me for so long and why he struggles now. This is everything he has wanted to keep me safe from.

"Get your hands off of her!" he orders, trying to wrestle free from the guy holding onto him.

"We'd be happy to," Liam agrees as a woman who looks like a secretary enters from the side, carrying a pen and a stack of papers. "As long as you sign everything over to us."

"I can't. I can't do that," Emmett insists in a weeping voice.

"Then your girlfriend dies," Malcolm hisses, cocking his gun.

"Mom, please don't make me do this," Emmett begs. "You know the Hendersons will only use Jameson to wreak havoc. I thought you wanted me to run things differently than Dad."

"You're such a fucking idealist," Bernadette retorts, standing to take her mother's side behind Liam. "That's not how things work. Every word you say just proves Liam right. You're too soft for this!"

All at once, I receive the confirmation I needed, just as Emmett receives one of the worst blows of his life. This whole time I have wondered who the real Emmett is. Is he good, is he bad? Is he an Elite or is he just some kid born into their world, fighting with all of his might to break free? I have even wondered if it was a little bit of everything. Emmett has seemed like a swirling tornado of all of it, and I never know which part of it will touch down or when. Or what kind of damage will be left when he's done.

But his family is telling me everything I wanted to know. Emmett is nothing like them. They know it, and that's why they're casting him out. He isn't evil enough to be one of them. He won't value money and power over human lives. Everything I have seen in him before now is what was demanded of him. He was always telling me the truth.

I feel terrible for making him work so hard to prove it to me. The pressure I put on him probably only made things worse, but I didn't know what else to do. I know as we walk out of this room, that we will be leaving the worst parts of him behind. And I don't have to be afraid of him anymore.

"What would you have done if I hadn't ended up here tonight?" Emmett's eyes tear up as he looks at the stack of papers waiting for him.

"Originally, I thought I might have kept the company for myself," his mother explains in a weary tone. "But Bernadette came to Liam and the two of them were able to talk some sense into me."

"Your mother is a beautiful woman and an excellent partner," Liam says with a creepy sweetness. "But she doesn't have the head for running this kind of operation on her own."

"I could have run things with you," Emmett argues.

"Really, son." She smirks pityingly. "That's laughable. This is how things should be. Now hurry and sign the papers. Liam can be a very impatient man."

Malcolm straightens his gun and lurches, making me think he might pull the trigger at any second, causing me to scream. Emmett looks to me in desperation, knowing his time is running out.

He gapes. "It's like you've brainwashed them. What is wrong with you!" he screams at his mother. "You could have had a chance at a better life! One where you weren't always cowering down before Dad! If you wanted to help run the company, we could have done it together. Things could have been better!"

"Your father was the way he was for a reason," she says with a cool voice as she pulls a cigarette from Liam's desk drawer and lights up. "He ran everything the way he did for a reason. It's just how things have to be, Emmett." Her tone turns condescending. "Don't take it so personally. Sign over everything, and we'll let you and your little girlfriend go."

"Now you can be penniless and directionless, just like your little white trash whore," Bernadette snickers heartlessly.

With a heavy sigh, Emmett nods, prompting the guy who had been restraining him to shove him towards the stack of papers and force the pen in his hand. In a painfully slow process, Liam flips through each page, pointing out where Emmett needs to sign and initial. It's ridiculous. Like he's selling him a car or a house. You'd never know by looking at Liam that I was being held at gunpoint in the corner of the room and that Emmett was signing away absolutely everything his father had left him.

Malcolm shoves me into Emmett's arms with violent force once everything is signed. He leads me towards the door, stopping only once to turn back and look at what's left of his family.

They barely even look up to acknowledge him, much less say goodbye. It's like he's invisible now.

"Are you okay?" he asks me softly. I nod and look back at all of them, standing there and flipping through the newly-signed papers.

"So now what?" Emmett asks from the doorway.

"So now nothing," his mother responds, waving her hand dismissively. "I've left a little bit of money in your bank. Not enough to survive on, but it will get you by until you figure something else out."

"Maybe Ophelia will loan you some money," Bernadette cackles.

"What…you're disowning me?" Emmett asks earnestly. "You already have everything you wanted. Why cast me out like this?"

The snide grin fades from his mother's face, turning into a cold, dead, and serious stare. She flicks her cigarette into an ashtray and prances evenly over to him, stopping near his ear. "Oh, son. You think I don't know?" she hums quietly. "You think I don't know about what you did to your father?"

"What are you talking about…" he stammers.

"Your little deal with Theo Nickelson," she hisses. "You might as well have been holding the gun yourself. You killed your father."

I can't take it anymore. I can't stand here while she tries to make Emmett feel bad after everything she's done. "Well, if you've been up Liam's ass this whole time anyway, just waiting for your chance to run the company," I chime in, "why do you care what Emmett did? You said you were glad Thomas was gone."

She shrugs cavalierly. "It doesn't change the way things work around here. You can't just take out the crown of the hierarchy around here and expect not to suffer the consequences."

"You people are all seriously fucked up," I blurt out.

"I knew what you did, Emmett," Bernadette grunts resentfully. "I came and told Liam. He was the one who let Mom know."

"I thought you were smarter than that, Emmett," Liam scolds. "You know what happens to people who mess with the Elites. You know a thing or two about that yourself, don't you, Ophelia? So now you'll walk away with nothing."

"And if I were you…I'd get out of town," Malcolm adds.

"Now the Elites will rise back to where we belong. And once the entire town is under our control again, the police, the school, everyone you pass on the street will know you're blacklisted."

"I thought you hated the Elites," I remind him, feeling stupid for ever buying into his act that he was so different.

"Only because I wasn't one of them." He shrugs.

Liam nods in agreement. "We refused to be under Thomas Jameson's rule."

"My father and I have always known we could run things better than him," Malcolm explains. "We planned to take your father down the same way everyone else was going down. But then Theo stepped in and started messing around. But thank him for us, by the way. Killing Thomas turned out to be a much more convenient outcome than just sending him to jail."

"Why help me look into Bernadette's phone data, then?" I ask in confusion. "If you knew she was here the whole time!"

"You two are a fucking mess." He smirks. "It was too much fun playing with you. You made it so easy. You were so convinced Vivian was behind everything and that she was trying to steal Emmett from you. Pointing you in her direction was too entertaining to pass up."

"The picture!" I gape, turning to Bernadette. "You took the picture!"

"Malcolm helped me doctor it," she beams proudly, blowing at the file against her nails. "Like I said, we really did think you would figure things out sooner, Emmett. We were getting bored waiting for you to piece it all together. We decided to have a little fun with you in the process."

"It just made you look that much more desperate to the cops," Malcolm adds.

He pulls out his phone and begins playing a video of Emmett having his meltdown in the motel room. At the same time, Bernadette pulls out her phone and begins playing a video taken from outside the Jameson manor. It was right after the fake photo of Malcolm and I had been sent out over the Elites' blacklist app. You can see his silhouette through the window flailing around his room like a madman, breaking everything in reach.

"Sooner or later, we figured we'd gather enough evidence of you cracking," Bernadette explains. "So, if you did refuse to sign everything over, we could just tell our lawyers you were too mentally unstable to run Jameson Automobiles."

"And rest assured, we will use that defense if you ever decide to come back after us for the company somehow," his mother adds indifferently. "And since your father committed suicide… you know it runs in the family." She suppresses a laugh. "It wouldn't be that hard for people to believe you would take your own life, too."

The weight of it crashes over both of us. Bernadette and Malcolm were just playing with us, taking every opportunity they could to make Emmett look like he had gone crazy. If we never barged in here, giving them the chance to use me as leverage, they would have gotten the company anyway. And now there's nothing Emmett can do, or they will kill him and make it look like he did it to himself.

"Ironic, isn't it, brother?" Bernadette sneers. "You helped Theo kill our father and passed it off as a suicide. And now that's the exact same thing that will happen to you if you try to get what you were promised out of that deal."

"So, this is all punishment for Dad." He shakes his head in disgust.

"You punished him for your own weaknesses," she scoffs. "He shouldn't have had to die just because you weren't man enough to handle him, to face up to who you had to be to fill his shoes."

"Mom even admitted it…you didn't know him the way we did," Emmett defends. "If he had treated you the same way you…"

"I would have done exactly this," she snaps. "Whatever it took to uphold our family's legacy. I'm nothing like you. Never have been. I can do what needs to be done to protect our position and everything our family has worked so hard for."

"You mean you can treat people like shit to get what you want," I thunder over to her, which she meets with a dismissive smile and shrug.

We stand there in stunned silence at how cold and calculating they all are. Like it's just a game of musical chairs with lots of money and power being thrown around, everyone waiting for their turn to sit in the biggest chair. Only lives are carelessly taken along the way, and no one seems to bat an eyelash. No wonder Emmett wasn't more affected by his father's death. Not only did he hate the man, but this is apparently an ordinary part of business in his family.

"Let's go, Emmett." I tug at his arm. "There's nothing we can do."

"Mom?" He hesitates one more time as we're halfway out the door. He sounds like a scared little boy. My heart breaks for him as she flips through the newly-signed rights to her company and who knows what kind of money. She doesn't even look up.

I pull Emmett along, wanting to take him as far away from them as we can get.

As soon as we're outside, I look up and release a huge breath. My eyes shine over at Emmett, and of course, he looks at me like I'm crazy. He doesn't think there's anything to be happy about right now. He's hurt and shocked and has every right to be. But I can see how this is for the best. The Hendersons would have always been waiting to strike, to take everything away from him. His mom and sister, too. Now it's over and he can walk away.

His biggest problem is that he'll have to worry about money now, like the rest of us. But with his charm and good looks, I don't think he'll have too much trouble figuring it out. If he was capable of running Jameson Automobiles, he can do so many other things just as well. I'm excited to watch him figure it all out.

"They can't do this." His voice cracks as I rush him back to the car.

"Here, let me drive." I yank the keys from his hands. "I'll take you wherever you want to go."

Emmett doesn't answer, so I just drive. I know it doesn't really matter where we go. He's too upset right now to care. But I drive to the motel he had been staying only because it is far enough outside of town. It may not be far, but we both need to be out of Jameson right now.

The one thing we can be relieved about is that Bernadette wasn't working with my dad, but I don't know that the Hendersons are any better. Definitely not for Emmett. Just a little less traumatic for me.

I remember what I learned about the Elites. The town was built around them and everything in it is theirs, and has been for centuries. When one person is struck down, it seems the remaining family members merge with another so that they can rise to take back their rightful place. Nothing is going to change that.

I remember Malcolm telling me he and his father were

merely tolerated by the Elites. Being tolerated is better than being blacklisted, but I guess it was still enough to build up this much resentment. He once told me their money couldn't touch the money of the Elites. I don't know if that was a lie, or if it's changed now that everyone is being investigated and their assets are being seized. One thing is for certain, the Hendersons aren't going down with everyone else, no matter how guilty they are.

When Emmett took over Jameson Automobiles, I worried Liam and Malcolm might do something drastic in a panic. The change in leadership and the fact that Malcolm and Emmett did not like each other put the ties between Jameson Automobiles and their software company at risk—a profitable alliance their company surely could not afford to lose. But I also thought Malcolm was supposed to be better than the rest of the Elites. I was so very wrong, and I never saw this coming.

# CHAPTER TWENTY-FOUR

BOOK 2

"I can't believe they would do this to me," Emmett laments from his new room at the motel. "Just cast me out like this."

"I'm so sorry, Emmett," I try to console him. "I feel like it's all my dad's fault. If he hadn't roped you into that deal with him, your dad would have gone to jail with everyone else and your family wouldn't have turned against you."

"It doesn't matter." He shakes his head with a bitter smirk. "I could have never stood by and let Liam and Malcolm take things over. It would have happened this way regardless."

"I don't know what to say," I whisper. "I can't believe this is happening."

"I went from having everything and the chance to run things right…to having nothing at all," he moans.

"You're not left with nothing." I perk up, running over to wrap him in my arms "You have me."

"Ophelia." He takes my face in his hands. "I can't believe you've stayed by my side through all of this. I've tried so hard to change. And I do wish it was easier for you. I would give anything to make that happen. I'd burn this whole town down if I thought that would fix things for you. I can't take anything back. I can't go back and make myself be better in the past, because the truth is, Ophelia…I never had a reason to be better until I met you. It wasn't just about my father or Vivian or any of them. It was about you. I found you and that's when I realized I could be better. I had to be better…to have you. And I know I'm not perfect. I know I'm not there yet. But I will spend the rest of my life trying to become the man you deserve. I'll do whatever it takes!"

"I can't believe you gave everything up to save my life." I sigh.

"I guess they were right. I can't make the hard choices my father always went on about," he muses. "I could never lose you just to keep Jameson. I hope you don't think for one second that I would have. I wasn't hesitating to think it over, I was just trying to make sense of it all."

"I know," I assure him. "It's going to be okay, Emmett. We're going to figure everything out."

"You promised me you didn't want easy," he reminds me. "Do you still mean that? Because things just got a lot harder."

"I don't know." I smile lightly. "Did they? You're free now. You don't have to play their games anymore, or walk around with the weight of your father's legacy on your shoulders. You can live your life however you want to now."

He grins. "I can finally take you to that concert, that band I was telling you about. There's nothing to worry about anymore but normal stuff like school and college. And us."

"The concert…sure." I laugh. "But also Ritzville. The Ferris wheel at Ritzville."

"What?" He smirks and wrinkles his brow.

"It's a thing for me." I shrug. "Just promise me we'll go."

"I'll take you anywhere you want to go," he says before pulling my lips to his.

"I don't know about where I want to go…but I know I need to go home." I look at the time on my phone. "My parents are going to be worried sick…again."

He nods and looks at me intently. "I think it's time to tell them everything, Ophelia."

I have always known that anyone outside of Jameson would never be able to understand the full extent of the Elites and this fucked up little society, and that is what has always kept me quiet. That's why I've never talked to my mom or Brendan about it. But my biggest hesitation was over Emmett. I didn't want anyone to know that I still fell for him after everything he did to me. Maybe now that he has redeemed himself, I can find a way to tell them a very edited version of the story. It sure would make things easier the next time things go crazy, as they always inevitably do. I can't help but feel like my parents will be the types to say fuck it, and move us right out of this town.

"I don't know if they can handle all of that, Emmett," I reply with dread, trying to imagine their reactions. "But you're right. I might have to. It might be the only way to convince them you have to come sleep on our couch for a while."

He pulls me into his arms. "I love you, Ophelia Lopez," he says softly against my lips.

"I love you, Emmett Jameson." I smile. "You know I'm not going anywhere, right?" I tease him. "You wanted me and now you're stuck with me."

"I wouldn't put it that way." He grins and reaches over to twirl his finger in my hair.

Emmett's wrongness is almost what makes me want him more. The fact that I can't tell anyone about everything that has happened between us makes me feel like we live in our own little secret world that only we can understand. I embrace his darkness in a way that I think only I can. I hate it and am afraid of it, but he's still here, so obviously some part of me has accepted it.

"I can't pull myself away from you no matter how hard I try," I tell him.

"So, you've tried to get away from me?" he asks, sounding both hurt and intrigued.

"I've wanted to try," I confess hopelessly.

As I look into his eyes, I know everything is so much more complicated than I'm willing to say out loud right now. Emmett had talked about flying out to see me if I went to college somewhere else, but now he won't have that kind of money at his disposal. He'll have to figure out work, and I doubt his mom has any plans to provide for his college education—the real kind that he actually has to work for. The kind that can't be bought. Those days are over for him, and while I can't quite bring myself to feel sorry for him about those things… I know how scary it must be for him.

I shake it all away for now. If we can overcome Emmett's fucked up childhood, kidnappings, murders, hostage deals, and the surrender of a giant company coupled with millions of dollars… I'd like to think we can figure out things like college and a long-distance relationship.

# EPILOGUE

## BOOK 2

I walk through the halls of WJ Prep feeling better than ever. Nothing around here has ever felt this consistently normal, and for the first time I almost feel like my old self again, the way I did before I came to Jameson. Only better. Because now I have Emmett.

I've spent the past month catching up on my college applications. The essay questions were ridiculous, wanting to know all about what has shaped me in life, what struggles I've faced. Obstacles I've overcome. I didn't know what to say. The hell WJ Prep has put me through is indescribable, and not something I can talk about in an essay. But it has made me who I am. Enough that I know I deserve a track scholarship, because I have proven to myself that I can push through any kind of pain. The fact that I'm still here and with Emmett proves that I don't give up, and that I can work my ass off and persevere. Instead, I wrote about my mom and Brendan, and how they taught me what it means to work hard, and about how I wouldn't be where I am without their love and support, which is true. But it's only half the story.

It's the last day of school before winter break, and there's a tingling of excitement in the air. All of the students are high on an adrenaline rush of expectation, with two weeks of sleeping in and partying to look forward to. The teachers are being especially lax, and classes are flying by like a breeze.

"Hey, gorgeous." Emmett's voice rings out to me from

behind my locker. I slam it shut and fly into his arms for a long kiss, relishing in the softness of his lips against mine.

"Hey, handsome," I hum with smile. "Are you excited?"

"For the concert tonight." He nods and grins. "You have no idea."

"I don't think it can beat the Ferris wheel." I shrug. "But we'll see."

He laughs. "Oh, it'll beat the Ferris wheel. Just you wait. You're gonna love these guys."

We continue down the hall, arm in arm, as envying students watch us pass. The Elites aren't back in full force yet, but we know they're coming. Liam and Malcolm will make sure of that. And since they're coming back at everyone who shut them out before, they'll do so with a vengeance. One we're not looking forward to.

But for now, we're trying to enjoy the quiet, doing all of the normal teenage things we've been denied these past few months —things I think Emmett has been denied his entire life. He hasn't lost his temper once since the night we left his family at the Hendersons. I know his heart is broken, but overall, I think it's a relief to be free from the pressure of his father's legacy.

All this time I have wanted things to go back to how they were before I came to WJ Prep, but suddenly I realize I am happier with the way everything turned out. I always thought I was tough, but nothing could have made me stronger than what I have experienced these past few months.

And while some couples may have had a road a lot less bumpy than Emmett and me, I can't imagine any obstacle we can't withstand together at this point. We are stronger than I ever thought we could be.

Malcolm, of course, got off on any charges relating to Coach Granger's son, just like I knew he would. His father's expensive lawyers stepped in and argued that everything was Lily's idea and that they couldn't be blamed for what his son chose to do with the drugs they left for him. Even with Coach Granger's police contacts, the case was open and shut.

Coach Granger and I had a chance to sit down and talk about everything that happened. He wasn't happy that the charges against Malcolm went nowhere, but mostly he was just glad that he tried. It brought him some sense of peace, knowing what happened with his son. I told him I felt relentlessly guilty, thinking none of that would have happened if it hadn't been for me, but he made me promise to let go of my guilt, swearing that his son's addiction was one of his family's biggest weaknesses. The Elites prey on people's weaknesses, and if it hadn't been for my situation, they would have struck out in the same way the moment it became convenient for some reason or another.

Lily, however, was not so lucky. Thanks to Malcolm's lawyers, the same logic was applied to her case and she escaped criminal charges. But the psychological evaluations she underwent didn't make her parents very confident of her mental health and ability to return to normal life. They put her up in a prestigious facility where she has to stay for "rest."

Vivian transferred to an expensive private school in New York with her aunt. Judging by her social media, the change has been good for her. She's thriving in the big city as some kind of trendy fashionista, and doesn't seem nearly as angry and miserable as she once did in Jameson.

With things back to a sense of normalcy, I've been able to refocus on my running career. I've applied for all of the top schools, and Coach has been welcoming scouts to our track meets from every one of them. He's confident I'll have several scholarship options to choose from, most from some of the best athletic coaches in the field.

Emmett and I race through the cold to the warmth of his car after school. A fresh snow has just fallen, and the campus has been transformed. The blinding, pure white glow all around brings me hope that maybe when we return in January, the Elites won't come at us with the force we're expecting. But mostly, I try not to think about any of it at all.

The weather in Massachusetts is beautiful, especially in Jameson. It's a small enough town with a historic square in the middle that gets decorated with lights, greenery, and bright red bows every November, and stands through the holidays. It all looks so beautiful with the snow and the sparkling salt on the cobblestone sidewalks. It's so scenic that horse-drawn carriages park in wait for people who want to pay to ride around.

The orange and red autumn leaves have shriveled to dried, brown, crunchy dead things that are frozen and buried deep beneath the snow. In some places where the snow has turned to slush from cars or foot traffic, you can see the black mush of the soggy thawing leaves underneath. It's a gross contrast to the pure white snow, and a reminder that just beneath the beautiful surface of everything winter has brought, there are remnants of the fall still lurking. Secrets and bad memories that will inevitably surface in the spring.

I have a newfound gratitude for my family. I always knew that they were loving and supportive in ways other kids at WJ Prep did not seem to have at home. But now my appreciation has only grown since I've seen the cruelty of Emmett's family in full force. The sting of what they did isn't just that they forced Emmett to sign over everything he had inherited, it's more about how they went about it—lying and tricking him into thinking they were in danger to try and make it look like he was mentally unstable just for caring about where they were and if they were okay.

Emmett and I have spent a lot of time listening to music in his motel room. One of us always plays something on our phones before we make love. Both of us like brooding, sad songs, and the band Emmett wants to take me to see has a heartbreaking, sort of ethereal sound to it. But lately we have both taken to listening to happier songs. Anything to help build the momentum of how we've been feeling. Maybe if things can feel happy and simple for just long enough, we won't completely crumble when the next wave of the Elites' drama strikes.

Emmett has been spending a lot of time with my family, and he has just enough money to keep his room at the motel for a little while longer. My mom knows something happened at his home that is making him come around so much, but explaining it requires so much backstory that I'm not ready to give her just yet. But sooner or later, he will have to figure something out for money. What little bit his mom left him won't last much longer, and I hate her for putting him in that position. He never had time to think about what he might want to do with his life when he was growing up because it was always planned out for him. Now all of that has been taken away, and he has to decide all at once while he is starting over again from scratch.

The snowflakes cling to my cheeks and melt against my warm skin, getting caught in my eyelashes. I love seeing them accumulate in Emmett's curls, reflecting in Emmett's gray eyes. His cheeks blush from the cold, rounding out around his playful smirk. I like seeing him this way. He looks happy.

He catches me by the door and brings himself close enough to pin me to the car. He grips my face and brings my eyes to his, lingering for a moment before pressing his lips to mine, urging my mouth open with his tongue. I moan into his kiss, suddenly feeling burning hot even in the snow.

"I've got plans for you later tonight," he warns.

"Oh, yeah?" I smile devilishly.

He swoops his mouth over mine again, biting at my bottom lip with always the perfect amount of roughness. Enough to keep me on my toes and keep me burning for no one else but him. The kind of roughness I never expected I would like, but that he does so well.

The cold air carries with it a new hope. A hope for these unexpected changes, and that they can somehow work out better than we ever planned. While what happened to Emmett seems awful, we both know things might be better this way. Before, he only had one possible path in front of him that he just had to make the best of. Now he has the opportunity to do anything he wants. I call tell the crash of choices scares him, but it's exciting at the same time. The hope of possibility. And while I promised I didn't care if things with him weren't easy, the hope of it all being simpler in the future is refreshing.

We're both smiling and grinning in his car, relaxed against the lingering warmth of the heated seats. My fingers loosely grip my phone in my lap, and I see Emmett close his eyes and tip his head back with softened features. It's something I see him do a lot now, as if he is breathing in as much of this peaceful time as he can before it slips away again.

Emmett smiles at me from the driver's seat before he blows into his cold, red hands and rubs them together. The car smells like burnt lint as he turns up the heat, which is strangely comforting. He hasn't talked to his family since the night they officially cast him out, and Malcolm and Bernadette have yet to return to school. But he seems happier this way. More at peace. I don't think he could have ever turned his back on his family. Loyalty to them above all else was too ingrained in him for that. But when they disowned him, he was freed and it gave him permission to wash his hands of it all and walk away. I know there is an emptiness left in him, but not for the family he had. It's a gaping hole for the family he should have had. The one he deserves—much like how I feel about my own father.

As we drive off, my phone buzzes in my bag. "It's my mom," I tell him. "She's probably wondering if you're coming over for dinner."

"Hell yeah, I am," he shoots back without hesitation. "I love your mom's cooking. I'll come any time she asks."

Emmett and I have decided not to tell them everything for now. We know we need to, but we decided we needed time to process it all ourselves first. Plus, we don't want anything else to change right now. We want to get through the holidays with a sense of calm, and plan to catch them up to speed in the new year.

"Mom?" I answer, still shivering as the car heats up.

"Ophelia," she huffs back, sounding worried. "Are you on your way home?"

"Yeah, Emmett's driving me," I tell her. "Everything okay?"

"I need to talk to you," she says sternly.

"Okay, sure," I answer pensively, afraid of what this could be about. "What about? Care to give me a hint?"

"It's your father," she replies grimly, stopping my heart cold. "He called me today. I haven't talked to him since I left him when you were just a baby."

"Uh-huh," I stammer, unable to breathe. "What did he want?"

"Just come home," she says again. "I need to talk to you before he gets here."

"Gets there?" I demand. "What do you mean 'gets there'?"

"He's joining us for dinner," she says plainly, but with an obvious tinge of anxiety.

I hang up and stare straight ahead, wishing the afternoon hadn't taken this unexpected turn. I want to go back to how I felt just minutes ago, when everything was going well for once. I don't want my dad in any part of my life, even the dark, distant part my mom doesn't know about. I can't stand the thought of those two worlds merging. My mother, who I love. and the man who beat and left her. I hate him enough as it is. I can't bear to see him with her and let the rest of it slide so easily.

"What was that all about?" Emmett asks.

"My father," I reply breathlessly. "It seems he's coming over for dinner tonight."

My blood boils. I grew up hearing my mom refer to him as the scum of the earth, and now he is coming over for dinner. He was completely absent for most of my life, and then became responsible for the torment I had to endure at the hands of the Elites.

"I forgot to tell you," I remember suddenly. "I got pulled

over. The night Lily got arrested. The cops were asking me about him again."

"Did you tell them anything?" He looks at me questioningly.

"No," I reply. "I didn't know what to say. I wish you had never made that deal with him Emmett. Now I feel like he's never going to go away."

His face contorts. "You know what would have happened if I hadn't made that deal. One of our fathers would have killed you, and my dad would still be reigning over everything."

"I know you were desperate to get rid of him." I sigh in acceptance. "But it's like making a deal with the devil. I'm not convinced my father would have been any better than yours…if he had been around."

"Well, it sounds like you're about to find out," he says ominously.

I remember my father defending his decision to kidnap me if Emmett hadn't stepped in. He claimed he just needed to 'remove me from the game.' Like I was just some kind of gambling chip in his mind, one that was swinging the odds out of his favor. At the time, I didn't know if I was better off with Emmett or my dad. Now it seems I'm getting both, whether I like it or not.

We've come so far since then. When everything about Emmett and my dad came out, I couldn't imagine ever trusting Emmett again after everything he had put me through. I certainly never thought we'd be where we are today. But I can't help but feel like the lingering presence of my father threatens what we have. I don't know how, but I know it's not good.

"Do you think he still keeps tabs on my mom and me?" I ask Emmett nervously. "You remember what he said after everything happened with your father. About my mother belonging to him before anybody else. You don't think he's…trying to get her back or something…He wouldn't, right? Not with Brendan around."

"Despite what you think…your dad and I aren't buddies, you know," he reminds me. "My guesses about this whole thing are as good as yours."

"I don't understand why he's still around!" I lament. "He said he was going to leave me alone now that Thomas is dead."

Suddenly, I wish I had told Mom everything. Then maybe she would have known better than to let Dad join us for dinner. I'd like to know how he talked his way into this one, anyway, especially since my mom hates him. Not to mention how Brendan must feel about it. I cringe to imagine what kind of smooth talk he must have laid on them to make this happen.

"What do you think he wants?" I ask as Emmett continues driving.

"Maybe he just wants to be closer to you," he suggests innocently.

"Oh, come on," I scoff. "You know better than that."

"Well, there's only way to find out," he says. "I guess we're going to have dinner with your dad. And Mom. And stepdad. All at the same time."

I swallow hard, wishing there was some way out of it. Maybe if we can get there in time, we can talk some sense into my mom. But I don't see how we can do that without telling her everything.

"I guess we need to start working on our story." My voice cracks. "Decide on a version of it my mom can handle."

"Your house is only fifteen minutes away," he retorts. "I think it's going to take a lot longer than that."

I press my head to the window and look out longingly. I knew things couldn't stay simple and easy for long, I had just hoped that we could have until the new year before everything went haywire again. But I guess that's just life in Jameson.

# Game Changing RULES

# PROLOGUE

## BOOK 3

I can practically hear dramatic trumpets playing a funeral march as my boyfriend, Emmett Jameson, drives me straight into my worst nightmare. My mom has just called to inform me that my biological father, Theo, will be joining us for dinner.

It's a scenario I've never prepared myself for. I grew up hearing her refer to him as the scum of the earth. And I had never met the man until my life came to depend on him in the midst of being taken hostage in the sick and twisted game of the Elites, which he was more of a central figure in than I ever could have imagined.

I don't know how he's charmed his way to our dinner table right alongside my stepfather, Brendan, who has been more of a father to me than he ever has. All I know is that when he shows up, everything goes wrong. And this is definitely not the way I wanted to spend my first afternoon of winter break.

"I'm sure it will be fine," Emmett offers, reaching over from the driver's seat to squeeze my hand.

My eyes dart over to him in desperation, wanting to believe he's right. But his own view of Theo has been skewed ever since they made their demented little deal to kill off Emmett's monster of a father together all in the name of bringing down the Elites once and for all.

My cozy, comforting suburban home suddenly looks like a haunted castle with dark, ominous clouds looming overhead and crows cawing as they fly by. As Emmett's car rolls to a stop in the driveway, I'm frozen for a moment. My hand slides along the seat belt, but I'm unable to bring myself to actually unbuckle it and get out of the car. All I can do is stare at the front door with dread, knowing that behind it, the man I hate so much is putting on his best face for my mom and stepdad as we speak.

"Let's just get this over with," Emmett says as he opens my door and tries to lure me out. "It'll be over before you know it and everything will be back to normal. We can watch a movie later."

I can't help but snort at the word "normal." He doesn't even know what that means. I don't think I do anymore either, not since the day I arrived in this fucked-up little town. But I take a deep breath and force myself from the car.

The house smells delicious as we step inside to see Theo sitting with Brendan at the kitchen table. My mom is busy behind them preparing dinner. I do my best to hear what they could possibly be talking about, but the moment we round the corner they both stop and perk up.

"Ophelia!" Theo chimes, looking especially pleased with himself and this position he's managed to talk himself into.

"Hi, sweetie!" my mom sings with a big smile.

She looks calm and happy, maybe even a little excited, but it seems naïve and dangerous to me. Emmett is quick to take a seat with both of them and soon they are chattering on about sports. Once again, I'm frozen. Staring at the scene in bewilderment. It's like they're a bunch of helpless gazelles grazing away in ignorant bliss, completely unaware of the lion stalking from just a few feet away. Only it's worse than that. The gazelles *invited* the lion to dinner.

I join my mom in the kitchen and do my best to corner her. On the phone, she sounded panicked and had wanted to talk to me before Theo arrived, but we didn't make it on time.

"You sounded upset on the phone," I whisper with my eyes still glued to Theo's back at the table. "What's going on? How did this happen?"

She scrunches her nose and waves her hand dismissively. "I was just nervous is all. But as soon as he arrived, I knew everything would be fine. Not nearly as awkward as I expected."

My heart races in frustration. None of this makes any sense. My mom hates Theo as much as I do and she doesn't even know the whole story. But she's humming to herself as she continues cooking away, cheerful as can be like she's preparing a meal for a king.

"Mom," I hiss more sternly, pulling her to rapt attention. "What the hell is going on!? Why is he here!?"

"We'll talk later," she replies through clenched teeth, breezing right by me to place a dish onto the table. "Sweetie, grab some plates and silverware, please."

I want to refuse. The last thing I want to be doing is serving Theo, but I know that making a scene won't help anything. Everyone is bizarrely calm and cheerful, so I take another deep breath and hope that Emmett was right. Maybe if I just play along for a little bit, he'll go back to where he came from before I know it and everything will be okay.

My mom and I set the table and put out all of the dishes, filled to the brim with the makings for building your own tacos. She made way too much food, which means she's nervous. Even though she already admitted that much, it's a relief to see proof of it. I need to know that anyone feels even a fraction of the tension that I do.

"This looks delicious, Lala," Theo announces gratefully as he piles fillings into a tortilla. Brendan and Emmett let out grunts of agreement, but I still find myself looking around the table wildly, feeling like I've stepped into the twilight zone.

"Ophelia," my mom blurts, jerking me to. "Aren't you hungry?"

I nod blankly and slowly begin putting some things on my plate. I can feel Theo's eyes looking at me every so often, but mostly he smiles politely and looks around at everyone with a friendly gaze. His grin reminds me of an outside dog who conned his way into the house and is sitting on the sofa like a throne.

The dinner carries on with small talk and polite conversation. I'm on edge the entire time, expecting his real motive to surface at any moment. But no. We eat, we talk, and then at an appropriate time once the table is cleared, Theo thanks us for the invite and goes home.

Brendan and my mom show him out, but he stops and turns in the doorway with an appreciative, humble smile. "I can't thank you two enough for letting me into your home...after everything. I'd...I'd like it if we could do this again sometime."

Brendan looks to my mom who smiles and nods hesitantly. Just before starting down the front steps, Theo looks over their shoulders to me with a wave. "It was nice to see you, Ophelia. I hope to see you again soon."

All of my questions and fears have been bubbling up for hours. The moment the door closes behind him, it all starts to spill out.

"Can someone tell me what the fuck is going on here!?" I shriek, causing everyone but my mom to freeze and look at me like I'm a madwoman.

"Theo called and apologized. He asked if it would be possible for him to be more involved in your life. In our lives. That's all, Ophelia," she explains casually as she starts on the dishes.

"He *apologized*!?" I fume in laughter. "Can he even do that!? Just call up out of the blue and say 'I'm sorry' after what he did? Mom! He beat you! I had never even seen him until we came to Jameson!" She stops and looks up to me with a wrinkled brow and I immediately realize my mistake. As far as my mom knows, tonight was my first time ever meeting him. "Until tonight," I quickly correct myself. "And anyway, don't I have any say in this!? Shouldn't he ask *me* if he can be a part of my life!? Not just use you to force me into it…"

Truthfully, he has asked. Or rather implied. I have shut him down each and every time.

"Enough, Ophelia," Brendan grumbles from the other side of the room. "This isn't just about you. Theo and your mom have their own baggage to sort through too, you know."

"And you're okay with that!?" I gape, flailing my arms dramatically.

Emmett appears at my side, placing a hand on the small of my back in comfort. He doesn't say it out loud, but I know he's begging me to calm down. But the calmer everyone else is, the more enraged I feel. I press the issue throughout the night as my mind races through the possible disastrous outcomes of Theo hanging around.

"People change," my mom insists, sounding tired. Not by our dinner guest, but by *me*. "I don't want to keep hanging on to old grudges. If he wants to try and make amends, I'm ready to let the past be the past. And you should too, Ophelia. You may think you hate him now, but one day when you're older you'll regret not taking this opportunity to get to know your biological father."

"The sperm donor as you called him!?" I huff back, but she

ignores me. She may think I'm being too dramatic or bratty, but she doesn't realize that Theo's worst offenses aren't so far into the past. It's easy for her to let go of things he did eighteen to twenty years ago and the absence that followed. But once she knows the truth about what Theo has done in just the past few months, I know she'll feel differently.

# CHAPTER ONE
### BOOK 3

There is still a light snow lingering on the ground outside as I look out my bedroom window, waiting for Emmett to pick me up. Just as he promised, the dinner with Theo came and went. We haven't heard from him since, thankfully. But it didn't stop me from feeling on edge for the rest of winter break, worrying when he might pop up again.

But now there are bigger things to worry about. The first day back to school. Even in a normal town at a regular high school, I'd be teeming with anxiousness over today. It's my last semester in high school, which means in just five short months, I can finally put WJ Prep behind me forever. There's college, prom, and graduation to think about. But that's overshadowed by the fear of not knowing what we're walking into now that everything in our school's everchanging hierarchy has shifted once again.

Emmett's beat-up green Toyota pulls into our driveway. A downgrade from his expensive, luxury sports car that he sold to have more money to live off of now that he's on his own. It's a reminder that he's probably going through just as much anxiety as I am over this first day back. I feel guilty over how comforting that is for me. I'm used to a new semester at WJ Prep feeling ominous, but for once, I'm not facing it alone.

I bound out the front door and into his car, eager to escape the crisp, cold morning air. He smiles as I jump in, but I can see the worry in his eyes.

"Good morning," I lean over for a kiss, avoiding stating the obvious.

His lips linger against mine for a moment, as if he needs to soak up a few extra seconds of comfort before we take off. His fingers gently trail against my cheek before he finally pulls back with a deep sigh and puts the car into drive.

There's an awkward silence at first. I don't know if we should get it over with and just put all of ours fears out there right off the bat, or if we should try to ignore them together. Maybe naming them makes it worse.

"He'll be there today," Emmett blurts. "All of them will be."

I nod and shift against the seat, feeling relieved that we don't have to dance around it. "Better than them being absent any longer, I guess. We get to dive right into the new order of things."

"New order," he scoffs under his breath resentfully.

From the moment I arrived at WJ Prep, I was informed of the hierarchy. The town Jameson was founded by the predecessors of Emmett's father, Thomas Jameson. And at the center of it all was Jameson Automobiles. A luxury car manufacturer that only the richest of the rich could ever dream of buying from. But that's exactly what the Elites were. The wealthiest, most powerful people around. Everyone in town bowed to them. The police, teachers, doctors, lawyers. No one dared to question them.

Emmett's car pulls into a parking spot near the back of the lot, trying not to call attention to us, but there's a group of students gathered around front who notice us and stop to gawk. The school has assigned parking, which has of course also always been controlled by the Elites. I've been used to parking in the back. My assigned spot has always been as far away from school as possible. If they had their way, they probably would have had me parking in a different lot altogether. But Emmett once had one of those spots up front. He used to be the ringleader of them all. A painful fact neither of us wants to think about right now, even if our reasons are different.

His eyes dart across the huddle of staring, snickering students, then over to me with a look of dread and acceptance. Before the end of last semester, he at least still had his old car. Now he has nothing left to hide behind, and there's been the passing of the entire break for rumors to fly around. We're certain everyone knows now.

I offer a comforting smile and squeeze his hand tight just before we finally force ourselves out of the car. We can feel everyone's eyes burning into us as we make the long walk to the front doors. It's as if they're surprised to see us. Maybe they thought we'd run away and never come back. That's what the rest of the old Elites have done, either by choice or by force.

Emmett's ex-girlfriend, Vivian, lives in New York with her aunt now that her parents are in prison. Trey and Vincent, the twins from hell, have vanished. I heard their relatives sent them off to some military school as an attempt to erase the poor job their parents did raising them. Parents that are also now in prison. Lily used to be a friend to me, or at least pretended to be. But the absurdity of the Elite hierarchy got the better of her, and she now rests in a high-class mental facility. No one survives the Elites it seems, except for Emmett's sister, Bernadette. The only remaining original member. In that context, I guess Emmett can be glad he's at least still here, even if he is black-listed right along with me now.

We do our best to ignore them and brush past, but we're not far into the halls before we see him. Malcolm Henderson. Leaned up against his locker with a hoard of worshippers around him. He stands where Emmett once stood in every sense, and he has a new group of minions surrounding him.

I squeeze Emmett's hand tighter as we walk by, feeling him glaring at us. The muscles in his hand tighten, and I know it's taking everything in him not to turn around and pounce. But we do what we're supposed to. We keep walking. If we keep our heads down and ignore him, things will be much easier for us.

We part ways for our respective classes and thankfully the morning is uneventful. We've both had time to adjust to being in the same building as Malcolm by the time lunch rolls around and things feel slightly less tense.

After going through the line of ridiculous food that gets served here, including steak and an array of other gourmet dishes, we settle into a table by ourselves at the back of the room. We eat in silence for a while, but I can see Emmett staring at them from the corner of my eye.

The Elites always sit at a table in the middle of the cafeteria. For a short time last semester, seating was free reign around here. But now things have been restored with new faces to assume the role of school leaders.

I try not to notice how hurt Emmett looks as he glances over at them, mostly looking at Bernadette. His sister. For him, this isn't just about school politics or who the popular kids are. His entire family has betrayed him and Bernadette sits proudly at Malcolm's side, ignoring her outcast brother.

My father was one of the first Elites to ever be blacklisted after he squandered tons of their money to bad gambling debts. They banished him, but shortly after I arrived at WJ Prep, he came back with a vengeance. In a whirlwind of events, which I was held hostage in the middle of, he murdered Emmett's father, Thomas. The rest of the Elites went down with charges for a sex trafficking ring they were all running for profit. Briefly, it seemed like things would be better. Emmett stepped in to take over Jameson Automobiles and was determined to toss out the old ways of the Elites altogether.

But his mom and sister had something else in mind, and the Hendersons were whispering in their ears the entire time. Waiting in the sidelines for their chance to pounce and take away everything. They backed Emmett into a corner and gained control over every aspect of Jameson, both as a town and as a company. Now the Hendersons and the rest of Emmett's remaining family sit on the town's throne, leaving him with nothing.

I can see all of this rolling through his mind as we sit and eat, but Bernadette looks pleased with herself without a care in the world. Not an ounce of guilt, regret, or shame. I marvel at the new faces sitting around them, already looking comfortable in their new roles. It makes it all feel more impossible. When one round of them are taken out, a whole new bunch pops up in their place practically overnight, like daisies.

"Who are they?" I gape, shaking my head. "Where did they come from?"

"Liam and Malcolm fired most of the old executives and key players in the company after they took everything from me," he explains through lightly clenched jaws. "They probably thought they couldn't trust them. So they brought in new people from all over the place." He tips his head to the guy sitting on the other side of Malcolm. "That's Skye Liang. One of the youngest, self-made millionaires in the tech world. He's been working on the sidelines of the Hendersons' software company for years now."

Sitting across from Skye is a smarmy looking pale guy with slicked back blonde hair. His cheeks are round with bright red lips, making him look much younger than he probably is. Everything about him spells out spoiled, rich brat.

"Who's that one?" I snarl.

"Miles Hartford," he replies, rolling his eyes slightly. "They're like the Jamesons of Connecticut. They were always big competitors of ours on the stock market. I guess Liam decided they'd be better off joining forces."

"How amicable of them," I huff bitterly.

Emmett smirks, but it quickly fades. I see a wave of heaviness wash over him as he stabs into his food without taking a bite.

"They're having a grand opening," he says softly in a pained voice.

"For what?"

"Jameson Automobiles," he answers.

"But...it's *been* open," I stammer in confusion. "It never closed. They can't even have a re-opening. Definitely not an opening."

His face tightens, but he doesn't say anything else. For as messed-up as his father was along with everything his family has always stood for, Jameson Automobiles was still his family's legacy. One he was born into believing he would inherit. With his father out of the way, not only did he think he would inherit it, he thought he'd finally have a chance to make it a clean business, free of the dirty underbelly full of things like rape, murder, and the sex trafficking rings the rest of the old Elites went down for.

Not only did Emmett lose his chance at turning his family's legacy into something clean and decent that he could finally be proud of, but he also has to watch the Hendersons take over everything that had always belonged to him. The money and power hurt to lose, but for the first time I can see the deeper side to it. Emmett was prepared to work hard and make Jameson Automobiles a success that was built on honesty and ethical operations. That's gone now and being flaunted in his face. And the Hendersons are even more greedy and corrupt than his father was. It's like Emmett has lost his chances at redemption.

He lets out an uncomfortable grunt and digs back into his food. Our silence is overshadowed by the cackles of the Elites echoing through the cafeteria. An outsider might think we're making too much of their whole display, but we know how they work too well, Emmett better than anyone since he used to play the same games. They're being obnoxious on purpose, to rub everything in his face. It's a show of dominance.

Once lunch is over, we walk slowly and quietly through the crowded halls towards our next class. That's when things get worse. It's as if Malcolm has sent out the pecking order and everyone has to be sure to reinforce it.

"I can't believe he bothered to show his face here again," one girl whispers to her friend as we walk by.

"I heard he lost his mind and tried to kill his mom and sister and pin it on Malcolm," her friend hisses back. "He was too mentally unfit to take over Jameson. He had to turn everything over to them."

"Just as well. Malcolm is better looking anyway. And smarter."

I can see the rage boiling under Emmett's skin, so I quickly grab him by the arm and yank him into an empty doorway. I pull him into a deep kiss. He's stiff at first, but soon melts into it, letting everything else fade away.

"We're in this together," I remind him as I pull back. "I've always been at the bottom of the totem pole around here and I've made it by just fine. You can too."

Some of the tension escapes his face as he loosens into a smile. Slowly a sense of revived hope begins to show through, and he leans back in to kiss me again. Once he walks away for his next class and is out of sight, I break into a determined march for the hall we just passed through. I go right up to the pair of whispering girls.

"Hey," I bark, catching them both by surprise. "If you're going to talk shit behind his back, at least get it right. Emmett isn't crazy, and he didn't try to kill anyone. Malcolm and Emmett's backstabbing sister stole everything from him."

Their eyes grow wide, amazed that I would dare to question whatever story WJ Prep's new king has sent into rotation.

"Are you crazy?" one of the girls asks, almost as a warning. I can see her secretly pleading with me to shut up for my own sake. Everyone knows what happens to people who are dumb enough to question the Elites.

"I'd be careful what you say about Malcolm," the other girl adds, taking on a snarkier tone to save face. She says it loud so the others around her can hear. She wants no mistake about who she's aligning with.

"Malcolm can go fuck himself," I declare confidently. I have my own story to set straight. I'd like to think I've established my own gray area in this whole order of things. They'd like to think I'm blacklisted, but I only have five months left here. And even when I was the Elites' number one target, I survived. I'm not backing down to them anymore.

My defiance terrifies them. One girl leans in close, grabbing my arm. "Shut your fucking mouth," she begs. "Do you have any clue what they'll do if they hear you talking like that?"

I can't help but laugh. Not only at her assumption that I'm unaware of how things work around here, but at the absurdity of it all. This is a high school, not some medieval kingdom where people who commit treason get carted off to the guillotine. But unlike my first day here, I know better now than to question the very real danger of it all. The Elites have nearly killed me twice now for ending up on the wrong side of their games.

But since that's where I keep ending up anyway, I might as well own it.

"Oh, I know all too well," I tell her. "I just don't care anymore."

Suddenly the girls straighten, looking alarmed at the sight of something over my shoulder. I glance back and see Malcolm watching closely from the other end of the hall.

"Get the fuck away from me," one of the girls shouts suddenly. They look me up and down with disgust and quickly walk away. I've been blacklisted, right along with Emmett. If anyone is seen talking to either of us for too long, or god forbid acting friendly towards us or helping us in any way, they'll pay the price for it.

With them gone, I turn back to Malcolm and look him straight in the eye from where I'm standing. He studies me with a questioning look, wondering if I'm going to behave and step back into line, or if he's going to have to teach me a lesson. I flash him a defiant smile before moving on to class. A move I'm sure I'll regret eventually, but at this point, I don't know what they can do to me that they haven't already done.

# CHAPTER TWO

BOOK 3

Emmett and I meet back at his car after school and exchange heavy sighs of relief and a smile. We survived the first day back, and at least now we know what the new gang looks like, even if we have no clue what they have in store for us.

"It's their last semester too," I think out loud as we get into his car. "Maybe they'll be so busy getting ready for everything that happens after WJ Prep, they won't have time to fuck with us."

He flashes an unconvinced smirk, as if to say 'Yeah, that'd be nice.' But he's not buying it.

"Let's not talk about them," he replies. "From now on, when we walk out of those doors at the end of the day, I want them to be the furthest thing from my mind."

"Deal!" I agree enthusiastically. "So, what should we do then? Movies? Pizza?"

Emmett and I have delighted in enjoying regular teenage pleasures these past few months. Being a former Elite, he never really got to have fun. He was always being forced to carry out some mission for his father or the WJ Prep crew. I hadn't known real fun from the moment I arrived here. The Elites made sure of that. But once Emmett was stripped of his place in town, we both got some time to fly under the radar and finally just act like normal teenagers for once.

"I have something better planned," he says with a grin.

The days are still short from winter, and it's dark by the time we pull into the parkway. Emmett drives to one of the highest overlooks with all of Jameson sparkling underneath us. He leaves the car running as we climb out onto the hood of his car, pressing ourselves against the heat of the engine.

Looking down at Jameson from up here, you'd think it was like any other town. It looks completely normal. Beautiful even, with a sprinkle of white snow clinging to the rooftops of houses and buildings. The lingering Christmas lights draped across gutters and trees and the glowing warm lights shining through windows.

The scariest thing about Jameson is how untrusting it has made me of the world. If Jameson could look so normal and inviting from the outside, even though it's malicious and cruel, I have to wonder if every town has the same underbelly without most people even realizing it. Maybe most of us just manage to skate by on the outskirts of it all enough not to realize.

"How are your college applications going?" He asks me, reaching for my hand as we turn from the town below to the stars overhead.

"Done!" I announce proudly. "Application fees paid. Essays written. Everything's sent off, and Coach Granger has been getting a lot of feedback from scouts that have been visiting our track meets."

"That's my girl," he hums. "You know, the good thing about being cut off from everything here is that we can go wherever we want. I can follow you to just about whatever school you decide to go."

My heart swells with the promise of us being able to stay together, but a nagging feeling quickly steals it away. There are several schools on my list that would be hard for me to get to financially, and Emmett would find it nearly impossible to find his place in those cities where the job markets are so competitive.

"But what about what you want to do?" I ask. "Aren't you going to apply anywhere? Even try to get in?"

"You know they won't let me get in anywhere," he replies grimly.

Emmett's grades are perfect. Even if at one point he didn't have to earn them. Teachers never give Elites bad grades. Their parents would make them pay if they did. Now he gets the opposite treatment. Teachers are waiting to give him bad grades, even if it's not entirely deserved. It's almost expected of them. But Emmett works twice as hard to make it nearly impossible for them to sabotage his GPA.

But it doesn't matter. Lily once had everything going for her too, and the Elites still made sure she couldn't get into any of the schools she wanted. Each and every one of them rescinded their interest. Around here, it's not just about surviving this nightmarish high school. The damage they do goes well beyond that into the rest of our lives.

When he was Jameson's golden boy, even after his father died, Emmett was set up to receive the same college education all the men in his family had. A private tutor from the Ivy League school of their choice would come around enough to justify the sense of them earning their degrees. But it was all a show. Jameson men didn't have time for school after all. They were running a multi-billion-dollar corporation. Their degrees were bought and paid for, so they'd have something to brag about at business dinners and the golden ticket Ivy League degree that was expected of them to hang over the desk of their private study in the Jameson manor.

Now even if Emmett can get into some random school, he'll have to figure out how to pay for it. And once he's in, he'll have to work for it the old-fashioned way. Like the rest of us.

"But surely there's something you want to do," I insist, not wanting to let him slip away into a sense of hopelessness in the face of all this. "This is a fresh new start for you, remember? You can do anything you want! You're free!"

His eyes light up as he rolls over to me. "Exactly. And what I want is to follow you. You're the one who will get a scholarship. Coach Granger won't let the Elites fuck that up for you. I'll go wherever you want to go, and then I'll figure out what I'm going to do once we get there."

I lean in to give him a big kiss, thinking I am one of the luckiest girls in the world. Most high school romances like ours are doomed once college rolls around. But Emmett and I just might have a shot at figuring all of this out.

"Well, wherever we go, I think it should be far away from here," I suggest as I look back at the lit-up town below. "As far away as we can afford to go."

"I like the sound of that," he smiles wide. "But what about your mom and your step-dad?"

"They'll deal with it," I quip back. "I love them, but if they knew what I've really been through here, they'd never blame me for wanting to get the hell out."

His face grows serious again. "Are you going to tell them?" he asks with a daunting tone. "We decided we would. Before Theo popped up again."

After the Hendersons took everything from Emmett, we knew it wasn't a matter of 'if' some new craziness would pop up, but when. To stay on top of things before the next disaster struck, we decided we needed to finally tell my mom the truth about Jameson. About Theo's part in it all. About my part in it all. Something I should've done long ago, but I was too afraid. It seemed like a story too crazy to believe. Then, before I knew it, I was in over my head and it was too late to tell her anything. I don't want to end up in that spot again.

I consider everything we've talked about carefully, biting my lip. "I guess I've put it off long enough," I admit reluctantly. "I should go ahead and get it over with. You never know what could happen tomorrow. Everything could change again."

"Want me to come with you?" he asks with assuring devotion.

I almost scream out that of course, I do. But as much as I want him there, it's too complicated. Emmett's role in everything that's happened to me is too big of a thing to even try to explain to my mom. That's the part I can't bring myself to tell her the whole truth of. And I just can't navigate that kind of lie with him sitting across from me.

"I better do it alone," I sigh.

We drift back into admiring the starry sky above for a while until we finally decide it's time to go. If I'm going to finally have this talk with my mom, I'm eager to get it over with. Once and for all. I peel myself up from the warm hood of his car and start psyching myself up for it. But as I slide back into the passenger's seat, Emmett stops.

"Wait," he says, leaning into the backseat. "I have something for you." He pulls out a small wrapped box and hands it to me.

"You shouldn't be buying me anything," I scold him. "You have to save your money as much as you can."

He cuts his eyes to the side, ignoring me, then watches eagerly as I open the present. Beneath the paper is a small, black velvet box. I open it up to see a necklace inside. I take the fake gold chain into my hand and hold it up to the light, revealing a little running shoe charm that dangles down.

"Emmett!" I gasp. "I love it!"

"Of course, it's worth nothing," he admits, sounding embarrassed. "But I knew it was perfect for you. In the scope of what I can afford."

I hand him the necklace and turn my back to him, flailing my hands in a rush for him to put it on me. "It *is* perfect," I insist. "No matter what you can or can't afford, I still would have wanted this one."

I admire the sight of it resting across my chest. Out of all the things he could have bought me, he picked this necklace with a running shoe charm because he knows how important track and running are to me. Between this and his willingness to follow me to whatever school I want to go to, I realize just how big of a shot we really do have at figuring all of this out. He supports my dreams, and I can't think of anything more important to find in a man.

"Thank you," I murmur as I wrap my hands around his face and pull him close.

He kisses me softly and slowly, knowing we have to go, but soon we're unable to pull away. We are caught up in the taste of each other and the kiss deepens. My body sparks with excitement as his tongue rolls across mine, and I can't stop myself from climbing over to his seat, straddling my legs around his lap. As I lower my hips onto his, our kiss growing more urgent, I can feel the hardness rising beneath his jeans.

His hands quickly grow more daring, spreading across my thighs, squeezing them and pulling me against his erection. Then they drift upwards, gripping my breasts tightly. We're both panting with need and before long, we're flinging every article of clothing we can get off of each other to some other part of the car. The steering wheel is an obvious obstacle, but he quickly pulls the lever on the side of the seat to send it back, giving us more room.

Half-naked and overwhelmed with arousal, I lean down over him, finally having enough of my clothes off to push my panties to the side and slide him into the wetness between my legs. He hisses and claws into my ass with excitement, just as a satisfied moan breaks through my lips. I'm always surprised by how deeply he fills me and how good it feels. I move up and down slowly, relishing the feeling of how easily he glides in and out of me.

My mouth hovers over his as we both let out heavy breaths and groans. But finally, he mutters words, broken up by grunts of pleasure, "We have to… hurry…the cops…if they find us… out here like this…"

"Shhhh," I grin, holding one finger up to his lips as I move faster, pushing us both to the edge. He holds on for as long as he can, his eyes lighting up as he watches me ride him until I am yelling out with the crash of my orgasm.

As it fades into whimpers and I slow down, he grips my hips and begins moving me up and down, picking up the pace again until he cums. I love the way he digs his fingers into my skin as he growls through his climax, pulling out just in time to spill out onto my thigh.

We giggle as we clean up and awkwardly work our way back into our clothes. It was just the release we needed after our first day back, but I soon remember the promise I've made. When I get home, I have to tell my mom everything I've been avoiding telling her for so long.

The laid back, relaxing feeling of our time together fades the closer we get back to my house. There's been a dark cloud looming over this place for too long now and I'm hoping that coming clean will make everything start to feel a little better. If nothing else, Emmett and I will have another person to turn to if things get bad again.

But then a scarier thought pops into my head. What if the other benefit of this is that I will have a person outside of Emmett to turn to? Half of what got us to where we are now was him being the only person in the world who understood what I was going through, even when it was because he was the person putting me through it all. While this is good for me, I hate that part of me still wonders if that dark side to Emmett I've seen in the past is still lurking in there somewhere, waiting to rear its ugly head again.

I push all of that down for now as we pull into my driveway. Emmett gives me a slow, lingering kiss goodnight, mixed with soft, mischievous laughter. We're still high on lust for each other, and we both know we could easily go for round two if we had a place to go and the time. But reluctantly, I pull myself away and go inside.

I stop just inside the door and take a deep breath, gearing

myself up for this inevitable talk. My mom is sitting on the couch alone, watching TV.

"Where's Brendan?" I ask as I curl my legs up next to her.

"Working late," she replies, shooting me a sweet smile.

Mothers are usually the ones protecting their daughters from the harsh, cruel realities of the world. I know my mom is by no means sheltered or naïve, but sometimes she just looks so content and hopeful, I hate to spoil it by letting her know she's unknowingly thrown me into a hell hole by bringing me here.

"Can we talk?" I finally blurt with a sharp breath, needing to get it out there before I change my mind.

"Sure," she perks up with concern, quickly picking up the remote to turn off the TV, giving me her undivided attention.

"About dad," I force out with another nervous breath. It's not just about him, but he's a big enough player in all of this, I figure it's the best place to start.

To my surprise, she immediately rolls her head with an almost agitated expression. "Oh, Ophelia," she groans. "Do we have to get into all of that tonight? Look, I'm sorry. I should have been more sensitive to you meeting him for the first time..."

"No, Mom," I cut her off. "That's just it. That wasn't..."

"But sometimes certain things just have to be like a band-aid, you know? You and I could have sat and talked and worked ourselves up into a frenzy over him coming here for hours, and maybe chickened out of the whole thing altogether. But we just jumped in and did it, and now you can say you know who your biological father is," she states optimistically.

"Oh, I know who he is alright," I grumble under my breath.

But she's quick to keep talking over me, ignoring my remark. "Ever since we had that dinner...everything just feels... a little lighter. You know? There's no more big bad skeleton waiting in our closet. He's just your dad who comes and has dinner sometimes. That's all."

Her eyes are wide and looking at me expectantly. It's not like her to be so adamant about something without even hearing me out first. Normally she's begging me to talk more and resents having to be the one to say everything. Maybe I've trained her into being this way. But then I look deeper into her eyes and realize she's asking, begging for my permission to feel this way. She's worked hard to get to this place, and she's terrified of me stealing away this peace of mind she's finally achieved.

"You're right," I exhale, settling back into the couch. "I'm sorry. I shouldn't have been so resistant to the whole idea. It's a good thing that he came."

She scoops me into a big hug and then turns the TV back on. I watch with her in silence until I'm ready to go to bed. The fact remains that I still have to tell her everything. But tonight, I know she's not ready. Which is fine because, truthfully, I'm not either.

# CHAPTER THREE

BOOK 3

The crisp winter air burns in my lungs right along with my muscles as I blast through another timed round across the track at practice. For all that I have gained and lost in Jameson, running has remained my constant. They may have tried, but this is the one thing the Elites were never able to fully take from me.

The cold races across the skin of my bare arms and legs, but I'm moving so fast and pushing my body so hard that my skin is burning hot and numb to any coolness around. One thing I can thank the Elites for is that everything they put me through has made me a better runner ever. I could already hold my own before coming to WJ Prep, but the mental endurance I had to learn from their charades translated perfectly into a new level of performance on the track.

As I rush through the last lap, Coach Granger stops the timer in his hand with a pleased look on his face. I try to remain humble and ignore it, but inside I am giddy over how well I'm doing and how happy he looks with my performance. I keep my smile hidden, not wanting to appear too pleased with myself, and join the rest of the team as we gather our things and head for the showers.

I reach for my towel, but there's a tug on the other end of it. I look up and come face to face with a pale, brunette girl with big blue eyes. She's new here and I recognize her from our first day back. She's part of the new Elites and has been sitting with them at lunch. Her face is blank as she glares at me, still clutching the other end of the towel. I wait for the inevitable outburst to ensue.

"Sorry," I offer lightly. "I thought this one was mine."

She keeps staring me down intently for a few seconds, not moving or speaking. It puts me more on edge as I wait for her to chastise me for living or something worse. No one should ever dare disrupt an Elite.

"It's okay," she shrugs and grumbles suddenly, and without another word, she turns and vanishes around the corner.

I'm silent and stunned for a moment, in complete disbelief that she didn't pounce or scream or cuss me out at the very least. Maybe she's too new of an Elite to know how things usually work with them.

"Ophelia!" Coach Granger calls out from the other end of the bleachers, snapping me out of my trance.

"Coach," I answer dutifully, jogging over to meet him.

"Come into my office for a few minutes," his head bobs towards the door. "I need to talk to you."

I follow him into his small office resting a short distance from the track field. It's dimly lit but lined with trophies, medals, and photos from all the school's wins over the years. I can't help but feel proud at the sight of the more recent awards that I helped us win.

"Have a seat," he barks dryly. He comes across as cold and harsh, but Coach Granger is the nicest, most loyal adult left in WJ Prep, and he's always had my back. A position that the Elites have made him pay dearly for. Not even the teachers and coaches are above their wrath.

"You know we've had scouts from all the top schools watching you over the past few months," he continues in a serious tone. "And as your guidance counselor may have already discussed with you, many of those schools are ready to start extending scholarship offers, contingent on an in-person interview, of course."

I shift nervously over the topic of interviews. They can watch me run all day long, but the moment my presence and words come into play, I'm void of all confidence.

"There's one school in particular that's shown interest and I'd like you to check it out," he explains. "It's only a couple of hours from here. The track program there is outstanding and has churned out a handful of Olympians over the years. To boot, I have plenty of colleagues there and my recommendation will hold a lot of weight for you. They'd like to meet with you next week. Just an informal interview and some paperwork so they can finish the admissions process to let you know if you'd be accepted along with your scholarship offer."

"Wow, Coach…that's amazing," I gasp. "I don't know what to say…thank you!" My face drops for a moment. I bite my bottom lip, wanting to express my doubts, but I hate to sound ungrateful.

"What is it?" he questions knowingly.

"Well, it's just…you said it was only a couple of hours from here," I respond hesitantly. "I am pretty set on getting as far away from Jameson as possible. I'd think you of all people could understand that."

He nods in heavy consideration as his eyes drift to the window with a pained stare. When the original Elites threatened my life over my father's promise to take them down with evidence of their illegal sex trafficking ring operation, it led to Lily and Malcolm targeting Coach Granger.

Coach was the only person in the school on my side, and they wanted to make sure I had no one to turn to. They planted heroin for his son who was a recovering addict and the poor guy couldn't resist the bait. He died of an overdose, but of course, neither of them suffered any consequences for it. Other than Lily, but knowing what I know now, she probably would have ended up in a mental health facility regardless.

"It's a shame what they're able to get away with," he finally responds with a somber tone, then he straightens and turns back to me. "But you can't let them win, Ophelia. Once you're out of here and even just a couple hours away, they'll leave you alone. This is a good school. Don't let them continue ruling your life."

I scoff lightly but do my best to keep it well hidden. It seems overly optimistic to think they'd let Emmett and I off the hook so easily. I'm convinced the only option is to get far away from them where hopefully they won't bother looking for us. But Coach is right. At some point, I have to stop letting them dictate how I live my life. And if nothing else, the more acceptances and offers I get, the more choices I'll have. It may even encourage other schools to increase their offers to compete.

"I'll do my best at the interview," I assure him. "Thank you for everything."

After my chat with Coach, I meet Emmett in the parking lot. I tell him all about the upcoming interview along with the others I can expect to schedule in the coming weeks. He's happy for me, but I can see the faintest hint of sadness in his eyes. He would never admit to it or show it to me, but I know this is hard for him.

Everything that's happened in the past six months has left him clueless as to what he wants to do with his life. He wouldn't even begin to know which colleges to apply for right now or what for. He didn't spend the last three and a half years preparing for that the way the rest of us have. If the Hendersons along with his mom and sister hadn't taken everything for him, he'd be too busy preparing to take over Jameson Automobiles to feel left out of everyone else's college preparations.

Nonetheless, he keeps all of his despondency well hidden. I doubt anyone other than me could see it at all. He spends the next week helping me prepare, practicing interview questions with me and helping me gather everything else I'll need. Maybe this is how all couples should do it, I think. One person takes a year off after high school so they can devote all their time to helping their boyfriend or girlfriend get in. The demands of the more prestigious schools are so high, it feels like it requires an entire team of people to properly prepare for it all.

The following week, I make the two-and-a-half-hour drive to the campus for my interview. The neighborhood around the school is a lot like Jameson with giant, pristine houses and perfectly manicured landscaping. But there is something more wholesome about it all. There are people jogging down the sidewalks, dodging kids on bikes or moms pushing baby strollers. There are dogs barking from their leashes and little kids in heavy coats trying to scrape up remnants of snow from the grass to play with. The houses may look the same, but the people seem more relaxed. Normal. Happy. There isn't an air of fear weighing everything down.

The campus is lined with massive, old trees, and I can already imagine how beautiful they must look in the Spring with fresh green blossoms or in the Fall with gold and red leaves. I watch students shuffle by, bundled up in scarves with bags and arms full of books. My heart leaps with anticipation. Whether it's here or another school, soon I'll be starting a whole new life. One that is hopefully more normal than the nightmare I've found at WJ Prep.

The stark difference I see between here and my school is solidified as I get so caught up in taking in the sights that I accidentally bump into a tall guy walking in the opposite direction down the sidewalk. I expect him to go off on me, but he simply apologizes with a big smile and carries on his way. The Elites have traumatized me to the point that I've forgotten there's a whole world outside of Jameson without a circle of a select few who think they are so much more entitled to the air they breathe and the ground they walk on than everyone else. It will be a hard thing to get used to once I'm gone for good, but I'm more than ready for the change.

I made sure to arrive early for the interview. I know Coach called in some favors to get this lined up and I want to make sure I don't let him down. There are a few other students anxiously waiting in the sitting area as I make my way in. The floors and walls are deep mahogany wood with a flawless shine. The upholstery and drapes are deep jewel tones of green and burgundy, and the walls are lined with cases and frames of trophies and black and white photos.

The excitement in my chest builds as I catch glimpses of the shrines to their Olympian alumni. I notice one of the bronze medal winners smiling out from their photo. I've read that runner's stats and mine are pretty on par with how they did in high school. I feel a rise of giddiness at the thought that one day, that could be me.

The possibilities only make me more nervous, but at least I know I'm not the only one. There's a cluster of students sitting nearby who are plotting their interviews. They discuss questions they assume we can expect to be asked along with rumors they've heard about interview sessions that have happened before.

We're each clutching onto folders of important documents in our sweaty hands. The goal of the interview is to be able to extend a scholarship offer along with our acceptance letter. Demographics and place of birth make a difference in those things, so along with the interview, there's a round of paperwork and document checks that has to be done. The list of what to bring was lengthy and a little ridiculous, but I assume part of the goal was to test us on following instructions. They can immediately rule out less than ideal candidates that aren't responsible enough to follow the directions and gather everything that's asked of them.

I flip through my papers, double-checking everything, as one of the other people waiting spouts off the list of required items. Suddenly, a sinking feeling jolts through me. The other people mention a birth certificate, which I know I remember seeing on the list. More than seeing it, I know I remember getting a copy of mine and putting it into my folder. Yet somehow as I flip through it now, it's nowhere in sight.

My eyes dart to the clock as another person is called in for their interview. Judging by the time, I am likely the next one to be called, giving me less than half an hour or so to figure out what the hell has happened to my birth certificate. I can't stand the thought of blowing this over something so small and simple after what Coach has done to set it up. He's done so much for me, and the last thing I want to do is disappoint him. I look back to the Olympian's photo on the wall and wonder if they would have forgotten something so important.

But I didn't forget. I know I didn't. I look around the floor surrounding my seat and retrace my footsteps through the room. I dig through my backpack and check the folder three more times. Still no sight of it. The others sitting nearby start to whisper as they watch me search. They can see the panic on my face and know I've shown up without something. Their mouths twist into poorly hidden satisfied grins. This just knocks another competitor off the list for them.

Finally, one of the other girls comes over and tries to help me search. A gesture that never would have happened back in Jameson where the Elites keep everyone at each other's throats.

"Is there anyone nearby who might have a copy?" the girl suggests as we continue looking with no luck. "Did your mom come with you?"

"No," I sigh, breaking into an awful sweat. "I know we put a copy of it in there. I don't know what could have happened to it."

"It's not here," she confirms grimly. "Well…what about your car!?"

"Good idea," I shoot back nervously, checking the clock again. "I'll hurry but if they call me, will you tell them I'll be right back?"

"Of course," she nods, but I am already racing out the door to the parking lot.

Times like these are when it comes in handy to be a trained runner. I break into a full sprint across the pavement until finally my car is in sight. I don't even have to unlock the doors to know my birth certificate isn't inside. I can see the empty seats and floorboards plain as day. But I open it up and search anyway.

I'm huffing and panting for breath as I frantically search everything one last time, partly from my run over here but mostly from panic. It's still nowhere in sight as I flail my head back against my car seat, feeling dangerously close to bursting into tears. I tell myself I will just have to march back in there and own up to my mistake, hoping and praying that I can somehow charm them enough so that it doesn't matter. But I know there will be some other star athlete with excellent grades who will march in there with everything they were asked to bring. It's game over for me.

Just as I'm starting to give up, I hear the faint blow of a boat whistle from the distant shore, sparking an idea. My dad lives near here. A fact that crossed my mind more than once on the drive up here, but I kept pushing it down, telling myself it didn't matter. Although now it could matter quite a bit. His house can't be more than five minutes from here.

I hesitate to reach for my phone, but quickly snap myself out of it. There's no time to have an emotional crisis over this. It's as simple as he's the only person within a few miles who could possibly have a copy of my birth certificate, and even that's a stretch. It's highly unlikely that he'll answer the phone, have what I need, and be available to get it here in the next ten minutes. But I have to try.

My heart pounds relentlessly as the phone rings, and I'm not sure if it's because of my urgent predicament or my nerves over talking to him again. Not just talking to him but asking for his help. Something I've always been convinced I would never, ever do.

# CHAPTER FOUR

BOOK 3

By some miracle, not only did Theo answer the phone, he had a copy of my birth certificate on hand and was able to show up with it just in time. I was in such a rush by the time he arrived that it barely phased me to see him again and accept his help. I took the document and raced back inside, barely stepping foot into the waiting area just as my name was being called. I saw the girl who had been helping me with her lips parted, ready to defend my tardiness. But I was able to breeze right past her and into the interview on time.

I was so flustered and relieved by the time I sat down that I didn't have time to be nervous about the questions being thrown my way. The essay in my application cited my mom and stepdad as my inspirations in life, being the only people in my corner to set an example and help me along the way. I felt a slight tinge of shame as I backed up the sentiment in my answers, knowing it was Theo that helped me out today. But I quickly remembered everything he's put me through up until now and swallowed down any feelings of guilt.

I walk out of the interview feeling like I did my best, reliving the sight of the panel's pleased and impressed expressions. I'm more than ready to get into my car and go home and forget about all the pressure until the next one of these interviews pops up, when I will bring five copies of my birth certificate just to be safe.

"Ophelia!" Theo's voice calls out from behind me just as I

unlock my car doors.

I cringe and slowly turn around to see him running towards me. "Oh," I huff. "You're still here."

"How'd it go in there?" he pants as he shuffles over.

"Fine," I answer curtly, wishing he had just left after he handed the copy over to me.

"Thatta' girl!" he smiles, stopping just a few feet away. "Where you rushing off to now?"

"Home," I shoot back, having to hold back a groan. Why does he care where I'm rushing off to? Aside from when his vowed vengeance against the Elites wasn't on the line, he never once cared about where I was before. Why now?

"Ah," he nods, looking slightly wounded. "Well, listen. While you're here…why don't we grab some lunch? Ice cream? I want to celebrate!"

"There's nothing to celebrate," I grumble. "It's not like I got in. It was just an interview."

"You'll get in," he announces confidently. "Whether it's here or somewhere else, I know you'll have your pick of the best schools. I looked you up, you know. Saw the articles about your races and things from your last school. And some of your competitions with WJ Prep. You have quite an impressive record."

I stare at him blankly, feeling a twist in my gut at the thought of him researching me. I'm convinced his only real reason to do so would be for some ulterior motive. It was likely just so he could track me down and use me as a pawn in his battle against the Elites. One that he would just as soon throw out the moment I didn't serve him anymore.

"Thanks," I respond half-heartedly. "But I really should get back. Mom will be waiting."

"I'm sure she'll understand if you stay a little longer to catch up with me," he insists. "She's hoping you and I will get to know each other a little better."

I'm frozen as he stares expectantly. I want to get away from him as fast as possible, but he is right about my mom's high hopes for me to give him a chance. Maybe to relieve her guilt about him being my biological father. But her innocent optimism only makes me angrier.

"You're right. She has a lot of hopes for you being back in our lives," I bark. "But only because she doesn't know the whole story."

He recoils with a pitiful little grimace. "I deserve that," he offers. "And anything else you could say to me. I know…I wasn't around and then when I did show back up…It wasn't exactly under the best circumstances."

I laugh scornfully, thinking back on the split second I had to look him over for the first time when he showed up on the doorstep of Jameson manor just as I was running for my life. No sooner than I recognized his crooked smile he pulled up a gun and shot Thomas Jameson to death. Not to save my life, but to finish his own little wicked game of vengeance against the Elites.

"I may not be everything you hoped I would be," he continues.

"I didn't hope for anything about you at all!" I cut him off. "You weren't around, and I was prepared for it to stay that way. I figured if you cared about me at all, you would have never let so much time pass without finding me. Brendan has been around since I was ten and has been more of a father than you ever were. I'm glad things turned out the way they did." My voice cracks in exasperation as I rant, prompting me to turn back towards my car and pull the handle to get in. I refuse to let him see me get emotional.

"It's not so simple," he says quickly, stepping closer to keep me from leaving. "Didn't she ever tell you?" His brows raise. "I did try to see you, Ophelia. I may not be perfect, but I was prepared to be around for you. Everything that happened between your mom and I…it was too much. And still too painful for her when I tried to see you as a baby. She was afraid and I can't blame her."

I start to argue but stop myself. I can't imagine my mom refusing to let Theo see me without at least mentioning his attempts when I got older. Even if a parent is absent, knowing whether or not they tried makes a big difference in a young girl's life. But anger boils in my gut as I consider why she would be afraid to let him see me. He beat her. Of course, she was afraid of him.

Theo did think my mom had cheated on him, but it turns out that was just another stab from the Elites trying to put him in his place after he squandered so much of their money. Regardless, his reaction was inexcusable. Emmett may be fucked-up and I don't doubt that he would beat up the other dude in a heartbeat if I ever cheated on him, but he'd never lay a finger on me...right?

That thought catches in my throat as I remember all the times Emmett has harmed me, threatened me, and a long list of other offenses. He claims he had no choice under the pressure from his father and the other Elites. I quickly remind myself that they seem to have a knack for making good people do horrible things.

"Why do you think your mom is so insistent on us having a relationship now?" Theo says. "She feels guilty, I think, for shutting me out all those years before. She made a choice that should have been yours."

My inner conflict over Emmett has my guard down as he speaks, and I can feel his guilt trip taking hold. I look down at the envelope of documents in my bag. Deciding who is good or bad or what did or didn't happen is too much to process on the spot like this. But for now, Theo did save my ass at the last minute. The least I can do is have a quick lunch with the man.

"Fine," I groan. "I'll come with you. But not for too long. I want to get home before it starts getting dark."

He lights up before motioning for me to follow him back to his car. I can't help but feel paranoid that something terrible could come out of me being so trusting and riding off with him. I can't forget everything I do know about Theo. No matter what he says, if it were in his best interests to kill me, he'd do it in a heartbeat. And with people like him, there's always some larger game at play that I don't know the details of.

Things seem normal enough aside from the awkward silence as he drives me to a diner towards the center of town. I slowly start to relax, telling myself that this will be over before I know it. It's like Brendan's yearly family dinners with his senile grandparents. They're inconvenient and seem like a waste of time, but they go by fast and make everyone else really happy. I just have to grit my teeth and smile and get through this.

"I love this place," he says as he opens the front door for me.

A bell chimes as we step inside and a waitress greets him by name. He leads me to a corner booth, citing it as his usual spot. It's crazy to think he's been so close long enough to have a regular hangout spot with a preferred seat. It breaks into my resolve, making me wonder if he really has been trying to keep an eye on me all these years. Is that why he ended up so close to Jameson?

"Order a milkshake," he tells me as I look over the menu. "Doesn't matter what flavor you pick; it'll be the best one you ever have."

"The usual today, Theo?" the waitress chimes as she pulls a pen and pad from her apron. "And who's this young lady!?" Her eyes light up across me.

"This is my daughter, Ophelia," he beams. "She just had an interview over at the university. She runs track and is hoping to get a scholarship."

"Ophelia!" she sings back with wide eyes. "It's so good to see you here! I've heard so much about you!"

I'm too stunned to do anything but stare up at her wildly, blinking in shock. She takes our order and vanishes off into the rush behind the counter, and I can't help but notice the pleased look on Theo's face. I'm not sure if he's genuinely proud to show me off, or if he just knows I've been proven wrong in some small way.

"Did you pay her to say that?" I quip, only half-joking. I'm convinced Theo doesn't care enough to have ever mentioned me to anyone.

"How's Emmett?" he asks, ignoring my jab. "I heard about the Hendersons taking over the company. He got gypped."

"I'd think you'd know how he's doing," I remark bitterly. "I thought you two were good buddies. I know you have a tendency to meet up behind my back."

"Don't hold that against the boy," he grunts, looking annoyed that we even have to talk about it. "You two weren't even an item yet. He was just a poor kid in a fucked-up situation and so were you. He helped you in the only way he knew how."

"And who were you helping?" I sneer, fidgeting a plastic straw between my fingers. He sighs and lays his hands flat across the table, looking lost. It may be a ploy, but it works. I start to feel bad for holding onto my grudge so tightly and have to remember that isn't the point of this lunch. Laying into him will only make it worse for me. I know he doesn't have the answers or explanations I'm looking for, so it's better just to let it go. At least for now.

"But you're right," I add, trying to swallow down my frustrations. "He did get gypped. It's a shame he made the sacrifices he did and still got everything taken from him. He would have done amazing things with Jameson Automobiles. He was going to make it a legit, honest company." I stop myself from adding that that's more than Theo could ever dream of doing with anything in his life.

He nods and looks away. I see his wheels turning, likely over some new scheme. He never stops looking for some new way to get rich or take advantage of a situation. But he's interrupted by the arrival of our food. I do my best to participate in tense small talk as we chew through our burgers and fries.

"You were right," I concede as I sip the thick milkshake through my straw. "This is a really good shake."

"I told you!" he laughs proudly, as if he had made it himself. "Just think. If you get into that school, you'll be able to come here and have these all the time! Maybe we could even make it a regular thing."

My chest tightens at the thought. Me and Theo meeting up for regular lunches as if we have anything close to a normal father-daughter relationship. I could never let go of everything that's happened up until now to let that happen. Him living so close is one of the things that makes me not want to go to that school at all.

"I haven't made up my mind about where I'll go yet," I reply politely, thinking its more kindness than he deserves. "I applied a bunch of different places. All of the top collegiate track teams across the nation. Coach Granger will help me decide what's best for my career."

I almost hate to even bring Coach up to him. After what the Elites did to him and his family, I want to protect him in any way I can from Theo and people like him.

"Well, whatever he suggests or whatever you decide…you should be able to go wherever you want. You've worked hard and earned that much. And I know I haven't made it easy on you, when I was around just as much as when I wasn't," he admits. "Money shouldn't be a factor. I may not have the fortune I once did, but I'm certainly not hurting for anything and neither should you. Once you decide on a school, you just send me the bills."

"That won't be necessary," I shoot back, sounding a little snide. "With my grades and track record, Coach expects me to get plenty of full scholarship offers."

"But what if you don't get one from your top pick?" he suggests.

"Whatever scholarship money doesn't cover, I'll get a part-time job to pay for the rest," I shrug. "Plenty of people work to pay their way through college."

"Don't be so stubborn," he sighs in an irritated tone. "You're an athlete. You need to focus on training, not killing yourself to work and go to school full time when you don't have to. You'll need to keep your body in shape and keep your grades up. Why add the extra stress of a job if you don't have to?"

Rage starts rushing through me as he talks, sounding like such a concerned father all of a sudden. I told myself I'd stop being so resentful just for the sake of getting through this, but there's only so much I can take.

"And just how do you think being kidnapped last semester helped me?" I bark, staring him down intently. "Being held hostage? Threatened to be murdered? My life suddenly depending on my absentee father that I've never met who can't even bother to respond to the hostage notes."

"I had a plan," he hisses defensively, leaning over the table in a hushed tone. "You made it out of there, didn't you? Because *I* showed up."

"Is that what you tell yourself?" I sneer. "You were planning to kidnap me yourself. Maybe even kill me. Just so the Elites wouldn't have the chance to use me against you. If Emmett hadn't talked you into letting him take me as a part of your little agreement, how do I know you wouldn't have shot me just like you did Thomas Jameson?"

He sits back, running his hands over his suddenly tired face. Once again, I have to remind myself that he's not going to have the answers to satisfy me. If he did, he would have played them long before now.

"Look, just forget it," I add curtly, grabbing my bag to hint at how ready I am to get the hell out of here. "The past is the past or whatever. You can come around for these little dinners to ease your guilt and make my mom happy. I'll let the rest of it go enough to play along. And thanks for helping me out today, but beyond that...I don't need anything from you. I'm fine, okay?"

I'm too mad to care that he looks hurt, even if it means anything beyond hating that I can see him for what he really is. But I force myself to thank him again as he drops me off at my car to drive home. I'm more than ready to go back and be with the people who really care about me. The ones who were around long before he showed back up again.

# CHAPTER FIVE

BOOK 3

Everyone was excited to hear the interview went well, and my mom was especially excited to hear Theo was able to help in some way. I resisted the urge to ask her if what Theo said was true about her turning him away when I was younger. We have enough on our plates without letting any more of his drama seep between us. I trust that whatever she decided then was for the best. And she was so happy to know that I attempted to have another cordial meal with him that it almost made the whole ordeal worth it.

"Coach Granger thinks it might be one of our top choices," I explain to Emmet in excitement over lunch one day. "But…I don't know." He looks at me questioningly. "It's awfully close," I add with hesitation. "Just a couple hours away. I don't know if it's far enough from Jameson for me to feel comfortable."

He doesn't try to talk my fears down the way Coach did. He's just as eager as I am to get the hell away from all of this.

"Well, the Theo complications aside, I'm excited for you," he beams as he chews through a sandwich. "My college girl! Wherever you decide to go, it'll be great. A whole new life for us!" He leans over and plants a playful, sloppy kiss on my cheek, getting mayonnaise on me.

"Gross!" I squeal out in laughter, pushing him away.

We both freeze as we catch a glimpse of Malcolm and the others glaring at us, as if any momentary sign of happiness from us is an affront to them. We reign in the display a little, but the closer we get to freedom, the less daunting the new Elites seem.

"Soon we'll be far away from that kind of bull shit," I grumble, nodding slightly towards them.

"How do we know there won't be a new version of the Elites waiting for you at college?" Emmett asks grimly.

I cut my eyes over to him, saddened by how little perspective he has. He's never known anything outside the fucked-up bubble of Jameson. He's plagued with a very real inability to imagine any other kind of life.

"Movies," I quip. "There's plenty of stories of college and life that don't involve corrupt millionaires or death threats or hostages or any of the crazy scenarios that are so common around here."

"There's plenty that do have those things though," he defends himself as if it all really could be so normal.

I want to remind him that those are usually things people dream up for excitement or entertainment and that the average person doesn't experience them firsthand, especially before the age of twenty. But I don't want to steal away any weird sense of normalcy he has left to cling to. More than that, I'm ready to talk and think about anything but the Elites.

"I don't have practice today," I tell him, grabbing his hand under the table as I raise my eyebrows suggestively. "Want to go back to your place?"

We've both been busy with the start of school, and I'm eager to get him into bed to blow off some steam.

"I have something to take care of after school," he replies, looking disappointed. But he quickly recovers and leans in close to my ear with the hum of his deep voice that drives me mad. "But soon enough I'll get you alone and make up for lost time."

His hand snakes up my thigh, teasing dangerously close between my legs, causing me to tense up with desire. My cheeks blush as I look around to see if anyone is watching. But truthfully, I want him so bad I'm tempted to drag him off to a closet before next period.

We run out of time before I have a chance to suggest sneaking away and before I know it, we're both rushing off to our next classes. The Elites are gathered in their usual huddle in the hall, taking up more space than they need as a show of dominance.

"Who's that girl?" Emmett asks, nodding to the brunette.

"Bridgett," I reply. "She's in track. Do you know anything about her?"

He shakes his head no and we quickly look away before they catch us staring. I'm still puzzled over the fact that she didn't freak out on me at practice the other day. Whatever the new Elites are busying themselves with these days, it seems to have been enough to distract them. I expected some sort of backlash for my show of power in the hall the other week, but it has yet to happen.

"I'll see you after school," Emmett says, leaning in to kiss me. I notice him shooting one last look over to the Elites before he walks away.

I can tell he's just as confused by the silence as I am. We expected them to come back with force. Malcolm has to prove himself as their new ringleader after all. Especially after I acted so defiantly on two occasions, even if one was only an accident. But things have been chillingly calm. It almost has us more on edge than we would be if they were attacking like we expected.

The rest of the school day is lost in a haze of taking notes and preparing for exams. With the Elites mostly staying out of our way, I can focus my energy where it's needed. My transcripts may be good enough leading up to now, but it's all worthless if anything happens to screw up my last few months of high school.

After my last class, Emmett and I meet up in our usual spot near the lockers. He sweeps me up in a slow, deep kiss that only makes me more impatient for some alone time with him. We're interrupted by a bouncy girl who bounds passed us to put a flyer up on the wall. She tells other students around us that tickets for prom go on sale tomorrow but intentionally ignores us. Likely something she's been instructed to do by Malcolm and the others.

Senior Prom. Another totally normal high school experience that I haven't had time to think about since coming here. I immediately push down any urge to go. If the Elites would even allow us to attend, I doubt it'd be something Emmett would want to bother with.

"I'll get our tickets during lunch tomorrow," he announces casually, catching me by surprise.

"What?" I gape. "We're going?"

He looks down at me and wrinkles his brows. "Of course, we're going," he answers. "Why do you look so shocked?"

"I…I don't know…," I stammer. "I guess I just thought… that you wouldn't want to. Or…that we couldn't."

"Couldn't?" he asks in confusion.

"I wouldn't be surprised if they didn't sell you tickets," I explain. "Do you really think Malcolm and the others will let us go?" My face drops as a scarier thought pops into my head. "And if they do, you don't think they'll try to do something to ruin it for us?"

I shudder, thinking back to Lily's story about what they did to her at the dance years ago. Only that time, Emmett was one of the Elites. I don't like to think of him as one of them, but at least it gives us the advantage of him having a pretty good guess at what they may or may not try to pull off.

"Knowing how conceited Bernadette and Malcolm are, they'll probably be so wrapped up in it for themselves they won't even have time to care about us," he insists, not seeming worried.

I want to give in and feel a little excited, but I'm not entirely convinced. "You really think so?"

"A chance to get dressed up in expensive shit and parade around in front of the whole school? They wouldn't pass that up for anything," he scoffs. "I'm not going to go try to win prom king or anything, but they'll let us go. I know that much at least."

I catch the slightest glimmer of something in his eyes, even through his optimism. Up until a few months ago, he was on track to be prom king with Vivian as his queen. It may be silly, meaningless high school stuff that we'll forget about by this time next year, but it's just another reminder of how everything has changed for him.

"So?" he asks expectantly, snapping me back to attention.

"So…what?"

He smirks, looking somewhat shy. "Will you be my date?" he clarifies. "Will go with me to prom?"

It may be a moment that I had entirely forgotten to dream about ever since I started at WJ Prep, but all at once I remember that before this, I was a normal teenage girl with a typical life. Starting high school brought on giddy anticipation for a slew of milestone moments just like this. My hot, dreamy boyfriend asking me to prom.

I can feel the hormones and excitement surge through me as I look into his piercing eyes filled with the promises of a night to remember. Briefly, we get to be just two regular high school students feeling giddy over something as ordinary as prom.

"Of course I'll go with you," I snicker, wondering if he could ever really think I'd say no.

He swiftly slides his hand to the small of my back, yanking me in for an earnest kiss as if he really was surprised by my answer. I lose myself there for a moment, once again being reminded of how long its been since we've been able to sneak off to be alone.

"I'm going to make it perfect for you," he promises with a smile the moment his lips part from mine. "The whole works. A fancy dinner and limo and all."

I chew my lip with worry as he brightly announces his plans while we walk hand in hand down the hall. "Wait," I stop suddenly, cutting him off. "Emmett...," All at once, I shrink, realizing I don't know how to express my concerns without offending him. But he's wide-eyed and waiting. It's too late now. "Well, it's just," I continue hesitantly, almost in a whisper. "Money...How will you afford all of that?"

A look of astonishment washes over him as if he had momentarily forgotten about the loss of his fortune. He is still pretty new to living like the rest of us, after all. But he's quick to recover. "Don't worry about it," he assures me, stiffening with a wounded sort of defensiveness. "You just get all dolled up the way you want and let me take care of the rest. I wouldn't promise you the perfect night if I wasn't prepared to follow through with it." His voice darkens some. "Anyway, after every-thing...you deserve this."

"Any night with you is perfect," I insist, hating how corny it sounds, even if it is how I feel. "We could show up in rags after eating McDonalds for all I care. I'm just excited to be going with you."

He smiles slightly but doesn't look amused or relieved by my modesty at all. Emmett has had four years of his own dreams and expectations for these last few months of high school. I can only imagine what kind of expensive splendor he always assumed he'd have on his prom night. But suddenly it seems that affording even a fraction of that is some new mission for him to prove he can make it just fine without his family's fortune.

While he drifts off into a distant, worried stare, likely scheming over ways to make money, I try to force myself to do as he asked. I do my best to forget about how it will all happen and just fantasize about showing up that night on Emmett's arm, both of us looking better than ever, as I rest my head on his shoulder and dance the night away. Even when I did have time to think about these things, I didn't think I cared this much. But now that it's actually happening, I feel like I could burst with excitement.

We're lost in our separate thoughts as we walk hand in hand out of the school. He stops at the edge of the parking lot and pulls me in for another kiss.

"I've got to go," he says reluctantly. "Remember, I told you I had something to take care of."

"Oh yeah," I nod, yanking him back down for one more kiss. "I'll talk to you later," I smile, wishing I didn't have to let him go.

I still have a big grin plastered on my face as I dig my keys out of my purse and walk to my car. But all of that fades as it comes into view. I see what should be my car, but it's almost disfigured beyond recognition. I even look around for a minute, thinking I've made a mistake.

"*Fuck*," I murmur to myself, as a tight lump forms in my throat.

The red paint is keyed and chipped down to a patchy gray mess, and over that every foul word you could think of is spray painted in layers. Cunt, whore, slut, bitch, and so on and so on. Any insult you could dream up. A couple of the windows are even cracked in with big circles, as if someone took a baseball bat to them. The only thing that isn't completely fucked-up about it are the tires. By some miracle, they neglected to flatten them.

I look around cluelessly as if someone would help or tell me how this happened. But even the security camera hanging from the nearby streetlight means nothing. I know exactly who did this, and whether there's footage or not, no one is going to do anything about it. I knew the Elites had been too quiet. I should have figured they were waiting to strike just when I let my guard down.

With a heavy sigh, I look around one more time, confirming my assumption that no one is going to help or offer me a ride. Emmett is nowhere to be seen, probably already gone.

"Well, I guess it's still drivable," I shrug as I unlock the doors. "Even if it's fucked-up in every other way."

But my heart sinks even more as I realize the doors aren't locked. They got inside somehow, and the seats are shredded as proof. As I open the driver's side door, I quickly realize cutting into the seats is the least of what they did to the interior. An awful ammonia smell slaps me in the face, causing me to gag and turn away as my hand rushes to cover my mouth and nose.

Urine. They've managed to drench the seats in urine. I immediately think I should call for someone to come and pick me up, but then I realize one way or another my car will have to make it home for clean up and repairs. And the cost of a tow truck is the last thing any of us need right now. I have prom to save up for after all.

I reluctantly press my fingers to the seat, trying to determine if it's still wet. There's a lingering dampness that makes me want to puke, but I force myself to accept that I have to get in this thing and drive it home. I brace myself and pull my sweater over my head to lay it across any part of the seat that will have to touch my body. As I get in and start it up, I'm quickly close to vomiting again as my fingers clutch the gearshift and land in something wet and sticky.

*"Chewing gum,"* I groan as I pull my fingers back to look. "Disgusting…But I guess not the worst thing they could have stuck under there."

The longer I sit in the car, the worse the smell gets, and I'm terrified to find out what other kinds of surprises are waiting for me in here. I have to talk myself out of calling someone all over again. Sticking to my guns, I flick away the chewed-up gum, using the passenger seat to wipe any lingering bits of it away. The interior is already fucked anyway. I check a few other spots where nasty things could be planted and finally put the car into reverse.

It's disgusting, and maybe I'm being too stubborn, but driving this car home is almost like another act of defiance. Once again, they tried to stop me, but they won't. I refuse to let them, even if it means driving home sitting in urine-soaked seats. Knowing them, they're hiding somewhere nearby just to watch my mortified reaction. I can't resist flipping my middle finger out the window as I speed off.

# CHAPTER SIX

## BOOK 3

I'm feeling pretty smug in my determination to drive my destroyed, urine-soaked car home. Nothing can stop me. I'll show those Elites they can't bring me down. I turn my stereo up full blast and speed off down the winding roads away from the school.

I get a little overzealous and hit a curvy hill too quickly, shrinking my feeling of invincibility. The car handles around it fine, but I decide to bring it down a notch and press my foot to the brakes to slow down a little before the next sharp turn.

I'm startled by the give of the pedal. It sinks straight to the floor with no reaction in the car. Without thinking I raise my foot and lower it again, but to my horror, it drops in empty motions over and over and my car doesn't even slow down a little. My heart pounds as the realization sets in that I have no way of slowing down and I am flying downhill, quickly approaching a series of sharp turns that I'll never make at this speed.

Panic brings tears to my eyes, blurring my vision, as my foot slams to the brake as hard as it can. Each time, there's just an empty push of air. The breath in my lungs becomes just as empty as I fully accept that the brakes are useless, and I hit another abrupt bend in the road. I barely manage to navigate around it before there is another one. The car is going way too fast and starts to shake with a frightening rattle.

With a loud bang that vibrates through my entire body, it

flies off the edge of the road, shredding against rocks and trees. It comes to such a sudden stop that my head slams into the steering wheel just before the airbags go off.

The airbag slams my body back against the seat with a stinging force that leaves me completely disoriented. I feel like I've been punched in the chest and my head is dizzy and aching. I blink through my blurry vision and try to look around, realizing that at least the car is stopped. But the hood is smoking and squealing, and I can hear the drips and pops coming from underneath, letting me know that it's completely fucked.

I lean forward to try and get out, but the entire car creaks and moans, wobbling in the air with the shifting weight of my body. My vision quickly grows sharp as I look straight ahead with wide, terrified eyes. The car is wedged over the side of the cliff so far that the front two tires are hanging in the air. I try to move again, more slowly this time, and the whole thing see-saws, threatening to go flying off the edge.

My hands are shaking as I sob to myself for a second, still in shock. I have to get out of here. Being more careful this time, I try to sit up enough to get a grip on my seat belt, but the car groans and shifts forward again, this time creaking forward even more. I barely hear my own scream as it lunges toward the cliff-side with a steep drop down over giant rocks and trees.

There's a loud crack as the car barely catches on something underneath, maybe a tree. Whatever it is, it momentarily stops it from rolling any further. But the car is at a full downward tilt now and wobbling more with every tiny movement I make. Even the faint weight of my labored breaths seem to be pushing it closer to the edge.

I slowly and carefully inch my hand toward the seat belt buckle, but like the brakes, nothing happens when I push down. The belt is still pulled tight across me from the crash, but the release button does nothing no matter how hard I frantically push it. My urgency causes me to get sloppy, not being careful enough about how much I'm moving, and the car screeches forward another few inches. I freeze in terror.

Now without me moving at all, the car continues giving into gravity an inch at a time, as I accept that the seat belt isn't going to unbuckle. I take the risk of trying to wiggle out of it, but it's too tight across my lap and I only make the car teeter even more. A loud snap echoes around me, causing me to take a deep breath as if I'm about to crash into water. But there's no water below. There's just a steep drop to certain death.

Still deaf to my own screams and cries, even though I feel them burning through my chest, I try to come to terms with the fact that I am about to die.

A gush of air from my left snaps me out of it just as a pair of hands fly into the car around me and make desperate attempts to loosen the belt enough to rip me out. With a sharp tug to my arms, I feel the seat leave the bottom of my thighs. I go flying through the air, tightly wrapped in someone's arms, while the sound of whining, twisting metal cries out from a few feet away.

When we hit the ground, I shoot straight up, not fully aware of what's just happened. The cracking leaves beneath me give the assurance that I'm back on solid ground again, but I look up just in time to see the car slide over the edge and crash down below with a terrible sound.

My chest heaves with adrenaline as my eyes shoot up, finding Coach Granger's face towering above me.

"Are you okay!?" he huffs.

But I'm speechless. My eyes tear up again, and I am completely unable to wrap my head around anything that just happened enough to form words. It all happened so fast, but in eerie slow motion at the same time.

"I could have died," I murmur breathlessly as I stare at the spot where my car was lodged just moments ago.

"What the hell were you doing going so fast!?" he scolds, his voice booming with anger.

In shock, I have to ask myself the same question at first. Then it all comes flooding back to me. The Elites. They did this. I thought they had just graffitied my car all to hell, but they obviously tampered with the brakes too. And possibly the seat belt.

"Malcolm," I stammer out finally through sharp breaths. "And the others. They keyed and slashed my car. The brakes...they..."

Suddenly I'm overcome with the urge to bolt to the edge of the overlook to try and see my car. Coach Granger races behind me, holding my arms to keep me steady on the edge. It takes what feels like forever to finally spot it. It's so far down it's almost a spec, and what I can see of it is completely crushed and folded in on itself. Just as I feared when I was still trapped inside and dangling there, I would have never survived that fall.

"Those bastards tried to kill me!" I shriek, half hyperventilating as I stare down at the mangled mess below.

Coach Granger pulls me in tight and drags me away. He shuffles me into the passenger seat of his car. Once I'm sitting inside, I become aware of the pain shooting through my head and limbs all over again. My fingers touch lightly against the wet ache on my forehead, and when I pull them back, I see they're bloody.

"We need to get you to the hospital," he says as he watches me with concern.

"I'm fine," I heave in disbelief.

"Doesn't hurt to get checked out," he insists. "That's a pretty nasty gash. You could need stitches. Anyway, you don't want some hidden injury popping up next time you start running laps."

I laugh lightly at Coach's focused concern on my ability to run track, even after my near-death experience. But he's right. As much as I'd love to pretend none of that just happened, I need to see a doctor. And beyond that, my car is gone. Completely crushed and mangled. Which is just what I need as I near the end of my senior year.

Coach drives me to the hospital for a check-up, where they determine I don't need stitches. But they do give me a prescription of muscle relaxers from the aches and pains, which I can expect to be worse tomorrow. I'm waiting to be officially dismissed when two police officers walk into my room. Jameson police are terrifying to me. They're corrupt and with all the changes in the structure of the Elites lately, it's impossible to know whose side they're on.

"Ophelia Lopez?" one of the officers questions as Coach takes a cross-armed stance in the corner. He knows all too well about the corruption of local police and is just as skeptical as I am. "We're sorry to hear about what happened to you today. Mr. Granger filled us in, but we'd like to ask you a few questions if you're feeling up to it."

"Okay," I answer blankly.

He nods and pulls out a pad of paper and a pen from his coat pocket. "He told us you suspected someone tampered with your car before driving it. Can you tell us what made you think that?"

"Ha!" I laugh out accidentally. "I didn't just suspect it. It was obvious. They spray painted it, keyed it, and shredded the seats! I thought I could get it home to be fixed, but when I started driving…the brakes wouldn't work. Then the seat belt was jammed."

"Was it an older car?" he asks suggestively.

I have to fight back a spark of rage before answering. "What does that have to do with it? You're saying it was just a coincidence that it was vandalized right before I discovered the brakes weren't working?"

He shifts his feet, looking slightly offended by my tone. "Well, if you're so certain someone tampered with the brakes, who do you think might have done such a thing? Has anyone threatened you in any way? Someone at school maybe?"

Once again, I can't contain my laughter as I consider all the ways in which the Elites have threatened me since my first day at this school. I try to keep it together. My laughter trails off into suppressed snickering as I cut my eyes over to Coach Granger, unsure how honest I should be. He nods his head in encouragement, pushing me to tell them more.

"Malcolm Henderson," I blurt finally. "It's a long story, but I know he hates me. Him and the whole clique he runs in." I try to avoid using the term Elites. If these officers aren't already bought by the new leaders of the circle, the phrase alone will scare them off from actually doing anything about this.

"Malcolm Henderson?" he echoes in surprise. "Didn't he and Liam Henderson just take over Jameson Automobiles?"

"From my boyfriend, Emmett Jameson. Yes. He's the one who rightfully inherited it," I shoot back firmly.

I see the wheels turning in the officer's eyes. He perks up and tries to pin down what question to ask next. But just as his lips part, the officer behind him whispers something in his ear. They mutter things back and forth for a moment, and finally I see his pen click shut before he puts it back into his pocket along with the notepad.

"Thank you for your time, Ophelia," he announces suddenly. "We'll let you know if we have any more questions."

I'm not surprised, but the blatant calculation of it all enrages me. They're obviously trying to get a handle on who's off-limits around here now, rather than pursuing all crimes and criminals equally.

"That's it?" I huff. "Will there be any consequences for Malcolm over this?"

I notice Coach Granger's eyes darken. I should know the answer to that. We had DNA evidence that Malcolm maliciously planted heroin into the hands of his recovering addict son and nothing happened to him. He's definitely not going down for this.

"We'll look into it," the cop assures me half-heartedly, already halfway out the door.

"Yeah, I'm sure," I grumble sarcastically, thinking he won't even hear it. But he stops abruptly in the doorway and whips back around, looking angry.

"Look, Ms. Lopez," he snaps. "I understand this was very scary for you. But the fact is we have no way of proving who vandalized your car or if they were also the reason the brakes malfunctioned. There's a big difference between vandalism and attempted murder, and we can't make that leap with no evidence. Your car is at the bottom of a valley, completely crushed. I just don't think we're going to get the result you're hoping for out of this."

I'm quiet as I process everything. I know part of what he's saying is true, but I also know it all comes down to how hard they're willing to try. And with Malcolm being the accused culprit, we all know they're simply not going to try that hard.

"Thank you," I finally mutter, knowing it's useless to argue with them. With that, he finally turns and walks away without another word. Once they're gone, I turn back to Coach. "This is bullshit. You know Malcolm and the Elites were behind this."

"I'm just glad you're okay," he offers, his eyes still haunted by the memory of what Malcolm has put him through.

"Ophelia! Oh my god!" my mom's voice cries out from the doorway.

My mom's worried voice and face instantly remind me of the car accident that Emmett and I got into last year. I may never know what the Elites expected him to do to me that day. Whatever it was wasn't good, and in my desperate attempts to get away from him, he slammed the car into a streetlight. And somehow that's what led to our first kiss, right here in this hospital.

My mom rushes over and showers me in kisses and hugs, each one causing me to wince in pain.

"Mom! Stop!" I rasp as I cringe.

"Sorry, I was just so worried when I got the call about your accident!" She cups my face in her hands, looking down at me with a relieved expression. "Coach Granger, thank you so much for everything."

I listen to her tone and realize whoever called her must not have told her the whole story. She is obviously thanking him for picking me up and driving me to the hospital but has no idea he saved my life. And maybe that's for the best. I'm learning to accept that my mom may never know the full story of anything in Jameson.

"I'm ready to go home," I moan as I brace my stuff body against the back of the bed, eagerly pushing myself to my feet.

She wraps her arms around me and guides me out of the room. Coach Granger says goodbye at the front doors of the hospital. I almost want to run after him. The corruption of this town has a special way of making you feel alone, making you want to flock to the arms of anyone who fully understands it. That's part of what brought Emmett and me together after all.

The Elites have threatened to kill me plenty of times. Thomas Jameson and the Hendersons have all put guns to my head. The ways I've been injured and humiliated have almost been as bad as the death threats. But they've never come this close to actually killing me before. If Coach Granger hadn't shown up on the side of the road like that, I would be dead right now.

The harsh reality of it makes me feel sick as I press my aching forehead to the window of my mom's car, relishing in the coolness of it against my skin. All I want is to graduate and get the hell out of Jameson, away from the Elites and WJ Prep. But I'm starting to wonder if they'll ever let that happen.

My father and I are the ultimate insult to them, after all. Between his past transgressions against them and the murder of Thomas Jameson. That only left Emmett standing in their way of ultimate power, and he's hand in hand with me. Plus, I've never been good at bowing down to any of them the way everyone else does. I swallow down a hard lump in my throat as I begin to wonder…if maybe I will have to start treating them the way everyone else does just to survive. Like unquestionable gods.

## CHAPTER SEVEN

### BOOK 3

Between the muscle relaxers and the exhaustion from my adrenaline crash, I sleep like a rock. When I wake up the next morning, I somehow briefly forget about the whole thing. Enough that I spend a minute or two wondering where my purse is before I remember that it's down at the bottom of a cliff.

As it hits me, there's a knock at my bedroom door. "Ophelia?" my mom calls out, just as she barges in. "Are you ready?"

"No, I just got up," I reply, rubbing my face in confusion. "Ready for what?"

"I'll have to drop you off at the DMV so you can get a new license," she says. "But we have to hurry. I can't be too much later for work than I already will be."

"But…school," I murmur through my grogginess.

"You'll have to miss part of the day," she insists. "You can catch a bus to WJ Prep when you're done. They're only open weekdays and you'll need your ID."

"For what?" I sneer. "It's not like I have a car to drive."

She ignores my pity party and disappears down the hall, but I know it's her way of rushing me. If I want to sulk, I'll have to do it in the car. We have to go. I throw on some clothes and follow along. As she drives me to the DMV, I reach for my cell phone five or six times, thinking I need to message Emmett, only to remember it's in my mangled car right along with my driver's license.

"Did anyone tell Emmett what happened?" I ask her, amazed that I was too tired to think about it the night before.

"Yes, I talked to him last night," she assures me. "He was worried sick, like the rest of us. But I told him you were okay and that you'd be at school later in the day. He wanted to come over, but I told him you were asleep and needed your rest."

I'm suddenly overwhelmed with the need to be in his arms, and I'm almost angry that she didn't let him burst in on my sleep in the middle of the night. Aside from Coach Granger, he's the only other person I really feel safe with right now.

She drops me off at the DMV, feeling completely naked without my phone or anything else. I can only hope that I don't have any problems and that I catch the bus afterward because otherwise I'm screwed. It's at least a three-mile walk to any place where I could reach someone to come pick me up, and everyone will be at work or school.

Those Elites really do know how to fuck a person over. I'm sure they'd be happier if I died, but survival means I'm stuck facing down all of these inconveniences. I guess I should be grateful for. But it's all overshadowed by the fact that if Malcolm and the others tried to kill me once, who's to say they won't try again?

Thankfully, I get my new license with no problems. I catch the bus to school in time to make the last couple of class periods. I manage to meet with teachers for the classes I missed that morning, pass a test I should have studied for last night, and survive the school day without any more brushes with death.

I barely have time to see its Emmett as I meet up with him at the end of the day. The moment he sees me, he rushes up to me and pulls me in close, squeezing so tight I can barely breathe. The moment he lets go he crashes his lips into mine, reminding me how badly we need to sneak away together as soon as possible.

"I'm so glad you're okay," he says passionately, pressing his forehead to mine. "Your mom wouldn't let me come over last night. I almost drove over anyway and snuck in through the window."

"You should have," I smile. But really, I wonder if I would have slept right through it.

"I want to kill those fuckers," he fumes suddenly, pulling away from me with clenched teeth and seething anger. "I can't believe they did that to you."

"Well, the police don't seem to think we have any way of proving they did it," I shrug.

His eyes cut over to me, full of as much disbelief as mine were when I first talked to the police. But there's also a look of acceptance. He knows as well as I do how things work around here, and we're better off not holding our breath for the new Elites to ever suffer any consequences for their actions. Conveniently, all the evidence is crashed down in the valley anyway. Right where I would be lying right now if it weren't for Coach Granger.

"Well, all that matters is that you're okay," he softens, pressing his lips to my cheek again. "I don't know what I would've done, Ophelia…if…"

"Shhh," I whisper into his ear. "Don't think about that. What are you doing right now? Let's get out of here. I need to see you…like, *really* see you…alone…" I playfully trail my fingers down the front of his pants, teasing between his legs.

"Don't you have practice?" he asks reluctantly.

"Shit!" I remember suddenly. "You're right. Ugh…I want to skip it. I'm sore and I'd rather be with you."

"You better not," he insists, looking just as disappointed as me. "You're in the home stretch now and you need to be in tip-top shape for all those scouts that have been sniffing around."

"I know, you're right," I sigh.

We linger there getting in as many long, deep kisses as we can before I force myself to leave him to go to practice. Despite my aching joints, I do surprisingly well. I figure it's from all the anger boiling in my veins. It pushes me to fly past all the other girls on the team. I make a special point to show up the brunette who is one of the Elite's newest members.

Coach Granger is nice enough to give me a ride home. But when I get there, Brendan and my mom are in a panicked state of planning. They can't afford to get me a new phone or a new car right away, and their work schedules prevent them from being able to drive me around everywhere until we can afford everything. I assure them Emmett will help at times they can't, and there's Coach too. As for money, I suggest getting a job, but they insist that the only things I should be focusing on right now are school, exams, and track.

Somehow, we manage to figure it out, but each day I feel like more of a burden to everyone. I'm feeling particularly bummed out one day as I step out of my last class and pull out my cheap refurbished flip phone to text Emmett. I thought he'd take me home, but then I remember he said he'd be busy this afternoon. With no other choice, I walk to the bus stop and wait. By the time I finally arrive home, I'm angry to see my mom's car sitting in the driveway. She could've saved me at least a half-hour by coming to get me if she was free.

But I quickly realize why she didn't pick me up when I step inside the house. I find her at the kitchen table with none other than my good old dad, Theo, sitting across from her. Great, I think. I'm already in a terrible mood. This is just what I need.

"What the hell are you doing here?" I blurt out, too tired to play nice.

"Ophelia!" my mom scolds. "Language! Please!"

Theo just smirks. "That's okay, Lala. I guess it is still a shock to see me pop up, which is my own fault."

A bitter, suppressed laugh sneaks out of me. He still hasn't answered my question, and I'm in no mood for any of this.

"Ophelia, honey. Come sit down," my mom beckons, making this little meeting of theirs sound important, which only makes me more nervous.

"What's going on?" I ask impatiently as I join them at the table.

She looks to Theo who nods and pulls a slender white box from his pocket. He slides it across the table into my hands.

"What's this?" I raise a brow at him, feeling skeptical.

"Open it," he commands with a grin.

I pull off the thin lid and gasp at the sight of it. A brand-new smartphone. I'm instantly excited and imagine tossing my old flip phone into the fireplace. But it all fades quickly as I remember who handed the box to me. I look up at Theo who has a huge, smug smile plastered across his face. He's getting way too much satisfaction from rushing in to help when I'm in no position to say no. It irritates me so much that, for a moment, I forget my mom is sitting next to us. I slap the lid back on and slide the box right back to him.

"Ophelia," my mom gasps in disappointment and embarrassment.

"Thanks, but no thanks," I bark.

"I appreciate your independence," he responds slowly, biting back anger. "But you need a phone, Ophelia. One that can access email and other things. Now more than ever while you're deciding where you'll go to college and taking your final tests. Graduating. People need to be able to get in touch with you."

"The flip phone works fine," I quip back stubbornly. "We've made it this far without your help, Theo. We'll be okay without your handouts."

My mom lets out a heavy sigh, gearing up to lecture me. But Theo raises his hand to silence her and gets ready for his own speech. I hate seeing them together like this. Like two parents working together. Which I guess is what they are, but I still have a hard time seeing Theo as anything beyond a sperm donor.

"It's not for you. It's for me," he explains, almost looking choked up. "I can't do anything about the past, but I do think about it all the time. All those years I let go by without making more of an effort to see you. To help you two while you struggled…"

"It's fine," I cut him off. "Brendan helped. We didn't need you."

"As I was saying," his voice tightens. "I can't do anything to take all that back, but I do owe you. I owe you more than I could ever repay, but the least I can do is help you now like I should have been helping all this time. Take the phone, Ophelia. And more than that, I'd like to give you a new car."

"What!?" I shriek, feeling like someone knocked the wind out of me. "A new car!?"

"Well, new for you," he adds. "It's used, but in great condition. All ready for you to drive."

I'm filled with so many conflicting things that I don't know what to say. On the one hand, Theo is right. He does owe us. And since he's so insistent on showing up now and redeeming himself somehow, I might as well use it to my benefit. It's not like I asked him to do any of this. And living without a decent phone or car has been hell.

But I also wonder if he knows what really happened to my old car. If he knows the Elites tried to kill me. He can't, not by hearing the story from my mom. I never would have been targeted by them in the first place had Theo not been blacklisted by them all those years ago. Or even if he would have just let things be instead of coming after them for revenge. In that light, it's really his fault I don't have a car right now in the first place.

"Come outside," Theo begs suddenly.

"Why?" I shoot back, my mind still racing.

He doesn't answer. He just heads for the front door with my mom following behind. I hang back for a moment, taking a deep, frustrated breath. I don't want to go with them, but I'm not sure it's worth arguing.

Reluctantly, I peel myself from my seat and huff out the front door. Theo and my mom are waiting in the driveway. The moment I round the corner, the garage door starts to rattle. Behind it is sitting a shiny new car. It's incredibly tempting and even has one of those big corny bows tied around it. I admire the sheen of the red paint job, and the fact that it isn't keyed, spray-painted with obscenities or drenched in mystery bodily fluids. Most importantly, it's not crushed on the side of a mountain.

"It's very nice," I admit quietly with my jaw tightened.

"It certainly is," my mother chimes in. "Could you give us just a moment, Theo?"

"Of course," he replies before strolling away down the sidewalk.

"Mom, I'm sorry. I just don't…," I start before she even has a chance to lay into me. But she raises a finger swiftly, demanding me to be quiet.

"I know, Ophelia," she shoots back sternly. "I know this is uncomfortable for you. I raised you to be independent. And unfortunately, I also raised you believing you should hate Theo. But things change. People change. He's trying to make amends. Why not give him a chance?"

I squirm under her gaze, immediately thinking of about a hundred reasons she's unaware of that more than justify not giving Theo a chance. But once again, I'm struck down by how hopeful and eager she looks.

"I'm not asking you to love him or be best friends with him," she continues. "Just let him help us this one time. We need it. Brendan and I already talked about it, and if he has the means to provide these things for you, we should let him. Like he said, he owes it to you. And you really don't owe him anything in return, except to say thank you."

I let out an exasperated groan as I accept that she's going to force me to do this, one way or another. And the more of a fit I throw about it, I'm just making myself look like a brat. No matter how good my reasons are. But I know Theo. At least I know how greedy and calculating he is. And she's wrong about nothing being owed to him in return. That's not how he operates. All of this is for an end goal, and sooner or later he'll expect all of us to pay up.

Then an exciting realization hits me. Taking the car and phone would make Brendan and my mom feel better. It'd be a huge weight off of their shoulders. But as for me…just as soon as I agree to take the things, Theo will leave, and I will be free. In my new car. I could drive over to Emmett's before dinner and get him into bed. A need that has been so terribly neglected for a while now.

"Okay," I announce. "You're right, Mom. I'm in no position to turn it down."

She smiles and nudges me over to Theo, who's kicking little rocks around on the pavement up ahead. I march over, burning into him with a knowing glare. He knows this is just a small part of a much bigger conversation that we can't have right now with Mom around. But for now, I'm going to do whatever it takes to make her happy. And then I'm going to go get laid. Finally.

"Thank you," I call out to him as I walk closer, but my expression does not match the sentiment.

"It's my pleasure," he grins, ignoring the anger written all over my face. "Every teenage girl needs a car and a phone. And it's not just about finishing high school. You'll need them for college too."

I nod my head and bite my lip. I don't know what to do next. Even if it would delight my mom, there's no way in hell I'm going to hug this man. But a handshake feels awkward too. Mostly I just want the keys so I can go speeding off. If I'm following through with this, I want to take full advantage of the opportunities it affords me.

"Would you like to stay for dinner?" my mom yells from over my shoulder.

"I have a study date with Emmett!" I shout back instantly.

"I'll get going," he answers so quietly that only I can hear. He slides his hands into his pockets and looks at me with a humble, bashful expression. He looks sorry for everything, but I still think it's all just an act. Guys like Theo don't change overnight. But for once, at least I have something to show for it besides a bunch of father issues and the trauma of being held hostage at gunpoint.

And those are all the things it feels like I'm driving far, far away from as I hop into my new car and take off down the road. Only after carefully testing the brakes, of course.

# CHAPTER EIGHT

BOOK 3

I park my new car in front of Emmett's apartment and try to push down any resentment I feel towards it as I hop out and lock the doors. It's a favor to my mom. Being the bigger person. Or any number of other excuses I make for it, but nothing seems to shake the sinking feeling in my gut that comes from taking anything from Theo.

But I do my best to shake it all from my mind as I knock on Emmett's door. This last semester has had a rough start for both of us and I am more than ready to forget it all for a little while.

He looks surprised to see me when he answers the door. His lips part, likely to ask how I got here, but I immediately crash my lips to his and push him inside, slamming the door behind us. I roll my tongue into his mouth, not giving him the chance to talk. Soon he melts into our kiss and matches my urgency, squeezing my ass as he pulls me in closer. We fumble through his mostly bare apartment, frantically pulling at each other's clothes.

Somewhere in the shuffle, the backs of my thighs find their way up against a countertop. Or a table or some kind of flat surface. I don't really know or care. I just know it's been too long and I need him inside of me as quickly as possible. He grips me from behind and hoists me up onto the surface before quickly snaking his fingers between my legs. He doesn't even bother sliding my panties off. He quickly swipes the thin, wet fabric to the side and slips in.

Pushing his tongue deep into my mouth, his fingers caress me, with one thumb circling around my sensitive folds. I am already shaking with need by the time he starts kissing down my neck and chest, biting at my nipples through my shirt. I've already lost my bra some time after charging him at the door. He sucks and licks at them through the fabric until he grows impatient and slides his palms underneath, stretching around them with a firm squeeze. Soon the shirt is flying over my head, our lips barely parting for a second as he quickly tosses it aside.

His tongue sneaks across my skin, all the way down to his hand and he lets his mouth take over for his thumb. The minute his hot breath teases me, working alongside his fingers gliding in and out, I thrash my head back with an eager moan. I needed this so badly.

It's almost more than I can take as he expertly rolls his tongue around my folds, sucking them into his mouth with just the right amount of pressure. His fingers hook against my g-spot until I feel like I might explode. It's so intense I find myself pushing him back slightly, but he fights against me and relentlessly pulls me further into his mouth until I am erupting with pleasure. My legs shake in his grip as it slowly fades, and I am still somehow left wanting more.

I clench my fingers into the curls of his hair and yank his mouth back to mine, relishing in my own taste on his lips. I quickly find my way between his legs and pull the hardness from his tight boxer briefs, stroking it as I urge him to slide inside of me. He's just as worked up and impatient as me, and quickly uses my dripping wetness to guide himself in.

He pulls at my legs to angle my hips upwards, moving in and out of me at the perfect angle. But soon we're lost in each other's mouths again. He lifts me back into the air, not breaking our kiss or his thrust, and lowers back onto the nearby couch. I rear back, admiring the view of his gaping mouth and clenching muscles as I start to ride him. He's impossibly hard and throbbing inside of me as I move up and down, gripping the bottom of his shaft with one hand to match my motions.

He hisses and digs his nails into my thighs. The nerves I feel pulsing through him tell me he's close. I lift my arms above my head, running my hands up through my hair, giving him a good view of my body as I go faster. But he suddenly grabs my wrists and grips them behind my back, holding me in place as he gyrates his hips, doing all of the work for me. Taking complete control over our pace. With one hand securely wrapped around my arms, pinning them out of the way, he sneaks his other hand back to my clit.

"What are you doing?" I moan, quivering from the sensitivity.

"I won't cum until you do," he grunts, thrusting harder and faster.

"I…already..did," I stammer out slowly in between the intensifying waves of pleasure.

"Cum again," he commands, writhing against me and fingering against my tingling folds. I didn't think I would cum again, but the moment he says the words and begins moving so skillfully, I instantly feel myself plummeting into another orgasm. It catches me off guard, leaving me trembling and limp as I crash down over his chest.

He lures me up, keeping his arms gripped behind me, as he turns me around on the couch. With one perfect slap to my ass, he slides back inside of me from behind. I'm so tight around him that in no time at all he is groaning in a way that tells me he is so close to cumming. He quickly pulls out and spills onto my back, rubbing along every inch of my skin within reach with his breathless moans.

After cleaning up, we reluctantly put some of our clothes back on and lay around on his couch for a while, wrapped in each other's arms.

"How did you get over here?" he finally asks, now that he has a chance.

"You'll never believe it," I huff. "My dad bought me a car. And a phone."

"Really? I thought Brendan didn't have the money for any of that right now."

"No…Not Brendan. My quote, unquote real dad bought them for me," I explain.

I feel his chest flex as he strains his neck to look down at me, studying the expression on my face as if I must be joking. "No shit…" he rasps.

"You don't believe me?" I chuckle, still hardly believing it myself.

"I believe he'd try to do something like that," he replies. "I just can't believe you let him."

"I didn't have much of a choice," I tell him as I roll off of his body and look for the rest of my clothes.

He gets up and walks into his kitchen, throwing some kind of frozen food into his microwave. Emmett always gets hungry after we have sex, which has been an endearing quirk to learn about him. As sexy as it is to have a boyfriend with his own apartment, sometimes I miss the days when he was hiding out in a cheap motel. Things felt even more scandalous and romantic then.

Emmett's mom let him back into the manor long enough to pick up a few things from his room, but she made sure he had no way to collect his bed and other furniture. He's tried looking for a job, but as he expected, he hasn't had much luck. His mom and sister, as well as the Hendersons, made sure everyone in town knew better than to hire him.

He's been living off of whatever money he could make from selling his car and a few other heirlooms he retrieved from his room. He picked up an old sofa and mattress from the thrift store, but other than that the place is mostly empty. A poster from one of his favorite bands hangs crooked near an old television set. The rest of the walls empty with an almost taunting sadness.

Every time I think about how empty and gray the whole place is, I'm amazed he manages to stay in as high spirits as he does each day. But I know he's just banking on us leaving town right after graduation. Once we get to a new place, hopefully before his reputation in Jameson catches up with him, he'll be able to get a job and start figuring out the rest of his life.

"What's that?" I ask, pointing to a large box plopped near the front door. One that I am positive we tripped over at some point in our mad rush to get into each other's pants.

"Another box of shit from the manor," he answers despondently as he slides it over to the couch. "That's what I was doing the day of your accident. I had to go pick it up. They brought it to the gate of course. Wouldn't even let me pull up to the door."

"That was…nice of your mom I guess…to give you more of your things?" I wince awkwardly, knowing very well that there's nothing nice about any of this. A box of stuff? Great. How about a bed or the rest of his clothes. Money for food. Or any number of things she could still be providing her son who's barely eighteen.

"Oh, it didn't come from my mom," he grunts. "The house staff of course. I guess they felt sorry for me." He rummages through it, pulling out random items. A baseball, a t-shirt, and a few books. "It's all pretty useless."

One leather-bound book with no words on the front catches my eye just as he grabs it and tosses it to the ground. I quickly snatch it up and open it out of curiosity. There's handwriting on the front page, in perfect cursive, that reads *Property of Marissa Vanderbilt.*

"Who's Marissa?" I ask, trailing my thumb over the old ink.

"My mom," he shoots back curtly as if it stings to say it. "I don't know why they threw that in there. Must have been a mistake."

"Her diary," I gasp, rolling over to my stomach at rapt attention. "Did you read it?"

"Hell no," he groans.

I can tell he wants nothing to do with it, but something about it seems important to me. Nothing about his family makes any sense. They're corrupt, greedy, and heartless. But reading his mother's private thoughts seems like the perfect way to try to make sense of it all. It could provide some insight into what goes through her head that allows her to treat other people so terribly. I can't resist stashing the book away in my coat.

With the diary hidden away, I look back up to Emmett. He's standing over the kitchen counter chewing on his microwaved burrito, but he's staring ahead in deep thought.

"You okay?" I ask.

He barely moves, making me think he didn't even hear me at first. "Yeah," he says blankly. "Just tired I guess."

But I know he's lying. What his family has put him through and the position they've left him in is still a big, raw wound in his life. I know it hasn't been easy to go from being a spoiled rich kid living in a manor with his whole privileged life laid out before him down to the slums. A crappy apartment with nothing in it and no job. All while still walking through the prestigious halls of WJ Prep where any student would be literally disgusted if they saw the way he was living.

He was almost relieved at the thought of withdrawing and going to a public school, but Thomas Jameson had paid his tuition up long before his death. I think the only reason his mom didn't make a point to have him kicked out was so Malcolm would be able to fuck with him up until graduation.

"I should probably get going," I announce as I pull myself to my feet, still feeling dizzy from the amazing sex. Emmett nods slightly but still seems as if he's off in another world. "Unless you want me to stay," I suggest with concern. "Keep you company?"

"Nah," he shakes his head, pushing around the last bite of his food. "Like I said, I'm tired."

"Well…then…I'll see you tomorrow," I nudge my way into his arms, pulling myself against his chest. "I'll meet you there. I finally don't need a ride."

"Hey. I gave you a ride plenty of times even when you did have a car," he reminds me playfully. "I kind of liked our morning drives before our first class."

"I know," I smile fondly. "But I'm so excited to have my own car again, I'm looking forward to driving myself. At least for tomorrow."

He kisses my forehead and walks me to the door. After I've driven home, I plop down onto my bed and am almost half asleep before something brings me back to life. I see the diary on the floor, poking out from underneath my hoodie. I grab it and slide under my comforter, thinking I'll be asleep in no time. Marissa's private thoughts may be disturbing, but I can't imagine them being entertaining enough to keep me awake. I switch on the lamp next to my bed and turn to the first entry, dated January 1995.

"January, huh. Same month it is now," I muse to myself as I start to read.

*Dear Diary,*

*Today my parents informed me that I'd be attending prom this year. I thought I might have to wait until my junior year, but the family they have decided I will marry into has a son who is a senior. The Jamesons. The founders of the town and the automobile company that this whole place revolves around. Their son's name is Thomas. He is one of those untouchable kids at school. I've seen him and his friends picking on the other students a lot. The only reason they haven't bothered me is because my parents befriended the Jamesons as soon as we arrived. They know we are old money and therefore in the club.*

*I'm excited to go to prom, but I'm scared about what it means. I know there's no use arguing with my parents about it. But I don't want to rush off into marriage and kids as soon as I'm done with school. And with Thomas being next in line to take over the automobile company, it means that if I'm married off to him, I'll be stuck in Jameson forever.*

*I want to travel and see the world! I know my parents will never allow me to do that on my own. Not when they're determined for me to secure the future generations of our family. The only way to do that is for me and my siblings to marry into other families who are just as wealthy. I have always known that this was expected of me, but I had secretly hoped I would by some miracle be married off to a man who would show me the world. Someone I could travel and have fun with.*

*Maybe I shouldn't be so quick to judge. Who knows what Thomas will be like. I guess I will find out tomorrow when he officially invites me to prom.*

*~Marissa*

I force myself to close the book as my eyelids grow heavy, but I am already sucked into this time capsule of Marissa's life. I have to double-check the date to make sure it is actually Emmett's mom's diary and not her mother or grandmother's. Arranged marriage? It seems like such an ancient practice, but I guess the ultra-rich do have different ways of doing things.

My mind drifts back to the moment Emmett asked me to prom. How good it felt to hear those words and the flurry of butterflies it set off in my stomach. I can't imagine having that stolen away by not even getting to choose your own date and being informed of the decision before the guy even has a chance to ask. The Elites sure do have a strange way of running their kids' lives, but I guess I'm not surprised given everything I already know about them.

I shrug and drop the book to the floor, sliding it under the bed so Emmett doesn't see I've stolen it the next time he comes over. Maybe it's wrong of me to pry into his family's life, but he didn't care to read it. If I can find some glimmer of humanity in who his mom used to be, maybe it would help him feel better about who she has become. To know that once upon a time, his mother was a kind and decent person.

# CHAPTER NINE

## BOOK 3

It's an especially cold and snowy Saturday evening as I finally park my car in the driveway at home. I can see the freshly shoveled snow piled into the yard and almost feel bad that I wasn't here to help. It seems unfair that after working such long, hard days all week, Mom and Brendan still have so much housework to tend to.

I want to help more, but they keep insisting I just need to focus on school and track. Part of me wonders if they're banking on some far-fetched dream of me having a successful athletic career to fund their retirement. I have my own dreams about the same thing, but I try not to get my hopes up. The pressure is too distracting.

"Mom!?" I yell out as I rush inside, desperately needing to warm up.

"Dining room!" she yells back.

I hear a man's voice and for a brief moment am terrified Theo might be back. But thankfully, it's just Brendan. They both look exhausted and have a pile of papers spread out in front of them, but they quickly sweep it all up into their arms and stash it away as I come in.

"How was your interview?" my mom's face brightens.

"Great," I shrug, half-surprised. "I've gone to so many of these by now I barely even get nervous anymore."

"That's fantastic, sweetie," she answers warmly, but there's a worrying distance in her voice. "There are leftovers in the fridge if you're hungry."

"Thanks, but I grabbed something on the way home," I tell her, already turning for my room.

"Ophelia," she stops me. "Could you sit down for a minute? We need to talk to you about something."

"Okay…" I answer slowly, pulling out a chair, feeling afraid of what could possibly be wrong now. No good talks ever start with that tone.

"It's about college, actually," she explains. "We wanted to wait until later to bring it up, but…well…now is as good a time as any."

"What about it?" I blink from the edge of my seat.

They shoot each other a hesitant glance, but finally, Brendan takes a deep breath and starts talking. "We've never kept our financial situation secret from you. You know we've struggled over the years to make ends meet."

"Of course," I nod with wide eyes while I am instantly hit with a heavy feeling of guilt. "But you've always taken good care of me. I've never really wanted for anything, and I can't tell you how much I appreciate it. Really I…"

"Thanks," he blurts, cutting me off. "You really don't have to say any of that."

"It's our job to take care of you," my mom smiles, reaching over to squeeze my hand.

I stare blankly ahead, thinking if they don't get to the point soon, I might have some kind of panic attack.

"But there's one thing we haven't been able to do," he adds.

There's a heavy silence that makes my heart pound in confusion.

"It's your college fund," my mom announces with a heavy sigh. "We had some money saved but moving here to Jameson depleted some of it. And it's just been one thing after another since then."

"I'm afraid we don't have much of anything to give you for college," Brendan states, looking ashamed and disappointed.

"Phew!" I exhale in laughter, clutching my chest. "Don't scare me like that! I thought something was really wrong!"

They shoot another concerned look at each other before turning back to me with baffled expressions. "Something *is* wrong," my mom urges. "We have no money to give you for college. Do you understand?"

"I don't need it though," I insist cheerfully. "Coach is certain I'm going to have plenty of scholarship offers to choose from."

I feel slightly offended that they're not more aware of how much of a reality that is. Have they been keeping track of my grades or athletic record at all? Have they even been listening to me? Of course, I've got this covered.

"Ophelia, you know Brendan and I plan to stay in Jameson no matter where you go to school," she explains. "At least for a little while. We can't afford to move again so soon." I bite my lip, holding back from spitting out that they'd never want to stay here if they knew the whole truth about this town. "Which means you'll be doing more than just starting college," she continues. "You'll be living on your own. There's rent and groceries and all your other living expenses that will have to be covered. A full-ride scholarship is great and all, but I'm afraid that doesn't quite cover all your bases."

"So...I'll get a job," I shoot back dismissively. "What's the big deal?"

"You can't go to school full time and work and keep up with track all at once," she asserts, looking at me like I'm crazy. "I'm afraid...you may have to consider...going to school somewhere nearby. So you can still live here with us."

A million things flash before my eyes at once. Every moment in WJ Prep when I first came here and the Elites tortured me. All of my worst memories of Emmett before he was free from their control. My destroyed car and the sight of it flying off the cliff. Emmett's apartment and the hopelessness in his eyes that grows every day we're forced to stay here.

"No!" I exclaim too quickly and too loudly. "Absolutely not. I appreciate everything you did to get us here so I could go to WJ Prep, but after I graduate, I have to get out of here. I just...I have to. I'll figure it out. I'll work however hard I have to."

Her hand reaches for mine again. "Honey, I know it's been a rough year. You and Emmett found his dad's body...and then you disappearing those few days. The car accidents and your dad coming back into the picture..." I bury my face into my hands, thinking while that sounds like an awful lot to deal with, those are just the things she knows about. They're only the tip of the iceberg. "I can understand why you'd be anxious for a fresh start."

Brendan clears his throat, grabbing her attention for a

moment. He nods as if there's something else she's not telling me.

"There's one more thing you could consider," she offers with a lingering uncertainty. "To ensure you have plenty of time to focus on everything you need to without stressing over money. And so you could attend any school you want to."

"What?" I ask anxiously.

"When your dad visited and brought your new car and phone…," she says slowly. I immediately start shaking my head 'no' before she even has a chance to finish, which just makes her speak louder and more urgently. "He offered to pay for whatever expenses your scholarship wouldn't cover. An apartment, miscellaneous funds, textbooks, supplies…whatever you need. He said he'd be happy to take care of it."

"No!" I shriek. "Are you crazy!? This is getting to be ridiculous!"

"That's enough, Ophelia," she barks sharply. "Theo has made a lot of kind offers to be the dad he should have been all these years, at least financially if nothing else. And you've been nothing but rude and ungrateful to him every step of the way!"

I fly up from my chair in exasperation. "I faked a smile and sat through his surprise dinner visit! I let you talk me into taking that car and the phone. I even had lunch with him one day!" I fume. "I've tried my best to go along with all this…for your sake. But you…you don't understand who he…," I catch myself as naïve faces burn into me. They don't know Theo like I do. So, of course, they can't understand why I'm acting this way. It dawns on me that this may be the time to tell them everything. I'm not ready and it hasn't been planned, but I don't know if I have a choice. It may be now or never.

I take in a sharp breath, feeling a million different explanations and reasons bursting from the tip of my tongue. But just as I am about to lay everything out for them, my mom's phone rings. She immediately answers after looking at the caller ID, making me lose my nerve.

"Yes, hi," she speaks quietly into the phone, stepping away to the corner of the room. "I'm talking to her now."

I groan to myself as I hear her talking to who I can only assume is Theo. They must have planned this whole conversation out. I can imagine her telling him it'd be better if they talked to me alone. Maybe I'd be easier to convince without him around.

"No, no. Don't worry about it," she whispers. "She'll come around."

I slump back into my chair and dramatically plop my head against the dining room table. Brendan shifts in his seat with a heavy sigh and I can picture the look of exhaustion that's probably plastered on his face. He hates dealing with arguments between my mom and I. Probably because he's so kind-hearted he can't bring himself to pick sides. He loves us both too much.

For a moment, I wonder why Brendan can't be the one with all the money. I'd be more than happy to accept his help and I know he'd be just as happy to give it. But I guess that guys like him rarely get rich. The Jamesons and guys like Theo climb to the top by stepping on everyone along the way. Brendan doesn't have the heart or stomach for screwing people over just to make a fortune. I guess that's the same kind of softness that Emmett's family saw in him. And that's exactly why they cut him off and kicked him out.

"You're just like your mom," Brendan grumbles with a smirk. "In a good way. You're both so stubborn and independent." I lift my head and look to him, feeling completely lost. "I know it's not easy to accept help. Especially from someone you don't like. I mean…hell, I don't care much for Theo either."

"I wouldn't give you all such a hard time about it if I didn't have good reasons," I urge him. "You just have to trust me. Call it a gut feeling or whatever you want. I just think it does more harm than good to accept Theo's help."

"But if it gets you into college and into a position where you can focus on running," he pleads. "Or whatever else you may decide you're into in a year or two from now, then wouldn't that really show him? To really make something of yourself so you never have to take anything from him again?"

I groan and slam my head back down, desperately wishing that I could just bring myself to scream out that Theo is a murderer and a liar. They think those few days I went missing was me and Emmett just being irresponsible and running off together. But really it was Emmett trying to save me from Theo in the only way he knew how. Without him, Theo would have kidnapped me. And I might not even be sitting here today if that had happened.

Taking deep breaths, my fingers trail up to the running shoe charm hanging from my neck. I rub it gently, wishing more than anything that he could be here right now to tell me how to handle this. He's one of the only people who really understands Theo the way I do. And he's so good with people. He could think of the perfect thing to say on the spot.

"Sorry," my mom chimes as she slides back into her chair.

"I need some time to think," I blurt, feeling like I can't sit at this table for another second. "Is that okay? I'm tired from the drive and I kind of just want to be alone for a little while."

"Of course," my mom tilts her head. "We didn't mean to spring all of this on you. But I'm glad it's all out in the open now. You go ahead and think it over."

I race from the kitchen table, desperate to escape the pressure of accepting Theo's help. Taking a car or a phone or even sitting down for the occasional dinner is one thing but signing up to be intertwined with him and dependent on him for at least the next four years is more than I can bear. I lock myself away in my room and pull out my phone to call Emmett.

"You get it, right!?" I fume after I've caught him up on everything. "He's no good, Emmett. Guys like him never put it all out there in the open. There's always some ulterior motive in hiding, waiting to come out. If we give him an inch, he'll take a mile. He's already done that! First, dinner. Now all this."

"Mm-hmm," he grumbles, listening carefully. "No, no. I know. I get it." His silence is not the reassurance I was hoping for.

"You know him, Emmett," I press. "I can't give him that kind of power, right? He'll find some way to ruin everything for me. I just know it."

"Maybe if he could just give you one lump sum of money and be done with it," he suggests. "So you're not forced to run to him for every little thing you need."

"Then he'll still have something to hang over my head. No, I just can't do it, Emmett. I know my mom and Brendan are stressed, but the easy way out isn't always what it seems," I explain. "He's just trying to prey on their biggest fears about providing for me. It's their weak spot and he's using it to weasel his way back into our lives."

He's quiet for a moment longer. "What do you think he wants? Why try so hard to get to everyone?"

It's a reasonable question, but not the one I want right now. Because it leaves open the possibility that I am just being paranoid and that all Theo really wants is a chance to be the father he should have been all along. As much as he knows how to be.

"I don't know," I mutter. "I just know things never end well with him."

"I'm sorry, Ophelia," Emmett says slowly. "I feel…guilty… or responsible in some way."

"What do you mean?" I ask, assuming he thinks his little deal with Theo might be part of the reason he's still lingering around.

"If my family hadn't cut me off from everything," he continues, sounding pained. "I could fix all of this. I would have more than enough money to take care of both of us through college."

I try to be open and appreciative to his words, but it just makes me want to scream into a pillow. I feel like some helpless damsel from the 18th century. No one seems to think I'm capable of working and keeping up with track and school enough to take care of myself. But the guilt of knowing everyone I care about is stressing so much over their ability to take care of me just makes me feel stuck. It's too much pressure on me to do whatever it is they think I'm going to accomplish. And now I'm falling deeper into this rabbit hole of worrying so much about how everyone else feels, my own desires and dreams seem to be falling to the backburner.

"It's not your responsibility to pay my way through college," I tell him curtly. "It's nice that you would, but even if you had the money…I couldn't have accepted that kind of help from you."

"Sure you could have," he insists. "We're a team, Ophelia. Partners. Your problems are my problems."

Part of me wants to melt. The idea is so sweet and tempting, but something about it makes me feel like a big hand is closing around my neck.

"I know," I reply half-heartedly. "Listen, I'm exhausted. I'm going to go to bed. Goodnight. I love you."

"I love you, Ophelia. So much. Goodnight."

I crash down on my bed, laughing at myself. Now I look like some corseted damsel too, fainting across my bed like this. Poking out from under my bed where I stashed it last, Marissa's diary calls to me. I pick it up and flip through the next few entries. She talks about a feeling of having no say or control over her own life, but all of that fades away when she officially meets Thomas. He's good-looking, charming, and the kind of guy she would want to be with even if she had a choice.

It's frighteningly relatable. Being surrounded by pressure on all sides, everyone telling you what to do and how to do it. Then the charming knight sweeps in and makes you forget you ever wanted anything different.

# CHAPTER TEN

## BOOK 3

I knew it was going to be a bad day when I woke up to the ding from my phone. It's a special notification that only sounds off when the dreaded Elites app of shame has been used. It's a special thing they designed and use to torment black-listed students or anyone else that's crossed them in some way. I myself have been a victim of the app more than once, which texts every single student at WJ Prep.

But this morning Emmett is the victim. I open the message to see Emmett's drooping face looking incredibly sad. There's a caption that reads: *What a poor rich boy looks like when he loses all of his daddy's money.*

I look at the photo closer and realize it was taken the night that we cornered his mom, sister, and the Hendersons. For weeks, we thought Bernadette was missing, but she had been hiding out at the Hendersons' manor the entire time. Their mom soon joined her there. It was all a ploy to drive Emmett mad so they could set it up to look like he had lost his mind after his father's death. Then they held me at gunpoint and forced him to sign all of Jameson Automobiles over to them. His family cut him off and took every penny left to his name.

The sting of this mass text and the words along with it is, of course, that Emmett wasn't hurt because he lost all that money. He was hurt by the principle of it. That his mom and sister were so cold, ruthless, and greedy that they would squander his inheritance just because they could. It was a power play. They could have taken the company and left him his trust fund and he would have had enough to live off of. He would have surrendered everything else and let them carry on with their corrupt little business deals while he lived in peace.

But no. His mom and sister cared so little for him, and even hatefully resented him in a way, that they would rather leave him with absolutely nothing. Completely cut off and cast out from the only family he has simply because Emmett had something they didn't. Empathy. And an inability to prioritize money and power over human lives.

For me, it was a good experience. I thought it was better for Emmett to be left to make his own way without any ties to his evil family. It also proved to me that Emmett was different from his family. That he had a heart and the ability to be good.

I'm thinking it all over as I get ready for school. Even with my own car, Emmett still picks me up some mornings and this is one of those days. I peak anxiously out the window every few minutes to see if he's pulled up, wondering how he'll feel about the latest blow from the Elites. Whether it can be seen as good or bad in the long run, that night was when Emmett lost what was left of his family. Even if they weren't good people, it was hard for him. And now the Elites are using it against him to try and humiliate him. Definitely not a great start to the day.

Just as I'm sliding into a hoodie and throwing my shoes in a gym bag for practice, I hear the gentle honk of his car as he pulls in to park. Even though Emmett seems like a changed man these days, many parts of me aren't over the trauma of how he was before. I know he has a temper and I'm not looking forward to seeing how he behaves with the Elites adding insult to injury.

It's cold enough outside that I don't even bother hesitating to read how he's feeling before I jump right in and begin blowing on my hands, warming them against the heated vents. But within seconds I notice the tight, blank expression on his face. He's stern and silent as he jerks the car into reverse. He handles turns with a sense of agitation, but he drives slowly down the streets. As if he's putting off arriving at school as long as possible.

"So…I guess you saw it?" I ask gently after a long and heavy silence. He nods with nothing but a grunt, obviously not wanting to talk about it. But everything in his expression and body language tells me it's eating away at him.

"Fuck them," I offer with a shrug. "Way worse things have been sent out over that app about me."

My comments only make things more tense and awkward. Especially as I am left remembering how it was Emmett who once stole my phone when I was the old Elite's number one target. I find myself instinctively inching closer to the car door as the memories flood over me. The vile things he sent me, both sexual and predatory all at once. The nude photo they found of me and sent to every single student and teacher in the school.

I'm lost in all these things I'd rather forget as Emmett puts the car into park at school and waits. I start to unbuckle and grab my things but freeze as I notice him not moving at all.

"Aren't you coming?"

"No," he huffs. "I'm going back home today."

"Then why did you pick me up? How am I going to get home?" I ask in confusion.

"I picked you up because I promised I would," he explains tensely. "And I'll be here to pick you up after school too, just like I said I would be."

The tone of his voice sounds almost condescending and resentful, making me angry. I could have driven myself to school and maybe would have preferred that if I had known he was skipping today.

"Is this because of the text?" I ask with a sigh, tired of dancing around it.

"I don't want to talk about it," he grumbles through clenched teeth. I can see his knuckles turning white as he tightly wrings his hand around the steering wheel, causing the leather to creak.

"Emmett, you can't let them have that kind of control," I urge him, speaking from experience. "You know better than anyone...that's what they want. You have to march right in there with your head held high, so they know they can't hurt you. Even if they do hurt you, you have to carry on anyway. Otherwise they'll never lay off."

He shakes his head and looks out his window. I can see the torment twisting inside of him. He's humiliated, but safe hiding here in his car. Walking through those double doors puts him right into the hands of unkind, snickering assholes who will use the text as ammunition. Messages through the Elites app is like an arrow pointing to the person everyone is supposed to give shit to. Anyone who doesn't make their best effort at pouring salt on Emmett's wounds could become the next victim.

"Maybe we should get revenge," he perks up suddenly. "Find something on Malcolm to put out there and get back at him. I have some old embarrassing photos of him from when we were kids."

"It's just a waste of time," I insist. "Even if we do manage to strike some kind of nerve with him, it's only going to make things worse. He'll retaliate with something much bigger. They've already tried to kill me this year, Emmett. I don't have time to wage a war against them right now. I need to focus on school and getting into college so I can get us the hell out of here."

He's immediately turned off by my refusal to play their games, shaking his head and growing more irritated by the second as I talk. "Well, who says you have to help at all," he shoots back begrudgingly. "I'm not worried about getting into college right now or anything else really. I'll go after him myself."

That thought scares me even more. Emmett humiliated and desperate, feeling like he has nothing to lose, going after Malcolm for revenge. Two entitled, fucked-up high school boys going head to head with millions of dollars and a disregard for human life on the line. It'd be a nightmare. One in which I can't see everyone surviving.

"What happened to what you said last night?" I argue, even though it still causes a huge lump to form in my throat. "Partners, remember? Your problems are my problems?" He softens a little but still seems insistent on clinging to all this bubbling rage. "Let's just walk in there and get through this together. I'll hold your hand the whole way and march you right up to your first class. Like I said, Emmett. Fuck them. Don't let them send you running off and hiding."

He lets out a long heavy sigh before finally, slowly turning the key in the ignition, shutting down the engine. He's still a while afterward, gathering up all the energy he has to go through with this. Or maybe he's just turning himself to stone. Compartmentalizing and shutting down. His upbringing forced him to become very good at detachment.

But he must still be feeling something because he squeezes my hand tight as we walk inside. When the doors swing open, it's as if everyone has been waiting for us. They all go completely silent and turn to us with wide eyes as we make our way through. All of the students are divided up against the lockers, leaving plenty of room for us to go right past them down the middle of the hall. But it also puts us in perfect view and we're all too aware of their growing snickers and whispers as we walk by.

I can feel the muscles in Emmett's hands tense the further we go. His heart pounds through his wrist. The further we go, the louder and more blatant the taunting becomes. As they grow bolder in their insults, directing them at Emmett rather than each other now, the crowd seems to be closing in. The students push out from the lockers lining the walls on either side of us and put themselves in our path. We're forced to zig-zag to dodge them, but as they close in on us, each time we avoid bumping into one of them, another is waiting just behind them.

Emmett's hand twists in mine, growing damp and I see beads of sweat forming on his brow. Everyone is shouting at us and cackling, jumping all around like crazy people, not letting us move any further. It's so loud and suffocating that we can barely make out their words, but every once in a while, an awful jab will stand out among the rest. Terrible things about Emmett and his father. They throw Thomas's death in his face and blame him for it, all while making fun of him for being poor.

I'm not immune to the insults, of course. If anything, I give them more ammunition. Vivian coined me as the white trash girl who didn't belong here and needed to go back where I came from. The fact that we're a couple only spurs them on more. They mock Emmett for having found a poor, white trash girl just like him to fuck in whatever dirty shack we come from. The worst part is, knowing how these kids live, my little house and his little apartment are like uninhabitable shit holes to them.

As the shouting worsens and the crowd folds over us, we both begin to duck and shield ourselves with our arms as fruit and opened packets of condiments fly at us. I feel something soggy splash against my cheek just as a packet of ketchup smears across my jacket. They sound like a mob of crazed monkeys on the attack.

I grip Emmett's hand tighter and begin fighting our way through, dragging him along. He's stronger and scarier than me, but I can feel the panic coursing through his veins. He's never experienced anything like this before. Even I have to admit this is more dramatic than some of the shit the Elites pulled on me.

Finally, we pierce through the bulk of them enough for me to hear his hyperventilating pants. I shove the remaining stragglers out of the way and pull him into the closest closet, where we can find some peace. His nostrils are flaring in and out as he heaves. I grip his shoulders and try to get him to look at me, but he looks lost. I've seen that empty look in his eyes before. It's from whatever scary place he goes into when he's put into a position he finds himself unable to handle.

"Hey!" I bark, trying to snap him out of it as I firmly shake his shoulders. "Hey, Emmett! Look at me!" I try again, but he's unresponsive. He looks in every direction, doing his best to avoid making eye contact with me, still breathing wildly.

"Stop it!" I scream again, become afraid. The shrillness of my voice causes something in him to snap and one of his hands rears back above me. I flinch, throwing my hands up and whimpering slightly, convinced that he's so out of control he'll actually hit me. But when nothing strikes me, I slowly lower my hands just as he starts coming back to reality.

His face softens and fills with remorse. His brows wrinkle and he looks like he's about to start crying. He collapses against my shoulder with a breathless series of gasps. Short, shallow cries with no tears to back them up.

"I'm sorry," he groans listlessly, clinging to my body. "I don't...I don't know what happened...I just...I couldn't take...that."

I hesitate for a moment, still feeling afraid. But I finally wrap my arms around him and rub his back gently. "Shhhh," I comfort him softly. "It's okay."

We rock back and forth like that for a few moments. Then all at once, he straightens, pulling back to wipe his nose. He seems like himself again and looks embarrassed for whatever just happened.

"Sorry," he says again. "I just kind of lost it for a moment. I couldn't...I couldn't *breathe*."

"I think you just had a panic attack," I suggest with concern, studying the change in his face.

"Those fuckers," he sneers, wiping his nose again with a sniffle.

I let him calm down some more, knowing I can't process any of this for myself until I'm alone again. Away from his deep, mournful eyes staring back at me with his twisted pink lips that I love and yearn for always, even in fucked-up moments like this.

We hide out in there for a while until after the bell has rung and we hear the hallways grow silent again. Then I walk Emmett to his class as I promised. As I walk on my own after delivering him to the door, I am horrified to have such a recent reminder of that side of Emmett. The side of him that is so lost and confused, it's almost inhuman. That used to be the only side of him I saw, and he did awful things to me when that part of him was in the steering wheel. I can't help but wonder if these new Elites will find a way to crack him, bringing the old demented Emmett out again for good.

Something else stirs in me after the awful morning. It's a strange, new way of seeing Emmett. He suddenly doesn't seem as strong as he used to. Not that breaking down or having a panic attack is anything weak in itself. No, it's something else. Just as I try to quietly slip into my class, ignoring the teacher who chastises me for being late, I realize I'm having a hard time feeling sorry for Emmett right now. I have walked in his shoes before, only the difference was…he was usually the one tormenting me.

In a sick way, it's like the new Elites are exacting revenge on my behalf. Emmett is getting a dose of his own medicine. I wouldn't say I'm enjoying it, but part of me feels like Emmett is getting what he deserves after all those years of being on the other side of this, doling out punishments to anyone who crossed him or questioned his position. And if that's how I really feel…should we be together?

# CHAPTER ELEVEN

BOOK 3

I bound out of school at the end of the day, eager to get to practice. Emmett usually walks me, but today I rush over to the locker rooms without him. I feel bad leaving him to fend for himself, but there is still some resentful part of me that thinks he should be able to tough it out on his own. I hate feeling that way and it only makes me more impatient to run it all out of my system.

Once I'm changed, I join the others on the field and try to start warm-ups. But Coach Granger blows his whistle and asks us to huddle together. We groan and form a group around him. It's freezing cold and the only thing to warm us up is to get moving, but first he says he has an announcement to make.

"Everyone, I'd like you to meet Jada," he announces, nodding to the petite, dark-skinned woman at his side. She's nearly half his height, as most people are, with a cute button nose and little black curls pulled into a bun around her bright face. "She'll be working with you all this semester as my new coaching assistant."

I expect Jada to smile with her introduction, but instead, she stands firm with her arms behind her back, practically scowling at all of us. Which is for the best. My favorite coaches have always been mean and stern, more concerned with pushing us to be the best runners we can be rather than pretending to be our friends.

After Jada is introduced, the other girls and I line up on the track field, waiting for the whistle to blow. I feel like a bull waiting to charge as jets of steam shoot out of my nose and mouth against the cold air. I'm freezing in my thin running gear, but I know soon my skin will be burning hot once I get a good way into the laps. And I am in serious need of the release. I could barely stand to make it through warm-ups. I bounced through the stretches and exercises, impatiently waiting for the chance to take off.

The whistle shrieks and I start running, leaving the others behind me by a long shot. I break into a fast and even stride, leaving everyone and everything behind me. I'm so desperate to run away from the complexities of my life that I don't even have to get through the first mile to get that runner's high. The pumping adrenaline hits me instantly.

Practice flies by as I slip into a sort of trance. I run through a mindless meditation, basking in the peace and quiet. There is nothing but me and the building pain in my body and chest as I round the final few laps. I notice Jada eyeing me intently as I slow down into the covered bleachers where we always gather at the end of practice.

Coach makes a few announcements about upcoming competitions but keeps it brief. Now that we're all motionless and sweaty, the cold quickly sets back in. We're all dismissed, but Coach asks me to hang back for a moment. Just long enough to spout off some of my times for the day, complimenting me and reminding me of my training commitments to keep it up.

"Good job out there today, Lopez," Jada concurs with Coach as they walk away, heading for his office.

I'm feeling good from their praise, but mostly just relieved from how therapeutic today's run was. As I gather everything up to head into the locker room, I remember that Emmett is supposed to drive me home. Practice helped me get some things off my mind, but I'm still feeling conflicted enough about him to not want to see him. I consider running home, which would give me an excuse to avoid him, but would also give me more opportunity to run everything out of my system.

"You okay?" a voice interrupts my thoughts suddenly from the corner of the bleachers.

I whip around in surprise to see Bridgett standing there, watching me closely as she reaches for her gym bag.

"What do you care?" I bite back.

"Don't be like that," she scoffs. "No one's around, you know. We don't have to pretend to hate each other."

I blink in shock, realizing that she is aware of the expected dynamic between her as an Elite and me as someone who is blacklisted. She knows how she is supposed to treat me, obviously. But does she know what will happen if she doesn't obey?

"I'm Bridgett," she says suddenly, ignoring my frozen, blank expression as she marches right up to me with her hand out.

I shake it lightly, unsure of what to say. "Ophelia," I answer slowly. "But I'm sure you know that."

"Well, sure…but we've never officially met," she smiles, but it fades as I continue staring at her with wide eyes. "I'm not going to bite," she huffs.

"You don't seem to know how things work around here," I defend for her own sake. "I'm blacklisted. If Malcolm or the others see you talking to me or being nice at all, they'll make you pay."

"I'm not scared of them," she insists with a shrug of her shoulders. "Anyways, I grew up with Malcolm. We're cousins. It's hard to see him as a threat when our moms used to throw us in kiddie pools with each other as naked toddlers."

I want the image to be humanizing enough to make him less scary. But then I quickly remember the time he overpowered me on his couch, trying to force himself on me. Or the way he looked when he was ganging up on Emmett with his dad and the others. Maybe Emmett would have thought Malcolm wasn't so scary either. They had grown up together too, after all. But he was quickly proven wrong.

But her defiance of their rules is admirable, even if it does seem suicidal. It's the same kind of rebellion I'd be bolder about if there wasn't so much at stake right now.

"You were great out there today," she adds. "I heard you would be, but man…you were even better than I expected."

"I had a lot on my mind today," I explain resentfully. "Nothing pushes me harder than a bad day. So I guess I can thank you for that."

"Thank me?" she laughs. "What the hell do I have to do with it?"

"You're an Elite," I remind her. "So little stunts like that mass text this morning and the big show in the hall…You're a part of all that whether you want to be or not."

"What stunt? Texts? What are you talking about?" she stares at me with her mouth twisted and brows wrinkled.

Her ignorance makes me angry at first, assuming this is all a part of some trick. But I look at her more and realize she really doesn't know what I'm talking about. "Were you not in the hall this morning? When everyone started harassing me and Emmett?"

"I listened to Malcolm rant and rave about the kinds of things kids did at this school for years," she tells me. "Up until recently when it turned into him bragging about everything he's done or what he plans to do. People around here are crazy. When my parents told me we were moving here from California so my dad could start working with Uncle Liam, I made a plan right then to follow along but keep my head down. I get here early in the mornings and go straight to class. I prefer to stay out of it all."

"Good luck," I jeer, remembering when I once thought it was possible to just keep my head down and stay out of their way. "You'd be surprised how easy it is to offend them. And then they'll make you sorry."

"It's different now," she argues. "The old Elites felt entitled to their roles in this town. The new ones are more focused on money and business. They'd much rather sit around and get drunk coding some software than go after some kids they don't like at school. Not to say they won't. I'm just saying they have bigger things on their mind is all."

"I don't know if that's better or worse," I shudder in the cold.

"It's freezing," she hisses. "What are you doing after you shower and clean up?"

"What am I doing?" I ask blankly, genuinely confused as to why she would care.

"Yeah. Wanna grab something to eat? Catch a movie?" she asks innocently, but I'm still too thrown to answer. "We can go to the next town over, so no one sees us," she insists. "I get tired of hanging out with my family all the time. I could use a new friend."

I squint my eyes at her, trying to discern if this is some kind of trick. Everything I know about the Elites tells me there's no way this won't end in something horrible happening to me. But there is something different about Bridgett. A certain laid back, down to earth vibe about her that matches her claimed sentiment of wanting to stay out of all the drama. Hanging out with someone besides Emmett does sound great. As much as I love him, I have been craving some time with a girl my age. Something I haven't experienced ever since Lily turned on me and went off the deep end.

"I don't have my car," I tell her, hoping that'll ruin what she had in mind. It'd be easier if I didn't have to make the choice of whether or not to trust her.

"We can take mine," she offers. "I can take you home afterward. But whatever we do, let's get into the locker rooms. It's too fucking cold to stand out here and talk about it all night."

I nod and run in after her. Once the others are around, Bridgett does what is expected of her and ignores me completely. But the moment I'm dry and bundled up in regular clothes outside again, she finds me around the side of the building with no one else in sight.

"So, what do ya say?" she asks again, looking hopeful.

So much of me screams to play it safe and turn down her invite, but I do so desperately need a friend who isn't my mom or my boyfriend. Bridgett is close to my age and she's a runner. I want more than anything to be able to put all the dumb Elite bull shit aside and just have some fun with a girl from school.

"Fuck it," I exhale finally. "Let's go."

"Sweet," she smiles back at me. "My car is just over there. I don't think anyone will see us walking together if we go right now."

I nod and follow behind her, but of course, a figure appears around the corner as we get closer to her parked car. At first, we turn in different directions, putting distance between us.

"Oh wait," I call over to Bridgett. "It's okay. It's just Emmett. Come over and say hi." I announce it casually but really my heart is pounding. I was hoping to avoid him altogether this afternoon.

Bridgett runs over and catches up to me before we're within earshot of Emmett. "Hey," she grabs me and whispers into my ear. "Are you sure he's cool?" she asks nervously. "I'm not afraid of Malcolm or anything, but…well…I'm not stupid either, you know. You sure you two aren't just going to punish me for whatever my stupid cousin has done to you?"

I sigh with relief, realizing all at once that Bridgett is just as wary of us as I am of her. "I promise it will be okay," I assure her. "Even if he's weird about us hanging out, he would never do anything to you."

Emmett's face wrinkles as he gets closer and I have to hope my last promise to her is one I can keep. The Emmett I have come to know would never maliciously hurt another person, but with everything that happened this morning, how things used to be are too fresh on my mind.

"Hey," he grumbles, staring Bridgett down.

"This is Bridgett," I put my hand on her shoulder, hoping to defuse everything. I shoot him a look as if trying to communicate telepathically – this one's okay, I promise. Just be nice. "And this is Emmett," I nod over to him.

"Hey man, what's up?" she says coolly, embodying her Californian roots.

He lifts his chin briefly in a half-hearted greeting, but mostly just keeps darting his eyes back to me in disbelief. "I waited for you after school," he says dryly. "I thought I'd walk you to practice like always. And then I thought I'd drive you home."

"Oh, sorry," I answer awkwardly, wishing he could have saved the interrogation for later.

"Hey, I'm gonna go heat up the car," Bridgett tells me. "I'll wait for you. Nice to meet you, Emmett."

"Okay, cool," I smile towards her just before she runs off shivering. I want to go running after her, but Emmett's eyes are burning into me expectantly.

"What the fuck?" he scoffs.

"She's nice," I instantly defend, knowing what he's thinking. "Or she seems nice anyway. She knows she's not supposed to be friends with me, but we're just gonna keep it on the down low."

"Have you lost your mind!?" his voice strains. "She's an Elite, Ophelia! Did you forget that they just tried to kill you a couple of weeks ago!? And what about everything they did to me today!?"

"You used to be an Elite too," I snap coldly. "I doubt she had anything to do with either of those things. She doesn't want to be wrapped up in their bullshit…just like you didn't."

He looks over at her car as it starts up, blowing heaps of smoke into the air as the sun begins to set in the distance. "It's different," he insists.

"How?" I grimace at him. "How is it different?"

"You don't understand how they are," he mumbles.

"Oh, I don't!?" I fume, feeling my heart throbbing with

anger. "Have I not been just as wrapped up in everything as you ever since I came to Jameson? You don't think I've learned anything by now? Or are you saying Elites can never change? Cause if that's the case…I shouldn't be standing here talking to you either."

His lips part to argue back, but he stops himself, seemingly tripping over his own defenses in his mind. "I don't want to fight," he says instead, still looking defeated as his lips tighten.

"Me either," I agree, inching closer towards him. "I love you, Emmett." I know that much is true, even if everything today brought back old feelings of how fucked-up our love might be. Even now.

"I love you, too, Ophelia."

"But sometimes…I just really, really miss hanging out with other girls my age," I explain, my voice dripping with so much desperation I'm practically whining. "We're just going to hang out for a little bit. Outside of Jameson so no one will know. If she turns crazy on me, I'll call you right away."

I stand on my tiptoes to kiss him, but he's stiff and it takes him a minute to fully kiss me back. I can see his mind racing with more arguments or comebacks, but I meant what I said about not wanting to argue. And this has already been blown into a bigger deal than it should be, bringing back my feelings of being some 18th-century maiden…royalty that's not allowed to socialize with certain people.

"I'll call you later," I tell Emmett before quickly bouncing backward and running towards Bridgett's car.

"Everything cool?" she asks as I jump in.

"He'll be fine," I tell her, hoping I'm right. "He's just a little untrusting…which I'm sure you can understand."

"Maybe not as well as you'd think," she frowns. "But we've got twenty minutes until we get into the next town. Why don't you tell me about it?"

I spend the rest of the ride filling her in on everything that happened that day. Once I start talking, I can't stop. Soon everything is spilling out, including our complicated past and how all of those old, awful feelings between Emmett and I were dredged up today. Bridgett is a great listener and extremely nice, but it's almost like talking to a therapist. It almost doesn't even matter what she says. I just needed to talk to someone new about it all without having to lie.

# CHAPTER TWELVE

BOOK 3

"Mmmm," I close my eyes and grunt as I take in big, hurried bites of my mom's enchiladas.

"You're supposed to chew your food. Not inhale it," Brendan chuckles.

I ignore him and continue shoveling the fork into my mouth. Both him and my mom stare at me with wide eyes as I go.

"What's the rush?" my mom asks finally.

I pull a napkin to my face and attempt to swallow enough to talk. "Emmett is picking me up," I reply. "Date night."

They grin and glance over at each other. "Date night?" Brendan questions with a teasing tone. "You sound like an old married couple."

"They will be before you know it," my mom taunts.

Their jokes make me stop for a moment, but I'm quick to roll it off my shoulders and get back to cleaning my plate. It's not the kind of thing I want to get into with them right now, but the assumption that Emmett and I will be together forever is making me more uncomfortable every day.

Of course, I love him and can't imagine life without him. But I'm not naïve. I've heard less than stellar reviews about high school sweethearts who got married. Aside from the grim odds of our relationship actually surviving college and the early adult years after that, there are all the other reasons I have to be wary about where this is going. All the things Brendan and my mom know nothing about. But thankfully, it's all weighing on me a little less ever since I was able to vent to Bridgett.

I jump up the second the doorbell rings. "That's him," I announce, my voice still muffled with food. "I'll be back later."

"Have fun!" my mom calls out to me as I bound for the door. "Don't stay out too late!"

Regardless of what happens five or ten years from now, tonight I am just excited about going on a normal date with my boyfriend.

"Hey you," I smile as I hop into his car and lean over for a kiss. "What's on the docket for tonight?"

"A big surprise," he grins. "Something we've never ever done before."

I buckle my seat belt and brace myself for whatever mystery thing he has planned. As he drives, I study his face as the passing lights move across it. Sometimes the sight of Emmett takes my breath away. Especially now that he's out from under the expectations of his family and he's become more down to earth. His shaggy curls and crooked smile, all leading to those piercing gray eyes that always spark with something dangerous but alluring. I can't stop myself from sliding my hand across his knee, teasing toward the top of his thigh. He responds with a smirk but is quick to cup his hand around mine, stopping it from traveling any further.

I shrug it off, hoping we'll have some time for that kind of thing later in the evening. But it's hard not to let it get to me. Ever since his family disowned him, we've been having sex less and less. The tinges of anxiety I feel about it only worsen as he pulls up to our destination.

"Bowling!?" I shriek.

"Yup!" he beams back proudly.

I shift in my seat, remembering my parents' jokes about us being the old married couple. Sure, bowling is fun. But for date night? Maybe we're even closer to being in some middle-aged, sexless relationship than what I thought. But Emmett looks so excited, I can't bring myself to give him too hard of a time about his choice.

I follow along as we go in to rent a lane and some shoes. We order pizza, wishing we could have some beer along with it. Each turn I take is comically bad, and I start to think goofing off with rolling the ball in ridiculous ways will be more fun than I originally gave it credit for. But then I notice how serious

Emmett is taking each of his turns. He poses carefully before rearing his arm back and skillfully gliding it across the waxed floor. Each time it pummels towards with pins with good aim, usually getting him a spare or a strike.

"Have you been skipping school and coming here to practice?" I ask skeptically, only half kidding.

He looks pleased with me noticing his good performance. "Not exactly," he smirks. "But I have been practicing."

I feel him watching me as I shrug and bite into a slice of pizza that's dripping with cheese. I shouldn't have any room for it after dinner, but a good pizza is too hard to pass up.

"I've been thinking of joining a league," he blurts, sitting back in his seat casually.

"Huh?" I shoot back. "A *bowling* league?"

"Yeah," he rolls his shoulders defensively. "Why not? I mean, you'll be busy with college soon and I feel like I need a new hobby."

"But…once we move…Aren't you going to think about college? Or work or something?" I ask lightly, trying to hide my rising panic.

I've been understanding of Emmett needing time to figure things out after all that's happened, but now I'm worried he'll get too comfortable and lose all ambition. As he leans back and adjusts the waist of his pants, I suddenly see a flash of him twenty years from now. I imagine him with a gut and a mustache, drinking away in the bowling alley several nights a week while working some dead-end job.

"On that note…," he answers slowly. "I meant to tell you…" He winces slightly, hesitating to finish his thought.

"Yeah?" I stare back expectantly.

He looks around and shifts uncomfortably as if he's struggling to spit it out. "Well," he stands, taking a few steps back towards the revolving line of bowling balls. "I talked to Theo the other day."

His words stop my heart cold and were so cleverly planned. Before I can get over being tongue-tied from shock, he's already stepped up to the line to take another turn.

"What!?" I bark, but I know he can barely hear me over the echoing crash of pins.

He calmly strolls back to the table as if he didn't just drop a huge bomb. "Your turn," he states.

"What is wrong with you? Do you think I'm stupid?" I

seethe, not moving from my seat. "You just casually announce that you talked to Theo and then act as if it's not a big deal? You think we just talk about other things now?" He recoils from my ranting, leaning across his knees to stare at the floor. "Talked to him how!?" I continue. "Phone? In person?"

"Phone," he replies. "For now."

I'm too afraid and enraged to keep doing this dance with him. As my anger boils, I fly up from the table towards the door. I can't just sit there and try to coax the details out of him. I'm not sure I want to hear them at all, much less beg to know what it was all about. I just wish they hadn't spoken at all, especially not behind my back. The last secret meeting they had resulted in me being taken hostage before Theo shot Emmett's father to death.

"Ophelia! Wait!" I faintly hear Emmett calling after me as I storm out of the building. I'm halfway across the parking lot by the time he catches up to me, pulling my arm to stop me.

"I'm not playing around, Emmett," I snap as I whip around to face him. "Either you tell me what you two talked about right now or I'm running home."

"I'm sorry," he answers quickly. "I did a horrible job at bringing that up, I know."

"There is no right way to bring it up! Because you shouldn't be talking to him at all!" I scream. "Spit it out. What did he want?"

His mouth opens, but nothing comes out at first. "Well… he…actually…he," he stammers slowly, making me impatient. I spin on my heels to get away from him again. "Okay, okay," he darts after me, gripping my arm. "He offered me a job."

My brain freezes with confusion. A job? What kind of job does Theo have to offer anyone, much less my boyfriend who hasn't even graduated high school yet?

"What?" my face scrunches up. "What the hell do you mean!? A job?"

"I don't know much about it yet," he explains. "That's why he called. To set up a meeting about it."

My nostrils flare as I glare back in silent anger. I try to speak, but my jaw is locked up. "Yet?" I growl finally through clenched teeth.

"Huh?"

"*Yet*," I hiss. "You said you don't know much about it *yet*." He blinks at me with a blank expression. "Implying you actually plan on meeting with him to find out more!?" I let out a shrill groan of exasperation, turning away again. I can't stand to look at him right now. I'm so angry I'm starting to shake.

"Hey, I didn't say that," he defends. "Look, I couldn't keep it a secret from you. But talking about it makes me nervous, so everything's coming out wrong."

I stand in the cold night air with my arms crossed, shaking my head as I stare off at nothing in the distance. I came to know Emmett as a master manipulator. It's not even his fault. It's just how he was raised to be. Even after everything that's happened, I can't imagine that trait just disappearing overnight. It's hard not to feel like every word he says and action he takes isn't carefully calculated with every possible outcome considered.

"All I know is that he wants to start his own company," he continues. "A new car manufacturing company, but with more energy-efficient models to compete with Jameson. Obviously, I have the qualifications since my entire upbringing was devoted to preparing me for running Jameson Automobiles."

"Ha, of course," I scoff, as my throat tightens. "How convenient. He weasels his way back into Jameson and our lives and suddenly he has a passion for cars and the environment?" He shrugs cluelessly as I glare at him. "Get fucking real, Emmett. All Theo cares about is competing with the Hendersons and the new Elites. I knew getting rid of Thomas wouldn't be enough for him. He's the greediest person I've ever met. He's not going to stop."

"I don't know," he answers nonchalantly. "Does it really matter what his motives are? All I have going for me is what my dad taught me about running the company. But with none of the actual work experience for it to matter to another car manufacturer. Whatever Theo wants out of it, it'd be the start of a career for me..."

His defense knocks out what little bit of wind I have left in my chest. "Wait...so you are actually considering this!? What the fuck..." I let out a shaky exhale and start to pace in the dark parking lot.

"I don't know! I didn't say that! I...I just don't know."

"What about everything we planned!?" I cry out. "All we've talked about the past month is getting the hell out of Jameson. Now not only are you actually considering getting a job here, but you also want to work for my father!? What was the point of everything we've been through!? You scheming to have your monster of a father taken out of the picture…hoping you could run a legitimate company with some sense of ethics and morals. I know everything changed when your mom took everything and cut you off, but it was supposed to be a fresh start! Now you're just going right back to…to…"

"Taking my father out wasn't just about gaining control over Jameson Automobiles," he defends with that familiar haunted and wounded look in his eyes. "It was much more than that and you know it."

A streak of guilt cuts through my rage. I firmly believe there's little to no difference between Theo and Thomas, but I didn't have to grow up with Theo. A fact that has probably left me better off. Emmett has suffered horrible abuse at the hands of his father. Killing him wasn't about money or power. It was about survival and getting rid of a sick and twisted man who did nothing but cause harm to others.

"I know, I'm sorry," I offer. "But that's just it. Why put yourself into Theo's hands? And right back in the same situation you had to go through so much to get out of?"

"Hey, come here," he demands, intercepting my manic pace to wrap his arms around me. "It's okay. I'm not really considering working for him, okay? Like I said…I had to tell you, and it felt like there was just no good way to go about it."

I give into his embrace, still reeling with fear no matter what he says. My chest and arms tremble against him, and I can't tell if it's from the cold or lingering anger.

"No matter what happens…I just can't stand to see you slip back into that life," I explain gently. "Too much has happened for you to end up working in Jameson with a corrupt company the rest of your life."

I want him to agree and reassure me, but instead he's silent as he strokes my hair. I know that look on his face. It's the same one that everyone's been giving me lately, especially my mom and stepdad. The look that implies I'm holding too much of a grudge against Theo. But I can understand it from them. They don't know him like I do. Emmett does though, which is exactly why he should be more adamant about refusing his proposal.

"Let's get back inside," he coaxes, nudging me towards the door. "Wherever we move to is sure to have a bowling alley and I want to show up looking like a seasoned pro."

Referencing our planned move out of here should comfort

me, but it feels half-hearted. I can see Emmett's wheels turning and I'm terrified about just how seriously he's considering this meeting with Theo. The thought twists in my gut, leaving me nauseous by the time I lay down for bed later that night.

This new bit of information put a dark cloud over the whole evening, prompting me to refuse Emmett's invitation to his place after the bowling alley. Once again, something has killed our sex drive. I toss and turn on my pillow and get mad all over again. How could he say there was no good way to tell me about Theo's proposition?

*Your dad actually thought I would consider a job offer from him. Can you believe it!? Isn't that absurd!? Unthinkable!? Completely out of the question!?*

Followed by dismissive laughter and then a change in subject because the idea is too ludicrous to even waste our breath on. *That* would have been a *great* way to bring it up. The fact that Emmett can't see that only worries me more.

Believing that men like Theo and Thomas are the same...is that why it's so hard for him to see my dad for what he really is? Is that why working for him seems like a logical option? Some of my biggest fears about Emmett come bubbling up to the surface once again. Is he a lost cause? Maybe being raised by that monster left him too damaged and fucked-up to ever really be able to live the kind of life we've been dreaming about.

Unable to sleep, Marissa's diary calls to me once again. I roll over to my nightstand drawer as I flip the lamp switch.

*Dear Diary,*

*As mortified as I was about this whole arrangement with the Jamesons, now I feel like the luckiest girl in the world. My parents were going to dictate who I married regardless. If it had to happen, I can't believe I ended up liking the guy they picked for me. More than like. I think I am falling in love with him.*

*We spent the day with our parents going to lunch and then a show. But Thomas was so smooth and charming, he convinced them to let us sneak away afterward. We walked through the park hand in hand while he talked about all of his big plans for Jameson Automobiles. It was all so fascinating and Thomas knows when he takes over, he will do an even better job with it than his father.*

*His ideas are interesting, but his dreams for life are even better. The Jameson Manor is stunning and impressive, and Thomas talks about how he imagines raising a family there. Such a big beautiful house with all the finest foods and clothes. Not to mention vacations around the world. I always thought that the kind of life my parents envisioned for me would dull, but something about picturing it with Thomas by my side makes it incredible. Suddenly, I want it more than anything.*

*Just before we turned around to walk back home, Thomas pulled me off under some trees. He passionately pinned me to one of the trunks and kissed me. I have never felt anything like it. I melted into him completely and would have done absolutely anything he asked. I would have given myself over to him right then and there. But like a true gentleman, he pulled away and walked me home.*

*I can still taste him on my lips and smell the faintest trace of his scent lingering around my neck. It's intoxicating. After our first couple of dates, I couldn't stop daydreaming about prom. But now prom seems like a footnote. Now I spend all day fantasizing about being Mrs. Thomas Jameson. I've practically planned our whole wedding already and have even started picking out baby names.*

*Can I really be this lucky? Will this really be my life?*

*- Marissa*

# CHAPTER THIRTEEN

BOOK 3

I race into my house with my hands full of mail, flinging my backpack to the corner of the room as I begin frantically shuffling through the envelopes. I've been watching the mailbox like a guard dog on high alert for the past week, knowing that acceptance letters and scholarship offers would soon arrive. They have finally started trickling in day by day.

I flip through each piece of mail, tossing bills and other things for my mom and Brendan onto our table by the front door. Once I have weeded out a total of five letters from colleges addressed to me, I run up the stairs to my room and lock the door.

I sit on the edge of the bed with my hands shaking as I run my thumbs across the envelopes, feeling the current of excitement surging through my veins. It's possible that none of them have accepted me at all, much less extended a scholarship offer. But Coach Granger and even his new assistant, Jada, have assured me that's unlikely.

Unable to stand it anymore, I start tearing into the first one at random. The first one I open is from the campus a couple of hours from here. The one where Theo had to rush in and save my ass with a copy of my birth certificate at the interview. It's Coach Granger's top pick, but it's not as far away from Jameson as I would prefer. And it's definitely too close to Theo.

The thought of distance makes me stop. I suddenly have an idea. I line the envelopes up across the bed, arranging them according to how far away from Jameson they are. I imagine them being like a map. A line across the country, each acceptance a pin signifying just how far away I can get.

I finish opening the first one with the nearest campus. Accepted. Full ride track scholarship. I pound my feet on the carpet in a little dance and squeal as I read the words. Placing it back down on the bed, I think: *Okay. There it is. I know I can get at least two hours out of Jameson.*

The next school in line is several states away down south and is the most prestigious institution I've applied to. I rip the envelope open and see another acceptance. I dance and squeal again, but quickly notice the letter doesn't include any mention of a scholarship. It doesn't mean one could not come later, but for now that pretty much rules it out. *That's okay. At least I know I got in,* I think as I place the envelope back in line.

I reach for the next envelope, my heart already swelling with pride and accomplishment. This one is several more states away and even further down south. I read over the letter, now too impatient to take in each word as carefully as I did with the first two. Once again, accepted. Partial track scholarship. And this one is nearly 800 miles away.

The next letter offers another acceptance and scholarship, and it's over 1,000 miles away. A full twenty-four hour's drive. Then I come to the final envelope. The furthest campus all the way in Southern California. 3,000 miles from Jameson. My hands still shake as I rip it open, knowing it is my top pick, no matter how impractical it may be for me to dream of moving to the other side of the country.

But the moment I see the words of acceptance followed by yet another full-ride scholarship offer, something in my heart swells in a way it didn't with the others. Almost as if I intuitively know this is the one I will choose even before I've had time to seriously consider it. The track team has an outstanding record, and like the school that's two hours away, it has turned out a handful of Olympians. The campus and area around it are beautiful from what I've seen in photos. Beyond school, I can imagine weekend trips to the beach or trail running in the mountains. Shopping in the city and maybe even a local coaching gig when my own running career is no longer my main focus in life.

I sit on the edge of the bed and look at the line of envelopes leading away from me. Away from Jameson. A tinge of sadness hits me as Lily's face flashes before my eyes. I can remember sitting across from her in her family's restaurant sipping on cocktails. We talked about this very thing. We counted down the days to our escape from Jameson, but now it seems like she may never make it out of here.

First, the Elites destroyed her chances at getting in anywhere. Emmett eventually fixed that, but her obsession with him landed her in the looney bin. She may have done terrible things, but I still wish she could have had the chance to know what I am feeling right now. Without Jameson, she may have been able to move on and live a normal life. Vivian sure seems to have found that.

I let out a big sigh, suddenly feeling anxious about the threat of the Elites. Why haven't they ruined my chances of getting into college like the old Elites did with Lily? Maybe Bridgett was right and ultimately, they have bigger things to worry about. Or maybe they still see Theo as a threat and want me out of Jameson just as bad as I do.

"Ophelia?" my mom calls out from behind my bedroom door with a light tap.

"Come in!" I answer, scrambling to collect the line of letters. My eyes start to tear up as I prepare myself to tell her all the good news.

"Hey sweetie, you left your backpack in the middle of the floor," she scolds as she comes in and hangs it on my closet door. She turns back to me with a look of disappointment, but she perks up when she sees me standing there with watery eyes. "What do you have there?" She points to the papers in my hands.

"Acceptance letters," I reply, my voice cracking with happy tears.

Her eyes grow wide and also start to well up, but she quickly snaps out of it and rushes over to give me a big hug. "Acceptances!?" she beams. "Where did you get in!?"

We plop down on my bed as I hand them all over, letting her inspect them for herself. "Everywhere so far," I tell her with a deep and shaky exhale. "With scholarship offers at almost all of them."

She skims over each one, shaking her head with overwhelming emotion. "This is amazing," she murmurs as she reads. "Ophelia, I am so, *so* proud of you." She sweeps her arms around me again, squeezing tight. "We have to celebrate!

Dinner anywhere you want tonight. You pick the restaurant. Brendan can join us when he gets off work and you can invite Emmett."

"Uh, let's just keep it down to you, me, and Brendan," I suggest, awkwardly rubbing my arms. "We hardly ever have time with just the three of us anymore."

She looks down at the letters more thoughtfully. "I guess you'll be leaving us soon," she says sadly, trying to hide her dismay with a smile. "We should get in as much quality time as we can."

I lunge forward to hug her again. "Don't worry," I assure her. "We will."

"So…which one do you think you'll pick?" she asks, wiping her eyes. "Or do you know yet?"

"I don't know yet," I shake my head with wide eyes, still stuck in some disbelief.

"Whichever one you choose, we'll find a way to make it work," she insists. I know she's thinking back on our conversation about accepting Theo's financial help, but I'm not ready to broach that topic again.

"Well…I do have a favorite," I explain hesitantly. "I haven't made up my mind, but there is one in particular…"

"Which one!?" she asks excitedly. I pull out one of the envelopes from her hand and hold it up as if I'm too afraid or nervous to say it out loud. "It's in Southern California," she whispers to herself. "That's so far away!" The sadness in her eyes shows through again, followed by a panicked look. But she's quick to swallow it all down for my sake. "Tell me about it. Why is it your top pick?"

I start getting ready for our dinner as she sits on my bed and listens carefully. I ramble on and on about the school in California and all it has to offer.

"It sounds amazing," she beams once I've finished. "And perfect for you. I think you should go. Trust your gut. Of course, I'm not thrilled about you moving to the other side of the country. But it's only an eight-hour flight, I think. And it gives me an excuse to move there when we can afford it," she winks.

"Well…I should wait until I hear from the rest of the schools I applied to before I decide…and…," I trail off, feeling worried about even seriously considering California.

"What's wrong?" she asks. "What is it?"

I sigh and collapse back down to the edge of the bed. "It's Emmett," I confess with my heart feeling heavy. "He wants to move with me when I go, but…it's *so* expensive there. And when I was researching it, I learned it's really, really hard to find a job there. Like almost impossible. He's running out of money and has no work experience. I don't know what he'd do. I don't know if he could come with me."

I avoid telling her that secretly I wonder if he'd be better off staying here and working with Theo. It's not the life I want for him, and definitely a life I want no part of. But condoning it is almost easier than my constant fear and panic of it coming true whether I like it or not. And I'm still worried that maybe that's all Emmett has the strength to settle for at this point in his life.

"I know you two love each other," she nods in deep thought. "It would hurt to leave him, but Emmett isn't your responsibility. You can't put your life on hold or settle for less than what you want just for him."

"I know," I answer softly. "I have a lot to think about anyway. For now, let's go eat! I know exactly where I want to go!"

My mom freshens up as well and then we hop into her car and head downtown to the restaurant of my choice. Gusto's is an Italian restaurant. My favorite kind of food second only to Mexican, but I don't dare ask my mom to go to any Mexican restaurants around here. We quickly learned within our first few weeks in Jameson that none of them are authentic and can't hold a candle to what my mom cooks at home.

Brendan meets us at the restaurant a half-hour later after he finishes up at work. They both rave about how proud they are of me, making me blush. I'm proud of myself too but doing my best to stay humble. We laugh and joke and, for a moment, I forget we're in Jameson at all. The Elites and everything with Emmett feels a million miles away. I smile every time I remember that by Fall, I will be many miles away from here.

But then I look across the table and my mom and stepdad and realize how much I will miss them. Part of me wants to tell them to accept Theo's offer to help just so they can follow me wherever I go. I swallow down a hard lump in my throat realizing it never occurred to me to consider that option for helping Emmett to follow me.

After dinner, they ask me if I want to watch a movie with them at home. I politely decline and step away to my room to call Emmett. I'm not ready to talk to him about Southern California, but I do want to share the good news with him. He says he's just watching TV at his apartment, so I ask to come over. Once I arrive, I tell him that I received five acceptance letters that day, all but one offering a scholarship. As I say the words out loud, it's still hard to believe.

"I'm not surprised at all," he beams as he takes me in his arms with a flurry of kisses up and down my neck and face. "Of course, you'd get into all of them."

As I pull back, I want to ask him if he has spoken to Theo again or if he has given any more thought to what he might want to do after graduation, aside from following me wherever I go. But the spark in his eyes pulls me in. The last thing I want to do with him right now is talk.

I lunge forward, crashing my lips into his. His hand rakes up into the back of my hair with a deep moan as he leans back, pulling me on top of him. I breathe heavy with excitement as I look down at him and the crooked, sly grin on the corner of his lips.

"I've missed this," I whisper as I press into the growing strain against his jeans.

All at once he sits straight up and kisses me more deeply, running his hands up my thighs and around to the small of my back. He guides my hips back and forth across him until we can't stand it anymore and start ripping off each other's clothes.

The moment he slides my panties down and tosses them to the side, he slowly runs his fingers across my upper thighs before finally reaching my pulsating folds. He slips inside of me enough to feel the pooling wetness, and then uses it to massage in soft circles over my clit, causing me to hiss and groan impatiently.

"Oh, Ophelia," he hums in his deep voice against my ear. "I want to feel you cum." He works his fingers faster and harder, knowing all the right ways to push me to the edge.

With his fingers still moving over me, I grab onto his long shaft and begin massaging it up and down, relishing how hard he feels. I love how much I turn him on. I guide him inside of me and begin riding him, keeping his fingers pressed against me.

"You're so wet," he murmurs, his voice cracking.

I collapse across his chest, muttering into his ear. "I'm close."

His eyes burn into me, his chest rising and falling as I claw into it. I pin his wrists against the couch and roll my tongue into his mouth. We explore each other's mouths with our hands clutching and grabbing at every inch of skin they can find. We move greedily with labored breaths and pained moans.

I throw back my head with the intensifying satisfaction, trembling with ecstasy as he pushes in harder against my tight and aching muscles. He lunges his hips, his skin growing hot and sweaty. Almost too hot to touch. I yell out with unintelligible strings of words and exclamations as a violent wave of ecstasy crashes over me. The moment my own rippling orgasm fades, he quickly pulls out. I take him into my hands and grin as I work him to his own climax with him trembling beneath my touch.

Once it's over and we've caught our breath, we can't help but look at each other and start snickering over how good everything just felt.

"I needed that," I laugh as I lay my head across his chest.

"I'm sorry," he says in a more serious tone as he strokes my hair. "I know I haven't been…in the mood much lately. I guess I'm just stressed."

"I know," I offer. "Me too."

As I lay across his chest, slowly rising and falling, moving my whole body up and down with it, I feel closer to him than I have in a while. For a moment I think maybe I should just come clean about the prospects of me moving to California, but everything feels so perfect. The room is dark with only the light of the moon shining in through the window. All I can hear are his breaths and the pounding of his heart. My naked body is pressed against his warmth. I just want to fall asleep right here and forget about everything else for a little while.

# CHAPTER FOURTEEN

BOOK 3

"You'll have to decide no later than June," Coach Granger urges me as he looks over my collection of acceptance letters and scholarship offers which has only grown in the past week. It should make me ecstatic. But it is starting to get overwhelming. "Have you at least narrowed it down some?" he asks.

"Sort of," I nod intently, not wanting to seem indifferent. "I'm trying to."

"Anything we can do to help?" Jada adds from her seat at the other end of his desk. "These are some amazing offers. You don't want to wait until the last minute and miss out on anything."

"I know, I know," I respond with a sharp exhale. I know they are just trying to help and have my best interests in mind but having so many options has only made me more indecisive. I feel panicked every time I consider making a final decision. At this very moment with my leg bouncing like crazy as I try to sit still, I really just want to take off running.

I've been running even more than usual lately, and when I'm not running, I'm usually thinking about it. Which means when I finally do pick a school, I'll be in top-notch shape by the time I get there. At night I go to sleep imagining that I could just start running and see where I end up. Wherever my legs take me, that's where I'll go to school.

"I'm sorry," I add, snapping back to the conversation. "I'll do my best to start narrowing it down. Anything else? I told my mom I'd be home in time for dinner tonight."

"No, nothing else," Coach sighs, seeming disappointed. "But let's talk again next week. I'd like you to have made a short list of your top picks by then."

"I can do that!" I announce confidently, but inside I'm dreading the deadline.

I'm relieved to finally be dismissed and out from under the pressure, at least for a moment. As I start walking to my car, I hear someone call out to me.

"Hey!" Bridgett smiles as she comes running up, carefully looking around to make sure no one is watching us. "I was hoping I'd catch you. What did Coach want?"

"Hey! He just wanted to talk about colleges and stuff," I explain.

She nods, seeming thrown by my short response. "Which ones have you been accepted to?"

My lips part to answer, but I quickly stop myself. I have come to see Bridgett as a friend. I've trusted her enough to tell her the whole story about Emmett and my time in Jameson. And being related to the Henderson's, she understands more about it than the average person would. But it doesn't change the fact that she's still one of them, even if only in appearances. They have a way of getting what they want from people, and they're especially skilled at pretending to be your friend.

I think back to Lily and how clueless I was to what was really going on in her head the whole time we were friends. Then I think about the Elites calling in their contacts to make her top choice schools rescind their interest. I don't know which end of the spectrum Bridgett falls on, if any. But it seems smart to keep some things to myself for now.

"A good number of them," I answer finally. "I don't want to talk about it. I feel like that's all anyone ever asks me about anymore. What about you? How are you doing?"

"Good," she answers sincerely, no longer seeming too bothered by my unwillingness to share more. "Practice was good today. I'm dreading dinner tonight though. We're supposed to go over to Uncle Liam's."

"Ugh, I'm sorry," I wince at the thought of having to sit down at a dinner table with Liam, Malcolm, Marissa, and Bernadette. And it still seems so strange that Emmett will be eating at my house, while what's left of his family will be dining with Bridgett. "It's so crazy...," I muse. "The way things turn out."

"How so?" her brows raise.

"That you're so nice," I shrug, not knowing how else to explain it.

"Thanks...I guess," she laughs.

"Well, you should blow them off and come to my house for dinner instead," I suggest. "I guarantee my mom's cooking will be better than any chef Liam has hired."

"That is tempting," she grins mischievously, thinking it over. "Do you think your parents would mind?"

"Nah, they'll be relieved to see me hanging out with someone new," I reply. "A girl at that. Emmett is coming too, though."

A strange look washes over her face. "Do you think he'll be okay with me tagging along?" she asks hesitantly. "He didn't seem to like me too much when we were hanging out the other day."

"He's just wary of you is all. I'm sure you can understand why." I drop my eyes and kick some rocks around awkwardly. I hate the way the words sound, but I don't know how else to put it. She may be one of the good guys, but how can any of us be so sure after what we've been through?

"Okay...," she says slowly. "If you really don't think it'd be any trouble..."

"Not at all!" I assure her. "Come on. Let's get out of the cold before someone sees you leaving with me."

We start walking as I search for Emmett's car in the parking lot. Once I spot it, I see the dimmed lights and steam billowing out from the back, telling me he's already heated it up and is waiting on me. I can't see his face through the windshield, but I can only imagine how he must look as he sees Bridgett walking up with me.

"Hey baby, Bridgett's coming with us. Okay?" I warn him from the driver's side window, but I don't give him much of a chance to respond before we both jump in. "Whew, I'll be glad when it starts warming up!" My lips shiver as I rub my hands together and rock in the heated passenger's seat.

"Hello again, Bridgett," he grumbles, eyeing her skeptically through the rearview mirror.

"Hey, Emmett!" she says cheerfully. "What's up?"

"Oh, nothing," he replies as he puts the car in reverse. His voice is dripping with disdain, but I shoot him a threatening look to play nice.

We don't give him much of a chance to be mopey or weird on the drive back to my house. Bridgett and I chatter away. We're both students and athletes, and don't have much time to laze around watching the latest movies and shows. You'd think we'd have trouble finding anything to talk about. But we get by just fine discussing our favorite running gear or shoes we've recently purchased, or weird things we've learned in class the past few weeks.

"Alright, ladies," he announces as we approach my house. "Your chauffeur has…"

"Shit!" I cut him off, eyeing the expensive car parallel parked in front of my house.

"What is it?" Bridgett asks from the backseat.

I look over to Emmett who recognizes the car too. "It's her dad," he tells her. "Looks like Theo has come around for another visit."

"Shit," I say again, thinking the timing couldn't be worse. But really there's no good time to come home and find him here.

"Should I go?" she suggests politely. "I could call Malcolm to come pick me up."

I want to tell her it's not the best time, but I don't want to send her off in a car with Malcolm either. She shouldn't have to spend any more time than necessary with those assholes. And anyway, I can't let Theo ruin everything for me.

"No, it's fine," I sigh, gathering the determination to make the best of it. "It's better this way actually. Extra support for me. If you're still okay with joining us, that is."

"As long as Malcolm and Liam don't find out," she smirks. "But then again, if they knew I was here, Theo wouldn't be their only issue."

I laugh lightly, but it is a scary thought. It's still too easy to forget that she's taking a risk by being around us, just as we feel like we are with her.

"It's like Romeo and Juliet!" I jest dramatically as we unbuckle our seat belts. "Let's hope this dinner has a better ending."

"Let's aim for no suicides…or deaths at all," Emmett adds, still looking wounded by Bridgett's presence.

We step inside the warmth and aroma of my mom's freshly

cooked food. Brendan is helping her in the kitchen while Theo reads a paper at the table.

"Hello everyone," I announce, eyeing my bio-dad with hatred. "Mom, I hope you don't mind, I…"

"Hello!" my mom shouts enthusiastically as she turns to see Bridgett standing there. She doesn't even bother letting me finish my sentence before running over and giving her a big hug.

"I…invited my friend Bridgett to join us," I chuckle as I notice how happy she looks. I knew she was concerned about me not having any girlfriends, but I think I underestimated just how much.

"Well…I think you must be the first girl Ophelia has had over since we moved here," she gushes. "This is my husband, Brendan. And this is Ophelia's dad…Theo."

I notice my mom tense up slightly as she turns to introduce Theo, but she's quick to smile and play it off before returning to the kitchen as if it's all completely normal. Theo sits proudly at the table with that same old annoying grin, like the cat that ate the canary. Always looking so pleased with himself as if each time he talks his way back into this house it's like summiting a mountain.

"Can I help with anything?" Bridgett offers, but my mom shoos her away to sit at the table and make herself comfortable.

Emmett and I take our seats next to her, and I'm left sitting across from Theo not knowing what to say. I can't hide my discomfort or anger as I glare at him, but he seems completely unmoved by it.

"So, what brings you here this time, *Dad*?" I ask with a sarcastic emphasis on the title.

"Oh, you know," he leans back arrogantly. "Just wanted to check in and see how things were going."

"They make these things called telephones you know," I snap back.

"Let's eat!" my mom announces quickly as she and Brendan bring an assortment of dishes over to the table.

Emmett and Bridgett seem relieved for the brief interruption as they glance tensely back and forth between Theo and me.

"Thank you, Lala. This looks delicious as always," Theo proclaims as she heaps food onto his plate. "Ophelia, your mom tells me that you've been accepted to quite a few schools already."

"Every single one she's applied to," Emmett boasts, shooting me a wink.

"With scholarship offers," I add.

"And have you thought any more about my offer to help pay for your living expenses?" he asks snidely, but in a way I think only I can detect. "I hear you're top choice so far is the one in Southern California. I live there for a time, you know. That city is expensive. And jobs are really hard to come by."

"I'm aware," I murmur. I see Emmett freeze in the corner of my eye, but I try not to look at him. Instead, I glance up to my mom, silently scolding her for telling Theo something like that.

"Southern California?" Emmett asks. "You didn't tell me about that one. Or that it was your top choice."

I drop my fork and turn to him, feeling ashamed. "I…I'm sorry," I stammer. "I meant to…I…I just…"

"And what would you do in SoCal, Emmett?" Theo shoots out abruptly, intentionally stirring the pot. "I know you didn't want to come work for me so that you'd be free to follow Ophelia."

Emmett stabs back into his food bitterly. "I don't know," he sulks. "I obviously haven't had any time to think about it."

"I really haven't decided anything yet," I defend with an awkward laugh, looking around the table, begging for someone to diffuse this.

"Work for you?" My mom questions, staring Theo down.

Theo looks smug as ever as he prepares to tell her all about his big eco-friendly car plans, but he freezes suddenly and cuts his eyes over to Bridgett. "Where did you say you were from… uh…what was your name?"

"Bridgett," she replies with an innocent smile. "Bridgett Henderson. We're from California actually."

"Uh-huh," Theo straightens, rolling his tongue across his teeth. "Henderson. That wouldn't be any relation to…Liam Henderson?"

"He's my uncle," she nods, studying my reaction as if she's asking for my permission to admit it.

A heavy tension falls over the table. Everyone looks deep in thought except Brendan who looks like he's a million miles away. Most likely just trying to survive another dinner with my mom's ex until he can finally relax in front of the game with a beer. My mom looks puzzled, probably trying to figure out what kind of new thing Theo is starting now and why he'd try to rope Emmett into it.

Bridgett looks apologetic, like she's worried she has said something wrong. Or that *she's* wrong simply for being related to the Henderson's at all. Theo keeps his mouth shut, eyeing her every so often like she's a traitor over enemy lines.

And Emmett is silently stewing, still stabbing away at his food, and is probably getting more salt in his wounds from this dinner than anyone. He hates the Henderson's for stealing everything from him, yet he's sitting right next to one of them, even if she's only related by blood. With her family's ownership of Jameson Automobiles and Theo's big plans to start his own thing, I can see how he'd feel like the only one without a piece of the pie. Even though it was his birthright.

"Well, this has been pleasant as always," I scoff under my breath.

"What was that dear?" my mom asks with a naïve sweetness.

I shake my head and practically hold my breath, impatiently waiting for this whole thing to finally be over.

"Spring will be here soon," Brendan announces randomly in his deep, gruff voice. "I'm already seeing termites all over the poles around town. We've had to treat everything. They'll be bad this year. Which reminds me, honey. We need to go ahead and treat the house too."

Theo darts his eyes between them, looking oddly jealous. "That's right, Brendan. You're an electrician, aren't you?"

"Mm-hmm," he grunts, not looking up from his plate.

"Maybe you could teach Emmett your line of work," he suggests snidely. "He'll need something to do to take care of our Ophelia. Since she won't take any help from me."

There's a loud clanking noise, and it takes me a second to realize it's my own fork crashing to my plate. "I'm driving the car you gave me and using the phone. Isn't that enough?" I bark, throwing my napkin over what's left of my food. My appetite is completely gone now. "And Emmett doesn't have to take care of me. I'm not his responsibility." I pull my chair out from the table and turn to Bridgett. "Hey, do you want to see my room while you're here?"

"Ophelia!" my mom scolds. "She's not even done eating yet. Let the poor girl finish."

"No, it's okay!" Bridgett says quickly. "I'm full. Thank you, though. It was delicious." She pushes out of her chair and jumps up to follow me.

"You coming?" I ask Emmett.

"I'll be up in a little bit," he answers, looking stiff and rigid.

I shrug and lead Bridgett to the stairs. It feels weird to abandon Emmett down there, but I can't stand sitting across Theo for another second.

"Phew, and I thought my family's dinners were tense," Bridgett exclaims when we're finally in the privacy of my room.

"I'm so sorry," my cheeks blush. "You probably would have been better off going to Liam's, huh? If I had known Theo would be here…"

"No, it's okay," she assures me. "I understand. Trust me. You don't have to apologize for the crazy shit your family does." She looks around my somewhat messy room. "Hey, what's that?" she asks suddenly, reaching toward the old journal on my bed. "Do you keep a diary?"

I panic and snatch the book up, quickly throwing it into my dresser. When I turn back around, Bridgett is frozen with a stunned sort of look.

"If I tell you what that is, you have to promise not to tell anyone," I sigh, figuring I've told her all my other secrets just about. Why stop now? She nods and agrees. "It's one of Marissa Jameson's old diaries. They gave it to Emmett for some reason, but he didn't want it. So…I took it. But he doesn't know," my voice drops to a whisper, realizing he could walk in at any time.

"Whoa, I bet that's quite a read," she gapes. "Marissa scares me."

"She always did me too," I agree as we both sit on the edge of the bed. "But…reading that diary…I don't know. It's from when she was about our age. And she doesn't seem so bad. It's almost scarier to think she used to be just a normal girl. But then Thomas and the life of the Elites…something about it must have broken her along the way."

She gets a distant look in her eye as if she understands all too well. We go back to talk about normal things, and by the time Emmett joins us it actually seems perfect that she's here. Of course, I would've preferred my mom not telling Theo about SoCal or him not announcing it at the dinner table. But if all that had to happen, Bridgett turned out to be the perfect buffer. I can tell he is itching to talk about it, but after a while, he has to offer to drive Bridgett home instead. I just stay hidden in my room, hoping Theo left in peace without doing any more damage.

# CHAPTER FIFTEEN



Emmett and I sit in awkward silence with nothing but the sounds of us quietly chewing our food, which seems louder with the absence of words. Beyond our little bubble sits the rest of the high school cafeteria, filled with laughter and everyone trying to talk over each other.

In the middle of it all is the Elite table. I have started a daily habit of studying Bridgett as she sits with them, but she's smart enough to know not to stare back at me. She always sits, eating quietly, seeming completely detached from whatever the rest of them are talking about around her. She wasn't kidding about preferring to keep her head down and stay out of their business the best she can.

I turn back to Emmett who seems determined not to look at me. "You okay?" I ask finally. He nods with a grunt, not saying anything. "I'm sorry Theo blurted that out about California," I add. "I was going to talk to you about it, but I've been stressed and nervous about it all. Coach is putting a lot of pressure on me to make a decision…not to mention all the money stuff with my parents."

"So, it's true then?" he perks up. "That's your top choice so far?"

"I…I don't know yet," I reply, feeling frustrated. "You know…I just said I was under a lot of pressure. It's not exactly the response I was hoping for…For you to add to that feeling."

"Whatever," he grumbles. "Sorry. Forget I said anything."

"What the fuck?" I mutter, wondering where the attitude is coming from.

"Hey, I'm leaving early today, so I won't see you after school," he states casually, still seeming irritated with me.

"Oh…okay…well…what for?" I ask in confusion.

He barely lifts his head, scrunching up his face. "Huh?"

"What are you leaving early for?"

Commotion rises from the corner of the room, distracting both of us. Our heads whip around to see that Malcolm has left his lunch table and is pummeling some guy against the wall. Everyone watches in discomfort, but we all know better than to try and interfere. Their fight dissipates after a few minutes and everyone goes back to pretending everything is fine and normal. Who knows what that guy did to bring on Malcolm's wrath.

I look back to Emmett, always feeling uncomfortable with any reminder that those are the kinds of things he used to do. Then I'm eager to hear why he's leaving early, but before I can ask again he quickly stands and starts gathering his things.

"I'll talk to you later, okay?" he blurts coldly before walking away with his tray.

He's too far away for me to yell after him, and with Malcolm already riled up, I don't want to draw any attention to us. I'm not done eating yet, but I can't just let Emmett walk away and leave things so tense. I leave my food and go chasing after him.

"Hey!" I call out just as he's rounding the corner in the hall. "Wait up!" He stops and turns towards me, but his eyes dart all around, still avoiding me. "What's going on with you?"

"What do you mean? Nothing," he shrugs.

"You're acting so weird," I point out, annoyed that he seems to think I'm too stupid to notice. Or that I would let him get away with it.

"Just a lot on my mind," he says quietly. "I have to go, okay?" He kisses my forehead and takes off again, leaving me with a nagging feeling in my gut.

It doesn't seem like it'd do any good to chase after him again, so not knowing what else to do, I slowly turn and begin making my way back into the lunchroom. I walk with my brows furrowed and my head down, muttering under my breath the whole way. I hate it when I know something is going on with him, but he refuses to tell me what it is.

I can't ignore how guilty I feel. I should have talked to him about California rather than treating him like some pity case who wouldn't be able to work it out with me. Who am I to say he wouldn't be able to find some kind of job there? Furthermore, what kind of job am I going to find there? I'm not ready to give up on the possibility just yet, but I don't know if I can bring myself to take Theo's money if it comes down to that.

As I get closer to the cafeteria, I see Bridgett coming through the double doors. She's making her early escape to class, like she always does, avoiding whatever new drama could erupt in the hallways between periods.

"Hey!" I smile, knowing no one else is around.

But she breezes right past me like I don't exist, ignoring me completely. It scares me at first, bringing back memories of the times Lily turned on me, but then the doors behind her swing open again as Malcolm and a few of his other cronies come filing out. They're pumping fists, likely congratulating each other on their little show of dominance in the cafeteria. Malcolm doesn't see me standing there at first and bumps straight into my shoulder.

"Watch where you're going, whore," he sneers, shooting me a look of pure hatred and disgust.

I ignore him and go through the doors, feeling relieved to know Bridgett probably ignored me because she knew they were right behind her. I sit back down at my tray with a heavy sigh, knowing my food is probably cold now.

I take a sip of my water, thinking it tastes a little weird. Then just as I am about to take a bite of my burger, I notice it has some kind of weird powdery substance on it that wasn't there before. I throw it back down to the tray. Maybe I'm just being paranoid, but it definitely seems like somebody tampered with my food. Not wanting to take any risks, I decide to just throw it all out.

*Great, first they tried to kill me in my car, now they try to poison me.* I think to myself as I return to the hall, still feeling hungry. It's almost time for my next period now and the rest of the students are beginning to spill out to the lockers. I stop at my own to switch out the textbooks in my backpack, but I immediately notice that the lock is undone.

I look around over my shoulders, trying to determine if anyone is watching me. If there is something gross in my locker or anything that could jump out or spill over me, the Elites would likely be waiting nearby to watch it happen. But they're nowhere in sight as far as I can tell. I consider not opening it at all just to be safe, but we're studying for an exam in my next class and I need the book.

Bracing myself, I pull open the metal door. I jump slightly at the sight of a barbie doll hanging there by a noose. There's a note dangling beside her. I yank them both down and quickly grab my book, not wanting anyone to see me freak out over the sight. I don't want to give whoever did this that kind of satisfaction. I march off towards my next class, tossing the doll and noose into the garbage on the way.

I stash the note away in my backpack, refusing to let myself read it until after school. I just want to forget it even happened so I can focus on my schoolwork. Through some extreme form of dissociation, I manage to block the letter's existence out of my head. By the time I'm walking to practice I think, I've made it this far without knowing what it says. Why not go a little longer?

The mystery of the letter is the perfect fuel for practice, spurring me on to run faster and harder. Once practice is over, I figure I've waited long enough. Brendan's prediction about Spring coming soon was spot on, and the evening air is less chilly than usual. I sit on the bleachers alone after everyone else has gone inside to shower up and pull the folded note out of my backpack.

"What's that?" Bridgett asks suddenly from over my shoulder, causing me to jump.

"It was in my locker today," I reply. "Along with a doll on a noose. Do you know anything about it?"

"No," she scoffs, looks offended. "Why would you think I'd know about it?"

"I didn't mean to…accuse you or anything like that. I just didn't know if you had overheard any of the Elites talking about leaving something like this for me," I explain.

"I would've tried to warn you if I had," she says, sitting down next to me. "What does it say?"

I hand the note over to her, more than ready to get it out of my hands. She reads over the cut and collaged letters spelling out a warning for me to watch my back and that I might not be so lucky next time.

"What the hell does that mean?" she winces.

"It has to be from whoever fucked with my car and almost

killed me," I tell her. "We can both take a pretty good guess at who might have done that."

"Can we?"

"Oh, come on," I huff. "You know Malcolm and the Elites are behind this. No offense, I know you're technically one of them. But they're not like you. They're cruel and heartless, and they hate me."

She nods and looks thoughtfully out over the track field. I wish I knew what she's thinking, but it definitely doesn't seem like she's hiding anything. I believe her when she says she didn't know anything about it.

"I don't know," she says slowly. "Uncle Liam has been keeping Malcolm so busy with Jameson Automobiles and their software company. I can't imagine him taking time away from all that to send you death threats. Not saying he wouldn't do something like that. It just doesn't make sense right now… timing-wise."

"What about Bernadette or one of the others?" I suggest. "I mean, Malcolm had time to beat that guy up in the cafeteria today. I can't totally rule it out." We sit, quietly contemplating everything for a moment, when suddenly I remember my food being tampered with after I chased Emmett down. "Hey, did you see anyone near my tray before you left the lunchroom today?"

"No, why?"

"It looked like there was something on it. Something that wasn't there before," I divulge, thinking I must sound crazy and paranoid.

"Holy shit," she shakes her head in disbelief. "Someone's really out to get you, Ophelia. Are you scared?"

I consider the question carefully. I feel on edge and nervous. But scared? When I think of scared, I think of Emmett holding me while his father groped me or having a gun shoved in my face. Recording a hostage video pleading for my life. Maybe my perception is too skewed now, but it takes a lot for me to feel afraid these days.

"At least they warned me this time," I laugh darkly. "Now I know to be on the lookout for someone trying to kill me. It's considerate really…if you think about it."

"Girl, that's fucked-up," she smirks. "That's what I like to call Jameson humor."

"Ha! I'm sure Emmett would appreciate that term," I cry

out, thinking it feels good to laugh. No matter how fucked-up the situation might be.

"Hey, I want to ask you something, but I don't want you to take it the wrong way," Bridgett says cautiously. "You don't think…well…Emmett. He wouldn't…would he?"

I stare at her blankly, not knowing what she means at first. She nudges the letter in my hands and then it clicks. "Leave me death threats!?" I shriek. "No, no way!"

"Oh, okay. Good," she answers quickly. "I just…I don't know. The way you described him before…I know he's changed and everything, but…If you don't think he could do something like that, I believe you."

"Of course, he couldn't!" I proclaim confidently, but a seed of doubt bounces around inside. The memory of all the torture and humiliation from before doesn't just disappear, even if it does seem like it came from an entirely different person than the Emmett I have come to know and love. It's hard to replay those images in my mind without thinking he could be capable of something like this. But why?

"Huh," I blurt suddenly, panicking as I think it over more. "He was being so weird today. And he left early. The day of my accident…he left early then too." I look over to Bridgett who is shooting me a sympathetic look, seeming to say: *that doesn't sound good.*

"I'm sure you're right though," she offers. "He wouldn't do something like that. He loves you. I shouldn't have said anything. I just know how fucked-up people in Jameson can be. Sometimes it's hard to know who you can trust."

I try to ignore the fact that it could be just as easy to think Bridgett did these things or that maybe I shouldn't trust her. But Emmett's behavior around these events is all I can think about now.

"No, it has to be the other Elites," I insist. "They hate me because of who my dad is. And they want to destroy Emmett's life. If he lost me…he'd officially have nothing left."

"Maybe you're right. But what if Emmett doesn't actually want to kill you? What if he just wants to scare you so you'll get the hell out of Jameson?" she asks.

"I don't think he has any doubt that I'll be leaving the first chance I get, and hopefully taking him with me. Besides… whoever messed with the brakes on my care definitely wanted me dead." The thought tightens my chest, as if the whole accident is happening all over again.

"Well, I'm here for you…whatever happens," she squeezes my hand, noticing the growing worry on my face. "I'll do my best to help keep an eye out. Protect you in any way I can."

"Thanks, Bridgett," I smile, wondering how the hell I'd be navigating all of this without a good friend who is someone besides Emmett.

The paper rattles with a gust of wind, pulling me back in. I read over the words one more time and then crumple it up.

"What are you doing!?" Bridgett shrieks. "You need to save that! For evidence!"

"Evidence?" I laugh. "Anyone around here who would do something like this wouldn't get in trouble for it anyway, no matter how much evidence we had. I don't want to keep it around. It's only going to make me overly paranoid."

She jerks the crumpled paper from my hands and begins straightening it back out. "Then I'll keep it," she insists. "Just in case you ever need it."

"Well, at least I know it's not you," I joke, watching her bury the letter into her backpack. "You'd never stop me from destroying the evidence."

"Glad you've ruled me out as a suspect," she smirks. "Now, let's get out of here. It's too pretty a night to sit around yammering."

We decide to go on a short run from the school to Bridgett's house, which is only a couple of miles away. She assures me no one is home and that she knows a back way where no one would see us. There are acres of sprawling property around her parents' manor, which is pretty small for a manor, at least in comparison to Jameson manor and the Henderson Estate. We hop on a couple of bikes stored near the pool house and ride around in the woods, soaking up the crisp but warm evening air. As we ride, she tells me all about her favorite places to run in California and says she may even consider going back there herself after graduation. Even if it does piss her family off.

When it gets too dark to see, we walk the bikes back to the yard that's well-lit with decorative lights mixed in among the landscaping. The sparkling blue pool glows orange from all the hanging lights and I find myself hoping that Bridgett and I are still friends by summertime so I can dive in. Just like tonight has been fun, and almost made me forget about the death threats entirely, I hope I can enjoy just one month of summer in Jameson before I go. Without anything crazy happening, so I can walk out of this hell hole with at least a handful of pleasant memories.

# CHAPTER SIXTEEN

BOOK 3

The next night, I turn back to Marissa's diary as an escape from my own scary life for a moment. She talks about how excited she is for prom and how she plans to lose her virginity to Thomas that night. It's easy to forget that I know the rest of the story. Reading her young and innocent teenage words, you'd never guess how corrupt and evil both her and Thomas would become. At this point, they're two seemingly normal teens caught up in the throes of their all-consuming lust.

The hormonally charged writing makes me miss Emmett. I decide to call him and ask if I can come over. He still seems distant and weird on the phone but wants to see me. I start to rush out the door after hanging up, but then a dress catches my eye from the closet. It's a tight, red dress that I bought for a Valentine's Day dance at my old school. It pops against my dark eyes and skin and hugs my figure perfectly. I haven't worn it since the dance, but it looks so good on me it seems like a shame to just let it sit there in my closet.

I decide to slip into it and take a few extra minutes to fix my hair and put on some matching red lipstick. Then I slide into my long leather coat that I only wear on special occasions. The next trick is sneaking out without my mom and Brendan seeing me. They'd tease me to no end if they saw me all dressed up like this for no reason.

Emmett's face drops when he answers his door. His jaw goes

slack as his eyes look me up and down, drinking in every inch of me.

"Holy shit," he murmurs. "You look *incredible*. Get in here. Now." He swoops his arm around my back and pulls me inside, instantly pressing his lips to mine as all tension between us seems to fade.

Keeping his mouth against mine, rolling his tongue in and out, he walks us towards the bedroom. I can already feel his excitement growing, especially as he pushes me against the door, deepening his kiss and pressing into me. Without taking his attention off of me, he fumbles for the door handle behind him and finally opens it up.

His hands slide under the dress, grazing the fabric of my panties across my ass, sparking a heightened surge of desire in both of us. "I want your body so bad," he hisses. "But I almost don't want to take this thing off of you...you look so good in it."

"So don't," I suggest mischievously, guiding his hands up to my breasts without removing my dress.

He slides them around to my back, unfastening my bra before moving his thumbs back to my nipples. He massages each one and then takes them into his mouth, working his tongue over the red satiny fabric. The urge to feel him between my legs grows, prompting me to grab one of his hands and move it downward. He slides down my lace underwear and flings them to the side, then teases the dripping wetness.

I roll my head back with a moan as he flicks his tongue over my nipple and teases me with his fingers. I grab his hips and move him closer to the bed. Before he can throw me down onto his comforter, I turn around and press my back into him while he runs his hands all over my body. As he pushes his erection against me, I bend over and lift the dress up, giving him the perfect view of my ass. He gives it a quick and playful slap before undoing his belt. His pants fall to the floor, and I soon feel the soft skin stretched over his hardness teasing around my folds.

I reach back and grip his hips, jerking him closer and begging him to enter me as I lean over the bed. He guides my legs up onto the mattress, angling me around him. We both cry out as he slides inside of me. I'm so tight from this angle and he fills me up to the brim, caressing against every last tingling nerve as he slowly moves in and out.

He pounds into my g-spot and the pulsating tissue inside, coaxing me to climax. I'm so close and can tell he is getting there too. I arch my back, pressing into him more before I start rocking back and forth, matching his rhythm. He moves faster with me, our bodies slamming together in unison. He groans out in strings of words I can't understand, his voice deep and straining as he grows impossibly hard inside of me.

"Yes, that's it, baby," I whimper as we pick up the pace more and more. I dig my nails into his thighs and any other flesh within my reach.

Just as I start to feel the build of overwhelming pleasure coarse through me from inside, he reaches his fingers around and begins massaging me, pushing me over the edge. I cry out through my orgasm, feeling him pulsing inside of me as he grows close. As I come down off of my own wave, he pulls out to cum. He grabs at my back, but I quickly turn around and pull him into my mouth, wanting to drink him in. I feel the hot liquid spilling out in my mouth as he makes noises unlike anything I've ever heard from him before.

"Well, *that* was unexpected," he pants, smiling down at me.

He reaches down and pulls me up to my feet, kissing me softly before I press my head to his chest and wrap my arms around him. We crash down onto his bed and lay there for a long time, tangled up in each other's skin.

"I've missed this," I whisper as I twirl my fingers through his curls.

"What?" he asks.

"Feeling close to you."

"Is that what this was all about?" he teases, tugging at the fabric of my dress.

"Sort of," I smirk. "I guess. I didn't think about it too much. It just seemed like it couldn't hurt to spice things up a bit. It seems like you only ever see me looking frumpy."

"*You* never look frumpy." He rolls me over and spreads his hands across my curves. "Even when you're in sweats, I know all of this is waiting underneath and it drives me mad."

I bite my lip, thinking of how strange he's been acting. I want to say he has a funny way of showing it sometimes if that's how he feels, but I don't want to spoil the moment. And I definitely don't want to slip and accidentally blurt out that just yesterday Bridgett and I were wondering if he is responsible for all the recent threats to my life.

"There is something I need to tell you," I confess, realizing I never told him about the letter. "I think the Elites are threatening me again."

"What are you talking about?" he jerks up with concern. "What happened?"

I tell him all about the strange tampering with my food followed by the hanging doll and death threat letter. His face tenses up with anger as I speak. He clenches his fists, and I wonder if I might have to keep him from storming out to beat Malcolm's ass when I'm done explaining everything.

"Do you think Bridgett has anything to do with it?" he suggests almost immediately.

"Funny you should say that," I laugh bitterly.

"Why? You think it's her?"

"No, never mind," I try to hide my smile over the irony of his accusation. Of course, my only friend and boyfriend don't like each other. Things would just be too easy otherwise. "I'm positive it has to be the Elites. All of this started happening after I told this girl in the hall that I wasn't afraid of them. I know Malcolm heard me. We have to get out of this stupid fucking town."

He leans back across the bed, propping his head up on his arms as he stares up at the ceiling. I expect him to agree with me. For us to start scheming about the big beautiful lives we'll have as soon as we get away, like we used to. But instead, he's silent, and it makes me terribly uneasy.

"What's going on up there?" I ask, caressing my hand across his forehead.

His eyes meet mine and it looks like something is just on the tip of his tongue. But it fades away into a smile as he leans forward to kiss me again. "Nothing," he says. "I'm sorry I wasn't there when all that happened. But you know I'll do anything I can to protect you. You're safe with me."

He pulls me against his body, reminding me how much I love the warmth of his skin when I'm stretched out next to it. I want to believe I'm safe with him, but sometimes the looming danger feels so big and mysterious that I'm not sure anyone can really protect me. Emmett may have been able to save my life before, but there were so many other things that happened during that time that he couldn't protect me from. So many things that were done by his own hands.

I push it all from my mind and let out a big sigh as I roll

over and slide to the edge of the bed. "I guess I should start getting ready to go," I groan. "I can't be out too late or Mom will start to flip out. They've been extra fussy about my schedule lately. I guess they don't want me to be dealing with all this preparation for college while running on no sleep."

"They're right," he insists as my hand slides from his. "Now is not the time to be running on empty."

I start to gather my clothes from the floor, feeling sad about how things have been between us before tonight. "Hey, you know…we will talk about all of this college stuff soon. Coach helped me narrow it down to a handful of schools and I want to discuss it with you before I decide anything."

"Don't worry about me," he says as he stands up and slides into a t-shirt and boxer shorts. "I want you to pick a school based on what's best for you. Not what you think will work for me. Whatever happens, we'll figure it out."

His words instantly lift some of the heaviness I've been feeling lately. "Thank you. I really needed to hear that."

I turn around to slide back into my boots, looking aimlessly around his room as I go. I notice more clutter on his desk than usual, and then a sheet of graph paper grabs my attention. I step closer and see schematics for some kind of car. From the notes scribbled around it, I can see it's an energy-efficient model.

"What's this?" I ask in shock just as he bounds over to try and keep me from seeing it, but it's too late.

"Nothing!" he defends, snatching it from my hands and shoving it into a drawer. He even goes so far as to brace his body back against the drawer, as if he has to physically stop me from fishing it out and seeing it again.

"It's obviously not nothing," I laugh awkwardly. "You're… you're designing a car?"

"I mean, I know how," he shrugs. "I thought I'd put together a portfolio or something, you know? Maybe I can find a job in the automobile industry after all."

"Ah," I nod suspiciously. "But that's an environmentally friendly car, isn't it?"

"Yeah…lots of companies are trying to produce more of those now," he answers, trying to sound as innocent as possible, but his face looks as guilty as can be.

I put my hands on my hips, growing bored with his charade. "Like the kind of cars Theo wants to manufacture?"

He rolls his head and groans. "Alright, fine," he sighs, walking over to plop down on the side of his bed. "I know you're going to hate me for this, but I met with Theo."

"What?" I hiss through clenched teeth.

"He was just so persistent!" He buries his face in his hands in exasperation. "It was starting to get awkward…turning him down so much. I finally thought it couldn't hurt to go meet with him just so he'd shut up about it, but then…"

"But then he magically convinced you he had all these grand plans and sold you on the whole thing?" I jeer. "Oh, what a surprise. Theo the master manipulator won you over."

"He actually has a really great business model and a lot of investors lined up," he explains. "It doesn't really matter what kind of guy Theo is. If I can design a car model for him, I can make us a lot of money and have a good start to doing something with my life. It's for us, Ophelia. You have at least four years of college ahead of you, and you've already said you don't want to live on Theo's dime. I want to be able to support us."

"I don't need you to do that," I snap. "Don't use me as an excuse to make a deal with the devil, Emmett. So, is that all it is then? You just sell him the design and walk away?"

"Probably," he looks away. "Maybe."

"Un-fucking-believable," I drag my palms down my face.

"Come on, Ophelia. Please don't treat me like an idiot," he begs. "I know you don't trust your father, but I'm not some helpless little sheep prancing off to be slaughtered. I know what kind of man your father is, but for all the trouble he's caused… if something good can come out of him being around again, then it might make things feel a little better, you know?"

I want to storm out without listening to another word he says, but then I remember how it felt to be lying next to him just moments ago. It seems like we can't get through a single day without things feeling messed up again.

"If you would just sit down with us and see what he has planned, I think you'd feel better," he insists. "When I finally did, I saw him as a businessman. Not just your crooked father."

"A crooked businessman who embezzled money!" I shriek. "Did you forget about what the police said after your dad was shot? They told me Theo was being investigated by the FBI. I was supposed to tell them if I saw Theo again. I didn't know he'd be showing up for family dinners all of a sudden! Do you really think he's going to be able to start a clean business without those things coming up to bite him in the ass!?"

"Come with me to see him tomorrow, Ophelia. Please? After school." He folds his hands together and looks at me with the most pitiful puppy expression. "I want your honest opinion on all of it, but you have to walk into this with an open mind. If I do some work for him, it could solve all of our worries about moving out of Jameson. It could make it easier for both of us to go to California."

Any mention of California has become like a golden ray of sunshine that goes off in my head every time I hear it. A big, bright shining beacon of hope that pierces through the mess that the rest of my life has become. It's a fresh start. One that I so desperately need, but I know Emmett needs it too.

"I'll think about it," I grumble finally.

I finish gathering my things and tell him goodbye. Driving home, I wonder what will happen if Emmett really does start working with Theo. What if he gets trapped in Jameson? Or thrown in prison for one of his illegal schemes? I can see Emmett giving in more and more. That's what Theo does. Give him an inch and he takes a mile. Will Emmett keep giving in until all of our dreams to move away are shattered? If we can even get that far, considering all the death threats looming over me.

# CHAPTER SEVENTEEN

BOOK 3

"Where are we going?" I ask Emmett as he pulls off into an industrial park on the edge of town. "I thought we'd be meeting up at a restaurant or a coffee shop or something?"

I slump down in my seat as I stare out the window, still in disbelief that I let myself get talked into this stupid meeting at all.

"He's rented out a big warehouse space," Emmett says nonchalantly.

I do my best not to snap and start going off again, which would be the fifth or sixth time I've done that since last night. But every new thing I learn about this whole venture makes my gut twist more. First, they were just talking. Now Emmett is drawing up plans. And to top it all off, there's a whole building already in the works. This isn't just some pipe dream Theo is using to lure Emmett in. He's legitimately trying to get this thing up and running, whether it's a smart move or not.

I feel even worse as we pull up and park. There are at least twenty guys scrambling around in the warehouse which I can see through the open garage doors. They're assembling equipment as Theo comes running up to our car, wearing a hardhat with a walky-talky in hand.

"You made it!" he beams as we get out of the car. "Good to see you again, son." He wraps Emmett up in a hug, slapping his shoulder as if they're old pals.

"Son?" I mutter to myself with disgust. I'm sure Emmett

thinks nothing of it, but I know it's a subtle psychological jab. Theo is playing on his lack of a father figure. Even going so far as to make an entire damn car company, just like he inherited from his father before it was taken away.

"I'm so glad you came," Theo turns to me with his big, sneaky grin that always makes my stomach turn.

"Don't be too glad," I scoff. "He practically had to drag me here kicking and screaming."

They both ignore my comment and start walking inside. The building is massive with big corrugated metal siding and smokestacks up above that remain still and empty for now. There's a big emblem being raised to the side with a crane, promising what's to come.

I follow them through the doors and marvel at the big machines as we go. Emmett grabs a hard hat and hands me one as well. I like seeing him look like some kind of working professional, and he seems comfortable in this environment. For as much as I've heard him talk about his father's business, I've never actually gotten to see him in action firsthand.

What I don't like is seeing him walking side by side with Theo. One of my biggest fears is that he's going to get Emmett's hopes up with all of these big promises about what his company can be. And then the FBI swoops in and shuts the whole thing down. It's hard to imagine my father pulling off anything legit and legal.

He ushers us into an office towards the back of the warehouse, which is a lot nicer than I expected. There are two corner offices with a big conference room between them. The carpets are a sleek black, which goes nicely with all of the modern décor and furniture. It's minimalistic and chic. There are large windows with an impressive view of Jameson as sunlight streams through.

"This is awfully nice for a start-up," I mention as we sit down at the big marble tabletop.

"We have some very generous, optimistic investors," Theo boasts as he spreads big rolls of paper out before us.

"Should they be so optimistic?" I say. "Can you actually deliver on the promises you've made to everyone wrapped up in this?"

Theo laughs, looking surprised. "Should I put you in touch with the finance department?" he taunts. "Would you like to see the financial plans?"

"Yes," I shoot back coldly, looking at him with dead serious eyes to call him on his sarcastic bluff.

He straightens up, spreading his hands across the table with an insulted and offended smirk. "Well, I'll see what I can do," he answers dismissively.

"Please do," I add boldly. "You seem to think Emmett needs to take care of me. So if our futures are going to be depending on this in some way, I think I have a right to know how you're running things."

Emmett shuffles his feet awkwardly, directing his attention back to the plans. "This is what I wanted to show you," he blurts to break the tension. "This is the machine that will be manufacturing the first model I've designed."

He points out the different features and how it functions, pointing out the area of the warehouse behind us where it will go. I see his eyes light up with excitement as he talks. Something I've only ever seen when we were discussing our plans for the future.

As they drift off into their own discussion about what still needs to be done, I find myself looking around the office again. There are computers along one wall and printed research about production laying around. There are a number of electronic devices that look super expensive and like something I probably have no idea how to work. Drafting tables line the other wall.

"Emmett's been an invaluable asset in getting all of this set up," Theo brags, slapping him on the shoulder again with a proud smile. "Most of what you see here was his doing."

"I thought you were just sketching out a design for a car," I gape. "I didn't even know you knew how to do all of this."

After the two ramble on about all of the manufacturing plans and designs, we take another walk around the big open warehouse. Theo tells me all about the layout in great detail, and I can't help but feel slightly impressed. Even if I am still picturing men in black suits swarming the place as they shut it all down.

The space is open and well-lit, and nowhere near as dirty as I expected it to be. The floor is still scattered with shelving, pallets, hoses, valves, and an assortment of other tools as workers busy themselves with assembling everything. There's a painting booth and a plethora of safety signs, most not hung up yet.

Theo leads us up a spiral staircase in the far corner of the warehouse, which goes up to a metal walkway, allowing you to observe everything happening on the production floor below. The two men lean over the edge and look down with hopeful eyes. As skeptical as I am, I can see what they see. I can imagine the hissing and whirring of machinery echoing throughout while supervisors circle the room. There's already the faint smell of grease and motor oil in the air mixed in with the scents of Styrofoam and all the fresh and shiny things being unpacked.

After the tour, we go back into the fancy offices. I take a seat at the big table again, unsure of what to say. They're both so confident and excited, and I hate to burst their bubble. I couldn't care less about Theo, but I can see now just how much potential Emmett sees in all of this. I just don't want my father to disappoint him in the same ways he has disappointed me.

"I bought this just for your visit," Theo tells us excitedly as he pulls a bottle of champagne out of the mini-fridge.

I know nothing about champagne, but Emmett reacts strongly to the sight of the bottle. "That's an awfully nice one," he says, looking thrown. "You don't have to open that for us."

"You always seem to forget we're underage," I remind him, remembering our visit with cocktails when we saw him on our pointless search for Bernadette.

"Ah," he grunts and waves. "Who cares about those dumb laws? A little champagne never hurt anyone. Especially when it's celebratory."

I want to remind him of the kind of trouble ignoring rules and laws has got him into before, but I stop myself. Once again, I'm suspended between wanting to take Theo down a few notches and not wanting to spoil everything for Emmett.

He pops the bottle and pulls out three glasses. Each one fizzes to the top with the hissing, amber liquid as we clink our glasses together. I make a point to cheers with Emmett, avoiding Theo's glass as much as possible. It may be petty, but that's what I'm apparently reduced to now.

"So when does this whole operation officially launch?" I ask after taking a sip of the bittersweet drink. "You're a lot further along than I expected."

"We hope to be up and running by August," he exhales optimistically.

"August? Wow," my voice cracks, feeling like the wind has been knocked out of my lungs. "That's when I start school. *Wherever* I start school."

Theo doesn't seem phased by my remark and instead turns to Emmett with a strange look. "There's something else I wanted to show you while you're here," he says. "Come this way."

He takes us back to the corner office on the right and starts bragging about everything it has to offer. The view, the mahogany desk, and top of the line office chair. There are sleek, black shelves waiting to be lined with personal items from whoever claims the space.

Theo pulls out one of the desk drawers and takes a golden plague into his hands. "Ta-da!" he shouts as he slams it to the surface for us to see.

Engraved into the plaque reads: EMMETT JAMESON - Chief Manufacturing Executive and Senior Design Engineer

"What's this?" Emmett gasps with wide eyes.

"Yeah…what the hell is this?" I add sharply.

"That's your official title!" he shouts enthusiastically. "And this is your office. If you accept my offer, that is."

"O-o-o-ffice?" I stammer. "Office…offer…Emmett, what is he talking about?" I try to forget Theo is even in the room and race over to Emmett, taking his hands in mine. "Why do you need an office here?"

His head hangs in shame as he shoots an awkward glance back over to Theo. "We only talked about it briefly," he says quietly. "When I called to set this meeting up."

"Talked about what briefly?" I ask urgently.

"I want Emmett to be my partner," Theo bellows, as if it's the greatest offer in the world.

"Can I talk to you for a moment?" I beg him in a whisper, feeling my throat catch as my eyes start welling up.

"Of course," he nods, following me back into the conference room.

I slam the office door behind us, giving Theo the not so subtle hint to stay in there and give us some privacy.

"I don't understand," I say in disbelief. "Why the hell would you have an office and a job here!? I thought we were leaving Jameson!? It's all we've been talking about for *months* now!"

"Calm down. I know. I'm sorry," he puts his hands on my shoulders. I don't realize how loud my voice had become until I see him trying to quiet me down. "He only just brought all this up. I wasn't expecting it. I haven't even had time to think about it."

"He wants you to be his partner in all of this?" I continue, flying into a mad pace across the room. "And some kind of Manufacturing Executive? *And* a Senior Design Engineer!? Emmett, people go to school for a long time and have degrees for those sorts of things. Doesn't this seem strange to you? This whole thing. It's like he's just trying so hard to sell you on something, and we don't even know if any of its real or not."

"Ophelia, I was going to be an executive of a car company before," he defends. "I've been preparing for this kind of career my whole life. It's the only thing I know how to do. I probably know more about this stuff than most guys with degrees do. And what I don't know already…I can learn as I go."

"So, you're actually considering this!?" My eyes bulge out with rage.

"Maybe," he shrugs. "I don't know, okay? It's all happening so fast. I just need you to calm down and give me some time to process it."

"Exactly! It's happening *too* fast! Faster than things like this should happen if they're being done properly," I rave. "Theo has no fucking idea what he's doing here!" I hold back from saying I'm worried Emmett doesn't either. As far as I know, his father prepared him for a life behind a desk in the Jameson manor, signing papers and making calls, but mostly letting everyone else do the work while he reigned in the profits.

"I know what you're thinking," he glares at me. "You're thinking I'm not qualified for this."

I look away, trying not to blurt out how right he is.

"I know a lot more than you think I do, Ophelia," he says disappointedly. "I didn't want to do things the way my father did. I wanted to be a valuable part of Jameson Automobiles, so I prepared accordingly."

"But designing cars?" I ask, wishing I was more convinced. "Managing and supervising all these people? This whole operation? Are you sure that's the kind of thing you're prepared to do?"

"I like that it's more hands-on," he tells me, putting his hands over my shoulders again as his voice softens. "I want to be a part of this, if that's what I decide. To actually do something. Not just wear a suit and make millions for nothing."

I shake my head, wishing I didn't sympathize with him so much at this moment. I want it all to be a sham. I want him to see through it, and I want him to think there's something off about it. But no matter how hard I try; I can't seem to make anyone see Theo the way that I do.

"I am *not* staying in Jameson," I fume, not knowing what other points I can argue on right now. "You want to go into business with him, fine. But I won't stay in this hell hole. And frankly, I don't think you should either. There's a reason he picked this place to start this in, and whatever it is I don't think it's good."

"You don't have to," he assures me. "We'll figure it out, okay? What about that school that's just a couple hours away? Didn't Granger say that was one of your best options?"

"Didn't *you* say I should pick whatever college I wanted without worrying about you!?" I bark.

"You're right," he recoils slightly, pulling me into his chest.

I push myself against him, urging him to tighten his arms. I need to feel him around me right now to feel safe. Like everything I'd imagined isn't crumbling around me. All of our plans. Everything we've been dreaming about. It all seems more impossible than ever. I can't stay in Jameson, but the thought of leaving Emmett behind here makes me want to burst into tears.

"Can we go now?" I ask suddenly. "I'm exhausted."

"Sure. Let's just say goodbye to Theo."

"Can you just give me the keys!?" I spread out my palm to him. "I don't want to see him again right now. I'll wait in the car."

The moment he hands them over I bolt for the door. As open as the building is, it suddenly seems suffocating and claustrophobic. I want to get out of there as fast as I possibly can. I race to the car and get inside, locking the doors until Emmett comes out.

Hot tears stream down my face as I wait. It wasn't enough for Theo to be absent my whole life and then nearly get me killed when he showed up for his own personal gain and vengeance. He had to weasel his way back into our family, and now he's ripping the man I love away from me. I can't help but think it's on purpose. Like he'd do anything to hurt me, but I just can't understand why. I don't think I've ever hated Theo more.

# CHAPTER EIGHTEEN

### BOOK 3

I'm curled up in a ball next to my mom on the couch watching some ridiculous romantic comedy she picked out. I watch the couple on the screen, thinking everything seems so simple and clean. No matter what scandal arises or shenanigans they get into, it's oddly normal yet completely unfamiliar to me. I see nothing of Emmett and me in any of the couples in these movies my mom likes to watch. But I go along with it because I know it's close to what she and Brendan have.

The men in these movies have never humiliated their dates or shoved them up against walls, threatening them. Sure, maybe that's a distant part of our past. But it's there. And as for what we face now…I don't see them fretting over an estranged, corrupt father figure showing up out of nowhere and threatening to rip them apart.

I start to chew on what's left of my thumbnail as I come face to face with the reminder of the last time I remember feeling this way about these dumb movies. I sat on Malcolm's couch just before he tried to force himself on me and I lamented over why my life couldn't be this simple.

"You okay?" my mom asks.

I jump slightly and look over to see her staring me down with worry lines cutting across her forehead.

"Yes, fine," I answer quickly. "But I guess I should start getting ready. Emmett is taking me out tonight."

"Another date night, huh?" she teases. "What are you two going to do?"

"I don't know," I shrug as I peel myself off the couch, almost wishing I didn't have to get up. "He says it's a surprise. I just hope it's not bowling."

"Well, don't make plans tomorrow night," she requests with a twinkle in her eye. "I'm taking you dress shopping. We need some mother-daughter bonding time and prom will be here before you know it."

"Sounds great, Mom," I smile. "Looking forward to it."

I head for the stairs, thinking how excited I really am. Only these days less so about prom, and more so for graduation and getting the hell out of this place. But I'm still filled with resentment that it's all threatened now by the very real possibility that leaving Jameson might mean leaving Emmett.

I check my phone before hopping into the shower and see that Emmett has texted me. He asked if I could wear the red dress with a winking smiley face. I smirk, feeling amused that he must think that's the only dress I own.

"Boy, have I got a surprise for you," I muse to myself out loud as I picture the black velvet stringy number hanging even further back in my closet. We bought it for some awards ceremony, but it's about time to take it out on the town for something fun.

After showering, I spritz on some perfume and slide into the soft dress, pairing it with the only pair of heels I own. I've dressed up more times lately than over the past four years combined, but maybe I can just chalk it up as practice for prom. And maybe, just maybe, seeing this new vixen side of me emerge, Emmett will have no choice but to follow me away from here for college. That may be a long shot, but I'll take whatever hopes I can get my hands on for now.

He's waiting for me downstairs by the time I'm finished getting ready. I watch from around the corner for a moment as he talks to my mom and Brendan. He sure has worked his magic on them considering how much they used to hate him, but I guess I can say the same for myself.

"Hey," I announce finally as I enter the room.

Emmett's eyes grow wide when he sees me, but he blushes and clears his throat with a quick glance at Brendan. "You ready?" he asks, not wanting to start flipping out over how good I look right here in front of my parents.

"Yeah," I smile as he leads me to the front door.

The moment we're outside with the door closed behind us, he pulls me in for a long kiss. "I couldn't wait to do that," he says, looking me up and down. "Damn…you look good."

"So do you!" I chime, noticing his expensive shirt and pants. "Are these new?"

"Mm-hmm. I wanted to look nice for you too," he grins.

I take a moment to breathe in the spring air as we walk hand in hand to his car. It feels good for it to be finally warm enough that I don't have to wear a sweater. He drives me across town to a fancy restaurant. An *expensive* restaurant. So expensive that I assume the date is over after that, but I'm surprised when he insists on ordering dessert and then wants to see a movie.

"Don't take this the wrong way," I say lightly as he parks in front of the theater. "But how can you afford all of this? I can pay for the tickets, you know."

"No way," he insists. "Don't you worry your pretty little head about it."

I feel thrown by his comment. It seems out of character for him, but I do my best to roll with it. I can't quite put my finger on what's wrong anyway, aside from all the money he suddenly seems to have.

We only watch half of the movie, getting sucked into making out at some point. Before I know it, the credits are rolling, and I'm forced to rip my mouth away from his. The scent of cologne lingers on my skin, and I realize it's a new scent.

"Think we have time to go back to your place?" I ask once we get back into his car.

"Not tonight," he grins. "I'm taking you somewhere better. I've had enough of that dumpy old apartment."

I can't imagine where else we could possibly go for what I have in mind. All I know is I'm all worked up from our hour-long make-out session, and wherever we're going I want to get there fast. But all that pent-up lust fades when we pull up in front of one of the nicest hotels in Jameson.

"Wait…we're not…here?" I stammer as I watch the cars pull through the valet ahead of us underneath the ornate, golden pillars.

"I know we can't stay all night," he says. "But we can enjoy it for a little while at least."

Big, red, flashing lights are going off in my brain. Something is definitely wrong here. Emmett went from being completely broke to suddenly having money for new clothes, cologne, an expensive dinner, a movie, and now a luxury hotel room that we can't even stay the entire night in. He looks so excited that I don't know how to bring up all the glaring problems with all of this.

I can't imagine how much a room at this place costs, but as he leads me into ours, I have to assume it's not the cheapest one in the joint. It looks like a fully-fledged suite with a living room area and an adjoining bedroom. The carpet is plush and spotless, and the rooms are filled with only the finest furniture and linens.

Just as I am about to broach the topic of where all of this money is coming from, I spin on my heels and come face to face with Emmett. He's waiting there with a long velvet jewelry box in his hands.

"What's this?" I gasp. He opens the box to reveal what looks like a real diamond necklace that's stunning enough to instantly take my breath away. Before I can say anything else, he pulls it out and steps behind me to clasp it around my neck. He starts to remove the running shoe charm necklace he gave me at the beginning of the year, but my hand flies up to stop him.

"No, don't," I beg. "I'll wear them both. That one is too special to me."

"But it's cheap. It's turning your neck green back here," he scoffs. "I wanted to replace it with something nicer."

"No," I insist. "Please…it means a lot to me."

He gives in and adds this new sparkling diamond over top of the old necklace, but I can't get over how strange it feels for him to belittle such a sentimental gift.

"You deserve all the nicest things the world has to offer," his deep voice tickles against my neck. "But I haven't been able to give you much of anything lately, so I thought I'd make up for lost time."

His hands begin to spread over my body as he kisses behind my ear. I almost forget everything and melt back into his touch, but the necklace itches across my neck, urging me to try and figure out how all of this is possible.

"Wait," I tell him, pulling away. I go over and sit on the couch, hoping the distance will help push my arousal down again, at least until after we talk. Regardless of where the money is coming from, we already have the room. We might as well put it to use once we've talked.

"Where is all of this coming from?" I ask him in disbelief. "The clothes, the food, the room…This necklace!?" I run the diamond between my fingers, thinking I still prefer my little running shoe charm. "How can you afford all of this? Be honest with me."

He sits down next to me on the couch with a heavy sigh. I can tell he's not looking forward to whatever he's about to tell me. "I've already done so much work for Theo," he explains. "He's gone ahead and started paying me for my time."

"Wait…so…all of this…it's from Theo?" I question, my voice growing shrill and broken.

"No, it's from me," he shoots back, sounding irritated. "I earned the money."

"Well, shouldn't you be saving it or something?" I suggest, still feeling a gnawing uneasiness that all of this did come from Theo, no matter how Emmett wants to paint it.

"There's plenty. Don't worry," he leans back, looking smug.

Suddenly, all of my longing for him vanishes. He looks unfamiliar to me in his expensive clothes here in this ridiculous suite. And that smirk on his face…it's one I've seen before. On his father, Thomas, and on my father as well. It's a boastful sort of look worn by rich men who feel like they own the world.

"I don't understand how all of this is happening," I gape in disbelief. "You know what kind of man Theo is. But you're seriously considering partnering up with him…and you're already on his payroll, which is funded by who knows what."

"Investors," he snaps. "We've told you that. Investors."

I shake my head and cross my arms, looking away to keep from screaming, demanding to know who all of these mystery investors are.

"Everything's ruined," I mumble, holding back tears. "I can see it written all over your face. You're enjoying this too much. You want to stay here in Jameson and work with him. I know it. Your mind is made up."

I want him to immediately argue back, swearing he's still thinking it over. I need him to tell me I'm wrong, but instead, I'm met with a chilling silence. He leans forward, perching his elbows on his knees as he runs his hands through his slicked-back curls. "I want some solid way to be able to provide for you and our future," he says firmly. "That's what I was taught to do for a woman I love. And maybe working for Theo is my best possible option for doing that."

"And what if I'm not in the picture?" I ask, flying to my feet. "Because that's exactly what's going to happen if you stay here."

His face drops. "Are you giving me an ultimatum?"

"No, that's not what I meant," I argue, wondering if it's a lie. "I just meant…I can't stay here in Jameson. I've told you that. If you stay…what happens to us?"

"I'll have enough money to fly and visit you, or to pay for you to visit me," he assures me. "Just like we planned to do before I lost Jameson.

I want to believe him, but for some reason him staying here and working for my father feels like losing him to something more than distance. It feels like the Emmett I know will eventually be lost forever and I can't explain why.

"I want to go home," I sob. "I'm sorry. This is all so lovely. But I feel sick suddenly, and I just want to go."

It's painfully silent as he drives me home, but thankfully he doesn't seem offended that I had to go. I guess he really must have built up a really nice stack in this short bit of time, because he doesn't seem at all worried that the money on the hotel room went to waste. I'm quick to tell him goodbye in my driveway, feeling anxious to crawl into my bed.

Once I've tossed aside my little black dress, which I now hate by association with this night, I throw on the most comfortable pajamas I own and grab Marissa's diary before climbing under the covers.

*Dear Diary,*

*Prom is just a couple of weeks away, and I am so excited. And so very in love with Thomas. Really, I am. There is…just one little thing bothering me. The other night, my parents and I went to the Jameson manor for dinner. Everything was so lovely, and the evening was going perfect. Thomas's mother even showed me her jewelry collection, pointing out which pieces she'd give to me once Thomas and I are married one day.*

*But as I walked out of her room, I noticed the study door being slightly open. I stopped and listened for a moment, even though I know I shouldn't have. Thomas and his father were talking my dad into some sort of business deal they schemed up. I almost walked away because it seemed so ordinary, but then I began to realize exactly what it was they were really talking about.*

*It was some kind of crooked deal that I know is illegal and takes money away from a lot of hard-working, less fortunate individuals. I was so upset at the thought of my father being involved with something like that, but even more upset that Thomas would be involved and drag others into it.*

*Later in the evening, we took a walk. I know he was eager to get me alone so we could kiss and touch, which I normally can't wait to do. But I was so bothered by what I overheard, it's all I could think about. He asked why I was so quiet, so I tried to confront him about it.*

*He turned cold and angry. He pointed to the manor in the distance, telling me that all of it would be ours someday. But that the life he wanted to provide for me wasn't cheap. I argued that we could live a less extravagant life if it was the difference between swindling innocent people or not.*

*He snapped and told me not to concern myself with these things. It would be my job to manage the manor and one day have our children. He told me I'd never want for anything, but that I needed to stay out of his business when it came to our financial affairs and how he made his money.*

*I didn't know what to say. I had never seen that side of him before. But as awful as it sounds, I thought back on the jewelry his mother promised to me and thought maybe he was right. I wouldn't even know any of this if I hadn't been eavesdropping.*

*Is it okay for me to ignore anything bad he might be doing…and just sit back and enjoy the life he provides me? It's not like I'm the one running those bad business deals after all. I don't know, diary. But I do know I love him more than anything in the world.*

*-Marissa.*

I toss the book to the floor and flip off the lamp before rolling over in the darkness. I pull the covers around me tight, needing their comfort and warmth. I think about Marissa's comment on her future mother-in-law's jewelry and can see myself following Emmett into that expensive hotel, and again when I almost let everything slide after he put that necklace on me.

If I give in and let Emmett enter into this business with my father, will he one day become just like his dad? And will I eventually become like Marissa? So heartless and cruel that I'd turn my back on my own son out of greed?

# CHAPTER NINETEEN

## BOOK 3

The next day at school is long and tortuous. Emmett and I sit together at lunch barely speaking to each other, and I find myself avoiding him to rush home after school. Only what I rush home to is just as daunting. The excitement of shopping for a prom dress with my mom is lost in my anxiety about everything happening between Emmet and me.

I want to look forward to this big high school milestone. I want to daydream and fantasize about the magical night we could have together, making memories. But all I keep thinking of is what happens after prom. If we have to part ways when I move, what's the point? Why delay the inevitable? And even if we stay together, do I lose him to Theo's world? It's the world he was born to live in, after all.

I'm so quick to get inside and get the whole thing over with, thinking maybe it will be fun to spend some time with my mom regardless. I don't even notice the car parked out front until I hear the familiar voice echoing from the dining room.

Theo. Again. In my house. The last fucking thing I wanted to come home to. I try to be as quiet as possible as I peek around the corner to see him and my mom talking. I can't make out what they're discussing, but it's obviously so enthralling they didn't even hear me come in. I take my chance to dart upstairs and wait for him to leave.

My mom knocks on my door a little while later and asks if I'm ready to go. I resist even asking what Theo was visiting for this time. It feels like I can't get away from him no matter where I turn, and the last thing I want to do is talk about him any more than I absolutely have to.

She asks normal questions as we drive to the first shopping strip. How's school going? Stressful, but fine. How's track? My favorite thing in the world, as usual. College plans? Still freaking me the hell out.

I walk through the first boutique, doing my best to get into dress shopping, at least for my mom's sake. But none of the froofy gowns are appealing to me. My mom stays positive and suggests a hundred different cuts and colors. But after three more stores and still nothing I like enough to buy. We decide to take a break for burgers and milkshakes.

"Do you remember when we used to do this all the time?" she asks, swirling a fry in her chocolate shake. "I'd bring you to these little diners when you were a kid. You didn't believe me at first when I told you how good a fry dipped in chocolate could taste."

"It still surprises me," I laugh as I do the same.

We're mostly quiet as we eat. By the time my mom has cleaned most of her plate, she takes a stab at addressing the obvious.

"Everything okay?" she asks. "You don't seem too excited about any of the dresses we've seen so far. I think we're running out of stores we can afford."

I shrug and stare at my plate, unsure of how to explain the problem. "Emmett and I are kind of fighting," I confess finally. "I guess it will all be fine. It's just kind of putting a damper on the idea of prom right now."

"Ah," she says with a knowing smile. "I guess that would do it. It must be in the air. Brendan and I seem to be having some trouble ourselves these days."

She says it so casually, but my stomach drops. "What?" I blink. "What do you mean? What kind of trouble?"

"It's nothing to worry about," she assures me. "It's just normal couple stuff. I just wanted you to know it happens is all. Especially after you've been together a while and the honeymoon phase has worn off."

My mind drifts back to her and Theo sitting alone at the kitchen table and I immediately jump to all of the worst possible conclusions.

"Theo?" I ask, my voice filled with dread. "Is it him? God dammit! I knew it. He's going to fuck up absolutely everything."

"Ophelia Lopez! Language!" she scolds. "It has nothing to do with Theo. I promise you. All couples fight. That's all I meant."

"Well then how come you've never mentioned having problems with Brendan before?" I argue.

"Because it's private," she states bluntly. "But also…you're older now. Practically an adult. I feel like you and I can start talking about more things now. That's the beauty of an adult mother and daughter relationship. I don't have to be mean old mom all the time. I can be more of a friend now. Friends talk about their problems."

I want to feel better, but I don't. My mom hasn't been around Theo since I was a baby, and I can't help but worry that maybe she's forgotten just how manipulative he can be. He's won over Emmett. He could win her over too. I remember the flash of jealousy I saw on Theo's face at our last dinner and wonder if he really could be driving a wedge between her and Brendan without her even realizing it.

"Well, what do you think?" My mom asks once the last of our food is tucked away into leftover boxes. "Should we try one more store or are you over shopping for the day?"

"I'm down for one more," I tell her, still feeling heavy with concern. But the idea of avoiding home a little longer and spending some quality time with her is too good to pass up. Moments like this are becoming more precious since I know I'll be leaving soon.

I notice the other whiney teenage girls shopping with their moms, seeming bothered that their mothers have to be tagging along at all. Then I see other girls shopping in groups with each other, probably not even bothering to wonder if their moms would have liked to have been there.

I know as a teenager it'd be normal for me to be so annoyed by my mom that I can't stand to be around her. But we've never had that kind of relationship. We've both been through so much and it's made us close. My heart aches to think of a time when we'll live so far apart. I vow to myself right then and there that I will be one of those girls that calls her mom every single day.

Once we start digging into the next store, I'm immediately glad we did. After only a few minutes of browsing, I come across a dark blue gown that piques my interest. It's short but cascades down in the back. The fabric flares out from the waist, which is something I normally wouldn't like, but I can't resist the urge to try it on.

My mom tears up when I step out of the dressing room, which seems dramatic, but I honestly feel just as excited about it. The short front is somewhat revealing and emphasizes the muscular curves of my long, tan legs.

"This is it," I say confidently as I study my reflection in the mirror, turning side to side.

I can imagine Emmett in a nice tux standing next to me with my arm looped into his. All of the anger and worry that's been building up in my heart finally softens a little, even if there's still a lingering sadness. Whatever happens, when the time comes for me to leave Jameson, I'm excited that we'll have such a special night to share. I have that much at least.

We're excited but exhausted as we pay for the dress and head home. I'm just as eager as she is to slip into some comfy pajamas and veg out on the couch for a bit before going to bed. But I notice something odd as our house comes into view. Two dark figures are bouncing around on the lawn.

"Do you see that?" I ask, wondering if someone is trying to break into the house. But as we get closer, I realize one of the men is Brendan. And once we're parked, I can see the other guy is Theo. "Why is he here again!?" I groan.

"I don't know," she murmurs. "What are they doing?"

Just as soon as she asks the question, I see Brendan lunge towards Theo and clock him right in the face.

"Hooolyy shiiit!" I exclaim, unable to hold in a little bit of laughter. I hear the painful smacking sound against his jaw and feel an instant sense of satisfaction. But it doesn't erase the shock or confusion of why the hell the two of them are fighting on the lawn.

"Hey!" my mom shouts as she bounds out of the car. She rushes over to Brendan and tries to hold him back, but he's like a charging bull and is quick to rush forward again just as Theo is stumbling back to his feet with a mouth full of bloody teeth.

She puts herself in front of him and forces him to look her in the eye. "Stop it!" she demands. His nostrils flare with rage, but the longer she stares him down, the more I see him relax.

"What the hell is going on here!?" she fumes once Brendan seems somewhat diffused.

"I just came back to get my jacket," Theo defends before

spitting out a mouthful of blood. "Then this idiot attacked me…like a madman!"

Brendan growls and starts to run for him again, but my mom pushes him back. "Go in the house!" she orders before turning back to Theo. "And you! Just go home!"

I follow Mom and Brendan inside, shooting a quick pleased smile over to Theo as he stumbles pitifully back to his car. Ha, serves him right, I think.

I'm completely shocked as I walk into the house, realizing I've never once seen Brendan lose his shit like that. But if it had to happen, nothing makes me happier than knowing he unleashed it on Theo. Maybe I'm not so alone in my hatred of him after all.

As my mom starts grilling Brendan, demanding to know what happened, part of me thinks I should go upstairs to my room and give them some privacy. But then I think there's no way in hell I can go to sleep without knowing the juicy details of what caused him to snap like that. I linger in the doorway, wishing I had a bag of popcorn. Or even better, some kind of medal to award Brendan with as a thank you.

"He came knocking on the door like he has a right just to stop by anytime he likes," Brendan snarls, still looking riled up. "He started talking about some jacket he left here earlier today. Why was he here!?"

"To talk about Ophelia's college fund!" Mom cries. "What did you think!? That I was having an affair with him!?"

Brendan looks ashamed, giving away that it's exactly what he thought, even though he feels stupid for it now. "I tried asking him what he was here for," he explains, hanging his head. "But he just laughed and said, 'Wouldn't you like to know.' I just lost it."

"Oh goodness sakes," my mom huffs. "Is that it!? I swear… what a ridiculous reason to punch someone for."

By this point, I am itching to chime in, even though I know she'll probably banish me for it. But too much is building up for me to hold it in.

"It's not so ridiculous," I suggest. "In fact…that's probably why Theo showed up and said that in the first place. To get Brendan to attack him just as we were pulling up. How do you know he wasn't stalking us to time it all just perfectly?"

"Are you kidding me!?" she whips around to burn her eyes

into me. "That's the craziest thing I've ever heard. Do you hear yourself? Stalking us!?"

"He could've asked for his jacket back later," I reply. "He was trying to push Brendan's buttons. And he's right…He doesn't have a right to just show up whenever he wants."

"Go to your room, Ophelia!" she shouts, pointing her finger as if suddenly I'm ten years old all over again. "Stay out of this!"

"But you said I'm practically an adult now…so can't we talk about adult things?" I remind her.

She closes her eyes with a big groan. She hates having her own words used against her, but I couldn't resist. Sooner or later, everyone has to start understanding Theo the way I do.

"Your mom's right," Brendan caves. "You shouldn't have had to see that. I'm sorry. We've all been trying really hard to let your father be a part of your life, and I shouldn't have done anything to mess that up."

"Yes, you should have!" I cry. "I don't *want* him to be a part of my life! You're a better father to me than he'll ever be! I'm glad you punched him in the face!"

"Well, that doesn't sound very adult," my mom says condescendingly.

"Being an adult means understanding that not everyone is who they claim to be," I argue. "Why can no one else see what a loser he is!? He's done nothing but cause trouble from the moment he popped up."

"Giving you a new car? Your phone? Offering to help with college?" she rants. "All of that…You think that's trouble?"

"It's all just a part of his game to win us over!" I shout, feeling more desperate than ever to make them see. "Nothing he does is innocent or accidental. It's all planned out. We're just like little puppets in his game. Don't forget this is the man that got you both run out of town and then beat you."

"That's enough," she hisses, her jaw clenched tight. "I'm tired. We're not discussing this anymore tonight."

I want to keep arguing, but I hate seeing that look in my mom's eyes. That haunted painful look of being reminded of everything she's trying so hard to forget. I sink into guilt, thinking it's not my place to use past hurts to make her see this my way. Not knowing what else to do, I storm off to my room, shouting goodnight as I go.

With the door slammed behind me, I'm too hyped up to

even thinking about getting into bed now. I want to cling to the beautiful image of Brendan punching Theo out, but it's all ruined with his regret of doing it and their inability to see how Theo obviously orchestrated the whole thing.

It's like Theo is some kind of sorcerer that's cast a spell on everyone, but I'm immune to it. I wonder if when he showed up here for dinner the first time had really been my first time meeting him, I could have been just as easily persuaded to believe in him. But Emmett knows Theo from before then too and knows the full story of everything that's happened. And even he has been won over.

Then I think maybe it's Emmett that's behaving like Marissa and not me at all. He's so wrapped up in all the money he's making and the promise of this successful career, he doesn't even care if Theo is screwing people over in the process. As long as he's not the one getting screwed. But that is exactly what I'm afraid is going to happen if I don't put a stop to all of this.

I was pissed enough before with everything going on with Emmett and this new job offer, but now Theo is threatening my mom's marriage. Her and Brendan are the two kindest, hardest-working most genuine souls in the world as far as I'm concerned, and they're perfect for each other. I'm not about to let Theo tear them apart. That's where I draw the line.

If I'm the only one who seems to be immune to his charms, then I'll have to be the one to stop him.

# CHAPTER TWENTY

BOOK 3

I lay flat across my back on my bed, relentlessly tossing a ball against the ceiling and catching it again. For the past few hours I've been manically rotating between this and restlessly pacing around my room. Anything to help rack my brain for some way to bring Theo down.

As the ball plummets back down to me again, I'm a little too slow to catch it and it ends up bouncing off to the side, sending a flurry of loose change crashing to the floor. As the coins scatter, I think…chips. Poker chips.

The whole reason Theo was blacklisted from the Elites and ran out of Jameson in the first place was that he embezzled money to pay off his bad gambling debts. A gambling addiction doesn't just go away overnight, and while I could easily assume that high-risk business deals give him the thrill he's seeking, I have to wonder if he's still into gambling.

But what good does that do me? I don't know anything about gambling, much less how to get enough proof that Theo is doing something illegal enough to help me out. But it's a start and the only thing I have right now. The tricky part is that I don't know if there is anyone who could actually help me with this. Anyone who would be capable of helping me probably wouldn't. Theo has woven the perfect web of safety for himself.

Anyone who knows about the underbelly of Jameson might be able to point me in the right direction, but the only two people who fit that description, who don't also hate me, are

Emmett and Bridgett. There's no way Emmett would actively help me bring Theo down with this new career prospect on the line. And while I'm sure Bridgett would help if she could, she hasn't been living in Jameson long. There's also the lingering fear that I don't know how much I can trust her with. She is a Henderson after all.

Lily was once a friend, or at least pretended to be, but I can't imagine what kind of help she would be from the rehab center. I'd try to visit her, but I don't want to do anything to mess up her recovery from what Jameson turned her into.

Then it hits me. Vivian. Emmett's ex-girlfriend. The former queen bee of the Elites before her parents were imprisoned for running a human sex trafficking ring. While she probably does still hate me, we did have a moment of humanity right before she left for New York. It's a long shot, but every possible option is at this point. And maybe, just maybe, she's mad enough at Theo for exposing her parents and fucking up her whole life that she'll offer some assistance.

I open my laptop and send Vivian a message.

**Hey. I hope New York is treating you well. I know you and I were never actually friends...so this is an awkward thing to ask. But Theo Nickelson is back and needs to be brought down. Any ideas on ways you could help? I have no one else I can turn to.**

I sit and anxiously wait for her response, hoping and praying that she has become less of a monster during her time in New York. And that the Vivian who replies is the same one I saw a brief glimpse of in the hallway, hiding under the stairs at WJ Prep before she left town.

Vivian: **What are you thinking?**

Ophelia: **He probably is still into illegal gambling. Any clue where I could start from there?**

Vivian: **Just outside of Jameson there is an underground poker ring that goes on every Friday night. I'll send you the address. If Theo is still into that vice, he'll be there. Good luck.**

Wow, I think. Easy enough. I thank Vivian and resist the urge to try and press the conversation any further. Elites, past and present, are like landmines. You never know where or what they're hiding or when they will explode. Better not to push my luck.

Using Vivian's tip, I dress in my best top-secret spy outfit of all black and sneak off to the rumored location of the underground ring. It's the kind of thing the average citizen of Jameson would probably know nothing about, but of course, an insider on the shady world of the Elites would have some clue.

I know I can't just barge straight into an illegal gambling den. And truthfully, even if I spot Theo here, I'm not entirely sure what to do from there. I can only follow this trail of crumbs and hope it leads somewhere. There's a big abandoned building taller than the little spot where the games are said to be held. I manage to get inside and make my way onto the roof just as the sun is setting.

While I lay in the darkness, waiting, I look up at the slowly emerging stars and think what a beautiful night it is. It's a shame I have to spend it spying on my corrupt bio-dad. All the more reason to get out of Jameson as soon as possible. I've had countless moments of being baffled by the abnormality of life here.

I lose track of how much time has passed when cars finally start pulling up to the building down below. A myriad of characters start going into the building, each one knocking in a certain way and then entering after being prompted for some kind of password. Everyone from guys in fancy suits with beautiful women on their arms to nervous-looking suburban-type guys in polo shirts.

Just when I am about to give up on catching any glimpse of Theo, I see his car pull around to the side and park. But he doesn't go into the same entrance the rest of the people did. He has a key and unlocks a secret side entrance. I use my phone to catch the best blurry and dark shots I can of him going inside, then I snap a few of his car just to be safe. But it's not enough. I know I need more than that.

I look around the roof frantically, trying not to accept the possibility that I have hit a dead end on this little adventure. Then a door on the roof next door catches my eye. It's next to some old and broken poles and lines, which look like they were once used for hanging laundry. If someone were using that passageway to hang their laundry to dry, where would the door lead? The basement? A laundry chute? Even if any access point exists there, is it still safe to use?

I spot a few boards on the rooftop and know the only way to find out is to travel across and see. But there are a few guards waiting around outside, keeping watch. One wrong move and they'll catch me and then who knows what would happen to me. Theo has been keeping up this nice act when everyone is around to see, but I know if it came down to it, he wouldn't give a damn about what happened to me.

I quietly steady the boards between the two buildings, forming a bridge. A terrifying bridge that could get me killed in more ways than one, but a bridge all the same. The moment I put my weight on them, they begin to wobble too much for me to stand. The only way I can get across is to crawl on my hands and knees. I have to bite my lip to keep from screaming out in fear and alerting the men below. Somehow, after what feels like an eternity of holding my breath and bracing myself to plummet to my death, I make it to the other side.

I run up to the rickety old wooden door, but it creaks and whines when I pull it up just a few inches. It's too loud to open. If I was a guard, I'd definitely investigate a noise like that. Then I hear train whistles in the distance and sit back to wait for my chance. As the train roars past, sounding like a tornado, I fling the door back under the muffled sound and stick my foot inside to test the opening. It feels like hollow metal beneath my foot, and then I spot the pulley system. Feeling around in the black hole, convinced some rodent is going to bite my hand off, I manage to find a handle and pull the top door open.

It's definitely a laundry chute, but the box is small and terrifying. I have no idea what kind of condition it's in. I have to brace myself for a moment and face the reality that if I step inside, I am seriously risking my life. But if I don't? If I pass up my chance to gather whatever evidence I could find against Theo inside? He'll do everything he can to come between my mom and Brendan and to tear Emmett and me apart. And that's only the beginning. Who knows what shape the people I love will be left in by the time he's done.

The Elites are already out to kill me, I tell myself finally. So I might as well make a go for it in the name of a good cause. With a deep breath, I crawl into the small metal box and use the pulley to begin lowering myself down. I pass through several floors of nothing before finally hearing the laughter and noise of the gambling party growing closer.

Each new floor I come to only shows some empty closet or maintenance room that connects to the chute, so I have no idea where I should get out at or what will be waiting for me on the other side when I do. Thinking it's better to sneak my way into whatever is out there by foot rather than drop in on it from this little box, I stop before the sounds of people get any closer.

I quietly step out into a gray room with concrete floors and shelves lined with dusty cleaning supplies. A bright fluorescent light blinks from the ceiling. I stop at the door for a moment to make sure I won't be walking into a room full of people on the other side. It seems quiet enough, so I slowly crack it open. But the first thing I see in the distance is a pair of legs. I immediately shut the door and lock it, stepping back in a panic.

Okay, Ophelia. This is not going to work. You don't know your way around this building at all and you're going to get yourself killed. Maybe it's another dead end. But then I look up and see the opening for the air vents. I've seen this in movies. Sometimes it works perfectly, other times it goes terribly wrong. But it's a viable means of secret transportation through a building, so I'll give it a try.

Using a stack of crates and boxes, I climb up to the vent and pop it open before climbing inside. I army crawl through until I finally come to a series of rooms where various poker games and other forms of gambling are being held. But there's no sight of Theo. I've come this far. I can't give up now.

I keep crawling, studying each room as it passes. Until finally I've reached some back offices. I see a room for counting money and then another with a line of TV monitors for men to keep watch over the games, ensuring that no one is cheating. Whatever would happen to a suspected cheater would probably happen to me if I was caught in here, so I take it as an extra reminder to be as careful as possible. The guards in there don't look like the kind of guys you want to be on the bad side of.

As I'm passing an empty hall, I almost don't even stop to look out. But a figure catches in the corner of my eye. It's Theo, walking back to one of the offices. I wait a minute for him to walk past, then do my best to turn around in the tight space and follow after him. He makes the rounds through all of the important rooms, checking in on the TV monitors and then the money counting room. He pockets some of the cash in there and says something to the guys, but I can't hear what it is.

One thing is certain. He is moving and talking like he owns this joint or is at least very heavily involved in the organization of it. That's exactly the kind of thing I need proof of. It's even better than I hoped for. I wonder if this has anything to do with all of those eager, generous investors he's been talking about?

I follow Theo around on his business for a while, snapping pictures all the way. When I've taken as many as I dare, I try to remember my way back to the room I entered through. After a few wrong turns and panicked moments of thinking I'll be stuck in here forever, I finally find the closet where the laundry chute pulley is waiting for me. I climb in and pull my way back up, thinking the entire time that this is when the line will finally snap and send me hurtling through the building straight to the hard floor below.

But thankfully, I make my way back to the roof and even back across the wooden boards to where I started from, safe and sound. I go back into the empty building and I'm feeling pretty confident that I've truly managed to pull this off as I go out the side door. I start marching back to my car when suddenly, someone calls out to me.

"Hey! Miss! Stop!" a deep bellowing voice yells in the darkness.

I ignore it and start walking faster, but I can hear him pick up the pace behind me, still shouting for me to stop. My heart pounds as I think this is it. I've been caught. Just as I break into a full-on running pace, the man grabs me by the arm and whips me around.

"What are you doing here?" he demands.

"I…I'm just out for a run. Now let me go or I'll scream," I stammer, wishing I sounded less guilty.

He squints his eyes at me, trying to determine if he believes me or not. But finally, his face softens as he straightens his suit jacket, looking slightly embarrassed.

"Sorry, miss. I didn't mean to scare you."

"It's okay," I shrug, swallowing a hard lump in my throat before sprinting off back to my car.

I start driving as soon as I'm inside, not feeling safe again until I'm almost back home. My hands are still shaking when I pull off into a parking lot and pull out my cell phone to make a call.

"Ophelia? Is everything okay?"

"Coach Granger," I answer. "I need to ask you something. Do you still have that contact on the police force? The detective or whoever you said could be trusted?"

"Detective Williams?" he asks. "Yeah, but what's going on?"

I sigh, not quite sure where to start. "It's my biological dad.

Theo Nickelson. I have some information that ties him to this underground illegal gambling ring and I want to turn him in."

The line falls silent for a moment. "You want to turn in your own father?" he puzzles. "Ophelia…are you sure? Sure, it's illegal gambling. But do you really want to take the man out just for that?"

"That's not the worst he's done by far, believe me," I huff. "It's just the only thing I have any proof on. Can you help? Can you put me in touch with Detective Williams?"

Finally, Coach Granger is convinced enough to give me his friend's number. I call him immediately and find out where to send my photo evidence to. After hanging up, I go home for some much-needed sleep. I can hardly wait for the news to come that Theo has been busted.

# CHAPTER TWENTY-ONE

## BOOK 3

It's a blissful Sunday morning of waking up to no alarms, and the sun seems to be shining even brighter now that I know Theo will be going behind bars soon. He's obviously some kind of head guy for this underground illegal gambling ring, and with the FBI already keeping an eye on him, waiting for more fuel for their investigation, this is sure to bring him down once and for all.

I sit up in bed and stretch out my arms with a smile on my face, thinking how pretty the birds sound chirping outside of my window. I slip into a sweatshirt and head downstairs, thinking I smell bacon and eggs cooking. The perfect breakfast for the perfect morning.

But there's more stirring and voices downstairs than there should be, which only becomes clearer as I round the corner. I freeze when I make out one of the voices to be Theo's. What the hell is he doing here again? Especially after that fight with Brendan. Surely, he'll be arrested soon.

I step into the living room and see that not only is Theo here. Emmett is too. And they're all sitting around chatting, my mom and Brendan included. Everyone stops suddenly and grows very quiet when they see.

"What's going on?" I ask, feeling completely thrown. Not exactly the kind of thing I expected to walk into this morning.

"Oh, good morning, sweetie," my mom says softly with a

strange somber tone. "I'm glad you're up. We were wanting to talk to you."

"We?" I laugh nervously. "We as in all of you? Together?" No one answers and each time I look at one of them, they shift and fidget, darting their eyes away. "What's going on?"

Emmett walks up sheepishly and takes me by the hands. "Come here, have a seat."

"Okay, you're all really starting to freak me out," I exhale as he leads me over to the dining room table. Everyone seems to be bubbling up with something, but they won't say a word. "Is someone going to tell me what this is all about or…"

"We're all worried about you," my mom announces as Brendan grabs her hand in support.

"Worried about me?" I scoff, thinking I'm the one that's worried about all them. Especially any time Theo is around. "What for?"

There's a longer awkward pause until finally, Emmett takes a stab at spitting it out. "Theo told us about you talking to Detective Williams," he says.

I let out a big gulp, unsure of what to say. Why would Detective Williams give me away like that? He knew it could be dangerous for me. Now I don't know how much Theo knows or what kind of spin he has managed to put on this for everybody.

"Did he tell you *why* I talked to Detective Williams?" I sneer, growing angrier by the second as I look at Theo across the table. Why the hell am I the one being interrogated here? And why isn't he in jail yet?

"He's running an illegal gambling ring!" I blurt, unable to hold it in anymore.

But no one looks surprised at all. In fact, it only seems to make them more frustrated with me. They sigh and hang their heads in disappointment.

"I've been working with the FBI, Ophelia," Theo states plainly as if I should have known this all along. "Yes, I did get into some trouble with them a long time ago. But I made a deal with them and part of that is being an inside guy for some things. Like that illegal gambling ring."

"You could've gotten Theo killed, ratting him out to a stranger like that," my mom scolds.

"Have you lost your minds!?" I shriek. "You honestly believe this!? Detective Williams isn't a stranger. He's a trusted contact. And how am I supposed to know that I shouldn't turn him in for doing illegal things!? I'm just supposed to give him the benefit of the doubt and...what? Lie for him?"

"What you did was very dangerous," she snaps. "You weren't supposed to lie for him...but you shouldn't have been there in the first place. Honestly, Ophelia. Sneaking off into a place like that at night by yourself. Do you have any idea what could have happened to you!?"

I let out a big huff of frustration, knowing full well what could have happened to me. And it was worth the risk. "Do you have any idea what will happen to all of us if we keep trusting this guy?" I snarl towards Theo.

"That's exactly what we're worried about, Ophelia," Brendan chimes in. "I know I didn't set a very good example the other night. I think everyone can agree that making amends with Theo has been emotionally trying for all of us. But he's a good guy. At least now. And he's doing his best here. I've apologized and I think you should too."

"Apologize?" I gasp. "That's not going to happen. In fact, I can't sit here and listen to this bullshit. I wanted to save you all from him, but if you want to be this way about it...let him have at it. You hear that Theo?" I fume across the table. "They're all yours! My boyfriend and my whole family! Do you wanna invite Bridgett over too? Sweet talk her into trusting you? I see straight through it and it's not my fault none of you can." I leap from my chair and turn to storm out of the room.

"Sit down, Ophelia," my mom's voice booms, letting me know she really means it. "*Now.*"

"I don't want to," I insist. "What else is it you want to say?"

"Listen to your mother," Theo says, adding insult to injury.

My eyes grow wide, and I think I have never been more furious in my life as I stare him down with my blood boiling. It feels like hot lava coursing through my veins, and I wish I could spew it out at him.

"Oh, you want to parent now? Dear old Dad?" I snap back bitterly. "Why don't we tell them about the kind of parent you were we first moved here?"

"Stop it," Emmett warns.

"Don't you think they'd love to know how you and I came to meet the first time?" I continue. "The *real* first time we met?"

"What is she talking about?" my mom asks, whipping her head back around to Theo with concern.

Theo's eyes look straight through me with a cold blankness.

"I introduced them," Emmett exclaims. "Theo and I had a business deal. I introduced him to Ophelia when I realized the relation."

I can't help but laugh. It's not entirely a lie, but he's leaving out all the big important parts. Like Theo's plans to kidnap me. The way he blackmailed the Elites and brought them under investigation. He murdered Emmett's dad, however welcomed it may have been. But I guess I can't tell them about that. It could be just as damaging to Emmett as it would be to Theo. And knowing him, he'd probably spin it to be all Emmett's fault.

"Why didn't you tell me you had met him?" Mom questions, looking shocked and hurt.

"Emmett, can I talk to you for a moment?" I beg, motioning for him to follow me into the other room.

It's bad enough that they're all ganging up on me, but I'm not about to sit here and take the fall for Emmett and Theo's decisions just because no one can know what really happened. I'm tired of lying for other people. I haven't done anything wrong.

"How could you agree to be a part of this!?" I howl in a whisper once we're around the corner. "What am I supposed to say in there!?"

"Everyone's just worried, Ophelia," he insists with his big innocent, gray eyes.

"Bullshit!" I snap. "I don't want to hear that anymore. I wish everyone would stop talking to me like I'm a child. I haven't felt anything less than an adult from the moment I saw you for who you really were. And after everything you and Theo have put me through...I'd think you'd be a little quicker to defend me."

"That's just it though...I changed. Don't you believe I've changed?" he asks earnestly as if his whole life depends on my answer.

My mouth opens, but the only sound is a sharp inhale building up to words that won't come out. "I don't always know," I confess. "I believe you have, yes. But after all of that... sometimes it's hard not to wonder if...if the old you is still waiting to come out." I watch his face drop as the words sink in. "But that's why I don't like you being so wrapped up with Theo! If anyone can turn you back to the way you were before...it's him."

"Well, whether you believe it or not," he says slowly, looking heartbroken. "I *have* changed. And so has Theo. I know you don't like to see it this way, Ophelia, but your dad saved me. Whatever his intentions were then or are now…He helped me get rid of my father. A man who harmed me and plenty of others on a daily basis. If he hadn't…I don't know…" his voice cracks and trails off.

"I know, I'm sorry." I rub his shoulder. "I'm glad Thomas is gone, but…"

"I think you should come sit back down," he urges me.

My eyes tear up. I feel betrayed. Since when can Emmett not talk to me himself? He seriously thinks he needs my whole family and Theo as back up?

"Just hear what they have to say," he adds. "Then this will all be over, and…you can think whatever you want."

Before I can say anything else, he turns to walk back to the table. I reluctantly follow behind, telling myself I'll just listen and keep my mouth shut from now on. Soon I'll be leaving here anyway and whatever Theo does to them after that…well, they can't say I didn't warn them.

"We want you to let go of your grudge against Theo," my mom states as soon as I sit down, not bothering to waste any time. "You don't have to like him. You don't even have to give much of a chance. But turning down his help for school or anything else just out of resentment is only hurting you more. And you definitely have to stop dictating everyone else's relationships with him. Like it or not, he is a part of this family."

I laugh under my breath again. A part of our family. I get an all-out intervention for not wanting to trust someone who has given me plenty of reasons not to trust him. But he can waltz in and out of our lives whenever he wants, screwing over whoever he wants as he goes, and we're all expected to give him the benefit of the doubt. It's maddening.

"Do you have anything you'd like to say to me?" Theo asks, looking like a kid waiting to be apologized to on the playground.

"Where to start," I scoff. I look over to Emmett who is begging me with his eyes not to say anything else about what happened with Theo before. It's too incriminating for him. "I don't expect anyone else to understand it," I explain instead. "I thought Emmett could, but…that's what you do. You tell people what they want to hear and give them what they want to win them over. But I can't be bought, Theo. I know the truth about you. And I'm never going to trust you. I don't care what anyone says. Nothing is going to change that. And the saddest part is…I know the rest of you will be forced to face that truth eventually. I just hope it's not too late."

I wipe a tear from my cheek, wishing I could just bring myself to say what they want to hear. If I could just play nice with Theo and fake it, this would all go away. But I feel like I'm watching them all be led straight off the side of a cliff. How can I not speak up?

"Is that all?" I ask quietly. "Can I go now?"

"Suit yourself," Theo says grimly.

My mom doesn't seem to have anything else to say. Brendan and Emmett grow quiet as well. I excuse myself from the table and walk slowly to my room, still in disbelief. My heart aches as I consider the reality of it all. Had it not been for Theo and his bad ties to the Elites, I would have never been invited to WJ Prep. And all the awful things that happened after would still be distant nightmares or scenes from horror movies. They wouldn't be my reality. All of that would have been more than enough reason to hate him. But now it feels like he has stolen my entire family from me.

Doing all I know to do, I try to call Detective Williams to see what went wrong. Why did he tell Theo I was his source? The phone rings and rings with no answer. I think it's just as well since I'm a sniffling, sobbing mess right now. But a minute later, Coach Granger calls.

"Yes?" I answer.

"Ophelia, are you okay?"

"I've been trying to reach Detective Williams," I tell him in between my short, labored breaths. "He told Theo that I ratted him out. And now my whole family knows and…What happened? I thought we could trust him?"

"About that," he clears his throat. "He asked me…well…he doesn't want you or Emmett to contact him anymore."

"What?" I cry. "Why?"

"Your lead on Theo went nowhere because it turns out he was an inside guy for the FBI the whole time," he explains. "I don't know how Theo found out. But between that and Emmett's false alarm on his mother and sister's kidnappings… he'd prefer you go through regular police channels from now on."

"But those things weren't our fault!" I sob harder. "And the police here are all corrupt! If we don't have at least one person to turn to, what are we supposed to do?"

"Just stay focused on choosing which college you want to go to," he urges. "Keep your chin up, Lopez. You'll be out of here soon enough."

"Thanks," I murmur half-heartedly before hanging up. Sure, I'll be out soon enough. But the rest of them won't be.

As has become my habit for when I am alone in my room, upset with nothing else to do, I pick up Marissa's diary. But my eyes are still watering, making it hard to read too much.

*The more time I spend with Thomas, the more I see a side of him that no one else does. Not the sweet, charming guy that everyone loves. But a dark side. Something I've only seen glimpses of, but he has moments of being so heartless and selfish. I tried to talk to my mother about it, but she says all men can be that way and that I'd be a fool not to want to be Mrs. Jameson. So, more and more I am learning to stay out his affairs and keep to myself. And sometimes, I still feel like the luckiest girl in the world, but...*

I can't read anymore. I throw the book to the ground with a big thud, wondering what is different between Emmett and Thomas. Did I save Emmett in a way Marissa couldn't save Thomas? Or have I just been fooled? There has to be some reason he's so willing to choose Theo over me.

There's a knock at the door, making me jump as I quickly kick the diary back under my bed. "Go away!" I shout out. "I want to be alone."

"It's me," Emmett calls out from behind the door.

"Go away, please!" I try again.

But the latch turns and the door opens anyway. Of course, I forgot to lock it. Just my luck. I hear him come in, but he says nothing.

"What do you want!?" I moan, but as I turn around, I notice the pale ghostly look on his face. "Wha...what's wrong?"

"It's Malcolm," he says in shock. "He's dead."

# CHAPTER TWENTY-TWO

## BOOK 3

I stare down the black velvet dress crumpled up in the corner of my room. It's been laying there since the night Emmett attempted to flash all of his newly earned money at me, not realizing I'd inevitably find out where it came from. Now I have to consider putting it on for Malcolm Henderson's funeral, but something about it makes me feel sick.

"I'm not going," Emmett announces from the other corner of my room.

"I didn't think you would," I answer listlessly as I try to remember if I even own another black dress.

He can't face Liam, Bernadette, and his mom all while pretending to care that Malcolm is dead. He hates him even more than I do. Which is sad since they were childhood friends. Emmett should be able to say goodbye to that part of him at least, even if its been dead for a while now.

"Why are *you* going?" he adds.

"For Bridgett," I sigh. We've had this discussion twenty times already.

"But she can't even talk to you while you're there," he argues. "No one's supposed to know you two are friends, remember?"

"Does any of that even matter now that Malcolm is dead?" I wonder out loud as I dig through my closet.

"Another one always pops up in the old one's place," he grumbles.

The funny this is…Malcolm is the one who popped up in Emmett's place.

"Well who's next in line now, you think?" I yell out from the back of the closet, tossing out garment after garment. "Bernadette? One of those new guys?"

"Who cares," he huffs.

I finally find a pair of black dress pants and decide those will have to do. I'm not in the mood to dress up too much anyway.

"Anyway…even if I can't talk to Bridgett, I should at least be there as…I don't know. A sign or something. It might make her feel better to have me around," I explain as I slide on a dark, sheer sweater. "She didn't like Malcolm any more than we did, but he was still her cousin."

I leave him to sulk as I finish getting ready in the bathroom. He's still sitting there looking miserable when I come out.

"What are you thinking about?" I ask, walking over to drag him out of the chair.

"Jameson Automobiles," he answers quietly, looking almost shameful. "I guess I shouldn't care. But at least with Malcolm around, I knew things would be in his hands when Liam croaked. Even if Malcolm was just as messed up as his dad. Now who will it go to? One of those strangers they brought into town? Malcolm may not have been a blood relative, but we still grew up together."

"Why wouldn't Bernadette take it over?" I suggest.

"Yeah right," he scoffs. "She'd never sign up for something like that."

"I don't know…she seemed pretty concerned with the welfare of the company when she was working to rob you of everything," I remind him. "Why do you care anyway? Jameson was fucked the moment they stole it from you. I'd think you'd enjoy watching it crumble right before their eyes."

He stares off into the distance. "It's bred into me to care I guess," he shakes his head. "Even if it's not mine anymore, it's still my family's legacy."

I want to comfort him, but I'm still angry with the way he teamed up with the rest of my family to attack me. Pile that on top of everything else that's been going on, and I don't exactly feel like a top-notch girlfriend at the moment. I just want to get this funeral over with and pick a school so I can get the hell out of here. I don't care anymore about whatever happens with these car companies or the Elites after that.

"I better get going," I tell him. "You staying here…or…?"

"No," he snaps to. "I'm going home."

I head for the door, hating how lost Emmett looks. Ordinarily, I'd drop everything to try and help him find his way, but I just don't have it in me right now.

The funeral service is cold and traditional. As is the burial afterward. The men stand around in their expensive suits and the women in their big black floppy hats. Everyone in sunglasses, as if it'd be too awful to imagine anyone seeing the Elites and their friends and family showing real emotion. They have to hide their tears like ice queens.

I still feel out of place, even as I sit and stand among them. I wonder if I'm welcome at all, so I stand back a ways from the burial site. Once it's over, I wait for the rest of the crowd disperse before leaving. But as I wait, I notice I'm not the only one lingering in the cemetery. A tall, dark figure stands over the grave in privacy. As I walk closer, I realize it's Coach Granger. I want to leave him alone and get away without disturbing him, but a twig snaps under my shoe as I turn to go.

"Ophelia," he calls out for me.

"Oh, hey," I spin around in embarrassment. "I didn't mean to bother you."

"It's no bother," he says, looking back down to the grave. "I was wondering if you'd be here or not."

"I'm kind of surprised you're here, honestly," I confess as I step closer. "After what Malcolm did to your son…"

"It's sad any time someone young dies so suddenly," he replies. "My son…Malcolm…my heart hurts for both of them."

"But your son would probably still be here if it hadn't been for Malcolm," I blurt without thinking, quickly realizing it was probably a harsh, unnecessary reminder.

He nods with a somber sort of acceptance. We're both quiet for a moment as we stare down at the fresh dirt. I wish I had more thoughts on his death. I wish it brought up feelings about the meaning of life and the shortness of it, and why are we all here anyway? But all I can think is I know exactly why this happened. One way or another, Malcolm is just another victim of Jameson. I don't trust any event like this being a natural occurrence. Not anymore.

"You'll be the last runner I ever train, Lopez," he says suddenly. "Once you're gone, I'm retiring and leaving Jameson."

"You can't!" I plead. "You're such a great coach. You could help so many more students."

"I'm tired," he says sternly. "I knew what I was getting myself into at WJ Prep. I thought if nothing else I could take a few of the spoiled brats and be one of the only people in their lives who demanded genuine excellence from them. The only person who didn't put up with their twisted hierarchy and let them get away with their games. But I didn't count on finding people like you mixed up in it all. And then…my son."

I stare back down to the flowers piled on top of the grave and wish Malcolm's death would change something, but Emmett is right. When one goes down, another one pops up in their place.

"It's a shame," he adds somberly. "If Malcolm had been given a chance, maybe he could have changed eventually."

"People never change," I scoff.

"We all change," he turns towards me with an insistent look. "You've changed since you came here. I've changed. All we ever do is change."

We stand there quietly for a long time before I finally say goodbye and leave him alone to think. I decide to skip the gathering afterward, assuming I wouldn't be invited anyway since it's at the Henderson Estate. But as I'm driving out of the cemetery, I see a long black dress blowing in the wind up ahead. It's Bridgett. What is she doing walking out here all alone?

"Hey, need a ride?" I ask as I roll my window down, checking to make sure no one is watching.

"Yeah, thanks." She jumps in, looking happy to see me. "I was going to call a cab when I got back to the main road. My family was driving me crazy. I couldn't stand the thought of being locked up in a car with them."

"I'm sorry. You'd think they'd chill out for at least a little while…considering the circumstances."

"No way. They're too paranoid about what happened to Malcolm," she says.

"Paranoid?" I repeat. "So they suspect foul play?"

"Of course. As you would with any death around here, I guess," she replies. "But an accidental car crash? They're not buying it. They're convinced someone did this to him."

"No one told me it was a car crash," I blink, feeling certain their suspicions are right. "Where did it happen?"

As Bridgett describes the area of the crash, I realize it was the exact same spot where my car went spiraling over the edge.

"What was he doing before that?" I ask frantically. "When did it happen?"

"He was leaving school after some kind of study group," she looks at me with curiosity. "Why?"

"Did the cops happen to fish my car out of there while they were pulling him out?" I ask bitterly. "I'd say your family is right. If the brakes had been tampered with on the car, that'd be about the spot he'd lose control at. I know from experience. Which means…" I trail off as my mind races.

"What?"

"I assumed the Elites were responsible for all these threats to my life," I explain. "But if they were…Malcolm would be the main one behind it all, right?"

"Probably so," she nods. "But if the same thing happened to Malcolm, then…"

"You don't think one of the other Elites would have tried to take him, do you? Like some kind of weird power struggle or…I don't know."

"I guess it's possible," she looks out her window, thinking it all over. "But," her eyes cut over to me in hesitation. "Never mind."

"Tell me," I insist. "What is it?"

"Just…what I said before," she stares down at her feet. "You don't think Emmett would do this?"

I want to say he would never try to kill me or anyone. But that's not true. He did play a hand in his own father's death. And when he was told to by his father or the other Elites, he was capable of hurting me many times. If it had come down to it and they asked him to kill me, would he? And as for Malcolm, we all know he has plenty of motive for wanting to do something like that.

Then the words of Marissa's diary ring through my brain, and I'm filled with even more doubt. Is Emmett inherently fucked-up because of his upbringing and genetics? Does he have this dark side always lingering beneath the surface now that he's claiming to be a changed man?

"I can't believe he'd do any of these things," I proclaim, trying to convince myself just as much as Bridgett. "It'd be easier to believe that Theo would."

Once again, Theo has reasons for wanting to harm the

Hendersons. They stepped up to fill the shoes of the former Elites he managed to erase. I never did find it easy to accept that he'd stop there. I always thought he'd just keep going and going, power-hungry and aimlessly stomping out whatever new figure popped up in Thomas's place. And what about his deal with Emmett? They both wanted Thomas dead, but is Emmett indebted to him now?

"Well whoever did it," she continues, snapping me out of my rising mental panic. "If the same thing was done to your car that was done to Malcolm's, I'd say whoever killed Malcolm is probably behind your death threats. Which means your number one suspect is dead and the real culprit is still out there. And obviously thirsty for blood."

"I really am sorry about Malcolm," I tell her. "I know he wasn't your favorite person, but…"

"There was always something off about him," her eyes darken. "I could never put my finger on it when we were younger, but then he turned into a complete monster as we got older. I think he's a sociopath."

"Emmett would agree with you," I sigh, remembering his opinions of Malcolm and their friendship. But does that mean Emmett is just as messed up? Maybe that's why the two got along so well. And why he gets along with Theo. Could he be a sociopath too?

We're quiet the rest of the way, playing detective in our minds. But mostly we're both just exhausted. I feel bad for Bridgett. I want to go home and crawl into bed, but she still has hours of socializing to do among the grieving Elites and the rest of the school.

I drop her off at the iron gate lining the Henderson's property, shivering to remember the last time I was there. I'm quick to say goodbye and drive off, getting home as fast as I can.

I'm conflicted as I crawl back into bed at home. Part of me wishes Emmett had stayed and that I could curl up in his arms right now where I usually feel so safe. But there's a part of me that is losing all the trust I have built up in him.

I think over the past few months, all the way back to our first day back to school. His feelings about Malcolm and the new Elites were never resolved. He's been so shady and withholding, disappearing for all of these mystery errands I never know anything about. And each time he disappears, another threat is made on my life. Then there's his friendship with Theo.

Throwing me under the bus to protect himself when I wanted to tell the truth about my dad and how we met. Going along with that whole intervention even though he knows why I don't trust Theo.

By the time I get back to remembering his insecurities about money and his future, and the way he was so quick to start blowing through cash the moment he was put on Theo's payroll, I feel sick to my stomach. More so than I have all day.

And still my heart aches for him. Even with all of my doubts. How could one part of my brain seriously be considering the possibility that he'd threaten my life while the other part of me wants nothing more than to call him and be in his arms again? But I guess that's the way it's always been with him from the beginning. He hurts me, and somehow, I only love him more.

I give in to the side I always do and reach for my phone to call him. If I could just see his face and hear his voice, I can convince myself that none of these fears are true.

# CHAPTER TWENTY-THREE

BOOK 3

"Hi," I smile as Emmett opens his apartment door.

"Hey." He leans in and kisses me so deep and soft that I instantly get the relief I need. But a big part of me still wants to cry. I have to stop myself from bursting into tears as he brushes his hand to my cheek.

"How was the funeral?" he asks, pulling me the rest of the way inside before shutting the door behind me.

"Like any other funeral, I guess," I shrug. "Coach Granger was there. And I gave Bridgett a ride to the Henderson Estate."

"How's she doing?" He says the words, but he doesn't really seem to care what the answer is.

"They don't think it was an accident," I explain, wondering how much I should divulge. I'm terrified if I go into detail, I'll see some subtle admission of guilt on his face.

Emmett picks up on my hesitation and narrows his eyes at me. "What's wrong?"

"Nothing," I shoot back too quickly.

"Ophelia, I can tell when something is bothering you," he groans. "What is it?"

I've been caught, but I can't bring myself to say the words. I feel the tears rushing to the surface again as he stares me down. I look away and try to tame my trembling lip.

"Look, I know funerals are tough, but let's not forget what kind of guy Malcolm was. Do you remember what he did to you? To Lily? Coach Granger's son? To *me*?" he rants.

I bite my lip, thinking of all the people Emmett has hurt. "I haven't forgotten," I mutter, unable to look him in the face.

I watch him storm around his apartment, flinging things around. There's something different about him and it frightens me. I've seen this plenty of times before, back in the shitty motel he stayed at last semester when we were closer than ever. But even then, I knew how unhealthy this relationship could be at times. Should I have left then?

"Did you do it?" I ask finally with a sharp, shaky breath.

He freezes and looks to me with wide, raging eyes. "What?"

"Did you kill Malcolm?" I say again, more sternly.

His face shrinks into a soft laugh. "You've got to be kidding me," he moans, raking his hands across his face in exasperation. "You really think I could kill someone?"

I tilt my head, silently reminding him about his father.

"Ophelia, if that's the kind of person I was…I would've shot Thomas in the head myself," he argues coldly. "He deserved to die even more than Malcolm did and I still couldn't bring myself to do it. That's why I needed your father."

"So then you admit Theo is the type of person who could commit murder," I snap back. "But you still have no problems going into business with him?"

"Oh Christ, not this again," he fumes. "I can't get into this right now. I'm tired, okay? Is that all you came over for?"

I want to keep arguing, but then that soft part of my heart cries out, longing for him. That's what I came here for. To feel his warm skin against mine and forget all of the bad that is flooding my mind. Without saying another word, I march up to him and throw myself against his chest. He's tense and still at first, but slowly his arms wrap around me. His palms spread around my back, lowering to my upper thighs.

I look up into his eyes, and he lowers his lips to mine. Our kiss quickly deepens into a passionate, hurried frenzy. We want to make each other feel good. We want to forget about the complicated mess around us. We haven't had enough of this lately and our bodies miss each other. Not just the motions of having sex, but the primal connection that used to spark between us. For everything I don't know, I am certain so much of me still belongs to him and probably always will, no matter what kinds of crimes or wrongdoings he could commit.

He throws me onto the couch and begins to unbutton my jeans. I try to pull him back down to kiss me, but he pushes my hands away. I expect him to go down on me or slide his fingers inside, but the moment he takes off my pants, he starts to remove his own.

"Wait," I rasp, running my hands across his skin. I want him, but I'm not ready yet.

He ignores me and quickly throws the rest of his clothes to the floor. He touches himself and there's a mad look in his eye. His nostrils are flaring and he looks angry, but like he wants me just as badly as I want him at the same time. I *do* want him, but my body isn't responding. Has it finally caught up to the logical, rational side of me that never thought I should trust Emmett in the first place?

Emmett pushes inside of me, but there's a sharp pain. I wince and dig my fingers into the couch cushions, trying to go somewhere in my brain that forces my body to do what I want it to. To be wet and excited over him. I think back on how sure I felt of everything after his family cut him off. They knew he wasn't like them. That he wouldn't choose money, power, or greed over human lives. When did I lose that certainty? Where is all of this doubt and mistrust coming from?

My mind races as he moves, grunting with deep thrusts. I tense up, still not feeling any of the pleasure I am used to feeling at his hands.

"Stop," I whisper, pushing his hips back with my hands. "It hurts."

As if he's in another world, he doesn't seem to hear my words. He keeps moving, ignoring me completely.

"Emmett!" I shout louder. "Did you hear me!? Stop it! You're hurting me!"

He freezes and looks down at me with a mortified expression, but it melts away into something else. Something I haven't seen since long before I started to think I understood who he really was. Suddenly I am face to face with the Emmett I first knew at WJ Prep. The Emmett who bullied, humiliated, and threatened me.

"Oh, what?" he smirks with a cruel spark. "First you think I'd murder someone…and now you think I'd…what? Rape you?"

I shake my head, but I'm not sure if I'm telling him no or just asking for the world to go away. That's not what was happening, was it? I look into his darkened eyes and search for what I came here for. Safety. Assurance. Why can't he give me any of that? But once again, only the old Emmett stares back. I remember the times he used to grope me, force his lips on mine with the other Elites standing there to watch. The time in the car with Trey and Vincent when he blindfolded me and teased me. Only no matter how fucked-up it was, I wanted him. I wasn't just freezing and going along with it. My entire body shook with desire for him.

"Do you want this or not?" he demands, stroking himself again.

I should be furious with how cold and bossy he's being. That moments ago, he didn't stop when I asked. That he had to say that terrible word in the middle of all this. But the traumas that used to make me cringe are melting me from the inside out. I feel the pulsing sensation between my legs that longs to feel him inside, but I can't bring myself to tell him just how badly I do want it suddenly.

Unable to speak, I run my fingers between my legs. I tease the tingling folds and coax him inside. His eyes spark again as he thrusts forward with an animalistic grunt. Our nerves are shot and everything is tense, causing us both to sweat. But somehow it just makes it feel better. My brain wants me to yell at him, to push him away. But everything else just wants to get off on him. I need to.

I writhe underneath him as he pounds into me, and all the sharpness from before is gone. I dig my nails into his skin so hard, I'm certain I'm drawing blood. He deserves it, I think, for hurting me a moment ago. And again, the thought turns me on more. He hisses from the scratches but doesn't stop or ask me to stop.

The more I replay in my head, the more turned on but angrier I get. I grab his shoulders and pull myself up, forcing my lips against his. We bite at each other's lips and tongues as the sweat pools around my clit. His thrusting body rubs against the slickness in all the most perfect ways, swelling with pleasure. I pull on him so hard, he finally flips over, rolling me on top of him as he sits back against the couch.

With our mouths and teeth still nipping at each other's skin, I start to ride him harder than I ever have before. It's more than enough, but we're both feeling insatiable and greedy, so he thrusts up into me in return, our rhythms so rushed and frantic that we barely sync up. Our rush makes it sloppy, but we slip into some trance where all that matters is how it feels. We stop caring about what we look like or what kinds of sounds we make and lose ourselves completely in the feeling. Immense pleasure with a tinge of exquisite pain.

I don't realize we're on the floor until the orgasm is rippling through my body, with Emmett climaxing right behind me. I don't even know how we got down there. I feel like I've been floating up out of my body for the past half hour.

"What the fuck," I grumble under my breath as I lift my head to confirm I am in fact laid out on the carpet.

Emmett blows out a big gushing breath, then looks troubled. His eyes glint with worry as he rolls over and scoops me up into his arms. He carries me into the bedroom and lays me tenderly down onto the bed before kneeling at my side.

"I'm sorry," he says urgently. "I can't believe I…I should have never…"

"It's okay," I shake my head and run my fingers through his dampened curls. I don't know how it's okay. It should never be okay for him to keep doing anything when I ask him to stop. Not anymore, even if it did used to be a normal occurrence before he started trying to be his real self.

My heart twists in my chest as I finally begin to think maybe I have been trying to draw too many lines in the sand. There was the Emmett from before and the one from now, the good, the bad, the one who would do this thing or would never do that thing. The one who lies, the one who owns my heart, the one who loves me more than anything. It all starts to shatter as I think…It's all him.

I don't think people change. They're multifaceted. Emmett has all of these different sides, but just because I can only see the good now doesn't mean the bad couldn't resurface at any time. The same goes for Theo, even if I have been purposefully blinding myself to any good he has shown lately.

But as we accept all of the different sides to a person, can it all start to blend and bleed together? Maybe the good will somehow neutralize the bad. I don't know, but somehow, I mean it as I tell Emmett over and over that it's okay. Because it is. I don't know how or why, but it is.

"Can I get you anything?" he asks suddenly, desperate to redeem himself.

I shake my head no, and he finally peels himself up to get a towel and a glass of water. I wrap myself up in his sheets and realize I don't even remember what day it is. Wednesday, I think. We had the day off for Malcolm's funeral service and prom will be this weekend. I've still lost my excitement for prom, but now for completely different reasons.

Our sex trance seems to have woken up so many old feelings. I don't feel indifferent at all. The opposite. I feel too much. Maybe I have just been suppressing my feelings this entire time to be able to get through the days. I had to learn to control the all-consuming, obsessive love I feel for him. But now it rushes back over me and something like prom seems silly. Like we're above it. Our love is too big for stupid little high school dances.

The thought makes me laugh as I watch Emmett through the doorway, slipping into his boxers. But then there's a sudden, booming, violent banging on the door that scares us both. He looks to me with wide, questioning eyes, but I don't have any clue who it could be either.

"Emmett Jameson!" a man's voice yells out. "Open up. It's the police."

I shoot up in bed, clutching the covers around me. My clothes are still in the living room, but I don't know if I have time to get to them. Emmett tries to ask them to wait a minute, but they only bang on the door harder, demanding for him to open up right away. Instead he bolts over and shuts the bedroom door to give me some privacy.

My heart pounds as I hear him open the door followed by muffled voices. What are they doing here? Jameson police are corrupt and not to be trusted. But if they're trying to pull something over on us right now, I don't know who I could turn to for help. Detective Williams thinks we're crazy and asked us not to contact him anymore.

"Ophelia!" Emmett screams for me.

Practically forgetting that I'm naked, I fling a sheet around my body and race out to him. As I run into the room, I see they have him pinned up against the wall and are about to handcuff him.

"What's going on here!?" I shriek. "Emmett!"

"Miss, step back," commands one of the officers.

"Emmett Jameson, you're under arrest as a suspect in the murder of Malcolm Henderson," the officer handcuffing him announces before reading him the rest of his rights.

"What!?" I cry. "You're wrong! He didn't kill Malcolm!"

They ignore me and carry on. Emmett says nothing as they cart him away and leave me alone in the empty apartment. I don't even know how I was able to defend him so vehemently when hours ago I was partly convinced that he did it. I just never expected the police to think the same thing enough to arrest him. What do they know that I don't? Or is this the Elites' doing?

Feeling completely lost and heartbroken, I fall to the floor and pull the sheet to my face as I sob. I'm frozen like that for what seems like hours, just crying by myself. Every time I try to stop and stand up, I collapse in tears again, harder than before. By the time I finally manage to stop, it's dark outside. I have no choice but to get dressed, gather my things, and go.

# CHAPTER TWENTY-FOUR

## BOOK 3

*D*ear Diary,

*Prom is over, and everything went as planned. Well, almost everything. I am no longer a virgin. Thomas took me to the most exquisite hotel room after the dance. He sweet-talked my parents into lifting my curfew. I guess they figure we'll be married soon enough after graduation, so there's no point in trying to keep us apart.*

*But sex was…rougher than I expected. I did not get the sweet, charming side of Thomas I thought I would be going to bed with. He was cold and direct. I am so attracted to him and care for him so much that I enjoyed it, but it didn't match the romantic fantasies I had in my head.*

*Today at school, Thomas and his friends were picking on this poor girl who made the mistake of talking badly about them to some of the other students. It's the kind of thing I had always heard about Thomas doing. He and his friends are sort of like a little gang. They call themselves the Elites. The existence of this clique has been around as long as WJ Prep has. But it reaches far beyond the walls of our school. It's ingrained into the town of Jameson.*

*Thomas and any of the other kids whose families work with Jameson Automobiles basically run the school, while their families run the town. Only now that I am with Thomas, I am considered to be one of them even more so than before. I am one of the Elites.*

*Because I am one of them, they expected me to join in on their torment of this girl. They pinned her to the wall and threatened her and asked me to take a turn in making her regret what she had said. I looked in her fright-*

*ened eyes and wanted to run away. I don't want to hurt anyone. But I didn't want to disappoint Thomas or embarrass him in front of his friends.*

*So I spit in her face. I felt awful for doing it. When I tried to talk to Thomas about it, he said anyone who questions our position in that school, or this town deserves whatever happens to them. He told me I'll have to get used to defending our respected titles.*

So it begins, I think as I slam the diary shut and turn back to the news streaming on my laptop. The reports of Emmett's arrest have been blaring across every channel all day. When I got sick of hearing it all, I tried to turn it off only to find headline after headline repeating the same information. Then there's the endless gossip flurrying across every social media platform, coming from people in Jameson and all over the country. Everyone's eager to talk about the drama of the high society Elite millionaire world.

The police have reason to believe someone tampered with Malcolm's brakes, just as we suspected. Which is what caused him to crash to his death. They collected DNA evidence from Malcolm's car along with a few misplaced personal items, and it all points to Emmett.

Even though I had been questioning his innocence myself, the moment he was arrested I went into defense mode. I keep running through the reasons over and over again for how he could have never done this. He was right about one thing. I can't bring myself to be too upset that Malcolm is gone. He was a horrible person and has done so much harm to so many people.

But whoever killed Malcolm, likely tried to kill me too. That's why I can't bring myself to believe he did it. For all the time I have spent unable to erase awful memories of Emmett from my brain, now I can't seem to remember any of it. Everything has reversed. I can only remember the good, the sweet, the loveable side.

I keep reading Marissa's diary, thinking I will feel the same as before. That I'll see the glaring similarities between Emmett and his father and remember the potential for how messed up he might be. But it all feels distant and impossible. Like a dream. Like I never knew Marissa or Thomas at all. And what has happened between Emmett and me has been nothing short of a perfectly ordinary high school romance.

Then comes the dreaded knock on my door. My mom checking on me for the twentieth time today. I've been turning her away, begging to be alone. But I'm tired of fighting her. Maybe if I let her say what she has to say, she'll finally leave me alone. I march over and open the door before promptly returning to my bed without saying anything.

"I know you want to be alone," she says, making me roll my eyes.

"If you know…then why do you keep bothering me?" I whine.

"Because I'm worried about you!" The urgency builds in her voice. "This is such a huge, scary thing to be dealing with, and I don't want you to go through it alone."

"It's not scary," I state plainly. "He didn't do it. They'll figure that out and let him go. End of story."

She sits on the edge of my bed looking even more worried than before. Wringing her hands in her lap, I see new lines forming in her face. She suddenly looks older than I ever remember and it makes me feel guilty. It's my fault. I'm causing her to age so rapidly.

"You think he's guilty," I blurt.

She hesitates, but I know what she's thinking. "There has always been something off about him," she suggests. "That car crash when you were with him…and then the way you disappeared for those few days not long after that. I wanted to give him a second chance, but Ophelia…if…if anything ever happened with him…If he ever hurt you or scared you in any way…I want you to know, you can tell me."

I burst into uncontrollable tears, breaking down the way I did on the floor of Emmett's apartment. I want more than anything to tell her everything that's happened. Maybe what I really need is for someone else to tell me Emmett is bad. That I was wrong for thinking I could see good in him or trust him at all. The only other person who knows the whole story besides Emmett and me is Bridgett, and she also thinks he could be the one who killed Malcolm. The one who's been trying to kill me.

My mom takes me into her arms and cradles me as I sob. But I can't bring myself to tell her anything. I just can't. If I could have, I would've done it by now. And what if it turns out Emmett didn't do this? What if I'm right and they let him go, declaring him innocent? Then I would still be held accountable for everything he did before this. Even if he isn't a murderer, he did enough to have never deserved a chance with me in the first place. But I'm not ready to accept that.

She holds me and lets me cry for a long time before telling me that Theo and Brendan are downstairs. "You can come down to eat if you'd like," she offers sweetly. "Or just come down to sit and talk. Sit and not talk. Whatever you need."

For the first time, hearing Theo's name or that he's in our house doesn't fill me with rage. I feel nothing. Just cold, numb emptiness. I follow her down with a blank, dejected look. But as we approach the table, I suddenly feel like running away. I can't sit with them right now and pretend that my entire world isn't falling apart. And the only thing I can't stand to do more than that is actually talk about Emmett.

Without saying a word, I pivot and bolt for the back door. I feel instantly better the moment the spring night air crashes over me. My heart is still aching with an impossible hurt, but at least I feel less trapped. Less cornered.

There's a swing set in our backyard that was left by the previous owners. Sometimes the neighborhood kids come by and play on it. I stare at it under the glow of the distant street-lights and realize I have never once sat on this thing in the nine months that we've lived here. I slide onto one of the swings and rock gently, leaning my head against one of the chains in exhaustion.

I don't even look up at the sound of the screen door slamming. At first, I'm frustrated that no one can give me a moment's peace, but then I realize how dark it has gotten and think I must have been sitting out here longer than I realized.

I avoid looking at the manly figure approaching, taking the swing next to mine. I know it's not Brendan. I'm not so lucky. Instead I'm just a magnet for fucked-up men, romantic or otherwise.

"I'm sorry, Ophelia," Theo says softly. "I'm shocked and hurt too."

"Hurt?" I scoff. "Why the hell are you hurt?"

"I lost my partner in this," he explains. "I never would have thought Emmett could kill anyone…or try to hurt you at all."

I cut my eyes over to him. "What makes you think he tried to hurt me?"

"Your mom may not want to admit some things to herself, but I'm good at piecing things together," he tells me. "I know your car crashed off the cliff in the same place Malcolm's did. And I know how far that spot is from the school. I feel awful.

Here I was trying to give the kid a job, thinking he might be my future son-in-law…"

His words are frighteningly sincere. Maybe it's because I'm shocked or tired, but my stubbornness breaks down and I start to think he actually cares for me.

"I know I'm not your favorite person," he adds. "And I deserve that after being absent from your life and everything with how we finally met again. But Ophelia, you're my daughter. I may not always get it right, but I love you. I would never do anything to intentionally hurt you."

"Ha!" I belt out sarcastically. "Except the time you were planning to kidnap me so the Elites couldn't use me against you in your little quest for vengeance."

His face pans over to mine with a pained stare. "He never told you," he murmurs.

"What? Who? Never told me what?" I fire off impatiently.

A sad smirk slides across his face as he leans over and lets out a heavy sigh. "I was never going to kidnap you Ophelia. That's just something Emmett made up, and I went along with it because I could see how crazy he was for you. I felt bad for the kid. I know it's not easy to be a little messed up in the head, but to be in love with a good woman who doesn't deserve you. He wanted to be your knight in shining armor and I didn't want to ruin it."

I shake my head. "No…No, he said you were going to kidnap me and that he begged to take me instead. He said it was to protect me."

"Never happened," he assures me. "The Elites were going to take you hostage no matter what. I asked them to leave you out of it. I don't expect you to understand why I needed revenge so badly, but I never wanted you to get dragged into any of it. And I never planned to kill Thomas. I would have if it meant saving your life, but it wasn't the original plan."

"What was the original plan?" I ask, not really caring what the answer is. I'm still not convinced he even knows how to tell the truth and I'm not letting myself fall for this crap so easily.

"I just wanted to send them to jail," he insists. "Sure, they had a right to blacklist me after I took their money. I deserved to be cut out of Jameson Automobiles and stripped of my shares. I fucked up. But they didn't have to rip Lala and me apart…They didn't have to keep coming after me and destroy my family like that. Even after I made back my money, it still felt like I had lost everything because I didn't have you or your mother."

So much of me wants to believe him. I've been clinging to my hatred for him, and only now do I realize how much easier it would be to let it go. I almost don't even care if he's lying. It feels better to think it could all be true. Maybe this is how he really feels.

"I probably still would've left them alone to live out their poor, miserable lives…But then I found out about the sex trafficking rings," he says. "After everything they had done to me, I couldn't sleep at night knowing the harm they were causing to so many other people. I thought about you…and how I would feel if you went missing into something like that. It haunted me. I knew I wanted to come back into your life, to know you. But I had to put a stop to the Elites first."

I start swinging harder. The creaking chains get louder and almost drown him out, but I still hear every last word and feel my resolve slowly breaking.

"Emmett was the one who asked me to kill his dad," he says finally, stopping my heart cold. "I never intended to kill anyone. But Emmett told me about Thomas's escape plan. If it came down to it, he was going to take off with a hidden stash of money and disappear in some other part of the world. I couldn't let him get away with what he had done, and Emmett pleaded with me to kill him. He didn't want to wait for Thomas to die of old age before he could take over the company."

It all makes too much sense. And the more sense it makes, the more my heart cracks and breaks into a million pieces. I thought Emmett would be glad to be free of Jameson Automobiles, but if what Theo is saying is true, it makes sense why he would be so torn up about losing the company. Why he was so willing to work with Theo on starting a competing automobile manufacturer, even if it meant staying here while I moved away.

All this time…Was Emmett ever hurt by his upbringing at all? Or was he just trying to win me over and have Jameson Automobiles all to himself? It never occurred to me that might be the only reason he needed for killing his father.

"Why say all of this now?" I ask. "Why not tell me before? And if Emmett was so determined to kill his dad, why wouldn't he just do it himself? Especially if you think he killed Malcolm and tried to kill me."

"It didn't matter what Emmett's intentions were," he

answers. "Thomas was a terrible man who deserved to die. And if someone was going to do it, I thought it should be me. I knew if I told Emmett I wouldn't do it; he'd try it himself and get caught. Then who knows what would have happened to Jameson Automobiles. Of course, I had no idea then that the Hendersons were waiting for their chance to strike."

"I can't believe it," I mutter. I don't know if I actually believe it. It's more of a plea with myself, begging my heart not to take it all in. It seems it's impossible to have both of these men be good and loving. If I accept that one of them is, I have to accept that the other one isn't. Or maybe they're both bad. But right now, Emmett is the one sitting in jail with DNA evidence stacked against him.

"It's a lot to take in, I know," Theo shifts in his swing to take something out of his pocket. "But here...I got you something. I've been meaning to give it to you for a while now, but I didn't want to do it while you were so angry with me."

He hands over a small satin covered box. I open it up to reveal a necklace. It's the perfect combination of the two given to me by Emmett. It's a running shoe charm but covered in little sparkling diamonds.

"I've been holding on to that, but with everything that's happened...I thought you might want something to replace those two necklaces you've been wearing."

Theo gets up and slowly starts back toward the house. He stops a few times as if he still has a million things he could say, but each time he pushes himself forward. I am left in the darkness, sitting on my swing that has slowed to a stop, staring blankly down at the piece of jewelry. Part of me wants to toss it into a lake. The other part of me wants to wear it and cherish it forever. And no part of me knows what to do with the charms Emmett has given me.

# CHAPTER TWENTY-FIVE

BOOK 3

I stare down the dark blue fluffy gown hanging from my closet, feeling bad that my mom even wasted the money on it. Where else could I ever wear a thing like that? The more I look at it, the more I start to think I don't even like it at all. What was I thinking when I bought it? It's hideous and prom is stupid and, with or without Emmett, I never wanted to go at all.

"That's that," I slap my hands together and lay back on my bed.

I try not to think about all of the other girls who are giddy with excitement, slipping into their dresses, doing their hair and make-up. How many of them are like Marissa and will be losing their virginity tonight? Does anyone even wait that long anymore?

And how many of them are like me…thinking they're going to prom with the guy of their dreams but will soon discover that he's a murderer. Or some other kind of monster that threatens to destroy them.

And how many girls out there right now are with the guy of their dreams…only it's true love. They'll survive their college years together and live happily ever after, more in love than ever.

I fight back tears that threaten to start up again. They come and go, but each time I start crying again it's harder than it was before to stop.

My bedroom door flies open suddenly, making me scream.

Bridgett freezes there with big, apologetic eyes. And then we do the only thing we can do. We burst into laughter.

"Jeez," she giggles. "I was trying to surprise you, but I didn't mean to scare the shit out of you."

"Well you can't be too cautious these days," I tell her, only half-joking. "You never know when someone's going to try and kill you in this town."

She howls out with laughter again and I can't help but join her. "It shouldn't be funny because it's true! But why…why is that so fucking funny!?"

I want to say that if we weren't laughing, we'd be crying. But I'm buckled over on my bed, rolling around and unable to speak.

"What the hell are you doing here anyway?" I ask, wiping tears from my eyes as I finally manage to stop cackling hysterically.

"To pick you up," she says confidently. "You're my date to prom."

"No!" I argue. "No way. I'm not going. We can't go anyway, remember? We can't be seen together. The Elites would have your head on a platter for showing up to prom with someone who's blacklisted. Especially now. Emmett was already their number one enemy, and now he's killed their master not once, but twice. I'm not so sure I won't be killed stepping foot back inside WJ Prep for any reason at all, much less as your date to prom."

"Nope, we're going," she insists. "I've done some reconnaissance on the new order of things. Who knows how the Elites will evolve once everything settles, but for now…with Malcolm gone, they couldn't care less if we're friends."

I look back over to the ridiculous dress hanging there and think it seems to have regained a little bit of its appeal. No, nothing has gone as planned. Nothing has turned out the way I hoped and my heart is broken. But what remains is that I'm about to graduate from high school. I have worked my ass off for the past four years, and as a reward, I will be going to a college far away from here on a full scholarship. Don't I deserve to celebrate a little? Not with or for some guy. But for myself. For everything I've accomplished.

"This is our night," Bridgett declares. "We're two smart, strong women who are about to graduate from hell. You going to make me dance for that alone?"

I start laughing again. "No, I guess not." I admire how good she looks all done up. She's wearing a white corset and long black tutu, but when I look down to her feet, I realize she's wearing tennis shoes. "Did you run over here?" I snicker.

"Well, yeah, but that's not why I'm wearing these," she answers. "They're comfortable, and I like them. They look cute with this outfit and if I have to run away from some attacker at the school, they'll never catch me in these. You never know at WJ Prep. Besides, all those other girls are just wearing heels so they'll look tall while dancing with their boyfriends. Not something I have to worry about...I'm way taller than you anyway."

"Fair enough," I giggle. My dress is already revealing around the legs. I might as well top it off with some running shoes too.

"Hurry up," she adds. "It starts in a half-hour, and I don't want to be unfashionably late."

I scramble to grab the dress from the hanger. Bridgett helps zip me up into it before I throw my hair up and put on a little makeup. Just before we walk out the door, I turn to the mirror, catching sight of the necklaces Emmett gave me, both dangling around my neck and taunting me. I impulsively unclasp them and toss them on top of my dresser and grab the velvet box Theo gave me.

"Ooooh pretty!" Bridgett coos from over my shoulder. "Where'd you get it?"

"My dad gave it to me," I sigh.

"Whoa...did I miss something?"

"That's to be determined," I huff. "But what I can say is it's perfect for tonight. Never mind who it came from."

We rush out the door and decide that I'll be the one to drive. The theme is some kind of gawdy Great Gatsby deal, giving the wealthy parents funding it a chance to splurge on everything shiny and extravagant. The entrances are all lined with black and gold balloon archways and glittering curtains of metallic streamers. Strings of lights twinkle along the ceilings. Everything is draped with tulle and loose balloons.

As we reach the table where an attendant sits, taking tickets, I stop suddenly. "Shit," I grab Bridgett's arm. "Emmett had my ticket."

"I got this," she assures me, marching up to the table. "Excuse me ma'am...my friend here seems to have misplaced her ticket. But seeing as how I'm in mourning over the loss of my cousin, Malcolm…Surely you'd let her in with me anyway."

"Oh, right…Malcolm Henderson," the woman blushes. "You know what? Sure. Go on in."

Bridgett winks at me as she puts her arm in mine and pulls me inside. I'm not sure if the lady let me in because she feels sorry for us, or if it's simply out of fear since Bridgett is technically an Elite. For that matter, do the Elites even buy prom tickets at all? Their parents are the ones paying for all this anyway. They're probably exempt, like they are with everything else.

Music booms out from a booth where a DJ stands spinning records over the dance floor. There's a disco ball sending glimmers of light around the room, dancing across little circle tables with candles and confetti…a seemingly dangerous combination. I laugh to myself thinking how perfect it'd be if WJ Prep ended up going down in flames tonight. As long as no one got hurt, I wouldn't be sad to see it go.

Pretty girls stand around in their gowns and corsages, clutching their purses as they wait in line for the photo booth. Outside of the professional photos, there's a sea of phones going off around us with everyone taking their own pictures. Friends asking someone else to capture their group or everyone leaning in together with big smiles for selfies.

The prom at WJ Prep is laxer than the average high school dance, likely by request of the Elites. Small groups of students stand out front smoking for everyone to see and no one bats a lash at the kids pulling flasks from purses or suit jackets.

As Bridgett and I stand there taking it all in, I catch sight of Coach Granger and Jada standing off in the corner, supervising. I can't imagine why they'd have him chaperone this thing since he's the only one who would have the audacity to make anyone actually follow the rules. The bass from the speakers pounds through the wooden gym floor and up through my body as I continue scanning the room.

That's when I see him. Suddenly, I'm unable to tell the difference between the booming music and my own pounding heart. Emmett is here, lurking in the corner. I can tell he's trying to go unnoticed while looking for someone. He's looking for me.

I grab Bridgett's hand and squeeze tight. "Is he fucking crazy!?" I hiss in her ear, pointing my head in his direction.

"How did he get out!? And why would he show his face here? He's going to get himself killed!"

She leans in as if to whisper but has to shout over all the noise. "Didn't you hear? It was just on the news this afternoon. He made bail somehow. I don't know how he pulled it off, but you're right…It's dangerous for him to be here. Phew, he's got some balls."

Just as she finishes talking, Emmett spots me. His eyes focus in like a hawk as he runs over. I want to run away but I'm completely stuck. Frozen like a deer in headlights.

"Ophelia!" he shouts, getting closer. I try to force myself to move, but he yells out again. "Wait! Please! I need to talk to you!"

Bridgett studies my face and decides to step in. She plants one foot in front of me and holds up her hand. "She doesn't want to talk to you," she says firmly.

"Please, you have to listen to me," he begs urgently. "You have to know I didn't do this. I'm being framed. You have to believe me!"

I look deep into his eyes, wanting to see something I can believe in, but there's nothing. He looks like a complete stranger to me. My heart feels like stone, and the last thing I want to do is listen to him lie.

"Tell me you believe me, Ophelia!" he demands in desperation.

My lips slowly part, spilling out the only thing I can bring myself to say. "Theo told me everything. I know what you did."

His face drops with stunned confusion. "What?" he grimaces. "Theo told you what!? What are you talking about!?"

"I don't want to talk to you," I insist boldly. "I don't want to see you. Please leave me alone."

I expect my heart to break as I say the words, but it's still hard and cold. I feel nothing for him in this moment. I just want more than anything for him to go. But he persists, erupting into a string of pleas and panicked explanations as he drops down before, clutching at my legs and feet. Bridgett tries to stop him, but he pushes her away. I look around the room helplessly, wishing someone could do something.

That's when I notice Coach Granger catch sight of the scene, and he immediately runs over. He grabs Emmett by the arms and locks him against his chest, lifting him up into the air before finally carrying him out of the gymnasium kicking and screaming.

"You okay?" Bridgett asks, gently rubbing my arm as I stare off into space.

"Just a little embarrassed," I say.

"Let's not let that ruin the night," she suggests, pulling me toward the dance floor. "Whatever happens with him can be sorted out later. You deserve to have fun tonight."

I follow behind her, feeling apathetic to this entire dance all over again. But then I realize she's right. I do deserve to have fun. And why should I feel embarrassed? This school has seen all sorts of things from me including outbursts, emotional breakdowns, stolen and leaked nude photos, and fake images of Malcolm and I having sex. It's really silly to have thought I could have made it out without at least one more incident. I decide to think of it as my farewell gift and dive into dancing with Bridgett.

We both lose ourselves in the pumping music and after a while, she pulls her own flask out from the cleavage of her corset. We take turns tossing back bitter, burning swigs from the little silver bottle in between songs. Soon I start to feel lighter and freer than I have in a long time. That is until one of my sips from her flask hits me the wrong way, making me gag as I nearly throw up.

"Go get some punch to mix it with!" she laughs over the blaring music.

I nod and make my way over to the punch bowl. I pour myself a glass, but when I turn around, I nearly bump into a big burly guy. My heart sinks when I realize who it is. I have to set my cup down to keep myself from spilling it. I can't remember his name, but I'd never forget his face. It's the punk who gave me my oh so warm welcome to WJ Prep. He gave me a tour and a little taste of what to expect during my time here. I brace myself for him to snap at me the way he did on that very first day.

"Oh, sorry," he smiles lightly before disappearing back into the dancing crowd, as if nothing happened at all.

"What the fuck," I mumble to myself under my breath.

Even if he didn't remember me from my first day, he would know that I am blacklisted. Everyone does. The Elites make sure of it. And it is everyone's responsibility to make my life as difficult as possible. Everything that's happened with Emmett and Malcolm's death would only make their expected wrath even worse. It's hard to think of a single reason this kid would have the guts not to go off on me, much less apologize and smile.

Is everyone just that drunk? Or high on their quickly approaching escape from the hell hole? Or maybe we're in one of those short periods of time when no one is sure who is in charge. With no one at the top of the food chain, maybe we can all just be nice to each other. It happened once before after Thomas died and a chunk of the Elites went under investigation.

I shrug it off and turn to pick up my cup, eager to steal some more of Bridgett's liquor. I just want to drink and dance and keep thoughts about Emmett or anything else that's painful as far from my brain as possible. I throw myself back into dancing until I'm covered in sweat and my feet are aching.

"Wanna take a break?" Bridgett suggests finally, but only after her flask is empty.

"Absolutely!" I yell back.

I follow her over to a line of folding chairs where a few sad, lonely looking kids sit along with another couple of kids who look pale or green, like they're about to vomit. As I crash down into one of the chairs, still panting and out of breath, I start to feel a tinge of queasiness myself. I do my best to ignore it.

I stare around the room, laughing at how crazy some of the students are dancing. Bridgett and I point out our favorite ones to each other. But the more I look around, the more the lights start to bleed together. I feel my head bob slightly out of my control as it grows heavy. The sick feeling in my stomach grows and the only thing that seems to make it stop is closing my eyes. But the moment I do that, I feel like I could pass out within seconds. I quickly stiffen up, trying to stay awake.

"You okay?" Bridgett asks, looking at me with concern. "Did you drink too much?"

I try to answer, but my throat and mouth suddenly feel dry as cotton. But I know I didn't drink too much. I've drank plenty before and made myself sick more than once on a lot more than what we had tonight. This doesn't feel anything like that. This is something else entirely.

# CHAPTER TWENTY-SIX

## BOOK 3

I sit as still as possible, hoping this sudden sickness goes away. But the longer we sit, the worse I feel. The booming speakers swell in and out, sounding too close one minute and a million miles away the next.

"Want to dance some more?" Bridgett leans in to ask. "I love this song!"

"What?" I groan, thinking how much I do want to dance. But I can't even tell what song is on, much less how to stand up and flail around without falling over right now.

"I love this song!" she shouts louder, starting to dance from her seat.

I sway a little, wanting to join her, but I almost fall out of the chair. Thankfully she doesn't notice, but I know this is quickly becoming too much for me to hide.

"I don't feel good," I moan, feeling like vomit might come up with the words. My throat tightens and my vision vibrates. I'm overwhelmed with the need to get the hell out of here.

I shoot up from the chair, falling against her a little before taking off towards the exit. The music fades and everything suddenly seems distant, like I'm submerged underwater. My head sways to such an extreme that every step makes me feel like I'm going to fall over.

"Want me to come with you?" she calls out after me.

I think she calls out after me. Maybe I made it up. I can't tell anymore.

All I can manage is a dismissive wave back at her, hoping she'll just leave me alone. I may have decided I don't care what anyone else in this school thinks about me, but I don't want to look like the loser who couldn't handle her alcohol in front of Bridgett.

I'm suddenly very glad I decided to wear these tennis shoes because I'm positive I'd fall right over if I were trying to manage walking in heels at this moment. The smells wafting from the refreshment tables mix in with the scents of fresh flowers, hairspray, cologne, perfume, breath mints, and alcohol. It all swirls together, making me terribly nauseous.

I push forward with a weaving walk, my voice slurring as I try to give normal greetings to the people staring at me. My arms wave in front of me, but I feel like I have no control over where they're going. Then I nearly fall as I bump into the corner of a bleacher.

As I stumble past, I eye the tower of water bottles and think I should grab one, but I'm so disoriented, I'm scared of sending them all crashing to the ground. Then I notice the punch bowl and remember what happened when I filled up my cup. That guy distracted me, and I sat it down for a while. Did someone drug me?

I turn back towards Bridgett, wanting to ask for her help. But she seems to have disappeared back onto the dance floor. I know I'll never manage to hunt her down in the bouncing crowd. If I don't get out of here right away, I'm going to throw up or faint right here in the middle of everything. Part of me thinks if I've been drugged, it'd be worth it to humiliate myself and make a scene if it meant getting some help. But then again…what if whoever did this to me is watching? Waiting to swoop in and carry me off before anyone can see what's happened?

I don't feel capable of making any rational decisions right now, so I decide to follow my instinct to escape. My dress feels like it's constricting around me, growing tighter, and I just have to go. I have to get out of here. I'm hit with a gush of cold air as I stumble out the exit, escaping the swelling heat of the dancing bodies in the gym. I lurch to the side with shuffling steps, hunched over against anything to steady me.

I feel a little better once I can brace myself against the wall in the hallway. I take long, slow steps, my feet feeling like cement blocks, as I drag myself to the bathroom. I'm faintly aware of how sweaty my palms have gotten as I feel my way down the shiny, slick painted cinderblocks. But everything is starting to feel further away. Even the things that are only inches away from my face. But the bathroom door up ahead weaves back and forth, seeming within reach one minute and then when I extend my hand for it, it vanishes back to the other end of the hall, seeming miles away.

Just when I think I'll tumble down right here in the hallway, I reach the door. My hand fumbles across the handle and I realize it doesn't seem right. I don't remember any bathroom at this school having a handle like this, but just as I think it, I crash inside, falling to the floor as the door gives way in front of me. I hit the ground like a ton of bricks, but somehow don't feel anything from it. My body is completely numb, reminding me of the shots you get in your gums at the dentist, except every inch of my skin feels that way.

I try to lift my head and I swear it's shaking. But I can't tell if my head is shaking or just my line of vision. That's when I notice the buzzing fluorescent lights up above and the cold concrete floor against my arms and legs. The shelves lined with mops, buckets, and cleaning solutions let me know I'm not in the bathroom at all. I've fallen into a closet.

I want to get up, but no matter how many times my brain sends the command, my body won't respond. Unable to move anything else, I blink rapidly, trying to focus on anything I can. Then I hear voices coming from an open door at the other end of the room. My head falls back down to the floor against my will, and I can see the shadows of two people standing on the other side of the wall.

"Do you regret it?" a familiar male voice asks.

"No," a woman replies sternly.

At first, I'm unable to place them, but then I recognize the man's voice. It's Coach Granger and I'm positive the woman he's speaking to is his assistant, Jada.

"My brother made some mistakes, but he was a good man," she adds with a cold resolve in her tone. "He was trying to turn his life around, and had those assholes not planted those drugs right in front of his face, he'd still be with us today. I know he would've stayed sober this time or asked for help. Even as a junkie, he was never the kind of sick person these spoiled, entitled brats like Malcolm are."

"It's a shame," Coach replies. "But I think the world is better off without people like him in it."

"What about the other one?" Jada asks. "That Lily girl?"

"Let her be," he says. "She's suffering enough locked up in rehab and I doubt her parents will be signing off on her release any time soon."

"But Dad…" she argues.

"I said let her be. I'll keep an eye on that whole situation and let you know if anything changes," he barks, leaving no more room for debate.

My head is swimming as I try to understand it. Dad? Jada is Coach Granger's daughter? Why wouldn't he tell us that and what the hell are they talking about?

"What about you?" she asks him. "Do you have any regrets?"

"No," he sighs. "We had no choice. The police and the courts weren't going to do anything. We had to take justice into our own hands. My son deserves to rest in peace without the guy responsible for his death roaming around free, hurting anyone else."

"And what about that Emmett kid? How did that DNA evidence get in the car?" Jada questions.

"I don't know. I had nothing to do with that," he explains. "But I bailed him out. I'll find some way to make sure he doesn't take the fall for this."

I can't tell if the pounding in my chest and rising sickness in my gut is from whatever is happening to me or realizing that Jada and Coach Granger are discussing how they murdered Malcolm. I want to call out for them to help me but interrupting a murder confession seems like a terrible idea even in my impaired state.

But if they killed Malcolm…how *did* Emmett's DNA get on the car? Was he telling the truth when he insisted someone was trying to frame him? And what does this mean for all of the threats made against me?

"How were you so certain his car would crash that way?" Jada asks.

"I've seen it happen before," he grumbles. "And if I hadn't been there that time, she would have died. That's when I got the idea for how we would pull this off without getting caught."

When Coach Granger saved me from plummeting off the cliff in my car, it inspired him to get rid of Malcolm. So whoever tried to kill me wasn't connected to his murder at all. But there are still so many unanswered questions, and they swarm around in my head making me feel dizzier than I ever have in my life. Impossibly dizzy. Like my brain could explode from the spins.

My eyes start to hurt from the bright lighting, and once again I find that the only thing that makes me feel better is to close them. But each time my heavy eyelids fall, it gets harder to open them up again. I panic, wondering if I'm dying. My survival instinct starts to overpower my better judgment and I try to scream out to get Coach and Jada's help. Maybe they'll hurt me or kill me, thinking I know their secret, but right now I feel like I'm dying regardless. So I might as well take the risk.

But nothing comes out of my mouth. I can't even tell if my lips are opening at all. Any sense of tingling or fuzziness in my limbs fades as my vision tunnels. The disconnect between my brain and my body grows bigger and bigger until finally I'm left trapped inside of myself, completely motionless. I can't speak, scream, or move at all. And as their distant voices fade, I realize my hearing is disappearing too. I don't know when I stopped being able to open my eyes, but I become vaguely aware of pitch-black darkness just before I slip off into nothingness.

# CHAPTER TWENTY-SEVEN

BOOK 3

My mind wakes up before my eyes can open. I hear the whirring rev of a car engine and the sound of air gushing through open windows. As the wind bursts by, I slowly come to enough to realize how cold it feels against my skin. But the fabric seat beneath me is warm. I push my face against it and am relieved to be able to move again.

That's when the red flashing warning lights start rapidly firing off in my brain. I'm in a car. But who's car? Who's driving? This is bad. Somebody drugged me. I think I can assume that much. Did they follow me into the closet and capture me?

When I try to move the rest of my body, unsure of what I even hope to accomplish, the car hits a bump and sends me rolling into the floorboard. I groan with the harsh thud against my bones as I hit the floor, my body contorting into the tight, uneven space.

"You're awake," a guy's voice rings out from in front of me. I open my eyes and gather it's the driver speaking. I know that voice. I know the curls of his hair.

Then he turns around to look at me, briefly taking his eyes off of the road. Emmett.

"You okay?" he asks with concern. "I can pull over if you want."

At first, my heart calms with the sound of his voice. I feel safe. He'll take care of me. But then the memories of the past few days come flooding back. Everything that Theo told me replays in my mind.

I faintly remember the conversation between Coach Granger and Jada just before I drifted off. I know Emmett didn't kill Malcolm, but that doesn't mean he didn't try to kill me. Theo said he was the brains behind his father's murder. That he's only been motivated by money, greed, and power this whole time.

I start to squirm, half expecting to be tied up. But my hands and feet are free. I lift my arms and legs and climb back onto the backseat, still feeling heavy and unable to fully control my body.

"Pull over," I command him. "I want to get out."

"Ophelia, I need to talk to you," he shoots back urgently.

"Pull over!" I scream louder. I grow frantic and panicked as I piece it all together, assuming Emmett had to have been the one who drugged me. After Coach dragged him out of the dance, he found some way to sneak back in and slip something in my drink. Or maybe he had help. I don't know, but I'm positive it was him. "You did this to me," I mumble through my groggy voice.

"No!" he insists. "I would never do anything to hurt you, Ophelia."

"You and I both know that's not true," I argue back, refusing to minimize what he's done to me any longer. That's what got me into this mess with him in the first place. Always telling myself that it wasn't so bad or trying to convince myself that there were two versions of him.

"It was you all along," I tell him. "You're the one who has been hurting me all along, and…and I don't know why it took me so long to see it."

"No, please don't say that," he begs. "Listen to me…"

"No!" I cry out. "I'm not listening to you anymore!" I reach for the handle, not caring if I fly out of the speeding car. But nothing happens when I pull it. "Pull over! Let me out of here!"

"Ophelia, please…" he tries again.

"I don't care if you love me!" I shriek. "If you ever loved me at all, it hasn't stopped you from hurting me! It was your idea to kidnap me! To hold me hostage in your mansion! And then it was your idea to murder Thomas! You turned me against my own father, who was only trying to help and…"

"You've got it all wrong!" he swears. "I don't know who did

this to you, but it wasn't me. Where was Bridgett when this happened?"

"Stop it, Emmett! I'm not falling for your shit anymore! Let me out of here right now or I'm going to grab the wheel and force us off the road! I've done it before," I remind him. "I'll do it again. I don't even care what happens, I just want to get away from you!"

I imagine my dreams of college and everything after it slipping away into nothingness, just as I did when I lost consciousness. It hurts to think about. I don't want to die, but I'm not certain that won't happen anyway if I leave it up to Emmett.

"What if Bridgett was working together with Theo this whole time!?" he suggests. "Think about it…We don't know her. They just moved here. She comes from California where Theo used to live up until recently. What if he knew the Hendersons would steal everything away from me!? And he's working with her to try and get Jameson Automobiles back!"

"It doesn't make any sense," I groan as my head starts throbbing, trying to figure it all out. The only clear and resounding conclusion I can come to is that Theo is right about Emmett. My dad and Bridgett aren't the enemies, he is. No matter how much my heart wants to believe otherwise.

"I overheard something when I was locked up," he explains. "These detectives were talking about what they found in the car and said some of your DNA was there too. I think whoever framed me was trying to pin this on you too."

"What?" I ask in disbelief. "You're lying. I know you're lying. You'll say whatever it takes to get back into my head, but I'm not going to let it happen this time. And anyway…I know who killed Malcolm, and it had nothing to do with Bridgett or my father."

He's quiet for a moment. "Just because he didn't do it, doesn't mean he wouldn't take it as a chance to bring us down."

"You're not making any sense!" I scoff, wishing this decapacitating headache would go away. I curl into myself across the seat, shielding my eyes from the lights as they whiz past.

"He framed me so he could get his hands on my designs without having to give me any credit or money for them," he proposes. "And when that didn't work, maybe he thought he'd try to go after you. I don't have it all figured out yet, but I know they didn't find your DNA until their second sweep of the car.

And doesn't Theo have friends in the Jameson police force? He used them to help make sure none of us were blamed for my father's murder."

"But you were," I insist. "You were to blame. It was your idea to kill your father." I cling to Theo's words, but there is some possibility to what he is saying. Theo is one of the only ones who could have gotten both our DNA into that car after it had already been retrieved from the wreckage. "Why would he do it?" I ask again. "It still doesn't make any sense."

He grows quiet again. I try to open myself up to this possibility that Emmett isn't behind all of this. Could Bridgett or Theo have drugged me? Maybe to make another attempt at pinning Malcolm's murder on me or something worse?

"You swear you're not the one who put something in my drink?" I ask. My voice cracks from the dryness in my mouth and I wish more than anything I had some water. I spot a bottle in the drink holder up front.

Emmett's eyes catch mine in the rearview mirror. He sees what I'm staring at and picks up the water bottle, offering it to me in the back seat.

"I would never do that," he says firmly.

I grab at the bottle and frantically twist off the cap before chugging it down. Some of it spills out of the corner of my still partially numb mouth and drips down my neck.

"Theo's one and only goal was to come back for everything he feels the Elites stole from him," he suggests. "He went from being one of the main guys behind Jameson Automobiles, having almost as many shares in the company as my father, to having nothing. No job, no money. They ran him off to the other side of the country and then they made sure to rip you and your mom away from him too."

"Yeah," I nod, thinking we can definitely agree on that much. I relish in the lingering cool feeling in my throat from the water and start to wonder where Emmett is taking me. "Where are we going anyway?"

"I don't know," he admits. "I needed to see you and talk to you. I tried to come back and find you, but you were passed out. I just knew I needed to get you away from the school and whoever did this to you."

"And what's your plan now?" He shakes his head cluelessly. "Keep going," I add. "If I'm going to be trapped in here with you, you might as well finish your idea of what's really going on here." My voice is dripping with bitterness, causing him to hesitate as he continues staring me down in the rearview mirror, darting his eyes back and forth rapidly between me and the road. "Emmett, I want to believe you," I say softly. And it's true. Every piece of my heart would rather believe his version of things. "But I can't until you start making more sense of this."

"He tried to start this new car manufacturing company, right?" he continues. "But how was it ever going to be a success if everyone within range of the Elites still hated him?"

I stare out into the trees flying past the window, lighting up under out headlights. "But why offer you a job?" I wonder. "Why bring you into it at all if he didn't want to share the profits or give you credit for your ideas?"

"All he knew was that he needed to get back into everyone's good graces," he suggests. "First, with you and your family. Then Jameson. Bringing me into it obviously won me over, and it helped win your mom and stepdad over. The only person it didn't convince was you." A wave of sadness washes over his face. "I'm so sorry, Ophelia. We should have listened to you. You were the only voice of reason the whole time."

The sincere regret in his voice hits up against my heart, begging me to fall back into the trap of believing him. It's starting to work, but I'm so afraid of caving in and regretting it all later when I realize Theo was the one telling the truth. And there's still so much that doesn't add up.

"If he did win us all over…why frame you? Or me for that matter? And when that didn't work, why drug me?" As I fire off questions, some of it starts to click into place. "To win the town of Jameson back over," I mumble to myself.

"Huh?" he grunts.

"Maybe if everyone felt sorry for him…"

"He could rise back to the top. People might support his company," Emmett finishes my sentence for me. "A man grieving the death of his daughter. People might pity him and with no one left in town who remembers the old Elites' grievances against him…what could stop him from winning everyone back over?"

I go through it all again like a checklist. A timeline of events in my throbbing head. First Theo comes back into town and strikes this deal with Emmett to get rid of Thomas. Everything becomes up for grabs. The Elites are weakened. The future of Jameson Automobiles is uncertain. He uses it as a window to sneak back into our lives, building the foundation of Jameson's new competitor as he goes. He gets his hands on Emmett's expertise and ideas while worming his way back into our family.

"Family," I blurt out before I even fully realize why it's important. "Family!" I yell again, even more confident than before. "Theo didn't just lose Jameson Automobiles. He lost me and my mom. Maybe he really was trying to come between my mom and Brendan the whole time. If he got us back, and started a successful company, he'd feel like everything was made right again."

"But you wouldn't budge," he reminds me.

I wonder if it could really be true. Theo had gotten as much as he could out of his relationship with Emmett, so he could have used Malcolm's murder to get rid of him. It not only left him with all of his designs, it gave him a window to get into my head. When that still didn't work, maybe he did plant that evidence on the car, trying to take me down too. Maybe he panicked when Emmett was bailed out, not knowing who would have stepped in to help him.

If anyone would have defended Emmett's innocence, it would have been me. With me gone, Theo wouldn't have had to worry about Emmett anymore, whether the charges stuck or not. Everyone else would have thought he was guilty. He had the most motive for killing Malcolm after all. Not only would killing me have secured Emmett's fate no matter what the courts decided, it would have given him sympathy from my mom and possibly the rest of the town.

Theo already managed to drive at least a little bit of a wedge between my mom and Brendan. If something tragic like my death happened, would it bring my mom and Theo back together?

I feel myself giving into it all more and more. I feel a whimper in my chest, all of my rattling fears and anxieties. I don't know who to believe. I study Emmett from the backseat, or what I can see of him anyway. I focus in on all of our times together, trying to convince myself that he could be telling the truth. I remember his smell, the feeling is his skin, and the sound of his voice against my ear. I love him, so I have to believe him, right?

Then I remember the crashing, crumbling feeling that came with Theo's side of the story in my backyard. All of that made perfect sense too and I felt so stupid for not seeing it sooner. I ask myself what I really know. I know next to nothing about Theo, really, beyond my suspicions of him being a lying, manipulative snake. But Emmett…I've seen Emmett's destruction firsthand and I've been the victim of it more than once.

If Emmett was really bad, how could he have gone without hurting me for so long? He has made every possible effort to prove himself to me ever since he was freed from his father. It'd make sense that all the violence and rage stemmed from the pressure of the Elites, just like he said it did. And even his own family doubted his ability to do the necessary evil required of whoever ran Jameson, both the company and the town.

"What do you think, Ophelia?" he asks suddenly. "We can try to prove this. I can try to find something to make you believe me, but I don't want to let you go until I know you'll at least give me a chance."

Won't let me go. The words trigger another flood of memories. The other day when he almost didn't stop when I asked him to. The car. Being trapped in it with him.

"What were you going to do?" I ask, my throat closing up as I start to cry.

"What do you mean?"

"When I first came here," I sob. "That time I grabbed the steering wheel and we crashed into the light post. What were you going to do? You had those things in your backseat. The rope, the gloves. None of the other Elites were around. If I hadn't crashed the car…what would you have done to me?"

I collapse back down against the seat, completely overwhelmed with uncertainty and fear. All the trauma of Jameson and everything Emmett has done to me. My shame of believing in him and trying to let myself love him. He's rambling off an explanation from the front seat, but I can't even hear him. My brain shuts down and won't take in a single word of it.

"Do you hear me!?" he pleads. "Ophelia! Do you hear me!?"

"Just stop," I whisper, clutching my ears and pulling at my hair. I don't know if I'm talking to him or myself. I just know I'm tired and feel like I can't take another second of this. He keeps calling out for me, begging me to listen. Begging me to believe him. "Stop!" I scream again.

A set of headlights slice into my piercing scream. They back at us through all of the mirrors in the car, blinding us. I hear Emmett swear followed by the jolting crash of something ramming into the back of the car. We swerve, but he straightens out and tries to drive faster. Then another crash, and another. Until finally, the car flies off the road.

# CHAPTER TWENTY-EIGHT

BOOK 3

The crash snaps me from my state of shock, and I am suddenly impossibly alert. I shoot straight up and see Emmett shaking his head.

"You're bleeding," I announce as I notice the red stream coming down his forehead. My voice is frighteningly calm, almost sounding foreign to me.

He shakes his head again, and lightly touches his fingers to the gash on his forehead. We both jump as his car door flies up, revealing a figure crouching down in the darkness. Before I can see who it is, a bright light flashes right in our eyes. I wince and look away, only turning back when my car door flies open too.

Then I see the all too familiar sight of a gun barrel pointing straight at me. Before I can react, a hand reaches towards me. I squirm for the door, but a searing pain burns into my scalp. Another familiar feeling. My hair being pulled. I'm drug from the car. I kick, but my throat is still too dry, preventing me from screaming even though that's exactly what I'm doing on the inside.

I'm shoved forward into the darkness. I want to run, but I feel the cold pistol push into the back of my head. Then Emmett is shoved next to me.

"Start walking," a man's voice demands from behind. It's familiar, but disguised by an eerie, primal rage.

We shuffle forward into the night, barely able to see where we're walking. The man shines his light onto our path, but it's shaky and hard to follow. Then it starts to rain, and as the light bounces off of the drops that fall into our eyes, it's even more impossible to see where we're going. We walk like that for what feels like a mile before finally being pushed up to a tall, chain-link fence lined with barbed wire across the top.

The man's hand reaches around me, pulling at an opening near the top of the fence. He forces it down and shoves me through. I quickly decide that I'll try to run as soon as I'm on the other side, but I'm hit with the fear of being shot for trying. The instinctual hesitation causes me to trip. I fall flat into the muddy ground, sinking down into the wet earth with a big splash that covers me in thick, dark sludge. I feel a sharp, cold pain to my shin as it catches on the fence.

I scream as I'm lifted back up into the air, being pulled by my hair again which is now drenched from the pouring rain. Once I'm forced all the way over to the other side of the fence, Emmett's body crashes into me from behind, nearly knocking me over again. I try to turn around and make an attempt at identifying our assailant, but his bright light, along with the downpour and the pitch-black night, keeps me from being able to see his face.

Big tire tracks begin disappearing from the ground as they rapidly fill up with water, turning to slush as we're pushed through them. Our feet sink more and more with each step, causing us to stumble every few feet. We come to rows of broken-down vehicles with dirty windows and raised hoods with exposed wires and hoses poking out of the rusted engines. I feel hard pieces of debris that litter the ground beneath my shoe, but they all sink into the mud and puddles as we traipse through.

We're pushed on through the vanishing roads that weave through mounds of scrap. The man keeps shoving the gun back into our skulls every so often to remind us of the threat. My sense of smell heightens with my lack of sight. The drenched air is filled with wet earth, motor oil, grease, gas, and rusting metal. There's a pungent smokey taste seeping onto my tongue from the polluted smell.

Emmett hisses and winces suddenly, holding up his hand to reveal another bloody gash from something he's scraped up against in the darkness. The man doesn't let us top, and every-thing around us continues flooding at an alarming rate.

I take another step forward and shriek at the emptiness

beneath my foot. I nearly topple forward and am saved at the last minute by a quick tug to the back of my hoodie. I'm flung back just enough to keep from sliding off the edge of a steep drop that overlooks a pit of rusty, shredded cars. The sharp, twisted metal gleams, and I immediately know that if I had fallen, I would have died in the razor-sharp sea of crushed vehicles. I whimper through my labored breaths as I watch the floodwaters rise around the cars. Whoever goes down there is either impaled or drowns. And as more water rushes past, forming a mudslide, I feel dangerously close to sliding in.

"Turn around," the voice growls.

We slowly turn. Theo stands there staring back at Emmett with flaring nostrils, but his face softens when he looks at me.

"Ophelia!" he shouts, seeming surprised. We stare back at him blankly, unsure of what to do next. "I...I'm so sorry! I thought...I thought you were Bridgett."

"Bridgett!?" I exclaim in confusion.

"When I saw a girl in the backseat of Emmett's car, I thought for sure it had to be Bridgett!" he explains. "If I had known it was you...I would have never...Come here," he reaches his hand out suddenly. "Come here to me."

"Don't do it," Emmett begs with a deep, commanding voice. "Don't listen to him, Ophelia. What the hell are you trying to do, Theo!?"

"You," his voice turns dark again. "You're the one I wanted. Not her."

"What's going on?" I plead, feeling my heart being ripped in two again.

"I can explain everything," Theo insists. "But I don't want you to fall. Come to me so I can make sure you're safe."

"Don't, Ophelia!" Emmett yells more urgently.

I start to run towards Theo, thinking that getting away from this slippery edge is the most important thing. I can figure the rest out after that. But as I stare at his face, my old feelings of mistrust bubble up. I look down at the gun in his hand and I'm frozen in fear.

"No," I decide out loud. "I won't come to you until you explain all of this. Were you the one who drugged me? And what were you going to do to Emmett out here if I hadn't been with him?"

"When I heard he was released from jail, I went to the school to see if he'd be there," he insists. "I pulled up just as his car was driving out of the parking lot, so I followed him. I had no idea you were in the car with him. What do you mean… drugged? Someone drugged you!?"

I nod my head in confirmation, still unsure if I can believe him or not. "Why did you go looking for Emmett? Why did you bring him out here?" I ask again.

His face twists with rage as his gaze turns back to Emmett. "Did you drug her!?" he barks. "Did you try to hurt my beautiful daughter!?"

"Cut it out, Theo!" Emmett cries. "We both know you're full of shit. Tell her the truth! You're the one who framed me, aren't you!? And you were going to frame Ophelia too, weren't you!? But you panicked when I got released and started to worry that wouldn't be good enough to cut us out of the picture for good. Admit it!"

"You're crazy!" Theo laughs before turning back to me. "Ophelia don't listen to him. You remember everything I said? You remember everything I told him?"

I shiver from the cold rain and start to cry. I repeat his story in my head again. "It was Emmett's idea to kill his father," I spout off, telling him what he wants to hear, but I don't know what to believe anymore.

"That's right!" his voice is shaky and high-pitched, as if he's speaking to a scared dog. He's desperate but I don't know if it's to save himself or to save me.

"But Emmett didn't kill Malcolm," I remind myself.

"I don't know anything about that," Theo says. "What I do know is that I was not about to let Emmett weasel his way back into your life. I trusted him once and I refuse to do it again. After I saw how hurt you were when I told you the truth, I hated myself for ever pushing you into his arms."

I think back to our talk on the swing set and almost want it to be the truth. I don't want to believe that Emmett is truly evil or menacing, but if I'm honest with myself, I don't want my father to be those things either. Am I only choosing to believe Emmett because of how much I love him? If Theo had been around for me to know and love while I was growing up, would it be easier for me to trust him instead?

I feel overwhelmed again and all I can do is scream. I bury my face in my hands, wishing I could be anywhere but here in this dark, wet nightmare, being torn between these two men. But I am here. And if something doesn't happen soon, we're all going to slide off this drop off into the watery pit of shredded metal below. I take a deep breath and try to cling to any ounce of strength left inside so I can calm down enough to figure this out.

"So…what were you going to do?" I ask for the third time, steadying my voice. "Bring Emmett out here and kill him? Shoot him the way you shot Thomas Jameson?"

His face drops, and he suddenly looks crushed. "I have so many regrets," he starts sobbing suddenly. "I don't know what to do any more than you do, Ophelia."

"Shut up, Theo!" Emmett yells, but I hold out my hand to silence him.

"It's true," he continues. "I'm a desperate and lost man. I have been ever since the day your mother walked out on me and took you with her." He stops crying suddenly. His face turns to stone and he looks back over to Emmett. "It's all your fault. Your fucking Elite family. You're the ones who destroyed my life! You made me think Lala had cheated on me and it was all a lie!"

"Emmett didn't do that!" I argue. "His father did! Your problem is with Thomas and he's gone now…so let's just go home! Please!" I grow more frantic as the water around us rises. I feel my feet sinking more, and I'm almost afraid that any attempt to move away from the edge will only cause me to slip.

"You really think he's so different?" Theo questions. "Wake up, Ophelia! The apple doesn't fall far from the tree. Emmett is just as awful as Thomas was. All he cares about is being the king of Jameson, and he'll do whatever it takes to make that happen and line his pockets along the way. Especially now that everything has been ripped away from him…just like it was from me. Trust me, I know what it feels like. And I can see the desperation in his eyes." He wipes his hand across his eyes, and I can't tell if it's to brush away rain or tears. "Don't make the same mistake I did, sweetie. Please. Don't waste any more time trying to see something in him that's not there."

"What if Bridgett had been the one who was with him?" I ask. "If you brought Emmett here to kill him…would you have killed her too?"

He thinks for a moment. "I don't trust any of them," he admits. "But no, of course not. I could have never killed her for that alone. I promise you, Ophelia. Now will you please come here!? Before you fall!"

It's getting harder and harder to hear over the roaring sound of gushing water all around us. I hear the distant crashing of trees as the flowing waters eat away at the soil around their roots. More and more debris shoots past as the flood overtakes everything, and the rain shows no signs of stopping. If anything, it only falls harder with each passing second.

My clothes are heavy and completely drenched, sticking to my shivering body. My eyes are gritty and swollen from stress and lack of sleep. Every one of my muscles aches. Chills and shivers ripple through me, up from the puddles of water in my shoes as I'm sucked down further into the mud. I wipe my eyes again, feeling the pruned grooves of my soggy fingertips.

Another big cracking sound startles me from the side. I cut my eyes just in time to catch sight of a shed on the other end of the junkyard being yanked off into a stream of floodwaters. Steady rain continues pounding against everything around us, pinging off of the old cars that are still clinging to solid ground.

"I don't know what to do," I mutter under my breath. I'm desperate but stuck in the crossfires of Theo and Emmett.

I start to wonder if it even matters who I believe. Why should I die out here with them? Maybe Emmett really can't be anything more than an Elite who was doomed to be a monster from birth. And maybe Theo really is every bit as greedy and manipulative as I have wanted to believe from the start. What does any of that have to do with me? I didn't ask for any of this.

"Please, Ophelia!" Theo begs again.

Emmett grabs my hand suddenly, squeezing it tight. I look into his gray, piercing eyes. Water streams down his flattened hair that spiders along the edges of his face.

"Don't go," he pleads quietly, so that only I can hear. "Stay with me. Trust me."

It's all he has ever asked of me all along. To stay with him. To trust him. Even when none of his words or actions made him deserving of those things.

"I have stayed," I cry softly. "I have trusted you. And look at where it got me?"

"We're almost out of here, Ophelia. If we make it through this night alive, we can get the hell out of Jameson and never come back."

"What were you going to do if you got away with me in your car that day?" I ask again. I stare into him longingly, desperate for an answer. Desperate for the truth. "Tell me the truth. What were you going to do?"

A sad smile flashes across his lips. "Drive away," he answers, his voice cracking. "Drive away and never look back. Take you somewhere far away from here. Tell you everything and get us out of Jameson, so I could give you everything you deserve. It's all I wanted to do then, and it's all I want to do now."

"But my family," I whisper. "You would've taken me away from Mom and Brendan?"

"I didn't know what else to do," he shrugs. "I didn't see any other choice. I knew what was about to happen and I wanted to save you. I couldn't let them make me keep hurting you."

My heart shatters as deeply as the dissolving ground around us. I wonder what would have happened if I would have gone with him that day. If I hadn't grabbed the steering wheel and sent us crashing into the pole. Could we really have driven off into the sunset and found some kind of happy ending? The kidnapping. Being held hostage in Jameson manor. Meeting Thomas. Every single bad thing that happened from there… I've blamed Emmett for it this entire time. Maybe he did just want to save me all along.

I lose myself in Emmett's eyes as Theo continues yelling, pleading for me to come to him. I barely hear him anymore as we stand there in the dark, looking at each other hopelessly.

Suddenly, his hand drops mine. His face stiffens with a strange, new resolve. "Go," he says. "Go to him."

"What!?" I cry. "Emmett! I don't know what to do! I don't know who to believe!" I look back at Theo, then back to Emmett, hoping at any moment some answer or sign will come to me.

"Go to him," he insists again. "None of this is your fault. You have a chance at a big beautiful life outside of Jameson. I wanted to have that with you, but it may be too late. I'm not going to let you die out here with me. You don't deserve that."

"Don't make me do this," I sob, wishing there was more time. If the water wasn't rushing around us so violently, we could stand out here and argue all night. They could debate and tell their stories, and maybe somewhere along the way I would find some shred of truth that I could believe in beyond a doubt.

"I love you," Emmett whispers.

I feel something shoving into my back. I'm flung forward,

plopping down into the mud. Not knowing what else to do, I slip and slide my way back up and run for Theo's arms. He reaches for me, crying as I rush to cling to him for safety.

But just as I am about to fall into him, he goes toppling over. Emmett pummels into him, tackling him to the ground.

# CHAPTER TWENTY-NINE

BOOK 3

Just as I have wrapped my head around the idea of abandoning Emmett to die, still feeling no closer to knowing who is telling the truth, I watch Emmett plow into Theo. They crash into the flooding ground, splashing around in the mud and water.

After they hit the ground, with Emmett on top pinning Theo down, Emmett rears back. I watch in shock as his arm hangs in midair for a moment before thrashing into Theo's face. He immediately pulls back to get in another punch, but he's thrown off. They roll around for what seems like an eternity, throwing relentless punches and kicks.

I stand there, completely paralyzed and feeling like I'm going mad from being wet and cold for so long. They can't keep track of where they're going in the midst of their desperate attacks on each other, and I'm stuck watching in horror as they move dangerously close to the edge of the drop-off.

"Look out!" I cry, not entirely sure which one of them I'm trying to warn. Maybe it's both of them at this point.

That's when I remember that I'm free. With them fighting, no one is stopping me from running away from all of this. I could take off and never look back, completely free from the decision of who I'm supposed to trust. My feet start to run, then stop again. I am stuck in that motion for a while, pivoting back and forth between fleeing or staying behind to see what happens.

If I run away from this, it's not up to me to decide anything. But both of them could die. If I stay and whoever the bad guy is here lives, I'm in danger. If I run and one of them catches up to me, I could be in danger. If I don't get out of the rising flood-waters, I die. There is no good option. No right decision. Every path before me is scary, unknown, and dangerous.

I remember how I felt when Bridgett showed up and convinced me to go to prom with her. For a brief moment, none of this mattered. The scene playing out in reality before my eyes now was happening in my head then. I was just as torn. Just as conflicted. But I put it all aside and let myself be free to celebrate myself. Can I do that just as easily now with both of their lives at stake?

All I've wanted to do from the beginning of this was walk away. And now I'm free to do it, and I can't. I look out into the darkness as the rain pours down. If I keep running, I can go home. I can tell my parents everything once and for all. Maybe they go to the police. Maybe they leave with me? Does it really matter at this point?

If Emmett or Theo come back with me, I run the risk of them destroying our lives. The only two factors of this equation that did not exist in the life I knew before, when everything was normal and happy, are Theo and Emmett. I didn't know either of them nine months ago. I can keep running and go back to that, forgetting they ever even existed.

The two continue grunting and thrashing behind me. I close my eyes and focus in on the sounds of my own breath. In and out. Inhale, exhale. What are you going to do, Ophelia? What are you doing to do?

My instincts take over, and I do the only thing I am certain I know how to do. I run. I run like mad in a way I never have before. I slip and slide in the mud every few feet and flail like mad to get back on my feet and run some more. The sounds of the fighting men grow more and more distant behind me.

Steam billows out from my mouth and flaring nostrils against the cold, dark, rainy air. My muscles burn and ache, and I don't know where I'm going. Everything around me has become unrecognizable, completely changed from how it was when we passed through here before. With each passing second, the rain washes away more. A car here, a tree there. It seems like the entire world is disappearing into this flood, and I know soon Emmett and Theo will be washed away in it.

A tinge of guilt pangs against my heart, but I force myself to keep running. It's not my fault. I didn't ask for any of this. I never would have come to Jameson if I had known this is what waited for me here. All I wanted to do was exactly what I'm doing now. To run. That's still all I want. And once I am really free, I can go to my safe, warm, dry home where my mom and stepdad are waiting for me. Everything can go back to the way it was before.

I'll get the hell out of Jameson like I have been dreaming about all this time. Maybe somehow, I can even avoid the news long enough so that I never know what happened to Emmett or Theo or Jameson or whatever new Elites pop up. I can forget all of Marissa's words that I've read. I can forget the sound of Emmett's voice and the features of his face. I can forget that I ever loved him at all.

I keep running and running, but my body starts to lose its strength. It wasn't that long ago that I was drugged and completely unconscious. Since then I have been under more emotional and mental stress than I thought possible, which is saying a lot considering everything I've been through. There was a car crash and all those scrapes against the fence and the surrounding junk. I'm dangerously cold and soaking wet. It's all catching up to me and I feel my batteries running out.

My run slows to a jog. Then a fast-paced walk. I feel like every step could be my last and I'm so close to just falling over and letting myself drown out here in the flood. But I didn't come this far to give up. I'm a runner. Pushing myself is muscle memory. It's in my veins. I take in a deep breath and take off again. But I quickly find myself in an area void of any light. I stop, heaving over in panic before desperately looking around for some sense of where to go. My eyes strain in the darkness. We had Theo's flashlight to guide us through here before, but now it seems as dark as some deep part of a cave, miles below the earth.

Don't give up, I tell myself again. I break off into another delirious sprint, not noticing the faintest shadow of something in front of me. I ram straight into the side of a big, broken-down semi. The ground around it is flooded and weak, and I feel the big hunk of metal give way under the force of my body. But it's still enough to knock me backward off of my feet.

I shake my head and climb back up, feeling even more disoriented and lost now. I take off running again. I carry on like that for a while, but then a frightening sound echoes through the night. Voices. Screaming voices. I keep running harder and faster, and the voices get closer. Finally, I make something out of the panicked yelling.

"Ooooopphheeelliiaaa!"

My name is called, over and over again. What have I done? Did I take off running in the wrong direction after I fell? The screaming continues and gets louder as I go until I'm certain I'm headed right back to where I started from. I stop and consider turning around to try again. But more of the surrounding areas of growing unsafe. It's too late, I think. I don't know if I can ever get out of here now.

Is this bad luck? Or a sign…the hint that I've been waiting for. No matter where I run to, no matter how hard or fast I go, I can't get away from them. And now I might die out here with them. I keep pushing forward, preparing myself for the possibilities of whatever I am racing towards.

I think I start to recognize some of the things I'm passing. I'm getting closer to where I started from. Or at least I think I am. But as I approach the spot that I am certain I ran off from before, Theo and Emmett are nowhere in sight. I can tell now that the voice calling out to me is Theo's. He's yelling my name over and over, and it sounds like it's right next to me. But I can't see him anywhere. I look around in the darkness, unsure of what to do next.

The aches and pains burn through my shivering body and I'm growing delirious. My eyes pound with the need for sleep, but I am so hyped up on adrenaline, I wonder if it will ever be possible to sleep again. My body is just as conflicted as my heart is.

Then I notice a strange splashing up ahead, and I realize it's coming from just beyond the drop-off. I carefully approach it, praying that the current doesn't overpower me. I get close enough to see that the splashing is coming from a pair of hands. Two pairs of hands. I drop to my hands and knees and crawl forward, finally getting far enough to see both Emmett and Theo have fallen over. But they're each clinging to their own shard of debris poking out from the ledge that shrinks underneath the flooding waters.

I really am right back to where I started from. I have no choice but to decide. I look down at their desperate faces, both looking half convinced that they're about to die. Why did it have to be so dark? Why did I have to get lost? Why couldn't I have escaped this and stumbled back out onto the road? I would've kept running all the way home, never looking back again.

But here I am. With no way out and both of them pleading for me to save them. It occurs to me that even if I am able to choose between them, I still may not be able to help. And I might die out here regardless. I hope that being faced with that will give me some sort of clarity. Some sort of nudge to what I should do. But I know now that I am all the way back here, I can't run away from this again. I can't leave them both to die like this.

I look around, thinking I have to make a plan for how to do this before I can do anything else. A clinking noise a few feet away catches my attention. A chain is caught on one of the old cars nearby and is rattling against the rushing, rising waters. I race over to it, unwrapping it from the twisted piece of metal it clings to. I return to the edge and look over and they're both still miraculously dangling there.

"Help me, Ophelia! Please!" Theo cries, nearly falling as he tries to reach for me.

Emmett is oddly quiet, grappling onto what looks like a bumper sticking out of the mud. I wait for him to join Theo in calling out to me. But he says nothing. He just looks up at me in between his attempts to hold on. The waters rise and I know if I'm going to try and save one of them, it has to be fast. A few seconds more and they'll both fall to their deaths or get swept up in the rushing flood. And the more time I waste in indecision, the more I risk dying out here with them.

What would my mom do? She and Brendan are the only good, honest people I have left in this world. Who would they want me to save? I think back to what my mom said about something always seeming off about Emmett. She wanted to trust and believe in Theo's ability to change and give him a second chance. Does that mean that I should too?

You're out of time, Ophelia. I look over to Emmett. His face softens with acceptance as if he knows what I have to do. And he's okay with it. Just like when he told me to run to Theo. He just wants me to make it out of here alive.

"Ophelia!" Theo sobs, slipping further down towards the put below.

Without wasting any more time, I swing down the chain. I

hear crashing waves all around as he climbs and the moment he claws his way back onto solid ground, I turn to take off running again. This time, I'm smart enough to stop and look around for the bobbing beam coming from Theo's flashlight. It's trapped among a cluster of debris. I race over, snatch it up, and take off. Not even caring if he's following behind me. I did my part. I made my choice. Now I have to survive this and get the hell out of here.

By the time I reach the darkness I got lost in before, I am nearly swallowed up by a gushing stream of water. I manage to grab onto something sticking up and use it to climb to slightly higher ground. The rest of my escape is a blur. All I know is that eventually, I find my way back out onto the road. My feet stomp across the flooding pavement. A few of the dips in the road are so flooded I have to swim through them, using passing sticks and logs to propel me forward.

As the lights of Jameson finally come into view up ahead, the rain stops. The downpour grows silent and all that's left is the sound of trickling water all around. I never thought I would be so happy to see this fucking town again. I hate it with every ounce of my being, but in this moment, I've never been happier to see anything. That is until I finally arrive home. I burst through the door and crash into the arms of my mom, still sopping wet.

I drag her down to the ground, crying the whole way. She holds me and rocks back and forth until I calm down. Not asking any questions or demanding I tell her what happened. She just takes me in and lets me get it all out.

# CHAPTER THIRTY

BOOK 3

As the band wails its way through Pomp and Circumstance, I am amazed that I am actually sitting here. I think back on how many times over this last year of school that I was certain I was going to die, and it seems unbelievable that I actually survived every time. Even the bout of pneumonia that I had after the flood couldn't kill me.

I smile and nod my way through the ceremony, mostly just feeling impatient to get to the pizza party Mom and Brendan have promised me once it's over. I zone out through the speeches and the assembly line we form to collect our diplomas. The only person I would be anxious to see here would be Bridgett, but I already know she was planning to skip this whole thing. She was too ready to take off to whatever comes next.

As another round of music blares and we all excitedly fling our caps up into the air, I think how funny it is that this seems like such a crucial moment to so many high schoolers. Every teenager laments their way through those four years, convinced they'll never make it out alive. But none of them can really appreciate this in the same way I and everyone around me can. At WJ Prep, it is a very real fear that we'll never make it out of the walls of this school. Not everyone has.

The thought makes me all the more eager to bound through those double doors with the crowd of students around me. I flip a bird over my shoulder as I pass through, back out into the fresh, free air. I did it. I actually lived. I survived the Elites of

Weis-Jameson Preparatory Academy. And I can honestly say their mission statement is true. Nothing could have better prepared me for whatever life has to throw my way after this.

I make my way out onto the school lawn, watching the groups of hugging and crying friends bid each other farewell. I listen to them congratulate each other and shout out in excitement. I marvel at how shockingly normal it all looks. Like any other high school graduation. Is this all it took for everyone here to become ordinary people? Is it just the status of being a student at WJ Prep that makes them all evil and crazy?

But then I notice the fear lingering in the haunted eyes of the younger students glaring at their older siblings with envy. They know what I had to learn the hard way. Emmett and the rest of the Elites of our graduating class may be gone. Malcolm may be gone. But someone new is waiting in the wings to rise and unleash the fury of the nightmare they've been silently living in. It'd be nice to think that with each new death of a round of Elites, the whole hierarchy could just crumble and be gone forever.

But that's not how human nature works. One soul will be so hurt and twisted from the wrongs done to them that they'll be waiting for their chance to seek revenge. They'll claw their way up, doing to others what has been done to them all along. I do feel sorry for those left behind and everyone that will come after them. But it's not my problem now. I'm done shouldering the burden of WJ Prep and Jameson.

I scan the crowd, looking for the smiling faces of my parents. I spot my mom and Brendan waiting patiently for me under the shade of a nearby tree. They wrap me up in hugs with the perfect blue sky and vivid green grass all around us.

"Can we please get out of this hell hole now?" I beg in laughter.

"You bet," my mom winks, scooping me to her side as we walk to their car.

A couple of hours later we're at home, digging into the boxes of delivery pizza scattered across the dining room table. We ordered way too much, but I think they're both just so happy I'm okay that they went a little overboard.

"I can't believe it's really over," I say with a content sigh after I've polished off another helping.

"I can't believe any of it," Brendan grunts.

"I can," my mom groans. "I'd go back and live through it all in your place in a heartbeat if I could. But I'm not surprised. WJ Prep has always been a living nightmare. I just wanted so badly to believe that it could be different for you."

I see a look of guilt flash through her eyes, prompting me to take her hand into mine. "You couldn't have known," I assure her, squeezing her fingers tight.

"Just promise me if you ever find yourself in that kind of trouble again, that you'll just tell us right away," she begs. "I don't care what you think will happen, or if you think we can handle it. Tell us."

"Deal," I nod.

But truthfully, I don't know that telling them would have helped. The forces at play in this town are so much bigger than them. I learned that quickly. And the scary thing is, I know they would have done anything to protect me. Which is likely what would have ended up getting them killed. Miraculously, that never happened. And now that I'm on the other side of it, I don't know if I'd change anything.

"No regrets," I add.

"What?" my mom laughs in disbelief. "I can think of one or two regrets I would have if I were you. None of it was your fault, of course. You were just doing your best, but…what if we had never come here at all?"

It's the thing I've been wishing for so long now. That we had never come to this stupid place. The moment Vivian and Bernadette first came speeding up in their fancy, expensive car, knocking me over and warning me about what was to come, I wished I could go back home. But then who would I be? What kind of person would I be right now if I had made it through high school without everything that's happened?

My old idea of home is distant and foreign. I realize now that this is all home was all along. Laughing and eating pizza with my parents. With Brendan, who I now refer to as my real dad. My mom happily goes along with it, probably wishing that's what we had done all alone.

"So, where's Coach Granger headed to now that he's retired?" my mom asks with a mouth full of food.

"Florida, I think."

I never told anyone about what I overheard Coach and Jada talking about. I didn't even tell them I had heard their accidental confessions of killing Malcolm. He helped me at times when no one else would. I figure I owe him my silence. Anyway, he's a good man at heart. He's about to leave here forever, and I don't imagine he'll ever commit another murder.

I can't say the same for Jada who decided to stay here and take over for him, coaching the girls' track team. That's the thing about this place. It makes people do all sorts of things they would have never dreamed of or thought they'd be capable of doing. I don't really care if she becomes some lone vigilante of WJ Prep though. If the Elites and everyone else here can play dirty, why rat out someone who stands a chance at giving them a taste of their own medicine?

Soon, it will all be behind me. And I have never been more ready to get out of this town.

A couple of months later, I have managed to cram all of my essential possessions into a few small boxes that are stacked up next to my door. Mom and Brendan assure me they're eager to get out of Jameson too now that they know the truth about everything that's happened here. Whatever I haven't packed up is donated or sold. And before long the room is empty. Except for one remaining thing that I'm not quite sure what to do with.

Sitting in the middle of the empty room is Marissa's diary. I smooth my hands across the cover, almost feeling tempted to open it up and start reading again. But I stop myself. I already know how the story ends. Marissa becomes one of them. Not by choice really, but as a means of survival.

I wish she could have seen other ways out. I wish it were just some novel where any number of other endings would be possible. But I know that's not the story written across the remaining pages, and maybe that's why Emmett never wanted to read it. Would it have been better for him to read firsthand of how his mother used to be before Thomas and his world changed her? No, probably not. Because that person is long gone, and what's left was too sad of an ending for him to stomach. I don't think I can handle it either.

I tuck the diary underneath a loose board in my closet. Maybe one day some scared and lost newbie to Jameson will stumble across it and see it as a warning. I don't know that there is any right way to respond to the wrath of the Elites, but these words could do something for them. Maybe one day someone will find a way to change things around here. It's a nice thought. I say a little prayer over the book that it could be a catalyst for such a thing just before closing the loose board back down over top of it.

I take one last look at my room. For all that's happened within these walls, I don't feel attached to this place at all. It was a refuge in the hell of Jameson, but really, we only lived here for one year. I've learned to look beyond places or things for a sense of security, safety, and belonging. I have found those things deep within myself and in the arms of my parents.

"You ready?" Brendan asks from the doorway with a proud smile.

"More than ever."

My mom comes up behind him and we each grab a box to carry down to my car. I may have thought the hardest part of all of this would be surviving, but as I hug my parents goodbye, I realize I was wrong. Leaving them behind here is the hardest thing I've ever been faced with. The reality of it causes me to break down crying.

"I hope those are happy tears," my mom says as she smudges her thumbs across my wet cheeks.

"Promise me you'll leave here as soon as you can," I beg through my tears.

"We're going to be fine," she assures me. "Don't you worry about us."

I peel myself away and let out a deep sigh, but it's harder than I expected to actually get in my car and drive away.

"You'll call us when you get there?" she asks. I nod and start crying again. "Enough of that. Everything is okay now. And not only do you have your first day of classes to prepare for, you have that new job waiting for you."

I was determined to make my way to the school in California, my top choice, without Theo's help. Even though everyone kept saying it would be impossible, I scoured the city's job boards relentlessly. Nothing feels impossible to me anymore. And my persistence paid off. I managed to find a part-time coaching gig at a community center. They had been wanting to expand their after school athletic programs and had never been able to offer track as an option before.

I completed a couple of phone interviews and a video chat, the whole time trying to hide my desperation for the job, so I didn't scare them off. Without that job, my chances at making it through my first year in California would have seemed dire. So much so that I might have had to settle for a different school.

Which is why it was such a relief when they finally agreed to hire me.

I try to focus on my excitement for everything to come, but I still find it hard to leave my parents. They finally shuffle me off into my car, giving me constant reassurance that they'll be okay.

"This is crazy," I laugh at them through my car window. "I have wanted nothing more than to get out of here, and now I can't seem to leave."

My mom smiles in a way that makes me believe that everything really will be okay. I know they'll make it out of here soon. But if I don't leave now, I might not. I've learned the hard way to never underestimate what this town could throw at you any given second, and I won't feel safe or convinced that I really am finally free until I am several states away.

With one final push from them, I take off. Once I start driving, I don't stop. I feel like a scared family fleeing a house full of poltergeists in the middle of the night. I don't check my rearview mirrors, and I don't stop for anything. For many miles, I am convinced that some part of Jameson is waiting in my backseat. The moment I glance back, it could jump out and kill me.

But that doesn't happen. By sunset, I am zooming out of Massachusetts for good. I have already warned my parents that any visits will have to take place somewhere else, or they'll have to come to me. I am never stepping foot back in that state again, and definitely never getting anywhere near Jameson ever again.

The next day, I am hit with a wall of survivor's guilt. It haunts me with each passing mile. I wonder why I was the lucky one to make it out and not Lily. What if Malcolm would have decided to leave? Vivian seemed to become a normal, happy person when she made a new life for herself in New York. Would he have managed to do the same if he could have just made it out of Jameson? I have to accept that I'll never know.

As I drive, it's impossible not to think of Emmett. My heart breaks in a new way each time the memory of him washes over me. All first loves seem big, important, and magnificent. At least that's what people say. But I feel certain that what we shared would be considered deep and meaningful by any standard, young or old.

Sometimes I worry that soulmates are real. Because if they are, I'm convinced he is mine and that I will never know that kind of love again. How else could I have loved him after everything that happened? No matter how I doubted him in the end, I continued trying to love him in every way I could well beyond what anyone else would have been capable of.

I can still see the look on his face. The way his eyes burned into me the last time I ever saw him. And I know that he loved me in all the same ways, even if I never put it to the test the same way he did with me. It was a selfless love that devoured and consumed, yet never lost its fuel. Even when I was certain I could not go on with him or was convinced that I hated him, there was still part of me that loved him endlessly. I tried my best to run from that part of myself, but it always caught up to me. And I'm glad.

For all the things I survived and learned along the way, nothing made me grow more than my love for Emmett. And I don't know that I will ever know another pain like what I feel living without him. I hope not, because I don't think I could stand. Sometimes I am still surprised when I wake up each morning, still feeling half convinced that my heart should just stop beating without him around.

But as my car flies down the highway, I know I am doing exactly what he wanted. He may not have been able to whisk me away from Jameson the way he dreamed of, but above all else he just wanted me to get out. It was all he asked of me in our final moments together.

The clouds hover across the open roads in the setting sky, and I swear I can still see the silhouette of Jameson haunting me from their shapes. They morph into the outline of WJ Prep. They shift and turn into Emmett's face. His eyes. His mouth. All the times I wanted so badly just to get away and now I think the only way I am able to keep driving forward is the mirage of him up ahead. I don't know what life could possibly hold for me beyond him, but I know I have to find out. I have no choice.

And so I keep driving, pushing forward. Pretending that my feet are carrying me away rather than the wheels of my car. I pretend that I am running straight towards him with his embrace waiting for me on just over the horizon.

# CHAPTER THIRTY-ONE

### BOOK 3

I step out onto campus, sucking in a deep breath of the fresh California air. The weather here is unbelievably perfect. The temperature reaches a level of heat I never felt in Jameson but is still somehow soothing and refreshing. And at night it gets chilly enough to make you long for a nice, cozy sweater, but never gets cold enough to compare to the bitter winter nights I've grown accustomed to.

Everything I became accustomed to over the past year fades more and more each day. The fear and anxiety I came to consider normal is a distant nightmare. A thing in my past that I am glad to forget. I ease back into normal, everyday life. And time passes quickly as I keep myself busy with classes, track, and work.

I smile at the passing students and forget that I ever knew to fear any random person I might come across. When I bump into someone, we say our sorry's and carry on our way. It's unbelievably easy and simple. Whenever I hear other students complaining about how stressed they are, I laugh but keep my thoughts to myself.

I am a couple of months into college life and already feel like a brand-new person. It's a perfect sunny day as I walk along the winding sidewalks towards my favorite coffee shop, planning a weekend run on the beach in my head.

Jojo's is a small eclectic joint just on the edge of my new school's property. The small lawn is lined with swaying palm trees, and there's always some acoustic tune ringing out from the speakers hanging near the patio. I walk inside and relish in the scent of fresh coffee.

As I wait in line, which is always long but fast-moving here, I admire the doughnuts and pastries in the tall glass cases. My stomach growls at the sight of cookies and paper-wrapped muffins. There's an assortment of Danishes, scones and biscotti. Chocolates, cakes, macaroons, and eclairs. All sprinkled in with bags of coffee on advertisement.

When it's my turn I walk up to the stainless-steel counter, ignoring the chalkboard menu that hangs behind it because I already know it by heart. I place my order and when I turn to walk away, I swear I see someone I used to know sitting in the corner.

I look away at first, thinking it's impossible. But I can't help looking back and taking a closer look at the long, brunette hair draping over the girl's shoulders. She looks a little different, but I know those features. The longer I stare, the more certain I am.

"Bridgett?" I ask nervously as I step over to her table.

Her eyes meet mine and nearly burst into tears. She jumps up, almost spilling her coffee, and takes me in her arms.

"I can't believe it's you!" she exclaims so loudly that the whole joint grows silent for a minute and stares.

"What are you doing here?" I blink, still suspended in disbelief.

"I moved back," she says, pulling me down to sit across from her.

"I had no idea," I reply softly, trying to hide my trepidation.

"I wanted to tell you…but…you never said goodbye before you left," she explains, looking somber. "I didn't know what happened. I thought maybe you were mad at me for something. Where did you go to that night anyway?"

"What night?" I ask, but I quickly sort my way through the haze of memories enough to realize the last time I saw her was at prom. Thinking back on it all now still feels like trying to dig up pieces of a dream that vanished the moment you woke up. "Oh!" I quickly correct myself. "I…I don't even know where to start," I laugh.

An awkward silence falls between us. I don't know whether to be happy or afraid to see her. If Emmett and Theo agreed on anything, it was that they didn't like or trust Bridgett. I'm not sure if I should either. After everything was over, I realized I never had any real reason to think she was bad. But Emmett was so convinced she was working with Theo. And Theo was so convinced she was just another Elite through and through. I'm not sure what to believe.

"Actually," I continue slowly. "I wanted to ask for your help that night. After I stumbled away, I realized I had been drugged. That's why I got so sick all of a sudden."

Her face melts with concern and sadness all at once. "Oh my god!" she gasps. "What...what happened? Are you okay? How did you..."

"Emmett found me," I tell her. My heart shatters, knowing this is the first time in months I've actually said his name out loud.

"How come you never told me!?" she scolds. "You just disappeared and I didn't know what to think."

"You never tried to find me," I shoot back, surprised by how angry I feel.

"I did!" she insists. "When you didn't come back, I looked all over for you. I told Coach and he was looking for you too."

"No, I mean...You never tried to find me after prom," I clarify. My suspicions of her grow as I remember that with each passing day when I didn't hear from her, I became more convinced that Theo and Emmett were right about her. "You never called or came by my house. You never tried..."

"Ophelia, you never know what's going on in Jameson," she defends. "I'm sorry I hurt you, but things are so rough there...If someone vanishes and you don't hear news of them being dead or hurt, it's usually because they want to be left alone. How come you never called or visited me? That's all I was waiting for."

I shake my head in confusion, rapidly losing sight of what I think is right or true. It's funny how one reminder of Jameson can do that to a person. "They had me convinced...I thought maybe..."

"What?" she asks. "You thought what?"

"That you were the one who drugged me," I confess.

I expect her to be mortified by the accusation, but she tilts her head with sympathy and a knowing frown. Suddenly she seems to understand everything, and like a true Jameson survivor, nothing shocks her. She does what I need her to do the most, what I'm secretly hoping and praying she will do, and simply reaches her hand across the table for mine.

"I didn't drug you," she states. "I promise. I know it's hard to know who to trust there, but I'm your friend. I would never hurt you."

I instantly know she's telling the truth. We sit there for hours and talk about everything that happened after prom.

"I knew I should have told someone what I saw," she says after a while with a haunted look in her eyes.

"What do you mean?" I ask.

"As we were walking into the school that night, I saw two guys lurking at the edge of the building," she tells me, shaking her head. "One was a student. The other was Theo. I knew you were trying to make amends with him, so I didn't think it was anything to worry about. But something always nagged at me, telling me it was off."

I think back on Theo and Emmett's stories. Theo claimed he went to the school after he heard Emmett was released from jail and got there just as he was driving off, with me in the backseat. But according to Bridgett, he was out front hours before that. Was he getting that guy to drop something in my drink? The absence of my former tour guide's outburst had nothing to do with prom or the change in hierarchy. It was all on purpose to distract me from what he slipped in my cup, and it was from Theo's direct orders.

I tell Bridgett every last little thing. She confirms what I always hoped was true. Emmett was telling the truth. She listens in horror as I describe the flood in the junkyard and how I was forced to choose between them.

"How did you know to choose him?" she asks, taking another sip of her coffee.

"It was something that Coach Granger said at Malcolm's funeral," I reply. "He thought it was a shame for any young person to die because no matter how bad they are, they stand more of a chance at changing their ways before it's too late. No one would ever know if they would find some way to turn their lives around and become a decent person." I pause as my heart swells. I realize just how much I miss Coach and wonder if I would be sitting here now without everything he did for me along the way. "I figured if he could bring himself to feel that way about Malcolm, after what he did to his son, I could feel the same sympathy and hope for Emmett."

"So your dad is...?" she asks.

"Yep," I answer coldly. "I decided regardless of who was

telling the truth, my dad had spent his life doing terrible things, and for all I knew, he'd never stop. But Emmett could walk away from it all…and maybe change. Live a decent life."

"You made the right choice," she assures me.

It's something I always hoped I would hear. I've done my best not to let it haunt me, considering I could have just as easily tried to run away again and let them both die there. Choosing between two evils is never easy.

Our conversation eventually drifts off into normal things. She tells me all about her classes and where she's living now. We exchange numbers before we part ways, because of course the first thing we both did when we got here was change our numbers. It was just another way to reduce the likelihood of someone from Jameson coming back to haunt us. We promise to stay in touch and hang out soon, letting the tension that grew between us become a thing of the past.

She turns to me with a big smile on her face just before she walks away. "Do you think you'll go to the ten-year reunion?"

I gawk at her like she's out of her fucking mind, but then she laughs and I realize she was only kidding. I think we both agree that someone would have to drag us kicking and screaming before we'd ever step foot back in that town.

As I walk home, I wonder how I would feel right now if the opposite had happened when I ran into Bridgett. What if she knew something that indicated Theo was telling the truth instead? Sure, I felt justified in my choice at the time, but how would it feel right now to walk away knowing I let my own father die when he was telling the truth all along? Or what if Bridgett didn't know anything that confirmed things one way or the other, and I had to spend the rest of my life never really knowing who had lied and who hadn't.

Now that I have the relief of knowing Emmett was telling the truth, it's hard to imagine it being any other way. I don't know how I would have handled another outcome.

Later that night, I lay in my bed, unable to sleep. I stare up at the ceiling, squirming with the awareness that the memory of how Emmett's body once felt curled up next to mine is still so vivid. I swear I can hear him, smell him on my sheets even though this is a new world he's never had any part in. My heart still aches for him the way it has since we first met.

I close my eyes and see his staring back at me. I roll over and think I brush up against his skin. I think I see him in the corner of my room or hear him call my name. Knowing the truth has summoned his ghost and it's back stronger than ever.

But maybe he's not a ghost. Maybe he's still alive out there somewhere and if he is, I can only hope that he's okay. I never looked back as I ran out of the junkyard that night. I watched him climb back onto solid ground and left, still not knowing who to believe. If he did make it out, I hope he got out of Jameson for good and found something that is making him happy. I can't imagine what he would be like without the constant threat of that town. What if he was so unrecognizable that I didn't know him anymore? What if I didn't love him anymore?

Part of me is tempted to know what that looks like, but mostly I'm just terrified. I don't know what I'm scared of anymore. Maybe I'm just clinging to fear out of habit. One glimpse back into that old life at WJ Prep and I almost unravel. I know I have to pull the covers over my head and go to sleep. Tomorrow will be another day in my new life. My life without Emmett. And I will survive it just like I have survived every day here and every day before I came here.

But as I drift off to sleep, I wish more than anything that I knew where he was or if he was alive at all. I think I would have heard if he had died, but if he did, it's possible no one even found him out there. No one would have thought twice about him disappearing. If anything, people were surprised he stayed for as long as he did after everything was taken from him. I know he stayed for me.

I wish I could tell him I know he was telling the truth and that I forgive him for everything. I toss and turn to the images of him dancing through my mind and even as I wake up the next morning, I swear I see him walking out my bedroom door. Maybe these visions are proof that he didn't survive. And now I will spend the rest of my life with what remains of him lurking in the corner.

# EPILOGUE

## BOOK 3

A few weeks have gone by since my run-in with Bridgett, and while I go through the motions of my new life, nothing has felt quite the same since. Not knowing what to make of the haunted feeling, all I can do is carry on. Bridgett and I have already hung out a couple of times since then, and I'm glad to have her back in my life.

She may be Jameson's only redeeming quality. For all the people I met there, no one ever ended up really being who they claimed to be. I can't help but think it's only because she was only there for such a short amount of time. If she had grown up there, or even just been stuck at WJ Prep for a couple of years instead of a couple of months, she might have been turned into a monster like the rest of them.

For the hundredth time that morning, Emmett's face flashes through my mind. What is a monster anyway? Just some unknown thing lurking in your closet. But if we turn on the lights and face it, does it lose its power? That doesn't seem quite right, or if it is, it proves Emmett wasn't a monster after all. Because nothing ever lessened the power he had over me. Even it faded briefly, it'd soon come crashing back with a fury.

I shake it off as I run, knowing that sooner or later I have to start letting all of my questions go and move on with the rest of my life. I have to move on without him, no matter how much it hurts. I'm thinking all of this over as I sprint down the sunny sidewalks near my apartment just like I do every Sunday morning. But no matter how many times I remind myself I need to move on, it hasn't happened yet.

Suddenly, I freeze, not even really knowing why at first. The hair on my arms stands up and I feel a nostalgic fluttering in my gut. I haven't felt it in so long, but only one thing has ever made me feel quite like that. But I know that is not the thing causing it this time. Only he could do that. It can't be.

Something makes me stop and turn to look at the figure I just brushed past. When I do, my stomach drops. A familiar pair of hungry eyes met mine.

It can't be, I think again. I drink in the sight of him, wondering if it's real. I know the strain of those muscles and every last mark across that skin as well as I know my own body. The gray eyes burning into me, pulling me in with the magnetic force I know all too well. Then he smiles and I think I would cry if I wasn't so overwhelmed with a million other feelings, all canceling each other out yet intensifying at the same time.

"Looking good, Lopez," Emmett says with a wink. His voice shatters through me like a crack in the earth.

I step over to him, still gasping for breath. Beyond my control, my hand reaches for his face. My fingers graze across the curl of his lips and his slightly crooked, charming nose. His thick lashes blink, sucking me into the storm of his gaze. I want to stay there forever.

But something pulls me back, remembering that even though I may be overcome with relief to know he's alive, I have no idea what he's doing here. For all I know this could just be his ghost haunting me again. Becoming more vivid to demand my attention, true to his living self. Am I losing my mind? Have I been running from the haunting memory of him for so long now that it's causing me to hallucinate something more real?

"You stalking me?" I blurt out, trying to sound normal, but I don't recognize my own voice. I don't know where else to start but from what I remember of our beginning. And my pitch slips right back to what spilled from my lips all that time ago.

He seems just as speechless as I am and we're frozen there in silence for the longest time. I swear everything around us moves in slow motion. I gasp as he reaches for my hand suddenly. The touch of his fingers lets me know that he's real. He draws the back of it up to his lips, kissing it with a smile. The moment my hand drops from his mouth, I'm filled with that old familiar feeling of disappointment that comes from never having enough of him.

"What are you doing here?" I ask breathlessly.

"I work just over there," he points to a building a few blocks away.

"Work?" I repeat back in disbelief, feeling like a zombie. "You have a job here?"

He nods. "I'm in school too," he adds casually. "I'm mostly just saving money, but for now I'm taking a few night classes. I was thinking I'd get those degrees you said I needed. For design and plant management."

"Oh," I exhale. "I…I don't know what to say."

We both laugh nervously and then he finally wraps his big, muscular arms around me. "It's good to see you," he chuckles.

"So…you're here?" I blink as he lowers me back to the ground. I need to feel the solid earth beneath me. For a brief second, it felt like I might keep going up until I drifted off into space. "Like…here here? You live here?" I hate myself for how stupid I sound right now. Just because he loved me once doesn't mean I won't scare him away by suddenly being a babbling, wordless idiot.

"Yeah," he smiles, melting me like always. "With Theo gone, I figured I could follow through with the original plans I made for him. Maybe start my own company one day or start selling my designs."

I can't believe that he's standing here in front of me on the other side of the country, talking about ordinary things. But none of its really so ordinary considering what we had to go through to get here.

"You did it," I grin, marveling at the sight of him in front of the California sky. "You made it out."

"So did you," he nudges my arm.

My mind races with a million things I want to say, but I start to get angry as I realize why it's so hard for me to find the right words. The smile runs away from his face as my brow furrows.

"How long have you been here?" I ask, afraid to know the answer. "Why didn't you try to find me sooner? Were you just counting on randomly running into me on the street in a city filled with hundreds of thousands of people!" I get angrier with every word and suddenly have to stop myself from slapping him across the face.

"To be fair, I'm used to Jameson," he defends with a smirk.

"I don't think I was quite prepared for what hundreds and thousands of people really looked like."

I cross my arms and stare up at him, not feeling the least bit amused. "I didn't even know if you were alive," I growl.

"I didn't know if you wanted to know I was alive," he quips back, his eyes matching my intensity. He never shies away from my bark and it never stops leaving me completely dismantled.

That's when the tears come. My bottom lip quivers and I have to look away as my eyes burn with the stinging wetness. He's not a ghost, and I know it by the way my emotions ping back and forth and rage all over the place with an effect only he can have.

"Don't cry," he says softly.

"What are you really doing here?" I huff. "Why are you in California?"

"I don't expect anything from you," he assures me, but the fear in his eyes gives him away. "But it's like I said all along…I'll do whatever it takes to prove to you that I can be the man you deserve. I'll be here, waiting, hoping that you'll find it in your heart to trust me. Again."

I'm overwhelmed and think of running away. I was finally free from him and then all I wanted was to have him back. To be pulled back into his current. Now he's standing here out of the blue, saying everything I never thought I'd never hear again. He's waiting for me. The pressure of it is terrifying and beautiful all at once.

"I'm sorry I didn't know you were telling the truth," I tell him, still doing my best to fight back my tears. "But I know now. I saw Bridgett, and she told me everything. I just wish I had known sooner…Emmett, I thought you were dead."

I collapse against his chest and I'm relieved to feel him envelope me. "I didn't know what to do," he confesses. "I'll be honest…part of me thought about just leaving you be. Letting you go on without me. I wondered if you'd be better off."

As he says it, I realize no part of me is better off without him. I don't even know what I've been doing since I last saw him. I thought I did, but now it seems like a foggy mess of waiting and hoping and trying to convince myself that he wasn't still out there somewhere. But as I take in a deep breath of his scent and all the other intangible things about him that I somehow understand perfectly, I realize my soul has been calling out to him this whole time, longing to be made whole again in his arms.

"I'm glad that didn't happen," I say truthfully. "But what happens now?" Everything around us seems to go back to normal and I am painfully aware of the passing traffic around us. None of them have any idea how monumental this moment is for me and I find myself resenting them for it.

"Whatever you want to happen," he replies, almost as a dare.

My hand slips into his as if it never left. I don't know what I'm doing. I just start walking, urging him to follow by my side. As we walk, I look back and forth between him and the city around me, unsure of which one I want to look at more. The sight of him and the feeling of his flesh…I didn't know if I'd ever know the feeling of it again. I'm afraid that if I blink or look away for too long, he'll vanish like a puff of smoke.

But as I look at everything around us, it feels like I'm seeing it for the first time. As if I never really arrived here until this moment, with him taking it all in by my side. We walk down to the beach with the waves dancing around our feet. I've looked across this ocean a hundred times by now, but with him next to me, it feels bigger than it has before. And scary almost, like it could burst at any moment and wash me away.

Each time I glance back up at him, towering over me and seeming even taller than before, his eyes stare back. I steady myself in them and wonder if what I was really afraid of the whole time was losing him. All those moments of doubt and mistrust that crept over me relentlessly, constantly demanding to know if I could really count on him, were really just my fears of losing something so great.

When my legs feel like they could give out and the sun starts to hang lower in the sky, I stop and know that it's time to finally just let myself accept that he's real. He's really here and he's not going anywhere if I don't want him to.

I lay my head against his chest as his hand raises, pressing his palm against mine. Our fingers mirror against each other, like two halves of flesh becoming whole again. There are a million things to say and do, and even after all this time of just walking and adjusting to him being here, I still don't know where to start.

"I know," he smirks, like he can read my mind. "It's okay. We have the rest of our lives."

"If we're lucky," I smile back.

Finally, he lowers his head and presses his lips to mine. I lose myself in his kiss as his tongue rolls across mine with the same rhythm of the crashing waves behind us. Against all odds, we broke all the rules and found some way to be together.

I take him back to my apartment where he lays me down and makes love to me for hours. It's pure and gentle and everything I always knew it could be once we finally got away from Jameson. Everything I always thought I saw in him was right there the whole time.

---

Thank you for reading THE ELITES OF WEIS - JAMESON PREP ACADEMY trilogy. Don't miss my DIAMOND IN THE ROUGH SERIES, and be sure to join my SMS list below to don't miss any of my future books!

**Want to read an exclusive FREE novella from Emmett's point of view? Check out book 1.5: RELENTLESS**

**Get an SMS alert when Rebel releases a new book:**
Text REBEL to 77948

*If you want to support me, consider leaving a review on Amazon. I'd love it!*

# ABOUT THE AUTHOR

Rebel Hart is an author of Contemporary and Dark Romance novels. Check out her debut series Diamond In The Rough.

**NEVER MISS A NEW RELEASE:**
Follow Rebel on Amazon
Follow Rebel on Bookbub

Text REBEL to 77948 to don't miss any of her books (US only) or sign up at www.RebelHart.net to get an email alert when her next book is out.

authorrebelhart@gmail.com

CONNECT WITH REBEL HART:

# ALSO BY REBEL HART

For a full list of my books go to:

www.RebelHart.net